Song of the Hills

Hannah read through the letter four times slowly before folding it carefully into her pocket. Well, she'd just keep working at it. "Love and remembrances" ... Would he be part of this big push? She *must* reach him; she'd try even harder next Saturday. She chewed the last bit of bread slowly, staring up into the dim cobwebby beams, remembering Harry's bright hair, his laugh, his lovely brown fingers. All the gaiety she'd loved so much in him would come back, surely, when he'd been home again for a while. And she would protect him somehow – she *would* reach him. She knew it was possible ...

Margaret Evans has lived in Wales or on the Welsh borders for most of her life. She has written four previous novels: *The Hall in the Field, And the Little Hills Rejoice, The Wild Sky* and *A Place of Eagles*, three of which centred round the historic manor house of Maesyneuadd where she has lived.

MARGARET EVANS
Song of the Hills

Mandarin

A Mandarin Paperback
SONG OF THE HILLS

First published in Great Britain 1995
by William Heinemann Ltd
and Mandarin Paperbacks
imprints of Reed Consumer Books Ltd
Michelin House, 81 Fulham Road, London SW3 6RB
and Auckland, Melbourne, Singapore and Toronto

Copyright © Margaret Evans 1995
The author has asserted her moral rights

A CIP catalogue record for this title
is available from the British Library
ISBN 0 7493 1917 8

Typeset by Deltatype Ltd, Ellesmere Port, Cheshire
Printed and bound in Germany by
Elsnerdruck, Berlin

To Chris, with my love.

My thanks and acknowledgements to:
Mr John Vivian Hughes, local history librarian,
Swansea Library; Mr Arthur Rees and
Mr J. Ivor Hanson of Taibach; Ray and
Georgina Day; and most especially Ted Albins,
for his tireless practical help and
his moral support, both crucial to the
writing of this book.

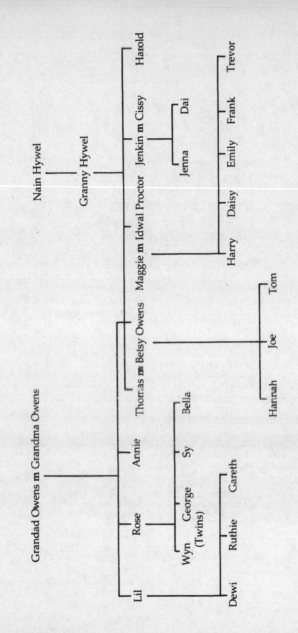

Prologue

South Wales 1768

Rachel Hywel heard the first shouts over the roar of the flooding River Avan. It boiled through its valley below the hillside where her cottage sheltered by a stand of sombre pines. As the ragged crowd approached, some holding aloft flaming brands to light their way, Rachel drew her toddler twins close.

"Stand by me, little ones . . . never fear."

They waited silently as the shouting crescendoed, and after a moment the first stone smashed against the low door of weathered oak. The little boys gripped their mother's skirts and their big slate-grey eyes sought her dark ones for reassurance. More stones followed from the wet and miserable rabble outside, their faces contorted by rage and grief. They had all lost kinsmen that day in the landslip at Llety Harry colliery; they held Rachel Hywel responsible and they wanted revenge, an eye for an eye. Rachel's man, too, had perished in the disaster. But that was her own doing. She had put a curse on her own man for his alleged misuse of her – had they not heard the witch? And that curse had brought down the rocks and earth upon not only Ben Hywel, but their own folk. A dozen men and boys now lay in the flooded mineshaft and their sons, daughters, wives and parents had toiled up the track in the stormy night to confront the perpetrator of their present misery.

As a stone smashed through the small window between door and hearth Rachel glimpsed the blazing brands outside. She knew why they were were there, her husband's brother had come earlier to warn her. She also knew that she had no power to bring down landslips, even had she a mind to do so. Her man *had* broken her finger just this market day, attempting to wrest money from her for drink when she was buying food, and she had rounded on him publicly for his sins. This oath was the reason for the mob about her home now . . . this and the fact that Rachel was a healer, a talent by its nature suspect. Some of the crowd outside tonight had doubtless benefited from her gift, with a cricked back freed, an arthritic joint eased, a boil swayed away. Now, they bayed like wolves for her blood.

A blazing brand was tossed through the broken window and she tried to douse the flames with a jug of water. But sparks had fallen on her basket of spinning wool and when it quickly fired, igniting the sheepskin hearthrug, Rachel feared for her children. She saw too that the thatch must have been lit, for thick smoke was drifting down the ladder to the sleeping-loft. Her twins huddled together, mute with terror; Rachel gathered them up, opened the door and deposited them on the muddied pathway. Then she stepped back to the threshold of her home and faced the crowd with her head high, the night wind blowing her dark hair about her face and the room behind her bright with flames.

"Are ye now content? This is more wickedness than ever I committed in my life!" Her voice rose strong above the wind. "Go mourn your dead like Christian souls, and lay not their deaths at my door. I've griefs aplenty of my own!"

A man whose only son lay dead in Llety Harry mine flung a stone and it struck Rachel on the temple; without a sound she fell back into the blazing cottage, leaving her babies crying on the path.

No one moved for a moment, no one spoke. Then a woman pushed forward and snatched up the children.

Within minutes the crowd had melted away. Increasingly heavy rain doused the thatch, the fire dimmed and died about the body of Rachel Hywel.

The twins survived. A Hywel cousin, indebted to their father for a favour once done, took little Joss with him to the Americas when he went to seek his fortune there. Thomas was taken in by another cousin, Marged, who had a smallholding in Taibach. Marged knew the benefit of another pair of strong young hands to hoe vegetable rows, to scrub out dairy pans, to feed chickens and pigs and cut wood. So Marged was charitable, and took over the infant Thomas.

Folk talked of the great floods of '68 for years afterwards. Those who knew the truth of Rachel Hywel's fate on the night of the floods would feel unease then, and keep silent. What could they do more? Two babes had been orphaned . . . but life was hard and brief, and children were expendable.

Chapter One

August 1914

Hannah Hywel, aged twelve years and two months, had known for a while now that she alone could see the drowned mariners on the *Amazon*. As she sat on Taibach beach on the Tuesday morning after Bank Holiday, allowing her brother Joe to spoon sand over her outstretched legs, her reluctant eyes were drawn again to the decaying, half-buried hulk . . . and to the shadowy figures moving slowly, dream-like, across its shattered decks.

It had been cousin Harry who'd told her the histories of the wrecks. Dada never would have, fearing it might add to her already deep mistrust of water. It had; yet still they fascinated Hannah, whilst other children seemed simply to accept them as part of the landscape of their little world. Listening to Harry, the oldest and best loved of her tribe of cousins, watching his bright hair lift in the wind off the sea as he bent toward her on the tide-scarred breakwater, Hannah shivered with an irresistible mixture of pleasure and fear. There was the steamship *Ethelwalda* rotting on Aberavan beach across the river, smashed on the breakwater whilst trying to enter harbour. That had been three years ago . . . not long after her baby brother Arthur had been buried in his little white coffin. Then only last year the *Broadland* had been driven aground – all efforts to refloat her had failed and she too had died, reared massively on her side in the sand that sucked at her. Whenever she saw

4

the dead ships, so pathetic with their ribs bared to the elements, Hannah wished they might decently be laid to rest like Arthur – or like baby brother Hughie last summer – away from curious eyes.

And then there was the *Amazon*. Harry most enjoyed recounting that tale, relishing the grim details. When Hannah was six, the year before Joe's birth, an autumn gale had forced the ship ashore at Taibach in huge seas, and would-be rescuers had watched helplessly as the graceful four-masted barque was torn and broken. Only eight crew had been pulled to safety, leaving twenty under ferocious, thundering waves. Hannah had listened in silence to Harry's account of the *Amazon*'s death, eyes fixed on a tattered remnant of her sails flapping feebly now in the breeze. She always seemed to live the tragedy as he told it; felt the wicked cold of the waves smashing like falling mountains on the black, jagged jaws of waiting rocks. And the men . . . she could not speak of *them*, intermittently materialising on those tilted decks, hazy as ribbons of morning mist. These men, these drowned mariners, she came to realise, were simply not *there* for Harry.

Quite often, she'd tried to talk to her father about those insubstantial figures – Dada was clever, he would explain it all. But this must be a private talk, and little Joe trailed her like a shadow, even walking the few yards to school with her and meeting her out again, face pressed to the playground railings with their terrier, Fly, on the end of a piece of string.

The sun had gone behind a cloud and suddenly Hannah shivered, legs chilly under the damp sand.

"Joe – you'll have to give up burying me now, they'll be getting the food out anytime."

Joe gave his handiwork a final pat. He was "finishing out" his old jacket for playing in and his flat little wrists poked uncomfortably from the sleeves. A stiff new one, a full size too big and with pockets stuffed with foul-smelling mothballs, hung ready on their bedroom door hook for him to start school in next month, when he would be five. He cocked his head, considering, and Hannah saw that his quiff of brown hair was already peppery with sand.

"What if I bury you *all over* so you can't breave?"

"Then I'd die, and you wouldn't have me to show you where the boys' lavvies are at school and you'd wet your trousers your first day."

Joe stopped considering; he was nothing if not practical. He flung himself across his sister's legs, squirming at the very thought of her threat – he tended to ignore calls of nature until the last possible moment and there was still the occasional mortifying disaster.

"Off, Joey Hywel!" Hannah pushed up her knees, which broke through the sand like two bleached moles. Joe, giggling, was thrown off as her legs and feet emerged; she grabbed him and they rolled laughing back and forth, Fly barking with excitement and diving in between them.

"Stop it now! Fly – *sit*!" Hannah fixed the terrier with a fierce eye and he sat, cocked ears quivering and tail thudding in the sand. "*Now* look at us both." She shook out her blue cotton skirt and the calico pinafore that was getting too short for her. "Make yourself tidy or you'll not be allowed your food. See, they're getting it out ready."

She knocked and brushed the worst of the sand off the little boy, setting his cap back on his head and rebuttoning the tight wool jacket. Then she put Fly on his lead, looking across the beach to where a driftwood fire was heating the kettle and women were setting food from deep baskets onto a checkered cloth, and calling

6

up their offspring. It was still scarcely eleven o'clock, but breakfast for most in Taibach had been hours ago, it was a district of early risers.

Hannah turned her back on the sea. Northward, inland beyond the docks, the railway sheds and shunting yards, Taibach's houses clustered around the coast road. They could not spread far; the shoulder of Margam mountain rose steeply behind them and rolled on eastward as Taibach merged into Margam with no perceptible boundary. To the west, separated by the river, the network of little streets became Aberavan, sloping gently to its golden sweep of sand.

Taibach beach was smaller, less impressive; close to the docks and the Port Talbot Steelworks Company, operating for seven years and lately prospering. There was indeed no call for any man in the district to be without work. Tin, coal and iron ore were ingredients for industry, and the sea was at hand to carry industry's cargoes. The first small dock built on the morfa below Taibach in the 1830s and named Port Talbot after the local landowner, quickly became inadequate, though it was later to give its name to the district. By the turn of the century it was enlarged beyond recognition and the docks were a forest of masts. With ocean-going vessels berthing on their doorstep industries burgeoned – although the port had still been considered no more than a creek of Swansea, its mightier neighbour west across the bay, until the last few years.

Though small in area, Taibach was highly concentrated, hemmed into the narrow strip between the mountain, the railway, the river, and the urban district of Margam. Shops, pubs and small businesses were in the main strung along the High Street, Station Road and Talbot Road which became Commercial Road, which became Margam Road and in thirty miles or so reached

Cardiff. A rich community life was interwoven with a thriving worklife; the houses may have looked grey, but that is the colour of Welsh stone and Welsh roof slates. The people were robust and vital as the mountains and valleys that swelled and dipped in glorious contours at their backs. They enjoyed their own theatre, the "New," that offered everything from opera through Shakespeare and music hall to broad comedy. The Electric cinema in Forge Road just off Station Road was always popular. A literary society met weekly in a room above a restaurant, there were rugby and football clubs, men's clubs, union clubs, choirs, and the Temperance Band. Chapels of stern grey granite abounded, but Hannah's family were church; St Mary's, which being just across the river was officially in Aberavan.

From where she stood on the beach, Hannah could pick out the spire of St Mary's beyond the tangle of masts in the docks, and the long mill sheds . . . she had lived very close to it, in Water Street, until they had moved to Incline Row last year. Aunt Rose, the second of her mother's three sisters, remained near St Mary's in Alexandra Street. Auntie Lil, the eldest, was in Mansel Street about half-way between Betsy and Rose and a few doors from Grandpa Owens and Annie, the fourth, unmarried sister. Hannah enjoyed her father telling the story of how he had first spoken to her mother in St Mary's. He had been in the pew behind her, and had observed a little blue butterfly settle on the daisy in her straw hat. It was still there when they filed out and Thomas had screwed up his courage to tell Betsy. She had unpinned the hat very carefully and lifted it off, but the butterfly, finding no refreshment in the cotton daisy had flown off into the sunlight.

It had been love at first sight for Thomas Hywel but for weeks he had contented himself with raising his hat and bidding Betsy "Good morning" each Sunday. When finally he had asked if he might walk her home, they had strolled awkwardly behind her parents who had turned at intervals to inspect the new suitor.

The courtship had taken six months, considered a seemly interval for young couples to assess one another. Thomas was regularly in work with the Port Talbot Railways and Docks Company before the steelworks opened, and Betsy's father, who worked for the same firm in the shunting yards, knew him by sight already. Thomas's sister Maggie lived at the bottom of Incline Row with her husband and five children but his two surviving brothers had strayed – Harold to Swansea and Jenkin to a smallholding two miles inland at Cwmavon. His father and youngest brother had both been killed in a pit explosion when he was eighteen. A miner himself until then, Thomas had heeded his mother's plea to quit lest she lose him, too. There were accidents aplenty in the steelworks . . . but Thomas was both careful and skilful. Once married he became even more careful, for he quickly discovered that Betsy's great fear was of being left without his support. A quiet girl, sometimes withdrawn, and lacking the facility to disclose her emotions, once he divined her fear Thomas accommodated himself to it, for he loved her deeply.

Hannah took Joe's hand now and moved across to join the picknickers. Three grandmas sat upright and stiffly corseted on kitchen chairs carried down for them, and one carried a paper sunshade with Japanese ladies and red and purple flowers printed on it. They were served first, with plates of chunky bread and butter glistening with a topping of gooseberry jam. There were around twenty picknickers of all ages, including a theology student from Aberystwyth who had stayed on after preaching the Bank Holiday Sunday sermon at

9

church – a plump red-haired young man perspiring freely in his tight black suit.

"I shall enlist, of course," he was saying earnestly to Alfred Phillips, the grandfather of Hannah's best friend, Florence. "I thought perhaps the Medical Corps . . ." He paused delicately, aware of the tender young ears about him, although the owners of these ears were in the main concentrating on the already sandy bread and jam.

"Fair enough, that is. You pick up the bits after the enemy's blown their guts out."

Alfred Phillips cleared his throat and spat into the sand, impervious to the woman's disapproving frowns. He'd seen too much blood spilt in thirty-odd years down Morfa pit to call a spade anything but exactly that. "I'd fancy a shot at that Kaiser meself if I'd a chance in hell of catchin' up with 'im."

He wiggled his right leg at the theology student; the foot that should have been at the end of it had years ago been sliced off by a runaway coal truck. Chewing her bread and jam, Hannah stared at the trouser bottom and imagined the severed foot forever walking back and fore through the now deserted tunnels of the pit, searching vainly for its leg. She pushed Joe's hand away from the sugared Welshcakes and nodded sternly at his unfinished hunk of bread and jam.

The knot was in her chest again. It came every time she heard threatening words like "Kaiser", "enlist", "war". Now, grownups were interested in nothing else. They didn't seem to like it – so why was it happening? She'd asked Dada why yesterday, after special prayers had been said so the war wouldn't start. He'd looked serious and Mam had stopped her knitting for a bit then started again faster than ever, lips pressed in a tight line.

"A sticky one, that, Princess." He pulled the hair behind his ear as he often did when thinking. Hannah had waited, confident that he would make it clear for her. Thomas was short on formal education having left school at twelve to work as errand boy at the steel mill. But he always read the newspaper passed round by his mates in the snap break, and his nimble brain had an above average grasp of world affairs.

"Well now. These Austrians and Germans have said they're goin' to fight Russia and France. Bully-boys they are! And if their ships come into the Channel, well, that's too close for comfort for us. So," he had spread his hands. "We'd likely say, oh no you don't, and sail out pretty nifty to stop 'em. But don't you worry your head about it, *cariad*."

Hannah had listened carefully and finally nodded. Dada had nodded back, smiling, and continued with his Sunday game of cribbage with his father-in-law, who lived alone since his wife's death and liked a bit of company.

Yesterday, everyone had gone on about an "ultimatum", and Germans marching through Belgium. Hannah hadn't asked Dada to explain that, but saw how serious it was by the lines that slashed down suddenly between his eyes. She'd felt the tension – had *seen* it, a dark web stretching over the room. She felt it everywhere today; the start of the summer holidays, that should have had a happy feel to it. The sunshine, the sandy shore and the picnic weren't changing the look on people's faces, or what they were saying. Mam had gone to wash Grandpa Owens' parlour curtains today, it being a good drying day. But she'd given them both a sudden hug along with a halfpenny each for sweets, and Hannah had seen trouble in her eyes. Mam's eyes were quite often not happy ... but today Hannah had seen fear.

"They couldn't hold out long, though, these Germans

and Austrians?'' one of the mothers asked now, passing the theology student an enamel mug of sweet steaming tea. He smiled reassurance with a dab of jam on his chin.

"I would think not, ma'am. And they may yet have drawn back, even at this eleventh hour, from taking the final step. So let us not give up hope.'' He beamed goodwill round the party and bit appreciatively into his *bara brith*.

Hannah didn't take her slice. She was certain, in a way she could not have explained, that there would be no turning back for anyone today. The same certainty drew her gaze back to the derelict *Amazon* along the beach. *They* were there, moving like trails of smoke over the wreck in the searching, restless way they had; shadows without substance in the sunlight. She was not afraid of them, funnily. But she *would* talk soon to Dada . . .

The slate-grey eyes so like her father's followed the skyline to the river mouth. The water lay flat and silver, pond-calm. But *now* she was afraid; her hands cold, her body stiffened with the fearsome power of memory. Joe gave her a nudge to whisper, could he have her *bara brith*. She looked up – looked through him; and the terror of the day Joe had been born welled up unbidden like vomit into her throat.

The night of the floods . . . the September when she was seven. That was the worst memory of her whole twelve years. Yet she never could work out *why* she had been so afraid. Everyone else had gone splashing around as usual but she had curled up behind the horsehair sofa on the cold lino of the parlour floor just praying for Dada to come home from work before the floods came under the door and she died of fear.

Hannah was pulled from her reverie by a thump from Joe, weary of getting no reply to his repeated request to go and dig a channel to the sea. She nodded absently, dazed by the clarity of her memories, and by a sense of impending ill. Silly, it was . . . she stood up and brushed the crumbs from her pinafore. And her a great girl of twelve, going up into Miss Probert's class next month. She gave herself a mental shake and helped gather up the plates, nut brown hair blowing across her face in the refreshing offshore wind.

There were games, after food. Cricket with a home-made bat, and quoits made of redundant rubber tubing. Some had brought their kites, and others stilts fashioned from driftwood. For Hannah, the day became increasingly burdened by the sense of foreboding, and twice she asked Florence's grandpa the time. She'd have felt better, she was sure, had Florence been here now, but she'd had to go with her Mam to see an aunt in Swansea. There was Dada though . . . his shift would finish soon and they could walk home with him. She was shaking sand from Joe's boots when a youth ran from the direction of Dock Street, shouting to them and waving his hands.

"War! It's war!"

Hannah laced up Joe's boots anyhow, grabbed Fly's lead and started for the steelworks. All might yet be well if she could reach Dada; he was the rock on which her world was built, no matter what madness was abroad.

"Han – ? What's the rush?" Joe tugged at her arm, struggling to keep up. "Bert Miles was going to give me a go on his stilts. An' Leonard's still got my best marble!"

"Sorry, can't help it." She headed straight for the short cut through the graving docks, banking on the dock police sergeant turning his usual blind eye. She and Joe often wandered here, fascinated by the noisy

13

life of the docks and adjacent steelworks, but now she kept up a fast trot – this was not a day for wandering.

"We'll get your marble back tomorrow, lovely. I need to catch Dada now . . . must be about his time."

They were past the throbbing hum of the hydraulic power houses. Joe dragged his feet when they reached the fuel works, demanding to watch the cubes of coal emerging on a conveyer belt behind a great mound of pitch. Not today she told him firmly, they might miss Dada. She heard the paper-boy's cry now, saw him waving the newest edition up by the tinplate works. Men eddied about him, snatching up papers. She could smell an urgency as strong as the smell of salt on the wind, as the smell of oil and rope and fish, and tangerines unloading from a Spanish vessel. It had come, the war, emerging from the gossip and speculation of weeks into dreadful reality. Waves of excitement were swirling down from the town, reaching Hannah as mixed shocks of pain and pleasure. She didn't understand that – surely war, for men, was all pain? Leaving people and places they loved, being cold, hungry, hurt and maybe dead? Men were proud to die for their country in a just cause, their headmaster had told them . . . But Dada would never want to; she felt certain of that. He wasn't a soldier though, praise be. He was a millman.

Hannah waved suddenly and called out, glimpsing the familiar figure leaving the gates in a knot of workmates. Smiling foolishly with relief, she grabbed Joe's hand and ran. Nothing could be so bad now she'd found Dada.

"Surprise, surprise." He bent and scooped up a child on either arm; a wiry man of average height, with light brown hair, grey eyes and a squared jawline. Joe knocked his cap awry but Thomas only grinned and

14

stuck it on top of the one already on his son's dark head. "An escort home, is it?"

"The *war*, Dada." Hannah whispered the word into his ear, it didn't seem right to say it aloud yet. "Did you know? The paper boy says it's a war."

"We got news in the mill, love." He set them down, no longer smiling, and they began to walk soberly, hands linked, towards the paper-boy.

Hannah and Joe watched while he read the headlines, eyes screwed up in concentration.

"I'm a soldier," said Joe, squinting along an imaginary gun barrel. "Bang! Got you!" Thomas didn't react in the usual way by clutching his chest and staggering around. He folded the newspaper and stuffed it into his pocket and Hannah, watching his face, was suddenly cold and hugged her arms across her body.

"Let's get home, eh?" Thomas started up the hill.

They'd moved from Water Street over the river to Taibach last year to rent a house on the terrace climbing up Incline Row, long coveted by Betsy. "Rain all it wants now, it can, no more balin' out for us, thank God," she'd said with a satisfied nod. That was not her only satisfaction. Incline Row was considered a step up from Water Street in every way. Outwardly the terraced cottages looked similar to other rows of workmen's homes, with front doors opening onto the pavement. But the two up, two down rooms were a few inches larger than the average, and those in Incline Row had a good sized scullery at the back. Number twelve was next to an entry; a passage which gave access to the door and small yard at the back of each house. It enjoyed the much prized bonus of a larger front bedroom, having the added space over the passage. Usually when such a house became vacant, the landlord or his agent would allow first refusal to the largest family among his

15

tenants so that the bigger bedroom could be divided. Betsy was envied the extra space for her small family. Some of the housewives of Incline Row thought it very unfair and were cool to Betsy as a result. Betsy insisted she cared not a jot and was cool back, enjoying her status, and kept her new home spotless.

Whilst only a good stone's throw distant from Water Street, the new house was higher, lighter, and very close to the paths leading onto the hill . . . and the newly built Eastern School was almost opposite. Looking down on railway sheds, ever fascinating docks, the steelworks, where Dada was, Hannah had felt safe in Number twelve Incline Row. Until now, when stricken with this unsafe day, she turned to Thomas for reassurance.

She examined his face again and it was bleak. No reassurance there. And if not from him, most certainly not from Mam.

"Dada?"

"Mmmm?"

"Where do all the soldiers live?" A silly question, when there were so many desperately important ones Hannah wanted to ask. But he was hurrying her, she couldn't think properly.

"Oh . . . all over."

"In houses?"

"Barracks. Then there's the Terriors – you've seen cousin Harry in his smart uniform?"

"So must Harry go to war?" Hannah sounded anxious; Harry was at the core of her life . . . always had been. He was a millman, too, anyway – only a Terrior in his spare time. That wouldn't count, would it?

"Shouldn't think they'd want youngsters like Harry, Princess." She had to be content with that; they'd reached home and Thomas was busy showing Betsy the paper and assuring her that it would all be over by

16

Christmas. Listening very carefully to his voice, Hannah still could not shift the sick lump of apprehension in her stomach. Dada did not believe what he was saying.

At dusk, the comings and goings of various relatives abated and, her evening chores done, Hannah came out on the cobbled pavement in front of the parlour window. Neighbours, standing about in shifting uneasy knots, were watching Territorials assemble at the corner before moving off to the drill hall to receive mobilisation orders. A woman began suddenly to cry in a quiet, hopeless way, leaning against the wall of her house with her face in her hands and for Hannah those tears crystalised the distress that had been building inside herself all day. The men forming into line on the corner seemed no more substantial in the fading light than had the shadows on the wrecked *Amazon;* their movements had taken on the same slow, dream-like pace, their khaki tunics were a colourless blur.

Hannah looked at her little house; seeking familiar reality in the blue parlour curtains, the aspidistra in the exact centre of the window as always. Her mother had gone to re-hang Grandad Owen's freshly-washed curtains but Joe was squatting on the pumiced doorstep, teasing Fly with a bit of string. Behind him, the parlour was a replica of the one in Water Street though slightly bigger, and had shiny new lino down in blue and fawn and a blue and brown hearthrug. And *there* – yes, now she saw her father, further down the street, talking with a big man whose bald head shone in the pool of light cast by the gas lamp.

Hannah ran, forgetful of not interrupting grown-ups' conversation. She threw her arms around him, pushing her face into the familiar smell of his old jacket.

"What's up then, *cariad*?" He put a steadying hand on

17

her shoulder. "Just asking Mister Maple if the Weston trip was still on for Saturday. Not goin' to let a bit of an old war spoil our treat, are we? 'Night then, Ellis, see you Saturday."

She whispered urgently as they walked back. "Dada? I want to talk . . . not for Mam or Joe to hear, though. It's secret."

He stopped, and Hannah knew this was the time to speak.

"Do *you* see the men on the wreck? You know, the *Amazon*? I see them, Dada . . . . quite often. No one else seems to."

"Go on," he encouraged as she faltered.

"They're not *quite* – not as real as *you* – " She put her hand flat on his jacket. "But they're *there*. They move around, only never leave the wreck. Joe says nothing about them, so I thought you might know if he sees them, too . . . or *you*?"

Thomas pulled at the hair behind his ear. Hannah waited. The sound of hammer blows on iron rang out from the smithy on High Street and, faintly, she smelt the fumes of red-hot metal being plunged into water. Caradoc Hunt wheeled his chipped-potato cart out of the street above, his peg leg thumping on the cobbles.

"Most likely Joe doesn't see the men, *cariad*," Thomas said finally. "Nor do I. You're special; that's what it is."

"How, Dada?" She felt half relieved and half nervous – but at least he *knew* about it now.

"I can't say why, Princess, but I know it can run in families. Second sight, it's called. Long ago, people who had it were called wise men, or soothsayers – an' ordinary folk were a bit afraid of 'em. The women were likely thought to be witches, an' got themselves a load of trouble!"

Hannah digested this, standing under the evening

18

sky with Dada. "Now I'll tell you something," went on Thomas. "My own Granma – old *Nain* Hywel up in Cwmavon – well, she's the gift, too, though you'll not hear it much talked of. Mam always seemed a bit put out by it as I recall. But my *Nain*, she'd the magic in her hands, too." He stopped, eyes full of memories. Hannah waited, intent.

"Used to ease off my toothache, did *Nain*. And when I fell out of a tree and sprained my wrist, she just held it, easy, with those soft hands. And soon the pain seemed to melt away." He smiled down at his daughter. "Would you credit that? Tell you what; we'll visit her, Sunday. High time we did. But she's been poorly, not well enough for visitors. She's old, Princess, nearing ninety. She'll die soon, will *Nain*," He added softly. "Lovely, she was, my *Nain* . . . On the go every minute. But always with time for us little ones."

They stood for a moment in companionable silence, united by their love for *Nain*, who could work magic. Then their noses were assailed by the hot, fragrant chips in Caradoc Hunt's approaching cart and the moment of intimacy was gone. But Hannah was content. She'd told Dada; and he'd said it was all right for her to see the men on the wreck. She began to feel pleased, being like *Nain* Hywel. Thomas pulled coppers from his pocket. "Here love, get us a penn'orth each – four bags, here's your Mam comin' back. Plenty of vinegar, mind."

The Taibach Temperance Brass Band came into earshot along the High Street playing a rousing march, and running to the chip cart Hannah was reminded again that a war had begun. But maybe *that* wouldn't turn out to be as bad as she had imagined either; the evening was taking on an air of celebration. The band was being cheered, she could hear singing, and a group of young men came down the street with linked arms, laughing, one with a Union Jack stuck in his cap. Even Mam didn't seem as worried as she had been earlier, taking her chips from Hannah and dipping into them at once.

"You'd not believe the goings on, Thomas! Queues, waitin' to enlist at the drill hall! And the Yeomanry, been ridin' up and down Aberavan – an' they've put up a marquee in Margam Park according to Mollie Roberts, for volunteers. And a special service at St Mary's – there, hear the bells?" Betsy put up a hand, her face flushed with momentous happenings which had over-ridden her fear.

"Young Harry's full of it, too, I bumped into him comin' out of choir practice an' he can't wait to get to France to have a crack before it all fizzles out. Half the choir's off there too if you're to believe 'em! Joe Hywel, you give one more chip to that blessed dog an' I'll – "

She raised her hand. But her son smiled and ran inside, followed by the ever hopeful Fly. Hannah, watching, knew that Betsy rarely carried out her threats to Joe. If only she didn't so often try to lay his misdemeanours at Hannah's door. She mustn't mind that, though, Thomas had told Hannah – she wasn't to take it to heart, Mam never really believed bad of her. She was only sharp because she still pined for baby Hughie, losing him had been a bitter sadness. And with little Arthur gone, too, likely she fretted that something might happen to Joe. Make her a bit soft with him at times, that, wouldn't it?

Hannah had nodded to please him and Thomas had given her a hug, saying she was his best girl. Actually, she *did* mind though; she quite hated being blamed by Mam for things she'd not done. But she'd gradually come to face that Joe was Mam's favourite, and that was that. His good luck for being a boy . . . it could only be that Mam must rate boys easier to love than girls, even though she could be sharp with Joe, too. No use worrying Dada about it, though.

Well past her usual bedtime, she climbed over Joe to her own side of the bed against the wall in the back room. There were still lots of people in the streets and more bells pealing. Joe was well away, yet tired though she was Hannah stayed obstinately wakeful, her mind full of the day's happenings. She heard the street door open and picked up a voice – Harry's. Lovely he'd been in his uniform, marching back from Terrior's camp last week so slim and smart with his gold hair, bright blue eyes and wide smile . . . then Hannah recalled a print of the Battle of Waterloo hung in the school hall, littered with bloodstained dead, and turned restlessly in the feather mattress.

She tried to think of something other than war, staring round the square little room with fawn trellised wallpaper and a green painted door with two hooks that closed at the top but not so well at the bottom. Saturday's boat trip to Weston-Super-Mare . . . well, that wasn't altogether good news. Dada had arranged for a full day out, two and sixpence for adults and children half-price, in a steamer with a big red funnel and rows of slatted seats on the deck. Their summer holiday treat, the money mounting slowly through the year in the blue toffee tin on the mantel. But Hannah knew Dada also meant it as a test of her courage, now she was twelve; her first time out to sea. Terrifying – but she *would* go. No one would call Hannah Hywel a coward. She could only hope that Dada was right; that it *would* conquer her fear once and for all.

Sunday was better, that would be lovely. A two-mile walk up the Avan valley to Cwmavon to see *Nain* Hywel. Cheeks like pink tissue paper, palest blue eyes, and a pink scalp through silver hair. A lovely voice had *Nain* Hywel, soft and wavy. *She* would understand about the shadows on the *Amazon*, Dada reckoned . . . maybe there'd be a chance to talk about it. Oh, it was hopeless – she couldn't get even *near* sleepy!

Suddenly she wriggled out over her slumbering brother and tiptoed across the boards. It *was* Harry. Hannah stood for a long time on the top stair, trying to find an excuse to go down, to join the warmth and the comfort of the family below. Only when she acknowledged the impossibility of facing visitors – even close family like Harry – in her cotton shift did she return reluctantly to her room. As she climbed back into bed the stair door opened and her mother's voice called sharply.

"Is one of you out of bed up there?"

Hannah didn't answer, curling in a ball with her back against the peacefully puffing Joe and closing her eyes tight. The door shut without further investigation; gradually she relaxed, drifting towards oblivion.

When light shot across her eyes she moaned sleepily, turning from it.

"Han! *Hannah*!"

Joe's voice held a note of terror that had her fully awake now. He pummelled her shoulder in a desperate tattoo as the shooting light became flames. Scrambling up, Hannah saw them licking over the rag mat, with the nightlight that stood on the chair in case Joe needed to use the pot, overturned on it.

Grabbing the wailing little boy, she pushed him down the bed.

"Quick, get *down* . . . come *on*!"

As he stood up to climb over the brass footrail his foot caught in his nightshirt. He teetered on the billowy mattress, overbalanced, toppled to the floor by the burning rug and in an instant flames fastened on the winceyette nightshirt.

Hannah dived for him. She hauled him back onto the bed, rolled his flailing body in the cotton coverlet and heaved the entire bundle over the footrail. Flames climbed the sheet as she did; she scrabbled after him, landing heavily on the floorboards. Her foot twisted under her and she yelled with pain, threw out a hand that was at once seared with hot agony.

"Christ almighty!"

Thomas loomed in the doorway, with Betsy peering over his shoulder. As her mouth formed a horror-struck round, Thomas shoved his candle into her hand.

"Water – *run* . . ."

He grabbed the chair and with its legs pushed the blazing rug toward the window. Hannah, patting hard at the struggling mound of counterpane that was Joe, could only watch as her father threw up the sash, fished the rug up and over the sill. The draught fanned the ignited bedclothes and he dropped the chair to pick up his son and make for the door.

"C'm on, Han, quick!"

Hannah hauled herself to her feet and limped after him, scooping up her frock and pinny and Joe's bundle of clothes off the footrail as she went.

From then, nightmare and reality became tangled. She stood barefoot on the pavement, clutching her unbuttoned dress bodice across her chest with a shaking hand. The skin across the back of her other hand had been burned by Joe's nightshirt and the pain from it flooded over her, worse than the throbbing ankle. Joe had been carried down the road to Auntie Maggie's still wrapped in the bedcover and Thomas led the line of neighbours passing buckets of water up from the standpipe. No one spoke to Hannah. She began to whimper with reaction and cold.

Then she turned, for someone had come to stand by her. Hannah saw her clearly in the gaslight, the lilac ribbon in her hair, the dimple in her cheek when she smiled. The calm simplicity in her eyes acted as balm to Hannah's turmoil, causing her to smile back. It was her friend. Five years ago . . . the night Joe had been born had been the last time. No time at all now it seemed, and how lovely that she'd come back. Her hand seemed easier already.

After a moment the girl smiled again, then was lost to sight as someone pushed past calling that the fire engine was coming. Hannah looked about her, up and down the street, but the girl was gone.

For a few seconds, past and present whirled together like the smoke whirling from her bedroom window. Dizzy, she clutched the lamppost for support as the fire engine swerved up Incline Row at a furious pace, the great dappled horses snorting and throwing up their heads. Yet straightening again, new strength seemed to seep through her tired body. That *was* her friend. She'd made her feel better that terrible night of the floods – taken away her fear; as now. Nothing seemed quite so bad.

The fire was contained in the bedroom and was quickly under control. Betsy rocked in silent grief, surveying her damp and smoke-grimed domain and Thomas, grey-faced, dropped on his bed for a couple of hour's sleep before starting his early shift – he couldn't afford a day docked from his wages, that was for certain. His sister, Maggie, made them all strong sweet tea, then took a look at Hannah, her handsome dark-grey eyes kind. She was a generous-hearted woman, quick to offer help and not known to bear a grudge. It

24

was a sore point with her that she could not get on terms as close as she would like with Betsy, but accepted that her sister-in-law tended to be "a close one".

"Come and bed down with our Daisy and Em, *cariad*, you look done up. Betsy, you get rested too now, we'll sort this lot out tomorrow."

Betsy turned suddenly on Hannah, pointing a quivering finger.

"And whose fault is all this?"

Shaken, Hannah stared at her. Her mother's dark eyes, circled now with khaki rings of exhaustion, bore into her own with accusing fury. "Don't play the innocent with me, miss, you were out of your bed. I heard you! *You* knocked the light over – all but killed your brother! And wrecked my house! A wicked girl you are and there will be retribution for you!" She sat down as though the bones of her legs had suddenly melted.

"Betsy, that's not fair, girl!" Aunt Maggie protested, shaking her head with its tight brown braid. "Leave it now, for heaven's sake, you'll see it different after a rest. Harry, *bach*, take your cousin to our place to bed down with Daisy and Em, eh?"

Hannah stood mute, staring at her mother with eyes like black holes in her blanched face. *Joe* had done it. He *had* used the pot, she'd seen it. He *must* have knocked the nightlight over. But she made no effort to defend herself against Betsy's tirade – she'd never told on Joe yet and had no mind to start now. What point anyhow, with Mam set on thinking the worst of her as usual?

Yet now a sudden, dreadful, unfamiliar anger flooded without warning into her throat, bitter as bile. It seeped through every tissue and nerve like poison, so alien that she could not recognise herself. The fury was not even directed against her mother, but boiled inside her with no obvious aim or outlet.

"Come on, Han," Harry spoke kindly. Chin at a defiant tilt, Hannah left the house, spears of pain piercing her ankle at each step. The burned hand, too, was making her feel ill ... But worse by far was this consuming anger that held terror in its depths. What was *happening* to her? Where was Hannah Hywel? Who else could be inside her, causing her to feel as *she*, the real her, never would?

She shivered under the gas-lamp. Then remembered the girl, her friend, and the fury and the confusion ebbed further, leaving her drained and very, very tired; more tired than she had ever thought possible.

Harry motioned to her. "Let's go down to Mam's, Han, you're asleep on your feet."

He reached to give her hand a friendly tug – her burned one. Hannah cried out; the street rocked about her, the gas-lamp wavered and seemed to crash on her. Harry's voice faded as she slid to the pavement in a fog of pain and dimly she thought she saw again the face of the girl, smiling.

But now, behind the fair head, she glimpsed another face, framed in the front doorway of her house. The features were indistinct in the pale oval face, which was framed by a cloud of black hair blowing wildly in the night.

Chapter Two

December 1914

Thomas Hywel spat on the floor, bending over the water pipe in a corner of the Light Plate Mill to ladle a palmful into his mouth. He was usually deaf to the racket about him with eleven years in the steelworks. But now he shook his head, trying to clear it of the din. The thundering of the great rolls, the hiss of water on hot metal, the loading instructions yelled by the Durham foreman, huge red fist cupping his mouth... today it all split his very brain apart.

He took a second slurp and wiped his mouth on his grey flannel shirt, catching the foreman's glance but refusing to hurry himself. Damn Durhamite, roaring away in his heathen tongue, another northerner brought in to lord it over good Welshmen. Rubbing his aching temples he walked back past the slab reheating furnaces to where his mate Sam Warburton was adjusting down the spray over the rollers, lips pursed in a soundless whistle.

"End of shift any minute, eh?"

Thomas nodded, squinting at the bright glint of spray hitting steel. Ten hours they'd slaved to get a load of ships' plating out for departure on the evening tide to Birkenhead. After feverish activity the consignment had just left the rollers for the shearing men, still to be marked, tested and loaded. There'd be a fight to the last minute, but he was done with his part, and emptied by the effort.

27

Sam Warburton nudged him, mopping at his broad face and impressive moustachios with his sweatrag.

"Comin' to choir practice tonight, man?"

Thomas shook his head. "Doubtful."

He gave the plating his full attention as it shunted back and forth between the massive rollers. The job of rollerman was demanding and dangerous, a man needed his wits about him every minute. He had dreams of making furnaceman one day, the highest paid job in the steelworks, but Sam chaffed him that he'd not the toughness for that pinnacle of ambition. Rawboned northerners or brawny Cornishmen like himself made true furnacemen, not your titchy home-bred Welshmen. But Thomas's sinewy hands wielded the rollerman's tongs with deft expertise – he knew ham fists weren't the full measure of a man. For now, he was grateful for his steady thirty-three shillings a week. At least he wasn't crawling underground on his belly for far less, like his father all those years in Morfa colliery, or buried deep and never found like his brother. Nor yet was he facing Hun machine guns in the freezing mud of France. Thomas counted himself lucky. All he asked was for a wage to see his family right, and a bit of peace of a Sunday to set him up for another week. Having that, he was content.

The end of shift whistle shrieked at last. He was among the first out, cap pulled down and jacket collar up as he picked his way over the soggy morfa towards Incline Row. Young Harry's last night – the battery was off to France tomorrow with a sizeable batch of local men. Over by Christmas, they'd said early on. Well, Christmas next week; and no more talk of an early end. Not after Mons and the Marne ... Not after Ypres and the old British Army cut to bits. Now, trenches ran from Switzerland to the Belgian coast. There'd been a free map in the paper and he'd pinned it on the kitchen wall, sticking in the coloured pins to show where the troops were.

Dead in the cold ground; that's where they were in their tens of thousands. And lads like Harry and Glyn, trombonist with Taibach Temperance Brass Band, and young Evan the best prop forward in Aber's rugger side for a decade – all this lot just down from their training in Shropshire – they were next.

He couldn't go of course Betsy would say, time and again, as if to convince herself. Not Thomas. But who could say where it would end? Who would go? Who would come back?

Ministry of Munitions . . . sounded important. He tried out the words in his head, taking the short cut over the rail tracks. Last week the railway taken over. Now the works. And this new Ministry of Munitions demanded steel and more steel – for shells, ships, bullets, bayonets. Betsy played this fact like a trump card at the least mention of recruitment. Couldn't win the war without steel, could they? Wouldn't get far throwing stones at the Hun? No, rollermen must stay put and make steel, nothing more certain. She would dare him to contradict; but Thomas would hold his peace, sidestepping for now. Time enough . . . always a great one for security, Betsy.

She was boiling the Christmas pudding, the spicy warm smell all-pervading. Should have been done long since she'd grumbled, assembling ingredients that morning whilst her family watched over the porridge bowls. An accusing stare at Hannah who'd tucked her feet in their controversial new boots under her stool and bolted her breakfast to escape Betsy's anger, for the new boots had delayed the buying of dried fruit for the pudding. The old ones had been rubbing Hannah's chilblains raw and Thomas had found her in tears one morning as she forced them on. He'd put a quick end to her misery, ordering new ones himself from Jones-the-Boot despite Betsy's protestations that it was a fuss over nothing.

"Keeps on growin' like this you'll be after a bigger house for her next. And hang out that wash 'fore you disappear, miss."

Hannah had directed a mutinous stare at her mother's back, caught the warning in Thomas's eye, and humped the basketful of clothes out to the yard's gloomy half light. Anything to make her late for school, she knew she was only there on sufferance.

Betsy had been put out to service at twelve years and saw no reason to spoil her daughter with useless education when she could earn her keep. Thomas was at present insisting Hannah got her chance in the top grade. Grateful, Hannah was stowing learning like an industrious squirrel, wits sharpened by the fear that father could lose – or give up – the battle for her schooling at any time. That would leave her to settle for a lowly position in one of the town's wealthier households; or worse, on a hill farm with further to walk home and back on her half-day than there'd be hours for.

She knew she'd no right to hope for more; yet hope she did. The world was big and strange, full of mystery – she felt its excitement like a thudding deep in her head when she thought about it. It seemed to be a box of treasure to which she must, *must* find the key. She had no idea, not the vaguest, about what she *should* do ever given a choice; was only certain that housemaiding would not be it. With this special thing she had, this sixth sense Dada called it, maybe she could *do* something just a bit special, too, in spite of her Mam being so certain she couldn't.

Hannah was cutting bread for tea, the burn scar on her right hand still vivid, when her father came in. She looked up to offer the slow wide smile, warming as the glowing coals in the grate. It revealed the chipped front tooth, souvenir of a fracas last month with a youth who'd tied a kitten to the rail track. It gave her a sweet vulnerability in Thomas's eyes, though Betsy would insist it had ruined any chance of her turning out respectable looking. Made thus conscious of it, Hannah would smile with her lips tight shut, or head down, until she would forget again. To her, the chipped tooth was just another of life's crosses, along with her summer freckles, the breasts that were defining themselves slowly but relentlessly under her bodice and Anwen Stokes who sat in front of her in school and had nits. Hannah would stare at the back of Anwen's head in horrified fascination, identifying tiny white eggs in the lank hair. Anwen had been given a note from the visiting nit nurse to take home – the deepest shame. Hannah would itch all over, imagine lice jumping across the desk to infest *her* . . . whatever would Mam say if *she* got a nit note?

For the biggest cross in Hannah's life – though she would confide it to no one – was her mother's antagonism, or at best indifference. It was worse since the fire. Nothing would convince Betsy that all the mess and expense was not her daughter's fault. Hannah's refusal to defend herself seemed only to outrage, as had Thomas's arguing. And since Betsy took care not to bring up the subject of the fire before Joe, he had no idea of the injustice. Apart from a couple of nightmares he seemed to have put the event behind him, the trauma of

31

his first term at school entirely taking over his small world.

"Smells a treat." Thomas nodded at the range, rubbing cold hands together before tweaking Joe's ear, who had his collection of coloured pebbles set out on the table corner. Hannah dropped the bread knife to help ease off his heavy jacket, hanging it with care on the door hook. She loved the small ritual; the familiar smell of the garment that had for years meant that he was home. Her friend Florence's father had died last winter of consumption; shocked, Hannah had been forced to contemplate life without hers, but the loss was too huge for her young mind to encompass. She had behaved as well as she possibly could for as long as she was able, to propitiate a vengeful God who might have designs on Thomas – had shadowed him for months, anxious-eyed, as though personal vigilance might prevent such a disaster falling upon Number twelve Incline Row. Time had eased her fear; but Thomas's hand on the door latch remained the high spot of her day.

He lowered himself into his chair with a grunt of satisfaction. Betsy poured tea from the brown pot on the hob and pushed the mug across the table before turning back to tend a pan of sizzling herrings. Her own face was sharply drawn in the fireglow ... high-domed forehead, a classic nose, with deep-lidded watchful eyes. Betsy had been the prettiest of the four Owens sisters; the prettiest girl in Aberavan in Thomas's opinion. When she had accepted his proposal and those soft little shoulders, that tiny waist and deliciously curving hips had become his, he had vowed always to do his utmost for Betsy. He had been unable to prevent the death of her babies but had been endlessly gentle, patient as her tongue and her sweet contours had

32

sharpened, the mouth tightened and the pretty shoulders muscled up with hard labour. The thick dark hair, dressed in becoming waves and coils in their courting days was screwed away now into a knot and she brushed impatiently at loose strands, turning the fish in the spitting lard with a practised flick.

"That's enough bread," she flung over her shoulder at Hannah. "We're not feeding the army. Joe, I shan't tell you again – clear off those stones, *now*."

Betsy was tired, too; bone-weary as Thomas after her day at the tinplate works. She'd been there a month, with women urged by the government to help supply their fighting men with the weapons of war. Not that Betsy felt any necessity to do her bit; this war was no doing of hers, let them get on with it! But the chance to earn money did appeal; she could not forget that cash in hand for a doctor at the critical time might have saved the lives of her infant sons. Money could buy anything. If she could earn just a bit they could put it by for emergencies she argued when Thomas had insisted he did not want his wife labouring at the Vaughan's place.

She had won, with the government behind her and several neighbours and two sisters already at Vaughan Tinplate. It was one of the better of several tinplate factories in the district in which to work. Mr Vaughan, who lived with his wife and two sons in a big house on Baglan Road, had actually had a privy built for women. But it was hard graft, standing all day in thick leather gloves and apron separating sheets of steel. Her hands and arms were sore enough to weep over by a Saturday. But Betsy did not weep or Thomas might make her give up, so she snapped instead, and was freer with a slap on Hannah's legs to relieve her feelings. Thomas did his best to act as buffer. But pressure was on him, too, with the works expanding to meet the needs of war – six new furnaces built and the coal hoists clanging twenty-four hours a day. He took to falling asleep in his chair after supper, sometimes only waking in time to wind the big-faced clock on the mantel and trudge upstairs to the cold bedroom, counting the days to Sunday and his half-hour lie-in.

Harry's imminent departure to France had charged the air in the little house with tension; war menaced the family personally for the first time. Eldest son of Thomas' sister, Maggie, Harry was a lad to stand out in a crowd, adored by Hannah and feared just enough to add a shivery zest to his aura which was, for her, golden as his thick bright hair. The hint of fear dated from a year ago, a hazy day in autumn. But how *could* she have seen . . . *that*, when Harry was the next moment turning to laugh at her, standing hale and wholesome on the valley footpath under birch leaves bright as his hair? How *could* she have glimpsed him for one frozen second of time like – *that*?

She jumped, knocking together the plates she was setting out, when with the rattle of the door-latch he was suddenly there. And the smell of fear faded, and with it the vision of blood overlaying the golden hair, the lean body melting broken into the mud. Harry was fine, Harry was *here*, in his new uniform, warm and glowing with life and she loved him terribly.

"Harry!" Flooded with relief Hannah flew at him, rough khaki cloth chafing the cheek pressed into his chest. He laughed, pretending to stagger under the eager onslaught.

"Act your age, girl, do!" Betsy rounded on her. "Make yourself useful and get out another plate – you'll have a bite now, Harry *bach*?" She smiled, as fond of him as was the rest of the family. He shook his head, giving

Hannah's shoulder a quick squeeze as she backed off, discomforted by the reprimand.

"Thanks, Auntie, but Mam's got tea waiting – my favourite, faggots. Last supper of the condemned man, see?" His grin took the sting from the words; he winked at Joe, who gazed admiringly at the closest he'd yet come to an actual soldier here in the house. "She says will you all come round in a bit – okay?"

"Sure, laddo." Thomas' voice was heavy as he accepted the plate of herrings held out by Betsy and sat down by Joe. The first departure of many . . . And when Harry had gone, the silence he left was heavy, too. Hannah felt it like a cold grey veil, and was no longer hungry.

She drank Harry's health with lemonade, the glass shared with Harry's sister, Emily. This set of cousins, Aunt Maggie and Uncle Idwal's five, were closest to Hannah not only because they lived at the bottom of Incline Row but because her father and his sister Maggie had always been especially close. Harry was nineteen; then came plump, easy-going Daisy, seventeen, then sharp, pretty Emily, born two years later. Next was Frank, now ten, always ready for an argument, and the youngest was Trevor, aged seven and young Joe's playmate. They were all crammed into Aunt Maggie's two downstairs rooms, the usual tomb-like chill of the parlour warmed now by the body heat of numerous relations. The grownups had beer fetched up from the Lamb and Flag in jugs decently covered with a tea-cloth, but myriad young cousins were relegated to Aunt Maggie's tart, flat lemonade and the kitchen cups.

Hannah had been inching her way towards Harry when his sister had pinned her against the wall. Two years Hannah's senior, Emily was clever. She'd won a scholarship to the Girls' High School last year – the summit of Hannah's own ambition – and never lost a chance to impress upon her cousin the superiority of her position.

"So, Miss Yates says I should get to teacher training college if I keep up my good reports." Emily gave her hair ribbon a satisfied pat and Hannah had an urge to pull it off the smooth brown tresses. To be a teacher – what dizzier heights could a girl attain? Even Mam would have to love her if she could bring such prestige to Number twelve Incline Row.

"I think that's boring, shut up with a bunch of snotty-nosed kids." She tossed off the last of her lemonade. "I shall do something *much* more exciting when *I* grow up."

"What?" Emily was reluctant to be taken in by the conviction with which Hannah made her pronouncement. But Hannah had already begun to elbow her way to where Harry was laughing at his Aunt Cissy, Uncle Jenkin's wife from Cwmavon, who'd perched his army cap over her carroty frizz and was offering him a cheeky salute.

"Harry . . ." She tugged at his sleeve, beckoned for him to bend so she might whisper.

"Will you come outside a minute? It's a secret . . ."

He raised an eyebrow, his fresh skin flushed with heat and excitment and beer. But something in the anxious face caused the flippant retort to fade before it left his lips and he guided her before him through the crush and into the back yard.

The cold hit Hannah like a blow after the fug indoors. The moon was full and Margam mountain reared black against silver, with ash tree twigs intricate as lace over scudding clouds. Their breath fogged in the sharp air to drift off like minature clouds towards the back fence;

Hannah shivered and her cousin rubbed her shoulder with brisk affection.

"So, out with it, Princess, or we'll freeze solid. Goin' to tell me where to find the Kaiser are you? A nice bullet between the eyes'd be just the Christmas present he needs."

She giggled, then rummaged in her pocket, shaking with excitement and cold. The package she held out was small, the brown paper liberally glued.

"I'd got this for you for Christmas."

He took it, weighed it in his palm, frowning. "Hmm . . . I know, a bar of soap to wash my mouth out when I cuss at them bloody Huns."

Hannah giggled again. "Wrong. It's chocolate . . . but you're not to have it 'til Christmas Day. After dinner, then I'll think of you eating it."

"That's lovely, *cariad*. Can I peep? Bet it's my favourite."

She watched him unwrap the bar with a smile of anticipation, for of course it was his favourite, milk chocolate with brazil nuts. She'd saved hard, it was the dearest sort; but worth it to see his pleasure. He bent, and for a magic second Hannah felt his lips against her cheek. Her arms were suddenly tight about his neck and she was clinging desperately; to life as she had known it, to life as it might never be again.

The moment was gone. Harry stuffed the chocolate into his breast pocket, blue eyes reflecting the frosty moonlight. "Do something for me will you, Han?"

She nodded, speechless with desire to do the hardest, biggest thing imaginable for Harry; to show him how she loved him.

"Brigid Davies." He paused, lit a cigarette. Hannah watched the smoke spiral past his bright hair, holding her breath. Let it be a really big thing.

37

"Will you write to me, Han? And – well, if you see Brigid about, maybe you'd let me know how she's gettin' on? She said she'll write, but I don't reckon she's much on letters."

Hannah felt as if she'd been trodden into the cold mud of the yard. Harry was sweet on Brigid Davies. Stupid of her not to have thought. He was going on nineteen; a man, off to fight in the war. *She* wasn't anywhere near old enough for – for –. He'd be married to someone else before she was old enough to – to –.

Swallowing painfully she smiled, really cold now. Lonely-cold. Brigid Davies was certainly good-looking with that red hair and big brown eyes. But . . . well, she was always walking out with a new boy . . .

He pushed open the back door, relieved. "Want a sip of my beer? Long as your Mam doesn't catch me, eh?"

The station was packed with well-wishers come to see the troop train pull out. Small children wove about the railings or perched on parents' shoulders, waving flags, calling and laughing, hands and noses red in the searching wind. But gradually they fell silent as a growing tension dampened slightly hysterical jollity. Standing on a slatted bench, Hannah could feel an undercurrent of bewildered anger driving in waves across the biting damp air, for today had come news that had shocked more deeply than the worst report from the Front. German cruisers had crossed the North Sea and shelled the English coast. At Scarborough, a girl cleaning her doorstep had been killed, one of almost a hundred and fifty, with hundreds more injured, their homes ripped cruelly apart. The war was no longer something happening somewhere else. It had arrived with unimagined ferocity on Britain's doorstep and the island was deeply shocked.

The great engine huffed and belched, almost ready. From every window blossomed posies of faces under khaki caps . . . smiles, determined last minute jokes and quips, promises to write. A contingent of Belgian refugee women and children billeted in Aberavan had brought baskets of food for the soldiers, fresh baked rolls filled with butter and cheese. They huddled together now with haunted faces, remembering the rape of their own land.

Hannah fixed her eyes on Harry. He'd kissed his mother, shaken hands with his father, and now stood with head poked from the carriage window, scanning the platform. She knew he was looking for Brigid Davies.

It started to rain without warning, hard and cold as chips of ice on the sea wind. Hannah still did not move. She was holding her breath, willing Harry to say something – anything – to her. Instead she was struck by a blow on the arm that toppled her headlong from the bench. She fell hard against a big man, who glared at her as she pulled herself to her feet again.

"Ruddy kids! No time for playin' around, this ain't."

"I wasn't playing around," flashed Hannah with an indignant face. She turned to confront a smartly dressed youth by the bench who was putting up a big black umbrella.

"You hit me with that." Her voice was stern.

"Sorry . . . You can come under it if you want."

They regarded one another; he from the shelter of his umbrella, Hannah with rain now channelling rivulets down her hair to run with an unpleasant chill down her neck. He was perhaps seventeen; face long and lantern-jawed with cropped, dark auburn curls well clear of high temples, brows straight and heavy over brilliant deepset eyes, cheekbones sharply angled, nose jutting from a narrow bridge, a long mouth with a cupid's bow. An arresting face; one that she would study longer but for it being bad manners to stare.

She knew him. Well, no, she knew who he *was* ... David Vaughan, eldest son of Vaughan Tinplate. Of course she didn't *know* him, how could you *know* someone of such a different class? But Mam worked at Vaughan Tinplate so Hannah heard occasional bits of gossip about the family. A story was circulating that he'd been thrown out of his expensive school, sent home in disgrace. Hannah's gaze became more interested. Then, louder huffs and hoots from the engine. Shaking her head in reply to the offer, she climbed back on the bench for a last view of Harry.

He was still searching for Brigid. He saw her as the train prepared to move amid a surge of waving arms and flags. Brigid had pushed through the station entrance and stood on tiptoe to see the train, the rich red hair an easy target. Harry leaned further out; his cap fell onto the platform just as the wheels began to roll, but an onlooker scooped it up and shoved it back into his fingers. Hannah's own hand came up in farewell. As his carriage drew level their eyes locked for a second ... the man on his way to war, the child left behind. Goodbye. Goodbye.

Then he was gone. Hannah's lips clamped shut, swallowing on her tears. Brigid Davies turned and left the station, a tall, full-breasted girl with creamy skin and treacle toffee eyes, and instinctively Hannah wanted to follow her, talk to her about Harry, to keep his presence vivid though he was lost to sight. But she had to get to school if she was not to be made to stand out at the front of assembly as a latecomer and have the ruler across her hand. And Brigid was clearly working by her outfit. *That* had recently created a stir; even

Hannah had heard about that, when Brigid had left her job as housemaid to Prys the baker and taken on Ted Conwy's milk round. Older folk had been scandalised by her uniform, no different from Ted's crisp white cotton coat and trousers, yes *trousers*, of brown corduroy tucked into leather gaiters. But it was starting to happen everywhere as women released men to enlist; Hannah's Auntie Lil said she'd seen a lady *coalman* in Swansea last week.

Hannah got down from the bench. The Vaughan boy had moved off to talk to a friend; she thought it would have been good manners to ask if she was hurt, but it could scarcely be expected that the heir to Vaughan Tinplate be interested in her welfare. As she passed him she took a good look; he certainly did have an interesting face. He caught her eye, lifted his cap. "Sorry about the brolly again. No lasting damage I hope?" His tone was easy, with an edge of banter that matched the quizzical lift of eyebrow and irritated Hannah, nerves taut from Harry's departure.

She gave him a level-eyed inspection. She may well be wearing her brown school coat and her fawn tammy was certainly a hand-me-down from Aunt Rose; but smart clothes did not necessarily – she was learning fast – make smart people. And did posh David Vaughan have second sight?

"No damage at all, thank you." Only to her pride and he would certainly not count that. Hannah gave David Vaughan what she hoped was a dignified nod and walked on fast, not looking back.

Easing her way through the crowd straggling from the station, she headed for school. She'd find Brigid on Saturday and introduce herself. She wouldn't enjoy it one bit, but it was what Harry wanted. In her imagination she tried to follow him on his journey ... to

London, down to the coast, across the Channel. And then? But Hannah could not part that veil, try as she would – she'd never been further than Porthcawl and shrank from the thought of the expanse of water he must cross. But she *could* write . . . and would when she'd talked to Brigid.

That first Christmas was best over. No shortage of food, yet, but seasonal treats would lose appeal when the telegraph boy was cycling through the streets with his orange envelopes, and every day more windows would show black ribbon wreathing the photograph of a young man in uniform. No word yet from Harry, of course . . . early days as Aunt Maggie would say with brisk good sense, and the family would nod agreement.

Everyone living near enough went to Granny Hywel's in Crown Street, between Incline Row and the river, for Christmas dinner. Nineteen sat down, grown-ups at two tables pushed together, children squashed round a card table borrowed from the Walnut Tree Hotel where Aunt Maggie did a bit of cleaning. The children were officially the under-fourteens; Hannah and her cousin Bella were the seniors here, and the smallest was Joe who, with Aunt Maggie's youngest, Trevor, was making enough noise for six. There was a goose sent from Cwmavon by Thomas's and Maggie's younger brother, Jenkin, who had a smallholding. It was served on a vast oval dish with a blue and gold rim, encircled with crunchy glistening brown potatoes and parsnips and stuffed with forcemeat, which Hannah preferred to the rich, fatty meat. The children were served last, but knowing their preferences, Granny Hywel would unobtrusively save them crispy bits of outside meat, over which she poured an unbelievably rich gravy thick with fragments of mashed up goose liver.

The Brussels sprouts were not popular with the card table contingent but they were chewed and swallowed with resigned stoicism, for only via the Brussels sprouts could they attain the nirvana of the brandy pudding with it's chance of a silver threepenny bit . . . almost a certainty really, for Granny Hywel had an unerring knack of fiddling one of these on to each child's plate. She saved them over the twelvemonth in a screw of paper in the top drawer of her chiffonnier, and on Christmas Eve would boil them up in her egg saucepan then rub them clean and shiny with a soft cloth. From one Christmas Day dinner to the next Hannah would remember the sensual joy of the hard thin disc against her teeth, and her tongue carefully removed every vestige of sticky sweet pudding from it before she would hold it up between thumb and forefinger with a smile of triumph. Her ninth Christmas, Hannah had been practically certain that Emily had stolen her threepenny bit off the table by her plate. Unable to prove it, and threepence-less, the loss had blighted the rest of the day.

This year Emily had joined the grownups being now fourteen, along with her sister Daisy and sixteen year-old Dewi, Aunt Lil's eldest. But you must be eighteen for the splash of whisky in the after dinner cup of tea, dispensed by Granny Hywel from an imposing copper urn, and Harry was the only cousin who had attained that great age. The urn looked to Hannah to be unbelievably dangerous but Granny Hywel operated it with unerring precision so that no splash of the scalding liquid marked the embroidered cloth with the hand-crocheted border, made by and inherited from her mother, great-grandma Hywel, known throughout the family now as *Nain*.

She was not at the table with them, nor had been for three years now. She was fading fast and had not left her bed for some weeks. In twos and threes the family went up to Uncle Jenkin's place at Cwmavon, where *Nain* had lived these three dozen years since being widowed, to pay their Christmas respects, very quiet so as not to tire her. Hannah went on Boxing Day afternoon with Thomas and his mother. She wore her Christmas gifts, a red knitted tammy and scarf which had delighted her. Snow was threatening as they wound along the valley road, purple clouds burgeoning over the mountains to dull the glow of dead bracken, the glint of little streams. She was glad to be outdoors after yesterday, crammed into her grandmother's parlour with tobacco smoke making her eyes smart. It hadn't really compensated for the balloon (quickly burst) or for the chocolate pennies. And she was weary of her uncles' and aunts' everlasting war talk. On Christmas Eve a single German aeroplane had flown over Dover, dropping a bomb. Just one but it seemed an omen almost, of unimagined things to come. Lights were dimmed by order and folk stared at the Christmas sky. They were not searching for the star of Bethlehem now, but for enemy aircraft. Not listening for street carollers and church bells, but for the drone of the new deadly menace, this foretaste of what the New Year might hold.

Thomas's sister-in-law Cissy let them in, flushed from sitting too near the fire. Old *Nain* Hywel lay in the box bed by the hearth of the cottage; a traditional longhouse with the byre for the livestock attached, built centuries ago in a fold of hillside. *Nain* was a Hywel twice over; she had married a first cousin in the face of her parents' disapproval. This had seemed to give her special person status in the family ... that and the glamour of her gift of second sight.

"Come in and welcome." Cissy kissed her in-laws, admired Hannah's tammy and scarf, put the kettle on the hob for tea and fetched a plate of *taisan* cakes from the oak dresser. "Jenkin and the children are out seein' after the sheep, gettin' them down off the hill. Smells like it could snow tonight."

Thomas peered at the lowering sky. "Dark before you know it. How is she, then?"

All eyes turned to the figure in the bed, so slight it scarce lifted the homespun woollen quilt. The old woman lay neatly on her back, hair silvered by the sparking wood fire. Hannah stared at the hand on the quilt. It was transparent, with an unreal quality of weightlessness. Even the swollen joints seemed unsubstantial, the blue veins lighter than air.

"Sinking," Aunt Cissy whispered "Won't make New Year."

Hannah looked at the calm face, the finely veined gossamer of her great grandmother's eyelids. As she studied them the eyelids fluttered and lifted; old, tired blue eyes met young grey ones. After a moment *Nain* smiled in recognition, and Hannah felt a small, perfect seed of joy swell to a bubble in her chest and float into her mouth. She bent to kiss the incredibly soft cheek.

"Well, then ..." *Nain*'s voice was low but firm.

"Well, Mam, and here we are to see you." Thomas's mother kissed her next and patted her hand, followed by grandson Thomas. But *Nain* Hywel's eyes remained on Hannah and Hannah's on her.

"See, a gift for you." Thomas unwrapped a small pillow of sprigged cambric, fragrant with lavender. "From the bush in our yard – it was a treat this year. You remember, years back, you gave me the cutting from

45

your own place? Betsy sewed it and Hannah stitched your name – see, here in the corner?"

The fragile hand moved, touched the pillow. "There's lovely."

"Lavender to help you sleep sound," Thomas's voice was gentle. "Such a one for herbs, weren't you, *Nain*? Something for everything you had, and what wasn't in your back garden you'd find soon enough on the hill."

His grandmother's eyes were still fixed on Hannah, who began to feel that there was no one in the room but the two of them. The beautiful transparent hand lifted just a fraction and Hannah slipped it into her own warm one. Fragile as thistledown, the fingers curled about Hannah's who stared at them, unable to comprehend the sensation of positive power those fingers were conveying. Returning her gaze to her great-grandmother's face, she looked again into the yearning, vibrating intensity of the eyes; the bed, the room slid out of focus and nothing lived for her but the urgent message of *Nain*'s eyes.

Aunt Cissy and Thomas's mother were making tea; in a moment Thomas laid the lavender pillow by *Nain* Hywel's head and joined them.

"The book, child." The voice was very soft, but Hannah nodded. "In my dower chest . . . under my bride gown."

Hannah crossed to the carved elm chest under the window and pushed up the heavy lid. At the bottom, beneath the muslin folded in yellowing paper, lay a small book with a blue marbled cover. Her hand closed over it with a sense of familiarity, as though she had grasped the hand of a friend. She took it to the bed.

"Yes . . ." Her great-grandmother held it for a moment. Then she pressed it back into the girl's hands and now her eyes were bright with concentration as she captured the child's entire attention.

"You do know that the gift has passed to you?"

"I do know, *Nain*." Hannah's voice was steady though she seemed almost to be melting with the strangest mix of fear, and a new, powerful exultation.

"You will need this. It tells of healing . . . what you must know besides what you yourself possess. And child . . . Rachel . . . do not fear . . ."

The soft voice faded and *Nain* sank back on the pillow, drained of strength. Hannah's grandmother came to the bed with a bowl of tea.

"Could you fancy a sip, Mam? Don't be talkin' too much now, you'll tire yourself."

"Foolish . . . You always were a foolish girl." No more than a whisper now; Hannah bent closer. "Hannah, *you* understand? You will learn – as I did. And those before . . ."

"I understand, *Nain*."

Hannah spoke with a conviction she was far from feeling, the sense of exultation quite gone now. How *can* I understand she cried in her head. I'm twelve and a half! *Nain*, don't ask me to!

She felt a hand on her shoulder and it was Dada. She looked into his face and there were tears in his eyes. Hannah tried to calm herself. Dada would help; he always had.

They stayed on, waiting for Jenkin and the children, but when daylight began to fade Thomas said they must go. Old *Nain* Hywel had drifted into sleep, her breathing easy and shallow; no sense disturbing her again Cissy agreed. Hannah lingered, clutching the blue book inside her jacket. If only she were older . . . if only *Nain* would tell her more about whatever it was they shared. Was it a burden to carry all her life? Could she refuse it?

Ignore it? Would folk hate her for it? No, that couldn't be so; no one, she was sure, had ever hated her great-grandmother. The turmoil in her mind subsided. She, Hannah, must make it come right . . . as *Nain* had.

"Come on, Princess. Dark soon." Thomas called from the door as she took a last look at the motionless figure of the old lady. At that instant she saw a small blue light, onion shaped, rise from the bed and drift obliquely up to disappear in the dark ceiling beams.

Hannah stood perfectly still. She did not doubt what she had seen; it had been no trick of her imagination, nor of the leaping firelight. And the happening seemed perfectly natural, utterly acceptable. Certainly nothing she need fear.

"What's keeping you, child, for heaven's sake!" Her grandmother poked her head back round the door. "We've a long walk back."

"She's gone," Hannah whispered. "*Nain*'s gone."

It was true. What was left behind, motionless under the quilt woven sixty years earlier by a bride for her marriage bed, was not Rachel Alice Hywel. Hannah knew that all that was important of Rachel Alice had slipped free, in the guise of an onion-shaped blue light, to another place.

That first winter the district geared itself for war. No more false hopes of a quick end, they had died with the old year and were buried deeper with the first zeppelin raid on Norfolk, with the army's defeat at Neuve Chapelle. On her way to school Hannah would see recruits marching down to drill on the beach, at first in civilian clothes and with broomsticks in lieu of rifles. Every child learned quickly to join in their marching song, swinging alongside.

Where are our uniforms?
Far, far away.
When will our rifles come?
P'raps, p'raps some day.

Soon they had both uniforms and rifles. Tailors from the local Jewish community disappeared into factories to turn out khaki uniforms by the mile, and every man in the industries huddled between the mountains and the sea was exhorted to give his all, followed quickly by his woman. Children, too. Hannah and Joe shared sixpence a week for war savings, queuing each Monday morning at teacher's desk to have a stamp stuck in their book. Girls knitted for the troops; on the way to school and home again, in the playground, whenever there was an unfilled moment for busy fingers. Tiny girls knitted blanket squares for the wounded, but Hannah worked on socks, her needles flying, imagining every pair going to warm the feet of Harry and his friends in their trench.

And soon, as his shifts became longer and more demanding, she had to take over her father's allotment. She would go early in the morning, digging over a little at a time for planting, Fly shivering patiently alongside for company. By April she was tending seedling vegetables, her working day lengthening with the daylight hours. Sometimes Joe would help, picking out the biggest stones to put on the paths between the strips of soil. But he would soon tire and wander off to look for snails under the rocks to race them, or attempt to teach an unwilling Fly to retrieve sticks. Hannah would gather catkins and sticky buds on the way home about which Betsy would speak her mind.

"Pollen droppin' everywhere," she would snap. "If

19

you've nothin' more useful to do than moon about pickin' rubbish, you'd better put the whites in the copper to boil, or turn out the bedrooms." And she again pressed Thomas for Hannah to leave school – there were good jobs to be had now in service she reasoned, with so many women going into war work. She was well trained enough for *that* if she never went to school again! Thomas kept his silence and Hannah redoubled her efforts to be useful.

Harry's first letter had arrived back in January, and with so many of the dreaded orange telegrams about it had been a huge relief. Aunt Maggie had brought it up the same evening to share; it was sparse and unrevealing but proved that he was alive.

"I could kill him for not lettin' us hear before," she'd insisted, taking the single sheet out of its envelope as if it were a hundred guinea note. Hannah had hung over Dada's chair as he read it; eight lines, to say that Harry was "all right" and trusted all at home were ditto. He asked for letters and cigarettes, said to tell Hannah specially to write, and added that he would shortly be somewhere "more interesting".

"And we know what that means." Thomas had folded the letter into its envelope. "How about a line to your cousin then, Han?"

'I've been writing bits for ages, I was just waiting to know where to send." Hannah had dropped her knitting and hurried to find her exercise book and pencil to copy down the address.

"It can go in with ours, save you the stamp," Aunt Maggie had offered, to show she was not offended by her son's special request, which in fact she was.

"Well . . ." What if they weren't supposed to know about Brigid? Discomfited, Hannah hesitated. Aunt

Maggie would be certain to look through it all; she was nice but nosey.

"You'll catch flies, gawpin' like that," Betsy had said sharply.

"Not in January." Hannah's reply had been swift and involuntary and she'd rued it as quickly as her mother's hand swung to give her a slap across the head.

"Cheeky madam!"

Hannah had dropped her exercise book and, head down to hide her shame, had run upstairs. She'd knelt by the window to stare out at the frosty night, close to tears but refusing to let them materialise.

"Harry . . ." She had tried so hard to reach him with her mind. But she could write now and that would make it easier to bear. With all the little notes she'd jotted down since November there'd be plenty to say. She wouldn't tell him that she'd seen Brigid going into the Electric cinema arm-in-arm with a sailor . . . she really must make a big effort to get on terms with Brigid now, to help Harry.

She went to weed between the vegetable rows before school on her thirteenth birthday. The June morning had a pearly midsummer sheen about it; metallic calm lay over the estuary and the hills beyond were simply shapes, lacking dimension. Hannah squatted by the peas, pulling out chickweed and young dandelion. She enjoyed the task, it left her time to think. And she was proud of the succulent green pods she'd grown, the onions in lines, the beetroot tops showing healthily red.

Harry had just returned to France after a week's leave. The six months had changed him radically. The old, positive Harry had become a man of hesitant speech and long silences; the corn-gold hair and blue eyes seemed duller. But at least he'd seen Brigid, several times. Her sailor had returned to duty and, Hannah hoped, was not mentioned to Harry. No point upsetting him . . . time enough for Brigid to sort out her beaux when it was all over. When she knew who was left alive . . .

Now he was gone; another painful farewell at the station. She would start again, scribbling snippets down as they happened. Hannah's thoughts were confused about Harry and Brigid. She *should* have been delighted that he had a girl to help keep up his spirits. Could she be jealous? Florence had told her that Mandie Andrews in their class had a big crush on the young man behind the counter in the Co-op, and that when he got engaged she'd cried her eyes out and eaten nothing for days. Was the love she felt for Harry simply cousinly love or did *she* have a crush, too? Certainly she thought Harry was wonderful and she would do anything to please him; but he was a man and she was still a child. So Hannah, bent over the rows of vegetables as the summer burst into glorious profusion all about, decided she absolutely must be sensible, help Harry all she could and not let her fancies run away with her. She had already approached Brigid this spring saying she was Harry's cousin, and though it had all been rather awkward with the differences in their ages, she had made contact and would build on that. Maybe give her a bag of these lovely peas . . . only she'd not have to let Mam know! Brigid had not seemed all that friendly at first; but she was unbending now.

She had finished hoeing the peas and the broad beans when Joe appeared with Fly, travelling as usual in small rushes and pauses whilst the terrier explored the new day's set of smells.

"Happy birthday, Han."

The little boy hugged her and she hugged him back, loving as she always did the sturdy friendly body, the familiar Joe scent and feel. She loved his freckled lively face with the Hywel squareness of jaw, his alert brown eyes, his hair that *would* part in the wrong place and his sudden radiant grin. She knew that Dada would love Joe hugely whatever he did – not only because he was, unlike his brothers, staying alive. She knew how devotedly Mam loved him, quietly, not really showing it much except in the perfect, laborious way she would darn the smallest hole in his stocking, the insignificant tear in his shirt – which was not to say he'd not have a telling off for getting the tear. Then sometimes she would touch his head in passing, so lightly, but to Hannah it would look like a prayer; a blessing. Joe was even popular with his school teacher ... not that he was always perfectly obedient, he had the enquiring mind beloved by any teacher and an ability to learn, not to curry favour or through fear, but because he enjoyed it.

She herself loved so much about Joe – his droll humour, his loyalty to her when she was in trouble, his willingness to communicate whenever she needed him to. Now he pulled a cigarette card from his pocket and a sticky little bag of aniseed balls.

"These are for you." He looked longingly at the sweets and she offered back the open bag, laughing. He shook his head. "You first ... it's your birthday."

"True." She popped an aniseed ball into her mouth, then one in his. They sucked and smiled at one another and admired the cigarette card, one from a set of new inventions and very much in demand he assured her.

"Thirteen's old, isn't it?" he said, having thought about it for a while. His aniseed ball was small enough to bite on now.

"Well, it's quite a bit older than five I suppose. But you'll be six soon."

"Yes." Joe felt in his pocket. "This is for you, too."

It was a stone, the size and shape of a pigeon's egg, smooth as glass and marbled with subtle greens, blues and browns veined with creamy white. Hannah closed her fingers over it; it was warm, oddly comforting for an object that had no life, and its compact weight had a reassuring quality in her palm.

"It's beautiful, Joe. But d'you really want to part with it?" She knew this pebble was the pride of his collection. He nodded emphatically, reaching for a bit of stick to throw for Fly. Hannah hugged him, keeping the stone in her hand, and tidied up her tools ready to go. She felt increasingly emotional, close to tears; aware that this was a time to remember . . . the first day of her teens, the special quality of the summer morning, Joe, the stone.

When Fly came back with the stick he was limping on a front leg. As they moved towards the allotment gate he lagged behind, licking his leg. Joe ran back and tried to encourage him along but the limp became more marked as the terrier endeavoured to keep up with the children.

"Han, he must be really hurting."

Hannah knelt by Fly, picked up the leg and he gave a small yelp. There was no thorn in his pad, no cut.

"Must be a sprain." She pushed the little dog gently onto his side. "Good boy," she whispered. "There's a good boy . . ."

Her hand moved very slowly up the leg, with no idea of what the exploration might serve. Fly lay perfectly still, gazing into the distance with liquid mournful eyes. Hannah became aware, little by little, of heat in her hand that appeared to fasten it to the skinny leg encompassed by her fingers. She was joined to the dog by a smooth peaceful flow of heat that seemed almost to be part of the peaceful morning that surrounded them. Joe squatted nearby, watching.

She had no idea how long it was before she slid her hand down the leg and released it.

"Come on then." She stroked Fly firmly on his warm flank. He stood up, shook himself thoroughly and trotted ahead.

"He's all right." Joe sounded uncertain.

"Seems to be." Hannah was unsure herself; uncertain whether to laugh or cry, whether to be afraid, or pleased or . . . anything. What she really felt was, in the end, simply calm and quite ordinary. She took Joe's hand.

"We'll have to hurry now, not to be late for school. Joe, would you like Ted? To keep, not just borrow?"

Joe looked up quickly, surprised. Ted was Hannah's golliwog, her lifelong best possession, knitted for her by Nain Hywel when she was a baby and treasured ever since.

"Are you sure?"

"Yes, I am. I'm thirteen now, that's quite old like you said. Too old for toys. Honest, you take Ted. I shan't need him again. I think I'm going to be quite busy with, well, with other things. Look after him, though. Don't get him all messed up or I'll be after you."

She swung his hand, smiling, suddenly loving him and the whole world enormously. "Come on, we'd better run."

55

Chapter Three

March 1916, and the war bit deeper into every life. In Port Talbot the steelworks were requested by the Ministry of Munitions not simply to increase their output, but also to build new facilities with all speed, to produce iron. This was the talk in every dwelling . . . a whole new plant was to be planned a short distance along the morfa from the present one, to be called Margam Works. *And* it was expected to double the present output of five thousand tons of crude steel weekly. Folk repeated these staggering facts to one another and marvelled; how could this ever be accomplished?

But it would be. Ships, guns, bullets, shells – those at home would provide for those fighting in France. Sleeves were rolled up with deadly intent on the little coastal strip crammed with small grey houses. Last autumn's carnage at Loos had drained the district of more fathers, more husbands and sons. By Christmas, the women of Incline Row had parcelled up drifts of mufflers, socks and mittens for the front and Hannah had taught Joe to knit, though with no outstanding result.

Now at the end of the bitter winter came the German offensive on Verdun. Harry's letters had become spasmodic and Aunt Maggie waxed pale as news of the Verdun casualties was given. They were largely French; but all Aunt Maggie knew was that there was fierce and deadly fighting going on somewhere out there – and that's where Harry was.

It was March when Hannah discovered what had become of Brigid. She'd known for weeks that something was wrong. Brigid's face had told her, even before she had begun to avoid Hannah, who had persevered with trying to strike up a friendship though Brigid was clearly indifferent. Hannah had at times felt like giving up, she simply had not the time to run around after a girl who had no interest in *her*. But . . . Harry was fighting to keep her safe . . . and she had promised him . . . So she would try again; and gradually, she and Brigid had reached a kind of rapport.

Now it had changed. "Can't make it Sunday – too much to do," when Hannah would suggest a walk to show her Harry's last letter.

"No, not after school. The milk round's bigger now, I'm late finishing." Or, "Mam's not well, I've got extra to do at home."

Hannah would watch her taking off her horse's tack and note that it was nowhere near as clean as it used to be. Earlier on, she'd helped Brigid saddle-soap it all before it was hung up, the leather supple and glossy, buckles and rings well burnished. Then they would groom Bluebell whilst she headed into her nosebag; Hannah unplaiting and combing the main and tail, Brigid brushing the liver chestnut coat until it shone like a freshly burst conker in sunlight.

"Oh, leave it," she would then begin to say. "It'll do." And Bluebell soon became less than immaculate, her tack sticky and dull, the cart not quite clean.

"I'll do it for you if you're tired, Brigid."

"Oh, give over do." Brigid took off her hat and pushed irritable fingers through the knot of copper hair. "You do go *on*, Han."

57

Hannah saw anxiety sharpen her face and a web of stress blur the girl's normally brisk movements.

"There's something wrong," she said doggedly. "Why don't you tell me? Maybe I can help."

"You can – just leave me alone!" Brigid swung on Hannah and her round, beautiful eyes were tormented. "I'm sick of you and your stupid cousin! Got it? Now, don't hang around me, I've too much to do as it is."

In late November, Brigid's sailor father was lost in a submarine attack. Her mother, known to be a feckless weak-minded woman, went to pieces, got behind with the house rent, and packing up her bits and pieces moved to Cwmavon to live with her sister. Abandoned, Brigid had lodged briefly with her married sister and then had disappeared, the first Hannah knew of it seeing a replacement milkman one January morning on the way to school. The sister would only say that Brigid had "moved away". Hannahs's efforts to find out where were met with stonewall silence. She had continued to put together chatty, diary-type notes for Harry, filling the gap left by Brigid's disappearance with titbits about school, the allotment, their myriad cousins; the prisoner of war camp set up in a disused celluloid factory at Margam.

Finally she was driven to ask Thomas. Sunday, after church, Betsy had taken back her father's washing and Joe was playing out in the frosty blue morning. Hannah was chopping meat and vegetables for a lamb stew, Thomas replacing a broken sashcord in the kitchen window. A rare moment's privacy.

"Why d'you want to know about Brigid Davies, Princess?" Hannah's unease grew, seeing her father's stern expression. He looked tired, too, and without the springing step she'd always known. Hannah was also tired, everyone she knew was tired. Women doing men's jobs, children doing women's jobs, homes run haphazard or left empty. She tried again.

"She's not on the milk round now. I wondered . . . we used to talk. She liked Harry – " The little rush of words tailed off. Why did she speak of Brigid in the past tense?

"You forget about her." Thomas's voice was curt. Hannah stared at him, knife poised over a potato.

"But Dada – "

"But me no buts, Han. Brigid Davies is gone. Like I said, forget her."

Hannah nicked her thumb on the knife and jumped, sucking at it with tears perilously close. She knew she'd get no more from him but that he'd clearly heard something about Brigid. It was really stupid, the way grownups acted. Why could Harry not have told his family he was sweet on Brigid anyway? Young men and girls courted and got married all the time, why not Harry and Brigid? She looked again at Thomas but he had turned his back on her, signalling blanket discouragement of the whole topic. Wherever Brigid had gone, whatever she had done, would not be learned from him.

It was Florence who told her, in March. Florence and she were classroom monitors for the week, staying behind after school to straighten up and take anything left about to lost property.

"My Aunt Bessie from Swansea was over to see Mam when I went back for dinner, Han." Florence's voice was hushed in the dim little room, filled with rows of pegs and lined with wooden benches and smelling stalely of damp clothes and much lived-in boots. "You know Brigid Davies? Used to be on the milk?"

Hannah looked up sharply. She'd longed for the luxury of telling her best friend about Harry's pash on Brigid; Florence was both trustworthy and goodhearted and would have kept the secret. But Harry had insisted upon her sworn word that it would go no further. She waited, premonition darkening her mind.

"It was in the Swansea Star." Florence's voice sank lower, colour brightening her round, fresh-skinned face, framed by the glossy brown plaits. She was only slightly taller than Hannah, only slightly heavier in build, but to Hannah she appeared to dominate the classroom at that moment. "It's awful, Han, Aunt Bessie cut it out to bring. Found dead she was, in some house in Madoc Street where she'd been lodging."

Hannah sat back on her heels, unbelieving. That couldn't be! Harry might die at any time, he was in the trenches, that's the way things were. But Brigid? What would a healthy young girl die of in a safe place like Swansea? But Flo's face gave the lie to all that.

"It was a – baby – " Florence broke off, the blush deepening. "Isn't it awful? There was a baby dead beside her, on the floor. Two days before the landlady even found . . ."

Her voice trailed off into silence. This was not something decent girls should be talking about, even to their best friends; the subject had quite overwhelmed Florence in its departure from propriety. Han must be agreeing that she'd overstepped the mark, she looked – well, winded, staring like that, not moving. "It's true," she added with a touch of defiance. "They were mad that I'd overheard only the kettle was singing and Mam stoking up the fire and they hadn't heard me come in. There was blood all over the floor, she bled to death – " A touch now of hysteria; Florence clung to a high peg feeling quite unwell herself at the picture conjured up by her description.

Hannah got awkwardly to her feet, holding to the bench like an old woman. "I have to go now . . . Mam's on late shift, I've tea to get for Joe." She wanted so very much to tell it all to Florence; to put her arms round her friend's neck and cry for Brigid, and for Harry. But she'd given her word. And no use telling now for sure.

She had not gone straight home. She had run through the shunting yards and fetched up on the docks, the March wind whipping her hair over her face in frenzied strands.

"Harry ..." her voice was carried off in the wind, drowned by singing wires, slapping sails, the creak of cranes, seamen and seagulls going about their business.

"Harry *bach* ... how can I tell you?"

Half hidden by a stack of empty crates Hannah emptied her mind and searched with her heart, head; wherever lodged that extra sense she possessed. Dimly, she eventually found him with that inner eye, watched him lift an enamel mug to his lips and tip back his head to drain it. Above his head puffs of smoke like little cottony clouds, below his feet, slime covered duck boards and the swollen body of a rat.

She leaned against the crates head down and hands restraining the wild hair. Impossible to tell him in a letter, in cruel black pen marks. Face to face ... on his next leave. Next month, Aunt Maggie had said. That would have to be the way of it.

Hannah turned and ran for home to make Joe's tea.

Now Harry was finally here, but how to find words? Could he know already? *What* might he know? It must have been his first leave when he ... they ... They meandered across the beach in the hushed time before daylight dimmed into the long, lilac twilight of late April. Behind them the docks were scarcely less active than at noon, and the steelworks' furnaces heaved flames up through grimed chimney stacks into the

61

empty sky. Ahead, gangs of German prisoners were digging the footings of the new Margam Works.

Hannah had said nothing of Brigid in her letters since the turn of the year – how could she, with him staying alive on memories and hopes? And she'd awaited the precious leave with growing dead. The pleasure of Harry's first hug drained all too soon into apprehension; then anger – it was the *war* to blame. And what use, to blame anything so all-encompassing and all-powerful?

"So, fourteen the month after next, *cariad*." He laid a companiable arm across her shoulder, watching gulls upending for their supper in the creamy wavelets. "A woman grown, before we know it!"

She knew it already; and to Hannah it seemed an age since her last birthday when Joe had given her his best pebble. She knew well enough about the monthly painful embarrassment, the rounding breasts straining under old bodices, about the confusion of bright joy and dark despair; the childish rebellions and sudden, mature compromises. She was unaware of other changes now manifest in Harry's eye . . . the defining of sculpted cheekbone and jawline, the newly graceful set of head on delicate stem of throat; firmer arch of brow, more generous curve of mouth. Hannah, Harry saw, was of a sudden all but beautiful, with subtlety beyond the usual seasonal blooming of a young girl.

She had known the next question must come and her mouth had dried. He faced her; no trace now of the teasing merry youth of two summers ago. A thin hard face, the corn-gold sweep of hair cut to stubble, "So the birds don't nest in it." He had grinned without humour.

"Brigid, Han – what's going on? I write but nothing's come back for months. Another fella is it?"

"No." Her lips felt too stiff to say more. She sank onto

a little rock; he hesitated then sat cross-legged beside her on the sand and watched her face.

"Brigid left the milk round after last Christmas, Harry. I didn't see her after that." Hannah took a deep breath. The summer dusk thickened and she thought what a terrible year 1916 was turning out. Two boys playing nearby knocked sand off themselves and ran up towards Dock Street, kicking a stone between them as they went. Harry waited.

He stood up when she'd finished, stumbling to the end of the dreadful little tale. He picked up a pebble and hurled it into the sea, staring after it, and his face was cleared of expression, carved stone-hard as the pebble he'd flung. Hannah remained seated on the rock, hugging her knees.

A strangled sound made her lift her head. He was still staring out to sea, but tears were rolling down the stony cheeks.

"Harry . . ."

Just a whisper; but it unmanned Harry. As she reached him he began to shake, rocking back and forth and keening, a low breathy moan not unlike the noise Hannah had heard a fox making when once she'd found one dying in a gin trap above Cwmavon. She folded him in her arms, crooning and rocking with him; she not a child, he not a soldier, but kinsmen. When later the wind had dried away his tears they remained enfolded on the darkening beach. Only when Hannah shivered did he stir and speak heavily as though the effort was great.

"It was mine . . ." She stroked his hand. "If she'd gone to Mam . . . she'd have done something. I know it."

"I'm sure her own Mam would, Harry, if she'd known." Hannah continued to stroke his hand.

"Not that stupid cow!" He gave a violent jerk. "Good

for nothing she is, never did a hand's turn for her kids. But *my* Mam would've. If she'd only written to *me*. Christ Jesus! On her own like that . . ."

She shivered as the wind cooled and he turned to lead her back towards the lights of Taibach.

"Harry? Why was it a secret? Why couldn't you let your Mam and Dad know you were . . . I mean, everyone has sweethearts."

"Oh, sure. Only preferably not born the wrong side of the blanket." Bitterness spilled out like bile. "Not a 'nice' girl, you see, Han. Her Mam didn't have her marriage lines tucked safely into her corset before she opened her legs. Sorry – " as she drew back, shocked. "But a spade's a spade. This bloody war's changed things a fair bit. They'll change a sight more before it's done. But it'll be too late now for *my* girl, and *my* baby."

Nearing Incline Row, Hannah turned to him. "Harry, listen. We mightn't have time together again before you go back – not alone, to talk properly. I want to help you. No, I mean it," as he gave a crooked smile. "Harry, there's not much more I want to tell you, but just try to understand a bit for now. It's important!" She gave his sleeve a little shake in her agitation.

"There are some things I'm able to do that other people can't," she went on earnestly. "Dada's Nain was the same. We've a second sight, that's what it's called for want of anything better."

She paused, half expecting a laugh. But Harry was silent, staring at his boots. "Well – from now on, whilst you're away, I'll think of you, try to be with you in mind. I really do think that I can do that. And if you do the same, maybe we'll reach each other – d'you see? And then you won't be lonely. You won't be alone. I'll be *there*."

Harry did not believe in magic. Or witchcraft; or

second sight. He hadn't before he'd gone to France, and if he had it would certainly have been knocked out of him by now. He believed in luck – he'd had it this far, unlike the poor sods trampled into Flanders mud or hung like dirty rags on barbed wire. Harry believed only in doing his damnest to get through each day; in trying to get an hour or two's sleep at night so he could forget what it felt like when you went to pick up your mate after an attack and he fell apart. Or forget the stench of decomposing horses strewn over the road after a transport column had been hit. Or forget the whole bloody winter ... always cold, usually lice ridden, often up to the knees in stinking mud, with braziers in the dug-outs whose fumes were so poisonous that you were driven back into the icy misery of the trench, where the combined smell of damp, and dead bodies made you retch.

What Harry believed in was killing as many Huns as he could manage and in having the best time he could whenever he got down the line for a few days' rest. He had seen most of the mates he'd gone over with killed, three gassed. He'd seen bits of men sticking out of the gaping earth of a village cemetery, clusters of corpses still hunched over their machine-gun nest. He'd seen hell opened up. It became hard to recall what real life had been like, but he had once, with Brigid Davies, had a taste of heaven; of that he was certain. It did not do to think too much of the future. If he had a future, though, Harry knew now that he had reckoned on sharing it with Brigid Davies.

He looked at his cousin whose eyes were glittering with tears in the twilight as if she could read his thoughts. He would have liked to please her, she was a good kid and this had been rotten for her. Maybe he could explain that he knew she wanted to help, but didn't think it would always be convenient to sit and think of her on a regular basis. In fact the idea made him bloody well laugh, only he'd no laughter left in him.

Harry was dog-tired now. He wanted to get to his bedroom, take a few swigs of his bottle of rum, and get his head down. He was too tired to explain anything at all at this moment.

"We'll give it a go," he said. She took a big breath and smiled, the deep, generous smile that exposed her chipped tooth.

"Harry, thank you! Which day shall we make it? When would it be convenient?"

Harry almost laughed. Oh dear, if Han only knew. *Convenient*!

"A Saturday? Our Saturday night date, eh?"

"Oh yes . . ." She gave his hands a little shake. "Right then; every Saturday evening around this time I'll send you my loving thoughts, and they'll reach you if you'll concentrate hard."

"Okay." He planted a kiss on her cheek. "Go on now, or you'll be in trouble, it's late even for a lady of coming up fourteen."

Betsy was waiting. Not long back from the corner Co-op she had dumped the heavy carpet bag of groceries on the table and was putting on a pan of water for washing Joe before bed. Hannah slipped out of her jacket and unrolled her pinafore fast, sensing antagonism; Thomas had gone to the Working Men's Club Friday darts match and Joe was in the yard feeding Fly his dinner – no buffers between herself and an over-tired, resentful mother.

"Had a good time, did you?"

Hannah began to put away the groceries; the bacon, cheese and margerine, the tea and sugar, soap, cocoa,

66

potatoes, eggs, flour, moving quietly in an effort to efface herself.

"I'm waiting. Weren't you taught to answer when you're asked a question?" Betsy's voice rose, her brown eyes boring into Hannah's, her cheeks glistening in the heat of the fire. She had lost weight this spring; the curved planes of her face had sharpened and two vertical lines had appeared between her eyebrows. Suddenly, she had begun to look older than her thirty-five years.

"Just went for a while to talk to Harry, after the allotment."

"How nice," cut in her mother acidly. "So the rent man didn't get his money – nor did the insurance man! Hung on 'til nearly closin' time waiting for you I did, and got the fag-end of cheese for it – and well you know when *I* go for groceries and when *they* come for their dues. But why should that bother *you*! You'd better fish to fry – a talk with Harry!"

Betsy leaned across the table, breathing fast as she got up steam. Hannah swallowed. It was true, she *had* forgotten she should be in Friday evenings to pay out the rent and the death insurance if Betsy wasn't back from her shopping. Friday was pay-out day, her mother would grumble, reluctantly counting out the coins into their respective tins. Now it must be taken round to the collectors' homes with an apology, which to Betsy's mind carried a certain stigma. Unable to defend herself – she couldn't possibly tell about Harry's baby – Hannah was tongue-tied.

Betsy glared at her daughter. There were still the flags to swill down at the front and Thomas's work shirt and trousers to scrub in the heated water left after Joe's wash, and the front step to pumice, only idle cats left that for a Saturday. She'd cut her thumb on a rough sheet at work and it was already sore and would be worse after the pumicing; her curse was two days late, her hair felt heavy and dirty and her head thudded painfully. All Hannah had done was sit in school, then help out at the greengrocer's for a bit before going to the allotment. At *her* age she, Betsy, had been on her feet twelve hours a day in service, seven days a week with every other Sunday off, and so done up some nights it was too much effort to eat her supper. One thing was sure, Thomas wouldn't win one more time over this schooling – it was not to be borne, with good jobs in service going begging. Fourteen and that was it! Scholarship or no scholarship; *anyone* could earn their living at fourteen.

Hannah picked up the last two items to be cleared away, the bag of flour and a small package of potted meat. Betsy felt guilty about that meat. She and Thomas loved it on a bit of bread for supper, but it *was* a luxury. She'd have resisted it, only that stuck-up Mrs Blair, new at Number two, had had some just in front of her, and Betsy had suddenly not seen why she should go without. But Thomas's trousers were through at the knee, and Joe's boots too small . . . and the children's bed needed a new blanket before autumn.

Suddenly the sight of the girl calmly going on as if things were all right maddened Betsy, more even than if she'd answered back. Things were *not* all right; life was hard, crammed with worries and dangers and injustices, especially for women, and the sooner Hannah learned that the better. Fourteen was a good age to start. What Betsy could not tell Hannah – for she had not the vocabulary – was that her anger was rooted in fear. She knew the value of what she had; a husband who loved her and was not ashamed to say so, who did not beat her or spend his wages on beer and betting. She loved her children; Joe more than Hannah because Joe was the only surviving son of the three she had borne, but Hannah, too. But this love was filtered through so many veils of her emotions – jealousy of her daughter's close relationship with Thomas, apprehension about this uncomfortable special sense of Hannah's that Thomas had tried to explain to her, and again, fear of the future – that it was scarcely ever shown. Valuing what she possessed, Betsy's heart seemed to crack open now with anguish of seeing it slip away. She knew with terrible, painful certainty that, barring a miracle, Thomas would go to war. The confidence that his loving support had given to Betsy's nervous, depressive nature was slipping away and leaving her shivering, naked in a wicked world.

Moving warily across her mother's path, Hannah looked up in spite of herself. Eyes met, hesitant grey no more than three inches lower now than furious brown

"You think you're special, don't you? Well you're not – you're as ordinary as all of us, and as long as you're in this house you'll pull your weight. Got that?"

Betsy fetched her daughter a sudden hard blow across the head. It knocked Hannah off balance, knuckles rapping painfully on the table edge; flour clouded out from the bag, dropped and spilt on the flagged floor. Both stared at it for a second, then at one another.

"Now look what you've done."

"She didn't do it. You did, hittin' her."

Betsy swung round on Joe standing in the kitchen doorway. He looked back, judging her. He seemed older now than rising seven, less because he'd shot up fast and was becoming sturdy than for the expression on his face that had, within the last months, lost its infant softness and taken on a hint of his father's in its sinewy squareness.

"If you hadn't hit her she wouldn't have dropped it," he repeated in the same level tone. Betsy, anger evaporating after her violent gesture, and feeling for the first time trapped by her children, put her hands defiantly on her hips.

"If you're so sorry for her you can help to clear it up before you get yourself washed and into bed. Any time now your dad'll be back and wantin' a bit o' peace with his supper, not a roomful of kids and flour. Go on then – " as they still looked at her. "Won't pick itself up will it?"

She drew the pan of almost boiling washing water off the fire with a jerk; a little splattered on her wrist and with a cry of pain and frustration she hugged it to her. Hannah glimpsed tears brimming in her eyes as her mother hurried into the parlour to blacklead the grate, another Friday night chore.

"Come on, love . . . you get washed, this bit of mess won't take a minute." She smiled at her brother and squeezed his shoulder. "It *was* my fault, I'd forgotten it was pay-out night, see?" She carried the steaming pan to the bowl in the scullery. "No mess now. And take your shirt off, how much d'you think you'll get clean with that on?"

"If my shirt covers it nobody can see the dirt," Joe pointed out with the uncluttered logic of the very young, but Hannah frowned and shook her head. By the time she'd swabbed up the spilt flour and funnelled the remainder into its croc jar he was washed and eating the bread and milk left warming on the hob. Betsy reappeared for brush, pan and duster to "set" the parlour in the unlikely event of its being used over the weekend and she hesitated, nodding at him as he spooned down his supper.

"Clean, are you? Off with you then – fold your trousers tidy. And don't forget your prayers." She touched his shoulder as she passed him.

Hannah looked up, surprised. Mam never mentioned prayers save in family emergencies or when she was feeling really down. They all went to church on a Sunday morning and that was that for the week. Betsy intercepted the look and stared back, colouring up.

"I've put Dad's things to soak," Hannah said quickly, anxious to avoid another confrontation. "I'll swill the back down now." Her mother grunted and turned back to the parlour, leaving an uneasy silence. Betsy was deeply ashamed of hitting Hannah, but found it impossible to apologise.

Hannah had sluiced down the scullery and tiny yard and was wringing out the mop when Thomas came along the dark little path between their houses and the backs of those in Somerset Street. She caught the smell of beer as he touched her shoulder affectionately but he was nowhere near being drunk – not like a lot of them who came home and made all sorts of trouble for their women and children. Hannah smiled at him, caught in the pool of light from the kitchen window. She was always grateful that she belonged to him, but tonight, even more so. He was – good. He would laugh to be called that and start teasing. But it's what he is she thought; just plain good. Her heart swelled with love. She wished him to have his heart's desire, whatever that was; would give it herself if only she might.

"What would you like most in the world, Dada?" She dried her hands, wanting more than anything to give it to him herself. He looked suddenly drained and old.

"I'd like the war to end, Princess . . ." He spoke softly,

71

Hannah could only just hear. "That's what I want most in the world."

"Oh. Oh, I'm so sorry. I can't give you that."

He smiled then and touched her cheek.

"No . . . So don't be frettin' about it, eh? Give me a while an' I'll think up something easier."

She nodded, throat tight with emotion. She wanted to tell him about Harry and Brigid, and about Mam being so upset; to talk it all through with him. But that would only add to his worries. They walked inside and she went to bed right away to avoid getting her mother more upset than she was already.

Lying motionless on her side of the bed, Hannah tried to empty her mind for sleep. After a while she got out and knelt down, head in her hands. She prayed for Harry's safety, and to be able to help him herself in any way that she was able. Then she remained still, eyes closed, and thought of her parents. Mam was so frightened. Poor, poor Mam, who knew that Dada *would* go to war. No one said the words yet, but she knew for certain this would happen. Hannah guessed it was only fear that made her mother so sharp; she saw the fear like a web and longed to be able to brush it away. But she knew this web must stretch over millions of women now. She could only do whatever she might to ease Betsy's hard path, and so she prayed for that. And, of course, for her father.

There was no chance to talk privately again with Harry before he left. But as she hugged him, Hannah whispered, "Every Saturday, don't forget now," and he nodded and squeezed her shoulder.

She was in school when she heard his train whistle its departure, struggling to deduce how many pails of water John would need to fill a tank of water of such and such a size, provided the pails were of such and such a size, the type of problem that confused her at the best of times. She sat very still, every nerve concentrating on the disappearing train. Logic told her that with every day his chances of survival must lessen, that each night may be his last. But *some* of them must come back . . .

"Having a nice nap are you?"

Hannah jumped at a smarting rap across her shoulder. Miss Probert was just behind her, her breath that always smelt of onions was close to Hannah's cheek.

"No, Miss Probert."

"That's what it looked like to me. What did it look like to you, Mabel Saler – were Hannah Hywel's eyes closed?"

"Yes, miss."

Mabel Saler had no idea what the state of Hannah's eyes had been but she'd learned more sense than to argue with Miss Probert when she'd a ruler at the ready.

"I was not asleep, Miss Probert. I was thinking." Hannah's voice was polite but positive in a way that irritated Miss Probert.

"Oh, good. Then you will have thought out the answer to this problem. Good."

"No . . . I'm sorry, Miss Probert." Hannah hesitated. "It was my cousin Harry I was thinking about."

"I see." Miss Probert said pleasantly. "Your cousin Harry. Then come to the front of the class and I will demonstrate why it is not the best idea to think of your cousin Harry during my arithmetic lesson."

Hannah walked to Miss Probert's desk, aware now of the vaulted windows of the classroom; the two blackboards tilted on their easels, the map of the world, the black unlit stove with the guard around it. She stood facing the class unblinking as the ruler came down hard six times on her outstretched hand. The first punishment for a long time . . . she was usually careful not to provoke the wrath of authority. She hated the sarcastic Miss Probert wholeheartedly and held her breath as she returned to her seat lest it turned into a sob, for her hand hurt dreadfully. Passing Florence, she saw the shocked red face turned to her in mute sympathy and felt better – dear Flo, it had probably hurt her as much as herself. One day she would tell Flo about Harry. For now, she concentrated on not crying. Doris Pearce who shared her double desk gave her a sidelong look and Hannah managed a little smile. Then she bent to her arithmetic again and a studious silence fell on the classroom. A fly droned lazily up the window by Hannah and left by the three open inches at the top. Glancing up, Hannah wished she could follow him out into the warm spring air and take the path, so tantalising close, on to the hill.

She found out that evening why Betsy had asked Joe to say his prayers, and why Dada had asked for the war to end right then. There'd been some act passed by the government, it said in the paper brought round by Aunt Maggie. Not only all single men between eighteen and forty-one must enlist, but now all married men must, too, unless specially exempted. Hannah had said nothing; had simply listened as she did the ironing on the end of the table, the flat iron hard and heavy in her sore palm. Aunt Maggie had rocked herself quite violently in the rocking chair, still distraught from Harry's departure after his brief leave.

"Not content with takin' our sons, they're after our menfolk now!" Her deep bosom heaved, straining the tightly crossed blue and red checked pinafore. "My Idwal's safe for this time thanks be – just had his forty-second. But you're in trouble, boyo." She nodded at Thomas.

The clock on the mantelpiece ticked unaccountably loud. Looking up from Joe's shirt front, Hannah saw her mother's face contort for a second into a mask of pure fear. Then she turned and made for the scullery, where she could be heard banging a pan about in the sink.

"We'll have to see," Thomas said quietly. Hannah bent over her ironing again. He was thirty-nine soon.

Soon everyone began talking about a "push" – a great offensive that would mean victory. Posters were stuck everywhere demanding more munitions and for women to make them. Hannah liked the one that showed a girl donning an overall with a soldier in the background waving goodbye and the caption THIS WOMAN IS DOING HER BIT. LEARN TO MAKE MUNITIONS.

Florence's brother Ronnie was a Navy cadet, he'd always been mad about boats. His whereabouts were a secret, Flo told Hannah worriedly, and her Mam was in a right state every time she thought it time for a letter and one didn't come – though when one did all it said was that the food was terrible and that he kept falling out of his hammock. Remembering plump, lazy Ronnie, Hannah caught Flo's eye then and they exchanged giggles.

Then talk of the big push intensified; already the Whitsun bank holiday had been postponed to keep the stream of munitions flowing unchecked across the Channel, and now Hannah was beginning to catch the mood of restlessness in the community – a sense of movement, purpose, change. She was fourteen in just a few days . . . she was always busy – Betsy saw to that – but other people were busy with a more vital business; that of waging war.

On the first day of June Thomas brought home the evening paper with the headlines of a big naval engagement off Jutland between the German High Seas

Fleet and the British Grand Fleet. Next day, Florence was absent from school. Hannah hurried round to Queen Street, Joe's tea and Chidzoy's the greengrocer must wait. The curtains were drawn at number thirty-seven and Florence's face when she opened the back door was blotched red and white, her normally crisp dark braids tousled. She glanced back to where low voices came from the living room, then stepped into the yard and pulled the door behind her.

"It's Ronnie . . ." she whispered. Her eyes brimmed and she squeezed on a damp hankie.

"Oh, *Flo* . . ."

Hannah felt sick. Ronnie was sixteen. She reached out for Florence.

"The man of the family since Dad died –" Florence sagged against Hannah, allowing herself the first luxury of being comforted since the telegram. Hannah stroked her shoulder, her own tears sliding down Florence's plait. "Our breadwinner, Mam would call him, we were a bit short you know with Mavis and Joyce married and Dad gone . . ."

Hannah murmured, still stroking. Florence relaxed against her.

"He'd wanted to stay on in the Navy. Said he'd get good promotion after the war, with signing on as a cadet. All planned out . . ."

It was later that they heard how the cadets had been sent to the ship's hold for safety and that a shell had driven straight through the deck to explode below.

"Mam's in a terrible way. I'll not be back at school, Han, I'm goin' after a job – the best pay I can get. I knew I'd have to soon anyway, with – with Ronnie away and Mam only part-time on account of bein' poorly. She was set on me stayin' til August even though I'm fourteen now, but not a chance. I've said so, flat." Florence stood straight again and blew her nose.

"I'm leaving too, Flo. We'll get work together if we can." Hannah felt better as soon as she'd said it. Silly not to have done it before, half the class had already left early to take advantage of the good money about, girls months younger than she were earning a pound a week in some factories. She hugged Flo. "I'll bring your things from school tomorrow and I'll ask round for jobs. Don't you worry now. You just see to your Mam."

She ran home to get Joe's tea and blacklead the grate before the fire was started. There was a performing seal giving shows outside the Walnut Tree in High Street Joe told her, brown eyes alive with excitment in his freckled face. A big tank of water on a red and green painted cart pulled by a brown and white horse, all done up with plumes and things. Freddie May's been allowed to pat the horse! Could he go?

"Why not, love . . . come straight back though."

Hannah cut bread and larded it thick with rhubarb jam she'd made last week from her allotment crop a mite runny but even Betsy had said not bad for a first try. She meant to make more later with wynberries from the morfa and wild raspberries from a cache she and Joe had stumbled across in a little hollow up behind the cottage hospital at Pencae when they'd been hunting for herbs. Time to go after herbs again . . . she loved doing that with Joe when she'd the time, scrambling about the hills and the morfa with a list from *Nain* Hywel's small blue book, and sketches she'd made from a botany book in the library. Some were easy to find, already familiar; goosegrass, shavegrass, meadowsweet and feverfew, heartshorn and bog myrtle and rosemary. She had collected some last summer and dried them painstakingly where she could. Betsy had found a bunch and

77

tossed them in the fire saying sharply that the house was too small for collections of children's rubbish and the place for green stuff was outside unless it could be boiled for dinner.

"Han . . . I said, I can't go. It's a penny to watch."

"Oh . . . right." She sprinted upstairs for her purse, kept at the back of the clothes drawer. "Here's one. Don't lose it before you get there. And here's another for sweets if you'll go to Chidzoy's first and tell them I can't come to help today. Family business, tell them."

Joe looked bemused. Tuppence had never been come by so easily. "You're savin' for Mam's birthday . . ."

"There'll be more tuppences by then," Hannah said grandly. Then she told him about Ronnie and how she and Florence were going to join the ranks of working women. "You're not to say a word till I've spoken with Dad now," she threatened. "It's to help win the war. Only I'll need to tell him myself." He nodded, looking suitably serious, mouth edged with jam and eyes bright with anticipation of the seal show. She wiped his face and hands before he went, combed his hair that would separate into unruly spikes rather than lay flat, and pulled up his grey wool stockings. Then gave him a final hug, thinking of Florence's brother lying cold at the bottom of the sea. When he'd run down the path, cap askew and the ever willing Fly bounding at his heels, she leaded the grate and started the fire, fetched in the coal and tidied the table all at double time, and was off down Incline Row herself, long nutmeg-brown hair streaming back. Instead of following Joe across the river into Aberavan she continued seaward, to the Light Plate mill. She had business with Dada.

The works spread across the morfa, between the docks and the streets of Taibach. Giant corrugated iron sheds, shuddering and roaring to the trumpets of war;

78

blast furnaces like convoluted monsters from pre-history; soaking pits and melting shops, rolling mills and coking plants, a massive railbank. A wilderness of scrap yards, screaming circular saws so full of menace.

Hannah halted then, shut her eyes and blocked her ears against the assault. She was a little child again, grasping tight at the security of Thomas's hand as he would tell her of this wonder of twentieth-century industry that was transforming the lives of the whole community.

"No hungry mouths now, Princess. See that big board up there? 'The Port Talbot Railways and Docks Company'. There's grand, eh? Fine new docks of our own. All the great ships we'll have comin' here now; an' steady jobs. Think on that, *cariad*."

He would squeeze the soft fingers, nodding towards the giant red-painted corrugated iron shed that was his work-day world. And Hannah would look up at his face and nod back, thinking how Dada was the finest man in the world.

"Wouldn't be there, any of it, y'know but for Talbot's dock. None of it. My old *Nain*, even she wasn't born when Mr Talbot said there'd to be a dock at Taibach – and he'd the land and the clout to get it done. There was the coal to mine, see, and the iron, and the lead. Rich, the land round about you, Princess. An' my *Nain*'s Mam told her of charcoal burners used to live in Margam woods; hundreds of years they'd been there." Hannah would nod again, captivated, wanting Dada to go on talking for ever.

"So we'd all we needed right here, under our feet see, Princess? And your Dada taken on amongst the first . . . But you'd not know that, you bein' in your crib when the first plate rolled from there."

He would laugh then. And she would laugh; because Dada was happy, and so all was well with the world.

The siren blew as Hannah skirted the engineering sheds. Thomas was among the first trickle of men from the Light Plate. He looked small beside the bulk of Sam Warburton, who gave him a robust nudge at some shared jest and laughed, a rough-edged bass roar that drew an answering grin from his mate. Waving, Hannah smiled herself, grateful to Sam for making Dada smile. He was too serious these days.

"Dada . . ." She kissed his cheek before being seized by Sam and scooped into an embrace redolent with the acrid smells of engine oil and cinders. Setting her down he caught the blush and roared again, clapping a great square fist to his brow.

"There – done it again! Kick my arse, Tom, next time I forget your girl's a young 'ooman these days!"

He doffed his cap with elaborate courtesy, blue eyes all but vanished in a grin that crumpled a face as undulating and weathered as his native moors. His nose had long ago been broken in some forgotten fracas but had once, he told Hannah, perceiving her interested inspection of the feature, been as fine and straight as that of the young Prince of Wales. Hannah preferred his nose the way it was. It fitted the rest of his face, which was to her a map, crammed with curious contours and fascinating detail. If she had not been so lucky as to have Thomas Hywel as a father, Sam Warburton would have done very well. Hannah knew instinctively that Sam could be trusted, and that he was kind – though he'd have died before admitting it. She dropped him a curtsey.

"Good day, Mr Warburton. Are you well?" They chatted companionably, making toward Commercial Road. When Sam left them for his lodgings Hannah told

Thomas quickly; of Ronnie Morgan, of Florence's need to get immediate work. And then in a rush of her own decision.

He looked up sharply then. She added nothing to her simple statement but put out a tentative hand and in a moment he took it, frowning.

"Not what I'd wanted for you, *cariad* . . ."

"No, Dada. But it's the war – it changes things more and more as it goes on, doesn't it? And there's always night school, you know; I *can* learn more. And there's sure to be lots of really good jobs for girls after the war. They'll not dare shut us all up in our houses again once they've seen what we can do!"

They walked on slowly. Each was aware of an ending; each grappling with their own emotions.

"Things *do* change; you're right, Princess. I may be takin' a different job myself in a bit." Thomas cleared his throat and Hannah looked quickly at the tense profile. Then she knew for sure; for absolute certain. With heart-stopping fear she wished him to be quiet, not to speak the actual words, so that she might be proved wrong.

She was not wrong. Although she wanted to scream and kick, throw herself to the ground and roll in pain, Hannah walked on with a dreadful calmness, listening to Dada bringing down her world.

"This new Act says married men, Han. An older man could do my job. Makes sense – the sooner we've won, got it over with, the sooner we can all get a bit o' peace. You want to do your share – you've just said. Well, so must I. You'll see that, won't you?"

Thomas would not hear of the shell factory. When she tried to argue he threatened her with being put to work in the kitchen of the Globe Hotel and, mutinous, she

81

subsided. Betsy ranged herself in favour of parlour-maid at the home of the two ancient Misses Harlow; Hannah had helped out there over last Christmas when their maid took ill with mumps and had been sickened by the all-pervading smell of stale urine and old flesh in the cold, dark house. Frantic, she had gone alone to Baglan Hall, recently turned into a convalescent home for troops, to ask for work; she had been kindly received and told she was too young yet to train for a VAD and on the small side for heavy cleaning duties.

Hannah consulted with Florence. Both would be munitions workers they agreed when they were old enough. The latest recruiting poster was compulsive, but Hannah and Florence needed no urging. One had the death of a brother to avenge; the other an ever lengthening roster of cousins bound for the Front who deserved her backup. Auntie's Lil's husband Griffith was just gone to training camp. Now, her own father.

But at this point Hannah's mind would stumble, turn away. He had not yet taken the final step; not confronted Betsy. But there was a rising pressure now in the atmosphere at Number twelve Incline Row. She prayed, a coward, that she would not be there – nor Joe – when that storm broke.

Florence was requisitioned overnight by her Auntie May, whose husband was an assistant in the steelworks metallurgy laboratory. The youth who had helped him tidy away after evening classes had been conscripted and his daytime job had been general help to the stocktaker preparing lists of plates for the test house. No earthly reason why a girl shouldn't do both jobs insisted Aunt May, and Florence had applied for the vacancies. She was snapped up. Just for a few months, Florence promised a somewhat depressed Hannah. Then no problems – they'd both be old enough for the shell factory. Except that the war should be over by then, in which case they'd think of something else.

Was there anything suitable for her at the works, she asked Thomas? He thought of conditions in the Light Plate and shook his head. But once she'd learned to book-keep and such there'd be jobs in the office for sure – clerks were getting scarce as sovereigns. Frustrated, she fled to the allotment to jab viciously with her hoe at the chickweed that would spring up overnight between the rows of vegetables.

Of course . . . Soldiers needed food to fight, as guns needed shells to fire; that was the answer! Hannah looked toward the hill, washed with the limpid brilliance of a June evening, and at the farmsteads dotted over it. Two days later she started work on Gideon Madoc's farm.

"It's yours now, Princess. I'll help you learn to play it, if you want."

They were alone downstairs a bit after five o'clock on the morning of Hannah's fourteenth birthday, standing by the little gas ring in the scullery and blowing on their tea to cool it. Thomas had gone to the cupboard under the stairs, the "dumble hole" and now held out his gift to her almost shyly.

She took it carefully. His bugle . . . his treasured, best loved possession. Choked by sudden tears Hannah flung her arms about his neck and felt the hard bulk of the bugle against her breast as they embraced.

"Dada . . . are you sure?" It had been his great-grandfather's, a bugler in the Crimean war. Thomas had mastered it by trial and error and when she was small they would take the instrument on to the hill, or down to the morfa, for him to practise. Hannah had counted these among the best times; the two of them together

with the old tunes he would coax from this temperamental piece of well-burnished brass. They had for
Hannah a powerfully haunting quality, evoking images
of romantic, long dead princesses and nobly courageous princes, to hover in her mind as the notes faded in
the wind.

"Sure I'm sure. Come Sunday we'll give it an airing,
eh?" His hand briefly covered hers.

Now they went quickly about the business of starting
the day. A cup of tea for Betsy; just rising, Betsy would
see to Joe and his breakfast at six, then take him along to
Aunt Maggie's till it was time for school with Maggie's
youngest, cousin Trevor. Then tea in Thomas's can to go
with the food in his snap-tin; the fire laid for the
evening.

Hannah went first; to the top of Incline Row for the
walk up to Madoc's farm, twenty minutes if she didn't
hang about. Only her fourth day . . . no surprise she was
feeling her muscles. She'd get accustomed . . . stifling a
yawn she bent doggedly into the slope. The new
"summer time" just brought in to help the war effort
meant an hour longer to work of course – old Gideon
Madoc didn't believe in his workers stopping till dusk.
But that was what she was doing it for, after all. The
Women's Land Army, Dada said they were thinking of
calling it. She was as necessary as any soldier, but
fighting from home rather than Flanders. Although
Gideon Madoc was already pressing her to live in,
which would be horrible.

It began to rain, lightly but with the feel of quiet
persistence she recognised. It would set in. But the
hillside was so beautiful in its lush early summer glory,
nothing could mar it. Each season up here had its own
magnificence, and appeared the more so to Hannah
against the man-made contrast below.

She'd kept a treat for her dinner break; a letter from Harry, his first since going back. She opened it lying on her stomach in the dim hay-barn, chewing bread and cheese and onion, with the rain outside doing its best to flatten this year's hay crop, now near ready to make. Harry wasn't the greatest correspondent; but what she looked for, what was important, was to know if he had bridged the miles between on a Saturday night. If it was *working*.

This leaves me well enough, as I hope it finds you, Han. Many new faces here, hope they all prove as fine fellows as the ones gone. I write this in a trench called Scottish Corner. Some Frenchies had it last and left bad smells, my mate Bernard says it is all the garlic. Now, I remembered our plan for Sat nights and did so, went off by myself (but for the rats) and shut my eyes. I was soon rapped on the head and sent on an errand up the line, but felt refreshed for it. I will do so next Sat also. Fourteen now, Han! I will think of you on the day. Must close now, with love and remembrances . . . P.S. Tell Joe I have a Hun's helmet for him.

Hannah read it through four times slowly before folding it carefully into her pocket. Well, she'd just keep working at it. "Love and remembrances" . . . Would he be part of this big push? She *must* reach him; she'd try even harder next Saturday. She chewed the last bit of bread slowly, staring up into the dim cobwebby beams, remembering Harry's bright hair, his laugh, his lovely brown fingers. All the gaiety she'd loved so much in him would come back, surely, when he'd been home again for a while. And she would protect him somehow – she *would* reach him. She knew it was possible . . .

Chapter Four

June 1916

Five months of slogging back and forth around the French fortress of Verdun on the Meuse and 700,000 casualties later no progress had been made. Verdun was still French; but if the Germans were to be defeated the offensive must be taken, and pressure on Verdun relieved.

To this end, since May the 4th Army had been preparing a huge offensive on the Somme front in the vicinity of Amiens. There had never been so much infantry and artillery gathered in one area before and ammunition dumps were everywhere, cleverly camouflaged to blend into the contours of the land. A network of German and British trenches zig-zagged across the baked battlefield and not a head dared be raised above them. For eight days, shells from 2,000 British guns saturated the enemy trenches, the infantry battalions marched to their assembly positions, backed up by massed cavalry.

"Gottcha . . . little bugger." Bernard slapped his neck and squeezed the offending louse flat between thumbnails. " 'Ope there's a delousing station at the end of this bloody 'ike," he confided in Harry. "That's my fourth since the last brew-up. If they're runnin' out in the open this fast, must mean standin' room only down my perishin' vest."

Harry scratched in sympathy, nodding. He'd have liked to talk, it made the time pass quicker on the march, but they'd no water left and he was saving his spittle. The last farm had padlocked their well. Hot, dirty, thirsty, the Tommies had been enraged, with one radical cockney ready to put a bullet through the lock, but Lieutenant Piers-Low had shepherded his platoon past without incident.

Harry recognised that in Lieutenant Piers-Low they'd struck lucky. Given that junior officers couldn't do much other than set an example to the men anyway, young PL was above half useful ... forever on the lookout for extra bits and bobs for the men to make the grind of trench life more bearable. And when little Clem Suter got the telegram saying he'd lost his wife in a shell factory explosion, he'd got him off to Boulogne on compassionate leave without even stopping to delouse. Too bad Clem had stopped a sniper's bullet in the throat a week after he got back.

Endless lines of cavalry horses covered the twenty miles or so of baked, undulating plains from south of Amiens northeast to Albert. "Wonder there's boats left for gettin' owt else 'ere when you reckon what it's tekkin' to fodder this lot," Jem Carler, a balding farmer from Yorkshire nodded at them.

"They reckon hay cargoes take up more ship tonnage than has been lost so far by subs." Geoff Nun was a great one for statistics, a maths teacher from Cardiff who'd once been caught writing poetry on the latrine and had taken a while to live it down. Jem Carler grunted again.

"Wouldn't care if the critters was ever used ... Never once seen them in action. Christ these bloody boots! Better shod'n us, them beasts'll be."

When they fell out for the ten-minute tea break Jem began to unlace his boots, sprawled in the sparse shade of a broken wall. Geoff Nun wagged his head, fanning himself with his peaked cap.

"You'll not get them on again. Best stick it out, this should be the last stop before Albert . . ."

They lay in a sweaty stupor. Harry propped himself on an elbow and lit a Woodbine; if he lay down he'd pass out . . . worse getting going again, then. He seemed to have been marching for ever; he'd no idea what day it was even. Couldn't be far off July . . . he didn't see how he could possibly survive 1916. Dust settled on them all from convoys of lorries moving to the front, from messengers' motor bikes, ambulances, marching troops, the occasional staff car with snapping flag. They must be getting close, by the great shell dumps beginning to appear. In the distance, over a ridge beyond the smudge that would be Albert, the regular faint thud of explosions punctuated the continual drone of spotter planes. A spiral of black smoke split the thick pale sky above the ridge . . . a brief orange burst then, as the plane struck earth. Harry looked away, drawing on his Woodbine. He's never seen such a circus on the move – Christ knows what they were in for. He felt the familiar griping spasm clutch at his bowels that he recognised as fear.

"Come on Christmas!"

Bernard punched his shoulder. Harry struggled to his feet and rearranged his gear for minimum discomfort. Mouth like a millman's crutch, he'd have done better without the Woodbine. They fell in behind the dust cloud of a French cavalry troop. Someone began to sing.

> *There's a long, long trail a'winding*
> *into the land of my dreams . . .*

Seemed funny, old Kitchener dead. No matter

though to the poor sodding Tommies ... Whoever was giving the orders made no odds, they'd doubtless make the usual cockup of it. The last letter from Han had given him a lift. A good kid, Han, you felt she actually wanted to do something for you. He'd give it a go next Saturday like she'd said; do no harm – if he could find out when it *was* Saturday in this bloody place ... his Saturday night date with a girl! Couple of years' time and Han might well be stepping out with her own fella of a Saturday night – she could easily turn into a little beauty, way she was going. And she'd lovely soft little hands ... comforting ... made him feel quite good.

He could do with something to feel good about at this moment. He was covered with flea bites, he had an unpleasantly painful sore on his finger from opening a bully beef can carelessly, he'd had toothache on and off for two weeks and he thought he'd got athlete's foot like half the battalion. He was sick to the stomach of marching through French villages that had been reduced to bits of walls sticking up from heaps of rubble. He'd seen part of a baby's pram sticking out from one heap and it made him feel literally sick for a while ... strange that; all the horrors he'd witnessed, and yet a messed up old baby's pram ...

Harry stared at the observation balloon ducking and swaying off to his left somewhere. Sometimes he and Brigid had walked out together on a Saturday night.

It had been a Tuesday though when he'd ... when they'd ... Harry, with a sudden vividly recollected memory of her soft, full breasts against his chest, her thighs creamy pale under the moon as they opened to let him in; missed his step. Bemused, he shuffled on towards Albert.

*

He hadn't meant to take communion; it could be taken as a sign of weakness. Yet again, maybe it wouldn't hurt for the platoon lance-jack to set an example. He eased up the line, wiping his hands down his trouser seams. Late evening, the last day of June. The ground still full of the day's fierce heat and light lingering on the endless mess of trenches – theirs, and the ones across No Man's Land they'd been ordered to take at dawn. How far ... four hundred yards maybe? The biggest thing of the war to date, that was obvious.

Harry, who had that afternoon been sent as runner to Gibraltar trench up on the ridge south of Albert, had seen nothing like it; men and artillery massed in their thousands everywhere he looked. But not a soul sticking their necks above ground on either side of No Man's Land, with every inch of the battlefield being ploughed up by gunfire directed by endless spotter planes buzzing around like wasps. On the way back he had paused, hidden in a bush to urinate. Below lay the remains of Carnois village. Rags of smoke-stained washing hung on a line behind a heap of rubble, the leg of a caved-in bed balanced over the gutted body of a goat. The smells of charred wood, decomposing flesh, cordite and old refuse were heightened by the force of the sun in the harshly blue sky. Gunfire had eased briefly to give a weird illusion of peace. Harry had watched a German observation balloon being hauled down and remembered feeling oddly relaxed about the whole thing. It was all too big ... out of his hands. Better get a letter home though; just in case. His luck could always run out. Another letter from Han would have been just the ticket for today. Strange that he could feel relaxed; as if a switch had been thrown in his head. Perhaps he was past fear?

Still capable of physical misery, though, on top of his ongoing discomfort he now had a dose of enteritis.

The padre was quick with the wine, no chance to get a decent swallow. Harry bent his head, the wafer sticking to his teeth. He remembered Jenkin's chip shop in Charles Street, the marvellous smell when the salt and vinegar went shooting onto his delectable penn'orth.

"This tastes of soddin' cat's pee." Jem forked over his bully beef afterwards in weary disgust. "You'd've thought they could have come up with summat decent tonight."

"Shut up complaining," said Bernard sharply. "It'll be rat pee, the cats are all dead long since."

"Your rum ration will take the taste away, Carler." Lieutenant Piers-Low had to yell over the screech and roar of heavy five nines passing over them towards the enemy lines. He smiled benignly, pushing towards them over fallen earth where part of the parapet had blown in. "It's on its way." Somehow, the rum hadn't tasted right either, though. Maybe it was them . . .

The whistling rush of shells burst nearer and nearer and these were coming straight for them. One pierced the next traverse and the world rocked. Choked and blinded and deafened, Harry doubled up, chin between his knees, trying to squeeze his whole body under his helmet. The next shell lifted over his head, following the course of the trench. The range was perfect, he had to hand it to the buggers. The joke was, they were supposed to be having a rest before they went over the ladders at dawn. He looked up to the sky. It was beautiful, a midnight velvet shot with sparkling clear stars. He found the Milky Way; and the Bear. He'd shown that to Brigid ... she'd not noticed it before.

The lieutenant pushed back the way he'd come; a few yards on, earth and burst sandbags spewed over shattered bodies and equipment, over bully beef and tin mugs and a shredded half-written letter on blue paper. The wounded bleeding in the further traverse, were propping each other up, grey-faced. The lieutenant, Harry and Jem got them into the next dugout then picked their way back to sort out equipment for the dawn assault, trying not to tread on half-buried, contorted shapes who moments before had been men with names, faces and families.

The pre-dawn bombardment turned to a hurricane in its earth-shaking ferocity. Minutes to zero, the parapet top appeared to quiver and slide forward like a grey undulating carpet. "Bloody rats..." Bernard hissed at his shoulder as Harry stared, paralysed, at the phenomenon. "Leavin' the sinkin' bloody ship. Jesus!"

Hundreds of them were taking flight together. Harry still stared, his bowels cramping with fear; he wanted to run blindly with the rats but in the opposite direction – *away* from the waiting enemy. Fiercely, as he faced eternity, Harry wanted to live.

He peeped between two sandbags, over the wire to No Man's Land. Leap from shell-hole to shell-hole, that's the way to stay alive. God knows there's enough of them. It's worked before; he'd gone over the top before and survived. He'd be okay. He squeezed into the shored-up earth as men filed past him from the communication trenches, a dark, mute stream moving to their allotted stations, to their fate. Were they like him, each struggling against sick panic? Units had crawled up between trenches now

and squatted soundlessly behind them in craters;
Lieutenant Piers-Low eased along his men, touching a
shoulder here, adjusting a strap there, whispering a
word to the first-timers. Next to Harry, young Perc
Bonner vomited down his tunic, adding to the stench
of unburied dead; his face glistening greenly in the
dark that was becoming, inexorably, dawn.

"Rum didn't agree . . ." He whispered, attempting
to salvage his manhood with a ghastly smile. Harry
nodded; tightened the strap on Perc's helmet.

"You'll be okay. And it's nice and warm – and dry.
At least we're not gettin' soaked." Harry suddenly
remembered it was a Saturday; the first day of July.
That was it then – he'd *have* to survive today.
Couldn't let Han down, she'd be expecting him! He
felt a small but unmistakable easing of panic.

Steel clinked as bayonets were fixed. Men began to
climb from the trench in single file to form the first
wave. Hundreds of guns opened fire from the valley
on the left, the French reopened on the right, a storm
of shells flew shrieking over their heads. Seconds to
go; Harry recalled Captain Brand's words – they
would have saturated the enemy lines with shellfire,
leaving nothing for the infantry to do but mop up.
Simple . . . was that the sun coming up, or flames
from Pozières village?

Right then . . . up the ladders and over. Move . . .
make your bloody legs *move*. Yell if it seemed a good
idea – if it helped.

The man in front tottered and fell. Harry leapt over
his body; the earth shook and roared, shells crashing
from every direction. The first wave had melted into
hot acrid smoke.

Flashes parted the smoke. Shouts from an officer,
bodies to trip over. Harry got stuck to a line of blown-

up barbed wire, pulling himself free as more men came behind; into a shell-hole and out. Into a trench, where German and British wounded were tearing open white field dressings, shouting for stretcher bearers over the unbearable din. Up again. He zig-zagged, eyes watering and throat dried out. More wire. He glimpsed Geoff Nun, lost him. The lieutenant's voice came from somewhere to the right, shouting encouragement. A hail of machine-gun bullets now – he reached the dubious shelter of a crater and fell into it.

"*Kamerad!*" Two Germans were crouching there; both were wounded, one dying. He had laid his gun, grenades, helmet neatly at his side and was stretched out awkwardly, the remains of a leg poking from beneath his hip. The other German stood up, repeated "*Kamerad*," and stared at Harry's bayonet. An unexploded shell was half buried a foot or so away from Harry. He was looking at it when the world burst open in searing, roaring chaos.

The reserve army and three divisions waited behind to exploit whatever breach in the enemy trenches the 4th Army could make. General Gough went to their headquarters in nearby Querrien to be kept in touch with operations as ambulances started rolling by with the first loads of wounded. Headquarters' windows rattled from the firing of some heavy artillery hidden in the park. The French, attacking simultaneously on the right of the British, were making a great deal more noise. Conflicting reports were coming in from the left; from the British.

Hannah longed for dusk today. First of July; a Saturday. She'd a half day off tomorrow ... time to get home, to see them all. She was sorry to discover that she simply could not take to the Madoc family. Gideon Madoc was a small grubby man with a dark port wine stain across one side of his jowls that gave him a threatening appearance. He bullied his three sons and his wife, who took out their frustration on one another, on Sarah the dairymaid, and on Hannah if she gave them half a chance. At first she had been cowed by their aggression but quickly reasoned that if she were to stay she must learn to stand up for herself.

George, the eldest son, was the most reasonable and she soon felt safe enough to appeal to him over any unfair treatment. The middle son was nondescript, a shirker who kept out of people's way lest they gave him a job to do; the third, Norman, was extremely unpleasant. A bulky young man with a thick short neck and the beginnings of a paunch, teeth that appeared to belong to an older generation and bristly little hairs emerging from nostrils and ears, he tormented people and animals alike. Norman was Hannah's biggest problem; he pawed at her whenever she came within reach and when she complained to his father, she was told not to be a dirty-minded madam and to get on with her work.

The Madocs were one of half a dozen families who had farmed on the mountain for generations. Rumours gave them good money salted away somewhere, but Hannah saw no sign of it. Their farmhouse was in poor repair as were their outbuildings; yet they had decent enough land, Gideon's sheep did well and he had laid a lower field down to vegetables that spring to sell locally. Hannah had to keep these hoed, an arduous job on the sloping stony ground, and help with the seasonal work. She had even tried her hand at repairing one of the dry-stone walls that crisscrossed the mountain in lieu of hedges. Now there was hay-making in a couple of the richer fields not occupied by ewes with their lambs.

Better to sleep in over hay-making, Gideon Madoc had urged ... the busy time. Before that it had been the shearing. But he was right about the walk night and morning – by the time she'd come back with the last cartload tonight she'd be grateful that her bed was no more than a step or two distant in the tiny room under the eaves.

There was Merry's flank to be looked at first. As weary as Hannah at the end of the day's haying, the great dappled mare stood quiet to be unharnessed, washed down and groomed, hoofs picked out under their curtains of pale silky feathers. Then a nosebag of oats in the dim, peaceful stable whilst Hannah, on the upturned crate, explored with sensitive fingertips the twitching muscles round the small, deep laceration high in the flank.

Nain's book said hypericum, St John's wort, for wounds involving nerves, so she decided to give it a try. Plenty in the front garden of Mr Mansel's ... she'd asked but had been told no, they could not allow one child to pick or the whole place could be stripped bare in no time. Deeply insulted, Hannah had gone back very late the same night to take what she needed – quicker than trying to reason with fools she told Joe, who helped her back in through the window.

Simmering the plant down was difficult with so little time at home now – Betsy had come back from her sister's before it was finished and had threatened to tip the lot down the yard. But of late, the heart for fight had gone from Betsy. She knew that Thomas would go in the end, that he would leave her; when fiinally his halting inadequate words had come, they had been no more than a confirmation of her dreadful fear. When tears and rage would not serve, and she knew that this time they would not, Betsy shored herself up with grim-faced silence which Thomas knew must be borne.

Hannah massaged in the St John's wort essence, talking quietly to the mare as she worked with rhythmic circular movements. When the twitching skin had become relaxed and quiescent, she laid both hands on it and closed her eyes. Familiar sounds of farm and hill receded, the steady munching of oats took on a beat akin to that of her heart. Faintly at first, a slow warm tide crept up her wrists ... the warmth of the horse became part of her connecting hands and girl and animal fused in one giving and receiving benefice. The girl looked small beside the huge creature. Her trousers were baggy on her slender hips and thighs and the old shirt of Thomas's slid off her shoulders. She rested her head against Merry for a moment and her hair, released from its containing cap, fell in soft, nut-brown waves against the pale oval of her face. The mouth in repose curved into shadowed little corners; the nose, short and straight like her father's with a smatter of summer freckles grew from a neat smooth bridge between wide-spaced brows. In an attitude of complete repose, Hannah seemed to rest against her patient.

"Coo-eee!" The crate was kicked from under her feet and Hannah fell heavily, her head mere inches from the massive iron shoes of the startled horse. The woman looked down on her as she rolled clear of the great hooves, hands on pudding soft hips which shook in silent mirth.

Matty Madoc was crazy. Hannah had asked Thomas about her after the first day.

"Intermarryin', *cariad*, that's what it is ... First cousins wedded once too often. She seemed well enough as a girl Mam says – she knew her from school, see. One of the boys is deaf, but that may be something other ..."

Hannah picked herself up, dizzy and shaken, and steadied the mare. The hypericum essence had emptied into the straw. She retrieved the bottle, angry enough for tears; all to be done again now. Matty watched her with eyes almost buried in a flushed balloon-fat face, not shaking with laughter now but with the smile still there, uncertain and suddenly pathetic. Hannah's anger melted to pity.

"You won't do that again, will you, Mrs Madoc? You could have killed me." The woman frowned worriedly, pulling at a strand of greasy hair that had escaped from its captive knot. "It's all right." Hannah added gently. "You didn't mean to – "

"Goin' to the fair on my birthday," Matty told her with a child's eagerness. "Goin' to buy a china dog. Money for it, I got." She pulled up her skirt to scratch herself and a smell of unwashed body assaulted Hannah. "You got money?"

"Not much." She settled Merry for the night, rubbed up the harness and left things ready for the morning, Matty standing idly by with vacant eyes now, lost in her jumbled day-dream. Hannah's legs shook with the fatigue of her twelve-hour day and she longed to curl into the straw by the mare's sweet warm flank for the night. But Matty would look for help with supper, a precedent set from the first day. Just get hay-making over; back home then with Joe's firm little body at her back in her own bed.

At last, the narrow flock mattress in the attic room shared with Sarah the dairymaid. Hannah hung out of the window under the eaves to let the still, hay-scented air caress her skin. A beautiful night ... stars were everywhere as the sky darkened from musky twilight to midnight blue. Could Harry see them? She'd work to do for Harry tonight for it was a Saturday, the first day of July. For days, papers had reported that gunfire from across the Channel could be heard in south coast towns and villages. As far inland as London floors of buildings were vibrating from the massive bombardment that was accompanying the big push. Over a million and a half shells, the papers said, so that when the troops attacked what remained of the enemy would give way quickly before the great advance. The final advance ... who knows ... then maybe Dada would not need to go?

But there would be losses ... every day until the struggle was won those dreaded telegrams would keep coming. So Hannah fixed her gaze on a little patch of night sky with its single star and began to centre down and focus her thoughts on Harry.

> *Dainty skirts and delicate blouses*
> *aren't much use for pigs and cows-es.*

The voice began faintly, increasing in volume as though blown by the wind through a tunnel. Finally it penetrated Harry's dazed consciousness to drag him back from blessed silence. He lay where he had fallen, enjoying the little song, but all too soon the girl's voice – it was Hannah's, he could swear – was overwhelmed by the infernal racket of war. Harry sighed and struggled to maintain contact with the voice as it faded.

Above him rocket lights burst and spread into vivid streamers of colour and he lay still a moment more, watching them. He felt disoriented, strangely detached; soon to begin to shiver, though the night was warm. Then he eased himself up to peer over the crater edge. As he did, he put his hand into a mess of something sticky.

"Bloody hell!" He put the hand to his nose, anticipating the smell, blood. His? Eyes accustoming themselves to the night, he saw that it was the remains of the German who had been standing. He also saw a fresh crater a few yards off, bordered by motionless figures. As close a call as he wanted, that . . . if he'd not stopped here those extra seconds, he'd have been just about *there*.

Harry eased himself over the edge of his crater and started to crawl, his head slowly clearing to allow the sickening, familiar fear to assert itself. He didn't fancy lying beside that unexploded shell all night, and he'd kill for a drink, throat dried now to sand. And that dismembered leg smelled something terrible – not that he could get away from that stink anywhere in this Godforsaken hellhole. He continued to shake, and in a moment stopped to vomit.

He inched on, rifle and ammunition dragging. Take two trenches, that had been the order. He hoped the others would be there, not a load of Huns lying in wait. Bloody daft order. Seemed hours ago he'd heard it . . . maybe it was. Funny, that song Han had been singing . . . she'd sounded so close by for a minute or two. Couldn't have been, though . . . just imagination. He'd reached a tangle of bodies in mixed khaki and grey uniforms when the ground erupted behind him with a hellish uproar and he was pushed flat, feeling the breath sucked from him by the blast.

Still in one piece ... that had to be the last of his luck used up. Harry increased his crawling speed, zigzagging over shelled and re-shelled earth, where earlier casualties were being thrown up to the surface again in crazy, disoriented glimpses of hands and feet, arms and legs. And over all, the sickening stench of death, cordite, and faeces. Christ ... that had to be the very worst of the whole hellish business.

What if his own mates shot him as he reached the sandbags? He began to call, but the shell barrage and ceaseless racket of machine guns drowned his efforts. He saw sandbags though the smoke, the metallic gleam of a rifle in a gap.

"God save me!" he heard himself yell, and he cast himself haphazard over the sandbags.

"Bernard didn't make it," Geoff Nun passed him a Woodbine. "Got it on the wire. And Jem – " He took a deep drag on his own cigarette.

They were cramped together with two other men on the slatted earth bench in the dugout, swallowing tea that tasted of dust and cordite. At a small table in the corner a captain was receiving despatches from a string of orderlies, who would then queue for a receipt before squeezing through the partly collapsed doorway and back up the steps, picking their way over the wounded slumped about as they waited for attention. Harry leaned back against the earth wall; he thought he would suffocate soon in this dank coffin of space under the devastated ground. He gulped more tea and chewed on a stale German oatcake from a tinful surviving the British shelling and the rats.

"So what happened to Jem?" He let the oatcake drop, it stank of rat pee. Seemed he never kept a mate past a month at most.

"Jack Prince brought him in with a chest wound. He was taken to Albert with the first lot some while back. Didn't look hopeful." Geoff Nun began to scratch with an expression of concentrated agony. "Christ ... these little sods will be the death of me ..."

"He said I could have his mouth organ," said Harry. "And I told Bernard I'd write to Nellie myself ... if he ..."

He felt sick emptiness, thinking of his mates. He'd lost count of how many had gone. What he wanted now was a woman, loving and warm and smelling of summer flowers, to hold him quiet in her arms; to stroke his hair, tell him it would be all right. Even though he knew it would never be all right again.

"Tell you what," Geoff Nun screwed his cigarette end into the wall with a ferocious movement. "They told us these Hun trenches'd be shelled to hell – said there'd be no one left alive, didn't they? Well they were bloody well wrong. As per bloody usual. These damn dugouts got dug so deep we could've shelled 'em for a lifetime and the buggers would've come up smiling. Not only that – looks like half the shells were duds. All over they are, sticking out of the bloody ground like daisies. So what went wrong?"

He glared at Harry, still scratching furiously. Harry shook his head, threw away his tea and eased free from the man next to him on the bench who had slumped on his shoulder. He didn't know what had gone wrong, except that he couldn't breathe down here one more bloody minute. He got up carefully because his legs were still shaking.

"Thanks for the tea, Geoff. I'm okay now; how about a stroll in the moonlight, sweetheart?" He hooked his hand through Geoff's elbow to steady himself, he felt suddenly light-headed. "Did I ever tell you about that French nurse in Amiens? Tall as a bloody street lamp? Used to put a bucket on her head and swing on the handles . . . Happy days."

Conflicting reports buzzed up and down the trenches. Things were going well with the French on the right; progress on the left was vague. Countless aeroplanes added to the confusion by exchanging signals with tracer bullets. One accidently shot down an observation balloon looming suddenly, bucking madly against the cable anchoring it to earth. The observer in his gondola disappeared as the blazing cloth collapsed on him.

"Roast Hun for brekkers," Jack Prince spat into the dust and stared at a bunch of prisoners being shepherded from crater to crater. They looked crumpled and insubstantial, ducking unsteadily as shells roared over them towards the German lines. "Wonder if they taste anything like pork?"

"Don't mention bloody food," snapped Geoff Nun. But Harry thought about it. He had a raging headache and felt as though he'd been used as a rugger ball. A big bowl of Mam's oxtail soup with wedges of crusty bread spread thick with yellow butter would set him up a treat.

He *was* alive, though. He squinted between the sandbags at what dawn on day two of the big push was revealing as the pearly, orangy-lemon light strengthened and the pale moon sank. Bodies and bits of bodies everywhere, in every conceivable attitude and condition. Many had been rotting in the sun for days; they were in the grey uniforms. But most of the newly dead were khaki – the lads of Kitchener's army, two years in the making and gone in a few hours last night. For a moment or two the dawn was uncannily quiet; somewhere behind him he could swear that was a bird singing. Impossible ... he was bloody lucky ... couldn't really believe it yet. Harry wiped his nose on his sleeve, took careful aim at a bit of grey cloth glimpsed between burst sandbags, just within range, and fired. At the same second shells began to whine over them again and started to find their range. Harry forgot about the birdsong and got his head down.

General Gough ordered the Reserve Army into the line on 2 July to replace the shattered 8th and 10th Corps, and cancelled orders to renew the attack. He sent out scouts to discover the situation at nearby Ovillers and La Boiselle, the ruined villages either side of the Albert–Baupaume Road. At least they could take the enemy's mind off Verdun. The immense difficulties of breaking through German lines in open country had been most tragically illustrated again as casualty numbers came in and the clearing station at Albert filled and refilled. All along the Front was the same story as the fatal tactics of attrition continued; those of trying to kill more of the enemy than one lost, and using reserves simply to repeat failed attacks.

They knew they had been badly checked, that seemed clear enough now. They knew the Reserve Army was drawn up ready behind them to exploit the small breach they'd made in this section, and by mid-morning fresh men were pushing into the trenches to join the few left from yesterday. But the orders for renewing the attack were cancelled. The enemy had the range of every trench and kept up a ceaseless shelling, with machine guns saturating anything that moved. They were to mount a small attack on the enemy-held ruins of La Boiselle that night though, Lieutenant Piers-Low told them – nothing large-scale but they'd have a go. Staring at the village, with smoke fogging over a chaos of bricks and ruined houses, Harry wondered what was going on in the minds of the men behind them; the enemy. Maybe if someone shouted to the Huns over the few yards between them that they were going to be attacked come dark, and as many killed as could be, they would quietly slip away to the next line of trenches and save everyone a lot of trouble.

It didn't work like that though – Harry had found that out early on. Both sides had to slog it out, get themselves bloody well blown to bits for the sake of a strip of torn-up French earth that could never be any damn use to God nor man again.

He began to clean his rifle and check over his equipment. He'd try for Han again next Saturday.

Almost every family in the district had someone "on the Somme". That first Sunday the big push was written up as a victory; the new armies had "surpassed themselves", men were "slightly wounded", losses were "by no means excessive". Hannah spent a precious hour of her half day writing to Harry before going to the morfa to try out the bugle with Thomas and search for more St John's wort for Merry's wound. The rare times with her father were doubly precious now – he was running in an older man to his job and would leave the works in a couple of weeks for training camp. Now, they did not speak of it. Only on the way back to Incline Row, with Joe running ahead with Fly, did he break the companionable silence to say abruptly: "You'll try to hold things together won't you, *cariad*? Your Mam will find it hard ... less money comin' in for one thing. And Joe ..."

"It's awful just to think of how we'll all miss you, and that's the truth, Dada!" Then she was in his arms, clinging tight. Joe turned at that moment, called out "Soppy ... our Han's a soppy date ..." Then he too dived back and burrowed into their embrace. Joe knew his Dad was going to fight the Huns; that other boys' Dads had gone and not come back. He'd no clear idea of what happened at the Front and thought of his Dad's going there with a mixture of pride and terror. His twin cousins Wyn and George were there now, and Harry of course, and cousin Dewi was training ready to go to sea, and now Uncle Jenkin from Cwmavon had gone, too, leaving Aunt Cissy to see to the sheep and everything. Mam seemed cross all the time and Han was hardly ever there. His small familiar world was melting away, ground shifting under his feet. Everyone was doing jobs they'd not done before, they were being told to eat less food which was daft because food was getting less anyway! Like coal ... and yet there were still great cinema shows, and the Red Cross Fête, and the bands, and games on the beach. He wriggled in between sister and father, and Fly scampered back to join them, barking.

"Will you buy us a cherryade from Old Peg's, Dad? Will you? Eh, Dad?" He may as well try to capitalise on the situation, and cherryade at old Peg's represented all that was good about the crumbling order of his life.

Thomas laughed and pulled his son's hair. "The limit, that's what you are." He jingled the change in his pocket, teasing. "Oh well ... and some mints for Mam, then, eh?"

"I'll get those," Hannah volunteered promptly. She wasn't used yet to having the shilling for herself out of her ten shillings wages; she bought a savings stamp with sixpence of it but still felt rich. Gideon Madoc had said nine shillings but Thomas had been adamant, insisting on ten at the very least after the week's trial period. This was hard work, long hours, and Gideon was not going to get Hannah cheap just because she was female. But he'd only pay a strong lad ten the farmer had objected, and Thomas had smiled. He couldn't get a lad though, could he? Lads were joining up, and if under eighteen they were in munitions for better money. And a lad might be stronger than his girl, but wouldn't help out Matty like Hannah was expected to as well.

And there were the trousers. Up and down the ladders on the haycart was hopeless in skirts; and when she'd been on top of the stack she'd caught Ned, the youngest Madoc son who was deaf, trying to look up her petticoat. So Hannah bought trousers in the market, not too badly used and only needing a good pin at the waist and the flies sewing up. With them she wore gaiters and on top a stout cotton work overall, pulled in with Dada's belt. The cap was Harry's, for her hair to tuck inside to keep it from dust and dirt. Thomas insisted that Gideon fork up the sixpence for the trousers and for the one-and-thruppenny gaiters – neither would be any use to Hannah once she'd left the farm he pointed out. Disgruntled, Gideon had parried by charging Hannah tuppence for her evening meal. Aware that he had a bargain in the somewhat unusual shape of this particular Land Girl as they were increasingly being called, yet he must keep his end up. Never pay out a penny if a ha'penny will do.

Betsy hated the trousers. Hannah was on no account to leave the farm wearing them or she'd be made to start in service in the town right away, which was where she should have gone in the first place. When Joe, winking at Hannah, sang the new Land Girl ditty under his breath:

> *Dainty skirts and delicate blouses*
> *Aren't much use for pigs and cows-es*

she clipped his ear before turning to give the stew a violent stirring, genuinely upset. Everything seemed to upset Betsy at present. Starting for the farm next morning, Hannah whispered to a sleepy Joe to behave himself and help all he could with the chores, or she'd be after him. He murmured, eyes still closed, then pulled her down with warm arms for a kiss.

"You comin' back tonight, Han?"

"Better stay just a few more nights, love, get the hay in before the weather breaks. Then I'll be home . . . we'll have a good talk then. Take care now." She crept from the room to hurry down Incline Row in the sharp dawn wind. She wanted to do her bit to win the war . . . but she disliked all the Madocs save for poor mad Matty. And she *hated* being away from home.

The attack on La Boiselle failed. The few men who survived the nightmare stretch of No Man's Land were pinned down in shell-holes on the edge of the village, but most lay still, soon adding to the stench of the earlier dead. Some wounded had dragged themselves to the aid posts; Lieutenant Piers-Low was one, with a shattered leg and a neck wound. Next day Harry heard he had bled to death waiting for attention.

Surprised each day to find himself still alive, Harry at least achieved the facility of removing himself from diabolically unpleasant circumstances by flicking a switch in his mind. Thus protected, the core of him stayed whole. Sometimes now the past was the only reality; the stinking sun-scorched present a nightmare from which he must wake soon. He could put up with it – the blood and death, hunger and thirst and weariness and lice, endless sapping discomfort and paralysing boredom – because it simply *could* not go on. Nightmares never did. And often he thought of Hannah; and that also helped to detach him from the unbearable present. He caught himself quite often humming that little ditty he'd heard that night.

He and Geoff Nun and Jack Prince drew close together after La Boiselle, they were all that remained of the old platoon. Jack Prince was sorting through Geoff's hair for nits now as Harry scratched himself, crammed with his friends into a wedge of shade. By peeping out at a certain angle he could just see the Albert–Baupaume road being heavily shelled, and either side of it the two enemy occupied ruins of La Boiselle and Ovillers. They'd made so little progress for all their casualties . . . a few hundred yards, less in places, of useless earth. He knew they'd have to have another go at talking those ruins, sooner or later. Later, he hoped. After Saturday. So's not to disappoint Han.

Beyond the Pozières ridge, big clouds were piling up fast to obscure the sun. The resulting half-light changed everything – the colour of the churned earth, the spiky charred remains of trees, even the gunfire had a different resonance in the charged air.

"How about this, then – "

Jack Prince left his nit-hunt to look at the sky now

turned to threatening purple and black. At that moment the dark mass was split by a fork of lightning and the trench vibrated under a colossal thunder crash. Harry thought that under it he heard the familiar "tick" of a bullet finding its mark. Jack slithered down beside him as great drops of rain peppered the dust, and slumped with his head resting against the boot of a long dead German protruding from the trench wall. His face turned white and a stream of blood oozed from under his helmet.

"Jack! Oh, bloody hell!" Harry went down by him as Jack's mouth opened like a fledgling waiting for food. He gasped and Harry slashed through the equipment webbing to take the pressure off his chest. It expanded once, twice; his eyelids quivered open, he appeared to look at Harry for a second before they fluttered down. With a last small tremble Jack subsided in a heap at Harry's feet, the now torrential rain washing the blood from his face.

Harry squatted by him, water swilling off his helmet. He put out a hand blindly to touch Jack's arm. As a shell burst a few yards off earth crumbled over the body and it seemed to settle further, the uniform now the colour of the mud starting to run down the trench walls.

"Fucking bastards." Geoff Nun was kneeling, too; the rain on his lashes could have been tears. A second shell, even closer, showered them with sand from burst bags and part of the trench caved in, pushing Harry over Jack's now half buried form.

"Christ, these buggers are gas!"

Eyes watering, they pulled off Jack's tag, snatched the contents of his breast pocket and his rifle and bolted from the creeping fumes, blinded by the ferocity of the cloudburst. They found Lieutenant Piers-

Low's replacement, a burly young man called Lincoln, giving a message to a runner in a communication trench, and handed over Jack's possessions. They did not speak of him again.

It rained for three days. The Somme dust turned to liquid mud that rushed off the slopes to invade every trench. Duckboards were buried ... a soft yellow paste stuck to boots, equipment, everything. Smoke lay like fog in the heavy air, clinging to the trees of Thiepval Wood so that they appeared to be rising from clouds. The attack on Thiepval had been beaten back to last week's front line, increasing the general depression. Harry was given his second stripe and wrote home to give the news, but when it was finished he made a boat of the letter and floated it down the trench.

When he heard that they were to be relieved on the following day, Sunday 8 July, he stared without comment across No Man's Land. He found that he was commenting on very little these days. It was a waste of energy. The broken ground hid machine-gun nests with clear views of their own lines; before them, the dead of a week ago still lay, flattened now by the rain. Some hung on wire, gnawed by rats so that bits were falling off – he'd gone out two nights back with a party to cut them free but they'd come apart with pulling.

Tonight an attack on Ovillers was planned. With that between now and being relieved on the morrow, there seemed little point in looking forward even to that ... to anything.

"They only told us about being relieved to jolly us along," Geoff said. It didn't jolly them along. Harry, knowing it was a Saturday, tried to think of Hannah, but this time his brain would not co-operate. Bits of him seemed not to be working properly now.

"There's a fresh division coming in," Lieutenant Lincoln told them, brisk and reassuring. They were not reassured. Only unbelievably tired, concentrating exhausted minds on staying alive an hour at a time; and often now, even that didn't seem worth the effort.

The barrage was short. They scaled the ladders, struggled forward in mud and water, fell into the first flooded shell-hole. Harry didn't leap obstacles and zigzag this time; the mud pulled him back, and any-way he was far too tired now for all that business. He stumbled into the enemy trench with a few survivors and was confronted by a bunch of Germans who at once raised their hands, shouting "*Kamerad*". Their rifle ammunition had run out explained their officer, pulling his emaciated form to attention, and their machine guns were out of action. Lieutenant Lincoln, grey-faced from an arm wound that he insisted was slight, hesitated; taking prisoners at this stage was inconvenient. He looked round, saw Harry, sighed and beckoned.

Harry and a skinny little private called Belper chiv-vied their Germans back across No Man's Land, all falling into the British trench like a mud-caked land-slide. Hustling the prisoners along the maze of trenches to brigade headquarters Harry became aware that for the moment he was reasonably safe. He had survived yet another night attack. And in only hours now the brigade was being relieved. He did wonder briefly if it had anything to do with it being a Satur-day night; and Hannah. But he was too tired to think. Too tired to do anything.

The officer was given a whisky by the interrogating major which he accepted with much heel-clicking whilst offering no information. When the major gave up and ordered the prisoners away to the cage, Harry pushed himself wearily back up the slippery steps and set off down the road again, Private Belper bringing up the rear. He wished he knew what had happened to Geoff. Wished he wasn't *so bloody tired*. Hoped to God Han had done her stuff. Because sure as hell he didn't feel in much shape to see after his own survival one minute longer.

The officer walked in silence abreast of him, the prisoners trailed raggedly behind. Several lorries had skidded into the roadside ditches, lying on their sides like dead elephants while men swarmed about them in the mire with ropes, yelling instructions to one another and cursing their generally abortive efforts.

At the cage his charges were delivered into custody, their arrival watched by dejected Germans peering through the wire. The officer was marched off with an intelligence officer, back still ramrod straight. Harry nodded at Private Belper.

"Right, old son. Back we go."

Private Belper sighed, nodded back. Christ, thought Harry, he looks no more than a kid ... nineteen? "Where you from then?" he asked kindly as they started back along the road. Not that he cared, but the poor young sod looked done in.

"Devon. Kingsbridge ..." Belper had to shout to make himself heard above the roar and rattle of lorries, the shellbursts, the planes overhead.

"Nice," said Harry politely. He'd no idea where that was. "I've not been to Devon. You ever been to Wales?"

Harry never discovered if Belper had been to Wales. A lorry was coming up behind. As he moved right in to give it space he heard the low whine of another shell. Instinctively he crouched. He heard Belper's frantic scream and the lorry's brakes shriek; felt pain explode in his head. "Han . . . Han . . . catch me." Lovely. Soft little hands; soft voice. Safe now.

Hannah sat up, screaming. The dairymaid shot up, too, knocking over her candle. Hannah clutched her head, gulped for breath, staring into the dark that was just greying into dawn. Then she began quietly to moan, rocking from the waist.

"Hannah?" Sarah called to her in a voice blurred with sleep. Hannah stumbled across the boards to the little window and pushed it further open with frantic fingers.

"Harry? Harry!" Tears trickled down her face as she strained to see south; battled to tear aside the veil hiding her from him, fought to span the distance between them. "Harry . . . oh, *cariad.*"

Trembling, weeping, she stayed there, staring southeast with anguished eyes as light strengthened over the hills and bay. When a worried Sarah tried to get her away she had to prise her fingers from the sill and found them icy as marble, as was Hannah's cheek where the dawn air had dried her tears.

Day by day, the truth of the Somme slaughter became clearer. Whole pages of casualty lists began to appear in newspapers; a grey mass of close-packed names, scanned with urgent impatience outside newsagents' shops, on the corner by the newsboy, or carried home to be read in private. An entire street in Taibach had drawn blinds. Black armbands were everywhere, and little wreaths of flowers round photographs of young men.

Cousin Wyn, one of Aunt Rose's twins, was posted

missing. "Where could he be?" She repeated time and again to neighbours and relatives, as though her son had been carelessly mislaid by the army. Wyn was a gunner. His father comforted Aunt Rose as best he could. After ten days the dread telegram arrived with its brief message and Aunt Rose, the most delicate of the four sisters with her small frame, her transparent pale skin, her pale brown hair and pale hazel eyes, disappeared into her bedroom to grieve alone.

Hannah came back home to sleep four days after she had the nightmare; the day Aunt Maggie got the telegram about Harry. Wounded. Not dead, then; Hannah had thought he *must* be dead. In fact she had thought of nothing else since the nightmare. She had felt stunned . . . so much of her life, especially lately, had been given over to thinking, worrying, planning for Harry. She had really been unable to envisage a world without him. Now she set about trying to raise Aunt Maggie's hopes of a recovery. When Aunt Rose's second telegram came she went out on the hill and prayed for her dead cousin's spirit.

"I hope you are happy now," she said, watching cotton wool clouds bouncing over the mountain tops. "I hope that where you are is beautiful, and that *Nain* was there to welcome you, and Zig." Zig had been Wyn's dog. To the shy boy who was not too good with people, his dog had been all to him. "And tell *Nain*, will you Wyn dear, that the St John's wort worked a treat on Merry."

Thomas heard the news of his younger brother Harold's death on the Somme two days before he went to training camp. Harold had moved to Swansea a few years ago and they'd not seen much of him. But Thomas had been especially fond of the "baby" of the family.

"You see!" Betsy faced him, arms akimbo, colour flaring in her drawn cheeks. It seemed she blamed Thomas for all these deaths. "Now you, too!" she cried out, beside herself, and stared round the room as though defying the furniture to contradict her.

Thomas stood mute, twisting his cap round and round. He wanted to cry for Harold, the little lad he'd taught to catch minnows in the long hot summers of childhood. He wanted to cling to Betsy and have her comfort him. He stood white and still while her helpless fury battered him. Then he put his cap back on and walked to Sam Warburton's digs, whistling to Fly to follow.

Hannah and Joe went to the station with him. Betsy had gone grey-faced to work; she couldn't afford a day off now, she said, with their money cut and all still to find. Joe carried the small haversack, Hannah the stiff unfamiliar greatcoat. Her father looked smaller in uniform . . . from behind she'd not have known him. He was going to be a sapper probably, he said, as they walked away from Incline Row. He told them what sappers did, talking cheerfully all the way to the station. Hannah was glad because when she tried to speak her voice had to work around a great lump of misery in her throat. She'd asked for the day off – she'd have taken it anyway, nothing would have stopped her.

It was mercifully quick. Thomas raked Joe up into a bear hug. "You be a good boy for your Mam, eh, son? Be back soon . . . Only up to Shropshire for a few weeks. Send you a card, that's what I'll do, a funny one . . ." He turned to Hannah, who was staring at him with a look of concentrated yearning.

"You mind now, Princess." He coughed and looked

116

away. Hannah laid his greatcoat over his arm with care.

"I'll play you a tune on the bugle when you're back, Dada."

Whistle blowing, doors slamming ... for a second the trio folded into one; unfolded, to let Thomas hurry to the nearest carriage door. He disappeared, but as the train began to move pushed to a window and raised a hand in farewell. Joe began to cry; Hannah squeezed his shoulder hard and hissed. "Smile – smile for your Dad, quick now!"

They were still there, with fixed smiles and tears coursing down their faces, as the train disappeared.

Wyn's twin brother George was killed in October as the battle of the Somme dragged on in a welter of mud and death, 1916 ... when would it end. Betsy drew the curtains and went to offer her sister what comfort she could, leaving Joe at his friend Leonard's and a stark note on the table for Hannah. Horrified, Hannah washed and changed though it was almost dusk and she'd had no food since midday, and set off for Aunt Rose's house in Alexandra Street across the bridge in Aberavan. The Electric cinema was just emptying; it had been showing the new documentary *Battle of the Somme* all week to packed houses. Some women were weeping. One was repeating "That was him, I swear it!" to her husband, who was hurrying her along with a hand under her elbow, saying nothing. Outside, a recruiting drive was in progress. On a small platform plastered with posters, with a gramophone playing martial music, an officer flanked by two sergeants and two privates was exhorting every man to do his duty without more ado.

"Now you have seen the men who are defending

your homes from the enemy!" The officer called strongly to the cinema-goers. "Will you not join their glorious ranks? Can you go about your business with a clear conscience, having seen their sacrifice on your behalf? Decide now that you *must* share their struggle!"

"He's right!" A woman clambered up beside him and raised her arm high. "They need you over there, you've just seen that! We'll keep the home fires burning, never fear. You'll be ashamed all your life if your son asks 'What did you do in the war, Dad,' and you have to say 'Nothing, son'!"

Hannah then realised who the young officer was, David Vaughan, the boy who almost two years ago had tipped her off the bench at the railway station when she was seeing Harry off for the first time. He had changed; broader in the shoulder with an air of assurance even more marked than she recalled. His cap hid the auburn hair, but the strong lantern-jawed face, the striking eyes that were brilliant aquamarine, deepset and clear beneath strong brows that almost met above a firmly cut nose. She watched him for a moment. He was arrogant; but with a magnetic quality that over-rode the arrogance. Hannah suddenly pushed forward.

"He might never have a son to ask if he does go."

Looking David Vaughan straight in the eye, she tilted her chin defiantly, and saw that his gaze too was now distinctly less than friendly.

"It's true," she continued quickly. "I have lost my uncle Harold, two cousins, and a third cousin is badly wounded and may not get home alive. And my Dad is already in training camp." She paused to steady her voice and the crowd was silent. "Those cousins had no sons, nor will have now! You should not be trying to find more young men to send to their deaths." She pointed an accusing finger at David Vaughan who was staring above her head with an expression of aloof superiority. "*You* should be persuading people to end this terrible war!"

She stopped, out of breath, pink-cheeked and trembling and quite unable to believe what she was hearing herself say.

"Little conshie!" The woman who'd spoken before shouted. "She ought to be shoved in jail along with the rest who're too yeller to give the Hun what for!" There was a murmur of agreement from the crowd, fresh from pictures of the game smiles and waves of the Somme heroes. Hannah turned to face them like a vixen at bay.

"That's a stupid lie, to say I'm afraid because I can't bear that more brave men must be killed! It's a wicked waste, *that's* what I'm saying. And if we all tried hard enough to stop it I bet we'd find a way!" She swung back to David Vaughan, now frowning down at her from the platform. "All *you're* doing is making it worse!"

"If I were you I'd keep quiet and allow those with knowledge and experience to decide how to run the country's affairs." His voice whipped sharp and cold across the spectators' increasingly noisy comments.

"I've got all the experience I need to know this war should be stopped at once – don't you think three cousins, an uncle, and now maybe my Dad, too, is enough experience?"

"We've all lost relatives," an elderly man called. "They'll 'ave gone for nothin' if we give in now."

"That's right!" The woman climbed off the platform and without warning slapped Hannah hard across the cheek. "You want a good hiding you do!" She began to shake Hannah, shouting "Conshie, conshie!" Others took up the call and made for Hannah, too. David Vaughan pushed through the jostling crowd, making a clear effort to assert his authority.

"Stop at once or I'll call the police. Stop, I say! Leave her alone!"

The sergeants looked uncertain, then dived to the rescue. David Vaughan emerged half carrying and half pulling Hannah and his sergeants pushed a path clear for them. As she stumbled, he swept her up and half-carried and half-dragged her round the corner to where a pony and trap were waiting. He dumped her in it, breathless and red with anger.

"If you're hurt, it's no one's fault but your own."

He flicked the pony and they trotted to the next corner where he pulled up and turned to regard her with his brilliant, icy aquamarine eyes. Hannah stared back with eyes equally cold, not in the least grateful that he may well have saved her from a hiding or worse. She pushed tumbled hair from her hot face and smeared it with blood from a scratched cheek. Dignified silence and a quick retreat seemed a good idea, but Hannah could not resist the last word. Climbing from the trap, still shaking, she faced David Vaughan head on. The misery of the mounting toll of her kin, the anguish of Thomas's departure, the stress of waiting for more news of Harry without even the comfort of her own bed at night, and the still vivid memory of her vision of him that dawn up at Madoc's farm welled up and found powerful voice beyond her years.

"You are *blind*, Lieutenant Vaughan, d'you know that? You don't care who's sacrificed to your senseless idea of honour, or whatever it is that makes you think it's better to die a hero than live a good man. My Dad doesn't know what he's expected to die for, and nor do I! You're blind and stupid – why don't you use your gift of the gab to stop the war if you're so good at talking folks into things! You won't talk me into being proud of dead cousins, dead uncle, dead father maybe, not if you talk for a twelvemonth! I tell you – if women had any say it would be all quite different!"

She stopped for breath. She'd shaken him, she could see it. She'd shaken herself! He looked at her with stern dignity, brows drawn straight and low over the deepset eyes.

"You know nothing. International affairs don't work in that simplistic fashion, I assure you. If you weren't just a silly child I'd be very angry at your thoughtless and damaging behaviour. As it is – "

"If governments *did* work a bit more like that we might not be in this terrible mess now," she flashed at him. "Has half the world to die before commonsense takes over? You try telling my Mam you want my Dad to die for international affairs!"

Choking with emotion, she began to run. Not to Aunt Rose's, too much agony there for her now. She made for the hill. And running through the dusk, hungry, tired, more alone than she had ever been, Hannah's world seemed dark indeed. *Nain! Nain! Nain*, come to me now. Talk with me, calm me with your soft voice. Help me, *Nain*!

Slowing at last, stumbling and trembling, Hannah thought then of the girl, her friend. A long time, since she'd come. How good if she could come tonight; she did so much need someone tonight.

Dorothea . . . where had that name appeared from? She'd no idea how she knew, but the girl's name was Dorothea. And she was out there somewhere on the hill; waiting.

Hannah paused for breath, then began to walk, more steadily now. She was past the last straggle of houses and the soft purple of trees and bushes lay quiet on either side, bird calls stilled for the day. Her cheeks were cooling, though the woman's slap still stung, and the wind came sweet at her, streaking back her hair. When she saw the girl by a young birch tree, waiting, smiling, Hannah lifted her hand in recognition and smiled back, though by then she was weeping.

Chapter Five

March 1917

Though Hannah had wished with all the force she could summon for it never to happen, Dada had come home on embarkation leave. Please let it be over before he has to go to France she had prayed each night. Please let America come in now and the Germans capitulate. But Germany, on the contrary, began that spring a policy of savage and unrestricted submarine warfare. Their intention was to sink such a quantity of British shipping that they would capitulate before America finally made up its mind to enter the war . . . and they were scoring an instant success.

No sign of capitulation in the trenches. When the Somme offensive had ground to a halt in late November with the onset of a blizzard, the British had gained only a hundred and twenty-five square miles of mud, at a cost of a million and a quarter men lost on both sides. Everyone had dug in for a long bitter winter. Only mid-February, with a thaw, was there a British advance – and that because the enemy had decided to abandon his dangerous salient. They had fallen back to the secure and heavily fortified Hindenburg Line and there, on 20 March, the Allies were brought to an immediate stand-still. The French countryside had been totally razed about them, there was not even an unmined road left passable to bring up ammunition or supplies; all they were faced with was utter desolation on a front of seventy miles.

Hannah had snatched precious minutes alone on the hill in the bitter cold of that winter. Fingers almost too numb to manipulate the icy brass, she had been determined to get this one simple tune right. There was so little else she could give Dada; she longed to give so much now he was going from his home, leaving everthing that had until now made up his life.

Now, on the hill with him on the last day of his leave, she stood braced against the wind of early spring, chin tilted and hair streaming off her face. Watching, Thomas saw how the last months had defined the contours of that face, with childhood curves shading off to fragile planes and angles. Not yet fifteen but appearing older, with a haunting, elusive beauty. Well, maybe not real beauty; the wide luminous eyes were smudged round with tired khaki and her old brown coat drained the delicate skin tones. Then she lifted the bugle to her lips with a sudden brilliant smile at him, eyes lit with love, and he drew a sharp breath. Of *course* she was beautiful. Beautiful!

It was no more than a few flickering, inexpert bars. When she'd done, holding the last note steady on a dying fall she waited, breathing fast, the bugle clutched across her body.

Thomas cleared his throat. "Lovely, that was. Just lovely. You keep it up, Princess. Write and tell me how it's goin'. You'll not forget to write, now?"

"Course I won't, Dada." Her eyes glowed with the pain of their imminent separation. "Every week, you'll see."

This time tomorrow he'd be gone. Hannah suddenly wanted to hold him, rock him as he'd once rocked her; comfort him. Tell him not to worry about them, just to stay alive. This was the true moment of their goodbye, not tomorrow on the railway platform.

In her misery she raised the bugle once again, throwing back her head. The single note poured across the quiet hills, a wail of pain, of parting between loved ones that sobbed away to die in far, deserted valleys. Stricken, Thomas reached to pull her to him.

Betsy's heavy cold hung on right through April and she began to cough. Hannah begged her to rest in bed a while; she'd see to Joe, to everything she insisted as her mother set out each day to work, hunched over with coughing as the wind hit her chest. No money to be lost on days off, Betsy would snap, not after the coal they'd had to buy this winter, and food going sky high. For the last cold months her dinner break had been spent queuing at the Maypole for margerine, or at Jepson's for a bit of meat or tripe, or hurrying down to the docks in hopes of fresh caught fish.

But now, with Thomas finally gone to France, Betsy's fight to keep the family fed lost momentum. She abandoned the hunt for an extra bag of sugar, a few more potatoes, and Hannah would come home to find her staring into the unlit fire with no sign of tea started and Joe round at Aunt Maggie's where he could rely on being offered a bit of whatever was going. And quietly, not disturbing the silent figure muffled in the grey kersey shawl, she would get a blaze going, put on the kettle and get out the bread. Rumours were about that soon there'd be no corn left in the country even for that.

"Could you fancy a bit of jam on this, Mam? We've still come of the blackcurrant." Hannah coaxed her mother as if she were a delicate child, but Betsy shook her head without looking up.

"I could do toast for you once the fire's taken. You like that."

"Don't tell me what I like. I already know." Betsy's

voice was without expression. She held one hand in the other, nursing it, and Hannah saw wheals of sore red skin across the fingers. She said gently.

"Mam, I'm so sorry you're feeling poorly." She filled a pudding bowl with cold water and put a pinch of salt in it. She found a soft little cloth from the bottom of the hearth cupboard and with the towel from the back of the scullery door pulled up a chair beside her mother. As she took the hand Hannah felt it stiffen with a gesture of withdrawal.

"Don't be daft."

"I'm not. Just let me bathe your hand."

Hannah kept her grip on the hand and for a second was aware of a battle of wills between them. Then her mother's shoulders sagged down, heavy eyelids dropped over the dark eyes and Betsy's fingers became inert, curling into the water in answer to gentle pressure.

"There . . ." Hannah said softly. "Looks to me as though your gloves are wearing thin. You should ask for new."

"Supposed to last a twelvemonth." Betsy's voice was still toneless as she allowed Hannah to spread the towel over her lap. Her hand floated on the water; Hannah turned back the blouse cuffs and began to massage the wrist in small upward strokes.

"You ask for another pair. They know you can get a job better paid in the shell factory any time you want these days."

"Nobody's going to do you down, are they?" Betsy's eyelids lifted and she regarded her daughter with a sudden sharp glint of humour. "You'd do well with that lot makin' all that song and dance in Russia."

"Time we stood up for our rights," Hannah agreed calmly. She took her mother's hand from the water and scrutinised it. "After this, I think they'll have to take more notice of us to say the least."

"Who's us?" Betsy suddenly turned her head and looked at Hannah.

"*Us.*" Hannah looked back, then lowered the hand again into the bowl. "Us women. Just give this a few more minutes while I get our tea then I'll wrap it up for you. It should be easier tomorrow, provided you get new gloves. Promise you'll ask?"

Betsy was still staring at her. Hannah measured tea into the pot, conscious of a slight but discernible shift in their relationship.

Hannah would look with anxious eyes over the bay these spring evenings hurrying down from Madoc's. Could that dark shape be a submarine in close? How many ships had been sunk today off-shore? How many men lost? How many tons of precious food? Would America declare war soon? She'd never seen an Ameri can but imagined tall, bronzed avengers, fresh and strong for a fight that had quite worn down everyone she knew. Except Joe; nothing seemed to bother young Joe for long. He was growing tall and sturdy, arms and legs shooting out of his clothes and grownup teeth fast pushing out his baby ones. He could even dig the allotment after a fashon and was always willing to run errands if she could catch him between coming in from school and sneaking off with Fly to play with Harry's young brother, Trevor.

She longed to see Harry. Aunt Maggie had visited him in hospital in London, staying with Emily who was doing her teacher training in Poplar. She had returned drawn and shaken from seeing her golden boy laid low; by nature a brisk realist, she was unable to accept the ill that had befallen Harry.

"Like a ghost, he was. Lying there . . . not even sure he knew his own Mam."

Hannah was saving for the rail fare. But it would take time, June at least with the stamp each week for Thomas's letter, an ounce of tobacco, too, when she could manage. Betsy had stopped buying a paper but Hannah popped round regularly to look through Uncle Idwal's, scanning the news from the Front with a frown of concentration and trying to guess where he might be. She tried closing her eyes and thinking of him, shutting out all else, but nothing came of it.

AT LAST! Big, reassuring capitals in heavy black newsprint. America was in! Now he would be safe; it would all be over quickly.

"About time, too," Uncle Idwal said. "Now we'll see some action."

Hannah thought there'd already been plenty of that but held her peace and read on. He might be at Arras. She wanted to talk to Betsy about it, but dare not; her mother didn't talk much anyway, these days. Questions put to her were usually lost like pebbles in the well of her deep, depressive silences.

It was cold, wet dusk as she rounded the corner into Incline Row and the strange woman grabbed her sleeve.

"Hannah Hywel?"

Hannah froze. A telegram? Dada?

"You Hannah Hywel?" The woman gave her arm a small shake; a frail intense Jewess, enveloped in black, eyes gleaming under the glow of the gas lamp as she regarded Hannah with a fixed stare. "The girl up at Madoc's? Who got that loose bull quiet?"

"Well, yes . . ."

That had been over a week back. The bull had broken out and cornered Matty in the yard. Hannah had heard her yell of fear and run from the dairy to see fat old woman and irritable old bull in head-on confrontation. No time to think; she'd walked with instinctive deliberation towards the sweating animal, speaking quietly as she moved between him and the near hysterical Matty. She'd seen the texture of the thick tongue, felt the heat of the massively compact body. Broken rope had trailed from the ring curving through the wet nose. Above it, hot pink eyes had stared back at her. Hannah had bent to pick up the rope without taking her steady gaze from the animal . . . ran a hand along the length of it until her fingers had touched the ring.

"Come on then, boy, good old boy . . ." Inches away now, Hannah had looked into the very soul of the bull, his breath hot and sweet on her face and his bubbly saliva dripping into the hand easing up the rope. And then, unaccountably, he'd allowed her to lead him away.

"It's my son." Not the bull's eyes now boring into hers but the strange woman's, hot and demanding. "You'll find him for me – my boy?" The sallow face was suffused with emotion. "I have to know – " She broke off, mouth working.

"Wouldn't the police be better? They'd know how "

The black straw hat broke free of its hatpin as the woman shook her head in vehement denial. "You're not understanding me, girl! Dead, the telegram said – gassed." The words were torn from some core of grief deep in the bony frame. "I've waited, hoped. Nothing. But you can find him, I know it. You've the power – "

"The power?" Hannah understood her then and shook her head in frantic denial. At that point, staring past the dark figure, she saw someone step from the shadow of the laburnum tree. Dorothea . . . She'd not seen her for a while; now the girl was smiling, welcoming, sweetly familiar and reassuring. Hannah became aware of a beautiful blossoming swell that seemed to ease her tired feet off the wet cobbles. She felt suddenly light enough to have floated on the evening wind; capable of accomplishing whatever might be asked of her. She *did* have the power. Suddenly she wanted to shout it out. It was inescapable, terrible, fearsome. Irresistible. Her fear was gone.

"Yes, I can help you. I'll come home with you now if you want."

They sat facing one another in the tiny parlour, airless and unused as any parlour would be. The brown cotton curtains were pulled across and the oil lamp turned low. Hannah folded her hands in her lap to stop them trembling and made an effort to relax. The room was cold, smelling of beeswax and damp soot and the horsehair seat prickled her legs.

"This is him." The woman clutched a photograph of a dark, thin young man in uniform standing to attention beside a plant on a tall stand. Hannah looked long and earnestly at the smooth sepia-coloured face, and her confidence began to drain away. What should she do now? What if she'd been quite wrong – if this dead boy was out of reach? What if she was being not only unwise but downright wicked? Across the room she saw now that Dorothea had arrived to sit on a footstool, and this calmed her.

"His name's Rowland." The woman's voice was hushed now as she stared with tragic intensity at Hannah. "Twenty-one he was, just. I'd made him up a parcel of food for it. Sent it off a few days before the telegram came."

Hannah nodded, swallowed, and looked at Dorothea again. She began to feel tired now, sleepy enough to nod off, and willed her eyes not to close . . . this was no time to fall asleep . . .

The old man had snowy hair and a beard, and knotted blue veins on the hand taking hers to help her over the stream. But he walked light and straight, and his eyes were blue and sparky like the bay in sunlight. They climbed from the valley where the stream idled through water meadows shining with buttercups, and bees and grasshoppers made conversation in clumps of white clover. The air was fragrant, resonant with the chatter of hedge-sparrows and with larksong. It was peaceful; beautiful. Hannah felt she had been here before, and had been happy. Maybe with Dada when she was small? She smiled, thinking of him, and the old man smiled, too, and offered his hand again.

"Nearly there . . ."

At the crest she stood with head thrown back, a delicious breeze lifting her hair before she dropped to the springy turf beside her companion. Before them spread another valley, shallow and broad with farm-steads in bright cornfields, little woods, the glint of a river. Watching the wind pattern the corn, the cloud shadows lying violet and blue over pale grass, Hannah felt heavy with a sense of peace and well-being.

"My home." The old man made a gesture that embraced the scene, and Hannah nodded.

He began to tell her about the valley. She lay on her stomach, hands cupping her chin, and listened to the soft voice, and to the larksong . . .

"I said, could you do with a cup o' tea?"

Her eyes opened with some reluctance. The woman was tapping her arm; Hannah saw tear stains on the flushed face and started up, apologetic.

"I'm sorry, did I fall asleep?"

"Asleep?" Rowland's mother looked perplexed. Then tears began to track down her cheeks again and she pressed Hannah's hand between hers. "How could you be asleep with my boy talkin' away like that?"

Hannah struggled to her feet. She'd no idea what had happened but something had for sure. Dorothea had gone; she felt suddenly alone and frightened. She wanted light, wanted her tea, she was hollow with hunger and stiff from sitting in her damp coat.

"No, I didn't hear him . . . I must have slept for a few minutes. I can remember dreaming." A lovely dream; the silver-haired old man, the peaceful valley, the larksong. But what had happened here whilst she dreamed?

"That can't be!" The woman sobbed. "His voice came out of your mouth! Don't say you didn't hear, don't say he never came. He did, he did! He said he was happy and content, said not to be sad. He said we'd meet again! You *must* have heard him.!"

Hannah leaned over, dizzy. A dead man's voice coming from her mouth? God, how could that be, what had gone on when she'd been dreaming on that hilltop? She rose, and the room was tilting sickeningly. "I must go now. I really must."

Blundering to the door she scrabbled at the latch, desperate to get outside, away from the weeping mother and the sepia photograph with the large black eyes whose gaze seemed to follow her. She ran home crying quietly for Dada, swearing that never, ever would she allow anything like that to happen to her again, not to help *anyone*! She had to see after herself now, never mind strangers in the street!

Leaning exhausted in the doorway of the cold kitchen, Hannah saw that the fire was almost past reviving. On the table, a scrap of paper with a couple of lines scrawled by Betsy to say she'd gone to bed early with a headache and would Hannah iron Joe's shirt for the morning.

"Oh . . . hello, sweetheart." A cold nose pushed at her leg. Hannah bent and scooped up Fly into her arms, pushing her face into the warm throat as he wriggled an ecstatic body against hers. The contact brought an unexpected release of tears and Hannah clung to the little dog as if her life depended on his proximity, whispering endearments. She lowered them into the rocking-chair, wiped her eyes on her coat sleeve and poked the fire into life.

"There's my lovely . . . find you a bit of something I will, see if I don't. Just give me a minute." Hannah rocked them gently, a foot on the brass fender. Fly licked her cheek then lay on her lap with his muzzle pushed into the crook of her arm, trembling a little with the pleasure and watching her face from the corner of his visible eye. She stared at the mantel shelf with its blue fringed chenille cover, the elaborately flowered red and blue tin tea caddy, the china spaniel with prettily drooping ears that Dada had won at the Flannel fair one year, the pair of turned brass candlesticks set precisely at either end and the carved wood clock exactly central below the print of Highland cattle drinking at the shore of a melancholy loch. The ceiling above was hidden by washing hung to air across to the wall by the stairs door and Joe's grey shirt hung at the end of the line.

Hannah stroked Fly's soft flank. She must get a bite to eat, she was ravenous. The ironing might as well be finished off then, save Mam doing it tomorrow. And she'd her snap tin to fill for morning. Lord, but she was tired.

Gently she put Fly down on the rag mat and and took off her coat. One thing she was coming to know for certain: no-one would see after her if she did not . . . not till Dada was home again at least.

By mid-June, by saving every half-penny, Hannah had enough put by for the train fare to London to see Harry. She had also saved her half-days off from Madoc's farm to make up two whole days; Gideon had pulled a face but she had been adamant. Betsy had made no objection, being fond of Harry; Aunt Maggie, who had seemed a touch jealous of the letters going back and forth to France between the two cousins, was now grateful for anyone caring enough to make the long trip and bring back news. She was uncomfortably aware that Harry's own sister, Daisy, had not yet stirred herself to go. But his younger sister, Emily, teaching in London, wrote that Hannah could stay in her room for the night after they'd gone together to the hospital for the evening visiting. The florin that was Betsy's fifteenth birthday present to her bought Hannah a lilac ribbon to freshen her straw boater, cream cotton gloves to match her best blouse, and a pair of white stockings from the market to set off her navy and white candy striped skirt. Joe's gift was what he himself would like to be given – a bar of chocolate for which he'd spent one Saturday morning queuing and which was now looking fairly well handled. Hannah put this into the small parcel, with her nightgown, face cloth and comb, to give Harry along with two oranges she'd saved for so long they were beginning to wither, some tobacco and a note from his parents and a sticky little bag of pear drops from brother Trevor.

Joe came to the station with her before going on to school. He was nervous that she might never return from London . . . so very far away, in another country; a foreign place. England, he knew, was not a bit like

Wales; and with the war on anything could happen. He fiddled with the string of her parcel, standing close, and he could just catch the faint familiar smell of her. A herby smell, nice, associated with comfort and affection.

"You'll have that string undone, Joe, leave off, do." Hannah gave his fingers a good-natured slap. "Promise you'll see after Mam, now? Don't skidaddle off with Fly and Trev til you've done your chores?"

"Will you see the Tower, Han? And the King's palace?" He bounced up and down on the spot, that always made her smile and she did so now and hugged him for it, for being Joe.

"Silly! I'll not be there 'til tea-time and I'm back again tomorrow! But I tell you, *cariad*, we'll both save real hard, then in a year or two Dada could come with us for a proper outing. And Mam of course if she wants. We could see the Tower, the palace, all of it. How'd that suit?"

She'd meant after the war of course, Hannah knew, as she leant from the window to wave to Joe standing alone and waving frantically on the fast receding platform in a haze of steam. And *if* Dada came back.

Paddington was more vast and more bewildering than she could have dreamed. Droves of people, frantic noise, steam, so many uniforms; another world, and perilously closer to the war than Taibach's little streets. What if she couldn't find Em? Hannah stood as arranged by the ticket gate and strained to see her cousin. The train had been late, with a long unexplained stop outside Oxford where Hannah had eaten her packet of brawn sandwiches as surreptitiously as possible, staring out of the window of the over-crowded, dirty carriage whilst chewing with small careful movements. Several nearby sailors had looked enviously at the food, but she resisted the temptation to offer it around, there being too many hungry mouths by far.

What if Em had been and gone? She tried not to fidget or panic. A one-legged ex-soldier with a barrel organ was playing 'There's a Long Long Trail a'winding' and holding out his cap. Hannah struggled not to look at the space where the leg should have been but her eyes were irresistibly dragged to it; she was still fighting the urge when Emily found her, waving as she pushed through a troop of artillerymen and their relatives.

"You'll see quite a change in him, Han. You must be prepared for that." They walked to the hospital through early evening crowds, Hannah bumping into people as each new sight grabbed her attention. She'd not thought how big it all would be, how busy and noisy; noise everywhere. Half a dozen khaki ambulances were chugging past with red crosses on the sides, back and top, carrying wounded from Charing Cross Station. Folk stood at the roadside and clapped and cheered as they drew near; a soldier with an arm in a sling and a bandage over his ears and under his chin was sitting alongside the first driver and, turning her head, Hannah caught his direct glance. And for that instant, the world stopped. The grey young face with its empty eyes blotted out the evening sun, silenced the roar and rattle of traffic, the cheering and clapping. Hannah, rooted to the kerbstone, was stunned by the glimpsed force of tragedy in the soldier's features.

"*Hannah*." Emily pushed her arm. "You day-dreaming again? I said, don't expect too much of him. I've visited every week for ages now and can't see much of an improvement, try as I will. They're talkin' of sending him to a place near home soon, did Mam tell you? That probably means they've done about all they can for him.

Still, while there's life there's hope.'' She looked prim in the face of admiring whistles from two Australian soldiers with springy strides and broad-brimmed khaki hats adorned with feathers.

Emily at seventeen seemed to Hannah to be quite grown up. Her hair was neatly coiled under her summer straw, pleated pink cotton blouse fastened at the neck with an enamel brooch shaped like a butterfly, navy-blue skirt at least four inches shorter than her mother would have allowed. She worked like a galley slave all day she'd confided over tea and toast at Lyons – her treat, she'd saved on dinners this week – and she needed to look nice to go up west. Hannah had nodded ... up west sounded quite a way off and a bit mysterious. As they crossed the road behind the ambulance convoy she judged that Em must be earning more than she let on about to go there, even though she'd not finished her training yet.

As for Harry; she tried to take in the thing about his being changed. She had of course seen him much quieter, on leave. And knew what the news of Brigid and her baby had done to him. But to her he was still himself; the favourite cousin with bright hair and a wonderfully infectious laugh who could do anything he set his mind to, and whom she adored.

They walked along corridors and up an echoing flight of steps to the first floor of the hospital, Hannah tense with excitement now. A young man was approaching with a nurse beside him, his hand tucked into the crook of her arm. They stopped by a narrow bench against the wall and clumsily, hands out in a searching gesture, the young man turned and lowered himself to sit on it. The nurse gave his shoulders a reassuring pat and hurried back the way she'd come while the man remained, hands on knees, motionless and dreadfully vulnerable.

"He's blind," whispered Hannah and stopped. The soldier was looking straight at her, a fixed unblinking stare that she found more than a little unnerving.

When they walked past him he drew in his feet nervously and flattened his body against the wall. Melting with pity for his plight, Hannah was not able to look back before they turned the corner of the passage, but he was none the less painfully clear in her mind's eye.

Harry was in a ward on the second floor. It held a dozen beds, had high windows on one side and dangerously polished floorboards. In the centre of the windowless wall an alcove housed a forbidding black-leaded stove with a support system of convoluted, massive piping. This monster was clearly taking its summer break and potted ferns had been set in a semi-circle between it and its ornate copper fender.

Emily walked straight to the bed in the furthest corner from where came the whistling tinny rasp of difficult breathing. A nurse caught up with them as they reached the bed, holding her head awkwardly tilted to accommodate the starched bow of her cap under her chin.

"Don't stay too long. He mustn't get excited, he's not been quite so well today." She rustled prodigiously as she bent to smooth the bedcover, then looked at the orange Hannah was pulling from her bag. "I'll take that, shall I? He wouldn't be able to manage without it being cut up."

"Nurse . . ." A small red-haired man with a cage over his legs called from two beds away. "I'd murder for a mug o' tea."

"Twenty minutes yet, Corporal." She glided away with more rustling of over-starched skirts and the corporal put his thumb to his nose and waggled his fingers at her rigid back.

Harry was propped on three pillows, face as colourless as the bandage that swathed his head and at close quarters his breathing was harsher. Watching, Hannah found herself breathing deeply in sympathy. Emily drew up a chair and sat down, frowning.

"Pity he's havin' an off day. He did want to see you."

"The bandages." Hannah kept her voice down. "What are they for, Em?"

"There was an operation last month. To relieve some pressure, they said."

"'E's like that on and off," volunteered the corporal, now staring at the ceiling. "Sometimes 'e'll start to shout. Near brings the roof in then. Bloke over there got up to clock 'im one, said 'Arry'd drive 'im bonkers." He nodded across the room at a curtained-off bed. "Didn't get far though. No legs." He winked at Hannah. Then he turned over with much sighing and groaning and closed his eyes.

The ward was quiet but for Harry's breathing. Hannah sat on the edge of the bed, lifted one of his hands to hold between hers, and found it dry and light as a dead leaf. She recalled how one birthday he'd carved a rough cradle for her rag doll with that hand, and used it another time to demonstrate how to skim flat stones to bounce across the river. Her mind began to home on him, and concentration gathered in her unblinking gaze. The nurse re-entered with another rustle of linen, sat down at the table near the door and began to write. A patient started to cough, two more visitors arrived, but Hannah noticed nothing. She continued to hold her cousin's hand and think of him.

Emily fidgeted. The middle-aged couple who'd just come in stopped by the bed of the man without legs and bent in turn to kiss his cheek, smiling and offering sweets. Across the room the coughing crescendoed alarmingly, causing the nurse to leave her writing and draw curtains round the patient's bed. Emily examined the front of her blouse, sighed, smoothed out the already smooth bedcover and shot an exasperated look at Hannah. Hannah continued to look at Harry.

"Looks like you've had your trip for nothin'."

Making it sound like Hannah's fault, Emily got up and bounced round the bed, hands on her narrow little hips. Hannah seemed not to hear, so intent was she upon Harry's white face. Then his eyes were suddenly open, looking at her.

"So there you are." Emily bent to intercept the gaze of cousin upon cousin. "About given you up, we had. Han's come all this way and then – "

"Shut up, Em," said Hannah clearly. "Just shut up and be still." She smiled at Harry. "Hello."

"Well, really," Emily flounced back to her chair. "He's only *my* brother. Pardon me for breathing." She stared past Harry's head and breathed quite loud.

"I came as soon as I could," Hannah said quietly, putting gentle pressure on the fingers lying inert in hers. "I'd like to make you feel a bit better if I can." Emily raised imploring eyes to the ceiling.

"You really are a daft cat, our Han. What you think *you* can do that all these properly trained doctors can't, I'd like to know. What's special about *you*? For heaven's sake! How can *you* make him feel better?"

"Does your head hurt?" Hannah ignored Emily. "Shall I put my hands on it?"

She searched his face for signs of the cousin she'd known and loved all her life. Her insides were hot and trembling with the shock of seeing him like this; it was terrible. God, if she really had any power to heal, let it come now, for Harry. God, you can't want to leave him like this.

Hannah put a hand on his bandaged head, making a huge effort to still her turmoil. She must be calm, for Harry. She touched the dressing; it felt stiff and inanimate.

No use ... there was nothing. It had all been wrong then; she seemed to be turning inside out until she was completely hollow. Harry did not even know who she was; he was looking through her as though she were no more than a shadow across the bed. If she could only concentrate ... no, that was clearly not the way. If she could let go; an empty vessel, that's what she should seek to be.

"*Cariad*? Harry?"

He looked back; unblinking, unrecognising. After a moment Emily leaned across the bed.

"Han, you're unlucky this time, I've seen him like this often an' all the askin' in the world won't work. He could be perky as a spring chicken again in a day or two ... no comfort to you though, back home tomorrow."

"No." She felt defeated. "Let's wait just a bit longer though, Em, in case."

Later, squeezed into the narrow bed with Emily's regular, bubbling breath warm in her ear, she lay sleepless and overtired and was merciless with herself. It had been so vain to think she had any special powers. Just a few coincidences, that's all there'd ever been: a way with animals; daft ideas about healing with herbs. *Nain* Hywel had been just an ordinary old woman and she was dead, anyway. As for Harry, either the doctors would make him well or he'd stay sick; nothing she could do would alter anything. Grow up, Hannah Hywel, and know your limitations. You're just an ordinary girl like millions of others. Like Mam said.

141

She stared into the unfamiliar dark of the London night, muggy and airless. That young soldier, a couple of months back . . . Rowland. How did she explain *him* away? And Dorothea? No one else saw Dorothea . . .

She walked with Emily to school, through Poplar's early morning streets, still stuffy with yesterday's air. It was as though it had no chance to cool and freshen overnight, trapped between the endless rows of close-packed houses and sunless courts. Eyes pricking after a wretched night's sleep, Hannah listened dully to her cousin's crisp light voice, thinking how she would hate to live in London. A grey pall of foreboding was falling over the day, becoming heavier with each corner turned. It surely could not be simply London . . . there must be something else. Harry? Would there be time to call at the hospital again on the way to get her two o'clock train? He might know her today.

"It's nothing like as lively about the streets as it used to be," Em was saying, patting a stray tendril into her neat coil of hair. "Not so many cars and buses, no hurdy-gurdy man, and there used to be some lovely street bands. And everybody's lookin' downright shabby . . . hardly ever see a lovely top hat these days or black cloaks with great red satin linings. Real smart they were. You come again when the war's over and I'll show you. It'll be a real treat." She buttoned her jacket. "There's my school. Come back at noon, I'll come out quick as I can. Plenty of time to get you to Paddington with this dinner hour I've wangled."

"You're sure, Em? I could get to my train all right on my own, I've a good tongue in my head!"

"Don't I know it. But it's settled now. An' I'll be glad of the jaunt, I don't often get one. Tell you what, we'll go by Underground. Lord!" Emily winced at the noise

142

coming from the crowded school yard running between the railings and the shabby Victorian building. "Little horrors! Don't get lost now, see you at twelve."

She hurried across the playground and disappeared through the doorway marked "Girls". Hannah did not hear her words. Neither did she hear the shouting, jostling children in their final moments of freedom before the bell rang. She was staring at the ugly, stained building, seeing flames tearing at the windows, smoke belching from a shattered roof. Hearing screams and frantic cries that came thinly through the roar and crack of falling timbers. Her hands went to her ears and she turned away but nothing could dull the assault on her senses.

It was the assembly bell that dispersed the nightmare. The children had lined up and marched indoors before Hannah dare turn again to the school: solid, four square, no damage anywhere. Whatever had possessed her to imagine . . . ? Tired – she was just very tired. Get back to Em's place, have a bit of a nap maybe, just half an hour. Be all right then; nothing but her imagination playing stupid tricks. Slowly, moving her legs with difficulty, she retraced her steps to Emily's room.

It was the first air raid siren she'd heard and thought at first it must be a practice. She'd woken from a heavy sleep to find it already time to meet Emily from school, scooped her things together and was letting herself out into the street when the warning shrilled over the houses. Almost at once Hannah saw them, printed clear on the blue sky; white aeroplanes, lots of them, in massed formation.

They were beautiful; quite magical. At the corner of the street she stopped to stare as they came closer, filling the sky with their powerful roar. Too amazed for fear, women were looking up from doorsteps with babies in their arms and toddlers clinging about their skirts and a little crowd gathered at the corner with Hannah, shading their eyes look up. A bus rounded the corner and the conductor hung out from the stair rail, head tipped back. The bus screeched to a halt.

"Take cover!" he yelled. "It's a raid not a bloody circus act." Passengers tumbled from the bus looking for shelter; there'd been no air raid since the zeppelins two years ago. Hannah began to hurry towards the school, the pall of foreboding clouding her mind again. It wasn't only worry about Harry . . . something else, something terrible was affecting her.

Now she was running; and the first bombs came down. She did not see them fall, her gaze was fixed on the pavement as she ran, but they seemed to be in the next street; terrifyingly close. The explosions sounded something like those in the slate quarry at home, but much louder, and she could feel the ground, the houses, tremble. Round the next corner as shrieking moaning destruction tore through bricks and wood and stone and flesh. A horse lay bloodily tangled in its entrails, its driver decapitated on the cart; the front of a grocer's shop blown out. An ambulance swept past Hannah, followed by a fire engine whose clanging bell added to the racket. She raced after them to the corner of the next road and her legs were shaking so much now she thought she must fall. Her heart knocked painfully, furiously, and she was sweating.

Then she saw it . . . the school, with smoke and flames belching from the windows at its far end. Sobbing for breath, Hannah reached the knot of people already gathered at the entrance and now she heard the cries again, the screams and wails of children. All was as she

144

had seen it earlier, in her head, even to the shards of glass under her feet.

Mothers jostled forward, crying out for their own, and Hannah went with them. Her mind was splitting apart between the old sick fear of fire, which like her terror of water lay ever in wait, and the instinctive urge to snatch helpless young from harm. But her body pushed strongly to get into the building even as her mind flinched away. She *must* reach the children she'd seen running and laughing in the playground. And Em, where was Em?

A policeman already stood between the crowd and the entrance doors. Hannah checked a moment, then darted inside as he pushed into the crowd to make way for a fire hose. Then she was in a cloakroom, pegs still holding children's coats and hats. Through to a classroom ... empty desks and forms knocked anyhow. Smoke was foaming through a doorway beyond the big black-leaded stove and a man was pushing backwards through it with a small boy in his arms.

"Outside with you girl!" He ran towards her door, the child like a dusty rag doll. "This door's to be kept clear, it's our only way out!"

Hannah ran through the far door into the smoke-filled hall beyond. Coughing, she stared about her. In the corner a Tommy, his tunic misted with fallen plaster, was at the head of what appeared to be the steps to a basement. He saw her and gestured wildly.

"They're down 'ere. Gawd 'elp em. Bloody bomb's gawn straight through an' exploded in the cellar, poor little perishers were sheltering there!"

Hannah ran across the hall, her eyes watering and smarting, and followed him into a pall of smoke and dust through which struggled choking, screaming children. Some clung distractedly to the legs of rescuers

145

piling in now, whilst from higher up a mother shrieked with hoarse urgency.

"Betty? Georgie? *Betty!*"

Whistles were blowing in the street, men shouting orders. But Hannah heard only the cries of the children in the inferno of the cellar. And now she glimpsed small torn bodies, severed limbs, dreadful fragments of humanity in the mess of wood and masonry. A little hand stretched from beneath a chunk of ceiling beam. Pushing frantically, Hannah uncovered a girl of six or seven, face down. Dead. So many dead . . .

Police now, and firemen, lifting the infant dead and wounded and shouldering back to the littered playground with their limp burdens. Here, women clutched one another, weeping.

"Nearly late she was, this mornin'," A smudged grey face turned each time a child was carried out. "Ran all the way she did, so's not to get the ruler."

"Bloody 'Uns, not 'uman, they're not!" One distraught woman shook a fist at the summer sky. Motor ambulances screeched to a halt by the stricken school and pathetic bundles shrouded in police coats were carried out to them.

In the cellar, Hannah was impervious to authority's orders to get out now and leave it to the men for she had found Emily, pinned against a wall.

"Come on, Em." She worked fast, clearing splintered wood and plaster from the skirt whose trim crispness she'd admired earlier that morning. "I've got you, not long now." But Emily was not listening. Her eyes were closed in her dusty face and one arm was doubled unnaturally between her body and the wall.

"Right, miss," A fireman's bulk overshadowed Hannah. "I'll 'ave her."

He eased up the unconscious girl and Emily fell

against him, limp as a broken doll as he picked his way through the cellar. Hannah followed, her eyes fixed on his back, but suddenly shaking with a sick uncontrollable violence so that she stumbled, overbalancing on the ruined stairs. Seeing blood on her once white stockings, she began at last to weep, quietly and painfully. She'd paid good money for those only last Saturday, with her birthday money from Mam.

Chapter Six

Autumn 1917

"Oi! You asleep up there?"

Hannah peered over the edge of the barley straw. "Course I'm not."

"Get a move on then, I want my dinner this week not next."

The podgy round face of Gideon Madoc's third son Norman glared up from the cart. The red kerchief knotted round his neck looked tight below the heavy jowls and Hannah wished for a moment that it would throttle him. He was the least likeable of the family, which wasn't saying much; either shouting at her for not doing the job to his taste or trying to get his meaty red hands on her breasts or bottom. She had the measure of him now though and mostly succeeded in denying him the pleasure of either upsetting her or pawing her.

She returned to ricking up the straw, working at a steady pace while refusing to be flustered by Norman into wearing herself out. She had asked for a pay rise a couple of weeks ago, prices were going sky high and her money just didn't go round the way it had. Gideon Madoc had refused at first, only adding a grudging shilling a week when she threatened to leave – he knew how pressed he would be to replace her at any price. But he was making every effort to extract his pound of flesh in extra work and his sons clearly had the same brief. It was up to Hannah to thwart them, she knew, to conserve something of herself.

She enjoyed this particular job atop the newly threshed straw, stacking it neatly before it was thatched. She was high enough to see right over the bay, over the smoking juggernaut of the works spread across the morfa, with the rising flanks of the mountains behind beginning to colour in a spectacular display; tone upon tone of siennas, ochres, hazy mauves and coppers as the year slid imperceptibly into autumn. Alone with her thoughts when some oaf wasn't bellowing at her, Hannah was content simply to get on with her work.

Only now was the memory of the tragedy at Poplar beginning to ease for her. For weeks she had jerked from sleep shuddering with the remembered screams, the sights in the cellar. Sixteen had been killed, she'd learned later, and twice as many injured. Emily had been burned on the neck and shoulder and had her arm broken. She had come home to recuperate and had only just gone back to London to start the autumn term in another East End school.

Sometimes Hannah was still afraid to close her eyes for fear of what she might see again. Then she would think of Dada . . . he might be enduring horrors such as she had known in Poplar every day. And then she would get out her paper and pen and however tired, clear a corner of the kitchen table and write to him; snippets of news about the people and places he must be missing, only good bits, though, nothing to fret him. Like how Joe was getting stars for composition, and how she and Joe had laughed 'til they'd fallen off their seats when they'd seen the Keystone Cops at Vint's Palace in Water Street. And she was giving Joe two-pence to see the weekly matinee serial about the terrible adventures of Pearl White and Eddie Polo at The Grand.

And how she'd found a lovely wild flower she could not yet identify, behind the engine sheds at the end of Carmarthen Row. Oh yes, and that she and Flo were knitting a pair of socks a week each now for the troops – they could almost knit in their sleep!

The letters back were sparse, and mostly said the same things. But it must be hard finding cheerful things to say about the Front, and all that mattered anyway was that he was alive to write anything, when names she knew appeared every week in the paper under "Killed in Action".

She thought a great deal about Harry, too. She asked Auntie Maggie for news of him so often that Harry's overwrought mother finally told her not to waste time asking again, she'd be told whenever they heard anything fresh. But though Daisy had finally made the trip to Charing Cross Hospital and Harry's father had also been a second time, the news was sparse and seemed mainly to be "no change". Hannah still felt there might be something she could do, something that no one else could, but she could not afford the fare again just yet. She contented herself by writing to Emily for any details that might emerge. In a way, Harry had to be in limbo for the present. She still loved him, but as she herself matured through her adolescence, so did that frantic sort of devotion lived out by the child for the young man. It seemed now, with the passing of the months, to be settling into the steady, loyal love of kin for kin, with the added dimension of care and pity for his being so cruelly struck down.

Norman's head appeared. His cap, an indefinable non-colour that may once have been brownish-blue or blueish-brown, was moulded permanently to his head, and straight tufts of equally nondescript hair stuck out above his ears in exactly the same place each day, so that they seemed to be put on with the hat. Privately, Hannah thought it likely that he slept in the hat. It was reputed that Norman was weary of life on his father's farm and had even, in desperation, offered himself for war service, but been rejected. Word also had it that he wanted a wife; but there had been no takers. Life in the Madoc household as a junior wife to Matty could hold no charms for any girl knowing the family, no matter how hard it was now to find a husband.

"Load done." Norman did not use two words where one would do. Hannah nodded and laid down her fork.

"Gettin' another now?" She hoped not, she was hungry and wanted a rest with her bread and marge and bottle of cold tea.

"Dunno. Let's 'ave a look."

He heaved himself off the ladder. "Steady on," Hannah protested. "Don't tip it, I've got it nicely squared up."

His arm shot out and grasped her ankle and suddenly she was on her back. She kicked out but his grip was firm. He grinned now, squatting back on his heels to watch, confident of his mastery over Hannah as she struggled to get free.

"Don't tip it," he mimicked. "I got it nice an' squared up."

"Let me be, Norman, or I'll tell your Dad of you."

She was still now; fighting back was what he wanted. And in this far corner of the field no one could see; the house was below them and Gideon Madoc and his eldest, Rhys, had taken down a dozen lambs to market so they weren't about.

"Come on," she made a great effort to instil a neutral tone into her voice. "Let's get something to eat." Don't show fear, that's meat and drink to him. Be casual and he'll let it drop. But her eyes belied her own advice.

They were anxious; and the blood had left her cheeks. Norman Madoc sensed her fear as an animal would and reached for her other ankle.

Anything in skirts would do for Norman. Females were simply objects, not in his book to be regarded as human beings. If one came into his orbit and he could have a bit of fun with her, that was what they were for anyway. This female riled him because she answered back, argued even. She seemed to think herself something a bit special, so he was always on the lookout to take her down a peg. And if he could have a bit of fun doing it . . .

"How about a bit o' slap and tickle first? To give us an appetite, eh?" He was drawing her closer over the straw, hands inching from ankles to calves to knees. Hannah began to fight like a demon, struggling to work her legs like pistons to kick him off and beating him with clenched fists. Norman continued to grin.

"Proper little ruffian, aren't you? Do well as a bantam-weight you would." He rocked forward onto his knees and forced her legs apart with a sudden savage jerk.

"That's a good girl . . . that's nice. Now then, want to please me, don't you?" He lowered his body onto her and Hannah arched frantically, feeling his erection hard against her. She twisted her head to look into his face; surely if she could look straight at him . . .

"Norman! Please . . . *please*, no – " But she could not see his face now, her head was pushed into his neck. She could only smell the old sweaty cap, hear the rasping breath, feel the roughness of his working jacket on her neck, the weight of his bulk pressing her into the straw. When he began to fumble with her trouser belt she cried out; he pushed a hand over her mouth and she bit it hard.

"Bloody vixen," Norman reared up and fetched her a blow across the head that all but took her senses, giving him time to yank at her trousers and fumble roughly with her underclothes. Dazed, Hannah was no match; when she gave a cry of pain as he drove furiously into her resisting body the hand was hard over her mouth again, cutting her lips against her teeth. The more she resisted, the greater the tearing, burning violation of his massive penis. Try to relax, lessen the pain . . . but her body refused to accept what was taking place. She screwed up her eyes and face and tried to remove her mind from her body but that failed, too. Please, God, make him stop.

When, after some incalculable age, he finished with a hoarse shout, bucking then collapsing heavily on her, Hannah lay inert. She felt ripped apart, too limp to move, half suffocated. When finally he rolled aside, sat up and began to fasten his trousers, she remained still for a moment, staring at the sky. Then she crawled slowly towards the ladder.

"Go on – bet you enjoyed it." But there was anxiety in his voice as she turned awkwardly to put an unsteady foot on the ladder. "Hey, don't you let anybody catch you lookin' like that, do your bloody self up, girl." His head disappeared as she made uneven descent, clinging to the ladder uprights. "You say a word to my Da' an' I'll 'ave you, right?" He called after her.

Hannah stumbled across the field, clutching at her heavy trousers. Not towards the buildings, no succour there, but down across ancient drystone walls, spinneys, outcrops that pushed icy streams into intricate loops . . . down to Taibach. She must get home. She was full of tears but they would not come; hoarse with silent screams. Something warm and sticky was running down her thighs; the sensation made her heave suddenly and, doubling over, she vomited. She knelt at the next tiny stream to splash her face and rinse her mouth. But nothing, she knew, not every drop of water in the world would wash her clean of Norman Madoc.

The house was empty, Joe at school and Betsy at work. Hannah stood in a bowl of water in the kitchen and scrubbed herself with carbolic soap until her flesh was red, using three lots of clean water, then towelled herself furiously. When she'd mopped every drop off the quarry tiles, tidied everything back to leave no trace she went upstairs to lie on her bed, staring at the ceiling. One particular stain, a damp one by the window, looked something like the outline of Norman's head with his cap on. She turned her head and fixed instead on the blank wall, eyes wide and dry. Her body was sore and bruised where he'd been, still throbbing from his onslaught. There'd been blood on her trousers – she'd rubbed it off mostly and they hung on the bedroom doornail now, blotched testimony to her shame.

She could have a baby! Her shocked mind faltered and tried to veer away from that dreadful idea. She and Florence had found out a bit ago how it happened, from Flo's eldest sister, Madge. Hannah was cold now, beginning to shiver; had Dada done that to Mam, to make *her*? It was too dreadful to contemplate – she would sooner not have been born!

She sat up then. "I hate you," she said to the wall and without a clear idea of who or what she meant, only aware of a great swelling pain and loneliness. "I'll never believe you again. Dorothea, don't you ever come back or I'll – I'll – " She paused; how could she harm someone who was, well . . . "You're just nothing," she finished. "I don't believe you're there. You'd have stopped Norman Madoc if you'd have been anything at

154

all." *Nain* Hywel was nobody either, just a stupid old woman. "And you went off and left me, Dada. Now I might have a baby . . . and I've no job. And I can't even go back to collect my wages for this week. Eleven shillings, I've lost."

That was when the tears came, flooding down her face like a burst dam. She was still sitting on the bed weeping when Joe came in, clattering straight upstairs to get out of his decent clothes, followed by Fly who was not allowed.

"Han?" He stood in the doorway, the summer's crop of freckles standing out as he stared at her. "What's up, Han?" Fly sat down beside them and cocked his head, waiting.

"Oh . . ." Hannah fished out her handkerchief from her blouse sleeve and wiped her face then blew her nose. "Well, I just let those Madocs upset me, love, that's all. They were worse than usual even for them, today. The pink limit!" She eased herself off the bed and slid into her working frock then reached on the chest of drawers for her comb. She began to tug it through her messed-up hair which still harboured bits of straw. "I'm not going back there. I'll get another job right away, don't worry about that." Joe stared at her, frowning, his mouth turned quite grim.

"I'll settle that bloody lot for you one day, Han."

Hannah gasped a reproof, shaking his shoulder. "Joe, where'd you hear that word! Mam'll tank you good and proper if she hears it."

"Well, I'll pay 'em back some way. You see if I don't." He still looked fierce. Hannah managed a smile then; whoever she'd meant to hate it would never be Joe. She smoothed down her skirt and laced her boots, feeling a little more composed but still nauseous.

"Forget it, *cariad*. Let's get on now, Mam won't be

long. I'll go see Florence later, talk over finding a new job . . . better money, p'raps, eh? I was worth more than *they* paid anyway."

She wrote a note to Gideon Madoc saying she would not be coming back and if he wanted to know why he could ask Norman. She posted it on the way to see Florence and prayed that she would never have to see any of the Madocs ever again.

She knew what had to be done before she got to Florence. She'd forbidden Joe to say a thing to Betsy before she was set up for work again, less chance of a row that way; though there seemed no peaceful way of admitting she'd lost a whole week's wages, since nothing would have forced her back to Madoc's place to demand it. And there'd be lies to tell. As she walked down to Florence's, Hannah tried to put a likely story together. It was never an option, to tell Betsy what had in fact happened.

Nor Florence, sadly. Her shame was quite terrible enough without anyone else knowing of it. Just carry on. As long as . . . the terrible possibility of having Norman Madoc's baby never entirely left her thoughts, invaded her sleep every night, and sometimes utterly overwhelmed her. A picture of Brigid's face flashed up for a second. Dear Lord, no.

"So I've decided I'm not putting up with that Madoc lot one more week," she told Florence as they walked to the bridge and back, the only way they could get privacy to talk – Mrs Morgan had given her lodger, a steelman from the Midlands, use of her parlour and second bedroom. Hannah stopped under a gas lamp and took Florence's arm. "Come to the shell factory with me, Flo, I'm going round to see if they'll take me on

156

fiirst thing tomorrow. Our Daisy gets over a pound a week there. Think of that!"

They were silent, thinking of over a pound a week, and the difference it could make to a household.

"If they take you, I'll come." Florence's voice went squeaky as always when she was excited. "We said we'd go when we were old enough, didn't we? You go and see if fifteen's old enough, Han."

It was. Not for a full pound Hannah was told next day, but eighteen and tenpence for a start. Dazed by thoughts of even that sum, so that yesterday's misery, pain and fear receded just a little, she was ready now to tell her mother. But Betsy had her own surprise to spring.

"Just as well." She was leaning over the flat iron, pressing the tucks of her good blue blouse and the steam hissed softly up into her drawn face.

Betsy Hywel had changed over the months that Thomas had been away. Bereft of the thing she needed as surely as the air she breathed – the security of a husband to stand between her and the poverty she always feared was waiting around the corner to wrestle her to the ground – her spirit had shrivelled. She saw shadow all round and was afraid. The community abounded now with women on their own, many already on their twenty-two and sixpence war widow's pension. But most found the support they needed in neighbours, the family of their particular street as well as in their own extended families. Betsy had moved to Incline Row only a handful of years ago and had not yet by her nature bedded down too tightly with its inhabitants. Her sisters would call in as they always had in the big family network spread over the district, but now Betsy, always the least gregarious, seldom called on them. She drew more into herself each day, sitting with her shawl hugged across in her rare moments of idleness and gazing into the fire with empty eyes.

She laid the iron back on the hob and folded her blouse. "I'll have to give up for a bit, pretty soon."

"Give up?" Hannah took over, thumping the second iron on Joe's school shirt which was going to need a patch on the elbow.

"At Vaughan's. I'm expecting, around Christmas time."

Hannah's head came up then. Her mother had turned away to put the folded blouse on the corner of the table; she looked quickly but Betsy's shape was hidden by the way she'd folded across her shawl. Six months ago. Dada's embarkation leave. She felt tears surge to her throat and, without thinking, reached over to touch the turned shoulder.

"Mam . . . Why didn't you say? I could've helped more."

The shoulder was stiff. Betsy's eyes flickered to her daughter's and her face worked; for a second Hannah thought her mother was about to burst into tears. "Does Dada know?" she asked quickly. "He'd be pleased, I know he would. Oh, Mam, you're not to fret about anything – "

Betsy's features seemed momentarily to crumple. Hannah put an arm about the rigid shoulders, forgetful for once of a possible rejection. But the woman seemed unaware of the advance and in a moment got up to rinse out cups in the scullery.

"He knows now." Her voice was muffled. "Anyway, you'll need to bring in what you can – every penny. There's all winter ahead, coal and things, and odd bits I'll need, for . . ."

"We'll work it all out, Mam. Maybe Dada will have his leave by then. Just think, we could be together for

Christmas. And Harry's coming to hospital here soon, didn't Auntie say?" Hannah hurried on with the ironing now to illustrate her willingness to pull her weight. "All together," she repeated, as if to convince them both. But Betsy did not reply; she was putting food into her snap box ready for morning and her face was empty of expression.

Had she looked at her daughter, Betsy might have been struck by the quite obvious signs of trauma written on the colourless, thin cheeks and the dark-ringed, lack-lustre eyes. But even had she asked, Hannah could not possibly have told her of the fear that seemed to be eating her away; a fear that Betsy's news had just brought yet again into sharp and terrifying focus.

Hannah felt part of the war effort now, though too young to operate dangerous procedures. It was hard, noisy, dirty, and the smell now was not of manure which she quite liked but the acrid stink of TNT. The first day she looked at Florence in her protective mask, face smeared with grease to combat fumes, and giggled. Florence put out her tongue and waggled fingers from her ears. End of shift at last, they both took great gulps of air coming out, rubbed at their faces and delighted at the mild west wind.

"I see now why the money's good." Hannah pushed her fingers through her hair, confined all day under a close cap and itching as if she had nits. Florence nodded.

"I feel sick. But we'll get used to it."

"Course we will." They ran across the morfa for the joy of being outside again. No situation could have been too difficult for Hannah to surmount today because her curse had arrived. She was safe, thank God. She had stomach cramps, a headache, nausea from the smell and itchy hair and skin, and was more dog tired than she'd been in her life. But she was not going to have Norman Madoc's baby and that one blessed fact dropped all else into perspective. She borrowed enough from Florence to buy fish and chips for three for supper, and even Betsy seemed to have a bit of colour by the time they'd picked every last bit of stuck batter off the paper. She cleared a corner of the table for Joe to sort out his collection of pebbles, got in tomorrow's coal and was scrubbing out the scullery when Sam Warburton walked across the yard with his heavy familiar tread.

"Still at it, young lady?" She always forgot how deep his voice was, deep and warm and rough textured. She scrambled up to move the bucket, wiping her soapy hands fast on the apron because Sam sometimes shook hands with her now in recognition of her adult status.

"Mr Warburton, hello." She ducked her head, smiling, then wondered if he could smell the awful stuff on her. "Mam's in." He stood for a moment, looking down at her with that wonderful interesting map of a face decorated with its great moustaches. Seeing Sam pierced her suddenly with sharp, deep longing for her father, so that for a moment she was dizzy with the pain of it.

"Right, m'dear. Everythin' all right is it? Not over-doin' it up at Madoc's? Your Dad said I was to get you from there if you did, y'know."

"Oh, well, no. I've something else now. You see – "

"Come in, Mr Warburton," called Betsy, hearing the deep familiar voice.

"I'll just finish up," Hannah said hurriedly. She swilled down the yard flags with the last of the water. She wished she could wash her hair but she couldn't in front of Sam, and she'd not be able to wash it every night from now on anyway, might as well get used to the smell. When she went into the kitchen her mother was pouring water into the shiny brown teapot and Sam sat in Thomas's chair, looking too big for it.

"I'll come Sunday first thing and see to it," He nodded at the sash window. "Bit o' putty'll soon put paid to that draught."

"I keep telling the rent man, but – " Betsy shrugged. Sam took his proffered tea and only one spoon of precious sugar with it though he liked three.

"Han's on munitions," Joe said suddenly, dragging himself back from his pebble fantasies to recall the big news. Sam turned the full weight of his attention on Hannah.

"Munitions? The shell factory?"

"A pound a week by Christmas." Now Hannah looked defensive. "What Mr Madoc wanted was a slave and I wasn't goin' to be one any longer."

Sam Warburton frowned and fingered his moustache into shape now he'd got it just nicely damp with the tea. "Your Dad wouldn't like that," he said heavily "He'd never've let you." Hannah stared into her tea; she'd no idea if he knew about Mam.

"She did right," Betsy spoke without emphasis, not looking at anyone. "Joe, give Fly his dinner then get on up to bed, when you've tidied that lot up. I'll bring your stockin' up later."

She bent to her darning again, the big hole in the stocking heel closing rapidly into a neat little trellis. Hannah found that she was blushing and bent her own head . . . the first time her mother had ever made such a positive remark about her. She stole a glance at Betsy, but saw only the top of her head as she went on with her darning.

Joe was awake when she went up; they had oil lamps upstairs now and theirs was turned up just high enough for him to read a comic swapped that day with Trevor.

"Why aren't you asleep?" The question was rhetorical and Joe did no more than offer a good-natured grunt. Hannah turned her back and undressed fast. She longed for the privacy of her own bed now, much as she loved Joe. Thomas had been adamant last winter that she must have one, then Betsy had said she'd have Hannah in with her while he was away. So nothing had been done . . . but nothing had been said about sleeping with Mam either. Hannah supposed she just wasn't wanted. She decided now to look round for a bed right away, her first household purchase as the sole, if temporary, wage-earner. Two pounds? No, less than that; probably she'd get a decent single for under a pound if she looked hard. Be a job to get it in the room of course, but she'd manage a way.

"Move up a bit, you're hogging it." She edged in and stretched flat for a moment, ready to fall asleep that second. She was a munitions girl. Hard to believe, really. A canary! She forced herself up with a sigh and reached under her pillow for pencil and paper; her father's letter was already overdue.

"You goin' to tell him about the shell factory?"

"Joe, go to *sleep*."

"He'll be glad, I'll bet. It's what they're asking girls to do, isn't it, there's posters all over. You know, *you* make the stuff for *them* to kill the Huns with? Oh, all right. I'm goin' to sleep."

Too tired to finish a tentative few lines, Hannah closed her eyes. But expected oblivion failed to come. Too much had happened, too much had changed, too quickly. Now Joe's words repeated themselves, forcing her to reason. This wasn't just a well paid job that was unpleasant and dangerous; she was going to be making objects that were designed to explode with the purpose of cutting men to pieces. She'd seen with dreadful

162

clarity what happened when metal met flesh in that cellar at Poplar. That barney she'd had with David Vaughan outside the Electric cinema – last year, was it? Dead now, most likely. David Vaughan, she'd messed up his recruiting speech nicely! But she'd liked his hair, those close auburn waves. And his eyes had been very nice. She hoped he hadn't been smashed up by a shell.

She twisted her head on the pillow. Men like her father would be overwhelmed and cut to pieces if they were without these shells that she and others were making. Funny how they'd found a name like that for them; she thought of the delicate shells on Taibach beach, curved, fluted, iridescent. So utterly unlike the weapons she'd seen today, the messengers of death. Who could say that one *she* might make may not kill the German who would otherwise kill Dada?

She'd wished Norman Madoc dead at first. He was the only living person beside herself who knew of her shame. If he died she could feel safe maybe; an ordinary clean person again. But terrible men like Norman had, she felt certain, the knack of living on when others . . .

She *must* get Dada's letter off tomorrow. And Harry coming home soon, would he be able to tell that something, something really bad, had happened to her? Certainly she'd die rather than him know about Norman Madoc. Or would he still be too sick to know anything?

Hannah put her hand under the pillow to plump it up and it touched *Nain*'s book, the small blue dog-eared legacy of a lifetime's work and wisdom. A long time since she'd opened it; somehow, none of it fitted with how she was having to live now. She remembered the mother of the dead soldier, Rowland, saying he'd spoken through her mouth. Hannah shivered and pulled her hand away from contact with *Nain*'s book.

Let it be. Time to think of things like that when the war was over.

The telegram came on the Saturday afternoon of that week: wounded, taken prisoner. Betsy's face was a dirty yellow-grey as she stood with the bit of paper in one hand, the other pulling across her shawl. Then she swayed and the telegram fell to the floor when she reached for the table to save herself.

Hannah was at the tub in the yard dollying the washing, not long in from the factory and thumping energetically at every stitch she'd taken off as well as Betsy's work clothes and Joe's school things. Joe called but she knew, even as she turned and saw her mother through the window; knew from the lump of lead where her heart had been.

"It's all right, Mam," she said over and over, hands still sudsy. "Only wounded! They call it getting a Blighty, you've heard, he'll be able to come home, it's good news, really! Like Harry."

She stopped chattering, horrified. Dada, like Harry? Lying stiff and senseless in a bed, maybe for ever? Or with no legs like the man four doors up? Or blinded . . . Hannah began to feel sick.

Betsy leaned over the table and whispered.

"All right, Mam. Don't you fret about a thing now." Hannah signalled Joe to go for Auntie Lil and eased her mother towards the stairs.

The big tent at the casualty clearing station was like heaven after the trenches. Thomas lay quite still most of the time, with no inclination to do other. Shrapnel had carved into his thigh and forearm and waves of agony washed out from the wounds to every nerve tip. He had been offered food, but with no appetite it was too much trouble to attempt to force a way past everything – the

164

pain and the enveloping smells of mud, damp, ether and decomposition – to the greyish mess of stew on the tin plate. His clothes had been cut away and he had been washed and dressed in a shift that tied down the front to allow for nurses' ministrations. It was coarse and stiffly uncomfortable and greyish like the stew, but this was the least of his worries.

They had certainly been good enough to him, and to other prisoners in the tent, British and Australians. There were so *many* of them. Between each camp bed was a stretcher, all occupied; it was dark due to the soaked tarpaulin but Thomas could hear groans about him and guns crashing in the distance.

He had been here some days he supposed and all of that time it seemed to have been raining. If the pain had allowed him to think at all it was to feel profound relief at being out of it at last. When the Huns had swarmed back into their captured positions in a sweeping counter-attack he'd seen at once that it was hopeless and dropped his gun into the mud along with the rest of his sector's survivers. Not that there'd have been much use resisting, laid out in a shell-hole bleeding like a stuck pig; a wonder they'd even noticed him there, layered in the mud of Passchendaele.

When their own casualties were cleared they'd turned to the British. Thomas had tried to lift a hand in thanks as he was hoisted from the glutinous mud that sucked at him with greedy slurps. Twice they'd over-balanced, knee-deep in the stinking mire. The second time he rolled off the stretcher face down and would have choked in seconds; pulled back, he had heaved and vomited. God, let there be an end to this.

Sometimes he sees outside briefly as the tent flap opens, catching glimpses of surgeons with bloodstained

165

aprons smoking cigarettes between operations. Always, the smell of the mud, stronger each time a new casualty is brought in and his clothes cut from him. One nurse who has a little English tells him apologetically that they are very short of drugs and dressings, she can only spare him something to help him sleep every other night. He drifts back and forth on waves of pain, sometimes seeing the long curved beach of Aberavan, feeling the fine dry sand run through his fingers. Had they read about Passchendaele in Taibach? When the man next to him is carried out every other day to have a bit more of his gangrenous leg cut off, Taibach and Incline Row seem far away.

The pain subsides a bit. Thomas knows he is lucky with no gangrene so far. Another day, the nurse tells him in fractured English, and he should be strong enough to make the journey to base hospital, beds here are needed for fresh casualties. Thomas tries to make a joke, will base hospital be a better hotel than this? Alas, she smiles, there is little left anywhere now of drugs, food, oil for heating. But he should look forward to being exchanged soon. Then he could go home. She smiles again and Thomas would like to kiss her in gratitude. Home, in time perhaps for the birth of his new child.

He asks for pencil and paper – at least he could let them know the good news. He is given a card that allows him to write a few lines. Afterwards, exhausted but content, he sleeps until a man nearby dies noisily of a head wound.

The rain stops and the tent steams. That night for the first time, the skies are clear; Thomas can hear British planes humming like bees overhead and sees through the canvas the big arms of searchlights trying to pick them up and flashes of bursting shrapnel. He makes an effort to rise on his good elbow to peer through the tent flap; glimpses the sky, lit with bouquets of light. He recalls the nights in the trenches, watching such skies, stomach hollow with fear. He thinks how it will be, telling this to his children when he gets back; imagines Joe's face rapt with attention and Hannah half-fascinated, half-horrified. But sparing them the worst, of course. And the fear, they'd not understand the fear . . . they'd need to be here to understand that. Thomas prays that never will his children know the like of Passchendaele.

A bomb explodes quite near and he lies back, waiting for the planes to pass. Then he hears a whistling unpleasant whine, getting louder, and seconds later the tent disappears in a blinding billowing light.

Hannah walked along the beach, the bugle cradled under her shawl. It was cold, a raw damp November cold, and the dawn was thick with vapour rolling in from the sea. She must have been down here for an hour or so, unable to keep still in bed and not wanting to disturb Joe. Auntie Lil had come to sleep with Betsy for the night and had given her a draught of something that had helped her to rest.

"Got to think of the baby, *cariad*." She'd rocked her sister as she would a child. "Thomas wouldn't want you to get yourself in a state now, would he?" Betsy had at last subsided into exhausted silence, leaning against the chair back with closed eyes and Lil had plied her with strong sweet tea, her panacea for all emergencies. The newly arrived telegram, the second one, had sat on the mantel shelf, watching them. Its powerful, dreadful mission accomplished.

Hannah had done her utmost to help Joe, holding him as he sobbed, and Fly had sat by their knees and quivered. Then she'd given him a bowl of warm milk with sugared bread floating in it and had fed him herself from a spoon, a bit at a time, flannelled his hands and face with hot water and got him into bed, cuddling and whispering until he dropped to sleep. She seemed unable to cry herself and unable to close her eyes; sometime later her leg muscles had begun to twitch and finally she'd eased away from Joe and let herself quietly from the house. Only when she was crossing the morfa had she become aware of having picked up the bugle from the top of her bedroom cupboard.

Her mind was numb from wanting her father, as her hands and feet were numb from cold. She'd tried to think it was a mistake, they'd only had that cheerful card a few days ago, saying he'd got his Blighty one and might even be exchanged in time for Christmas. Betsy had sniffed at that and said, "He'll be lucky," as though he were trying to swing a fast one. But she *had* smiled, a thing she did very rarely these days. She was stopping work at the end of the week, the heavy steel plates were getting too dangerous with the baby due next month. And she was worrying about money. They'd manage, Hannah insisted, she was on a pound a week now and more in the New Year. Her face was going a bit yellow, but it would wear off, and anyway she didn't mind that, she was actually quite proud of being a canary. Then Sam Warburton had said Betsy could do his washing and ironing, a few more shillings a week to come in. And Joe said he could find more errands about town. Dear Joe.

She was walking more slowly now, conscious of her legs dragging with tiredness. That newspaper headline, LORD LANSDOWNE PLEADS FOR PEACE, how futile; and all too late now. Why, *how* had men come to allow such misery? . . . Harry, Wyn and George, Uncle Harold, and now – now –

Her footprints were drifting towards the water line. The seaweed left by the tide straggling along it and ahead was a vague shape too soft in outline to be a rock. When she realised it was a body she halted for just a moment before approaching.

A sailor, the uniform German; several had been washed up on local beaches lately from torpedoed submarines. Mid-thirties perhaps, with fair hair and neatly trimmed moustache. One of the enemy. She hated him.

Hannah became aware of a cold more intense than that of the November dawn. Then anger, even more intense, so strong that she began to tremble. It transcended the cold, engulfed her, so that she lashed out at the body with her boot, again and again. Jerking upward with each maddened kick, Hannah felt she was towering over the beach rising up to meet the heavy rain-filled clouds.

"I curse you, I *curse* you!"

Not recognising her voice; it was deep in her head, blurred and distant. Only an increasing tightness across her chest finally slowed her onslaught and the silent cries until, dizzy and nauseous, Hannah returned to reality. Gulping for breath, she sank to her knees by the dead sailor.

What had become of her? Memory wavered, cleared to that other time . . . the first night of the war, the bedroom fire, the fury consuming her then as now. Hannah rubbed at the faint burn scars on her hand as if to rub away the recollection.

"Possessed . . . I am possessed!" Now she recalled the other thing; the pale proud face with its frame of wind-blown hair and dark eyes searching out hers in the crowd that night. She could see the face again now, clear and sharp in her mind's eye.

Her voice cracked, was blown away in the wind. Face buried in her hands, she began to pray. Gradually, mercifully, the image faded, leaving her drained as though she had run a great distance.

When she was calmer, Hannah bent to sort through the uniform pockets for something she might sell; money would be short with Dada gone and a baby coming. A thin wallet held a photograph, brown and sodden; a young woman with a baby in her arms and a toddler at her skirt, serious eyed. Hannah stared at it for some time before returning it to the wallet, and that to the pocket. Having folded the man's limp white hands over his breast, she stood up.

"I am sorry. Forgive me, I know of course that it's not your fault, any more than it was Dada's."

She saw a figure then, some way off. It was her father. So amazingly clear in his dark Sunday suit with the stiff white shirt collar starched so carefully by Mam, his good Sunday boots shined to perfection. His head was bare and the light brown hair freshly combed and parted just so.

"Dada!"

No tiredness now, feet flying over the wet sand. "Dada! Oh, my lovely —" But as she neared him the figure faded; was gone. Beside herself, Hannah ran back and forth in a frantic search for footprints. Nothing. She lifted high the bugle from the folds of her shawl and wailed her grief to the grey unfriendly sky, then threw herself sobbing onto the sand.

"Don't leave me, Dada! Please don't go!"

"I'll not leave you, Princess. I'm just a bit away, waitin'."

Hannah sat back on her heels and stared about her;

the beloved voice had been so close and warm. It sowed the first seeds of acceptance, although she could not possibly have recognised them as such.

"Come to me then," she pleaded. "Help me, I'm so afraid, Dada."

"Don't be, *cariad*. Be strong, not fearful. A long road you have, but there will be help, I promise you. Be strong, be what you are *meant*. Accept what you *are*. This is hard for you, but has to be."

Accept. Hannah waited, the word echoing around her mind, but Thomas had gone. Higher up the beach she thought she saw Dorothea and she was beckoning.

Hannah tucked Thomas's bugle back in her shawl where it lay hard against her exhausted body and started for home. Too tired to think now. That would come later, when there was not so much to be done.

Chapter Seven

December 1917

A son was born to Betsy on the last day of nineteen seventeen.

"The child that is born on the Sabbath Day, Is blithe and bonny, good and gay," quoted Auntie Lil, holding the bundle to the window for a better view in the brief winter light. "Turn up this lamp then, *cariad*, and get your Mam and me a cup o' tea, eh? And better put these sheets into soak." Auntie Lil had a penetrating voice and enjoyed issuing orders with it. "Well now, little fella. Image of your Dad, you are –" She broke off, shooting a glance at her sister. But Betsy lay still in the double bed, hands limp on her newly flat stomach and eyes closed. She had lain so since the arrival of a white-faced child with a note that had caused the midwife to hurry away to a bad miscarriage, only ten minutes after delivering Betsy's new son.

Hannah left the bedroom with the sheets, stumbling down the boxed staircase with a fatigue that threatened to fell her now the birth was safely over. She could scarce remember back to morning, this day had begun years ago. Betsy's face; the way she'd stiffened, clutching the table corner; Joe hovering by the door, daring neither to come in or to go and so abandon Hannah. They'd been dressed for church, a piece of oxtail simmering on the hob for dinner.

She pushed the sheets into the copper built across the scullery corner and poured buckets of water over the birth stains which paled as she poked and agitated. A shock it had been, seeing Mam like that, helpless with pain; a stranger. She'd done everything possible till Betsy had at last signalled for Joe to go to the midwife.

"And tell Lil on the way back," she'd called after him before her head had fallen back again to twist on the damp pillow, hand stretching with a compulsive jerk to fasten painfully on Hannah's wrist.

Over now, the bitter fight. A new life up there in the woven laundry basket that had been her first bed and Joe's; and the two dead baby brothers. Frightened by the thought of them, she hurried upstairs again.

Betsy was asleep, heavy dark hair spread on the pillow, small and lonely in the double bed she had shared with Thomas for seventeen years. Aunt Lil was tidying up, the steel-tipped heels of her laced boots clicking importantly on the lino. Little Tom snuffled in his shawl. He was invisible but for a button nose, but definitely breathing.

Hannah nodded, satisfied. Dada would want her to see after his new boy. And so she would, always; her word, unspoken, was pledged for life in the dim little bedroom where Thomas Hywel had begotten a new Tom Hywel on his last night in his home. I'll see after them, Dada, she assured the sepia photograph in the ornate little frame on the bedroom mantel. The man in a stiff formal pose appeared unfamiliar in khaki until she saw his eyes, and the set of the jaw so like her own. Mam, Joe, the baby . . . she laid a gentle finger on the man's tunic breast. I'll watch them for you, Dada.

"Where's the tea then, Miss Standabout?" Hannah pulled a face at Auntie Lil's back and ran downstairs to fill the kettle.

"Is she all right, Han?" Joe stood by the table, his face strained, older in the glow of the leaping fire.

"Course she is, sweetheart. She'll be fine when she's had a cup of tea and a rest."

Hannah damped down the fire, seeing the coal bucket almost empty. With coal rationing now she dared not risk them running out of it at this stage. "Joe, would you and Trev look for driftwood after school? I could leave out a good sack for you to fill. Only, Mam will be needing a bit extra fuel."

"We'll do that." Joe brightened at once. "We'll go to the best place, there's always some on Morfa Bank. Han, is it all right for me to see Mam yet? And . . . him?"

Hannah stirred the tea, then poured some carefully into two of the best cups, the occasion seemed to merit their being brought out. She set them on the tin tray that had bright pink roses over a thatched cottage in whose doorway a woman held her baby – Thomas's Christmas gift to Betsy a few years ago and much prized by her. She smiled at Joe and passed him tea also.

"I bet she'd love to see you now. And it's not 'him', it's Tom. Thomas Hywel, after Dada."

They were quiet as she arranged gingerbread squares on a matching plate and added that to the tray. Hannah's eyes pricked, knowing that Dada would not see his new son and, holding out the gingerbread tin for Joe, she saw that he, too, was blinking tears away.

"Come and see Mam, Joey, "she put a hand over his, clenched on the table. Joe looked steadily at his piece of gingerbread.

"Han, I liked it better before you bought that bed. I get . . . cold some nights."

"It is cold, some nights," she agreed softly. "How if I push the beds together 'til the winter's done? Then you can snuggle up."

Joe nodded. Hannah brushed his cheek with a light kiss and steered him towards the stairs.

Harry came back to Wales on a wickedly cold day in early January; to Baglan Hall, commandeered at the beginning of the war as a convalescent home for troops. Hannah went there straight from work on his second day, wishing she could have changed but knowing that once home it would be hard to get out again – so much to do now.

"You can come next time," she promised an impatient Joe, who just might have been spurred in part by a morbid curiosity to discover what his time at the Front had done to the admired eldest cousin. "The Front" was endlessly fascinating to Taibach's small boys – they included trench warfare in their games, writhing behind fences and bushes clutching themselves, or gasping "I'm gassed!" and choking horribly. Joe though had for the moment retired from these games; they smacked too much of reality in the raw aftermath of his father's death. He spent more time indoors now, hanging over his new brother's basket until Betsy would despatch him sharply on an errand. But it was to Hannah that he clung, waking from nightmares in the small hours and whimpering like a lost puppy for Thomas.

It was a long way in the icily damp dark, over the Avan bridge and out along the Baglan Road, glints of the railway tracks keeping her on course until the big house loomed through bare trees. Warm inside though, and bright, Christmassy still. Yet now she shivered, nervous of what she might find. She was almost dizzy with the mixture of emotions churning in her mind and making her tired body feel quite stiff and sore with tension. Partly she wanted badly to see Harry and partly she was afraid, afraid of what she might find, of not recognising him for the dearly loved Harry of the past. She knew that she would do *anything* to help him; but with her new maturity, knew also that she might be powerless. None of these doubts, though, would keep her away.

He was in a downstairs room, high ceilinged and painted in cool green with white shutters closed against the winter night. Seated in a group about the fire, he was watching a man speaking but had an air of aloneness, as though he did not quite belong. Hannah studied his profile for a moment, suddenly fearful. The once golden hair was duller, thinner now, laid flat to his head rather than springing back with the lively remembered vigour. His nose jutted proud of sharper cheekbones, and a hollowed temple was overlaid by a prominent vein.

Turning, he saw her. Their eyes locked, Hannah's willing his into recognition. She moved, the old remembered love welling up to choke her greeting.

"Harry! Oh, dear Harry." She started for him but checked herself before she touched him, apprehensive of her welcome. He pushed hiimself to his feet as an old man would, hands gripping the arms for leverage.

"Hello . . . er . . ." He stumbled, seeming to be at a loss.

It was awkward at first; small-talk, the others watching, listening, or making an effort to do neither. He was swaying a little on his feet and she sat quickly to spare him.

"So lovely, Harry, to see you home at last. Well, almost home," she corrected herself, colouring and tried again. "See, I made some oatcakes for you."

"Thanks." He took the paper bag and sat with it clutched on his knee as Hannah searched for a way to set him at his ease, her own dismay masked as well as may be. Did he not know her name even? His parents had called on their way home last night and said he'd seemed a mite tired and confused; probably the move from London they hastened to add. Perhaps she should have left it for a few days? Should she simply say goodnight and go?

"It'll feel easier soon, Harry, being here. You'll see."

She leaned to take his hand, no more than an impulsive gesture of affection. And Hannah felt a surge then, of . . . what? Sensation flowed down her arms and into the cold fingers lying inert in hers . . . warm, living energy for Harry.

Take it, cariad. Use it.

Harry looked at her. *Really* looked now; and truly saw her, smiling at him across their linked hands. Harry remembered her . . . little Han of the big grey eyes, the nut-brown hair that would fly over her face in the wind. Never still for long . . . yet you could feel quite . . . rested, yes, that was the word, when she was with you. And those hands . . . only little they were; but Han had lovely hands.

Soon he dropped the oatcake bag and reached for her other hand. "Han? Hannah?"

She nodded. Her hands warmed perceptibly as the healing force strengthened, blossomed and ran freely through her. The room faded, reality was her cousin's face and the bond uniting them was love. Silence spread like a silken mist through the space between them and it seemed to be golden and heavy with love.

How long before she was conscious of a rattling trolley, voices? Harry's face was tinted with colour now and she gently withdrew her hands, feeling them cooling from that charged enriching heat. He stretched as though from sleep, seeming more relaxed.

"Mam and Dad came last night. I'm real near to home here aren't I, Han? They said they'd come again soon . . . young Trev an' all, next time."

"That's so, love, we can all come often till you're well enough."

He looked down at his clasped hands. "Not over though, is it?"

He took the proffered tea from the VAD and Hannah gratefully accepted a cup herself; it seemed an age since she'd eaten her midday sandwiches and the brew was satisfyingly hot and strong.

"The war? No, Harry. Not over yet." She noticed his companions now, drinking their tea with various levels of capability. Two were in wheelchairs, one grey and shrunken with an empty trouser leg. The other was scarcely older than herself, watching her slyly over the brim of his cup. The war *was* over for some, for Harry and for these men. And for Dada. She knew that Harry could not have been told about Dada yet; she dreaded the moment of telling him because that made her father more securely, irretrievably dead.

God, she was sleepy now, and still with the walk back and the night's chores waiting for her. She set down the teacup.

"You'll not leave the oatcakes to get stale, now? I'll bring a bit of something else for you next visit."

Hannah picked up the bag for him and put it back on his knee. He made as if to hold on to her when she bent for a kiss, then leaned back in the chair and let go with quiet acceptance.

There was time to think, walking home. Hands pushed deep into her pockets, Hannah stepped out as her eyes became accustomed to the pale moonlight. Her head was full of images.

"Accept", Dada had said, that terrible grey dawn on Taibach beach. She recalled the shape of the German's body at her feet, the clammy feel of cold sand and her father's voice. "Accept, then be yourself." Dada had

178

come back from wherever that shell had blown him especially to tell her that. She should think about it at least.

She frowned at silver-edged clouds, concentrating. Could he have had Harry in mind? She'd thrown all that out as useless after – well, after Norman Madoc. Nearly thrown *Nain*'s little book away even as no more than the silly dreams of the child she'd lately been.

She'd *acted* like a child, wanting to destroy something because she'd been hurt. Well, perhaps that was very natural. And not being able to tell anyone made it so much harder. Since that dreadful day there'd been no time – or wish – to take her father's words from the corner of her mind where she'd pushed them. But what had just passed between herself and Harry; could *that* be what Dada had meant by "being herself"? This was the first time since the Poplar school bombing last June that it had happened; the gift. Would it happen again . . . pehaps more often as she grew up?

There; she'd thought of it not as a curse but as a gift. But which was it? Women had been burned as witches once. Yet tonight, what had passed through her to Harry had no part of evil in it, she would swear. Only of love.

"Dada, I *will* try to understand." She was terribly cold now, and began to run.

It was hard just making sure that the baby was warm enough. KEEP WARM. YOU WILL NEED LESS FOOD advised the economy posters. And IT TAKES FOUR MONTHS TO BUILD A MERCHANT SHIP AND FOUR MINUTES TO SINK ONE.

"Stupid idiots," Hannah would rage, out searching for driftwood with Joe on the frozen wilderness of the morfa. "How'd they think we can keep warm with coal rationed!" Little Tom slept muffled under old woollens, the yellow cap Aunt Rose had knitted him from an unravelled jersey burying his small features. Betsy would take him into bed with her at night for warmth, causing Hannah to lie sleepless for fear that he might suffocate. Betsy herself looked pinched and cold and seemed to make no effort to care for herself.

"Mam . . . Mam, can I get you a bit of that potted meat you like on the way home?" Hannah hovered by the door, anxious-eyed. Betsy looked up from feeding Tom, her breast wax-white against her dark shawl and dark hair. Even the baby's fist appeared rosy clenched on the white arc of breast. Betsy's eyes too seemed to have become darker in contrast, no longer the lively warm brown Thomas Hywel had known, but with a light-absorbing quality of darkness that could unnerve Hannah.

"Better to see if you can get a bit o' neck or shin . . . and I've found no potatoes about since Tuesday. You could try Chidzoys." Her voice trailed off as though it required too much energy to continue and she bent her head again to the suckling baby.

"I'll see what I can find. You just stay in the warm now with Tom."

Hannah went out in her midday break to forage, having swallowed her dinner in record time. She herself had a free pint of milk a day as a munitions worker and a hot dinner in the new canteen – mince and mash tuppence-ha'penny, beans a penny, rice pudding a penny – so ate frugally at home, the more for Betsy and Joe. She gained some small relief from the anguish of losing Thomas in guarding with single-minded determination the welfare of his family.

Joe was developing initiative of his own. Soon after Christmas he came home at dusk with a face bright with bottled-up glee. "I've got somethin' to show you, Han. In the yard!"

It was a handcart; sturdily put together from packing cases, sandpapered and creosoted, with an old pram handlebar neatly rivetted on.

"Mr Warburton helped me." He stood back to admire it. Fly inspected its wheels, selected one to pee on and was shooed off by the indignant owner.

"It's lovely, Joe." Hannah took time over admiring it, the first wheeled transport in the family. "Maybe you could fill it up with wood, weekends –"

'It's to help Mr Jacobi's stall. He says if I collect bits round the houses in the week, he'd see what's worth puttin' into Saturday's market. He's goin' to pay me!" His eyes shone, reflecting the light of the kitchen window. Hannah hugged him; her beloved, enterprising Joe who was having to grow up too quickly.

"Marvellous, Joe. That'll be really handy – we could get you a new jacket if you save for a bit." One of the Belgian refugees who'd arrived early in the war when their country was overrun, Mr Jacobi had a bric-a-brac stall. Only last week Hannah had lingered over a tiny pink lustre bowl . . . translucent it had been, like a shell almost. But he'd wanted sixpence for it and that was out of the question, the way things were now.

Betsy was disparaging about the cart at first. "Just one more thing to fall over out there." She frowned, pushing back the heavy hair that looked now as though it needed a good wash and brushing. Hannah had offered to brush it for her after the baby was born, but her mother had turned away, not replying; withdrawing further.

"If I had a daughter I'd be *pleased*!" Hannah broke out in despair on a visit to Grandma Hywel, caught on the raw by one rebuff too many. She bit her lip then and looked defensive; the first time she'd ever disclosed the distress Betsy caused her. Thomas's mother nodded and covered Hannah's hand with hers, smiling the half-smile so reminiscent of her dead son that tears suddenly welled and spilled down Hannah's cheeks. Grief for her father, anguish for her mother, or the blessed relief of knowing that she was still loved by Grandma Hywel . . . whatever the cause the dam was breached. Dropping by the old woman's chair she sobbed unrestrainedly, hiccuping out her misery for the first time, whilst her grandmother held her, rocked her, allowed her her tears.

"Hard for all of us, *cariad*. Takes us different ways, that's all." She stroked the head in her lap. Hannah clutched the warm body in its mourning black. "Very fond of your Da, your Mam was."

Hannah sat back and studied the familiar lined face through her tears. Worst of all for Grandma. Two sons now, lost to her in a year. She'd not known Uncle Harold that well, but both he and Dada would be equally dear to their mother. Another son, too, years back; Dada had told her about the young brother killed at the colliery. Three sons and a husband . . . Hannah dried her eyes then and put the kettle on for Grandma, ashamed of her own indulgence.

With renewed determination to bring in more money, she asked to be put on the monkey machine. Cousin Jenna from Cwmavon operated one and picked up almost twice Hannah's wage – danger money, Hannah knew, one girl had been killed and another blinded before Christmas when a shell had exploded in one. But someone had to operate them to compress the TNT into the shells.

"Too young yet, girlie." The supervisor was adamant. "Try when you're older if the war's still on, eh?"

Bitterly disappointed, Hannah grimly increased her output, checking then barrowing and stacking thirty shells a day was the record and she was still a way off that. Could it really go on till midsummer she asked Florence as they walked home together through the unlit streets? So many women in mourning now, and scarcely an able-bodied man under fifty to be found in the district; darkness everywhere, it seemed. Uncle Idwal was due to go for training in a couple of weeks . . . Hannah wondered if Aunt Maggie would manage any better than Mam.

She went to see Harry again on Twelfth Night, taking Joe and Trevor. She scrubbed her face until it shone to ward off the inevitable yellow tinge, freed her hair from the protective cap to brush it till that shone, too. No sugar now for oatcakes, but she'd finished a pair of socks for him in her dinner break – half the factory seemed to be knitting socks or balaclavas – and tucked a packet of Woodbines into them. If only her old brown coat wasn't so drab; but at least her hat was quite passable, with the new green velvet band and bow. Everyone looked drab nowadays but that didn't make it right, she reasoned that folk had a duty to brighten up their own corner. When the first snowdrops came she'd take him some – a few bulbs dug up wholesale into a pot so they would last.

In the big room the fire reflected a warmth to his face that made him appear more like the old Harry, and she thought the smile of welcome was more positive, too. The boys, tongue-tied, needed prodding, for they were quite over-awed at being in the presence of so many war heroes at once. What to say to a man who'd lived in trenches, been shot at with shells, seen his mates blown to bits? For all their war games, Trevor and Joe were at a loss to bridge the gap. Hannah filled it; but not easily,

183

and when she saw Harry tiring with the effort required for three visitors, she stood up and buttoned her coat.

"Time to go, boys. Glad you like the socks, Harry. And your Mam said to tell you that she'll be along on Sunday."

She pressed her cheek against his, then shepherded the boys into the entrance hall. It was bright with Christmas streamers and a candlelit tree, warm and inviting, but Hannah's eyes darkened. The first Christmas without Dada. Good job it was over and done with. Auntie Rose had wept right through with both Wyn and George gone, and no one could do a thing with her. Her spinster sister, Anwen, who had moved in with Rose when Uncle Griffith had gone to training camp last summer had told Betsy what their sister needed was to get herself a job now there were so many to be had. Leave no time for moping. But Hannah thought that Aunt Anwen was in no position to pass judgement, having had neither husband or sons to lose.

A young officer stood by the tree, lighting a cigarette. As the match illuminated his profile he drew on the cigarette then looked directly at her, deepset eyes an intense blue-green under straight, heavy brows. Hannah was checked in mid-stride. David Vaughan ... March of last year, just before Dada's last leave ... outside the Electric.

David Vaughan frowned, digging into memory. Then the long mouth relaxed, curved. "Ah, the young lady with the, er, strong political opinions, is it not?" He tilted the curly, close-cropped head and cigarette smoke momentarily veiled his brilliant gaze.

"Lieutenant Vaughan." Hannah managed a cool little nod. "You are well I hope?"

Memories of the debacle outside the Electric cinema flooded in and forced hot colour into her cheeks. At least she'd not lose her dignity this time, not get drawn into another argument with this arrogant person, especially with Joe and Trevor as interested bystanders. David Vaughan smiled then, though dryly.

"Not altogether first rate at present, Miss, er –"

"Hywel," Hannah supplied briefly. By the front door the boys were whispering together.

"Can we wait for you outside, Han?" They had their hands on the huge brass door knob.

"All right, but don't go far."

"Thank you, Miss Hywel." He walked to her side and, apprehensive, Hannah hoped they were not due for another argument. "I've been indisposed for a while, actually – a shrapnel wound – but getting on for fit again."

"I'm so sorry." She lost her nervousness now – close up it became clear that he was far from fit. His uniform was definitely loose on him, he looked downright skinny, and his eyes were ringed with dark shadows. He certainly looked older than she'd remembered him last summer. "Is that why you're here?"

"I was convalescent here, yes, but went home last week. I'm back to visit a friend. And you?"

"My cousin." Hannah nodded into the room she'd just left. "He's been very ill. We hope he will feel better nearer home."

"Indeed I hope that will be the case, Miss Hywel. A man's home becomes precious to him after experiences such as your cousin will have had." His gaze met hers directly again; no bantering now.

Hannah could only guess at his own memories of war. She'd heard gossip about this elder son of Vaughan Tinplate back in the autumn, she recalled. He'd been engaged to a VAD, but the girl had jilted him and married an Australian whilst nursing in France – a

185

whirlwind affair. He must have been wounded soon after.

They shared a companionable silence. Odd how this man was nothing like the curt, overbearing officer with whom she'd crossed swords so publicly that sad evening. She had no doubt changed, too. This war was changing everyone; doing terrible things to everyone.

"And you, Miss Hywel?" His voice held a note almost of intimacy despite a couple of convalescents lounging in another doorway. He stubbed out his cigarette into a potted plant. "How do you keep occupied these days?"

He proceeded to light another cigarette, giving Hannah time to think that one out, and something ridiculously like a giggle bubbled into her throat. Should she tell him about the washing and scrubbing and cleaning, about the endless hunt for food, the search for wood to keep the fire in, about grubbing around on the allotment at all hours to produce a few vegetables? Occupied!

"I make shells down at the steelworks," she finally said badly. "Can't you tell from my skin?"

Defiantly she tilted her face towards the light. "I'm one of the canaries, Lieutenant Vaughan. An apt nickname, don't you agree?"

He put down the cigarette, placed a finger under her chin and examined her face with such honest concentration that Hannah wanted to squirm. Serve her right for being such a forward hussy. She was about to break away from his scrutiny when he let her go.

"Without ladies such as yourself, Miss Hywel, this land would possibly lie already under the domination of the Hun. And for certain, I never shall be privileged to see a more beautiful canary."

Hannah burst into a peal of such delighted laughter that the man in the doorway turned and smiled, too.

186

David Vaughan, utterly serious until then, swept her an elaborate bow and his own eyes lit with laughter. He glanced up to the mistletoe bunch hung from the chandelier.

"I rejoin my regiment in two days, Miss Hywel. Will you permit me to claim a kiss from the prettiest canary in Wales before I go. It *is* Twelfth Night after all."

Giving her no time to object, he took her firmly by the shoulders and kissed her full and most sweetly on the lips. Surprised into silence, Hannah was at first shocked and then amazed by how much she had enjoyed David Vaughan's embrace. Her very first kiss from a young man . . . how could she ever have dreamed it would be from *him*. She let out her breath slowly. He was so close she could see flecks of green in the aquamarine eyes; smell his skin.

"My goodness," he said quietly and bent towards her again. At that point – and afterwards she never did understand why – Hannah stepped back and clutched at her hat which was threatening to come adrift.

"I – I wish you good night . . . and good luck," she stammered. She turned at once and fled to the door, pulled on the heavy knob and then was outside, her cheeks burning as the frosty night air hit them.

"Cor, Han!" Joe danced about her as she hurried down the drive, repinning her hat as she went. "Who was that? Fancy you talkin' to an officer. Who was it?"

"That was Lieutenant Vaughan. We know each other, that's all." Hannah slowed a little, still breathless with surprise.

"He was a *captain*," Trevor corrected her. "Three crowns, I saw 'em clear."

"Oh – well, he *used* to be a lieutenant." She sounded dismissive now. "Now come on do, both of you, or I'll not bring you again."

She was in bed before there was an opportunity to think about the kiss. When she did, a delicious warm melting went on in her stomach and she curled into a ball to keep it there as long as possible, staring into the dark to reconstruct the moment as best she could. *Captain* Vaughan. She didn't know what to make of him now. Was the real David Vaughan the one she'd had so much trouble with last summer at the recruitment rally? Or was *this* the real person, who'd kissed her so gently and had such lovely warm lips and smelled so exciting? She'd never known such a scent before . . . she was used to men smelling of the rolling sheds, of work and sweat. David Vaughan's scent was extremely subtle, and Hannah could not for the life of her dissect it. But it was intensely *interesting* . . . as was he. She went back to dwell again on the kiss. Later on she rolled out of bed and slid to her knees.

"God, I'd like to add one more to the list if you don't mind. I know it's already long, so many cousins at the front now, and Uncle Griffith *and* Uncle Idwal off as soon as he's finished training. And Mam and the baby and Joe and all. But would you please look after David Vaughan as well? He's already been wounded; and that's really enough for anyone, isn't it? I know he's a toff, not like us. But please, look out for him even so, will you? You'll find him back in France in a couple of days. Thank you."

Chapter Eight

April 1918

It surprised Hannah how often she thought of David Vaughan. She really wanted to tell Florence about the kiss. It seemed quite strange that Flo had not already spoken of it. Hannah thought that the event must surely have transmitted itself naturally through her skin, so all-pervading it was inside her head. Yet, somehow, she could not quite bring herself to speak of it.

For days afterward she had felt certain that they would meet again. After so momentous a happening how could he just go back to the war and never give her another thought? Then she gave herself a good talking to, telling herself that to him it was probably absolutely nothing . . . he had obviously kissed dozens of girls – had even been engaged to one. No, all it had been to him was a peck under the mistletoe and bye-bye.

Still, she regretted her hasty and undignified exit from Baglan Hall on Twelfth Night. It had been partly because of her sheer surprise and partly because of a kind of prejudice against someone who was different from her, socially superior. She had been, rather stupidly perhaps, fearful of breaking one of the strict rules that bound her society; that decent, self-respecting working-class girls did not allow men of higher class to make free with their affections. Hannah, of course, having had an appalling experience already of how a man could behave, was also quite terrified to have anything whatever to do with them, never mind what their station in life.

Pulling against this were her natural inclinations, which were to recognise as distinctly pleasurable the meeting of David Vaughan's lips with her own. And nervous as she may well be, she found it quite difficult to relate him in any way to Norman Madoc, who she regarded as far inferior to the most humble animal. In the end she decided that David Vaughan was an ordinary flesh and blood man like Harry, or her father, due to return to the war and wishing to take back a pleasant, harmless memory of a kiss under the mistletoe. She wished him safe and well and knew how she would love him to come back one day and do it again.

It was Aunt Rose's Bella who put the London idea into Hannah's head. Aunt Rose had not recovered from the deaths in France of her twin sons. Some days she would lay huddled in bed, not even coming down to make a hot meal for her man when he came in from work.

"Dad's set on gettin' to France if they will have him," Cousin Bella confided miserably in April when Hannah went round to Alexandra Street to spread the news that Chidzoy's had some potatoes in. Bella was Hannah's age, going on sixteen. She had been a bus conductress for three months and loved it, after an unpopular job cleaning for Mrs Jones the Boot.

"Dad says he wants a bash at the Huns on our Wyn's and George's account. But the way the war's going now, we might all be takin' in Huns as lodgers soon." She stared at Hannah with worried eyes. "Mam's not goin' to want to take any more of that – any more of her family gettin' killed – not after Wyn and George. And I'm not comin' off the buses to see after all this – I do plenty now, what with our Sy a real idle cat for gone eleven years old." Bella rearranged the fluffy bangs of dark hair over her brow with little prods of a deft finger. "It's good on the buses, Han. You get out and about, have a laugh with all sorts. An' if we really are goin' to lose the war I'd like a good laugh first. Two lovely sailors on leave, yesterday, they said had I got a friend to make up a four to go to the pictures."

"You are *never* to say we might lose the war. But you should've said yes to those sailors," said Hannah promptly. "I'd have come – I'm fed up with all work and no play and I can't afford the pictures. They could have taken us to the Electric, Charlie Chaplin's on there."

"I did think of goin' to London. An' d'you know what London munitions girls get?" Bella raised dark expressive eyes ceiling-wards. "*You* want to think about that."

Hannah thought about it, carefully and quite a lot, sometimes until her poor head spun. "I don't reckon it, girlie," was Sam Warburton's opinion when she consulted him. He was the nearest she had to a father now and he'd known Thomas well, knew how he felt about things. Actually, Hannah nursed a secret hope that Sam and her mother . . . well, he called regularly to see if anything wanted doing. Last week he'd turned up with half a bag of coal, saying it was "surplus to requirements" with a broad wink at Hannah and had slipped Joe a shilling. True, her mother wasn't all that good company these days. But with a steady income again and a man to look to in trouble, she'd be easier to get on with. And Sam loved little Tom, jiggling him on his knee till the baby threatened to throw up, and offering his watch to dangle before the bemused eyes. Above all, Hannah felt they could *trust* him as they had trusted their father. But he was definitely not keen on the London idea.

"Full of all manner of strange folk these days, London. An' you can hear the guns there now I'm told – and talk of invasion again, with this new enemy advance. Better here with your Mam don't you think, *cariad*?"

How to tell him that it was partly Mam she needed to get *away* from? That Betsy made her feel unwanted, unloved; that no matter what she did it was never right, or enough.

There was, though, very importantly, Hannah's last and sacred promise to her father ... to look after his loved ones while he was away. The dreadful fact that he was never to come back simply made that vow a long-term one and no less binding. But – if she sent home more money, every possible ha'penny she could scrape together, that would serve, would it not? Perhaps Mam could give up work and stay at home herself to look after the boys? Dada would have hated her taking his baby to a stranger to mind. She might perhaps take in Grandpa Owens instead – he'd more than pay his corner and his other daughters weren't keen to have him. Aunt Lil already did a lot for him but had gone to work in the munitions canteen now Uncle Grffin had gone, and her own hands full with Ruthie and Gareth still in school. And Aunt Rose; well, poor Aunt Rose really wasn't in any shape to take on an elderly father or anybody.

So much easier if families would arrange themselves neatly and conveniently – say *Nain* Hywel move in with Grandpa Owens and Sam Warburton marry Betsy for a start: save on rent and coal, practical all around. But folk were not tidy and obliging; mostly they were prickly, contrary and full of prejudices inherited along with the colour of their hair, or their chalky teeth, or their build.

Where was David Vaughan now? Dead in the enemy's March offensive as they overran the ground won at such cost last year and swept towards Paris and the Channel ports? Was the war really going to be lost after so many had died for it? Not really a time to dwell on how sweet that kiss had been with so many being killed, such sadness everywhere. But Hannah would stretch out in bed when the room was dark and relive it time and again. Ridiculous how two lips laid briefly upon hers could have been so – so –. Sixteen in June, Hannah knew that David Vaughan's kiss had made her fully a woman, as the mere passage of time could not.

It was a week after that birthday when she finally left, after weeks of agonising indecision. Joe in the end had been the one to make it so cruelly hard; for all his bravado, his success collecting up junk for Mr Jacobi and turning it into profit, she saw only the abandoned fatherless boy, waving gamely until her train rounded the bend and he was gone.

"I'll come back just as often as I can afford, and write every week," she promised, hugging the bereft figure in the jacket now far outgrown. Joe had nodded, body stiff with his refusal to cry babyish tears. "You'll see after little Tom, I know, *cariad*. And don't forget to feed Fly, do it before you take the cart out not after – and don't go taking time off from school to earn money. And *look after yourself*!"

Just as she was thinking she could not possibly leave him, the whistle had blown. Too late to change her mind; to do anything but stare out of the window to hide her tears as the train left Joe behind.

It was easier, with Betsy. Hannah had picked a quiet time with Tom having his last feed of the day. "Thank you, I'll not be told how to run my own house," she had snapped when Hannah had suggested having Grandpa

Owens. "Havin' a bed messin' up my parlour, easy for you to say. Dad's all right where he is and if you're goin' off he'll be none of your business – no more will I," she'd added cruelly, switching Tom so roughly to the second breast that he almost fell off her lap.

"I'm only going so I can get more money – I've *told* you that!" Hannah had said indignantly. Betsy had simply shrugged. The heavy hair seemed thinner since this last birth and was scraped away from the bitter, closed face.

"I'll send you every penny I can. And it can't be for that long, this war *can't* go on much longer even if it means we have to lose. Not that I think we will, with all those Americans going in. There's thousands and thousands of them, Mam, and they're fresh and strong, not worn out like we are!"

Betsy had shrugged again, as though that was no concern of hers. Her man had already gone, forever. Hannah wished hard for her to say, don't go; to say that she was needed, *wanted*, here at home, that they'd manage somehow about money. But there was nothing; only the critical, accusing silence, the turned head.

Emily was at Paddington to meet her, an infinitely more adult Emily than the cousin she'd laughed with on the eve of the Poplar tragedy a year ago. They threaded through troops weighed down by kitbags, gas masks, rifles, and the back-to-France parcels of the families clustering around them with strained smiles and forced, unfunny jokes. Outside, the rhythmic tramp of heavy boots drowned the clatter of buses and cab-horses' hoofs as another draft of soldiers marched towards Victoria.

"They don't sing these days," Emily said. "It used to be all 'Tipperary' and 'There's a Long Long Trail', smiles and waves and things. Now they just march away, lines and lines of them, tramp, tramp, tramp, day after day. They've got old men of fifty training now, and grandads in the militia. And the Military Police go round the music halls, football matches, all over, and check if there's any men in civvies that should be in uniform."

"Did you know Uncle Jacob's joined up? Because of what happened to Wyn and George, Bella says, Aunt Rose is in a state. And Uncle Griffith's already gone? So with Dewi in the Navy as well, Auntie Lil has – oh, Em! Look at *that*!" Hannah pointed, staring.

A huge tank was flanked by four Tommies shaking collecting boxes and a banner strung overhead bore the caption INVEST IN THE TANK BANK! in blood red ink.

"You not seen a tank before?" Emily nodded casually at the monster. "They've got 'em all over . . . aeroplanes too. And in Trafalgar Square there's the biggest gun you could imagine. Wouldn't be much fun havin' this rollin' over you one dark night, would it?"

Hannah saw the massive breadth of the treads and suddenly felt sick. Sam Warburton had been right – London was a terrible place and she wanted dreadfully to be back home. She must have been mad; the extra money couldn't be worth it. Her face drained of colour and she sat down quickly on a low wall that had been denuded of its railings.

"It's so – *big*, Em!"

"Can't be too big to flatten those blasted Huns." Emily sounded so cheerful that Hannah became angry. Couldn't the stupid girl see that there may be German tanks, too, grinding their own men into the earth?

She rummaged in her purse, resolved again. No use saying now what she'd told David Vaughan that time outside the Electric, that people shouldn't encourage this madness, should simply not allow it. All they *could* do now was hang on and throw everything into a last desperate blow. She walked across to one of the Tommies to put the shilling she could ill afford into his box with such a smile that he whistled after her. "Thanks, darlin', like a ride in it on my day off?"

"You want to watch yourself, our Han." Emily chivvied her along. "Give any boy in uniform an inch an' he'll have you in trouble before you can say no. You're not in Taibach now, you have to look out for yourself here. Come on, we might catch the last of the rally."

"What rally?" Already tired and hungry, Hannah was finding the bulging carpet bag heavier by the minute. She remembered now how bossy Em had always been, how set on getting her own way, and sighed; that didn't seem to have changed with her growing up.

"In Hyde Park. Millions of women, the papers said, all war workers. Well, *you're* a war worker aren't you, you've got a yellow face to prove it! So hurry up! It's to celebrate us gettin' the vote I think – not that *we've* got it. But it's a start if the older women have, I suppose. They'll probably take it back after the war – you know men!"

Hannah reflected grimly that she certainly knew some men, humping her bag along the crowded pavement in Emily's wake. Norman Madoc for one. Her stomach tightened, thinking of *him* – of that terrible day. Perhaps its nightmare memory would never leave her; it seemed to be a dark and savage beast always ready to spring on her in an unguarded moment. But then, Dada ... how very different he had been. She was sure Dada would have been pleased that Mam had the vote now. And after the war it was up to all women to make sure *all* women had the same vote. Would David Vaughan approve? She doubted that, remembering how he'd treated her as a brainless idiot in their argument outside the Electric. Then she thought of the kiss again; smiled. She couldn't possibly judge what category of man David Vaughan might fall into. She didn't really know the first thing about him. Except that he'd got a temper and could kiss well.

The rally was beginning to disperse, streaming across the park through golden evening sunlight in a kaleidoscope of colour – all ages, shapes and sizes of women, chattering and laughing together at the end of their celebration day. Hannah sank to the grass and watched, clutching her carpet bag. She was aware of witnessing history; aware that for her sex something of importance was taking place . . . boundaries were changing; old, well trodden ground was shifting, cracking.

"The ones with the green caps are Foresters," Emily said in her know-it-all voice. "Those in the long red robes are from gas mask factories, and the ones in brown and blue are bus and tram girls – you'll see lots of them around. Those are Post Office girls, see their delivery bags? And there's the VADS. I'm not sure of that lot, in the cream jackets and blue caps."

Hannah felt goose pimples rise as the war workers flowed around her like a bright noisy tide. She stood up, wanting to be part of it all; and then, knowing she *was*, even if she wasn't wearing her working oilskins and mob cap. She was *here*, right in the middle of the great war machine that must fight to the bitter end, however long it took. She shivered, strangely moved . . . and then between the women, she could have sworn she glimpsed her father for just a second, smiling at her. She smiled back at him and waved.

After that, Hannah felt exhausted with anticlimax. Emily was still in the same lodgings. "The devil you

197

know," she said and winked. "This one has no wall lice, no bedbugs!" It was over a little grocer's shop, a decent sized room with a bed under the window from which the view was of a row of roofs with little windows underneath. Cooking was on a double-ring gas burner on top of a cupboard on the landing, and Emily fetched up water in a large enamel bucket from a tap in the yard. An unobtrusive middle-aged man, a widower Emily thought, occupied the room on the other side of the landing, but never seemed to use the gas rings. Occasionally he could be heard shouting – presumably in his sleep – in the small hours. "But it doesn't bother me any more – I'm whacked enough to sleep on a clothes line most nights." Emily had shrugged.

There was a wardrobe, a chair, a small gate-legged table, and a wash-stand with a marble top on which stood a large blue-flowered bowl and matching jug. Mrs Piggot the landlady had brought up a truckle bed for Hannah with ample bedclothes and was only charging an extra two shillings a week, and for that Hannah could use the dolly-tub and mangle in the back yard once a week and hang up her washing on an arranged day.

"I go to the public baths once a week," Emily told her, pushing aside her clothes to make room for Hannah's in the wardrobe. "And we'll just about get this under here," she pushed Hannah's bag under the bed. "I know it's not exactly the lap of luxury, but I'm not throwing away my bit of salary on anything posher – I'm saving for better times. All we really need is another chair."

"It's fine, Em." Hannah gave a tired little giggle. "We can take turns eating standing up."

Curled up in the truckle bed pushed against Emily's she thought muzzily of home and the familiar quiet breathing of her brother in the dark. She also recalled that from their window she could see a bit of the mountain. There was an uneasy claustrophobic moment when she saw herself surrounded here by hundreds of thousands of houses, all of them filled with people. But Emily had managed, saying that when she'd finished her training she would look for a school somewhere really nice, and meantime she could save well here. Well, *she* could save well too . . . and if Em could manage, so could she. Just as well David Vaughan couldn't see her now, though . . . he wouldn't understand. Her eyes closed on the delicious thought of David Vaughan holding her in his arms beneath the mistletoe.

Paddington station two months later seemed an even grimmer place than it had in June. Hannah's two precious days' leave had just been used up answering a plea from Aunt Maggie to visit Harry, who'd suffered a set-back and demanded to see Hannah and only Hannah. The return fare had arrived with a note; and of course she'd wanted to go anyway, she was quite dreadfully homesick. The two days had been largely taken up travelling and now, according to the newsboy's placards, she was faced with walking back to Poplar through the blackout, because of a transport strike.

Another strike . . . it seemed the whole country was disintegrating under the stress of the last four years. Factories, miners, cotton workers, even the London police – and now both buses and trams. Nothing for it, then, she had the dawn shift tomorrow and must walk to that as well by the sound of it. A cup of tea first was a must, though; she pushed into the crowded station buffet, holding her own against rival travellers in a way she never could have done a couple of months ago. In London, Hannah was learning the hard way to survive.

"Tea please," she called over the shoulder of a naval uniform. No result. Seeing a space she dived for it and was jabbed in the stomach by a baton.

"Good grief!" Winded, she dropped her bag into a melee of boots and kitbags.

"I say, I'm –" the officer began apologetically, turning. "Why it's miss, er, Baglan Hall! Of all people to run into here."

"You've not run into me, you've more likely broken my ribs with that stick! And I'm Hannah Hywel not Baglan Hall!" Hannah explored her injury with a tentative hand. "I recall now that the very first time we spoke you poked me with your umbrella; that was on a railway station, too."

"Is that right?" David Vaughan steered her into a corner where the crush was less. "Then I apologise again, for I'm damned if I can recollect."

"Not surprising, I was only twelve."

"Ah. A long time ago. Even so, I should have remembered."

She couldn't be sure whether or not he was teasing, his face was serious but there was something about his eyes. "You'll allow me to get refreshment for you now at any rate – what d'you fancy?"

"Tea, please, I'm parched." She leaned against the wall to watch his determined progress towards the counter. He *was* a captain, she noticed; and had survived another seven months of war. One of the lucky ones.

Coming back with their drinks held high, she saw that, lucky or not, his face bore clear witness to the toll taken. A muscle twitched constantly in the sinewy cheek and Hannah had an urge to smooth it with her hand, to calm the jagged nerves. Instead she took the cup and smiled her thanks.

"That's lovely." She sipped the indifferent brew; saw how restless were his eyes, and how beautiful his hands; long and transparent almost. Hannah imagined Christ to have possessed such hands. She pulled herself up with an effort. "This will set me up for my walk to Poplar."

"What the devil are you going there for? What are you doing in London anyway?" He downed a large whisky in nervous gulps, frowning.

"I'm lodging with Harry's sister, Emily – my cousin. I work in a shell factory. Can't you tell – I'm even more canary-coloured than I was at Christmas!" She looked full at him, refusing to be coy about her fume-tinted skin. "I can earn better money up here, and my family need it," she finished in a rush; better to get it over with, and she had no cause to be ashamed anyway of such vital work.

He made no comment, but regarded her with those deepset, disconcerting eyes. "I have just finished my week's leave, I return to France tomorrow." He examined his glass. "I'm sorry we did not meet at the start of our journey. I should have enjoyed your company."

"I daresay you came first class," Hannah said honestly. "So we couldn't have sat together anyway." She was suddenly overwhelmed by their differences; defeated by a churning mix of emotions blocking her throat, so that she could not finish her tea. "Well, I'd best be making tracks –"

"We could sit together now, Miss Hywel." David Vaughan put that bony, beautiful hand on her arm. "Will you do me the honour to have supper with me? I shall see you safe home after – how would that suit? It would suit me enormously."

Hannah opened her mouth to refuse, to say she was very tired, was not suitably dressed, must be up early to walk to work, could not worry Emily by being late. But she said none of that, seeing the thin weary face, the brilliant eyes haunted by where he had been all these long months, years; where he must now return. She took his arm.

A sort of magic overtook them, then. London surrounded them as daylight thickened into dusk; a drab and shabby city devoid of light or laughter that August of 1918, full of grim-faced, sombrely-dressed people, many in mourning black. Shops were shuttered, houses emptied of their families, with men away or dead and women moving in together to economise. Forlorn "To Let" boards were everywhere. But Hannah and David seemed, briefly, to be untouched by past nightmares or the fearful future, each finding in the other an affinity that belied their separate pasts and present.

"We shall go to Durrant's," he told her, and, amazingly, managed to flag down a horse cab.

"It won't be too smart?" Hannah panicked briefly, brushing at her plain blue skirt and jacket and seeing how travel-stained were her white cotton gloves. He'd stilled the fluttering hand by trapping it between his as they clip-clopped through Sussex Gardens, empty now of homegoing traffic.

'Nowhere could be too smart for a young lady who makes the weapons to win us the war. Always remember that, Miss Hywel." He sounded so stern that she nodded meekly, and surreptitiously pushed stray bits of hair back under her hat until he captured that hand, too.

"Are you hungry? What do you like to eat? Not that we can expect too much these days. I swear I had roast artillery nag here last week. Managed a decent bit of mutton on leave though, smuggled in by a hill farmer I believe. But don't breathe a word or the family name will be ruined."

David Vaughan smiled then, so wickedly that Hannah glimpsed the wilful charming boy he must have been so few years ago. She thought fleetingly of how long she'd queued for a bit of sausage. Nice, to be a Vaughan. To be slipped luxuries on the side because of your name. Nice. But not all that fair.

"No matter how long I queued *I* wouldn't get a decent bit of mutton as you put it." The words were out before Hannah could judge if they would be welcome. She paused but she had to go on now if she meant to be honest with him. "That is one of the differences between your family and mine. It is not your fault, nor is it mine; it is, I suppose, simply how the world has become organised. Like the differences in the way we speak . . . but provided you don't pretend these differences are not there I shan't mind them and will be happy to have supper with you."

She stopped quite breathless and looked into David Vaughan's intent face. He still held both her hands.

"Hannah, I wish to pretend absolutely nothing to you – you are not a person for pretences. Everything about you makes them irrelevant, that is one of the characteristics that I find so – attractive, in you. And tonight, particularly, your honesty is exactly what I seek. So," he squeezed her fingers, "let us have supper together, and be simply two good friends far from home, and whatever our differences may be they will bother us not one jot."

He lifted up her hands and planted a light kiss on each. Hannah smiled. "Very well. That is just what we will do."

Durrant's was smart, but Hannah remembered what

he'd said and refused to panic. There were some gorgeously pretty girls in a party at one table; they wore lots of makeup and dresses shorter than she'd seen before, exposing slender legs in silk stockings.

"Are they flappers?" She was deeply interested. David Vaughan laughed outright, the first time she'd heard that.

"I suppose, yes. The name suits 'em, don't you think?" He gave his attention to the wine list until she said quietly:

"Wouldn't you rather have supper with a flapper, Captain Vaughan, on the last night of your leave?"

"Will you call me David?" He studied the girls across the room, squealing with laughter now at one of the officers in the party who was endeavouring to balance a lighted cigarette on the end of his nose. Then he looked at Hannah, and his eyes had become serious.

"Flappers can be great fun, Hannah Hywel. But tonight I am more than happy to be in your company." She was still, hands folded in her lap as he ordered wine. "It's, well, hard to explain." He gave her his full attention now, leaning across the table in his effort to communicate. "We know, I suppose, almost nothing of one another. So tell me first, how is your family? Your parents? Do you have brothers, sisters?"

Hannah stared at him for a moment. What was she doing, sitting here opposite this stranger who knew absolutely nothing of her, her family, her life? What was the point? Then she saw that nervous spasm again in the thin cheek and said quietly: "My father was killed in France last November. My baby brother was born a few weeks later. I have another brother, Joe, who is almost nine."

David Vaughan stared at her. He saw her now, for the first time, as a girl with a background, a family, with her own private sadnesses and small pleasures. He had a vivid recollection of her as a small firebrand outside the Electric cinema, intent upon ruining his splendid recruitment speech. Then again, with her unusual, haunting face turned up to his that night at Baglan Hall. And again, earlier this evening on the platform at Paddington, when he had seized upon the chance of her companionship for a few hours. On each occasion he had seen her only as an extension of *his* situation, and her effect upon it.

Now he answered in as quiet a voice as her own, and reached across the table for her hand. "I am so terribly sorry. That is quite dreadful. Would you rather not talk of it?"

"Probably not at this moment." Hannah frowned, struggling with her words. "Except to say yes, it *is* dreadful. I loved my father dearly and miss him more than I can say. My mother has been greatly affected, too, and is not well at all. I hated leaving them . . . yet it did seem that the best way to help might be to ease their way by providing for them as well as I possibly could. Now I am not so certain . . . my brother Joe is missing me badly I know –" She broke off; collected herself.

David Vaughan accepted the wine that came and when their glasses were poured, released her hand. "I hope you enjoy this, Hannah, you'll allow me to call you that?"

"Of course." She smiled; no one had asked her permission before to call her by her given name. So to the wine. "This is the first wine for me," she told him honestly. "How shall I know if I like it?"

He gave a small snort of laughter. "Try it and tell me, dear Hannah Hywel. She did and pulled a face at the unfamiliar burn of alcohol.

"That bad? Dear me." David Vaughan looked pained. "Try again, it may grow on you."

The second sip *was* an improvement. "But that will do for the moment, thank you." Hannah regarded him seriously. "Perhaps you would like to tell me something of your family now? As you said, we know almost nothing of one another."

She waited, watching him play with the stem of his glass; aware that he needed something of her but uncertain what it would be. The silence between them was filled by another peal of laughter from the party of officers and girls. David Vaughan began to speak, broke off, drank wine, shook his head in a gesture of impatience.

"My family . . . yes, of course." He played with a fork now with those nervous beautiful hands. "We come from the same place do we not; and that, tonight especially, seems to be important to me. Yet that is only the start of it –" He shook his head again and his words came jerkily, with clear effort being made to express himself. Hannah listened attentively.

"You know, I do recall quite clearly the way you took on both me and the crowd that time outside the cinema. I realise only too well now that what you said was perfectly logical, and events have in fact turned out in such a way. When we met at Baglan Hall I was pleased to have the mistletoe as an excuse to kiss a very lovely young lady. Now, by a strange chance, our paths have crossed again . . . this evening seems to me perhaps more than just a coincidence."

He took a long drink of his wine, whilst Hannah sat perfectly still, waiting for him.

"I can't tell you how pleased I was to see you again. You are, for me, everything I am fighting for – and please do not think that a perfectly fatuous remark. You

are . . . wholesome. Clean and clear; sort of rooted and –
certain. Whilst I may be just – bits, soon. Nothing left,
really. But *you*, and the hills, the place where you come
from will still be there; and *real* – so very real." He
smiled, rueful now. 'Sorry, does this all sound unutter-
ably stupid? Truth is, I'm not by any means looking for a
riotous time tonight. Flappers, good time girls, would
simply not interest me. You see –" he was almost
pleading now for her to understand, "I am looking for
something to hold on to; because I feel my luck is due to
run out and I'm scared yellow. Damnably scared. There
. . . never expected to hear an officer and a gentleman
admit that, did you?"

David Vaughan sat back after the awkward rush of
words and Hannah saw his forehead glisten with beads
of sweat, the cheek muscle twitching again. But it was
all right because she knew then what he needed and
knew how to give it. She was deeply affected by his
words and by their sentiments. She began to tell him –
and once begun it was surprisingly easy – about her
family, her childhood; of Dada and how she missed
him. And just a bit about herself. Slowly he relaxed.
Food came, they ate and enjoyed it. Hannah was
ravenous anyway not having eaten since breakfast, but
this food was delicious . . . halibut, moist and fragrantly
steamed in a creamy mushroom sauce with parsley and
lemon, and tiny sweet peas; rack of lamb that was crispy
and brown, yet fell from the bone, with baby new
potatoes and a wonderful platter of vegetables laced
with onion sauce. When Hannah expressed delighted
surprise, David Vaughan looked knowing.

"There are always ways to produce a decent meal,
Hannah, provided one knows where to look for the
ingredients – even in these stringent times. Or so I
understand. Of course, I have no first hand knowledge.

Left to myself I would indeed be pressed to find any of this." He gestured at the table.

"Of course, you never shop for food." She made a statement; was aware, then, that nothing could better have emphasised the chasm between their lives. "Who does the shopping for your family, David?" The first time she had used his Christian name; Hannah was surprised at how naturally it happened.

"I suppose, the cook." He made to pour some more wine for her but she shook her head, which was feeling just very slightly strange after one glassful. "Mama always decides what shall be served, though. Mama likes her own way in all things," he added drily, and his eyes flickered away as the waiter poured coffee into fluted narrow cups of translucent porcelain. "Although my sainted brother, young Desmond, has been known to thwart her."

"And your father?" Hannah had seen Mr Penrhiw Vaughan once, alighting from a remarkably large motor car to declare open a new rugby football club premises. She found it difficult to imagine the bulky, impressively bearded and moustachioed, frock-coated man in the role of "father". She recalled the Vaughan residence, the imposing solid house set back behind trees, and could not imagine that as "home" either.

"Well, I don't see all that much of him." David Vaughan downed the last of his wine. "Our paths haven't crossed terribly often; what with school, then the army. He's not too bad I suppose. A bit of a martinet, maybe."

"Will you follow his footsteps when you come out of the army? Into Vaughan Tinplate?" Where my mother works . . .

"Ah, the future! I would not dare tempt vengeful gods by presuming at present that I *have* a future!"

Another burst of merriment from the table added a bitter counterpoint to his remark. "But I shall not dwell on that tonight, dear Hannah Hywel," he added quickly. "Tonight I shall enjoy your company, and the devil take tomorrow, eh?"

When they strolled into the quiet street, lit only by the moon riding between puffs of cloud, it never occurred to Hannah to say she should be getting back to Poplar. Talking peaceably, they wandered into Bryanston Square. David tucked her hand into the crook of his arm and she moved closer, enjoying the friendly warmth of him. She was glad the night hid her discoloured skin, the cheapness of her clothes ... glad to be out of the discreetly opulent dining room where her inadequacies had been so apparent – certainly to herself.

"Good Lord!" He slowed in front of a white-painted house in an elegant Georgian terrace. "Spenlove's place ... yes, Number eighteen. Lord, that brings back –"

"Who is Spenlove?"

"Oh, a bit of a toad, really – not a reliable fellow in the least. But the thing was we ran away from school together. And *this* was where he insisted I come, to his mother's place. He was sure she'd see us right. She didn't, of course; packed us both straight back to Harrow."

"Why had you run away?" They crossed the road, paces matching easily.

"I loathed being there. Hated every minute. Five years of hell. I did it twice," he added casually. "Then was turfed out, thank God."

Hannah was shocked into silence. Taibach Eastern had been no picnic – particularly Miss Probert's class – but hell? Only if you behaved badly the whole time, surely: and that would be your own fault. Without warning, as so often happened here in London, she was deeply homesick for Taibach. "How awful for you," she said at last, aware of the inadequacy of the comment but at a loss to add to it.

"Forget it." He steered her towards the corner. "I say, ever been to Primrose Hill? Come on – let's scoot for that cab."

Breathless, they bundled into a taxi and collapsed laughing against one another, for no reason other than that they were young and pleased to be in one another's company.

"Where is Primrose Hill then?" Hannah set her hat to rights. "I hardly know London at all."

"Just through the park – Regents Park." David had quite recovered his spirits. "Wonderful views of the city – you'll see. We shall sit at the top of Primrose Hill and drink to us." He pulled out a slim leather hip flask, offering it to Hannah, and when she shook her head smiling, took a swig himself. "Very well, but I shall try again, later."

"Maybe. You should know, though, that I've not before –"

"Not been accustomed to strong drink, Miss Hywel?" David Vaughan's hand covered hers and she could see his eyes kindle to laughter. "I shall see you come to no harm – trust me for that. You are very young I know."

"I am sixteen." She tried not to sound defensive.

David took off his cap and pushed a hand through the strong close-cropped waves. Better go easy on the hip flask – he'd not thought that young. He looked at her in the moonlight. Sixteen, and she was on her own in London, wrecking her health in that damn arsenal. And her father gone, and mother labouring at *his* father's place. Her eyes, they were quite beautiful, a luminous sort of grey, big and clear as spring water. They watched him calmly; and yet obviously nothing like this had happened to her before. He really did feel quite remarkably fond of her. A quite special little lady . . .

"That *is* very young," he said finally. "I had thought perhaps seventeen."

"Sixteen is *almost* seventeen." She was firm on that.

"And how much older are you?"

"Not more than six years. But perhaps more in – some ways." This, almost to himself. Hannah pressed his hand, understanding. Enclosed in the intimacy of the back seat a wave of emotion became palpable. The faces were so close . . . their lips together then, warm breath intermingling.

Hannah sighed, the smallest sound but bringing answering pressure, an arm wound tighter. When the cab slowed at the corner she drew away, breathless, but his smile as he stroked her shoulder was warm and loving. Out for supper and a walk afterwards nothing more, that's all that was happening she told herself, for reassurance. And yet . . . she had never felt anything remotely like this before. Her entire body seemed to be melting so that she thought that she might end up no more than a pool of liquid on the cab's leather seat. But she did not want to melt, because then there would be nothing left for David Vaughan to hold, and there was nothing in the world more wonderful than that. His arm about her waist was both exciting and reassuring, which in itself was most strange. And when the cab stopped with a clatter of hooves on the cobbles and he handed her out, her legs were quite unsteady.

Soon they were climbing through trees heavy with August foliage, their passing stirring an occasional sparrow to a sleepy twittering. A patch of hawthorns blacked out the path with dense shadow; David Vaughan felt for her hand and did not lose it when they came out into the hill's lush, scented grasses that waved up to the dome.

"Not too far now." He stopped to take off his cap. Hannah pulled a head of rye grass to run through her fingers, blowing it away into the night.

"This is like Uncle Jenkin's meadow before mowing. Wonderful, the scent of grass . . ." It was easy to see now, the low hunter's moon seemed ridiculously close and the muted sounds of the city far off. They zigzagged past a stand of chestnuts and an iron bench where an elderly man sat with a dog, so resembling Fly that Hannah paused to stroke the warm head.

"Nice night, eh, miss?" The man sat with both hands on the knob of his stick.

"Indeed." She fondled the terrier's velvet ears. Then bent to rub with rhythmic, circular movements with the palm of one hand at its shoulder. It leaned into the hand, watching her face with moon-filled eyes. David and the old man watched also until Hannah straightened, caught their gaze and smiled, embarrassed.

"How d'you know she'd got a bad shoulder?" The terrier wagged her tail and stretched luxuriantly.

Hannah looked vague. "Oh, has she? All dogs like a rub, though. She reminds me of my own terrier at home." She started up the path again, the dog looking after her with ears pricked.

"What was that about?" David Vaughan caught her arm and pressed it as they fell into step again.

"Nothing, really." This was the part of her that she'd kept back; from not knowing where to begin, and also from fear of ridicule. It was always the same . . . once this came out she was "different". And for Hannah that was not a desired state, particularly now with David Vaughan.

"You are a white witch; I knew there was something." He was half teasing, but she could only laugh and evade. She'd been surprised herself when her hand had gone involuntarily to the dog's shoulder ... the heat flowing through had been brief but potent. Strange how for stretches of time she could forget all about it. She turned to David, laughing with a sudden touch of pure happiness in this one moment.

"That's right, a white witch! How clever of you to have guessed! Now I shall run to the top of the hill, jump up and catch the moon and, oh, ride away on it. Magic, that's what I am!"

Hannah began to run for the joy of it, for the wonder of the scented hill and the great golden moon that was surely close enough to touch, and the beautiful young man who was her companion for just this hour – and even for the little dog on her way home with an easier shoulder. David Vaughan set off after her, ran easily alongside, laughing himself and lifting her hand to swing it. When she stumbled on a loose stone he caught her in an instant; then they were a single shadow, wrapped close about and mouths stealing each other's quick breath.

'Hannah. Hannah Hywel." Heartbeats shook through his uniform, her own seemed thunderous from running, from exhilaration. He traced a line from mouth to ear with his warm lips, making her curl forward with delight and her arms came up to his neck, the crisp short curls springing between her fingers.

Nothing could have stopped it . . . sliding down to the hay-sweet grass, together still.

"Here, sweetheart," he slipped off his tunic and eased it beneath her, a button sharp on her hip bone and there it was, the marvellous scent of him again. He hung over her, easing off her jacket, stroking her breasts

213

before he unbuttoned her cotton blouse. When he cupped a breast Hannah tightened with the delighted shock of the warm firm hand on her cool flesh. There was just a second or two of – doubt, fear? But it was quickly gone, and in its place a great tumbling joy fell right over her like a sweet covering veil. It stole her breath, and every thought in her head but the one that sang "David, David, David."

"Hannah! God, let me love you. The first time –"

Of course it *was* the first time. As Hannah's spirit all but burst with giving, it was as surely the first time as though Norman Madoc's cruel invasion had been suffered by another person in a different dimension of time. It had no possible link with what was happening now, this willing and joyful exchange of loving bodies. It may have been that Hannah Hywel would as tenderly have lain with any soldier bound next day for France. But *this* was David Vaughan stretching skin to burning skin with her, whose hands were wakening every nerve.

"I won't hurt you, sweet. Oh, you are beautiful – I can't tell you . . ."

But he *was* telling her, with every touch of those long hands, and Hannah knew she was beautiful, made so by his ardour and desire. She whispered, "You are beautiful, too," and when he entered her, closed herself about him with a deep breath of pleasure, drew him up, up into the dark velvet centre of her. Hurting, pain – impossible, with the grasses sighing to their moving bodies and the great gold moon hung low above the hill.

After, when his head was damp and heavy on her skin and she touched his hair with butterfly caresses, Hannah stared at the moon and concentrated on memorising, stocking a storecupboard of sensation against the lean winter that would surely come. She stroked his shoulders; he stirred against her, murmuring, and Hannah lay still to retain the lovely weight of his relaxed body on hers as long as she might. They were warm, intimately alone in the sheltering dark.

"You never did show me this amazing view," she reminded him gently, after what seemed to be a long time. He heard the sleepy smile in her voice and after a moment rolled over to pull her down to him and kiss the warm hollows of throat and breast.

"All in good time. I need to say first that you are a wonderful girl. I shall remember – us – together, like this all the time I'm . . ."

His eyes closed and Hannah reached down to kiss each eyelid. On the hill above, a nightjar's flight call floated across the distant hum of London. Its lights were dimmed by war but she could see its shapes and contours under the moon. She hovered over David's still form, stroking his shoulders, his chest, running her hands into the narrow hardness of his waist, yearned to protect him from tomorrow; but knew that she could not.

"I know. And I am glad, David. I'll remember, too."

She had avoided thinking about the time, but knew now that it must be very late. Her skin had cooled and she shivered, pulling across her blouse. At once he sat up.

"Sweetheart, are you cold? Whatever time is it?" He took out his pocket watch and peered at it. "Good Lord."

"David, I must go now. I have to be up early . . . and there's Emily." Hannah stood up and began to tidy herself. She felt very tired now; the wonderful elation had gone and a measure of bewilderment had set in, and a worrying sense of insecurity.

"Let me help you." He shook out her jacket, held it as

she put it on then buttoned it carefully for her as she stood still before him. When she had tidied her hair she settled on the straw hat as best she could without being able to see and pinned it securely. For some reason she wanted to cry a little.

When David Vaughan had put on his tunic and brushed himself down he came to face her and took both her hands, and though it was darker now Hannah could see that his face was serious, the brilliant eyes intense.

"Hannah, there are things I want to say . . . you must know that?"

She waited for a moment, then nodded, afraid to speak lest he should discover her to be on the verge of tears.

"All I can really manage, I think, is, well; this evening has been very special to me. I cannot let you go without telling you . . . and also asking you to believe that I had not planned for . . . any of it."

"I know that, David. We met completely by accident. How could you have planned it?" Her voice was very low.

"I didn't upset you? I was . . . so . . . I thought you were . . ."

She touched his arm. Somehow the bewilderment was easing, though she would still have wept had she allowed herself the luxury. "I do not feel upset, I promise. I do understand. It was just as special, for me. I would not like you to think –" She broke off, too shy to say the words. David Vaughan folded her against him.

"I never could think of you as any but the dearest, finest person, Hannah. Come now, I shall get you home as quickly as possible."

They were quiet together in the cab, the horse trotting

216

sedately through the quiet streets. He tore a sheet from a diary in his wallet and wrote on it.

"This is where you can reach me. Will you write to me, please?"

"Of course." Hannah folded the paper carefully in her purse. "I will write first, and give you my address."

Outside her lodgings she would not allow him to dismiss the cab, to linger. "You would not easily find another about here so late." They parted with whispered words, small kisses, lingering hands intertwined. She watched their cab until it had gone, with the pale blur of his face through the rear window. The door squeaked as she let herself in.

"Whatever time . . ." Emily struggled from sleep as Hannah slid between the sheets of her small bed.

"Go back to sleep, Em. We'll talk tomorrow." She turned away and pulled the sheet about her ears; grumbling, Emily subsided.

She wouldn't, of course, tell Emily. Not about that. Wild horses wouldn't drag it out. Closing her eyes, Hannah began to rewind the pictures in her head.

It made Silvertown easier, through that last autumn of the war. The shells were for him in particular now, to give him covering fire, to soften up the enemy trenches before he went over the top. Her work was dangerous – she'd been told often enough by the other girls about their explosion last year that had flattened a square mile of dockland and killed seventy, many of them women. But if it could protect *him* . . . Most girls she worked with had men in France; would joke about grinding their husbands' swords. Now Hannah redoubled her efforts to raise her output. One last heave they said, after the massive counter-attack on the Marne at last pushed back the enemy. General Haig was marshalling all

217

forces, the Americans were pouring in 300,000 men every month. Keep up the pressure and the whole front will collapse.

So Hannah heaved. She walked to work to avoid catching the plague of influenza, the Spanish flu, that was killing and laying low by the thousand that autumn and seriously hindering factory output. She drank her pint of milk religiously, having before given it to Mrs Mount next door for the children, and ate all the canteen offered to keep up her strength. She wrote to the address he'd left, a cheerful letter that said nothing of how she worried, was dead tired and not infrequently sick with the toxic fumes that discoloured her skin. For a few days she had been so unwell that a fear had overtaken her . . . things could happen when a girl was foolish enough to give herself as she had done. Emily had been thrown off the scent by the tale of the very late train into Paddington and the long walk back to Poplar, but *Hannah* knew the truth. Briefly, irrationally, she longed for her fear to become reality. Should he not return, he would remain with her in his child. Next came panic; then anger with herself – a stupid wicked girl to wish for such trouble, her life was quite difficult enough. Did she want to end up like Harry's poor Brigid?

Hannah had plenty of time to think, walking back and forth to Silvertown. She thought of autumn at home, how the hills changed colour so gradually, so perfectly, and how the skies above them seemed to change, too. She wondered if Joe was picking blackberries and wynberries for Mam – she'd written him about that. She wondered if Tom was crawling yet. She would go home just as soon as this war was over. And she thought most of all of David Vaughan. She loved him, she truly did. Which was not only hopeless but entirely wrong in every way. She was the wrong age, the wrong class, the wrong everything. When her curse arrived she was dreadfully relieved and indescribably sad. Best forget the whole thing now. Wrong things do happen in a war; this had simply been one of them. And yet . . . *this* thing had never seemed remotely wrong, to her.

No answer to her letter. She wrote another; burned it. Reviled herself for not growing up to be more sensible and got on with the business of making shells. Each night she wept a little for him, quietly so as not to waken Emily, and remembered the night on Primrose Hill.

In mid-September, jubilant headlines announced that the Americans had annihilated the notorious St Mihiel salient, and were proving unstoppable. At dawn the next morning as Hannah was letting herself out of the house she felt hopeful, buoyant. She smiled at the baker's boy, sniffed the sooty air as though it might bear that tangy fragrance of autumn she was missing so much. She looked at the women already pumicing their doorsteps, lifting their heads now and again to acknowledge a neighbour. She saw the coalman's horse stop to emit a steaming pile of manure, and a woman dart out with a bucket and shovel to scoop it up. Then she saw David halfway down the street, walking toward her.

"Oh – oh, *David*!" She started to run, her shawl falling unheeded to wet cobbles. He lifted an arm, laughing. And then mist rolled over him and he fell sideways into it with a hoarse cry.

"David! *No!*"

She was crying, too, clutching at the gas-lamp for support and weeping with fear and with shock. A passing workman helped her back to the house where Emily, in curling rags and half asleep, took charge. Hannah, sobbing and shaking, drank hot strong tea and was sick. Half an hour later she set off again, having refused to explain the upset, and this time the street was no more than itself; a London street lined with identical houses, with rubbish in the gutters, cats hunched on fences and the milk girl filling jugs from her churn.

David was not there. Not ever again. The words drummed sickly in Hannah's head as she walked to work, head down. Not ever again. He had been wounded twice already, how could he possibly not be dead this third time – who would ever get a third chance? That smoke she had seen, rolling up to envelope him . . . could that have been gas? Dear God, please not gas.

She would write that very evening. She would try again. If there was no reply she would make enquiries at Vaughan Tinplate the minute she reached Taibach. Ivy Roberts in Vaughan's front office knew everything. Mam had said so time and again, and Hannah would not be too proud to ask. Perhaps even Mam would hear if . . .

Lord, but she was tired of making shells. She wanted to go home.

Chapter Nine

In Taibach, folk filtered onto the streets as the news spread fitfully from house to house. The day was raw even for November but the girls from Vaughan Tinplate were first out, dancing down the road without stopping for their shawls, beating the big tin sheets and shouting above the din. Youngsters pushed excitedly at each other, wrestling and pinching one another's caps; old men made for the pubs. Some women wept quietly in their doorways, clutching toddlers, or went to stand in silence before photographs of young men, deaf to the cacophany of works hooters and whistles spreading the message of the Armistice.

At Vaughan Tinplate Betsy carried on working, her face stony. At the end of the day she went to Crown Street to pick up Tom from *Nain* Hywel who was cuddling the sleeping child by the fire, red-eyed but smiling.

"A street party, they're sayin', only not till summer. Can't take it in, not after so long . . . Such a good lad this is, *cariad*, not one scrap of trouble." She laid aside her grandson and reached for the teapot but Betsy shook her head, picking up Tom to fold him in her shawl.

"Best get home, Mam . . . I've to get to the Maypole, too, before they close." Thomas's mother nodded, resigned now to the immovable object that was Betsy Hywel. How long since they'd sat comfortably over a cup of tea for women's talk – how long since any of them had got through Betsy's barrier?

"Han'll come home now, Mam, eh?" Joe rushed to her, stuttering with excitement. He had found a faded Union Jack from the under-the-stairs glory hole and tied it to his cart, in which sat Fly with a wisp of bunting around his neck. "Can I go for chips?" Joe was learning fast when to cash in on events and the Armistice must not be wasted. "She'll be home right soon then, won't she, Han? We don't want shells any more? Do we, Mam?"

Betsy's face was buried in Tom's neck as she held him. Joe saw that her shoulders were shaking, standing in the scullery doorway with her back to him. The hem of her old grey flannel coat dipped unfashionably almost to her boots . . . the coat Joe remembered from his toddler days. He liked her in her Sunday one, the navy serge fitted three-quarter length; but *this* was the mother-shape with which he wholly identified, this marvellously familiar shape topped by the squashy black velour hat. *This* was his Mam; and she was crying.

Joe was shocked, overcome now by a bewildering gamut of emotions. The day the war ended . . . he could scarcely recall life without it. And folk were dancing in the streets, waving flags singing . . . and his Mam was crying . . . because his Da was . . . wouldn't be . . .

Staring at his Mam's shaking shoulders, at his brother's round little face peering at him over them with his bonnet knocked over one eye by the brim of the black hat, Joe, for one dreadful moment, needed above all to fling himself at her and howl. He needed her to pick him up and cuddle him, tell him that it would be all right. But he was nine and two months now. He was too heavy now for his Mam to pick up, he was to see after her like

Han had said. Mam wouldn't want him blubbing, wouldn't want him scared.

He put a hand on the sleeve of the coat he knew as well as his own. "Mam, shall I go to the shop for you? Or I could mind Tom while you go? An' get tea ready?"

He relieved her of the baby who was getting heavy, almost one now. Betsy straightened her hat, nodded, sniffed back fresh tears. "I'll get my bag." Joe would have liked to prop Tom up in the cart and wheel him into High Street where they could join in the festivities; but knew better than to ask. He followed Betsy inside, sat Tom on the rug and saw to the fire. At least Han would be sure to come home quite soon now . . . be lovely, that would. He'd missed Han something fierce. But even Han couldn't make it right about Da. Nobody could do that.

Going home had been her goal from the time Hannah had heard the great peals ringing out over the city, soon to be drowned by shouts, singing and squeals of disbelieving joy. She wanted more than anything to be with Mam and Joe and Tom now; to sit quiet in her home and think about Dada. But she couldn't just up and run, she must work out her week until payday. Emily's school closed when the news came through and she ran home amid shoals of excited children, caught up with them as they shouted and eddied back and forth, stamping, skipping, released from a fear that for the younger ones had been a normal state of life. They had gone up west that night to dance in Trafalgar Square where a bonfire lit on the plinth of Nelson's Column by some Anzacs had got out of hand, scarring the monument and showering the girls with sparks. They'd tried to reach Buckingham Palace but the press along the Mall defeated them and Emily was knocked over by a boy scout who was pedalling furiously along the pavement whilst bugling out a final "All Clear". They joined a party of wounded soldiers dancing unsteadily to bagpipes, then strolled back along the river to Poplar, waving and throwing kisses to busloads of inebriated joyriders and singing "Everybody's doin' in, doin' it, doin' it." When finally they crawled into bed, Hannah's last thought before oblivion had been, "Home. In just a few days I can go home." That night she dreamed of walking with her father and David Vaughan on the great arc of Aberavan beach, laughing and kicking pebbles and singing "Lily of Laguna", and on waking her cheeks were tight with dried tears.

Joe was at the station to meet her. He hesitated just one moment, conscious of his position now as head of the family, then abandoned dignity to cast himself into Hannah's arms.

'There's my lovely boy!" She hugged him tight. He was taller, and when she took a long look, his face was leaner, harder cast. The war had without doubt left its mark upon Joe. He picked up her bag.

"We're to get Tom from *Nain*'s, then Mam can get straight home. Gosh, Han, I'm real glad you're back. It's been – funny, like, without you."

Nain Hywel had the kettle on ready. She kissed Hannah soundly but her eyes were misty, remembering her two sons who would not be coming home. Hannah swallowed the tea thankfully, it had been a long cold journey, ate half the slice of bread and dripping, then passed the rest to Joe who was trying not to watch her eat it. Tom sat on the rug, playing with screwed-up newspaper, and when Hannah picked him up he smiled placidly and studied her face with big unblinking eyes.

They almost ran the short distance from Crown Street

to Incline Row, the bag bumping against Joe's legs and Tom tucked securely into her shawl as the short afternoon faded towards dusk and it got colder. Betsy had started the fire and was leaning over the pan, stirring, her profile sombre as Hannah glimpsed her through the window.

"Well then." She turned as they came in, all red-cheeked and smelling of November twilight. Her dark eyes raked Hannah's face for a moment and Hannah thought she must be reading about David Vaughan, about Primrose Hill, on it. In confusion she went straight to her mother and put her free arm around her. Tom, pressed between them, grasped Betsy's pinafore and gurgled vaguely.

"Hello, Mam. Lovely to see you."

Betsy's arm came up round her daughter's shoulder for a moment. Kissing her mother's cheek, Hannah felt briefly a chasm of desolation in the tautness of the face. Oh, Mam . . . Mam.

Then it was over. Betsy turned back to the range.

"Put Tom down then set the table. I've potatoes and onions fried. And there's a sausage each. Joe, you wash your hands now, boy."

Joe grinned at Hannah and went into the scullery. Hannah sat Tom on the rug and turned up the lamp a little. Like *Nain*, she, too, was close to tears now. Dada was missing; she'd only have to set the table for three. God – God, what had it all been for?

"I've been taken on in the works canteen," she told Florence, two days after she got home, meeting her out of Stanbuckle's tailoring where Florence had just found work as an improver. "Aunt Maggie's Trevor helps out there Saturday mornings and he heard about this woman leaving. Not much money, nothing like the shell factory! But better than nothing for a start!"

Hannah hugged Florence, nose red with cold but happy to be back with her oldest, dearest friend. Warming up with steaming cocoa in the tiny cluttered bedroom in Queen Street, she said wryly: "Joe reckons he'll match my wages soon, the rate he's going – and him only just past nine! He's come on so much while I've been away . . . almost as if he's determined to take, well . . . Dada's place."

Florence sat on the bed beside her, blunt little fingers curled round her mug for warmth. "We've all changed, haven't we? *Had* to. I mean, how could things be the same? Ever again . . ." The air was charged with painful memories. Then Hannah said quietly:

"We only heard yesterday, my cousin Dewi – his leg, they said. Only days before the Amistice, Aunt Lil says. She's in a state about it."

"Tell you what," Florence said soberly. "We'll be lucky to find husbands, Han. When you think –" They thought, and the brightness left their young faces.

"I'm not that bothered. If we start that night school class for office work we can earn our own money, decent money in a little while, and be independent." Hannah sounded almost defiant. "We could get a little place for the two of us if – you know, we don't . . ."

"Hook a husband?" Florence grinned. At sixteen, neither could really believe they would end up that most despised of beings, a spinster. The unmarried daughter, general skivvy as a rule, with at best a corner in a sibling's home once her parents were gone. Spinsters had the lowest pecking order in the community; not an option to be considered. But now perhaps it *must* be. Perhaps unmarried women might even come to be thought of as normal women who simply do not marry, rather than sad spectacles of failure.

Three quarters of a million British dead. Two and a

half million wounded, many permanently disabled. Hannah realised the cold fact of a corresponding generation of women without men was forced to be considered as the grim figures emerged. Once the euphoria of the Armistice died down and the people of Port Talbot's little streets took stock, they realised that almost every household had suffered a loss. Nothing would be the same again. There was a grim set to many women's lips now; those that *could* welcome a man home from the war found them strangers as often as not – wounded, shell-shocked, some gassed – shadows of the men who had waved goodbye.

Hannah ached for the loss of her father. Some nights she would creep downstairs to get his bugle and would hug its hardness to her in the dark. Dada, cousins Wyn and George; Harry, Dewi, and Uncle Harold from Swansea who she'd not known that well but had been Dada's true brother just the same. Poor *Nain*, with only Uncle Jenkin left of her sons. And then, always, there was David Vaughan . . . short of going to his house and asking there seemed no way of knowing . . .

The day she heard that David Vaughan was alive her heartache turned to a swift clout of joy. It was while she was in the canteen kitchen mashing potatoes for the meat pie – Ivy Roberts had let it drop quite casually, as though it was of no importance.

"I told Edie I was sure it was that David Vaughan of Vaughan Tinplate, but she said his hair was more auburny. Anyway, I was sure – he *has* changed but there's no missin' eyes like those! And it was the Vaughan's car, that big black one. Waitin' for someone in the station yard . . . wish a smasher like that'd be waitin' for me!"

Hannah had gone on mashing the potatoes automatically until Ivy snatched them off her. "You gone to sleep, Han? You'll be through the saucepan in a minute."

Hannah moved on to making custard for the treacle sponge, ignoring Ivy. She was almost angry, now. How had she not known? That September morning in London . . . the smoke, the falling figure? She'd been so certain he was dead; wounded perhaps? But alive . . . David was alive. And actually *here*. Not that his whereabouts could ever be her business. Yet always, always, she was aware of looking for him, hoping that one day she would turn a corner and he would be there. She told herself firmly, time and time again, that she must *never* allow herself to believe that David Vaughan could have any part in her future. But at least the fearful ache of imagining him dead was gone.

The miners came back first, desperately needed, giving their delighted families Christmas treats with their war gratuities. Harry's brother, Frank, started at Bryn colliery on his fourteenth birthday and his sister, Daisy, finished at the shell factory, found a position in Williams' Emporium, haberdashery department, and could not credit the fearsome drop in wages. Dewi, Aunt Lil's eldest, came to Baglan Hall to convalesce in April after a series of operations had left him with a stump instead of a leg and a back scarred by shrapnel. Visiting him there, Hannah remembered the one-legged man she had seen playing a barrel organ at Paddington and wondered what Dewi's future would hold. So many were coming home now, wounded in body and mind. Some were limping about on crutches or being led sightless or being wheeled by a mother or sister or wife in a cumbersome invalid chair. Dewi was lucky in his two arms and his head being in good working order . . . he could train for clerical work at least. And at least he was *alive*. Uncle Griffith, too, still waiting to be brought home from the ammunition depot at Boulogne and his letters ever more gloomy as the months dragged into spring.

"Could've been back home on a good wage since Christmas!" Auntie Lil complained bitterly. "Instead, all they did was send him a coupon to vote on . . . poor man; likely without any idea of who was standin' even! Should've brought em' all home to vote, that's my opinion. Lord knows we should've had enough ships for that little job with all the steel we've been makin' here these four years! We could've gone together to vote then." Auntie Lil was proud of casting her first vote ever, but full of ire about the way demobilisation was being bungled by Lloyd George and his new government. "Wasted no time gettin' them out there did he – but certainly takin' his time about gettin' 'em back. An' dear knows if our Dewi'll ever work again, and the bit Ruthie brings in don't buy the groceries. We'll all starve if my Griffith don't get home soon." She made her protest in her usual forthright manner by bringing her youngest, Gareth, out of school a term before his fourteenth birthday in defiance of the new regulation on school leaving age, and packing him off to Bryn pit with Aunt Maggie's Frank. The two of them walked there and back together everyday, passing the time composing smutty new verses to "There's a Long Long Trail a' Winding".

"Done the trade unions a power of good, though, these new votin' powers," said Harry's dad, Idwal, who had been demobbed in January having got no further than training camp before the Armistice. "Eight million payin' their dues now, if we're to believe the papers . . . double at least what it was before this little set-to."

Harry listened quietly, staring at his boots. With his paralysing headaches that lasted sometimes for days, there seemed little possibility of his ever needing to join a union of working men. He seldom complained, helping with household chores when Aunt Maggie would allow. He carved a new, beautifully balanced wooden top for Joe when the one Thomas had made finally split. And he took Trevor's iron hoop down to the forge near the Colliers Arms at Pantdu to be repaired, and actually made him a new skeeter with which to bowl it along.

"Thanks, Han," he would say quietly, when she came at Aunt Maggie's request to work on a bad headache. They would go up to the bedroom he shared with Frank and Trevor, he would sit on the chair and Hannah would stand behind him, her back to the window. Relaxed, quiescent, she would endeavour to become the empty vessel she now knew was necessary for healing, closing her eyes and clearing her mind of chatter. Soon the warmth would spread down through her fingers, through her thumbs where they rested at the base of Harry's skull. Then she would be aware of black viscous pain, streaming from his head in a channel to disappear into the ground. Afterwards he would move his head gently from side to side, then turn it to smile at her and say again, "Thanks . . . that feels quite a bit better."

Hannah's canteen job, like Florence's, was a come-down in wages but must serve for the moment. They both began the office work night class with whole-hearted commitment, enjoying the work when not too tired to grasp what Miss Williams was saying through her formidable buck teeth. The book-keeping was after all only commonsense, as Florence pointed out. And they'd soon get the hang of the typewriter even if they couldn't understand a word Miss Williams said. Betsy was still at Vaughan Tinplate, resisting all attempts by

Hannah and Joe to persuade her to give up and stay at home with baby Tom.

"He's not liking it at Mrs Pinker's," Joe said, worried, when Hannah first came home. "Three days every week, an' I can tell he's been cryin' when I go to fetch him." He gave his brother a paternal thump on the back to help down the porridge he had spooned into the reluctant mouth. "Never cries as a rule, he's lovely an' quiet."

As spring advanced Hannah began to notice just how quiet Tom was. It was easy sometimes to forget he was there, sitting on the rug by the hour and gazing about with his usual genial expression. He had the look of a dimpled monk, sparse fair hair stuck out over large ears, with a bald patch at the back where he would rub it against the bars on his cot. An overlong bleached cotton smock that had been Joe's hindered his efforts to crawl. "Shouldn't he be walking soon?" Joe asked, balancing his brother against a chair.

"They go when they're ready, not before," Betsy said briefly. When she was out, Hannah began to encourage Tom, who would soon collapse with a lop-sided lurch and continue his bottom-shuffle around the limited space available. Hannah would hug him then, wipe his sticky hands and face, croon to him, loving his pillowy warmth. He *would* go when he was ready.

A late vicious wave of the worldwide influenza epidemic hit Taibach and Aberavan in May, just as it was thought this small corner had escaped the scourge that had rampaged out from the East across every continent. "Thought we'd been lucky," said Betsy dourly as the illness crept through the rows of houses like a killer tide. As the toll mounted the cinemas and pubs were closed, then the schools, as Hannah recalled had happened last autumn in London. Buses were sprayed with disinfectant and the elderly hurried about with masks over nose and mouth, whilst babies were kept indoors.

Aunt Maggie's Trevor, twelve now, went down with it.

"He's all right isn't he?" Joe asked anxiously of Hannah. Though three years his senior, cousin Trevor had been Joe's best friend since infancy and he could not envisage a world without Trev to make mischief with, with whom to share secrets. Hannah reassured him, Trevor was young and strong and had not seemed too ill until pneumonia developed late one evening. Hannah was there, helping Harry with one of his headaches, when Aunt Maggie all but fell down the stairs into the quiet kitchen.

"He cannot breathe. An' his poor face looks quite blue! Daisy, run for Doctor Reed, girl. Hannah, bring up the kettle soon as it boils."

She clattered back upstairs, moaning under her breath. Daisy, halfway through the ironing, ran without stopping for her shawl out into the rainy dusk, flinging back the old gate into the back lane so that another slat fell out. Hannah, standing behind Harry's chair to massage the nape of his neck, felt a cold shadow fall over the little room that moments ago had been full of peace.

Trevor died as early summer dawn roused the house martins nesting outside his window. A steaming kettle to ease the labouring lungs, wet towels to break the fever, a linctus sent by the doctor with the promise to come when he could. But Trevor slipped away with no more than a tremble of the hand curled into his mother's fist. Daisy fell keening to her knees by the bed but Hannah saw Aunt Maggie become rigid, immovable, joined to her dead child by the clasped hands. Harry, seated against the wall on a kitchen chair brought up when he refused to go to bed, watched his brother's face smooth into stillness; looked across at Hannah. When she reached him to cradle his head, Harry's cheeks were cold and smooth as the steel shells she had made last year.

"I've seen so many die." His voice was a crushed whisper. "But my kid brother . . . little Trev . . ." Hannah held him as though he too was a child, murmuring comfort, though she knew there was none to be had.

Ten days later Hannah got in from the canteen to find Betsy shivering by the fire. "You see after Tom," she said hoarsely. "He's not to catch it." She began to cough, temples held tight between her palms. When Hannah helped her up the stairs she leaned heavily for support; allowed herself to be undressed and eased into her bed, where she shivered so violently that Hannah wrapped a heated brick in its piece of flannel and slid it against the icy toes.

"Tom . . . fetch him – it's past time."

"A cup of tea first for you, Mam, warm you, eh?"

The cup was clutched thirstily, some tea slopping over the sheet but Betsy did not notice, coughing again. "Tom –"

"I'll go right away. Just stay warm till I get back."

Running through Taibach, she just caught the chemist before closing. "What helps the flu, Mr Price? Mam's poorly . . ." She clutched her purse anxiously. Mr Price sighed, offered her a packet of Beecham's Powders from a big box at his elbow, already almost empty.

"Somebody on the wireless said that snuff was good," he offered, trying not to sound too positive so there'd be no comeback if it did not work. "Kills the germ, they said."

Hannah opened her purse. "How much?" Then added quickly, "I'll have some anyway."

It was one of *Nain* Hywel's days for minding Tom. "Mam's poorly," Hannah said briefly. She went to pick up the baby, then recoiled, remembering how she had held Betsy. "It's the flu I think."

"I'll keep him." The old woman nodded, brisk. "Bring me a few things round for him. Get as much liquid down her as she'll take." They were both quiet, both recalling young Trevor's funeral last week. "Try to keep Joe away, *cariad*."

"Yes." Hannah felt despair then. Joe was already inconsolable about losing Trevor. "I'll be round later, then." Hannah turned to the door and gave her grandmother a tremulous smile. "Thanks, *Nain*."

Betsy took the Beecham's Powders. The snuff was abandoned, the sneezing too much for her head pains. Hannah went early to the canteen next morning, assured that Betsy was feeling slightly better and would stay quietly in bed. A shocked, subdued Joe got himself off to school, quite unable to swallow any breakfast. He took up a cup of tea to his mother made with half lukewarm water – he'd tired of waiting for it to boil – and half cold milk and swimming with tealeaves. Mrs Rees at Number ten, alerted by Hannah, took in soup at midday and found that Betsy had attempted to dress for work but had fallen by the door, having a severe nosebleed. She was shivering violently again and unable to keep down the soup. When Hannah got home she went straight back to the chemist and this time brought back some antiseptic gargle. She held her mother whilst Betsy made weak efforts to use it and spit into the chamber pot. She twisted hot fingers about Hannah's wrist.

"Don't go." Hannah looked up, startled. When had her mother ever asked that before?

"I'll be here. You lie back now. A drink, soon as the fire's set."

Joe was quiet, back early with his cart. "Mam better?" Hannah saw fear stark in his brown eyes; peat brown like the morfa pools in February.

"Not too bad, love." Hannah was gentle. "I'll not go in tomorrow, shouldn't have today really. Only what with Mam's money stopped as well . . ."

"Han, I'll try Court Farm, Sunday. They've early potatoes an' loads of bean rows. I've our own hoe, even."

He got four hours hoeing and came home triumphant with a florin, and blisters on his palms that Hannah salved with hypericum and bound before he ran to see if *Nain* Hywel was managing with Tom.

Betsy, ill, had strangely lost her indifference. She lay meek, amenable to Hannah's ministrations; even allowing her hair to be brushed. And when her face was sponged gently with warm water and patted dry with a soft piece of flannel, said "Thank you" in a cracked voice. She would cough all night, a tearing rasping sound that Hannah longed to smother by pulling the blanket over her ears. The noise even woke Joe, who would usually have slept through an earthquake but had already suffered nightmares from the shock of losing his cousin.

"She'll be all right soon won't she?" He looked at Hannah with big weary eyes, his knuckles white with clutching the sheet. She stroked the hair back from his forehead, high and round like Betsy's.

"I hope so, Joey. Would you try to sleep now and I'll see if I can help her. Maybe a drink."

Hannah went for help to her great grandmother's

dog-eared book; boiled up rosemary with feverfew and fed her mother sips of the cooled distillation from one of Betsy's six good china cups in the parlour cupboard. They were painted with pansies and had been a wedding gift; they had not been used since Joe's christening.

The headaches were relentless, causing painful vomiting. Nothing to do but wait for them to pass said the doctor, stupidly unsteady from lack of sleep. And take the mixture, three times daily. Desperate, Hannah went again to *Nain*'s remedy book. It was full early for meadowsweet, but she knew the hedge along by St Mary's church sheltered the first creamy blossoms – the scent of them guided her and as she gathered them, she was unexpectedly filled with joy. June, summer. The earth breathed, blossomed, each blade of grass renewed as it pushed strongly towards the arc of blue shimmering light where a skylark hovered, singing. Beyond the sheds and chimneys of the morfa factories, rising hills shook themselves clear of the last straggling dwellings to reach upward like the lark before they must drop again to smoky little Cwmavon.

"It is beautiful," Hannah said aloud. "Thank you."

Betsy nodded to her chest of drawers. "Top one . . . a box, quite little."

Hannah left the meadowsweet tea she had been spooning down, touched the dry, burning cheek. The box was tight at the back, under a cotton petticoat and a bodice threaded with narrow lemon ribbon.

"You can look."

The box was pink, the faded colour worn off the edges of the cardboard lid. Inside was a cotton wool nest holding a locket the size of her forefinger nail, on a thin gilt chain.

"Our wedding day . . ." Betsy's voice was cracked and dry as her cheek. Two tiny sepia faces, the bride's hair frizzed over big dark eyes and the mouth tight with nerves. Thomas looked stern and very young, his own hair sleeked severely across. But Hannah knew the sure jawline and flaring nostrils in the short straight nose, and the level stare.

"Oh, Mam, it's lovely. How pretty you look." She put it into Betsy's hand and watched a spasm of emotion shake the gaunt face. Then the locket was dropped into her palm.

"It's for you. A good girl, you are, watchin' after the boys. All right, are they?"

"Yes, Mam. They're perfectly all right. Truly."

Utterly overcome, Hannah clasped her mother's shoulders and raised her to cuddle her close, tears running over the limp, stringy hair. After a minute Betsy moved feebly away.

"Don't you catch it. A good wash mind, before you get Joe's tea." Hannah nodded, speechless, and ran downstairs to sob into her mother's coat hung on the stairs door hook.

Betsy seemed to give up then. She was quiet, except for coughing; made no fuss or argument, swallowed every remedy Hannah could devise. But the will to live was missing. She looked quite blue one morning with her breathing shallow and painful, and Hannah could see her fading. She died that night, three days before Hannah's seventeenth birthday, and Hannah could not wish to keep her when Betsy was so ready to go. There was a moment when she hovered, struggled to raise her head. Then she smiled, and Hannah saw with a sense of strange peace and relief that her father was standing, smiling, at the foot of the bed. After that it was easy; and soon both were gone.

She tried to tell this to Joe, curled against him in his bed as he sobbed. But he could not be comforted.

"I want them *here*, that's where I want them! I don't care about this daft stuff, they're not *here* and what'll we do now? They don't *care*, they've left us and I shan't forgive them not ever! What about *us*?"

Holding his heaving body tight, Hannah, in truth, did not know what about them. Except that they would go on. There was nothing else to do.

She insisted on a good oak coffin. Dada had had none; she'd no idea if Dada even had a grave. Betsy's, with brass handles and plaque, emptied the funeral fund, and she bought a bunch of white roses to go on top with a card written in her own painstaking copperplate: "From Hannah, Joe and Tom with all our love, for ever."

There were flowers from each of Betsy's sisters and a wreath of lilies on behalf of her father, too confused himself now to attend the service. Aunt Maggie sent a mixed bouquet of early summer flowers, delicate pastels, and the women of Vaughan Tinplate had had a whipround for a bunch of pink roses. It seemed a long walk down Incline Row into Commercial Road, Talbot Road, across the river bridge to St Mary's. Hannah had never queried why they were church not chapel – they always had been, Dada had said once and that had been enough for her.

Uncle Griffith organised two relays of six bearers, all family, and the mourners followed on in twos and threes, Hannah leading with Joe stiff and scrubbed at her side and Tom settled easily on her hip, thumb in mouth and new bonnet working askew to allow one ear to escape. Joe had offered to scrub out his cart to accommodate Tom but Hannah had thought not on this occasion, though said it was a good idea. The day was gusty and fresh, huge skies alive with running clouds and grasses swept and dimpled, the hills chequered blue and green. As the procession moved into Church Place Joe's hand stole into Hannah's; she felt her heart begin to jolt against her ribs with each slow step. Church Place . . . *Heol y Corff*, the Way of the Corpse. Belief was that to approach its resting place by any route but this would leave the soul to wander in torment for ever. She did not believe this, Hannah decided. She believed that Betsy was already at peace, with her husband and two baby sons.

There were half a dozen fresh graves . . . more were expected before the epidemic burned out. Betsy's was not far from the freshly covered mound where Trevor lay. Seeing it, tears spurted from Aunt Maggie's eyes and she turned into her husband's broad shoulder for comfort. Hannah had asked that they sing "Shall we gather by the river" and Tom, taken aback at first, joined in on the last verse with a high tuneless croon that made Aunt Lil, red-eyed, turn round and frown at him.

Joe held himself in, scarcely breathing, until the coffin was lowered, then began to shake so hard with suppressed tears that Hannah handed Tom to Aunt Maggie and led him a few yards away into the shelter of an ancient yew.

"There now, sweetheart. Mam's not *there*; she's away with Dada, happy and free. Hang on, *cariad* . . . *I'll* not leave you, ever. And it will feel easier soon, I promise. You'll not always hurt so."

With Joe's face buried in her stomach, Hannah watched the first clod thrown onto her mother's coffin by her Uncle Griffin. It was then that she saw her father, standing a way off by the hedge. He raised his hand and smiled at her. She bent to tell Joe but, looking again, saw that he was gone.

Two days later she heard that David Vaughan was home on a visit; but somehow it no longer seemed important.

Nain Hywel could not take them. Two weeks of looking after baby Tom finally convinced her that the only sensible thing to do was what her surviving son Jenkin in Cwmavon had been urging for months – move in with them, as her own mother had done before the war: abandon the struggle to find the rent each week with the new increases, let alone buy food and coal from her minute colliery pension; give up trying to keep her own place going with her dicky heart. When she fell on the wet stones of the back yard she had just washed down and put her knee out she agreed to go, and handed Tom back to Hannah. "You see how it is, *cariad*."

"Course I do, *Nain*. And you're not to fret – you've done more than enough, having him this long. And we'll be up to see you at Uncle Jenkin's, so don't you fret."

"If you've anythin' you'll not want in the way of furniture up at Uncle Jenkin's I'll sell it for you," offered Joe. "You know, on my cart?"

Sam Warburton was upset that he could do little to help. He had finally decided to marry again – a war widow, a comfortable woman with a spotless little home in Velindre Row and a son who had been gassed on the Somme and would not work again. "But I'll be round regular, like always, and you're to let me know if there's anything –"

Hannah hugged him, a thing she'd not done before, and felt the warmth of tears starting; the truth was that she had dared to hope for Sam to come as a lodger and ease their circumstances. "Shall I move your bits an' pieces round to Mrs Elm's on my cart?" Joe asked, and Sam said certainly, and he would pay handsomely for the job.

Aunt Maggie felt trapped. So difficult, not knowing from one day to the next about how Harry would be . . . and Frank on day shift and Uncle Idwal on nights. Then all this trouble with Daisy. Hannah knew about what was happening to cousin Daisy and did not see why there had to be trouble. Daisy had fallen in love with Albert Mens, one of the German prisoners of war from the battleship *Blucher*, interned in the disused celluloid works at Goytre. No one had managed to wring from her exactly how they had met, but Albert had been one of those sent to work on the site for the new Margam Steelworks along from the existing mills and Daisy had worked nearby in the shell factory for two years. Nothing had been said about the gangs of prisoners until a couple of months ago, when men returning from France and unable to find work protested that the hated Huns were taking bread from their families' mouths. There was a heated local outcry, a formal protest to Parliament, and the Germans were withdrawn. At that point Daisy had admitted, with some defiance, that she wanted to marry Albert who was asking to stay in the district rather than be repatriated, and whose ambition was to rent a bit of land and farm it with Daisy. Outraged, her parents had forbidden her even to speak to Albert again on pain of being put onto the street. Daisy had retreated into sullen silence but told Hannah privately that she would never give up Albert, even if she had to sleep under a hedge. They wanted to be married; they really loved each other.

Now, Hannah told Aunt Maggie not to worry, they would manage. She knew that most of all her aunt was grieving for her last baby, Trevor. There was no possible way the three of them would have fitted into the house anyway, and when Aunt Maggie finally said she would take Joe, Hannah said gently that it was a very kind offer but that they were going to stick together as a family.

When Auntie Lil heard this she gave voice – Hannah was daft, thinking she could stay on in that house when rents were on the up and up, men from all over pouring into the district to the steelworks and collieries, and houses being promised but not built? If Hannah found a nice cheap room for herself, and Maggie took Joe, maybe they could all find a way to share Tom out. A baby *was* harder, of course. Maybe the Board of Guardians, just for a bit . . .

Hannah was suddenly shouting, cheeks flaring scarlet with fury. "Tom's not going to any Board of Guardians! I'll work twenty-four hours a day before he'll go there! And I won't have us split up at all! I'd have thought you'd *know* we must stay together now!"

"Very nice, I'm sure!" Aunt Lil's beafy fists settled aggressively on her hips. "But we can't always have our own way, Miss – beggars can't be choosers."

"We're not beggars!" Hannah screamed back. "I can earn money – Joe can help out – and Tom's lovely, no trouble."

"But you can't take him out to work when you go, daft Madam, can you? Nor pay for a minder for him!" Lil looked satisfied at playing the trump card.

"Then I'll find work I can do at home!" Hannah countered sharply, without thinking. "We're staying together and that's it. Any help will be welcome," she made an effort now to simmer down. "But that's it, Auntie Lil. *Together* and we will *never* beg."

When Aunt Lil had gone, Hannah's heart was still thudding as though it would burst her rib cage. She picked up Tom and held him close, rocking him back and forth on her shoulder. He twined sticky fingers into her hair and made small contented noises; Tom loved to be loved.

"And so you shall be, *cariad bach*." Hannah stroked his back. "You'll *always* be loved, Han will see to that, just like your Dada and your Mam would want. We shall think of something, never fear."

She carried him from the house and up the road and soon was on the hill. Tom was getting heavy but she went on and up, driven to escape. When she was far enough away she sat on a grassy hillock and put Tom down at her side.

It was a perfectly lovely day. Strange how she had been too upset to notice before that the sky was such a gentle blue, with a few of the sort of clouds she had always imagined were reserved for angels to sit on. The hill was in full summer dress, foxgloves thrusting everywhere through freshly uncurled bracken and choruses of grasshoppers under the yellow gorse. In the distance, the hills of the Gower snaked blue and mauve beyond the silver bay and to the east the sandhills glimmered. Even the works below looked beautiful on such a day.

Hannah knew that she must be strong now. It did not occur to her to admit at this point that she could not cope – that she had lost father and mother and could not take their place for her two brothers ... that she actually wanted some care herself, and time to grieve for her loss. This may have been why she was here at all – her actual purpose in the scheme of things. Perhaps her gift would help her, give her the power to carry her load. She knew that she loved her brothers dearly; and now Hannah prayed with all her heart that she could give them all they would need of cherishing. She stroked Tom's little arm.

243

"We'll be fine, sweetheart. I'll not let you down."

She swung him onto her hip again and started back to Incline Row.

They were on their way to buy potatoes at Chidzoy's when she saw David Vaughan. He was driving a smart new car along the road to Margam. The girl beside him was beautiful, long ashen hair streaming behind her; remote and ethereal like a fairytale princess. Hannah had heard about her, too; some well-connected debutante of the current London season. Hannah longed to run into the road to speak to him, know how he was, what he was doing with his life. She certainly would have had he been alone – it would have been impossible to let him just – go. But she drew instinctively against the wall and he and the lovely girl, that she was surprised to find she quite hated, were quickly gone.

Hannah walked on home, Tom on one arm and her basket on the other. Her head was dizzy with thoughts of him. She felt wretchedly alone; lonely, hopeless. Even so, better not to try to meet him . . . a shame to spoil the memory of that magic night on Primrose Hill by finding that he did not even remember her face. Really there was no special reason why he should; not because he was selfish or spoilt or unkind, but because their loving had quite likely been for him no more than the transient need of a man seeking comfort before returning to war.

Hannah swallowed hard, then closed her eyes for a second in the dusty street. She felt a little better, having thought that through. Goodbye, *cariad*, and God bless you.

She changed direction suddenly and went to see if Sam Warburton was in. She had had an idea about how she and her brothers might survive.

Chapter Ten

July 1919

It was hard for Sam to accept that she was not still
Thomas Hywel's little girl, that she could take on the
responsibility for her family's well-being. But yes, he
would see she got someone decent in – no one would get
past Sam Warburton to diddle her. Aunt Maggie kicked
up; scarce seventeen and renting out her upstairs
rooms! What if they fell behind? If they were dirty? Stole
bits of things? But Hannah squared her jaw just as
Maggie recalled her brother doing when he'd been set
on his way. She sighed, which the usually brisk Maggie
did often lately, for her youngest son's death had been a
grievous blow. She went every day to Trevor's grave,
coming home red-eyed and silent. Now she offered to
give a hand sorting out stuff that must be changed
around. And she'd a spare rug somewhere that could
serve upstairs.

Five shillings a week for the two upstairs rooms, use
of the yard tap for water and use of the copper and
mangle once a week. Fair shares of cleaning the lav
shared with Number ten; half the pegging out space.
Back door only and quick through Hannah's kitchen to
the stairs – that was certainly the worst part, never
knowing when someone would barge in on them, either
going out or coming in. But not for long; just till they got
the money sorted, Hannah told Joe cheerfully. She felt
extremely nervous about the whole project, but it
would never do to let Joe know this. It was tricky,

getting their beds downstairs into the parlour – would have been easier to have done it through the window, Uncle Idwal told them after. The aspidistra took more light off the room each year but Hannah could not bear to get rid of it, it had been Betsy's pride. Betsy and Thomas's bed was left upstairs for the lodgers; Hannah hated that above all, but saw no alternative.

Joe came into his own finding things for upstairs, which helped lift his melancholy over his mother and Trevor. A good table and two chairs for six and eleven pence and a reasonable cupboard for four and six . . . lots of bargains about he said confidently, if you know where to look. Hannah earned the cash for these and a bit of new lino, a little paraffin stove and two pails, one for clean water and one for dirty, by doing washing and ironing for Mrs Jacobi who had just had her fifth and was taking time to get over it. Joe fixed that job up for her, it was clear Mr Jacobi thought highly of his small but enterprising assistant. That brought in another four and sixpence a week minus the wood and coal needed to heat the copper. Not enough. Then, would she do a day's baking? Joe was proud, bringing the message. Mr Jacobi had thrown a fit on being given fish and chips off the cart three days in a row and was threatening to leave home.

Hannah said yes at once; borrowed cookery books from the library and decided to make a thorough job of it. Experimenting here and there with herbs she already knew of, she discovered a natural flair. Mr Jacobi was enraptured by his sorrel soup, the touch of thyme in her rough scones, the tarragon that *Nain*'s book had told her grew on the morfa, mixed into the coating for fried chicken drumsticks. Another four and sixpence for the full day's baking. Still not enough, with threepence every week for school books for Joe and a penny a day for his playtime milk. His boots were letting in badly and Tom had no coat. And she was sick of living on bread, potatoes and porridge.

Sam's well-vetted tenants turned up and to her enormous relief handed over the first week's rent in advance. Mr Peplow, a small pale-faced, out-of-work silversmith had a ginger-haired wife who looked as though she was coming down in the world, and a toddler daughter. Two older boys were left with their granny for now, Mrs Peplow explained, bobbing her head like a chicken; Hannah nodded back, hoping they would stay there. Joe said he could lay his hands on a cot for two and sixpence that only needed a good scrub down and the woman looked defensive and clutched her purse tight. Nothing to spare there.

That first night, Hannah lay tense and sleepless in the little room that to her could only ever be the parlour. She listened to the unfamiliar noises from above, only slightly masked by Joe's gentle snoring and the regular creak of Tom's cot as he tossed back and forth. She hated the thought of strangers in her parents' bed . . . in her room and Joe's; felt panic swoop to stop her breath. What if she couldn't manage, couldn't make the money go round? Silly . . . her aunts and uncles would never let real harm come to them; the ultimate horror of the orphanage. They would simply have to split up and fit into what corners could be found for them till times got better. If only Dada and Mam were still here . . .

She sat up suddenly, clutching her sheet. Little Tom *was* slow. No one liked to mention it but she could not deny it now. He was not quite as he should be for almost two. Should she take him to the doctor? No, no money for that; not yet. Soon, maybe. If he still didn't, well . . . God, let it be all right . . .

She heard Joe's smothered, half-asleep sob, and was in with him at once.

"There, there, *cariad*. No fretting, now. Hannah will see after you, sweetheart. We'll do fine, you'll see."

She cradled him until he slept again; then did not want to leave the warm comfort of his sturdy body. But Tom seemed to be getting cold, too. She carried the baby into Joe's bed and the three of them cuddled together, fitting close into one another's curves, till dawn.

It was Joe who came by the typewriter. She'd worried a bit that he might have stolen it, but he insisted that he had found the monstrous old thing out back of the stock-taking office. Certainly it looked weather-beaten. Hannah strangled her conscience, she could no longer afford one anyway.

"That's marvellous, Joe." She wiped it carefully over with Vaseline, but failed to make it work. So Joe carted it round to Sam who had it functioning within a week apart from the last three lines running up the sheet of paper, and a temperamental attitude to capitals. He paid for a new carbon ribbon and cadged a wad of scrap paper from the print office to enable Hannah to practise.

"So, if I bring my night school stuff to you once a week, you can keep up with the lessons for free!" Florence said, only too happy to find a way to help. "Then soon as Tom starts school you can look for an office job. Good money, that'll be."

Hannah stared at her little brother sitting contentedly on the floor playing with his bootlace. Hard to imagine him ever being ready for school. But she would do her utmost to help him work towards it. And if he really was going to be a little slow, she would simply have to coach him a bit, evenings.

His young brother's death had set Harry back. He had grown more fond of Trevor since he had been at home these last couple of years and got to know the boy more intimately. Before the war, Trevor had simply been "the baby brother", and Frank, the brother who always liked to argue. As the eldest, with two sisters and two brothers, Harry had felt secure, confident of his position as head sibling. The others would consult him over childish difficulties, look up to him as one wiser than themselves but more accessible than their parents.

Now it was all different. Emily was away teaching, a superior young woman who had done well for herself. Daisy was at work all day and sometimes out in the evenings, though Harry was never clear what she did then. But he simply accepted that she was a grown woman and as such had no further need of him. Young Frank was a miner, who mixed with other miners despite his youth. He had grown closer to his cousin Gareth now they both worked at the same pit, and he seemed to have no time to talk to Harry. His mother tended to treat him like an invalid – in truth he had been exactly that for so long that he could not blame her for it. But Harry was still struggling to regain at least some aspects of the nature that had been his before the Somme. He resented, when he felt well enough to resent anything, being pushed for good into the role of the war-wounded son who would never again join the rest of the world. His father did little more than pass the time of day, kindly enough but clearly embarrassed by what had become of the eldest of his children, the one who had once been such a proud young fellow, the best there was.

No longer the best ... on the scrap-heap. Thinking that, Harry's headache would start up again; the unpleasant clawing at his scalp that would go on to become full-blown crashing agony. Then he would turn to Hannah.

He began to come regularly for help and Hannah developed a simple routine that appeared to ease them. He would sit on her bed and she would stand behind him, rubbing gently until she could feel the muscles and sinews begin to relax. Then, with eyes closed, her fingers would move over his head until she located what she sensed was a hole, round and quite black. Once her thumbs were pressed to this hole she would empty her mind of everything but her own image of it. Quite soon, pain would begin to flow, black and viscous, through her thumbs, arms, trunk, legs, until it spilled into the ground and seeped away. When the hole was drained, Harry would usually curl up and sleep, and she would cover him and get on quietly with her work until he woke, refreshed and out of pain.

"How d'you do it, Han?" He sipped his tea, smiling over the top of Tom's head. Tom adored him and Harry loved to amuse him with simple games and stories. Now Tom pressed against his chest, sucking his thumb and kneading the knobbly wool of Harry's jersey.

"Not sure, Harry." She finished up Mrs Jacobi's ironing and set it to air, folded neatly over the old wooden clothes horse. "Just natural, really; that's how it seems." Then, "He should be walking by now – Tom – shouldn't he? And talking – Joe never stopped at his age. D'you think he's all right, Harry?"

The words had tumbled out unbidden. Now Hannah bit her lip and looked sideways at Harry, cheeks pink from the heat of the flat-irons. To her surprise he nodded, matter-of-fact, stroking the back of Tom's hand with one finger.

"I'd thought to say, once or twice. I do think he's a bit

slow, Han. He's what, two at Christmas? Only another three months."

She drew in her breath hard, staring at him. "What will I do, Harry? I can't –"

Into the silence Mrs Peplow upstairs scraped a chair back, coughed. A moment later she clattered down the stairs and pushed open the door and crossed the room with the baby tucked into her shawl and her basket on her arm. She smiled vaguely above their heads and scuttled across to the scullery door, slamming it behind her.

"I hate that," said Hannah forcefully and burst into tears.

"He may catch up." Harry ignored them but began to look nervous, he could not cope with tears. "Anyway, he's good with me – I'll help with him, Han, honest." He set Tom down, pointing him at Hannah. "Come on now, boyo, you try walkin'."

Hannah wiped her face with her pinny. "Here, lovely. You come to Han." She bent and patted her knees invitingly.

Tom stared at her with big uncertain eyes; rolled them back towards Harry. Then, as Harry released his hands, he wavered, wobbled, and staggered with legs wide apart and arms stretched sideways the four paces to his sister.

"There's my clever little fella!" Hannah hugged him then turned him straight round.

"Back, now. Hold your arms for him, Harry." And back went Tom, rolling like a drunken mariner and grinning broadly. Back and forth, until he and Hannah fell together on the mat, and laughter and tears were all the same, and Joe came in from school and it must all be done again to show him and he had to be delighted, too.

That night Hannah went to tell Florence. Tom *was*

slow, but he was walking at last and she held tight to that. If only the money would go round. Florence was pinning up her freshly washed, glossy dark hair, frowning into the little swivel mirror on her chest of drawers.

"I shall get this bobbed next birthday." She jabbed in her hairpins, impatient with the long braids. "I've warned Mam, the minute I'm eighteen."

She inspected Hannah through the glass. "You've not put your hat on . . . *or* your good skirt?" She noted the puzzled frown. "Han, you've forgotten! The Flannel Fair!" She clucked impatiently, took up her everyday beret and pulled it over Hannah's hair, tucking it in, pulling it out until she was satisfied. "Here, my red brooch on your collar –"

"I've no money, Flo," Hannah protested. "And I told Joe I'd not be long."

"Nor will you be. And how much money d'you think I've got, idiot, after Mam's done with my wages? We'll just take a stroll round, that doesn't cost anything."

The site at the back of the station was crowded, shrill with blaring music, brilliant with coloured lights in the windy September evening with huge purple clouds massing over the bay: hawkers shouting over the cries of excited children, the screams of girls on the round-about, the heaving switchback, the helter-skelter that creaked alarmingly in the wind. Stalls were piled with red-cheeked gaudy dolls, cheap trinkets, pot figurines and fancy tea-caddies, feather dusters, huckaback towels and stiff sheets folded in cellophane. Hannah saw Auntie Lil bearing down in her formidable best hat and dodged, giggling, behind the orange-striped tent of Madam Orski the palmist – this precious bit of leisure was not to be wasted on a probing catechism from Auntie Lil on how she was managing her household and finances. The lady sailed straight by. But for some unaccountable reason, Hannah remained uneasy.

Florence had threepence to spare and they made it last. It was whilst they were arguing about whether the last halfpenny would do better hazarded on the gamble for a goldfish for Joe, or on the uncertainty of a bar of sticky toffee that Hannah began to feel even more uneasy.

They were not far from the swingboats. She felt increasingly compelled towards them, soaring up and down, higher and higher, the girls squealing in terrified delight and the young men laughing as they pulled harder on the tassled ropes. Hannah moved, slowly at first then faster, pushing through the knots of idling families until she saw that just below the first boat three small boys squatted over their cigarette cards, swapping to get their sets complete.

Hannah stood beside the boys, then looked up. There were four in the boat, which now swung towards her and paused at the end of its arc. It swung down and away from her so that she could clearly see the heads and stretched out legs of the occupants. Her intent gaze followed the movement of the boat, then continued upwards to focus on the top of the framework from which it was suspended. Again the boat returned, its underside looming over Hannah and the boys, then down and away again.

"*Move* boys! Get away!"

Surprised by the ferocious pitch of her shouting, the boys dropped their cards. At the same time Hannah ran at the boys, dragging two of them away from the swing. The third boy, making to escape from Hannah, leapt off in the opposite direction. She sprawled on the grass with her two captives when the boat that had fascinated her returned on its next swing. But this time there was a sharp cracking sound and the boat, instead of climbing, broke completely free, smashed a bar of the framework and came to rest with a terrific thud on top of the boys' abandoned cigarette cards.

Hannah thought she had got away with it when she did not figure in the major press report of the swingboat drama. But a local reporter arrived at Number twelve Incline Row intent upon a "human interest" interview and she was no match for the bright-eyed ferret of a young man. He turned out to be naturally sceptical of strange "powers" and it was not too difficult to persuade him that there had been an element of happy coincidence in the incident. There resulted a short piece headed TAIBACH GIRL'S PREMONITION SAVES BOYS IN FAIRGROUND ACCIDENT, including a report on the swingboat occupants who were all recovered after their shake-up.

Two of the boys saved by Hannah had been brothers. Their mother called on her to express her deep gratitude and offer payment; embarrassed, Hannah insisted that the part she had played was minimal and that she wanted nothing. The woman left, though still professing her fervent thanks for what she insisted was a miracle.

Among her familiars, reaction varied from admiration through faintly discernible ridicule to honest curiosity. Mrs Jacobi presented herself on the doorstep and quizzed her in detail. How had she known? Did she have a vision? Hannah, nervous that Mrs Jacobi might regard her as a witch and cancel her food order, explained as best she could about simply having a "feeling", talked again about a "happy coincidence". Mrs Jacobi eventually nodded doubtfully, accepting the offering as the best she would get, and asked Hannah if she could manage another three dozen oatcakes as she was having some ladies into tea. Deeply relieved, Hannah carried Tom down to the Maypole for extra floor, aware not for the first time that her "gift" could be a two edged sword.

The incident also affected her lodgers' attitude towards her. Mr Peplow took off his cap and squeezed it with nervous fingers when he passed her in the yard. Mrs Peplow scurried from her sight whenever possible; perhaps for fear of being turned into a frog, Hannah joked to Daisy. But Daisy stared at Hannah with her big round eyes, uneasy herself. Aunt Maggie said she was not to worry – that folk were always catty about others being clever. And her knee was giving her gyp again, would Han like to make up something for it when she'd a minute? She got a hug on presenting her aunt with a jar of finely chopped and dried dandelion tea and a bag of juniper berries harvested from Baglan Heath, one three times a day to start.

A month later Hannah was pumicing the front step in a scudding late October wind when a man in a trilby hat arrived: well set up with a neat moustache and eyes black as iced coal. He wore spats; Hannah noticed particularly because they were a few inches from her face as she scrubbed.

"Miss Hannah Hywel?" Not a Welshman's voice. London? She got to her feet, tidying her blowing tendrils of hair and found him to be short, heavy at the top but with thick little thighs. "My name is Webber, Maurice Webber. Can we have a chat?"

"What about?" Hannah was uncomfortably aware that their front door – their *bedroom* door now – was open to allow her to watch Tom playing inside on the floor; and of the piece of sacking tied, as always, to her waist when washing floors.

"Can we go inside?" He nodded towards the door.

She closed it firmly; shook her head, and picked up her pail. "It's not convenient." But he followed her through the passage into the back yard.

"I'm offering cash in hand, Miss Hywel, just to do me a small favour." He pushed open the back door for her but she turned to face him, angry now at the invasion. He lifted his trilby to reveal a creamy bald pate then smiled, and in spite of her anger she was starting to be intrigued. Cash, he said. God knows she needed that. Winter coming again, Joe and Tom to be kept warm and fed . . .

"Not a favour to me *personally*. It's to help other people really. I thought that idea might appeal to you."

Webber saw the hesitation and ushered her indoors, following closely. "Just a simple thing. I read of your, shall we say, happy knack in the paper. A real life-saver at the fair that was, eh? Well, I'm trying to help a little gathering –" He stood in the kitchen now, feet apart and knees braced back. Hannah fetched Tom from the front room and held him defensively before her, feeling threatened without knowing why. Tom patted her cheek, dribbling as he cut a back tooth, and she felt the little fingers cold against her skin. He *did* need more warm clothes.

"In Swansea. A few folk meeting together to ponder on the life hereafter, their loved ones, that sort of thing. I feel sure that a lady of your undoubted gifts could help tune them in . . . you know. Two pounds and your bus fare, just to give it a try – how would that suit?"

He took Tom's hand and jiggled it, smiling. "Hello, young feller, what's your name?"

Two pounds! Boots for Joe, a coat and hat and warm stockings for Tom. Hannah looked hard at Maurice Webber and wondered what she disliked about him when he was offering her two pounds, and her only earning a few shillings for a long day's washing and ironing.

The seance was held in someone's front parlour in Swansea's middle-class residential area, orderly streets of solid Victorian and Edwardian villas rising and falling with the hills, reached by Hannah via a goodish bus ride and a walk. Perhaps a dozen people were assembled, mostly women, and the atmosphere was tense enough to cut cheese. Mr Webber met her outside, repeating soothingly that all she needed to do was get them started, and paid her in advance to show goodwill. Hannah hesitated for only a moment before stuffing the money into her purse, lifting her chin, and following him to the door, fixing her mind doggedly on what the two pounds would buy and trying to rationalise the lie she had told Aunt Maggie who was minding Tom for her.

A plump breathless woman in black taffeta with rows of jet beads graduated down her shelf-like bosom seemed to be the hostess, and was marshalling the company into a circle. Viridian green velvet curtains were pulled across a tall bay, photographs of learned-looking gentlemen with large watch chains over their impressive midriffs were set at intervals about the beige satin-stripe walls. A marble fireplace supported a heavy over-mantle on which were arranged two china shepherdesses with over-large hats, a tragic clown, an improbably plump street urchin and a pair of evil-looking Siamese cats sitting back to back. Chairs were gradually being assembled into a rough circle and other furniture shifted to accommodate them on the red Turkey carpet.

Whilst people eddied and fluttered Mr Webber

introduced Hannah to the hostess, Mrs Leadbetter, murmured a few words and to her great surprise slipped away, leaving her with a fierce lump of nerves in her chest and a terrible urge to slip after him. But Mrs Leadbetter, still breathless with the rows of jet beads rising with every intake, motioned her to a chair in the now completed circle then coughed a warning, patting at her puffed-up wad of hair with nervous fingers.

"Are we settled, ladies and gentlemen? This is Miss Hywel, who will, I am sure, er . . ."

Her voice faded; she took her seat in the circle. Rustles subsided, someone gave a final twitch to the curtains. A dozen pairs of eyes fixed on Hannah from faces that were strained, at once sad and hopeful, questing, eager or fearful. She sat still, looking straight ahead, trying not to panic, unsure what was expected of her but hoping she could do it. After a time she heard only the thumping heart in her breast which gradually stilled. Finally she felt herself relaxing, closed her eyes and began to feel peaceful . . . tired.

The dream again, as she had had in the parlour of Rowland's mother; the lovely one with the old man on the hill, talking of his home, his valley. When her eyelids finally fluttered open again Hannah could feel herself smiling. She had no idea whether minutes or hours had passed, but as she stretched and looked up, felt pleasantly alert again.

Then she heard the weeping. Soft at first, it crescendoed hysterically as a tall bony woman in a purple and black ensemble flung herself back in a chair, beating at the air with a frantic fist.

"Where's Ted? I really thought he would come – where *is* he? God, help me!" Another cry from across the room where a woman slipped to her knees, moaning.

"William did not get through . . . my dearest son!"

A woman bent over Hannah, clinging to her husband's arm. "My dear Miss Hywel." Overcome, she sobbed into her already damp handkerchief whilst the man patted her shoulder.

"This is my wife, Mrs Peachy, Miss Hywel. She wants to say thank you," he told Hannah. "Gareth was our only son. When his ship was sunk by a submarine I did fear for her sanity. Now, hearing him speak like that, so natural, and obviously happy, well . . . We shall wait with quiet minds now, until we can all be together again in the life to come."

His wife nodded vehemently, weeping, smiling, and clutched Hannah's hand. "May God bless you for the comfort you have brought us, indeed."

Going home, after more than a little difficulty in extricating herself with everyone wanting to tell her of their loved ones they were trying to reach "on the other side", Hannah's mind ached with the jumble of received images. So much grief, so great a longing. Multiplied by millions, what a weight of sadness. She leaned against the bus stop, overcome by the experience; also by a sagging emptiness and isolation.

The war was over these eleven months but not its countless separate tragedies. They never would be. It had robbed her of both father and mother; changed her life for ever; and taken dreadful toll of almost every home in the land. She laid her head against the cold iron of the bus stop pole and, suddenly, need for her parents struck afresh like a physical blow – the need to share burdens that lay so heavily on her seventeen-year-old shoulders now. But now she also winced under the pressure of those tragedies just witnessed; knew, even as her mind shied away from them, that if what she had done had brought true comfort to even one family, she had been right to go with Maurice Webber. And the two pounds was lovely, she reminded herself honestly, and hurried on to the bus to relieve Aunt Maggie of her brother. Soon as Joe got from school tomorrow they'd go for new boots.

He came back within a week. Hannah knew he would, whilst half hoping he would not. More lies; this time she insisted that she could only come early evening. She asked Joe and Harry to sit in for Tom, saying she wanted to go to Cwmavon to visit *Nain* but not have to carry Tom all the way there and back. She also knew, bumping along in the bus through the driving rain, that she must stop after this, unless she told her family the truth. And why did she shrink from that? Why the reluctance to declare her – gift? Because she was unsure whether it was truly a gift or a curse? Might not this facility work equally for evil as for good? What dark power might she unleash?

Again, she was used, knowing nothing but the lovely dream whilst a young man spoke to his grieving widow through her. Again, she was persuaded by Webber to return. They desperately needed money, the wish to help ... in growing confusion Hannah could not tell which force drove her back to the darkened room in Swansea week after week through that long winter that ended in the spring of a new decade.

Florence called one bitingly cold evening in February to find Harry had been asked to sit with Tom again. She put down the shopping she had brought in for Hannah and warmed her numb fingers at coals in the range, glancing sideways at Harry. He had put Tom into his nightshirt and was helping him with a bowl of warmed milk and bread, tucking a bit of old sheet down his front to take the drips.

"D'you know where Han is?"

Florence was staring at Harry now, rubbing her fingers to restore the circulation. Harry concentrated for a minute on feeding his small cousin, at just two Tom still preferred assistance to independence.

"Not really," he hesitated, then smiled at Florence. "But she'll not be long now. We'll have a cup of tea while we wait, eh?"

Florence lifted the kettle over the fire and set the pot to warm, then knelt by Harry's knees to kiss Tom's warm little hand.

"Who's my lovely boy?" Then she looked at Harry with anxious eyes. "There's something not right, Harry, with Han. Where does she *go*?"

She watched Harry's face as he fed the last of the bread and milk to Tom with great concentration. Florence had loved Harry since she was twelve and had seen him go off to France, a bright and beautiful young man with corngold hair and wickedly blue eyes. No one knew this but Florence. She had watched with wretched but secret despair his final return as a different, shattered personality. She had no expectations of ever realising her goal; of being the one to care for him and make him as whole as it was possible for him ever to be again. She thought it enough to live within his orbit. She saw the shadows left by the Somme on his face now and longed to smooth them into oblivion . . . but if they were to be a permanent feature of him then Florence would love them, too. Though she had the oddest idea that if she could but caress his cheeks and brow the old, young Harry would reappear. But then, she was not yet eighteen, and still able to believe in miracles. Harry was alive – unlike her brother, Ronnie, who had lain at the bottom of the cruel sea these three years and could never change now – and while there was life there was hope; and Florence hoped.

"I don't think she wants us to know," Harry said now. "So I don't enquire too closely." He smiled again and saw how Florence's hair shone in the gentle light of the oil lamp. He thought sometimes what a lovely girl she was, so warm and loyal . . . some fellow would be lucky.

"No, well, I'm sure you're right. Maybe she'll tell us when she's ready." Florence got to her feet and held out her arms to Tom. "Shall I mop up his face? Then he can go down an' I'll make tea. Come on, sweetheart, let's get you pretty again."

Dorothea stopped coming. Hannah would catch herself actively looking for the small figure with the long fair hair; a glimpse in a crowd maybe, or a shaft of light across her as she worked. She began to rouse heavy and lethargic from her bed after restless, wakeful nights; with the extra cleaning job she had now at the Walnut Tree where she was allowed to take Tom, she found energy draining away alarmingly. She was awoken by a fierce sudden pain one night, to find herself hanging onto the kitchen table in her nightgown having struck its corner with her thigh. Joe was behind her, half awake.

"You were sort of blunderin' about, Han. I was comin' to bring you back to bed." He blinked sleepily, looking anxious.

"I'm sorry, love . . . just a bad dream I think. Come on, I'll tuck you up again before you get cold."

Worst was the sick, swinging sensation that would without warning confuse her mind, driving out peace and concentration. What was *happening*? What was wrong? Running out of lies and quite unable to admit the truth, Hannah took Tom with her the next week, asking if someone would watch him. That was the first time without a message; no one came through; no dream. Nothing.

"I cannot come again," she told Maurice Webber at the gate, clutching a sleepy Tom. He waved a hand holding an envelope he had just been given by Mrs Leadbetter.

"Nonsense. You are naturally disappointed today, it must be quite a satifaction helping those poor bereaved folk find their loved ones." He tucked the envelope into his breast pocket. "Why not, well, use your imagination a little? They'd not know the difference, would they now. They would simply feel good about hearing *anything*."

"You mean lie about messages?" Hannah stared at him and his glance slid sideways.

"It could be seen as a duty to them. Think of it in that light, my dear."

Walking to the bus stop with Tom heavy on her shoulder, Hannah for the first time began to figure out Webber's part in the seances. In the end there could be but one thing in it for him, and she'd been a fool not to have seen it before. He wasn't paying her two pounds a sitting from a desire to help anyone but Maurice Webber. And those wretched folk would be paying dear for his "services". It was not only wickedly cruel but, she was pretty sure, illegal.

Tom stirred in her arms as she jumped off the bus in Taibach. The night was rough, a north wind tearing down on the town from the dark mountain tops, and she tucked him securely across her hip, pulling down his hat against the cold. She was angry suddenly that the child should be kept out on such a night to help line that man's pocket. Well, he would not get her there again – she would find another means of earning two pounds. Something was wrong, anyway, the whole business was making her ill.

Harry was waiting, pale-eyed with a dreadful headache.

"I made him some tea but he was sick," Joe told her, turning her day's washing on the clothes horse. "And Fly's left his supper; I think his abscess is bigger."

Hannah touched his shoulder. "What a help you are, sweetheart. Sorry I had to go out again . . . just let me put Tom down and I'll see after that poor head, Harry."

"Where've you been, Han? You look awful tired." Joe looked so incongruous, folding sheets like an old housewife with his jersey on back to front and a sock falling down that Hannah wanted to hug him. But he was getting too big for that now, she must be careful of his dignity.

"Oh . . . I went to Flo's, about the night school work." Dreadful, lying to Joe; he deserved better. He looked seriously at her for a second, the eyes so like Betsy's and she knew at once that Florence had called. Cheeks bright, she scooped up Tom and began to undress him. She *would* tell him soon.

Harry's headache would not respond. A bit better, he said, but she saw by the way he held his head that he also was lying – only that was a different sort of lie, to be kind. Fly's cheek abscess was not responding either despite all her efforts. Was *that* happening, too; could she be losing her gift of healing?

Finding it impossible to settle, distressful sparks shooting through every muscle, eventually Hannah let herself out quietly. Incline Row had composed itself for sleep as she passed each small darkened house. She crossed Commercial Road with its one-man workshops, houses and "front-room" shops mixed up together, and began to run towards Margam and the long arc of beach beyond the mills and docks. Any direction, anywhere would do, to quiet her mind and body; to bring repose if only through physical exhaustion. She realised how badly she wanted to find Dorothea now – if she searched actively rather than waited, the girl might allow her the comfort of her presence.

Hannah stopped, breathless with running against the violent wind off the sea that snatched at her shawl and unleashed locks of hair to snap across her face. She cupped her hands and called, quietly at first and then loud and long, turning to every quarter as her voice was lost in the roar of waves crashing into the dark bay. "*Dorothea!*"

The sky above Aberavan was split suddenly by great tongues of flame as one of the steelworks furnaces was tapped. Fire and smoke unrolled in tortuous convolutions, blowing and belching up into black storm-clouds massing in powerful banks over the bay. In the unholy light, Hannah caught sight of the pitiful remnants of the *Amazon*; masts long gone now, only a few split bleached boards where dead shadows moved like aimless ants, lost in time, existing only in her eyes.

She stood transfixed, staring with a fascinated revulsion she had never before felt for the sad drowned mariners. And then, beyond them in the wild heaving water, she glimpsed something to make her stomach turn in horror: the black outline of a ship that reared and dipped helplessly in the massive turmoil of waves.

Pulling her shawl tighter against the rain that cut cold and sharp now, Hannah strained to see more clearly. A small ship, not so far out, possibly a coaster; but with no chance of making the safety of the harbour wall in these conditions.

When after a few moments a distress flare angled up

from it, she began to run – an instinctive action, a need to do something, anything. The harbour-master ... that was where help would be found. Stumbling, Hannah changed direction.

Another flare, the small vessel bucking wildly into the troughs only to be thrown up again at an impossible steep angle. A vision of the *Amazon* assailed her now – must another such disaster overtake this ship? She redoubled her efforts to reach the harbour-master's office but the storm clawed her back, dragging at her skirts to make a fight of every step.

Someone beside herself must have seen this. Surely the lifeboat will have been alerted! There might even be wireless contact. Even so, she had to make certain. But her boots were sinking deeper into the shingle as she turned up towards the harbour-master's office and she overbalanced and fell, grazing the hand she put out to save herself.

The night-shift harbour-master sat at his desk, his back warmed by a heavily stoked, round tortoise stove that gave out a palpable heat. At first Hannah could not speak, utterly exhausted by the battering of the driving rain and wind, the dragging, sucking shingle. Her chest was sore as she drew breath and her lungs responded painfully to the gulps of wet and icy night air.

"No mistake, I *saw* her, clearly!" The words came in agitated gasps. "Smallish – oh, get on to tell the lifeboat, *please*, she'll not hold long in that sea!"

"Where's she now then? I never saw no flares." Reginald Pickup was swinging his lantern to and fro and Hannah wanted to hit the old fool – what did he think he'd see with that? As he turned to make back to his office she caught his arm, beside herself now with anxiety.

"They'll not make the harbour, Mr Pickup. They were

266

being carried towards Mumbles – *please* call out the lifeboat!"

He scanned the blackness once again, a square, pedantic man with eyebrows that met in straggled profusion above a bulbous scarlet-veined nose. Then he turned with nerve-cracking deliberation to his telephone.

There was nothing. The Mumbles lifeboat combed the bay, its searchlight quartering the furious waters whilst Hannah, drenched and shivering, returned to where she had first caught sight of the foundering vessel. She could see nothing now but the massive, wicked sea churning and roaring in defiance and crashing over the sand as though to seize and destroy her.

Not even the *Amazon* was visible now with the tide at its height. Hannah sank to her knees, drained of all strength. The rain had eased but she was already saturated, colder than she had ever been before, and her chest hurt almost too much to breathe. She could give in . . . just roll over onto the wet beach, rest. Somewhere in her head, thoughts told her that if she did, that would be the end. Tom, Joe . . . she must get home.

It was Mrs Peplow coming down next morning to empty her slops who found Hannah, a sodden bundle on the floor inside the back door. And amazingly Mrs Peplow did the right things . . . she covered her with a blanket and ordered Joe out in record time to hammer on Dr Reed's door for help.

Florence came to look after Hannah, Tom and Joe. Mrs Peplow offered her services, but Florence realised in time that she would expect a rent reduction in return and knew Hannah could not afford concessions. Daisy also volunteered. Daisy was not awarded the highest points for usefulness in Florence's book, but Florence also knew that Daisy was having a hard time at home. So two birds were killed with one stone and she was allowed to come in for a period each evening while Flo went home to see her mother. Lung congestion, Dr Reed said, and for three days Hannah knew nothing, whimpering in delirium. Florence stayed for ten days in all, making soup for the invalid, caring for Joe and Tom and even doing Mrs Jacobi's washing and baking to keep the jobs, though she admitted, "My baking's not a patch on yours, Han."

"I'll teach you a few tricks of the trade when I'm up and doing again." Hannah smiled, catching her friend's hand as she was offered a drink. "We could set up together ... wouldn't need a lot to start with." She closed her eyes, not letting go of Florence's hand. "God, Flo, what a mess."

Florence gave her hand an affectionate shake. "It'll all come out in the wash, *cariad*. Not to fret, now; just get well, eh?"

"But that injured lifeboatman! He could have died. All of them – and *my fault*."

"You really believed you saw it, Han. I'd have done the same if I'd been sure I'd seen a ship in distress."

"Only you don't see phantom ships," Hannah finished wearily. "Only weird women like me do that. Are the whole family furious? Not that I could blame them. I can hear Auntie Lil now ... oh Lord!"

"Nothing they won't get over. Joe won't hear a word against you of course; he shuts 'em up pretty sharp. And Harry, Harry's really nice, isn't he?" Florence closed her lips tightly then looked away, but Hannah's eyes were shut.

"I'll make it up to them," she said quietly. "I shall

never let anything like that happen again, Flo. It just has to stop; it's too destructive."

Florence looked down at the white face. What could she say when she was not in the least sure what "it" was – what really had gone on in her friend's head that night; how exactly Han was different. She squeezed the hand, tucking it under the blanket.

"Sleep now. I shall take Tom out for an airing an' get a bit of somethin' for tea. Daisy's brought round a fruit cake, it looks pretty fair considering her Mam says she can't cook for toffee."

Hannah lay flat and still, hearing the Peplow toddler cry briefly in the room above before its mother soothed it. Everyday activities still appeared remote, unreal. Tomorrow she *must* get up – Florence could not afford to miss work on her account. She thought again about setting up with Flo. Maybe a stall to begin with . . . then who knows, even a shop one day.

She was not certain how long Dorothea had been there. Now she smiled and stretched out a hand to Hannah in a comforting gesture. But Hannah shook her head and turned to bury her face in the pillow. She'd done with that . . . Dorothea may as well leave her alone from now on.

She would make it stop. No more Maurice Webber, seances, premonitions. Disown it all; the best thing. Concentrate on keeping enough money coming in to survive, that must be her one aim. Maybe Aunt Maggie would help a bit with Tom once this wretched business had died down. A crushed arm, they said the lifeboat man had. Terrible; and *her* fault.

Disown it all. She had not asked for it, did not want it. Just concentrate on her family now; that was enough – more than enough! No more mooning over David

Vaughan either ... no time for stupid fancies. She opened her eyes and Dorothea had gone.

She needed at least thirty shillings a week to keep the three of them with the way prices were rocketing ... rent, coal, food, clothes. She *must* keep them going. And together. Above all, together.

Chapter Eleven

July 1921

Daisy came in quietly and had clearly been crying.

"Is it Albert, love?" Hannah looked up from her baking, brushed her cheek and left a smudge of flour. Daisy nodded and burst into tears whereupon Tom, regarding her from under the table where he was chalking on a slate, began to cry in sympathy.

Hannah bent to reassure him while Daisy sank into the rocker and blew her nose hard, rocking back and forth at a great rate. "It's Mam and Dad. There's no way round, Han, honest. I'm goin' to leave, it's the only way. You know how long I've tried to make them see sense. I mean, I'm lucky *anyone*'s asked me. We all know there's no men about unless they're like Harry or Dewi . . . not, well, right."

Daisy's big capable hands squirmed together in her lap, her blouse shuddering under the effort to contain fresh tears. Hannah reluctantly set down the pastry to sit opposite and Tom came at once to be cuddled, even if he was four come December, and show off the red chalk squiggles over his bare feet.

"It's – something else as well." Daisy's shoulders slumped. "I'm pretty sure a . . . baby." She turned, swimming blue eyes full on her cousin then, her expression a pathetic mix of pleading and defiance. "I'm twenty-four, Han. I want to be *married*, d'you see?"

Hannah nodded. "Of course. I'm only just turned nineteen, I know, but I can understand that. So, what

271

can I do? Does Aunt Maggie know? About the baby? Have you said anything to Harry?"

Daisy twisted her handkerchief. "Tellin' her wouldn't help. They'd only hold it more against Albert. An' I can't think our Harry would want to know. No, I think we need to get right away, to make a start on our own."

She got up to stand hunched by the window, staring at the dust-dry patch beyond the yard where Hannah's herbs leaned in profusion one against the other.

"Can I come here just for a couple of days, Han? It's the only way I can think to get all my things out," she rushed on, face red with distress. "I could bring them here then Albert could fetch me when he's got somewhere for us. He had it all worked out, he was goin' to Cardiff to get work, he knows a man there. Only now, with this awful strike; pits all shut an' everything ... well, nothin's certain now, is it?"

Hannah set Tom down with a kiss and went back to the pastry, she couldn't afford to leave it. The strike; tired of the very sound of the word she was and wary of it as a killer dog.

"You come," she said quietly, hands working deftly on the meat pies. "He can fetch you from here. As long as you are *sure*, Daisy."

Daisy let out her breath, hiccuped with relief. "He's a good man – Albert. We'll be all right, we really get on together. And later, we can move back here. When Mam and Dad are used to –"

"A German son-in-law?" Hannah smiled. "Time will change it all for the better, Daisy. Try not to worry."

Easy to say. Her cheeks were flushed with the heat of the baking oven and the July day, but Hannah's mouth was tight set as she worked against the clock to finish the pies. *What* would time change for the better? It was two years since Betsy had died. Every day had been a struggle; but until the last few months there had been work of one sort or another if you were strong enough, determined enough. But now – she caught the side of her hand on the fiercely hot oven and the shock brought a sudden spurt of tears. Knocking them angrily away, she spooned filling into the next enamel pie dish. Now, how many folk in Taibach apart from a few bosses and professional families could afford to eat pies like these, whose beefy fragrance was enough to drive *her* mad, let alone poor Joe, coming in after his grocery delivery to a supper of bread and scrape?

She looked up as the bulky shadow across the window turned out to be Sam Warburton. He leaned against the kitchen door, mopping his face which now bore an ever increasing pattern of contour lines, and the great shoulders had a defeated droop.

"Sam, hello; how nice." It had been "Sam" since Betsy had died and Sam had accepted that she had grown up. Tom hurled himself at the sturdy legs; usually he was hoisted into the air for a game, but today, distracted as he was, Sam offered only a pat on the head.

"We're stood off, Princess." Ages since anyone – Dada – had used that name. "Thousands of us, now. No coal to keep goin' with, see? But I'm sure your young Frank'll have put you wise on all that side of it." He sat down heavily as though he needed to.

"Sam," said Tom, happy, and climbed onto the familiar knee. Absently Sam offered his watch for the little boy to hold to his ear, head cocked.

"Been a losin' battle since the spring, really. Since Black Friday." Sweat shone in the crevasses of Sam's heat-toughened skin.

"Black Friday?" Her voice was absent, hand flicking the knife round another pie-crust edge to knock it up before she dimpled it with forefinger and thumb. She should get one more from this batch of flour.

"You recall, *cariad* . . . the time the rail an' transport workers reneged on the miners." Sam's voice deepened to a growl. "Betrayed they was, an' by their own kind; by union men who should've stood fair and square behind 'em." He shook his head and the sweat rolled into his neck where veins stood out in honest distress. "Who can a man trust in these times if not his own kind – you tell me that!"

Hannah nodded. Of course, Black Friday, back in April. The colliers had at the eleventh hour after a punitive national coal lockout, been promised a supportive strike by the two big unions, only to have them back down under harsh government pressure. Now the miners stood dangerously alone again, hopelessly vulnerable with their pits newly denationalised and owners scrambling to cut more coal for less and less money. Frank certainly *had* seen to it that no one in his family could be ignorant about Black Friday. Harry had told her that Aunt Maggie had threatened his young firebrand of a brother with eviction from home if he ranted on about the plight of the miners just one more time. Everyone knew about it already she pointed out and her son thinking he could right all the wrongs singlehanded was making her lose her rag.

Hannah floured the board for another roll-out. The harsh facts of too many men chasing too few jobs for too little money governed every life within her orbit now, as 1921 dragged on with strikes, wage cuts, grim-faced, ever-lengthening queues outside dole offices, soup kitchens, parish relief centres. The "land fit for heroes" had not materialised, instead many "heroes" were left without even a decent house to shelter their families.

"Lloyd George should have known what the blasted

owners would do once they was handed back the mines." Sam had to go over it all again; what other way to work out the poison? "Close down what pits they didn't want, cut wages of men left in t'others! God knows it'd still have been tough enough *with* government controls."

Sam mopped at his face with a huge red checked handkerchief, which Tom then borrowed to wipe his own. "See our works now, five furnaces shut down, all fifty-tonners, even afore this new lot of trouble – an' them buggers in Europe shovin' cut-price steel at us quick as they can make it!"

Hannah moved to the oven to check the last pies, saw Sam swallow as the scent assailed him, making his juices run. "And now you're laid off altogether? Sam, I'm so sorry." Stupidly inadequate words. She topped up the teapot for him, wanting above all to offer a plate of steaming meat pie and knowing that if she did there might not be bread tomorrow for her brothers.

Mrs Peplow came in through the yard, knocked and hurried across the kitchen, almost tripping over Sam's boots struck out in front of him.

"How're they managin'?" Sam nodded in her direction as Mrs Peplow closed the staircase door behind her.

"Not well at all." Hannah sugared tea for him. "They get behind with their rent ... and Mrs Peplow has a black eye."

Sam nodded wisely. "That's bein' out of work."

"I'm sorry for both of them." Hannah quite liked what she had seen of Mr Peplow, a stringy little man with a monkey-like face and a fringe of pale hair that would stick out comically from beneath his hat. He had told Hannah that he was by a trade a silversmith but, "There isn't much call for that at the moment". He continually tried round likely employers, but every firm was on short time. "He really *does* want work."

"I saw him last week. He's certainly a trier," Sam agreed. "He worked a couple of weeks, cleanin' windows up at the hospital, but was sacked because his trousers were torn at the crutch and Matron looked through a window at the wrong time an' swore he was exposing his privates. So it's not just me." He lifted Tom's dusty toes one at a time, wiggling them so that Tom squirmed with pleasure. "Nor Peplow. There's five thousand or so locked out down t'road. An' we get fifteen bob a week dole till there's work again! Not much good, that, to keep a family goin' – eh laddie?"

Tom offered his other foot to be played with, smiling in a way that reminded Sam with sudden breathtaking clarity of Thomas Hywel, his friend of the good years. The thin young woman regarding him with wide, serious eyes had been a bright-faced little princess then, held safe in loving arms. Sam's throat constricted. If he'd had a daughter, he'd have wished for one like Hannah Hywel.

"Come again, soon, dear friend," Hannah told him now, a gentle hand on his. "Any time."

Sam heaved himself out of his chair and gripped the small floury hand. "Tell you what, Princess. I'll see after a job or two here while I'm off work, eh? Fix you up a bit?" He surveyed the cluttered room. "Find a piece of wood mebbe, for an extra shelf?"

Two of the pies were for the wife of Dr Reed and one for Miss Harper, who enjoyed her food but was recuperating from an operation and could not face preparing it. There were little more than pennies profit from each item, but pennies were often now the difference between eating and going hungry. As she passed the house on the corner of Theodore Road a man in the tiny front garden was tending a fire that flared under a big boiler full of soup, dipping in the womens' jugs while they waited with toddlers at their skirts. Hannah knew they would share out the soup between their children, going without themselves ... she had done it herself, setting a plate before Joe and telling him she'd eaten already. At least they had not yet been reduced to queueing for soup, like the miners' families these past weeks.

Hannah looked towards the massive new steelworks between her and the docks along the morfa, begun when the country was crying out for ships, tanks, guns, railways. Now, damped-down furnaces and thundering rolling mills were silent, idle, as were so many men. Ironic how after the Armistice they'd demobbed miners first because coal was needed, yet now those same men were being starved into accepting wage cuts imposed by the powerful new mine-owners' combines. Where *was* the "Land fit for heroes" promised those who had survived the trenches?

She took a firmer grip on Tom, who'd just stubbed his toe and tripped. She knew why she felt so unsettled; it had been hearing that about David Vaughan in the Maypole last Friday ... that he had emigrated to Canada.

Always, a corner of her mind had been alert for a sight or just a word of him. But *Canada*, that was a whole world away; no possible hope now. That night she paced the little room, hugging herself, wanting so much to go to Canada, find him. He was somewhere in that huge, unimaginable land. Emigrated, the women had said. That meant never coming back, didn't it? In brief dreadful despair, Hannah had longed then to be rid of Joe and Tom, her sweet millstones ... longed with all her hungry heart to spread her wings and fly to freedom. Desperate for relief, she had finally reached to the back of the kitchen cupboard for the small precious bottle of brandy, kept as long as she could recall for direst emergencies. Hannah rated this as one, took a deep pull of it and choked as the cheap liquid raked her throat. Alarmed by what she had done, she sank onto the rug by old Fly, who pushed his muzzle into her palm by way of understanding, sighed deeply and went back to sleep. It seemed a long time before she got tiredly to her feet, fetched her father's bugle from the dumble hole and cleaned it until it glowed warmly in the lamplight. Held against her cheek, the warmth seemed palpable, and comforted her.

Of course she loved them. Would never leave them. "You know that Dada . . . But I did love *him*, too. I accept that I can never have him. Only that doesn't stop me wanting him. And I get so lonely deep inside, needful for a love of my own. Like Daisy has . . . even if it's only Albert!"

Daisy came soon, perspiring and overcome by the enormity of events and hurrying out to the privy to be sick almost at once.

"I left while they were all out." She stared at her bundled possessions, then at Hannah. "Albert sent a note by his friend yesterday, he's got a room for us, and a bed." She blushed deep scarlet.

Hannah nodded gravely. "What about work?"

"He didn't say about that. We could always manage on the dole for just a bit."

"Fifteen shillings a week? Daisy, are you sure you shouldn't wait a while? At least till you're certain he's in work?"

Daisy shook her head, full round breasts pushing

against their constricting bodice. "Mam's sure to notice," she laid a hand across her already round stomach in a protective gesture. "And I couldn't go on working at the Emporium for long, could I?"

"Does Harry know now? Or Em – have you written to Em about it?"

"Nobody knows but you, Han. Not Em . . . she'd just say I was a right idiot and why hadn't I done better for myself like her, up there teachin' in London. An' there's enough trouble without mine at our place with Dad laid off. And our Frank – he'll end up in jail the way he's goin' on."

They were silent then, thinking about Frank. They were brave men, the militants, but once marked down by the watchful bosses they would never work again in South Wales. Frank was so young, but full of fire and passion; so set on righting injustices. Hannah knew that Harry would have been out there in front with him if he'd been able – and her dead cousins George and Wyn, they'd not have suffered in silence either, she felt certain. She thought of Joe, going into his teens soon and a fine strong boy, not afraid to speak his mind either. God, let at least some of these troubles be sorted before Joe leaves school; her stomach clenched with anxiety. There'd still be Tom to keep and that could be a long job. If only she could afford to help Joe get to college; give him a start as his father would have wanted. Well, anything could happen yet.

"How if you lie down for a bit, Daisy? We'll have to squeeze in together tonight so you might not get much sleep." She took her now wilting guest into the already overcrowded front room. "I need to get on fast anyway now, while Harry's got Tom down on the beach. I'm doing a bookkeeping course and I have to be on my own to concentrate."

She was pulling back the sheet when the noise began with a loud thud from above. Daisy stared at the ceiling.

"What in heaven's name?"

"It's the little Peplow." Hannah winced as a flake of plaster shook onto Daisy's hair. "She fell downstairs a couple of weeks ago. Her leg's in plaster and her idea of entertainment is sitting on the floor and banging it up and down. Stuff your hankie into your ear, love."

She escaped. Daisy had had her quota of attention for now and must shift for herself; time was money, with baking for Saturday's market stall to start after her brief time with the accounting book. Impossible to make sense of it when she'd first unearthed it in the library, but there were glimmerings now, if she wasn't too tired. All part of the plan . . . clung to, nurtured. A raft of hope and resolve to get her through the rough sea of day-to-day survival: that one day she would have a shop.

The idea of the shop had grown slowly over the past year, as she had found a willing market for her baking. The stall was simply not enough, she needed to sell more to keep the three of them. She could bake evenings, do her accounts at home. She would be available for Tom's needs that way and he could help out with deliveries as he got older; Joe, too, he would enjoy that. A real family business. Nothing grand, just a small rented shop to sell her home cooking and simple remedies for common ailments. And Flo to help of course; they'd work so well together. They could bake together at night, Flo would love the extra money to help out her Mam whose lodger didn't bring in half enough to be comfortable. When she closed her eyes last thing, Hannah saw the lettering clearly above the sparkling clean window . . . HANNAH's. In blue paint picked out with gold, the colour of a summer sky with the sun glinting on cloud edges.

She glanced at the clock on the mantel. A good half hour before Joe came in from his grocery delivery and Tom from the beach. Disregarding her tiredness Hannah opened her books and gathered up concentration. This was the future she was working for now . . . *their* future.

Joe leaned over the old bicycle with the big loaded basket strapped to the handlebars. Pushing it up the mountain road in the sapping humidity had caused his hair to stick unpleasantly to his head and rivulets of sweat to seep down his ribs under his shirt – a bargain on the market stall two summers back but straining now across shoulders broadening into strong and healthy adolescence. Joe was big for twelve, as Hannah would explain in despair when he grew right out of things. And he knew he was pretty strong, too, by the amount he could push around on his cart.

He paused for breath at the gap in the foliage where a hint of breeze drifted from the sea that lay flat and pale as the sky. The horizon between them was bleached utterly of colour. The thick air muffled the sound of engines in the shunting yards; the huge, spidery transporter-unloaders on the dockside stood silent and still. A single ship lay in port. As Joe's gaze roamed along the strip between hills and sea that never ceased to excite him – a man's world of noise, fumes, dirt, heat – he felt fearful, for that world today appeared to lie crippled and still like a great wounded beast. Joe knew all about the miners' strike, the lockouts, the loss of steel orders and lay-offs, the open-air protest meetings; heard from his cousin Frank of bosses intent on squeezing the life blood out of workers and their families. He knew how Hannah struggled to keep a roof over their own heads, food in their bellies, shoes on their feet. And Joe played his part in this struggle with a willing heart. He attended closely to his lessons, tried his utmost in every direction. He was aware of the harsh truths of hundreds of desperate men chasing too little work; vowed that he would find the means to qualify himself for a decent job, come what may.

But now, for the first time, he felt puny, helpless, looking down on his world. How could he succeed where so many were not? Was determination enough? He sighed, then wiped his hot face on his shirt sleeve and started again up the steepening road. Joe took one day at a time and this day he had three loads of groceries to deliver before he could go for his tea or even get a drink. He really liked it up here, though. He loved the little sounds of small creatures going about their business, a whole separate world to his, yet running in parallel. He enjoyed the way everything looked just that bit different each time he came, yet he could count on nothing actually *changing*. His place.

Some way ahead a figure moved up the track, weaving an aimless erratic progress. Short, squat, in the hill farmer's uniform of greasy grey-green worn to its owner's particular shape by long usage. The figure now paused to vomit and Joe stared, leaning on his cycle. One of the Madoc brothers . . . Norman, he was almost sure. Han had always been so certain in her dislike of Norman Madoc, Joe had noted him especially. Once or twice he'd asked Han what she held against Norman personally. But she'd not said, just turned away, and he'd see her jaw square up like Dad's used to. There *was* something though . . . he just knew.

Joe pushed up the hillside. He hated *all* the Madocs, anyway. Not only had they cheated Han out of that precious week's wages when she'd left, he had no doubts but that they'd treated her rotten the whole time she worked for them. Maybe he'd give them all a hiding when he was grown – bullies like them deserved a taste of their own medicine.

Norman Madoc was shouting now and hopping, waving one of his boots about like the idiot he was. Drunk, too. Joe pulled a face, steering his bike clear of the vomit spewed on the track. The man had lowered himself onto a boulder where bushes masked the drop into an old quarry, and was shouting abuse as he struck it against the rock.

"Soddin' thing, no bloody good to God nor man!"

In a sudden drunken fury Norman Madoc flung the boot across the road, where it struck Joe's delivery basket hard.

"Hey!" Joe steadied his load with difficulty. "You nearly had this lot over."

"Did I now, Joey Hywel. Oh dearie me." Norman Madoc scowled at him and spat into the dust. "Pity it weren't your sister, I'd a' aimed better nor that an' sent her flyin', little cow." He got to his feet, overbalanced and lurched sideways.

"Don't you talk about my sister like that!" Joe rounded on him. "You're not fit to speak her name, a drunken lout like you."

Norman Madoc stood with legs apart, breathing hard. He had been to the market to sell beans and peas from the bottom field and had got well below the expected price; had assuaged his disappointment to some effect in the Lamb and Flag and would have to account for the missing cash to his father. The nail in his boot had been the final insult, the drink and heat had combined to give him the father and mother of a headache and, all in all, he was in no good mood to take lip from Hannah Hywel's kid brother. Those Hywels had always thought themselves a cut above.

"Not fit, eh?" He took a step towards the boy whose brown eyes glared at him from a flushed face. "Look who's talkin'. Bloody witch your sister is, she'd 'a been burned a couple a' hundred year ago. A witch an' a whore – bloody whore! Nothin' she likes more'n a roll in the 'ay wi' a good stiff cock up 'er fanny."

Joe saw the heavy jowls mouthing at him through a red haze of fury. How *dare* this foul mouthed little toad speak so of Han, his lovely, treasured Han. No wonder she hated him! Well he'd put one in for her, give the stinking bully a sore face!

Joe pulled back his right arm, well muscled from years of hauling his loaded cart around, and hit out with all his force. He connected with Norman Madoc's jaw. Joe was a sturdy lad for his age but even so, the punch would not normally have caused much damage. But in his drunken unstable condition, Norman Madoc tottered and tripped backwards over the boulder on which he had been sitting. Joe saw him disappear with a shout through an elder bush on the edge of the quarry.

Mouth dry and breathing hard with his exertion, he then set about retrieving the groceries from the fallen basket and sorting them into some order, knowing he would only get paid if the job was done properly. "Serve him damn well right," he kept muttering and hurried to rearrange himself and be on his way before Norman Madoc should climb back to the road to cause more trouble. He had taken a few steps before pausing to listen. No movement; no sound. Another few steps; he rested the cycle against a rock and crossed back to where the ground fell away.

"You all right?" His voice was absorbed by the high summer foliage and the still, thick air and nothing came back but faint rustles and scurries of birds and small mammals in undergrowth. Joe hesitated, sighed; began

284

to descend through gorse and brambles, birch seedlings and clumps of fly laden bracken, sliding down the scree and calling as he went.

It took some time to find Norman Madoc. He was sprawled on his back beneath a stand of foxgloves and his head rested against a boulder, but at a curious angle. Only when Joe saw the bloodshot eyes turned unblinking towards the sky did he bend over the man, and knew without doubt that he was dead.

"I got to go out again, Han." He looked a stranger, and years older than the twelve-year-old she knew and loved, standing twisting his old cap with frantic hands and not even acknowledging Daisy who was cutting bread. "Can't stay now; really I can't . . ."

He backed away. Hannah followed to find him moving uncertainly about the yard. She closed the kitchen door so Daisy should not hear.

"Tell me, *cariad* . . . you can tell me." Joe stood very still, drew his breath and stared at her, and Hannah became rigid with premonition of tragedy even as her eyes willed him to disclose it.

"He's dead. No doubt about it at all. Neck's broke."

"Who, Joe? Say right out now! *Who?*" Hannah grasped his shoulders as if to shake the bewildered boy.

"Norman Madoc. He's in the old quarry. I hit him," Joe added in a wooden voice and he began to shake.

It was almost midnight before Hannah judged it safe to go. The hot summer nights kept folk late on the streets, particularly the men laid off work who had nothing to get up for next morning. She eased out of the sheets without disturbing Daisy, who lay on her back bubbling quietly, and made sure Tom had a pillow alongside where Joe had been so he could not fall out of their narrow bed. They moved quickly then, up the back and onto the shoulder of the mountain. After Joe had told her the facts of his encounter with Norman Madoc they said little more. Both faced what lay ahead in their separate ways but were bonded close, and they walked with hands linked.

There was moonlight, which served both well and ill. Beginning the descent into the tough, pebbly under-growth of the quarry, Hannah's heart began such a thumping that she felt sick; her knees would have folded under her but for a sapling to grasp and she felt her body damp with sweat in the airless night. Looking at Joe's face, all she saw were huge dark eyes against startling white.

"Steady, love." Briefly they clung together and could hear one another's frantic heartbeats. "Now, lead the way carefully."

Joe had covered the face with fern fronds. Otherwise he was as he had fallen, a solid dark shape, fearsomely tangible. Looking down at him with Joe's hand clutched tight into her side, Hannah relived in a moment of anguished clarity that heavy body heaving and plung-ing on top of her; inside her. The utter degradation of the savage invasion swamped her afresh . . . the stale, fusty smell of his jacket reeked in her nostrils again and she seemed to shrink as the old sense of worthless, helpless failure repossessed her mind. At that moment she was *glad* Norman Madoc was dead. Had she not herself wished him dead that day? Now she must make certain that, being dead, he did not harm her or hers again. Joe was worth a hundred of him!

They lost all sense of time as they struggled and sweated frantically to bring the stiff body up to the level of the road. The task might well have been beyond them had they not searched for and found a rough path offering a more reasonable gradient than the one they had descended. Each grasped an ankle and grabbed at every available purchase to help them upward. The last few yards were almost too much and Hannah, exhausted, even considered abandoning the effort. Had she done the right thing? Should she have gone to the police? But now they had come so far the option no longer was available. They *must* get up to the road, then it would be mostly down hill to the river. One more big effort.

They *had* been right . . . the quarry would be the first place to look, the direct route to Madoc's farm. And who knew what clues to the death might have been uncovered from that? Even without detection, how could they have lived their lives knowing what lay there, so close to their home?

Back at last in the roadside undergrowth they rested, preparing for the next stretch of the journey. "About half an hour," Hannah told Joe, struggling to keep her voice normal despite the horrendously un-normal words it was uttering. "But at least it's all downhill now. The tide will be on the turn by then . . . it should float out to sea."

Joe nodded; turned away. Norman Madoc was "it" now; no longer "he". A chunk of carrion for disposal.

She was surprised to hear her own voice making these plans; the same voice that sang to Tom or asked for two pounds of potatoes in the market. But there would be time again to dwell on this. Now she must be occupied only with their safety.

They met no one, making their laborious way to the river. Both extremely tired. Their task became more dreadful with each step as they dragged the body from shadow to shadow like thieves in the night.

At last they were above the water. It curled in

rhythmic arcs toward the bay, its blackness broken by shards of moonlight between the sheltering trees.

"We must wade right in. Don't lose your balance, now."

"I'm takin' my boots off." Watching Joe pull at them, Hannah marvelled at the calm of this child. God, keep him from harm . . . he did this for me. Because he loved me, would hear no ill of me. And I love *him*; so much, so much.

They were up to their waists before they loosed the body, finding it hard to balance, feet sliding about on the icy pebbles. They pushed, and the mortal remains of Norman Madoc floated downstream. Seconds later there was nothing.

So exhausted now that she could easily have given way and allowed herself to float down river after it, Hannah grasped her brother's hand and struggled to the bank. Standing there, shivering and dripping, they looked at one another. No need for words now; each knew the other's heart.

"We must run home, *cariad*." Hannah's voice seemed not to belong to her, her body felt light and drifting away, unconnected with herself. "It's all done now."

Lies again, explaining the wet clothes to Daisy. Hannah had expected Joe to sleep on but he was up and away to school after spooning down some porridge. He glanced at her as he reached for his boots and she gave him a little smile. How on earth could he have actually reasoned, out there last night clutching the body of Norman Madoc, that he must keep his boots dry for school? He was a poor colour today with red-ringed eyes, had nothing to say to Tom who ran calling after him through the yard, puzzled by the rebuff. Averting her eyes from their clothes dripping on the line, Hannah tried to imagine last night as just a terrible dream. But bitter reason told her it had been rock-hard reality. It would not fade to a shadowy hallucination, like the figures on the old shipwreck. How could anything so terrible blur; become less terrible with the passing of time?

Albert came to fetch Daisy the next day to take her to Cardiff. He was a wiry little man with earnest pale eyes and a red ring about his brow, above which the skin was tender and white when he removed his cap. Albert Mens watched Daisy with the same proprietorial fondness Hannah could recall seeing on the face of her Uncle Jenkin, watching his Guernsey heifer win a rosette at the Neath Show. She would have liked to see them married, take the interest Daisy had counted on from her on this nerve-racking step into the unknown. But all Hannah's energies, every nerve and cell, were centred on the corpse of Norman Madoc. Where was it? Had it been washed to sea on the ebb tide? Did it lie caught up in weeds or rocks, awaiting discovery? Or was it even now stretched out under a sheet in the mortuary, the subject of a post mortem; a police report to trigger off a manhunt for the killer?

Daisy turned puzzled eyes to hers as they embraced, with Albert standing nervous by the door, cap safely in place again and weighed down with bags and parcels.

"I shall come to see you in Cardiff the moment I am able." Hannah forced herself to sound positive. "And when you want me to tell your Mam where you are let me know. I'm sure she will come round, given time."

Tears welled into Daisy's eyes and her mouth quivered pitifully. "I'd hoped you'd be there when I'm married, Han. There'll be nobody, nobody belonging to me at all." She began to shake with suppressed emotion. Hannah could take no more and stepped back.

"You'll have Albert there, won't you?" she said bracingly. "Go on now. If you're caught here you'll get dragged home by your hair and locked in for life." A last hug and she pushed her cousin through the door, to be grabbed by Albert and hurried to the station. And Hannah stood limp in the middle of the kitchen, wishing only to be boarding a train, too, and escaping from everything here.

"Han?" Tom's hand, warm and slightly sticky, pushed into her clenched fist. She looked down at the round face still smeared with porridge from breakfast, the shirt unbuttoned because she hadn't bothered.

"All right, pet," Hannah scooped him up and felt his arms go tight round her neck and stay there, holding fast. "We'll clean you up and then get on, shall we?"

Eyes closed, she pressed him to her, loving his soft compliant warmth. Just hang on. Get through this day first. And tomorrow, she could get through that one, too. She'd not be beaten.

Three tomorrows after she woke to find Joe's bed empty. On the chair where his clothes were usually folded overnight was a piece of paper torn from an exercise book and Hannah sat on the side of her bed to read this pencilled message, frowning in the poor light. She stayed there for some time, staring at it, then went through to kindle the fire and put the kettle on for tea. Her hand was shaking so that the matches fell useless from her fingers. She smoothed out the paper onto the table and read it again, so cold now that she shook all over.

Dear Han,
   I am sorry but I can't stay here. If they find out it would be too bad for you. I thought a lot about it. So I

have gone to London. They won't find me there, you tear this up and say somebody's got me work there. And you know *nothing about* NM. I'm nearly 13 and I will do fine. Had to take some of our money but I will send it back to you when I can, and more. I will write to you often. I will miss you and Tom. I will come back when I can. Love Joe. X X X

It was the kisses at the bottom that broke her. She burned the note, put down her head on the table and wept as though she could never stop. All gone. All gone. What left, now? Yet still she wept quietly, for a small clear corner of Hannah's mind knew that Tom was left and should not be wakened to see his sister in such extremity. When at last she blew her nose and made some strong tea and the Peplows were moving about overhead she knew that this day must be faced; the first dark terrible day of life without Joe.

Hannah felt quite dreadful. She must have failed to give Joe the assurances he had obviously needed. Not even thirteen, for goodness sake. She was nineteen and wasn't *she* absolutely sick with worry, waiting for something to come out about Norman Madoc? Could the cause of his death ever be traced to them?

He'd surely made things worse by going, though. So many more lies for her to tell now, why had he not thought of that? Go on, eat a slice of bread, you'll need food in your belly, girl, for this day. Summoning at last the will to move, she went through to put on her clothes.

For the first time she could ever recall she didn't want Sam to come in – for a second Hannah ducked behind the table as he came up the yard. No good, he was used to walking in. She straightened and waved through the window. Already there'd been Aunt

Maggie and Harry to lie to. Must remember to say the same to everyone. If only they'd all leave her quite alone. Thank God Harry had taken Tom to the morfa.

"Where's he gone, *cariad*? Young Frank just told me." No beating about the bush with Sam, he stood foursquare and demanded an equally direct reply. Hannah had herbs spread half-dried on their brown paper trays and was turning them, and the room was rich with their fragrance.

"I really don't know what all the fuss is about, Sam." Her tone was reasonable as she moved the pile of ironing from the chair for him. "He didn't want everyone knowing, they'd all have said their piece and maybe got him to change his mind."

"But he's not thirteen even. I don't see how you could ... I tell you, his Da wouldn't have allowed ..." Poor Sam, still trying to be the father Joe had lost. "Where *is* he, then?"

"His Dad's *dead*, Sam," Hannah said with such sudden force that he stared at her. "Joe must see after himself and that's the truth and that's just what he's doing! He's gone to board with someone I met when I worked in London and he'll stand a good chance of getting work there that's certain. There's nothing here for him, *you* know that!"

Suddenly she was crying. It was so dreadful to be lying to her dear friend who deserved better. Hannah stood with her back to him, fighting for control.

"There's more to it than that." He was behind her, his great fists heavy on her shoulders, and he spun her round to search her face. "I'm right, aren't I? I'm not a fool, Hannah! Is Joe in trouble? Hell, I've a mind to go to the police, report him missing. D'you even know where he *is*?"

At the mention of the word "police" Hannah's

mouth opened in a wordless cry. Sam pounded on. "You tell me then, and right now, or I shall go to the police. Okay? Summat's up and I mean to find out what, if I've to shake it from your senseless head!"

"Sam, please, *listen!*" Beside herself now, Hannah sat down hard as he released her. Then stood up again; very close to the big man who stared at her, breathing noisily. She'd only the one thing left to bargain with.

"Sam," a soft voice now and a hand against his chest. "Look, you do like me, don't you? I mean, really like me?" Her hand moved slowly over his chest, caressing it. "Well, you can . . . we can." Her hand went round his neck and she closed her eyes.

"Christ!" A sudden hard slap across the cheek caused her eyes to fly open again to meet the full force of Sam Warburton's wrath. Then he shook her till she was dizzy. "Now, you goin' to tell me what's goin' on? You will, if I stay here all day!" His eyes showed total bewilderment coupled with fury and Hannah knew she was beaten. She began to tell him.

Later, drinking tea, he put his arm about her shoulder and pulled her close for a moment, stroking her hair with his clumsy hand. "Nobody'll know from me, love. Rest easy on that. I still reckon it'd have been best to tell the law how it came about. But it's done now. We mun let it be. When I'm in work again I'll help out wi' cash where I can. But you're to give your word on one thing." Hannah nodded, too weary now to make conditions of her own. "Don't you ever do that again, offer yourself as a bribe for a favour." He frowned at the effort of speaking openly to a young woman on this delicate subject, but ploughed on. "Worth a damn sight more than that you are, Hannah Hywel, and don't you ever forget it! No more bargaining with your body – right? God, what d'you think your Da would 'a thought of that, eh?'' He shook his head in righteous affront. ''Now, I'll drop by tomorrow. You think on't, an' thank God you told me. A trouble shared . . .''

When he had gone, Hannah took the smooth, prettily marked pebble Joe had given her on her thirteenth birthday. She held it in her palm and let her fingers explore it and thought of her brother. Then she placed it under her pillow and every night would hold it, and still find it in her hand upon waking.

Chapter Twelve

May 1926

The dollar bill fell from the letter into Hannah's lap. Smiling, she smoothed it carefully before placing it with the others in the tea caddy on the mantel from where Joe had once taken the money he had needed to get to London. Five years ago now, almost. She could still feel the clammy heat of that day; Joe's face, his eyes, pleading with her to understand what he was telling her. And the hot July night; the dead weight of Norman Madoc's body, as they had heaved and pushed it up the side of the quarry, dragged it to the river bank. Five years ... Oh, Joe; and so far off now, in Pittsburgh, America. He'd described it in his letters, said it was a steel town on a river, only nothing like Port Talbot. She could not imagine it; or his life, so far apart from hers, so incredibly different. Jumping ship like that in New York, just on an impulse ... a terrible shock, that first letter with the foreign stamp. When the dollars had begun to arrive she had decided that if humanly possible she would save them, start a little account for Tom. A struggle, but reading the exchange rate every week in Sam's paper she reckoned there'd be around eleven pounds five and eightpence there now. A nice little nest egg.

Almost five years ... Hannah stared across the little room. She could still recall the letter she had written to Joe, sending him the news of finding Norman Madoc's body, and of the inquest, all suitably disguised: 'You recall that farming family I used to work for? Well, one of the son's body was found washed ashore way up the coast, he had been missing almost a month and the body had been badly damaged by rocks. There's been an inquest and a verdict of accidental death. They seemed to think he had fallen into the river when he was drunk.' She hoped that might have helped set his mind at rest; he had never acknowledged the information.

It had been a long hard climb uphill, these five years, and for much of that time Hannah had been desperately anxious about Joe's welfare. She knew he had worked on a building site in London, mostly running errands he had said, and lived in a room in Whitechapel above a cobbler's shop next to a derelict warehouse. It had sounded squalid; but he had never whined about it, just made a joke about the size of the fleas. After a year the work had dried up and he had cadged a lift in the van of a couple of plasterers down to the docks at Southampton. He seemed to have found fairly regular work there – general dogsbody mostly he had admitted, but his letters were cheerful enough. Then after a second year the news about the job on the liner, shoe-shine boy on the New York crossing. He had justified that by saying how work was drying up everywhere and that he was lucky to get this, the tips would be really good. Hannah had wondered then, if it was nearer the truth that he could never quite be left in peace by what had happened in the quarry, and was distancing himself as far as possible.

Perhaps that was the reason he had jumped ship in New York, too; that and the stark fact of over two million unemployed here. Hannah could not blame him for seeking hope of a better life in another country, for there certainly seemed to be none in Britain. Men who did still have jobs were hanging on to them even at the cost of cut-down wages, and the women were trying to keep food in their children's bellies on less and less and going without themselves to do it. Hannah knew all about that, with gaunt mothers coming up to her own stall asking for any broken pies or biscuits. What they did not know was that she would sometimes deliberately crack a pie in half to be in a position to offer it, but she could only do that these last couple of years as her trade increased. She was doing well now – not only with her stall but with private orders, accelerating by word of mouth: manager to manager, doctor to dentist to departmental head clerk; families not far enough up the social ladder to employ a full-time cook but sufficiently solvent to indulge in small luxuries.

Tom's tonsils had set Hannah back three years ago, just after Joe had gone to New York, when cash was still very tight. She had paid the bill off at sixpence a week, most had to do that. But there had been extra food afterwards to build him up again and her own working time lost nursing him. Harry had helped in every way he could. He had been like an elder brother to both of them, trying in his own way, on his good days, to make up for them losing Joe. When Tom had his tonsils out he had stayed all night; after she had scrubbed the table top for the doctor, scrubbed the floor, cleared away what she could, she had seen Dr Reed's face so clearly in the extra lamplight he'd asked for, bent over Tom's small still figure. Harry had slept in the rocker afterwards, while she had dozed on her bed, rousing often to listen to Tom's uneven breathing.

Harry had stayed the day Fly had died, too. She had held the fragile little frame gently, stroking the bony head, smiling into the dimming old eyes holding hers with perfect trust until with a last twitch of the paws he had gone. Then she had cried, long and hard; it had seemed to be the last link with her childhood snapped. She had wet the soft ears lying over her hand with her tears, and when Harry reached for her had clung as though she might fall off the edge of the world. Florence had come later and the three of them had gone to the allotment, Harry carrying Fly neatly wrapped in an old shirt of Joe's.

"He'll lie comfy in that." Florence had pressed Hannah's hand reassuringly. "Great mates, they were."

Hannah had nodded, her throat constricting again. Florence did not know the truth about Joe; no one did, save herself and Sam Warburton. Hugely difficult, keeping up the lies over so long; but there must never be a risk of – anything . . . Not so bad now of course; not like it had been earlier, when she had lived on a tightrope, guarding every word, every nuance, and could envisage no end to it, ever. Aunt Maggie had simply not accepted the story of Joe moving to London in such secrecy to a mythical "friend" who would give him a home. He wasn't old enough to leave school she'd kept saying, he'd be breaking the law if he started work. She had tried hard to connect his going with Daisy's defection to Albert and had become even more confused; especially when her son Frank, an increasingly militant seventeen-year-old said Joe had most likely gone to London to join the Commies. At last the miserable situation had inched back to normality, but only under Hannah's long perseverance. As for Florence, Hannah determined to tell her the truth about Joe one day; lies, half-truths, had fogged their clear-cut friendship and again long term tact and effort had been needed. She had loved Flo dearly, increasingly, for almost twenty years; for the last several they had pulled closely together to set up a viable business that in the future might support them both. Neither might be fortunate enough to find a husband among those of their own generation remaining alive, whole, and in the least capable of supporting a wife and family, and they saw the cooking project as an independent alternative. Always they had shared absolute trust and Hannah hated having this secret between them . . . the second one, actually, since she had been too proud to tell Florence what Norman Madoc had once done to her. Hannah's goal was to have a shop and cafe with Florence to help and *that* would entail full trust. One day, the luxury of truth . . . she would know when that time came; when no possible harm could come of the truth.

For Harry, too. Harry had certainly a right to the truth. He had supported her in every way possible since Joe's departure. Never strong now, he still relied upon her to keep his headaches under control. But if Hannah could do that, then he in return found things he could do for her; small ways to ease her burden of work. He did minor carpentry jobs, making her a second trestle table for the market as her produce increased. He delivered food to people, collected empty dishes, picked and hulled fruits in season, supervised her allotment, even cleaned her windows. When his younger brother Frank was arrested for assaulting a colliery under-manager and bound over to keep the peace, he took over the role of mediator between Frank and their irate parents. Frank was right, he argued; the man had tried to cheat a new young miner of his legal pay by inaccurately adding up his hours. Hannah had listened, and agreed. Frank could not be blamed for trying to protect his mate and Harry was right to support his brother.

She sighed now and looked at the clock. No time, really, even to read Joe's letter. But she'd been up since dawn baking and had earned a few moments' respite. Hannah sat in the rocking chair and opened the folded sheet with a smile of anticipation.

April 28th 1926

Dear Han,

Thanks a lot for your last letter and the note from Tom, he is getting good at writing. It is great to know how well your food is selling now. I remember that first lot you did for Mrs Jacobi! Yes, I can see that what you need is a proper shop, the market is not enough even with all your private customers. I hope you can find a good one to rent soon. Are all those new houses built now, the ones you told me about? I will see a big change when I come back – so many new roads built, so many more people. I used to know almost everyone in Taibach when I was about ten!

I'm sorry to hear about Cousin Dewi not being able to get work, with his miserable bit of pension and all. You say his tin leg gives him gyp – they should really pay men who were injured in the war a decent amount of compensation.

Are there still as many out of work? That sounds bad, I must say. And it is hard to see how things will change for the better in the near future. Seems to be plenty of work here still and I'm told the average wage is about ten dollars now. I'm real glad to be with Cline Steel Inc. And next month I get a raise, because I'm promoted to general assistant in the stocktaking office. Sounds good, eh? I'll mostly be helping produce copies of plates for the Test House. Just the first rung of the ladder, Han, but I'm definitely on my way! No more shoe-shine boy, newsboy, ice-vendor, I'm done with all that now I hope. And I've started night classes, because if you recall I did leave school just a *bit* early, so I've ground to make up there.

This new place I live in has an Italian-Jewish landlady who would love to know all my business (she darn sure knows everyone else's in this building!) But I never talk that way to anyone, not at work nor here. I reckon my business is no one's but mine. I'm the only British guy got a room here, there's about every other nationality on God's earth and half of them don't speak English!

Han, I have to close now. Thank you again for the good letters you write, I know it must be hard for you to find the time to do that. Take care of yourself, and buy something you would enjoy with this dollar. Soon I shall send more, and write again. My love to Tom, Harry and all, and most of all to you, dear Han.
Thinking of you always,
Joe.

Hannah folded the letter back into its envelope and put it with the others in the left-hand drawer. Reading Joe's words always made her feel choked up inside and on the verge of tears, even when he'd said something funny or nice, like his getting a raise in his pay. She just *missed* him so very much. When would she see him again? Ever? Oh, that was no way to think, of *course* she would. And yet . . . she had asked, begged, so often, for him to come home again, these five years, and he had steadfastly refused to. What would it take?

She took out his birthday pebble from beneath her pillow when she went through to her bedroom to change. Turning it in her palm she felt very close to Joe. She did not even know what he looked like now, at seventeen. A young man; the boy had gone for good. Like Dada? He'd resembled his mother more, the brown eyes, the heavy dark hair. But with Dada's open, cheerful optimism – she did recall that in him. He'd said about his business being his own ... it would be sad if he could confide in no one, feel unable to trust as a result of Norman Madoc. She wouldn't know if that had changed him and in what way until they were together again.

She was glad he was in America from the practical point of view; this general strike certainly looked disastrous, in its third day now and the whole country paralysed. The proposed miners' wage cuts announced by the pit-owners may have sparked it off and Hannah was aware of that injustice – having Aunt Maggie's Frank for a cousin she could scarcely fail to be! They must have a national minimum of twelve shillings a seven-hour shift he would insist; but the mine owners' only answer was that they demanded a longer shift *and* a wage cut as markets continued to fall. Mass meetings, protest marches; and still they got nowhere. Forty-five shillings for a forty-eight hour week ... and any miner complaining laid off right away.

Mayday just five days ago, but no celebrations round the maypole for the coming of summer. Instead, a strike order by the TUC chairman for all miners, rail and transport workers followed two days later by all affiliated unions coming out in support. Now, a state of emergency. Cousin Frank seemed to think they'd win through if no one wavered; he and his militants were all over the place trying to keep up morale and the atmosphere was almost festive. But Hannah already sensed the violent undertow ... there was too much at stake, too many hungry mouths, too little general hope of being able to change things.

Strike-breakers were already delivering mail, driving buses, trains, unloading and loading at the docks, and headlong clashes were inevitable.

"Dada . . ." Hannah whispered the word, looking out of the window at the knot of men in the street, at women standing with strained faces in their doorways. "What would you have done, Dada?" She supposed, obey his union and strike, like Sam, like all of them. But not Harry. Poor Harry managed on his tiny war pension and was perhaps well out of it, and Cousin Dewi, still struggling to pass his Civil Service clerk's exams and still having trouble with his tin leg. And Joe – Joe. I hope none of this happens to you . . .

She looked about the little room that had once been Betsy's pride and joy; the parlour. The aspidistra had finally gone to Mr Jacobi's market stall, allowing daylight to filter unhindered over her bed with the Welsh quilt given her by *Nain*, and over Tom's small one in the opposite corner. She had traded in the bigger bed she and Joe had once shared to leave room for a neat little chest of drawers and a small wardrobe that only needed a folded wad of paper under one leg to make its door close perfectly. A horse-hair seated chair by each bed – the last of the parlour furniture – and a shelf, put up by Sam for her books on herbs and natural medicines, and the room was full to bursting. At least the old gentleman no longer stared at her with his unforgiving eyes from above the black-leaded grate; he, too, had ended up on Mr Jacobi's stall. The walls were now papered by the good Sam with a warm pale-gold sprigged pattern, and Hannah had set a pretty fern on the bamboo plant stand in the window. Betsy, she acknowledged guiltily, would not have known the room.

She opened the wardrobe door now and her stomach lurched at the enormity of the step she contemplated. This was the day she was going to Porthcawl to see the estate agent about renting the vacant shop on Taibach High Street; the one she'd had her eye on for months. Was she a fool even to think about opening a shop? What would happen if she failed? Was twenty-four too young to open a shop? It had been her ambition since she was nineteen. So . . . now?

Hannah frowned, looking at her best dress, the one Flo had made her for Christmas. She *would* not fail – she would not even consider that possibility. This would be the first day of better things for her. She was already composing in her head the letter to Joe telling him of her venture as she took out the blue and white rayon dress, the blue shoes bought in the January sales with the Louis heels and T-bar straps. If only she had a full-length mirror. The white felt cloche fitted closely over her newly bobbed waves; it really was quite becoming, focusing attention on her large, limpid grey eyes. When she had carefully outlined her lips in Geranium Pink and dampened her well-shaped eyebrows with a finger to train them into shape, Hannah knew she looked good. She was "nicely proportioned" as Aunt Maggie said, which meant that her legs were a good length, her hips not heavy, nor her shoulders or back too broad. She was pleased about all this, but was always so busy that she never found the time to dwell on it.

She was staring worriedly at her old purse when Florence came through the yard carrying a big covered tray, pushed open the door with her shoulder and set down her load with a sigh of relief.

"They get heavier! There's four bakewell, four treacle, two apple. That's the last of the apples, they've done well to keep this long. I'll do jam next week." She sat down, her handsome, kind face flushed with effort. She, too, had had her dark glossy hair bobbed and it suited her. "Gosh, Han, you look a real swank!" She whistled in admiration. "Really, who'd ever guess?"

Hannah swung her purse onto the table. "That I haven't a bean? Well, I wouldn't be carrying a thing like this around if I'd a bob or two to buy a decent one, would I? Is yours any better?"

"Not really." Florence fished in her capacious pocket. "A better colour maybe, have it if you want it." She gave it a rub on her apron. She had lost a little weight lately and that suited her, too.

"Oh – what difference will it make! Thanks anyway, love; and for tomorrow's pies." She poured two cups of cool mint tea for them and sat opposite Florence, elbows on the table and chin cupped in her palms. "Doesn't seem the right time to start up a shop, does it? A general strike in full swing, unemployment, hunger marchers. I never see a child these days who doesn't need a square meal and a decent pair of boots."

"So, you make a bit of money and you can hand some out where it's needed. There *are* folk still in work. And they snap up whatever you cook for the market stall."

"There's undertakers," said Hannah with some bitterness. "They're booming. Pawnbrokers ... never done better! And police running baton charges into undernourished men at their wits' end to feed their families. And there's office workers pushing bits of paper around. That's what we should've been, Flo, nice safe civil servants!"

"We probably would be if there were any vacancies." Florence the pragmatist. "As it is we'll make out best we can. At least Messrs Stanbuckle, Tailors and Outfitters still keep me in work four days a week, thanks be. And you're sellin' out the pie stall every time – and we've doubled our table space! *And* helpin' with the cottage hospital catering, *and* helpin' out at the vet's."

"*And* doing his accounts for free." Hannah sounded grim. "*And* making up remedies for free." Suddenly she added, "God, Flo, but I still miss Joe something fierce. Another letter today, bless him, and I miss him more after one of those."

"I know, *cariad*." Florence's hand covered hers. "He'll be back, you see. Wants to prove himself out there first I suppose. Not much to hurry home for, after all. Just a dole queue! So don't fret about it, eh? Better where he is for the time bein' if he's in work."

Hannah had been told there would be one bus to Porthcawl and back each day, run by students from Swansea who were trying to keep up a skeleton service, and she waited for some time before anxiety began to nag. Such a perfect day, late spring bursting joyfully into summer. She forgot about strikes and lockouts, hunger and misery, sitting on the low wall on the Margam Road with her face turned to the sun. Clumps of gorse by the road glimmered yellow, alive with feeding bees, and beyond the stilled blast furnaces, the coking plant and paraphernalia of the docks, fishing boats crept like toys across the silver sheet of water. No one seemed to have called them out on strike. Three Model-T tin lizzies with "Food" scrawled across the windscreen crawled by driven by soldiers, and a horse pulling a cart full of bones and meat scraps for the soup kitchen set up in the Methodist chapel vestry. Then nothing, a Sunday silence, shops open but with no shoppers. Every factory stilled, locked.

The bus was late – worse; there was no bus. Hannah considered. Going home and taking off her best outfit after all that trouble was not to be borne. She hopped off the wall and stood in the road, determined that she would get to Porthcawl; when a car finally appeared heading her way she waved and beamed out a smile of encouragement. A lorry would have done, a horse and cart even. A sporty car was a bonus.

"Excuse me. Do you think you might . . ." Her voice faded. The driver had pulled up, removed his goggles, and it was David Vaughan. Hannah's smile fixed painfully. She felt dizzy with the shock of finding herself face-to-face with the man she had dreamed of for eight years, the man she had adored, had felt she could not live without. Now, her instinct was to mouth an apology, turn and run. She was utterly overcome. She took a step back, no more than a gesture, for there was nowhere to hide, nowhere to run. They regarded each other for what might have been hours before she spoke, raising her voice above the engine's hum.

"Good day, Mr Vaughan . . . David. Are you going as far as Porthcawl? There seems to be no bus."

David Vaughan continued to look. He would not have known, would have passed her, never connecting the immature girl of August 1918 with this fine boned young woman with a sensuously curving mouth, winged well-defined brows and beautifully clear, cool grey eyes meeting his directly with neither coyness nor bravado. Now he recognised that square little jawline; that long pure arch of neck down to delicate collar bone . . . remembered tracing the throat with urgent fingers, feeling the pulse in that warm hollow quicken under his touch. He remembered far back, a long, long way, to how it had been, that night on Primrose Hill with Hannah Hywel. He remembered that it had been exceptional.

"Hannah!" He raised his cap, leaned to open the passenger door, offered a hand to help her in beside him. She turned to smile then and he saw the clean peachy curve of cheek, a shaded vein under the transparent skin of her temple where a nut-brown wave disappeared under the little hat. David Vaughan turned off the car engine.

"Good Lord! After not so much as a glimpse in, what, eight years?"

"I saw you once, David, driving through Taibach with a beautiful fair-haired girl. Then I heard you were in Canada." Trite polite words saying nothing of how life had really been those eight years. She waved a hand as though in apology. How could the gap, the enormous chasm ever be bridged?

"Canada; yes." Then he gave a sudden smile that was utterly disarming. "The lady – Sophie – was never more than a passing ship in the night."

He sat half facing her now and Hannah saw how much older he appeared as the smile faded. The auburn hair, still tightly cropped, had receded in a deep V from his broad forehead and the eyes, the same startling, unexpected aquamarine, were set deeper under heavy brows that met in a stern line over the bridge of his nose.

"Do you – live there still?" Watching his face, Hannah saw the mouth she had remembered from so long ago, so beautiful to kiss, become thinner, drawing down in a firm line. He nodded.

"I'm over to see my mother, she's been unwell."

She remembered the estate agent then. "David, I'm sorry but I'm due in Porthcawl about now – an appointment. I'd been told there was a bus . . ."

He nodded again. "I'll get you there. Hang onto your hat."

No dialogue as the car roared through the quiet countryside, overtaking horses and carts, the food lorries, bicycles. Hannah sat speechless, breathless, clutching her hat and loving it all. He slowed to a more sedate pace as they entered the little town and finally drew into the kerb.

"Best I could do; hope you're not late. Here –" He pulled a small looking glass from his glove compartment and watched as she set herself to rights.

"I should do better without an audience," Hannah told him with a hint of tartness and then offered him her wide honest smile. "I am truly grateful."

"So, shall we meet again?" David Vaughan said quickly. "Tomorrow, for supper?"

Hannah paused no more than seconds. He was perhaps married. With children, too. Things were even more wrong now than they had been eight years ago. But he would soon be away again. Back to his own kind, for good. Just once . . . surely that could hurt no one?

"That would be nice."

Until the last moment she had tried to back out, but only in her head. The rest of Hannah was in no doubt but that she would go. She should have been exhausted: she'd baked a prodigious amount and sold every last crumb off her stall along with herb cuttings potted up for sale at tuppence each and some vegetables from the allotment. Most importantly, she had agreed to rent the shop. She had been to the farm at Cwmavon to ask Uncle Jenkin to lend her twenty-five pounds at current interest rates to paint and shelve it, and had visited Sam to ask if he would make the shelving and check over the old cooking range in the back room. She had fed Tom and helped him with his new sums, washed and ironed, told the Peplows upstairs as gently as possible that their rent was overdue again. Yet when Harry came in at seven o'clock to sit with Tom she felt fresh woken, churning with old memories and new desires. Yesterday's dress had been re-ironed, hair washed, white cotton stockings scrutinised for snags.

"You look smashing."

Harry so rarely made a personal remark that Hannah glanced up sharply from a last minute restitching of a button on her dress pocket. His smile had a melancholy twist that caught her breath with pity. Harry was denied the simple pleasure of getting ready to take out a girl. Harry, and millions like him, whose futures had been ordained by what war had done to them. Not for Harry the excitement lighting her skin now, glowing from her eyes, flowing through every nerve and muscle. To be young, in love, no matter how fleeting and how hopeless the joy – God, thank you for this. Many girls and young men of my generation will never be so blessed.

She remembered now that not too many years ago she had been ready to die of love for Harry; recalled the pain of knowing that he loved Brigid and saw her only for the child that, in truth, she was. She loved him still – but of necessity, with an emotion far removed from her girlish hero-worship. She would still have walked through fire for Harry, but for Harry the beloved kinsman now; Harry who had gone through fire himself and needed the strength and compassion of Hannah his devoted kinswoman. He had both taken from her and given to her and Hannah knew the value of the relationship that had evolved between them.

Impulsively, she kissed his cheek. "Don't know what I'd do without you, Harry dear."

Harry looked confused for just a moment before he gave her a slow smile. "Same goes for me, Han."

Tom, sitting at the table with chalks and slate, looked up and smiled, too. A calm, thin schoolboy with mild eyes and his father's squarely angled jaw, he was sensitive to atmosphere, reactive to anger or laughter, kindness or tears.

"Where you goin', Han?"

"To see a friend, love. And off to bed mind, when Harry says." A kiss for him, too; a word of praise for the picture he was drawing. Then she had gone, down to the corner where the white Lagonda was waiting . . . icy calm, utterly confused, recklessly joyful. Never more alive in any day of her twenty-four years.

He was there, smiling when he saw her and getting out at once to open the car door for her. "How good of you to come." He reached into the back and pulled a large box of expensive chocolates off the seat. "I hope you like these."

"I've never had them – but thank you, I'm certain I shall." She felt out of her depth for just a moment; disorientated. After eight years of silence it was all too fast, too much.

But as they sped along the Swansea road, almost devoid now of traffic as the countryside lay under the forced silence of the strike, she was soon feeling uncannily relaxed, at ease with this virtual stranger. She knew so little, their paths had only crossed briefly a couple of times: no, there was more than that to it – he alone had possessed her willing body. But nothing then for years but a glimpse, a car passing and quickly gone. Hannah had over the years inched herself up several notches by her efforts – caring for her appearance, learning to speak well, to expand her mind to further ambitions for herself and Tom. But still she and David Vaughan must be worlds apart; no possible common meeting ground that she could imagine.

And yet . . . here they sat now in the Georgian green dining room of the Talbot Hotel, Swansea, with the evening sun filtering discreetly through draped nets. And after he had ordered food and wine Hannah was relaxed enough to ask simply, but quite directly because it was by far the most important thought in her head, "David; are you married?"

His face became stiff; only momentarily, but Hannah thought she might have overstepped the conventions. Then he began to crumble his bread roll with nervous fingers. A fine clear Julienne arrived which gave him another couple of minutes until the waiter had gone.

"I am, yes, to the sister of my partner in the airline business."

"So, is she here with you? And what, then, am *I* doing here? I think I have the right to know this, David."

Hannah lifted her soup spoon once to her lips then laid it down, for suddenly the liquid was bitter as gall. How *dare* he. She had made the initial mistake of flagging down his car, but she *never* would have done had she recognised the driver. That had been an honest error, not calculated mischief as was his invitation to her. She stared at the table, the evening that lately had been so beautiful in ruins about her. A fool; she had been a simple fool.

"Hannah? Please, look at me." She remembered the voice from 1918, it had whispered that she was beautiful. Special, a special lady, she could recall every word. She lifted her head.

David Vaughan, watching her, saw the deep hurt clear on her lovely face, it had taken the natural colour from her cheeks. He sighed. How to explain, when he did not know the real truth of it himself.

"Neville wanted her looked after. She's – delicate. It was what she wanted, too, one big happy family." His mouth turned down in a bitter smile.

"So you married her to please your partner? How noble. For heaven's sake don't make it worse, David, you are under absolutely no obligation to me. All we shared was a few hours, after all, not an airline. What I'm asking is why I am here now. You have no business . . . cannot you see that?"

The waiter changed their courses, this time setting down a fragrant breast of duck, dark and rich, with cherries glistening in the sauce. Hannah stared at the wine in her glass and wondered what time it was. She should have been baking. She was simply making an idiot of herself here and if she ate any of this rich unaccustomed food would likely be sick.

"It must seem unforgivable to you, Hannah." He touched her hand lightly, feeling his way. "I do understand that. But it was such a wonderful surprise, seeing you. And I simply could not contemplate letting you go without seeking a few hours of your company. It was just like that; I could not do other

313

that ask you to supper. So will you really please me now by eating just one mouthful?"

She would not be drawn; her disappointment in him was too great, she felt sick with it. "If you had wished to see me at any time during these eight years you could have done so. I – I thought you must be dead when there was no reply to my letters. Do you not feel that was a cruel way to behave? It was some time after the Armistice that I heard you were alive."

Her pain was so apparent that he ceased even to think of making more excuses; wanted simply to hold her, comfort her for the hurt. "I did not receive a letter with your London address, Hannah. Many letters did not reach the lines you know, but were lost in attacks. And I was wounded again, mid September, and it all became – quite difficult. I came home briefly half-way through the next year ... I did remember you, please believe that. But, well, nothing seemed any use to me around that time. I went to Canada quite soon afterwards – a clean break, a new life."

He put his hand over his eyes for a moment then looked straight at her and Hannah could see he was tired. Her anger was evaporating ... what did it actually matter if he had no right to ask her out? He had done so. And she had wished to come. Now it must simply be for old time's sake that she was here. Auld Lang Syne.

She lifted her fork and ate a small piece of duck. "There," she said, and smiled at him.

She did eat a slice of wonderful summer pudding while David told her of his plans for the future.

"Passengers, freight – within a decade they'll use airlines as they use bus services now." He leaned towards her, long hand sweeping the air. "Distances are huge in my continent, Hannah."

314

She had nodded, but felt the shaft go home – *his* continent, not hers; and soon he would be back there. But not tonight; tonight he was in the dining room of the Talbot Hotel in Swansea with her. One day at a time, the way she had learned to live these past years. So this was just one more day, she *must* accept that now.

Neither seemed to have suggested walking along the beach but later they were there, the sea foaming across pebbles with the mysterious sucking and lapping that unnerved Hannah, so that she was grateful for the firmness of his hand, his body between her and the dark hungry water that pulled at the deserted beach. A part of her remained resentful at the way she had been taken for granted; another part was recalling that she had dreamed for years of this very night, of his coming back to her. She felt a need to let go, to accept that she could not get the better of the situation but only live through it in a way that was true to her nature.

"I have been afraid of it always," she said suddenly, and she was not surprised that he understood her at once. He led her higher to a sandy ledge between rocks and they sat in silence, hands linked.

"I'm afraid, too." His voice was low. "That was one of the reasons I left here. But my fear followed me . . ."

"The war." A statement rather than a question, for Hannah understood him also. He picked up a pebble, turned it about in his palm and she could feel the energy building up in the small movements.

"Nightmares. Christ! They drain me, reduce me to jelly. Not what you'd expect, eh?" David Vaughan threw the pebble with savage force towards the creaming wavelets. "I still smell it – do you know that? The smell of – everything; that was one of the worst things." He shook his head, staring seaward. "I thought if I got far enough from it all – new life, new country, new set of people – it might eventually fall out of my head. I do shake a bit less now. Used to think my bloody teeth would drop out!"

"David." Hannah put a hand on his arm and the contact remembered for so long had a warm reality that made her shiver. "It is exactly what I would expect. How could you not have nightmares after those appalling years in France? To me the surprise is that any of the survivors remained sane. And I can only imagine how it must have been, I was not even *there*. The reality, I know, must have been worse than my worst imaginings."

"I tried once to tell Julia – my wife – about the nightmares," he said in a quiet intense voice. "She countered by telling me how a pain in her left shoulder would sometimes keep *her* awake. We . . . do not share a bed, you understand, so would not know about these things. I would have liked a friend, if nothing more, to hold on to sometimes, in bed."

He was silent, head down. Then he let out a long breath and his shoulders dropped as though some of the tension had left him. "It's so easy, telling you. Do you know why that should be? There's not another living soul I could . . . oh Hannah. Hannah! If you knew how I needed you, some nights."

He reached out with a sudden turn and drew her across to kiss her hard and urgently. Surprised, Hannah made to draw back, but the long hands held her fast, one circled her throat and was cold against her warm skin.

"Hannah. God, I remember . . ."

The fingers shocked with their coldness, sliding

from throat to warm breast. Her breath drew in sharp against his mouth but it would not leave hers. Eyes closed, sensation swamped her as she slipped into a dark delicious pool. Now the fingers cupped her breast. David Vaughan sighed, his lips left hers to follow the caressing fingers. Desire streaked through Hannah's skin as he touched it to gather hot and needy in her stomach and she arched towards him.

"You are magic. Magic lady."

He pressed her back into the sand and his shape blocked the moon. Then warnings split through desire; she called out sharply and caught at his arm, straining to sit up again. For a second David Vaughan seemed to freeze, dark against the sky.

"David, no! Not here –"

He moved then, helped her to her feet. "God, Hannah. I am so sorry. I was – well, it just seemed that . . . oh, don't be angry. Don't go."

Shaking, she straightened her dress. She *was* angry; also ashamed of the desire that had ripped through her. What in heaven's name came over them both? She found that she was actually frightened, too; but of what she did not know.

They walked back to the car in silence and he drove off at once, presenting a stony profile to her miserable scrutiny. It was not until they had recrossed the river that he drew in under roadside trees and turned squarely to face her.

"I do apologise. I absolutely grovel, Hannah. Unforgivable of me . . . eight years ago there might have been some small excuse . . ." Hannah tried to speak but he put up his hand. "Tonight *was* unforgivable. But please will you forgive me just the same, dear Hannah Hywel?" He smiled then. "Truth is, you have a damned powerful effect on me. I've only got to

317

touch you and I seem to go up in smoke! You are not perchance a witch?"

David offered her a cigarette and she saw his hand shaking when she refused, lit one himself and leaned back to watch smoke spiral into the soft air. Hannah studied his face. "That's possible . . ." Her voice was serious. "David, are you really not happily married? Not in *any* way content?"

"Would I be here with you if I were?" The reply was so brutally direct that she was shocked. He threw the cigarette into the road with the same quick forceful movement that she had seen with the beach pebble. "My wife is . . . delicately balanced. Fragile, physically and mentally. No children, no taxing commitments. But there *were* other considerations; my partner put up a deal of cash up front and I got the message that it was conditional."

"Did you know, when you . . ." Hannah was feeling her way.

"Christ, we all make mistakes! Or wouldn't you recognise such messy facts of life!"

Shocked again by the anger spilling over her, she rounded on him. "Maybe I know more than you about those! If you want to know, since we last met I've been up to my neck in messy facts of life! Both parents gone, *and* a brother, *and* not knowing if the money I earn would keep me and my other brother from starving from one week to the next! You don't know you're born with your aeroplanes and your big cars and popping back across the Atlantic when you fancy seeing your Mam and Dad! And nobody *made* you get married, did they? No, *your* choice, so if it was a mistake, no one to blame but you and you must just get on with it! Not come expecting me to – to –"

Hannah faltered, then turned away, choking back a rush of tears.

David Vaughan's hand covered hers, clenched hard in her lap. "Expecting you to give what she does not?" he finished for her, so gently that her tears ran faster. "You're absolutely right, Hannah. I asked once before, and you gave. I never did forget that and never shall. Now it's different; of course it is."

"It's not that I don't want to," sobbed Hannah with painful honesty. "I'll never forget that night either if you want to know. But not *there*, not like that. I've got to think myself better than just someone you pick up and use when you've a mind, then drop again; don't you see that? You have a *wife* now, David. And I'm not just a body, I'm a *person*! And what if . . . if . . . oh, I shouldn't even have to say it!"

He turned her about. When she saw his face, so haunted in the cold light of the moon she wanted to give him everything he had ever needed. Instead she said in a tight voice, "Please will you drive me back now, David? Harry needs to get home, he's sitting with Tom while I'm out."

When he had gone, with a polite little embrace and thanks for the pleasure of her company, Hannah ran indoors with a knot of misery heavy in her chest. Yes thanks, a lovely time she told Harry; hurried him off before the knot melted into more tears.

"Mr Peplow's hitting his wife by the sound of it, Han." He sounded anxious, unsure about leaving her. Poor Harry. If only he had half of David Vaughan's advantages.

Tom was asleep, but no thanks to the row going on upstairs. Harry could be right about Mr Peplow. But now, just tonight, she couldn't take that on. It did happen when men were robbed of their right to work, to feed their families. When they might walk twenty miles to scratch on a coal tip for a bucket of nuggets and hope to sell them for coppers to buy bread and a few potatoes.

Suddenly Hannah was filled with righteous anger against David Vaughan. How *dare* he have so much, and then complain! There were delicate women around here aplenty and they'd no one to cosset and consider them, they just got on with it. She hated that pampered rich wife, half a world away. God, if only *she* had money!

No, if only she had David Vaughan, that was the crux of it – what she could not stand. She disliked all that he represented, yet loved the man. He could disappoint, hurt, enrage . . . but she may as well face the truth, even though there was absolutely nothing to be done about it.

Children of strikers were being fed three times a day in the chapel vestries, waiting in a self-conscious huddle until the number they had been issued with was called. Mothers who had nothing were given Parish Relief to be paid back after the strike. Some miners were given a shilling or two, part of a gift sent from Russian pitmen. The district struggled on for nine days, the poor helping the destitute; there was fury when a train steamed into the station using American coal and driven by university students.

"I *know* it's not good Welsh coal!" a woman screamed, shaking a fist at the tender. "Good Welsh coal don't turn the air black wi' smoke like this bloody Yankee rubbish!" Police were called to protect the scabs from injury and arrests were made among the maddened protesters. A group of men walked to London to sing in the streets and send back anything they could to their families. Two men cycled to London to look for work. Others would set off before dawn to pick coal on the colliery tips, some walking twenty miles there and back for one bucketful. The *South Wales Echo* published just one leaflet by strike breakers but were quickly put out of action; any household fortunate enough to have a radio had the only possible access to news.

Tom, not entirely understanding what was happening, asked if he might go and pick coal, too, his friends were going with their fathers. Hannah had refused; she had problems enough without Tom getting hurt as were some children by falling into pit holes as the tips came to resemble rabbit warrens.

"You stay, sweetheart." She waved a floury hand at him, deep into a batch of baking for Dr Reed's wife. "I've errands you can help with when you come home from school. I might just be a bit late with your tea, I've to go to Cwmavon see Uncle Jenkin when I've finished here."

Uncle Jenkin was stalling over the shop loan and she spent the precious half-day walking to Cwmavon and back, also searching for him as he was out with his ewes and lambs. Collateral – what was there? He had rubbed his stubbly chin, fingered his moustache with a doubtful frown. What security if the business failed? Money did not grow on trees for him, either. Pointing out that she had never yet been left with a single pie from her stall, Hannah finally persuaded her reluctant uncle by offering her furniture as collateral – or alternatively offering to sign an agreement to work off the debt on his farm. Drinking tea with Aunt Cissy and *Nain* afterwards, she told them of her difficulty. Catching a movement from *Nain* Hywel's corner she saw the old lady's eyes glistening, the frail hands flying over the knitting needles, hesitate for a second. She heard the words not with her ears but with her heart: I'd give it, *cariad*, did I but have it, Thomas's mother was telling her silently.

I know that, *Nain*. Thank you for having faith. She sent a loving smile across the room to her grandmother. How long it seemed now since the other *Nain* had been in the same corner; how long since that first Christmas of the war when she had given Hannah her little book of secrets and her blessing and had died, her spirit like a blue flame vanishing into the dark rafters. Oh *Nain*; I have no time now, I have to work. But one day . . . when life is easier, I will try to do as you wished.

David Vaughan was waiting at the end of Incline Row, a magazine propped against the Lagonda's driving wheel. He raised a hand in greeting as Hannah appeared, and jumped from the car. Shocked, for she had never thought of another meeting, Hannah tried to mask her emotion behind a composed expression.

"Just been to your place, met your cousin Harry," he told her cheerfully. "He said you might be back any minute so I hung on. Thought we should go for a spin tonight. We could celebrate the end of the strike if you need a reason." He was clearly hoping that she was over her anger of the evening in Swansea.

Hannah stared at him. "What end of strike?"

"You haven't heard?" His eyes were asking, she was sure, that she would agree to a friendly truce.

"We cannot all afford a wireless." Her voice was tart. He gave her a wide and irresistible smile, which had its required effect on her.

"Oh dear. Well, what I hear is that the government has threatened to sue every striker, having declared them all to be acting illegally. The railmen's leader has apparently backed down forthwith and the others have followed suit. But not the miners. They, I fear, are on their own."

"I fail to see that as any cause for celebration," Hannah told him curtly. "I sympathise one hundred per cent with them." David Vaughan screwed up his face comically and put up an arm as though to shield himself.

"What a terrible mess I have made of this conversation. Would it be at all possible to begin again from where you come round the corner?"

Tired as she was, Hannah was suddenly smiling. She had just won something of a victory with Uncle Jenkin. And there was no sense blaming David Vaughan for the collapse of the General Strike and the resulting plight of the miners. He could not help being born rich either – no sense holding that against him. She was reduced to such a state by him though that she could scarcely feel or act with commonsense.

"That's not necessary; I shouldn't have snapped at you. I really cannot manage tonight, David, but I will meet you tomorrow evening if you wish." As the words came out she could hardly believe they were hers. Would she *never* learn?

"I do wish, Hannah Hywel." His voice was serious now, but the remarkable eyes were sparking messages. "Tomorrow is my last evening here and I will be waiting promptly at seven if that is convenient."

"Yes, very well." She was suddenly breathless. "Now I must go. Good evening."

She hurried home, considering. Perhaps Flo would help out?

"Just for tonight, Flo? He's going back tomorrow. And I couldn't leave Tom by himself."

"I'll come," Florence said promptly. "There's pies

323

to do anyway. Leave out plenty of stuff for 'em. Tom can help, he'd love that; grease the tins, weigh up. Ask if your fella's got a friend," she added cheekily. "If I don't lose my honour soon I'll bust – not much goin' around here for us old maids, eh?" Laughing, she looked not in the least like an old maid and knew it.

"Do you think just anyone would do, though?" Hannah looked serious. "I mean, there's Daisy with her Albert now, expecting her third any day. Could you fancy Albert?"

"Not much. Only comes up to my shoulder from what I recall! But I suppose you could get used to that. D'you think they're all right?"

"As all right as anyone is now, which isn't very. Daisy still wants to come back here, you know, make it up with her parents. Aunt Maggie's ready to I know. Only, Uncle Idwal . . ."

"He should be glad she found *anybody*." Florence was firm. "Otherwise she could still be on his hands."

Working her way through all that must be done before she could meet David Vaughan again, Hannah had a sudden desperate wish to be on someone's hands herself; preferably someone with enough cash for her not to need to worry ever again about how to keep a roof over her head and Tom's. Small hope! But she would not think of that tonight. This might be the last time she saw him . . . she would try simply to enjoy it, not look forward or back. She knew now for certain there was no future in David Vaughan.

"A mystery trip. Sit back and enjoy the suspense." He grinned, settling her in the passenger seat, and for that moment looked as young again as on that night outside the Electric cinema, exhorting men to volunteer for the army.

"Ten years," she murmured. "I was fourteen . . ."

"Sorry?" David Vaughan guided the Lagonda up the winding road between scented aisles of cow parsley and honeysuckle.

"When we had our first barney. Remember?"

He grinned again. "Would I forget such a little fireball?"

"You were plenty unspeakable yourself." She smiled too now. They began to climb from the valley, eventually twisting along little more than a track. The May evening was still and fragrant, larks hovering high to pour their pure, liquid melody over the blossoming hillside. A single cloud, salmon-pink and edged with silver, hung over the Gower Peninsula beyond Swansea Bay. Gradually, the setting sun slid into view below it, flooding the hills and sea with mellow, shimmering light. Against this light the geometric shapes of the industries hugging the coastal ships spread darkly solid, intensifying in Hannah's eye the landscape's grandeur.

"All they want, you know," she said suddenly, "is enough to feed and clothe and shelter their families. And it is the worst, the hardest job possible."

David Vaughan glanced at her. "The miners? My dear I do agree. But – " He shrugged. "If the balance sheets fail to make economic sense, what are the owners to do?"

"I would not have had my father labouring down a pit shaft to feed me." Her voice was very quiet. "I am always glad that he was a foundryman and not a miner. He lost a brother and a father in colliery disasters."

"I think you loved your father very much." He placed a hand on her knee for a moment. Hannah felt the warmth of it through her dress and the contact

325

dispelled at once the melancholy that had threatened. Enjoy this hour . . . look neither forward or back. You will pay later, in loneliness and frustrated dreams, but it is worth that price to be with him now.

She turned her head to smile at him; then past his profile at a sombre arc of pines sheltering the tumbled ruins of a cottage, pale in a shaft of evening sunlight. Before it stood a woman, arms about the shoulders of two small children. Her head turned towards the car and terror cut the breath from Hannah's throat . . . the white, square-jawed face bore a faint but unmistakable likeness to her own. Her lips parted to cry out, so great was the impact of recognition. But she knew that David Vaughan had seen neither woman nor children. And then they were past, out of sight of the dark unblinking gaze.

"Good grief, what's up?" David's voice was sharp with anxiety, seeing Hannah slumped into the pale leather seat with eyes closed. "Hannah? Tell me!"

Stupidly difficult, to speak. When she did, her voice faltered, faded, seeming to reverberate sickenly in her head.

"Not sure, really. Just thought I'd seen . . ." Her face was stony, her lips too cold to move round the words.

"A ghost?" Teasing now. "Poor love, a trick of the evening light. Ghosts don't come out till much later around these parts, when it's good and dark."

Hannah, forcing an answering smile, knew him to be wrong. But with a huge effort of will she pushed the truth away as they drove off the track to halt before a small stone farmhouse. She and the truth were trapped together; how could she ever ask him, anyone, to believe her?

"The end of the line." He peeled off his gloves and

touched her cheek. "Ready for a drink, my poor haunted lady?" She nodded, trying another smile, but felt dangerously vulnerable outside the car and barely out of sight of the ruined cottage. She moved close to David, catching at his hand. He chaffed it between his own, frowning.

"Cold as ice. What is it, sweetheart?" Hannah looked back to where the remains of the cottage lay behind the trees and shivered.

"That place, David. What was it?"

"Just an old dwelling as far as I know." He turned a big iron key in the weathered door and Hannah followed him inside. "Been falling apart for years. The old man took some of its stones for this place when he did it up. Well tucked away; he wanted somewhere to bring his mistress."

He quickly put a match to the ready laid fire. The ground floor was a biggish room dominated by a beautifully carved oak dresser with a kitchen off one end and a deep inglenook fireplace across the other, and a small staircase climbing up the kitchen wall into the gloom above.

"Does he still – " Hannah paused delicately.

"Bring her here?" David Vaughan gave her a sour smile. "No. I believe it's rarely used now, though someone local keeps it clean. Though I'm surprised brother Desmond has not availed himself of it. Now see, a little refreshment, I chose it this afternoon when I came to lay a fresh fire."

He led her to a small pedestal table near the fireplace. On a cream linen cloth edged deeply with lace were set dishes with crusty rolls, sliced chicken breasts, a selection of cheeses, a crisp head of celery. A square of yellow farmhouse butter sat coolly on a bed of lettuce leaves, and in the centre of the table was a bunch of black grapes and a silver bowl piled with chocolates.

"Make yourself comfortable, Hannah. I shall open wine for us."

Hannah studied the table as he lifted the wine bottle from a silver ice bucket. The food looked quite delicious, he had gone to a great deal of trouble. Was his motive simply to give her pleasure? She did find this man an enigma.

"I do hope this is to your taste. I should like to please you."

He was watching her intently, brows drawn over the unusual eyes. Hannah said simply, "You have, David. What I do not understand is why, when we know we shall not meet again."

"Oh, dearest Hannah." His face was rueful. "Cold facts are such cold company. You are warm, so warm. Just for a little while, I beg you lend me some of that warmth. You may see me as fortunate, but the truth is that my life has little in it of true comfort. The comfort of love . . ."

They regarded one another with serious eyes. Then Hannah said carefully: "I understand what you say, David. I cannot take responsibility for your life that has to take place in another continent, among people I cannot ever know, nor have any wish to. But if my company this evening is what you want, need, then here I am." She felt a weight on her heart then, as though she knew already that he asked too much. But he smiled and touched her shoulder.

"Good. Now, try this wine. And tell me what progress you have made with your shop. Was your uncle willing to help?" He set her glass on the table and raised his. "I should like to toast the success of your venture, dear Hannah. And make a suggestion, if I may."

"Of course." The wine was cold, fruity, delicious. Hannah sipped, waiting.

"I want . . . I should be honoured if you would let me help." David Vaughan spoke hurriedly, then got up abruptly to put a log on the fire. He turned and bent towards her then, an arm along the back of her chair. "Whatever you need to set your business up in a proper manner – I should be only too happy –"

Hannah broke open a roll and began to butter it, struggling with the total unexpectedness of his offer. Then she put down her knife. "David, you must know that I could not possibly accept. Thank you for wanting to help. But, no. Uncle Jenkin has agreed on a small loan and that is all I need. I shall build up very gradually. The main burden will be finding the rent before I see the profits."

David Vaughan waited a moment, clearly wanting to argue his case. Then he shrugged his shoulders, sat down opposite her again and reached for her hand. "I did not have any great hope that you would agree, sweetheart. But I wish you had with all my heart. All I can say is that if you are in difficulties please contact me. For my easement, will you promise that at least?"

"I shall remember it, David. I cannot promise, though. But I will remember what you say."

They ate then; the awkwardness resolved they were at ease, companiably close in the quiet room as the last rays of evening sun left the lattice window and dusk gathered in the room's corners. When David pushed back his chair and lit a cigarette she studied the profile of the man who had brought her here. So little known, about him or his family. Would harm come to her through him? Was he telling her the truth

329

about how he felt? Why her rather than one of his own kind? What could she offer that was in any way special?

He looked directly at her, as though her thoughts had been heard, head turned with the remembered arrogance of ten years ago. But when he smiled and stretched out a hand there was no arrogance, only a yearning need, and Hannah's fear had gone when she walked without hesitation into his arms.

"Oh, sweetheart . . . Hannah."

They remained still before the fire, enfolded together. Hannah buried her head in his shoulder and there was the old remembered scent of him. He had taken off his jacket and his shirt was smooth to her cheek, and under that was a warmth of skin that reached her like a siren call, like Primrose Hill. The years fell away and she smelt the August grasses about them, and her arms came up about his shoulders to bring him tight into her.

"David. I have missed you."

He bent his head then and kissed her with all the tenderness of those lost years. Hannah wanted to weep for them, and for the empty years still to come. But she kissed him back instead.

"Will you let me love you, darling?" He nuzzled into her neck and spoke low in her ear. "I wouldn't take a risk with you this time. Last time I was careless; on Primrose Hill. Couldn't get that out of my mind. I wouldn't do that, not again, if you would trust me."

Hannah was silent for a moment. He'd come prepared, then; hoping she would give herself again. She wanted to, of course she did, she loved him and he was going away. And yet . . .

David Vaughan kissed her ear, then the white skin behind it. Hannah gave a little sigh and bent her head and his lips moved to the nape of her neck. Arms entwined, they climbed the stairs, leading into a small pretty bedroom with a sloping ceiling and lattice windows open to let in the scented dusk and the sound of the blackbirds' late song.

All she had remembered, and so much more. Time taken, care bestowed, gifts boundlessly exchanged in the little room under the rafters in the long May twilight. Not only passion but also laughter, as Hannah and David together discovered the joyfulness of lovemaking. And after, when they could no longer hold back, came the spiralling whooping throes of ecstasy as they fused shudderingly, clinging tight, straining ever closer. Then, another kind of joy to lie damply entwined, whispering, stroking.

"Must go soon," her head was in the curve of his neck, her tongue felt almost too heavy to move round the words.

"Take you soon. Promise . . ." Eyes closed, bodies curled together, drifting round the delicious borders of sleep before falling deep into unconsciousness with arms still about each other.

Her scream cut the dark with shocking violence. Bolt upright, Hannah was staring with horror at the rafters. Then she screamed again.

"What the devil, *Hannah*!" David struggled to consciousness, trying to hold her. But she shook him off, tumbled from the bed with terrified, incoherent sobs and attempted to crawl beneath it, wrapping her head with frantic hands.

"Coming down on us! Burning us!"

"It's nothing, my darling, nothing here."

He covered the rigid body with his arms. Her head twisted up suddenly and the anger he glimpsed caused his arms to drop from her. Pushing strongly away, Hannah flung out clenched hands then sprang to her feet, faint moonlight illuminating her nakedness to make her appear taller; vengeful, almost.

"Curse you, all of you! Never shall I forget, and now I curse you all!" She stayed there, head tilted defiantly and her eyes staring at nothing for a long moment, while David Vaughan watched, uncomprehending; recognising nothing of the woman lying so lately in his arms. Then he called her name, but softly. "Hannah?"

Hannah's fierce gaze wavered, focused. She drew a deep gulping breath and looked up. She saw the flaming thatch part, crumble, before it fell with a dreadful roar and she fell with it, into blackness.

Chapter Thirteen

May 1926

It was hard making their goodbyes.

"How can I leave you, after that terrible – thing – whatever it was? How can I know you will be safe?"

He held her face close between his hands. The air was like black velvet, but Hannah did not need to read his eyes. All she needed to know was there between them, unspoken but quite clear. They loved one another and she never doubted the truth of it. Her own hands came up to cover his and they remained still, heavy and quiet with that love.

"You must forget about what happened, David. I'm all right now, truly. A nightmare, no more."

"I'm not likely to forget."

She rested her forehead against his chest and her next words were muffled.

"What's that you said?" David put a finger beneath her chin, brushed her lips delicately with his. Hannah curled against his warmth, wishing never to leave the safety of him and knowing that was exactly what must happen now. In just a few moments she would be alone again. She needed to cry out, 'Stay, please stay'.

"I said, maybe one day you'll come back."

"Of *course*." He sounded almost angry. "Don't you know that?" Hannah thought then that he might shake her for being stupid. But he began to stroke her hair instead. He thought of how it had been up there on the hill, the happy eagerness of their love-making; he thought of how it would be going back to Julia, to life as it actually was. Without Hannah Hywel. He caressed the warm nape of her neck and she leaned against him, needing to believe that he meant what he said. After a moment she sighed, and straightened.

"I *have* to go, David."

He came round to open the door for her. She insisted he drive no further than the corner of Incline Row. They walked slowly, shoulders touching, and two doors from her house Hannah turned to him, catching his hand.

"You never did say, David. Why me? I should like to make sense of it I suppose. Not being the same, well – " She broke off with a vague gesture, aware of her own confusion.

"Class?" David Vaughan gave a curious little laugh. "Oh Hannah Hywel, nothing's that simple, is it? There's something 'twixt thee and me that defies sense – that's a fact. We fit, in a way that has damn all to do with sense or class. Don't you agree? Oh, I think you must agree."

He kissed her then, a long deep drink, and Hannah kissed him back with all the love that had lain dormant for eight years. It threatened, that last moment, to burst her body, to shower him with brilliant shards of herself, leaving no more than a shell to live without him.

"I will write. Bless you, darling. My dearest . . ." Then he was gone, striding down to the corner.

Hannah gave a great gasp of pain. Turning blindly to the house she saw a slight figure by the gas-lamp, watching her. Dorothea. She had stood in that exact place on the night of the fire: 1914, so long ago. Dorothea had smiled then, comforted and calmed Hannah; now she did so again. How long – five years since the storm? Since Hannah had turned from her, vowed to have done with it all?

"Hello." Her voice was tentative, still shaking from the misery of parting. She heard David Vaughan's car drive off and gave a desperate smile. "He's gone," she told the waiting girl, needing to say it to believe it. "That's it then. Gone."

Dorothea's hair gleamed in the lamplight and her face was full of compassion.

Hannah spoke to no one of the ruined cottage on the mountain, the shadowy figures, the "nightmare". She admitted to Florence that she and David had made love – Flo had, after all, been her best friend since they were five. But even so her instinct was to hug this to herself, too newly precious to be shared. Florence's face had been a study in both pleasure and envy.

"Suits you; love I mean." She'd looked up from covering the night's baking spread over the table. "All sort of soft, you look."

Hannah snorted. "Soft's what I am if we're truthful. In the head, I mean. I can't win after all, can I?"

"No-o. But you've had one lovely time, haven't you? Even if you never do it again. Looks like that's more than I'll ever get."

Hannah had put her arm about Flo's shapely waist, her own love spilling over and to spare.

"Lots of time yet, Flo, honest. We're only twenty-four! I tell you, any single man tastes these pies, he'll be after you like a dog after a rabbit!"

But alone, waiting for sleep in her narrow little bed, Hannah knew there was not lots of time, knew that their generation of single men lay rotting in Flanders. She ran her hands over her body, soft smooth breasts, warm curves explored so lately by David Vaughan's sensuous fingertips. Inflamed by memory, she longed afresh for his ardent body, the pulsing column piercing the dark core of her. Don't say that *never* again . . . ever? She had lain with tears on her cheeks, curled up with hands crossed over her breasts.

The other thing, the woman and the children on the mountainside, visible only to her; the nightmare of the burning roof and her helpless beneath it: Hannah locked all that away in a dark corner of her mind. She could not face it yet. One day, she already knew, she would be forced to discover more. That woman would not have appeared without purpose. But for now she tried only to forget it, for she wished to think of David Vaughan instead.

She seemed no sooner to have dropped to sleep than it was time to get up and begin what should have been a day of special merit . . . she was to take possession of her own business premises. Her mind should have been fully focused on this momentous event as she helped Tom get off to school in good order, checked yet again the list of items needed for the shop, forced herself to have tea and a slice of bread and butter. But still, images of last evening floated about in her head. What was *he* doing? Still sleeping? Thinking of her, of them together? Stop it now, do; Hannah frowned at her reflection as she put on her hat. Get on with the work in hand, more than enough to keep you busy. Let go of stupid, going-nowhere daydreams, they'll slow you down and drain the energies you need to *run your business*.

The decorator was waiting with the news that he would need to burn off all the old paint to make a good job of the shop front. Do that then, she told him; there was to be no compromising the blue and white facade with gold lettering. She saw now that some of the inside work might be beyond the scope of Sam Warburton, with one wall at least needing replastering. Sam had already cut the shelving to size and was coming today to

fiix brackets for it. So much to be done: as Hannah began
to clear rubbish from the back room, the kitchen, she
was soberly aware that Uncle Jenkin's loan would melt
like snow in June. Harry had said he would help, too . . .
even so, it was just possible that she may have over-
reached herself.

The letter was delivered by special messenger late that
afternoon. Hannah, just in from the shop, was nervous
of it, afraid to open it for several minutes.

Tom, spreading plum jam on his bread, watched her
in silence, aware of the tension. Then he said quietly:

"You goin' to open it, Han?"

His words broke the spell. She smiled and reached for
a knife. "That's the only way I'll find out what's in it,
that's for sure."

She slit it with care and saw the money at once, folded
inside a single sheet of thick cream paper. She sat down,
feeling strangely unwell for a moment as she drew out
the letter.

My dearest Hannah,

Aware though I am that last evening you declined
my offer of financial help for your new shop, I beg
you again to allow me this liberty. I thought long and
hard through the night and can have no peace unless
you agree to accept this small sum, perhaps to pay
your shop rent for a while until your trade settles
down. Hannah, please look on this simply as a hand
held out to a very dear friend, from one who values
that friendship enormously. I cannot prevent your
giving – even throwing – this away if you must. But
my deep hope is that you will use it, so that in some
small way I will be part of your courageous venture. I
shall never forget the time we have spent together,
and shall hope to hear of your success and happiness

when next I am in Wales.
                    With my love
                         David

Hannah folded the letter with care, then looked into the envelope again. There were five notes, white and important and worth fifty pounds each.

"Who's the letter from, Han?" Tom was watching her over his bread and jam. She slid the letter back in with the notes with a hand that shook.

"It's from that friend I saw last night, dear. He's had to go away now and wanted to say goodbye."

Hearing her voice crack uncertainly, Hannah put the envelope in the dresser drawer and went into the yard. She picked an early sprig of lavender and inhaled the scent of the blue spire, attempting to collect herself. There had been a first angry spark at the idea that he had as usual got his own way. Then confusion: she had never seen two hundred and fifty pounds before. She *could* put it straight into the Miners' Fund, God knows it would find a good home there. She *could* send it back to him to the address in Toronto he had left. Or she could keep it.

Hannah took a deep breath of lavender-scented air. As a loan, of course, to be repaid when the shop was in secure profit. She knew already that Uncle Jenkin's loan was nowhere near enough. It might shelve and paint the shop, pay the signwriter, buy some supplies; but it would not be adequate to turn the back room into a working kitchen, and without that her business could never do more than limp along.

Then there was the rent. She had used her meagre savings for the first quarter but knew already that it was going to be very difficult to find more. Her

produce sold out every day but the amount offered
for sale was still too small for real profit; too small to
pay the rent let alone have any over to build a
kitchen. She *had* perhaps aimed too high.

When Tom had gone to bed Hannah took out the
envelope again, read the letter, examined the fifty-
pound notes. She looked about the room that had
been home for so many years, now hopelessly over-
full with cooking utensils on every surface, bunches of
herbs hanging everywhere, lists pinned to the wall,
cartons of flour, fat, sugar under the table and washing strung about the fire. Then she put her hand over
her face for a few moments before fetching out her
writing pad from the dresser drawer.

Dear David
  It was a great shock to receive your letter, and the
money. It was wrong of you to tempt me with it after
I had already refused. But I have thought about it
carefully, and hope I now understand that your
motive was honest concern for my security and
happiness.
  Because I believe this, I will accept the money. But
only as a loan – when I am in a stable trading position
I must return it with my thanks. I have to confess that
I am feeling uncertain how things might work out
without this assistance.
  I shall use part of it to bring the room behind the
shop into use as a kitchen/bakery, and will put the
rest into a Post Office account towards the rent.
  Thank you, David. I promise to use the loan to the
best possible advantage. I wish you well in the future.
                              Yours ever,
                              Hannah

Her days were full now; there could be no time for

grieving, for missing, wanting. Yet from early morning when she tumbled half-asleep out of bed, to night, almost too dog-tired then to shrug off her clothes, David Vaughan was with her. Real enough some days for her to speak to, touch. Other days, seeing a man and woman walking arm in arm, or hearing of the birth of a child, Hannah would know that he was a dead and useless dream, and that she now craved reality. This was never more clear than on a hot July day when Harry told her about his sister Emily.

"Very sudden." His eyes met hers, slid away. "A teacher at her school, lost his wife a while back. Just a quiet weddin' where they live in London. Registry Office. Says she'll bring him down after end of term. Name of Geoffrey. A bit older, she says."

Not too old by the sound of it. Hannah's first reaction was a smile, recalling Emily's ascerbic remarks about her sister Daisy getting "caught" with Albert's baby. So now Em was the same, dependant on a man and with a baby coming. No more school-teaching for Emily.

Then Hannah realised that she was envious, just plain envious of Emily who had a man of her own and soon a child by the sound of it: fulfilled; fruitful. All the long-suppressed sexuality released by David Vaughan now tormented Hannah. She longed to hate him for breaking open her life so painfully, then leaving her to pick up the pieces and go on alone. But hatred was as impossible as indifference. However hard she drove herself through the daylight hours, a time would come when both heart and body ached for him.

His second letter stirred it all afresh when it arrived in late June. Hannah stared at the expensive-looking envelope almost fearfully, dropped without ceremony onto the cheap lino. She picked it up gingerly, laid it on her bed whilst she got Tom off to school, thoughts circling the rectangle endlessly until at last she was left alone with it. It was steamed open, a sacrilege to tear the fine vellum. A single, large sheet inside, with printed heading, covered with a strong sloping scrawl. Mouth dry, Hannah sat down and read.

What had she been expecting? She stared through the window. That he would be coming again soon? That his wife had died and now he was free to marry her? That he could not live without her? After a moment Hannah folded the sheet of paper, slid it back into its envelope and placed it carefully with his last one, under the newspaper lining of her bedroom drawer. What else *could* he have said? He had no right to send her a love letter. And tactfully he had not mentioned the loan. Of *course* he wouldn't come again for years. Of *course* his wife wouldn't die – much too well looked after for that. It was just a letter; more than she should expect anyway, really. It told her that he was very busy, quite well, that they were having a heatwave in Toronto. Oh, and that he was missing her. Fancy that. Fancy him even recalling that he'd written down her address!

Hannah buckled onto her bed then. She allowed herself for just a few minutes the luxury of tears, and remembering how it had been with him in May in the house on the hill. Maybe she would reply, if she could think of anything to say that he might find remotely interesting. Then she washed her face and set about collecting together what was needed for the shop. She would relieve Florence at midday behind the counter – lucky that Flo was still on half time at Stanbuckle's. Forty-eight hours to a day, that would help; but at least they were solvent. So, up to her to keep it that way. She heard Mrs Peplow coming downstairs to have her morning with the clothes copper and hurried out; she never would become used to sharing her home. One day . . . one day . . . when her business was flourishing.

She had been open a week now. Hannah was breathless with pride each time she approached the shop. The signwriter had done a good job of HANNAH's and it was very much as she had imagined it, dreamed of it these last five years. She knew now that David's loan had been crucial – all the help and goodwill of Florence, Harry, Sam, and her own unceasing effort could not have compensated for lack of hard cash. She had advertised the opening with notices on her market stall and brightly printed cards done with Tom's crayons displayed in any shop windows or doors allowing them. The shop front's gold name on blue was both pretty, and noticeable from quite a distance, drawing interesting spectators if not always buyers. She had been approached by several women to sell their wares, too, on a sale or return basis, and had accepted; it helped fill her shelves and make a few shillings more with no personal outlay.

"Han, these blackcurrant tarts just *walked* out of the shop – one lady visiting from Swansea took a dozen!"

Florence waved happily towards the empty tray. She had made the tarts from the first early blackcurrents bought from an aged lady in Constant Road who had become too arthritic to pick her bushes. Hannah's own crop on the allotment had been found picked clean two nights earlier – an ongoing hazard with so many hungry mouths in the district; some men had taken to sleeping on their allotments to guard their precious produce.

"That's good." Hannah took her white overall from behind the door opening into the kitchen and surveyed her domain. A long cast-iron cooking range installed with part of David Vaughan's money took pride of place along one wall. It was second-hand, from a place in Swansea that had gone out of business and had been a bargain. An old bread oven across one corner of the room had been repaired and Hannah had already started a service for women to have their own bread baked here, charging three-halfpence per loaf. The oven held a dozen loaves at once and more women each week were bringing their risen dough as shortage of coal stopped them firing their own ovens. Hannah had found Dai, a retired baker, very happy to put in mornings at the bread oven for twenty-two shillings a week – the problem was buying coal for their own baking as the miners' strike dragged miserably on. So far they had kept going; but Hannah was uncomfortably aware that without coal she could not bake. Unless she invested in a gas oven ... and cushioned as she had been by David Vaughan's loan, she was fearful of laying out money she might still need for rent if the district remained so depressed.

She washed her hands at the sink under the window and went back into the shop. Florence had to leave for work at Stanbuckle's and was hanging up her overall.

"Flo, I had a letter today – from Canada," Hannah spoke impulsively, always uncertain of her ground on this topic. Florence, putting on her hat, raised her eyebrows.

"Good news or bad?"

"Neither. Don't know why he wrote, really. It was, well, rather a nothing letter I suppose."

"Well," Florence opened the till to make a note of

her takings. "It's rather a nothing situation, isn't it? But at least his loan was a huge help . . . it's taken a lot of strain off you. See, quite a good morning's trade. Dai's bread sold out fast and he had an oven full of other people's afterwards. Shall I get some shin beef for the meat pies on the way home? I could cut it up and simmer it tonight – Mam likes a fire evenings, so the oven'll be just nice and slow. I *do* worry a bit about coal."

"Flo, so do I. We may end up beachcombing again." Hannah gave her friend a sudden hug. "I just wish you could work here full-time, you're such a treasure. Yes, some shin beef would be a big help."

A flurry of customers descended before Hannah had time to reflect. This business could not be cost-effective unless she could spend more time baking, to sell more. She needed someone full-time behind the counter *and* Flo and herself full-time in the kitchen, to do jams, chutneys and extras as well as straight baking. *Or* a full-time, trained cook . . . and she would never dare go that far, would she? That would cost twice as much as having a girl to serve. And then, the baking might not be to her own taste. Yet the shop was practically sold out already, so she *must* work out a way to produce more. She would give it serious thought tonight; try to sort out the money angle before she got too tired.

She looked round the shop, light and bright with the big display window, the glass panel in the door and the white paint. The quarry-tiled floor appeared rosy in the sunlight. It was a lovely shop and she would work all the hours she must to make it a success.

"Good, eh?" Sam Warburton nodded towards the

344

new bugle player in the brass band. Hannah, who had been looking for Tom to say it was time to go, paused to look. "Down from the North. Name of Bates, furnaceman, in Heavy Bar."

The band was playing on the vicarage lawn, a fete in aid of miners' dependents. It was packed tight on a stand alongside three stalls decorated with gaudy crepe flowers and bits of old bunting. The day was fresh and bright and crowds had come to support the fund, with children playing tic round the stalls and hide and seek in the shrubbery, and grownups drinking tea and eating fairy cakes on the terrace. The man playing the bugle – Hannah's bugle, Sam had asked if she would loan it out for the afternoon – was adept, the tone clear and strong when he tilted his head to blow. Of a little above average height, he looked more because of his powerful build; sturdy legs braced back at the knees, heavily muscled shoulders, big square hands. The features too were big, regular with a dominant slightly hooked nose and heavy black brows drawn together now in concentration.

The end of the piece brought applause. The big dark-haired man grinned, wiped the bugle mouthpiece thoroughly with a blue and white checked handkerchief and walked over to Sam.

"Right good bugle this, ta for t' loan. I'll get mine patched afore the next concert."

"Here's the owner, Miss Hywel." Sam put a hand across Hannah's shoulder. "Family treasure this, eh love? Her Dad gave it to her, an' his Dad gave it to him."

Bates nodded and turned handsome black eyes on her. "Thanks, then." He took Hannah's hand in a sudden firm clasp. "Decent tone to it, every bit as good as mine." His voice was pleasant, a rich brown voice matching his appearance. Hannah smiled.

"Is it? I only wish I could play it properly. Maybe one day I'll learn when I've the time." She touched Sam's arm. "Can I leave it for you to bring round, Sam? I've shopping to do on the way home. When I've tracked down Tom, that is. Oh, there, I'll grab him while I can. 'Bye now."

She included both men in her smile and as she hurried over the grass to where Harry and Tom were guessing the weight of a jar of liquorice torpedoes, was aware of Darrow Bates' black eyes watching her. Aware, then, that she was half enjoying the sensation while at the same time feeling unaccountably threatened. Daft nonsense; just another man, same as all the rest. But as she walked quickly up the road with Tom, Hannah would have liked to turn to see if he was still watching.

There seemed to be a strange inevitability about opening the door to him two evenings later. Freshly washed and combed, wearing his good dark suit and seeming to fill the cramped little yard, he held the bugle stiffly before him as though anxious to part with it at once. Hannah, her mind still on the first month's shop accounts spread on the table, was frowning, and Darrow Bates' polite smile faded. He thrust the bugle into her hand, knocking the pen she held to the floor.

"Oops, sorry."

Tom came out after Hannah, picked up the pen and regarded the stranger with his customary candid stare.

"Who is it, Han?" He tugged at her skirt.

"Mr Bates." The man offered a well scubbed hand

346

which Tom did not take. "And what's your name, sonny?"

Tom stared a moment longer and scuttled off to peep at him through the kitchen window. Smiling now, Hannah shook her head.

"Tom's a mite shy. Will you come in, Mr Bates?"

"Just for a minute, then." She had hoped that he would refuse, the shop figures must be finished tonight. But Darrow Bates stepped straight into the scullery, taking off his cap. Tom looked apprehensive as Hannah led the way into the kitchen but she laid a reassuring hand on his shoulder, put down the bugle on the paper-strewn table and shifted the kettle over the hob. The visitor lowered himself onto Thomas Hywel's old wheelback chair and looked about him, hands spread on his knees.

"Whereabouts do you live, Mr Bates?" Hannah asked politely, handing him a cup of steaming tea into which he ladled three spoonfuls of sugar before stirring it so forcefully that tea spotted the accounts. Bates seemed not to notice, sitting with feet planted wide apart and sipping with enjoyment through the dark moustache.

"Manor Street; Mrs Lauder." His voice had a resonance that filled the small room, the northern accent alien and attractive. "Does me well enough."

"Yes, not far from Sam's, then." Hannah perched on the rocking chair, aware of her faded cotton dress under the crossover pinafore, of the bare white legs to save her stockings. Darrow Bates' hands were brown-skinned, powerful, resting on the tightly drawn trouser suiting, which she noted was of good quality with a fine maroon stripe.

"Aye. Good man, that."

347

"He's been wonderfully kind to us. He was my father's best friend."

"Oh yes?" Bates looked at his teacup, slightly embarrassed. Then he touched the satiny patina of the bugle. "Your Dad's piece, Sam was saying; played much did he?"

"Hardly ever. Mam used to say it was a racket. You play well, Mr Bates. Were you in the band back home?" Hannah refilled his cup and discreetly slid her shop accounts further off. Tom sat quiet, watching the stranger's face.

"Aye. Tommy Talker bands we had there, too." The strong features relaxed into a half smile. "Have 'em here, don't you, Tommy Talker bands? Bits o' tin, holes in t' top and paper screwed in to get different sounds? The best could end up as good as a proper brass band though. Men had all day to practise, see, not bein' in work."

Hannah nodded. "We have them. They play round the streets, then come to the doors collecting, mostly for miners' families."

His mood changed then, the heavy-lidded eyes turning sombre. "All wrong, that. TUC'd no business callin' off General Strike ... all that pratin' about negotiations and what's there been? Damn all! Nor will there be, they'll starve t' miners back next, worse off than afore."

"I like Tommy Talker bands," said Tom unexpectedly. Darrow Bates, the flow of rhetoric stemmed, frowned at him. "Cousin Frank plays in one," added Tom. "And cousin Dewi when he can get his leg on." Taken aback by his daring, he darted past the visitor to the sanctuary of the bedroom, where he could be heard shuffling agitatedly through his pile of treasured comics passed on from Terry, his best friend.

348

Hannah looked warily at Darrow Bates. She never succeeded in feeling less than defensive about her brother; could never decide if strangers would notice his small inadequacies. To her he was simply Tom, a boy who could get as dirty and as hungry as most boys, and who was often in trouble at school because he had difficulty grasping hard facts like his times tables. She was so used now to helping him keep abreast that it was a natural part of their life together, not an extra chore. Only rarely, perhaps if she should find him poring over a word in his comic with a blank expression, would she wonder uneasily how he would ever manage without her, even when he was grown up.

The man drained his teacup and set it down, touching the papers on the table.

"What's all this, then? Not that it's any of my business," he added quickly, and shifted as though to get up.

"That's all right. It's the accounts for my shop." Thinking how pretentious this sounded she gave a deprecating little laugh. "Selling home-baked things, I'm only recently open. If I don't keep track of everything I'll end up in a dreadful muddle."

"Go on." He sounded impressed. "A shop, eh? Wouldn't't've thought there'd have been too much trade, funds bein' so short everywhere."

"Yes, I've been surprised. I think we could sell more if we increased the quantities and the range. Profits are very narrow yet though."

"Who's 'we'?" Darrow Bates asked shrewdly. "Got a partner in, have you?"

"Well, no. It's my friend, Florence." Hannah indicated a tray covered by a white cloth on the sideboard. "She was dropped to part-time at Stanbuckle's

349

so she's able to help with the cooking and serving for a while now."

"Smells good, anyway."

"Yes, fruit pies." Hannah lifted a corner of the cloth for him to see. "I told her she'll not stay single long once the right man gets his teeth into her cooking!"

"And you? Right man got his teeth into *your* pies yet?"

Shocked by the suddenness of the probe, Hannah stiffened. He'd no right; a stranger asking personal questions. As she searched for a remark to put him in his place there were footsteps on the stairs and Mrs Peplow pushed open the door, the toddler tucked in her shawl and a worn black purse clutched in a hand. She paused, seeing the man, then gave Hannah an apologetic smile.

Hannah smiled back. Mr Peplow *was* hitting her, she had been certain of that a couple of weeks ago when the old black hat had been pulled down over one cheek in an effort to hide a bruise. Hannah was still trying to think what to do about it; the only permanent solution would be to find the man work, and that was beyond her. She wondered if she should advise Mrs Peplow to hit him back – she was, after all, bigger than he was. Perhaps not though.

"Just goin' for potatoes, back in a minute." Mrs Peplow sidled head down round the table, shoulders hunched defensively. Darrow Bates watched her hurry through the yard.

"Who's that, then?"

"You ask too many questions, Mr Bates," Hannah told him crisply. "Mrs Peplow is my lodger if you must know." She cleared off his cup and stared with purpose at her paperwork. Bates got up, colour rising over his bold features and again she was aware of force, of checked-in power.

"No offence meant."

"None taken." Her tone was neutral as she opened the back door. He stepped into the yard and then turned to proffer a hand, which Hannah had no option but to take.

"Thanks again for t' bugle. We're playin' up at Neath, Saturday. Like to come?"

"Thanks, but I'm awfully busy, Saturdays. Goodnight, then, Mr Bates."

As he moved to go, touching his cap, Hannah closed the door firmly. She was tempted to turn the key; not sure why, unless because of that inexplicable scent of danger allied to the man. Stupid, a perfectly ordinary man, just a bit pushier than some.

She picked up the bugle, ran her fingers over the burnished curves, put her lips against the mouthpiece and blew, but gently, without a sound. Her father's face came to her clearly then – the tense pale look of him, the level slatey eyes and square jaw ... utterly different from the dark, bold appearance of the man whose lips had last drawn music from the old instrument.

Hannah saw Tom, watching from their bedroom doorway. She dropped the bugle and held out her arms. "Come on, love. How if you help me add up a few sums. Good practice for you, company for me."

Perversely, Hannah tried to believe that it was Florence he was – or should be – interested in when Darrow Bates would come into the shop for a meat pie or a jar of raspberry jam or a bundle of stick beans from her allotment. He was clearly not short of cash ... further sections of the mills had just shut down for lack of work but not the Heavy Bar, with enough rails for the GWR and the construction angle orders to keep going. Hannah recalled her father's own ambition to rise to furnaceman, the highest paid operative in the business. Special work, he'd told her, highly skilled. "You start off as third hand, Princess, and if you're lucky after few years you make it up to sample passer. Provided you've got the temperament; some haven't and they crack up somewhere along the line." Wherever along the line Darrow Bates was he looked solid and unmoveable, toughly confident as most northerners who had infiltrated the district in the last two decades to fill Port Talbot's need for more skilled steelworkers.

He never came to the shop straight from his shift, but always washed and changed.

"That Mr Bates was in again," Florence remarked, cooking with Hannah in the kitchen of Number twelve one warm evening in early August. "Wonder if his landlady pays him for the stuff he buys?"

"Why don't you ask him?" Hannah was testing a bubbling pan of blackberry jelly for a good set, touching with a delicate finger the glistening ruby mixture spooned onto a saucer. Harry sat at the table stringing beans for salting down at the tender stage and Tom was topping and tailing gooseberries, snipping laboriously before dropping each hairy red-green globe into the colander. Evening sun had left an afterglow in the little room, fragrant with ripe fruit and baking pastries. Looking up, Hannah became aware that all she most loved were gathered here with her tonight. All but Joe . . . in that moment she missed Joe as sharply as ever she had. And David, of course. But her love for David seemed always to be apart from everything, everyone. It lived in a special place, separate from all but her, like a deep quiet undercurrent in a river.

"He's likely to tell me to mind my own business, that's why." Florence crimped expertly round the edge of a bakewell tart, holding the dish high so that the pearly toned pastry with its brushing of milk gleamed. Turning to ask Harry to pass the tray of jam jars, Hannah intercepted the expression on his face as he watched Florence, and was transfixed by what she saw, spoon poised above the boiling jam.

She had never guessed. How long had he felt like this? Did Florence know? She might have been seeing him naked, so vulnerable was he as his gaze followed the lovely curve of Florence's arm down to her face, bright in the reflected warmth. Harry . . . come back to life after so long; all the old hopes and dreams blossoming again in the wounded mind. How beautiful if Florence . . .

Without warning, Hannah felt utterly alone. There might have been no one in the world but her. Harry and Flo, shutting her out, leaving her isolated. Her other cousins: Daisy, with her Albert; now even Emily the superior school-teacher, Em and her Geoffrey, together. Hannah, alone.

Late next afternoon she was wiping the almost empty shelves when Darrow Bates swung into the High Street. He paused to look through the shop window and clattered up the step in newly polished boots, dark eyes snapping into life.

"Afternoon, Miss Hywel. Not much left, is there?"

"That's the idea, Mr Bates, to sell out. All fresh tomorrow, then. There's just one steak and kidney left – I tucked it away or Mrs Pritchard would have pounced on it; it's her son's birthday today and she can't push together a decent piece of pastry to save her life."

"Put it in a bag," he said promptly. "And that currant loaf, that's a treat after my sandwiches at snap time." As she handed him the bags he added; "You'll be at it all night then, making fresh? Don't you ever stop?"

"I can't afford to," she said simply. "I've a roof to keep over our heads."

"Even so." He paused, looking down at her hand on the counter and for a moment Hannah knew he considered covering it with his. She removed it quickly. Their eyes met and subtle messages were transmitted, recognition made. Outside, the headmaster of Mountain School For Boys parked his bicycle, coming for his regular pot of jam and lardy cake. Darrow Bates made a restless movement, frowning.

"What about an hour on Sunday afternoon? Just an hour? A stroll by the sea, a breath of fresh air?" He saw hesitation and pressed home. "Do you a world o' good, the change. The world won't end for an hour now, will it?"

She held her breath for seconds, torn with an indecision unusual for her. As Mr Root came in and paused to blow his nose on a large checked handkerchief she spoke briefly.

"Perhaps. I'll see how things go."

He gave a satisfied nod and walked away.

"Mr Bates, your change." She held out the three-pence.

Darrow Bates turned at the door, setting back his cap at a jaunty angle. "Keep it towards tomorrow's beef pie, Miss Hywel."

Hannah was not in the least certain why she agreed to

walk out with Darrow Bates on Sunday. She was not sure that she even liked him. Perhaps the fact that it was a fine summer's day had a bearing after three dull cold ones, and she saw no reason why she should not allow a well set-up man to walk along to Kenfig Burrows with her in the early summer evening sunlight. It was a sad fact that it did not fall to every girl to be pursued in these post-war years. Hannah had had a couple of advances made, but from men she did not even consider in the least either personable or good company. Darrow Bates was certainly personable; she may as well discover if he was also good company. She had applied her lipstick with a flourish, almost of defiance, and had set her beret at a jaunty angle. She would not think of David Vaughan because this had absolutely nothing to do with her love for him – there was only one David Vaughan and he was thousands of miles away and married. *This* was reality, here and now.

What she discovered was that Darrow Bates was no talker. There were a few long silences on that first walk. But there was also a small, but definable frisson of excitement at having his masculine bulk shade her from the late sun, so closely did he walk by her. And when he asked before they parted if she would see him the following Sunday, Hannah said she might, if she could spare an hour again.

"Glad to see you with a bit o' proper company, love."

Sam Warburton watched her test the oven with an expert hand before sliding in two apple and cinnamon pies. He had just put up an extra shelf between the fireplace and the window wall at Number twelve; it was already packed with jars and packets, with piled trays and assorted bags. Herbs hung from hooks in the ceiling and baking dishes were stacked around the range; to find a place to sit was now a problem.

Hannah raised an eyebrow. "You don't call Flo and Harry proper company, then?" She stirred the next batch of early apples, the first she'd found, then returned to the measuring of ingredients, working with speed and economy of movement.

"You know what I mean." Sam frowned at her over the rim of his mug. "Get on wi' him do you, Bates?"

"He's all right. Is he liked at work?" She tried to sound casual.

"Well enough, considerin' he's a northerner. A bit of a loner, mebbe, keeps himself to himself. Just been given assistant foreman, meltin' shop, so he must be doin' well enough. But you'd know."

"Mm mm." Hannah had not known and now wondered why. Darrow Bates, she was discovering, was a complex man, and one who volunteered very little about himself. Not a talker at all in fact. And if he had not shared this news about his promotion with her, how honest had he been with other things? Would she ever know more than he cared to tell her? They had walked together three times now, and the last time he had kissed her goodnight. That was after they had sat on the hill and he had actually told her something of his past.

"I lived with my auntie till I was fifteen." Bates had stared down at the steelworks, turning his cap round and round in his big brown-skinned hands. "Mum had walked off years before an' Aunt Dot took to me. Only she died the year after I left school . . . couple of years before the war that was. So I went into lodgin's. Been there ever since, lodgin's in various places."

Hannah had digested this in silence; the barest

bones of a man's life over almost thirty years. Then she had said quietly, "When did you come here?"

"Oh, last year. A mate had told me they were tekkin' on skilled men still there," He nodded at the works below them. "An' the place I was at was foldin', nothin' on order books. I've been lucky so far in work right through."

"Yes." They had got up then, and when they reached home Darrow Bates had kissed her just as she was about to open the back door. He had said nothing; put his arms round her and kissed her full on the lips, then put on his cap and gave a small salute.

"See you, then. G'night."

Hannah had thought about him as she tidied the room and checked over things to take to the shop tomorrow. Tom's clean clothes for school were put on the chair by his bed, washing sorted into the copper. She felt disturbed, she supposed, also a little apprehensive. A relationship was developing; did she want it to? Any later and it might be difficult to back off.

Hannah was in fact assailed by so many conflicting emotions that it became impossible to separate one from another. Pity for his motherless childhood – fatherless, too, from what she could gather – and solitary state, living in lodgings rather than in a family circle. Admiration for his tenacity in climbing to the top of a skilled foundryman's ladder. Excitement mixed with apprehension about the kiss. She had liked it but was also nervous because she recognised that here was a man with whom one should not trifle. And she had no idea why Darrow Bates had not married before . . . this was like a marker on a strange road she was trying to follow. She felt it was important, but it was not clear why this should be so.

They were walking on the hill again when Hannah

made an attempt to ask this question. She hoped for an answer that might clear up doubts; but Darrow Bates clearly disliked being quizzed.

"I suppose I never found anybody I wanted to ask. See that big shed with a black roof, the one set at an angle?" He pointed down to the steelworks. "That's where I work."

He was determined to deflect the conversation from himself and Hannah had no option but to let it go. The query remained. Perhaps she should be flattered that he was taking an interest in her . . . or was it less straightforward?

A moment later, he drew her to him and kissed her. Sometimes now his kiss would stir an answering response in Hannah, the hungry need that David Vaughan had woken in the spring. And, as summer hung poised to drift into autumn, she became fairly certain that she would soon be asked for a decision. Cousin Emily had gone back to London with her respectable widower Geoffrey after an August bank holiday visit to her parents; Cousin Daisy had come from Cardiff to show off her third baby to a finally reconciled Aunt Maggie, though Uncle Idwal was still not beyond muttering darkly about having a Hun in the family. And Harry still watched Florence with a look on his face that made Hannah fear and hope for him in equal parts. Flo was certainly very fond of him; she had finally confessed that to Hannah. But Harry needed to build up his confidence if he was to declare his love to Florence, let alone to the rest of his family.

"It's really good, having the room behind the shop fully operational now," Hannah told Sam at the end of August. "It means we can sell quite a bit more. And with Flo starting full-time next week . . ."

Sam's features cracked into the great smile she

loved. "So, things really lookin' good, eh?" He captured one of her hands and squeezed it with such enthusiasm that Hannah winced. He added in a more tentative voice, "Done much on the other side lately? You know, remedies an' things? Still get up to the veterinary's place?"

"Not often, Sam. I'd like to, but it's the time. I do make up a few remedies. But I have to see us secure you see, me and Tom. That has to be my absolute priority. These days nothing is ever certain . . . and you do see that there's no hard cash in remedies!"

"Course I see, love. An' Tom's a lovely lad, he does you credit." Sam levered himself up and adjusted the greasy old cap. "Now, any more odd jobs, you let me know."

Hugging him, Hannah longed then to ask him what she should do, as she would have asked Dada. Not about her work or the odd jobs about the house. About Darrow Bates.

Darrow proposed to her one stormy evening in early October when he was drinking tea in the kitchen at Incline Row. Hannah was making false cuffs for Tom's shirt, he was growing fast now, and Darrow had been reading the paper until he put it down to look at her. Biting off cotton, Hannah met his gaze and smiled.

"A rough old night . . . Sam's fixed that window twice and it still rattles."

"I wouldn't need to go out in it if we were married."

She looked up sharply. He was staring at her with bold dark eyes.

"Would you marry me?" The newspaper slid down from the floor as he leaned forward. Hannah looked down at Tom's shirt.

Now you have to decide. Part of you wants to. Are you afraid? You could make him happy, secure in a home for the first time since he was little. He would give you love, protection, companionship. What was wrong with that?

"I'll need to think about it for a day or two, Darrow. It's lovely to be asked, but it's a big decision."

He nodded. "Okay by me. Give me a kiss, then." He came over and kissed her and Hannah closed her eyes and put her arm around his neck. He felt bulky and powerful. He *was* a nice man . . . he really was.

"Only you can decide, *cariad*," Florence told her earnestly next day. "Only *you* know how you feel about him."

"I never seem to feel the same for two minutes together," Hannah confessed. She was bottling plums and the Incline Row kitchen was fragrant with their sharp sweetness, and with the aroma of apple rings that Florence was spreading on a baking tray to dry. Tom was in bed, the lamp was lit, and the women talked together in the friendly harmony that had been theirs since childhood.

"Well, I reckon you should feel a bit more settled than that before you commit yourself. I mean, we're still barely twenty-five, we've both got a year or two to go. Is David Vaughan getting in the way?"

"He has to have some bearing on it, I suppose. That letter I had last week unsettled me again."

"But it wasn't a *love* letter, Han." Florence dipped one of the apple rings into a sugar bowl and nibbled at it. Her cropped hair was a rich glossy brown in the lamplight and her face, slimmer than it had been, glowed with attractive health. Hannah thought that if

Harry could not summon up the confidence soon, another man would be bound to discover the charms of this woman she valued so highly.

"No, he has no right to send a love letter, Flo. I realise that now and respect him for it. But it only takes the envelope – never mind the letter – to bring him back so very forcefully."

"Han," Florence touched her arm and her eyes were serious. "Don't you think you should let him go? I mean *really*, from your heart as well as your head? So long as you don't, he'll stand between you and, well, your chance of happiness with anyone – not necessarily Darrow Bates, but *anyone*."

Hannah stared at the jewel-rich Kilner jar of plums. To relinquish her dreams; to exchange it for ... specifically, for a Yorkshire foundryman who had a knack of staying in work, who was attractive physically but, if she was honest, still something of an unknown quantity. Yet with whom she could perhaps find companionship in a shared life and family. Who would put her first, as Dada had put Betsy first. She had seen through her childhood how Thomas had loved Betsy and, though Betsy never had been able to demonstrate it, Hannah knew that she had loved Thomas in return, completely.

Perhaps it could not be quite the same for her after David Vaughan ... but she *would* work at it, once she had committed herself. And she was lonely. Well, the label she gave the feeling was lonely. It was a small ache that was discernible most of the time. Was that lonely?

"I am thinking about it, Flo. Very carefully."

Hannah sorted out her thoughts as best she could. Darrow was an attractive man, a hard worker. He wanted her to be his wife. There was no other man about and available worth consideration. If she did not accept Darrow she might never marry, have children. Dear Flo would, she was certain, find happiness with Harry; it might be a way off yet, Harry had no job, no home, no security to offer. But one day it would come. And if she, Hannah, refused Darrow Bates, who would be *her* companion through life? Why should she not grasp this offer; believe that with goodwill on both sides it would work well?

They were married on a dark, mist-laden morning in early November at the Registry Office. Sam gave her away, creating umbrage on the part of the rejected uncles and threats from the aunts to boycott the small ceremony. Aunt Maggie relented first, never able to hold a grudge, finally inviting everyone back to her place for refreshments. Darrow Bates looked striking in a new suit, thick hair severely tamed and moustache freshly trimmed, and Hannah wore a simple blue dress and jacket with a navy cloche and carried a spray of creamy roses. She looked delicately beautiful, slender and fine-drawn beside the powerful breadth of her new husband. Florence was her only attendant – again causing family dissention – and Flo was to take Tom home with her afterwards so the couple could have one night alone. The Peplows had already moved out, Darrow insisting there would be no room now for another family to share the house, and Hannah was in full agreement.

When the food and drink had been consumed, when she had kissed the assembled company, and reminded Florence that Tom would need his milk money in the morning, Hannah left for home on her husband's arm. She suggested a breath of fresh air after the crowded, smoky little parlour and, walking with him along the damp streets, she looked about her, subconsciously taking stock of her territory on this first day of her new life.

Could be better: shabby men stamping their feet to keep warm on the street corners; women holding tightly to their purses, waiting for shops to mark down perishables before closing; pinched ill-clad children, many of them coughing. A determination rose in Hannah now to make things better for *them* at least. The shop could succeed, she knew it, once coal was available again – and surely that must happen soon. And with a man's good wages coming in she might even manage to start a little cafe in a couple of years.

As they turned into Incline Row a car came roaring from the direction of Margam. Hannah stopped to watch as it sped by with a man in a leather cap and coat at the wheel.

"What's that, then?"

"Oh, nothing." The gas-lamp gave her skin an unusual pallor. She had written just a week ago to David Vaughan: "I am sure this is best. We were just a dream, and I do not want to spend the rest of my life dreaming alone. I feel sure I can make Darrow happy. I shall not forget to return the loan to you as soon as I feel confident that I am managing. The use of the money has made things much easier, thank you again."

The car was gone now. The street was completely silent as Hannah Bates unlocked the door of Number twelve and followed her husband inside.

Chapter Fourteen

December 1926

The miners' strike had dragged on for eight months when it collapsed, first in Nottinghamshire, in December. A slow drift back to work followed, with no wage agreement, and the coalfields around Port Talbot suffered cruelly. Pits were acquired for tiny sums by unscrupulous owners' cartels who then closed them, thus forcing down wages in their nearby pits. Thousands were thrown out of work with nothing; men would walk six, seven or more miles over the mountains to seek work in adjacent valleys. If they were lucky they might rise at three to walk in darkness to their new pit by six. After an eight-hour shift they would walk back in their dirty and often wet pit clothes, unwashed and cold. On piecework, the coal-getters might, if they were allocated an unproductive section of the coalface, return home with no more than thirty shillings in their pocket for six days' unremitting labour.

At the Port Talbot steelworks large sections of plant were shut down due to lack of orders. Few ships were being built, there was little demand for rails, and quantities of steel from the continent were being dumped at below cost. Every factory in the area suffered and Vaughan Tinplate was on short time. Hannah saw David's parents and brother Desmond occasionally; Mr and Mrs Vaughan in the back of their forbidding black Austin Twenty; Desmond in a racy little red machine that made rather more noise. Their house, a substantial Edwardian residence well back from Baglan Road on the way to Swansea was staffed by, among others, Hannah's cousin Bella as parlour-maid. Along with so many young women who had been downgraded back into domestic service with the war's end, Bella had lost the freedom of a working day on the buses that she had so enjoyed. She cleaned the hearth and brought up coal; swept the crumbs up off the big carpets and shook the rugs, cleaned the silver and waited at table. And like so many other young women of her generation who had once been made to feel of value, and whose hopes of a husband and children might now be fading, Bella was determined that when she had just a little more money saved she would pay for a course in office work and apply for a position as a clerk. Women may have been dismissed from the factories and shipyards and farms, but they were gaining ground steadily in offices, a male-dominated area of work until quite recently.

Hannah had finally been forced to shut her shop for a month simply because she could no longer buy the fuel to cook her produce. She spent that month, the first weeks of her marriage, in making what jams, jellies and chutneys she could in the kitchen of Incline Row. She made up orders of mincemeat and Christmas cakes, charging what she must to cover the high cost of the coal. She was continually surprised by requests for her food but with so many industries both large and small in the district, she reasoned that there had to be a significant management class who were not on piece-work and not suffering as acutely as the working man. These managing and professional families lived cheek by jowl with those of the working class, their somewhat grander houses often popped in here and there in odd corners rather than congregating in a specific area.

When Hannah caught sight of members of his family it was impossible for her not to think about David Vaughan. This brought her no pleasure; she knew it never could. But her thoughts would not be disciplined entirely to her wishes, including some she recognised as disloyal to her new husband. She struggled to put the past behind her; to cement a partnership with Darrow Bates that would endure all and bring joy and comfort to them both. After the departure of the Peplows to Eagle Street, Hannah promising to keep in touch with them, Sam repapered the walls of her parents' bedroom. Hannah rubbed up the brasses of their double bedstead until they glittered, repaired the hand-made Welsh quilt with great care and bought fresh linen. Her own single bed, her first buy as an independant wage-earner a decade ago, she pushed against the wall into the extra space this room had above the covered passage. Tom's bed had gone into the second bedroom; the parlour, as a result somewhat denuded, would, for the moment, have to wait.

She realised in late January that she was pregnant. By then she also knew that for Darrow Bates the act of sex did not equate to "making love". He needed a certain amount of drink before he touched her, then he seemed to want suddenly to overpower her so that Hannah felt roughly treated, used. Love did not somehow enter into what occurred between them. He did not speak, not before and not after, when he would turn away from her, separate in every way once they were no longer physically joined. Even when they were; when he was circling her waist with his powerful hands and thrusting deep into her with a massive, mesmeric rhythm that could force her to the very brink of consciousness, Hannah experienced a sense of isolation that could leave her afterwards in tears. Darrow Bates never knew

366

of her tears, he would have turned away to lie alone until by his change of breathing she knew that he slept. Sometimes she would place a friendly hand on his hip; but he never acknowledged the gesture, the plea for communication.

A child perhaps would bring them closer – so Hannah told herself – and she was deeply happy, thinking of her own family becoming a reality. When she told him Darrow accepted it calmly but clearly did not see the news as any special cause for celebration. But a man would not naturally enthuse over what was predominantly the woman's sphere she reasoned, and refused to have her own enthusiasm damped.

She told Tom quite soon so he could digest the idea gradually. An uncle – he would help her look after the baby she said, and when it was born, in August, he would be moving towards ten and be able to do so much for his little niece or nephew. She was trying hard to instil confidence and at least some measure of self-esteem into Tom; he could just about keep up in school but was still behind for his age and Hannah regularly made time to coach him in basics. He was a sweet, patient boy, but lacked concentration. Punished often for what the master saw as inattention, he bore the cane and ruler stoically – more stoically than did his sister. She had for some months fought a running battle on his behalf and had now threatened that if he was caned once more she would remove him from the school. Mr Roach had replied in frigid tones that she had removed one brother illegally from his studies but would find it another matter entirely to repeat the error with Tom. Hannah was now praying that the issue would not be forced.

At first she was tired the whole time, and nauseous, but her happiness at the thought of the child made light of this and she discovered that eating small starchy snacks minimised both symptoms. She could no longer enjoy a cup of tea but developed a yearning for fizzy lemonade and would call for a bottle at old Peg's dim little shop on the way to work. Would the baby be addicted to pop? Hannah would smile to herself at the thought, swinging through the drab winter streets with her pop. The baby . . . how pleased Dada would have been . . . and she really must write Joe the news. So hard to fit in everything though when she simply wanted to sleep.

She knew that Tom was uneasy with Darrow – poor Tom, he had no clear idea what a man should do in a house. He had not known the pleasure of seeing his father's figure through the window, coming in from work: never known Dada. For Hannah that was the most severe deprivation of the child's life. It brought out afresh her most fiercely protective instinct, so that when Darrow complained about Tom's books being spread all over the table she pointed out to him that this had been her brother's home long before it had been his. Afterwards she had apologised, attempting to explain, but Darrow grunted, observed that where he came from children didn't rule the roost, and went to his band practice almost at once. Hannah waited up for him to return to supper, forcing herself to stay awake after Tom had gone upstairs. When the kitchen door opened she sat up, smiling and setting aside her sewing.

"Was it a good session?" She had served up his hot-pot which smelled wonderful but he had sat down with no more than a grunt and propped up the evening paper with the pepper pot, refusing to look at her.

After watching his stolidly masticating profile for a moment Hannah said quietly: "Darrow, if I sounded unpleasant I am sorry. Tom lost both parents, you see, he only has me to defend him. I always try to make him feel, well, as secure as possible."

"I didn't have parents," Darrow retorted shortly. "I just got on with it."

Hannah felt carefully for the right words. "But you are so capable. I cannot imagine you not being able to fight your corner. You know that with Tom, well, he's not so –"

"Bright." Darrow did not lift his head.

Hannah's head went back, almost as though she had taken an uppercut. Darrow continued to read and eat. After few moments she got to her feet, feeling almost too tired to stand.

"I think I'll go up."

He made no sign that he had heard. When he came up, took off his things and moved in beside her with his back turned he ignored her as completely as he had downstairs. Hannah stared into the dark and the knot in her throat was of unshed tears.

She missed Florence coming round some evenings to cook with her, and she missed Harry's company. Neither came now unless specifically invited, which was not at all the same thing. She simply had not thought that marrying would deprive her of the company of her lifelong friends; also, she was aware that Harry and Flo had seen her home as a congenial meeting place in which their own romance could ripen.

"Flo, you know you're still as welcome as the flowers in May," Hannah said with a note almost of appeal in her voice. Florence re-arranged some buns on their cooling tray in the shop kitchen before looking up with honest brown eyes.

"But it's not May, Han love. It's March. I mean things are different. Shouldn't think Darrow'd want a kitchen full of folk he doesn't know that well when he's tryin' to relax after work.''

"It's *my* home, Flo,'' Hannah had protested. "Why shouldn't I still be able to enjoy my friends' company in it?''

"Because you've got your husband's, Han,'' Florence said quietly. "That little room's not big enough for all of us now ... we were always burstin' at the seams anyway with all the cooking gear and bits and pieces. Couldn't turn round some nights.''

"I *liked* it like that.''

"We all did. But things change.'' Florence smiled then and touched Hannah's waistline. "Now a baby. And I do wish you happy, with all my heart.''

"And I you, Flo dear.'' Hannah kissed Florence's cheek. "And I have to wonder ... well, you and Harry; *that* would be wonderful.''

"Oh.'' Florence pulled a little face. "Not that obvious, is it?'' The firm lines of her features softened, her large brown eyes seemed to become luminous as she thought of Harry, whom she had loved so constantly for so long.

"Only to me; because I love you both. Has he – ?'' Hannah paused and Florence, dredging sugar over buns, gave her a broad smile.

"Declared himself? Not really. It's very hard for him isn't it, with no prospect of being able to support a wife? That matters nothing to me but it *does* matter to him and that's what is important. I know how much he wants to work, to feel as good as anyone again. But what work is there? And when are things ever going to improve again? Anyway, I'm happy to wait until he's ready – when he can feel more confident about his position. He's a lovely man,'' she added with touching sincerity, and Hannah nodded.

"I know that, Flo; he's the best. Haven't I loved him

since I was knee high? And I know he loves you, I've *seen* it, clear as daylight. But he was ill for so long. I think he needs to feel he's made a good enough recovery, as well as find some work he could do."

Darrow didn't touch Hannah after the third month of her pregnancy. At first she was anxious about this, but finally grateful, after being forced to admit to herself that their love-making was seldom a happy experience. Next she felt guilty; it had to be her fault. It never had been possible to banish David Vaughan completely from her thoughts; last May seemed sometimes to be as near, as clear, as yesterday. So what chance had she given her husband? It was up to her to make this marriage secure and it could not happen by recalling her bliss in the arms of another man.

Though working longer hours than before in the shop, and cooking at home most evenings, Hannah made the effort to go to Darrow's brass band concerts, knowing it pleased him to have her there, smartly dressed and pretty. It did in fact surprise her to see how proud he seemed to be of her when she was at his side in public. The waistless dresses of spring 1927 hid her pregnancy and Florence had made her two wonderfully becoming frocks for a few shillings with remnants from the market. Both had big white pique collars on scoop necks, showing off her lovely throat and the perfect set of her prettily bobbed head. Tom came, too, and afterwards she promised that if he wished, when he was a little older, he could learn to play on the bugle that had once been his father's.

"He'd not master it," Darrow said abruptly. Tom had dipped his head then turned away, demoralised, and Hannah, angry for his hurt, had walked away from

371

Darrow holding Tom's hand. *Why* could he not be more kindly . . . more tolerant.

Darrow had at first gone visiting with her; to Uncle Jenkin at Cwmavon, and to Aunt Rose, and to Dewi whose leg continued to spend more time under the bed than walking around. But by spring he was making his excuses and began staying out later at band practices or the Labour club. Hannah reasoned that this too must be in some way her fault, but could not work out what she was doing wrong for him. One warm May night, relaxed and on the verge of sleep when he came quietly into the bedroom, she watched him strip off his shirt with his back to her, then sit on his side of the bed to remove his socks. She touched his back gently with her fingers; he stiffened, then turned his head.

"Thought you were asleep."

"Nearly, had a nice evening? Was it darts match night?"

"That's on Friday."

He hung up his suit having put his loose change on the chest of drawers by his pocket watch, then pulled on the striped winceyette shirt he kept for sleeping in and rolled into bed. Hannah could see him clearly by gaslight filtering through the thin curtains; he lay on his back for a moment, hands behind his head, then turned away from her, sighing, and arranging his limbs for sleep.

"Darrow?" She moved towards him and touched his back again, fingers spread over the warm skin of his hip.

"What?" He did not move.

Hannah raised herself on one elbow. "Darrow, lately you haven't – " She checked, embarrassed. "I just wanted to say, it's perfectly all right, you know. You don't have to not – come to me because of the baby. I asked the district nurse and she said no harm could

372

come, it was perfectly usual right up to the last month provided I felt comfortable."

She drew a shaky little breath and waited, stroking his hip with gentle fingers. He remained still, then moved sharply so that her fingers fell away from him.

"Better not." The words came jerkily and Hannah could sense that he, too, was embarrassed. "Not with the belly you're gettin' on you. And up top . . ." He organised his pillow about his shoulder and drew up his knees. "Let's get a bit o' sleep now, eh?"

Hannah lay on her back, staring at nothing. He found her repellent. Her hand stole over the neat little round of her stomach. The breasts that were certainly fuller, but firm. Harry had told her a few days ago that she looked a real picture; and she could see for herself that she had become, well, really pretty. So was it the presence of his child inside her that he found unpleasant? If so, if he felt like that about it now, what would he feel towards it when it was born?

She turned, restless. She badly needed to talk to him, to have him explain whatever he was experiencing, so she could understand. But he never did want to talk . . . he did not wish her to know him, the actual man, Darrow Bates; Hannah saw now that she really knew very little of him. If he did not desire her body now, had he turned to another woman for satisfaction?

Lying rigid with the sleeping form of her husband suddenly dominating the whole room, Hannah swallowed the bitter pill of failure. She eased herself from the bed and crept down the black stairwell and into the kitchen. It was warm still from the evening's fire dying now in the grate. Betsy had always kept the range glowing with black-lead and the brass fender shone, too, in the soft pool of light from the paraffin lamp on the table. The whole road had had gas installed some time ago but Hannah still preferred the gentle quality of lamplight.

She laid her head on her arms and watched the fire's last embers grow pale. It could be that he was motivated by concern for her and for the child. So difficult always to divine his motives for anything. It would certainly be easier for her to believe the best of him; to learn to trust him. And surely she needed to conserve her energy for the amount of work she had to pack into each day, rather than dissipate it in useless doubts and imagined hurts?

Hannah pushed herself to her feet again, turned down the lamp and went upstairs, missing the tread she knew had always creaked. She opened their door carefully, closed it as quietly behind her; turned.

Darrow lay with his back to her in the single bed, rolled into the quilt. His side of their bedclothes had been neatly pulled up and he had taken his pillow.

Hannah was caught by a sudden wave of nausea and leaned against the door. It was like a smack in the face, a rejection clear enough to take her breath. She stayed still for a few moments, then walked round the bed and slid into her own side, curled up in a ball and pulled the sheet over her head.

"Do you want me to make up that bed for you?" She spoke quietly next morning when he was almost ready to leave for work, having waited in vain for him to say something.

"Might as well." Darrow shrugged into his jacket, not looking at her. "I need sleep for my job. An' wi' you up an' down all night . . . an' your condition. For the time bein' any road." He picked up his snap tin. As he lifted it their eyes met and held briefly before his gaze slid away. "I'll be away then."

When he had gone Hannah was still for a moment,

374

looking at the hook on the back of the door where Darrow's jacket had been; where her father's had always hung. What had happened to Dada's jacket? Had Betsy given it to the rag and bone man? Hannah wished she had that old jacket now . . . she wanted to bury her face in it and cry. At least she had the bugle, safely wrapped in an old towel in the stairs cupboard. She held it for a little while, its contours pressed comfortingly against her hands, before refolding the towel about it and going to call Tom for his breakfast.

By late July Hannah was finding the hours spent standing in the shop followed by cooking most evenings gave her backache.

"Here, you'll find this a help." Harry came in early one morning with a high wooden stool. "I've covered the seat. If it suits I'll take it down to the shop for you."

"Harry, you're a sweetheart." Hannah hoisted herself onto it, laughing. "Perfect. How do I look?"

"You look lovely, Han. And that's the honest truth." Harry was suddenly serious. He put his hands on her shoulders and his eyes, once as brilliant as a summer sky, were bright now with a hint of tears. "You're beautiful, in every way. I only hope Darrow appreciates what he's got." He kissed her gently on the lips.

Hannah, taken by surprise, was suddenly close to tears herself. She put her arms around him and they were still for a moment, cheek against cheek. "Thank you, Harry dear. Thank you."

Florence brought a bag round to Incline Row the next day. Hannah was helping Tom with schoolwork and Darrow sat by the table reading the paper and smoking.

"For the baby."

She took out two cream flannelette nightgowns embroidered round the tucked bodice, two lacy knitted

375

coatees threaded at the neckline with narrow satin ribbon and two pairs of bootees. Hannah held up each garment to admire it.

"They're just beautiful, Flo. See, Tom. Darrow, aren't these lovely?" Darrow looked up briefly.

"Very smart. A right load of stuff up there already, though, enough for six."

"Come up and see, Flo." Tom followed them upstairs, always reluctant to be left alone with Darrow. The baby's layette was in the top drawer, covered with tissue paper; the women hung over it with happy faces and Tom was allowed to touch the tiny satin bonnet.

"What's it going to be, Tom, boy or girl?"

"Don't know, Aunt Flo." Tom smiled back shyly. "Won't a boy look a bit daft in this?" He pointed to the dainty ribbon-trimmed hat.

"They all wear such things at first," Hannah explained. "But if it's a boy I promise I'll have it in trousers soon as I can for you, okay?"

It was not a boy. Hannah came home mid-morning from the shop a couple of weeks later, knocking on Aunt Maggie's door on the way up Incline Row. Aunt Maggie came right away and at tea-time sent Tom for the midwife. Baby Jonet was born just after Florence rushed in from the shop having closed it fifteen minutes early, and half an hour before Darrow came home. Aunt Maggie said she would fry him a couple of eggs, inferring that he was lucky to get that.

"Would you like to hold her?" Hannah, triumphant, offered up the baby but he shook his head.

"I'll not just now, not in my work clothes. After I've washed mebbe."

But when he had washed and eaten his fried eggs he had gone straight to the club, it being Friday. Hannah had tried to excuse him to Florence.

"He doesn't know what to make of something this small, Flo. You know men."

Florence had nodded, not wanting to rub in salt. "Men usually take more interest a bit later, when their offspring are more than crying, eating and nappy-filling machines. Well, I think she's lovely right now." She cuddled the baby close. Watching, Hannah hoped that Harry would make his move soon so Flo could have the child of her own she longed for. She smiled.

"I'm glad you like her, because I want you and Harry for God parents."

12 Incline Row
August 16th 1927

My dear Joe,

The big news is that you have a beautiful little niece, born three days ago and weighing six pounds fifteen ounces. She has dark hair and is perfect in every way. I am writing whilst I have these few days away from the shop because once I am back in harness goodness knows how I shall find time! Tom is thrilled, he hangs over the basket the moment he comes indoors and could not get over how she closed her fist around his finger and hung on! He is helping me so much, carrying things up and down stairs and going to the shops on errands. And of course, Flo is a tower of strength. A really nice woman, Mrs Jacobi's cousin, is helping with the baking for a couple of weeks, and Flo has struck up a very good rapport with her. We also have a girl, Connie, behind the counter – Flo cannot be everywhere at once. I must hope these extra wages do not sink our little ship when it has done so well this summer.

Thank you so much for the two dollar notes in your last letter, Joe. You really mustn't send any more now. I'd rather you put it towards your ticket home for a visit.

I did smile when I read that about the handcart! Of course you did well with Mr Jacobi. I don't blame you a bit for trying the same thing in Pittsburgh – though I am certain it is a classier cart than the one you had here! Anyway, it sounds as though you are developing a certain flair for buying and selling ... maybe you too will have a shop one day, selling beautiful antiques rather than pastries like your sister.

Not much more news here. *Nain* is still well, she has crocheted Jonet (do you like your niece's name?) a beautiful pale blue shawl. Frank talks of emigrating – I do not think he will ever get work here again now he is branded as a militant. Aunt Maggie hates the thought of his going of course. After all, she has already lost one son; poor Trevor, every time I write to you I think of him and how you were best friends. The employment problem here does not improve, though there was some work done on the docks lately – two transporter-unloaders built. But a rolling mill at Margam works has been dismantled and shipped out to Australia – even our machinery is emigrating! Thank Heavens Darrow continues in work so far.

Now, dear Joe, I must finish, for Jonet is waiting for her tea and her lungs are excellent. I do wish that you could come for a visit. But it will happen one day, I know. Whichever of us has the ticket money available will buy it, all right? Do look after yourself, and I send you greetings from everyone here.

All my love
Hannah

She lay back against the pillow, the closely written sheets of paper slipping from her hand. Tired ... she certainly was tired; so far Jonet was waking every couple of hours. The baby's fist had freed itself from *Nain*'s shawl now and was furiously beating time to her demands for a feed. Hannah reached over to lift her from the basket.

"I heard you the first time. You've inherited your father's appetite, that's for sure." She winced as the eager little gums fastened on her nipple, then deliberately relaxed, watching her daughter's tiny fist kneading her breast. She had inherited Darrow's dark hair, too. It was quite hurtful that he had taken so little notice of her so far; scarcely more than a glance into the basket. But there was time yet; he would relax soon.

She was quickly up and working again, anxious about the ratio of wages to profit. It had been apparent for some months that without David Vaughan's loan the business would have folded. Jonet's birth had been a temporary holdup but now she must produce and sell more. She would have liked to let David know how vital this input had been to her survival; but any contact would reopen wounds for her and make it harder for her to accept her life as it was. She would thank him suitably, one day, when she returned his loan.

Harry had taken to calling into the shop; she suspected it was because he felt wrong about going to Number twelve in the evenings. One afternoon in November he came to look at a faulty tap. Hannah and Florence were making Christmas puddings and mincemeat and the kitchen was warmly redolent with seasonal, spicy aromas.

"This is the place to be on a cold winter's day." He bent to examine the sleeping Jonet under her pram hood. "Comin' on a treat, isn't she? What's her Dad think of her now?"

379

"He never says. I don't think he's ever really looked at her."

Hannah glanced up from her mixing then and blushed, as though her remark had been unintended. It had; and yet why should she not speak the truth to her two dearest friends? "He'll take more interest when she's a bit bigger I'm sure," she added, seeing Harry's worried frown. Dear Harry ... he sensed something was wrong somewhere, but felt helpless in the face of it. He could not know, but that was exactly how *she* felt.

"Maybe he wanted a boy." Florence tried to help. "Next time, perhaps – "

"There won't – " Hannah closed her lips abruptly and there was a small electric silence. Suddenly, frightened of what she had almost divulged, she plunged on. "There won't be enough suet, Flo. I'll ask Connie to fetch some from the Maypole while we're quiet in the shop."

She hurried through, closing the door behind her. Harry and Florence looked at one another for a second, then Harry began to unscrew the tap and his frown had deepened.

When Connie had gone for the suet Hannah stood alone in the shop, staring across the murky November street at the shops opposite, with gulls hunched gloomily on the roofs. She wanted to tell them; that Darrow had left her bed many months ago and showed no sign of ever returning; that something *had* gone wrong, or perhaps never had been right. That he was not helping with the rent now, saying he'd many calls on his wages and she would have paid the same whether he was there or no. And he would not say *what* calls. And that no effort on her part to talk problems through with him met with any success.

380

Hannah straightened her back. No; she did not want to tell them. There was nothing they could do and anyway she felt too ashamed. Of what she was uncertain, unless of her having failed somewhere, somehow. Just a year they had been married . . .

She lifted her chin, the square balanced chin she had inherited from Thomas Hywel, and went back to the kitchen to face Flo and Harry.

Throughout 1928 the depression deepened and nowhere more so than South Wales, but Hannah's community welded itself together ever more tenaciously. With the miracle of talking pictures arriving, pennies were somehow scraped together for a visit to the Electric – sometimes one parent and child would see half a film show then come out to allow the other parent and child to see the final part. Concerts, plays and sports fixtures were regularly organised, circuses continued to circulate, fairs were held on traditional dates and sites. Children, many barefoot, ragged and skinny, still played whip and top, tag, marbles, hopscotch, or if they were lucky, football with a pig's bladder blown up by an obliging father.

Men would still struggle to find the coppers for their beer and cigarettes on a Saturday night, even if they had to wheedle it out of their wives. They sought the comfort of their Labour and British Legion clubs, their allotments, the Tommy Talker bands with their local competitions, the choirs and the brass bands. There was usually a knot of unemployed men down on the corner of Incline Row, chatting or staring grim-faced towards the docks and the bay beyond. For women there was only the worry of how to feed and clothe their children on either short time or dole money. They were at this point given the vote if they were over twenty-one, but it seemed at the moment to be a meaningless victory. More important to have money for food than votes. You couldn't put votes in a child's belly when it rumbled with emptiness.

After a low of twenty-eight shillings a week in 1921 farm-workers had to accept a still wholly inadequate thirty-two and sixpence, but that could now be as much as the wages of a skilled industrial worker reduced to part-time. The steelworks, determined not to go under as was rumoured might happen to the great Dowlais plant to the north-east of Taibach, built a new medium plate mill, but several other of their mills were closed temporarily. Darrow Bates remained among the lucky ones, still in work as Christmas approached. Hannah's shop was also still open; more, had increased trade gradually throughout the year. Many women were bringing their own tins of dough to be baked in her ovens, Dai's bread regularly sold out before noon, and she had developed an instinct for providing food that would be popular. Jonet at sixteen months, staggering drunkenly about under everyone's feet, was regularly wheeled off by Harry for long walks which were to the benefit of all. With increased freedom from headaches, thanks to Hannah, Harry was turning his hand to a variety of odd jobs. Gus Mantle, his childhood friend from Eagle Street, took him to help on rural delivery rounds of meat and vegetables twice weekly. He was also teaching Harry to drive the little van, with some success, so that the narrow horizon of the past decade seemed finally to be broadening for him.

As Christmas drew near and her marriage was two years old, Hannah was forced to acknowledge that the gap between herself and Darrow Bates was widening. He still slept in the single bed, with Jonet's cot at its foot. She had simply not found the formula of words to ask him why, and he never brought up the subject. He rarely brought up any subject other than to complain about Tom being too slow with his homework, or taking up too much space at the table, or not going early enough to bed. Also, occasionally, objecting to the mess Hannah's cooking made in the kitchen, which provoked her beyond endurance.

"When I'm earning enough to confine my work to shop hours, Darrow, no one will be better pleased than I." Her tone had a decided edge. "Until that happy day I've no option but to cook whenever and *wherever* I can. If you would contribute more equally to our expenses I would feel less pressure to work all hours God sends," she could not help adding in bitter frustration.

"You'd do exactly as you please as always," he had snapped back and, snatching up his cap and his jacket, went out, slamming the back door so hard the kitchen window rattled.

Hannah leaned on the table, tears pricking her closed eyelids. The situation was slipping from her control. *What* was wrong? If she had no idea, how could she even begin to try to right it? Did he in fact dislike her? Why would he not allow them to talk about what was happening here like two responsible, caring adults? *What* was happening? For some time she had felt certain there was another woman involved; but had there been she would definitely have been told by now, probably by some well-meaning member of her family with whom her husband was unpopular. Hannah opened her eyes now, wide to prevent the tears from falling. Keep working; that was perhaps all she *could* do. She'd kept her head above water through this terrible time and must not sink now, Tom and Jonet depended on her.

Joe . . . she wished devoutly that she could talk with Joe. A letter should come soon though and that would cheer her up, and she'd find time over Christmas somehow, to reply. Meanwhile she would take advantage of the season to sell what she could. The Chamber of Trade were organising an Empire Christmas Shopping Week in an effort to stimulate business; WHEN WORMS ARE SCARCE THE HENS SCRATCH! and THE TOWN WILL MARCH FORWARD TO THE GOAL OF PROSPERITY read the slogans. For a week up to Christmas Eve events were being organised, empty shops used for displays. Hannah was entering the window display competition, one of many, and she and Florence had been up late last night sketching possible ideas.

No time then for tears. Take one day at a time and keep working. Hannah reached for the washed dried fruit and candied peel and shook them on to the scales.

They came second in section C (flour confectioners) window display and won one pound. So tired that she felt light-headed, Hannah gave Jonet's blanket a final tuck in and fell into bed. They would decide tomorrow what to do with the pound; the only object in view now was sleep. Darrow was still out, but there was a Christmas do at the Labour club and he may well be later than usual. Hannah cuddled her flannel-wrapped hot water bottle, closed her eyes and lost consciousness.

She had no idea what time it was when she felt a hand on her shoulder. Struggling through a dense fog of sleep, Hannah made to push it away, only to have her arm grasped and pulled roughly behind her. Forcing open her eyes she saw the silhouette of her husband alongside her in bed. He was breathing noisily and she smelled alcohol on his breath as he bent across her.

"Darrow?" She tried to see his face. "What . . . what is it?"

He made a sound that was almost a laugh, but not pleasant, and as her head cleared of sleep she knew he had drunk more than usual.

"What is it? It's this." He forced her hand down until it touched his hot, engorged penis. "Good, eh?"

Hannah lay still, too shocked to speak. When he pulled up her nightdress she drew in a sharp breath but was compliant. It was Christmas . . . this was his right. Muddled half-thoughts chased across her tired brain. She lifted her arms, trying to welcome him.

"Not that way. *This* way."

He was pushing at her; on to her side, over again until her face was pushed into the pillow.

"Please – Darrow – " Hannah arched her neck. "I can't breathe!"

He snatched the pillow away and pulling up her hips forced it under them, grunting with the exertion. Before she realised his intention he had forced apart her knees and reared above her, pushing himself into her dry vagina with such force that she gasped with pain. He gave a long, low sigh; Hannah felt his powerful thighs knocking hers further apart as he pushed so far into her that she thought she would split, and cried out in fear and pain.

"Stop, please! Darrow . . . stop this!'

But he went on, harder, faster. To get it over quickly she ceased to struggle then and, grasping the mattress hard with outstretched hands, turned her

385

head sideways and shut her eyes. He slammed into her again and again, the drink resulting not in impotence but in a merciless onslaught of violence on her. The noise woke Jonet who began to cry, as finally he shouted in a mindless orgasmic frenzy, grabbing at her hair to pull back her head before collapsing his hot slippery bulk on her bruised body.

"You *know* it's too soon to come back, Han. Serena's only ten days old for heaven's sake."

Florence stared worriedly at Hannah, manoeuvring the pram, and her two daughters into the kitchen behind the shop. Two-year-old Jonet bounced up and down, demanding her freedom, but the new baby slept as serenely as her name, just a delicate curve of cheek and minute nose visible inside the shawl crocheted by *Nain* Hywel before Jonet's birth.

"I'm fine." Hannah spoke briskly but her face was too white for September, and she leaned for a moment on the pram handle before lifting Jonet to the floor. "How's Edith doing – where is she now?"

"Gone over to the Walnut Tree with their order of pies." Florence tucked her godchild's dark hair off her face and kissed her, but Jonet pulled away and ran to the shop door, pushing it open again to enjoy the jangling bell. "She's shaping well for a fourteen-year-old if only she'll learn to keep her hands washed and her fingers out of the till."

"Mm-m." Hannah's reaction was so unusually noncommittal that Florence turned from running a pencil down the day's orders for a closer scrutiny. Hannah was gazing across the room with blank eyes, every line of face and body signalling trouble. Then she pulled a hand across her cheek and Florence saw it trembling and went at once to her.

"Tell me, then. There'll be no more work till you have. Here, sit down a minute, I'll make a drink."

"Don't be kind, Flo, or I'll bawl ..." Too late, tears flooded down Hannah's face and splashed onto the baby's pram cover. Under cover of the jangling shop bell and Jonet's busy monologue Florence asked bluntly: "Is it his nibs again?"

"About Tom," Hannah's voice was jerky. She mopped up the flood with impatient dabs. "Not quick enough over his reading, books messing up the table, and so on. That was it, last night. There was quite a scene."

"More than that to it, though, isn't there?" Florence said gently. Hannah nodded, stuffing away the damp handkerchief.

"You know there is." Watching Jonet pattering in and out of the door she began to talk fast, words tumbling out as had the tears a moment earlier, released by Florence's loving concern.

"I don't want to go on living with him, that's the truth of it! I've tried everything ... giving in to him, ignoring him, trying to reason with him. Tom – the way he is with Tom – that's the thing I won't put up with! I vowed to look after Tom and I'll not see him put down in his own home. Darrow's never properly paid his way, you know."

"I did guess. I'm so sorry, Han."

"When Serena was coming I said he *must* contribute more. We had rows about that. They're his children, after all. But he said, I'd no more to pay with him there than without. Then I said, just before she was born, that I'd be better off without, then – " Hannah stopped. Her voice was quiet when she continued slowly: "I thought he was going to hit me. I could see it in his eyes, and I just thought – will he kill the baby? But he held back. His fist uncurled, he stared hard at me, then went out. It was past midnight when he came back. I lay so still, hoping he would think I was asleep. He – "

She fell silent. Florence poured cups of tea and put one into Hannah's cold hand; Serena stirred and whimpered and she rocked the pram gently.

"Han. I've done Mam's bedroom out now, nice and fresh. You and the children could have it for a while. I know I planned lodgers, but there's time enough. More important for you to feel there's somewhere . . . a bolt-hole, you know?"

Hannah's hand went out. "Thank you, Flo. I shall remember."

She cleared her throat and her voice became business-like again. "So, we'll start work, shall we? How is that wretched oven behaving?"

She wrote to Joe again that evening. Darrow was at the club, his usual evening haunt; Tom was picking beans on the allotment and the babies were asleep – unusually for Serena, born it seemed with a faulty time clock and preferring to wake at dusk, feed all night and drop off at dawn. Hannah was still sapped by deadening lethargy, frequently falling asleep with her new daughter at the breast. The birth had been harder than Jonet's though Serena was smaller; a doll-sized six pounds. Two weeks early, pale-skinned and fragile, she was ridiculously unlike her dark, burly father. Tracing the curl of tiny ear and jawbone as she fed, Hannah believed that she saw instead a likeness to her own father, and hugged the thought as close as she did the small body cradled beneath her breast.

Writing to Joe had become a lifeline. The paper was always the same blue, special, used for no one but him; when Darrow had asked for some once to send a rare letter to his brother, she'd answered firmly that there were a few sheets of exercise book in the sideboard drawer. The letters had also become longer. Hannah was re-establishing closer ties with Joe by the only means open to her. Not easy ... there were things she would never tell him, never could, even had there been any point in her doing so. He could not help; only be angry and upset that she had been such a misguided fool and was paying the price for it.

Now Hannah sat down at the scrubbed table behind a pile of ironing, where once Joe had nightly set out his precious box of pebbles. The one he had given her at the allotment on her thirteenth birthday was kept at the back of the same drawer as the notepaper. She held it in her left hand as she began her letter. Gaslight gave a gentle sheen to the nut-brown wave falling across her brow, deepening shadows about eyes that had become more like Thomas Hywel's; watchful, reserved behind the dark sweep of lashes. The planes of her face were delicately brittle as though suddenly she might shatter into a thousand glittering shards. But under the surface tension lay Thomas Hywel's wiry spirit of endurance; a core of resilience only fully discovered by Hannah in these three years of marriage to Darrow Bates.

My Dear Joe,

She turned the pebble slowly in her palm and stared at the paper. Then, her mouth drawn suddenly into a thin line, she dipped her pen and words spilled black and close down the page.

I would give the world to turn the clock back, Joe.

Such a mistake – how could I not have seen? This so called sixth sense I'm supposed to have – why did it not warn me?

For a start there's Tom. Picks on him one minute, deriding him for being slow to do this or that. Then sometimes I see him touch Tom's hand, stroke his hair, and wonder if he is perhaps sincerely fond of him. He can be a charming man, but there are two sides to him; I found that out in the early days. I get nervous, never knowing which mood to expect! Now he says the sooner Tom leaves school the better, to find himself a job and not leech on us. That angers me as he has never been asked for, or offered, a penny piece towards Tom's maintenance. Nor towards mine. Joe, I've no idea where his wages go, but it is not into this house. I do sometimes wonder – there is something, well, strange.

Hard to think of you as a grown man, Joe, with a life quite separate from ours. I want to speak with my heart completely open about personal things, but always pull back in my letters for fear of shocking you. I did know true love once, Joe. I gave myself to my dear one, and it was a great joy. But he has gone. And sometimes I still long for him. I do care for my babies, truly; but they were conceived in a – violence, which was no part of love. Can you understand? I was driven to hide inside myself, for there is no other sanctuary for a wife. But I work with every ounce of physical strength and mental resolution to make money enough to free myself. Then, if I cannot force my husband to quit this house I shall take Tom and the girls and set up on our own – yes, and divorce him too if I can find the means! Does this sound perfectly terrible to you, Joe? I pray not. You must still remember me well enough to know that I am not a wicked woman, I think.

Come soon, *soon*, Joe, for I do need you.

Hannah put down the pen and stared at the furious scrawl, breathing hard. No other sound but the old mantelpiece clock and the settling of coals in the grate; turning Joe's pebble in her palm, the warm little room wrapped her round with memories. When Tom came in with his bag of runner beans, bright-faced from the chill autumn dusk she started, then smiled.

"Hello, Tom dear."

With a decisive movement she screwed up the letter and dropped it into the fire. Tom watched the pages curl and fragment, then looked at his sister with calm, enquiring eyes.

"Joe's letter. I messed it up, I'll do another. We'll have a bit of supper first, though, before Madam starts shouting for hers, eh?"

Later, with Tom cross-legged on the mat stringing beans, Hannah pulled open the blue notepaper again.

Dear Joe

Just a few minutes to begin this letter before Serena's feed. I do write more often than I used, funny isn't it? But it's the next best thing to talking to you. We're all well, the baby is filling out already and has quite a look of Dada – isn't that lovely? I've started back at the shop today, just for a little while, to run myself in gradually again. Flo has been wonderful and it's all going along nicely. Tom is quite a help now, he just picked beans for me to salt down. You'd not believe how tall he gets.

Harry has struck a bad patch with his headaches, I must find time to help him with them again. He and Flo went on a day trip to Cardiff and had a fine time. Oh, and a bit of good news about my ex-lodger, Mr Peplow, remember? I heard he had found work with a man who owns two pawn shops, repairing broken

jewellery for resale. I was pleased about that and
hope he stops hitting his poor wife now!

She usually tried to be in bed when Darrow came
back from the club, but had sat overlong at Joe's letter
and was cutting food for the snap box when she heard
the gate clang shut. He stood in the doorway, scowl-
ing at the light and filling the room as always with his
powerful presence. Hannah showed a polite smile
then bent over the bread again; when he brushed past
her, smelling of sharp night air, tobacco and beer, she
shrank into the smallest target, smelling danger also.
Unnerving, this breath-catching whiff of a threat that
could hang about him. He opened his hands to the
dying fire and spat, causing the embers to sizzle and
smoke.

"Bacon was nowt but fat today." He nodded at the
snap box. "Any more o' that brawn?"

Aware of the belligerent undertone, Hannah kept
her own voice neutral. "That was finished yesterday.
Shall I just put cheese then?"

"Just cheese then?" He mimicked in falsetto. "What
bloody good's 'just cheese' to get a man through a full
shift, eh? You tell me that, Miss Smart-Arse."

"It's what my Dad took as often as not. And we
both know how many do their shift on bread and
scrape these days."

She kept her eyes on the food, but felt Darrow
Bates' anger bloom towards her like a choking
vapour. Still hoping to avoid combat she added
quickly: "I'll bring another end of brawn from the
shop tomorrow if there's – "

"All I'm good for is it, scrag ends your bloody
customers leave?" He leaned forward and she
smelled the alcohol on his breath. A quick wave of

anger left her cheeks hot; slapping down the lid of his food box she pushed it across the table where it hit his knuckles.

"I can only spare the scrag end for those who won't pay for their food, Darrow. That shop is my livelihood – and the children's, since *you* won't support us!"

"You little vixen!"

Bates lurched nearer and Hannah saw the bold, congested features clearly under the lamp. The same second she heard the first tentative wail from upstairs; still staring at Bates, she had a sudden total recall of that baby's conception. Hannah had been reluctant to confront the memory of that night; the coming child was innocent and the pain of her begetting must be erased. Only now, with the fruit of her ordeal crying upstairs and the perpetrator of it reaching for her across the table, did the horror of last December's violation grip her again to knot her stomach with revulsion.

"Don't touch me." Her voice was cold and thin. "I'm not afraid of you. I have an offer from Florence to take the children and live in her house. I shall do that, unless you decide to behave in a more civilised fashion."

Hannah turned to go up to Serena. Bates gripped her shoulder, swung her round and hit her hard.

"You've got a bloody nerve, going whining to that old maid about me! I've a damn mind to – "

"What, Darrow?" Gripping the table whilst her head cleared from the blow, Hannah confronted him. "What will you do? Rape me again to prove you have the upper hand? You'll prove *nothing* but that you are no true man!"

His eyes were big and hot now and he was breathing hard, chest rising and falling fast under the striped flannel shirt. Hannah was torn between desire to run for safety and a fierce urge to strike back at this now dangerously hostile person, to tear at the black glossy hair and mark the olive skin with blood. In that second, she wanted to kill him. Every muscle tensed to spring at his throat and choke that loud breath from his body; to stamp on him, bruise and defile him as he had her. Quivering with intent, Hannah failed to hear the stairs door open.

"What's up, Han? I was asleep. The baby's cryin'."

Tom stood on the bottom stair. Hannah pushed herself upright, forced her trembling voice and body into a semblance of normality.

"Sorry, Tom; woke you, did we? It's nothing; back you go. I'm coming up to Serena now."

Tom went reluctantly. Hannah closed the stair door at once and as she did, her arm was gripped and she was pulled backwards.

"I could break your neck, you know that?"

So close; she saw the beads of sweat, the evening stubble darkening his jaw. She stifled fear and stared right back. When she was suddenly released Hannah almost lost her balance and fell over the fender, but gathered herself up to stand with legs braced, not taking her eyes from those of Darrow Bates.

"I'd sooner do that than rape you." The voice slurred a little and something, a look she'd not seen before, secretive and strangely coy, alerted her. Bates' eyes flickered away from her. "If you want to know, I don't fancy you and that's the truth of it."

Hannah continued to watch him intently. Her husband saw comprehension begin to dawn then; and again, his own eyes slid from hers. He turned to stir

394

the spent embers of coal, the flush on his cheekbones deepening.

She *had* known. Not *known* precisely, but sensed that there was a – difference, about him. Hannah's mind shot back and forth, slotting jigsaw memories into the emerging pattern of Darrow Bates' sexuality. She remembered the times of too violent passion that had not rung true, the times of being, she now saw, punished for not being what he craved.

Then she remembered the times he had, unaccountably, displayed tenderness towards Tom. Touching him, once playfully slapping his behind.

"Why did you marry me?" Hannah's voice was dry as a dead leaf. "*Why?*" She felt suddenly strong, now she knew. "You didn't want a woman, children. Was it just a cover-up of respectability you needed? Is that what I am? A legal cover-up for your illegal relationships with your men friends!"

He came for her again, but Hannah sprang away to put the table between them. She faced him across it. "No, Darrow! Not any more. And *I'll* tell *you* what we'll do now. You touch me one more time – or Tom – and I shan't hesitate to spread the word about what you are. I've really no idea if many men feel as you do; but I do know it's not something you'd like to have broadcast, quite apart from the danger of prosecution. No one will hear it from me, if you *leave us alone*. I shan't speak of this again unless you force me to. Is that clear?"

"Clear?" Bates' voice shook. Hannah smelled the pungent mix of rage and fear, saw it in the suffused features of the man she had three years ago pledged to love, honour and obey until death.

"There's just one thing clear to me, you Satan's whore." He hissed at her. "What they say is right!

You *are* a witch! Duckin' pond's best place for you! Bloody fool I was not to take note what was whispered round – in league with the devil and no fit wife for any man!"

He stopped for breath. In the harsh little silence Hannah noted that the baby had gone back to sleep. Her mind sharp and perfectly clear now, she picked up her shawl from the back of the chair, raised her arm and smacked Darrow Bates across the cheek. Then she was out of the door and walking fast in the smoky autumn night. Anywhere would do. As she went, covering the ground fast and numbed by a certain light-headedness, she actually felt herself smile at the memory of her husband's surprised face.

The numbness had worn off by the time she reached the mountain road. Pulling the familiar shawl tighter, Hannah felt cold and tired. She sat on a boulder under a little oak tree and tried to think coherently about the past hour, frowning and smoothing the shawl fringe over her knee with nervous fingers.

So much had changed, so fast. Looking down on the lights of the mill sheds Hannah struggled to sort out exactly *what* had changed. Not her husband; he had been born this way. Herself, then? No, no one changed, snap, just like that. But there had been something – a refusal to go along with a bad situation, an assertion that she intended to change that. Battle lines drawn? The worst thing would be a long fight with Darrow, physically and emotionally draining.

David Vaughan's image was suddenly with her, so real she could have touched him. "It's been so long without you." Her voice was lost in the rustle of crisping leaves. "Dear Lord, how I do still want you, my dearest."

She hugged herself, rocking to and fro for comfort. Sometimes she did become angry ... the waste of love, that was the worst of it. But Hannah would try then to be still; search her mind for the good things in her life and the love she *did* exchange, and refuse to give in to anger. For she had learned that in anger, or in vengefulness, she was vulnerable to – to – what?

To some unquiet spirit. Of that she had become certain. Certain too, that the ruined cottage near the Vaughan retreat was involved. So often she had wanted to return there, to face and come to terms with what she should discover. But time ran on. One day, though. One day, she would go back.

So; she knew this now about Darrow. But she was tied to him. A vixen appeared soundlessly in a silver bar of moonlight, paused to scent the motionless figure beneath the tree, and was gone.

A witch, he'd said. Her head came up. Right then, Darrow Bates; see how you like this! In a sudden frenzied reaction, Hannah knelt to scrabble up the damp earth. Kneading a chunk of it with her fingers she fashioned a small misshapen man.

"Now we shall see." Unpinning the brooch from her blouse, she jabbed the figure with the point of the bar – once, twice, on and on until there was nothing left and she was crying.

"A witch, a witch ... So, this is what witches do when they hate someone! Got it right, have I? Good! *Good*!"

It needed a supreme effort of will to go home, fearful of what she might find. Only the fact of the baby needing a feed had forced her back to Incline Row and to the discovery that she had not killed Darrow Bates. He was asleep, a big warm mound in the small

bed, snoring. Easing herself into her own bed to lie
flat and still, Hannah had reflected grimly that maybe
she had lacked the right incantation to go with the
doll-sticking. Perhaps she should give it some attention . . . when she was not so . . . dreadfully tired . . .

He seemed almost to fear her after that. There were
no scenes; not even when she went ahead and had the
new baby christened Serena, though he had earlier
promised to throw the font water over her if she
saddled his child with such a name. Cradling her
daughter as she came out into the tranquil light of St
Mary's churchyard after the ceremony, Hannah
looked over to the yew tree in the far corner. Two
figures stood beneath it; shadowy, but to her perfectly
distinct: Thomas Hywel and his grandmother, old
Nain Hywel. Each raised a hand and she sensed that
they were smiling.

Hannah smiled back, peace flooding her like a
golden tide. She held up the baby for them to see,
before they dissolved into the shadows. She studied
the face of her sleeping child. Serena was exactly the
right name for this small newcomer. The bitterness of
her conception had been washed away – this was to
be a beautiful life just starting and her father and *Nain*
Hywel knew it and gave it their blessing.

Darrow was interfering less in Hannah's life, coming back late from the club to eat the supper she'd left
out for him. And once Hannah had begun to relax a
little, she slept reasonably well again. A day at a time
. . . situations changed, nothing stayed the same. That
was the thing to remember.

Sadness would take her off guard at times, perhaps
seeing Harry and Florence laughing together. It

needed just a small push now for Harry to propose, Florence told her in strict confidence.

"So why not give him a push? He'd thank you for it, I promise. And you've the room at your place with your Mam gone – and *he's* still crammed in with Frank at Aunt Maggie's."

Florence hesitated, her warm brown eyes serious. "It's the headaches. He's not spelt it out, but they're what's stopping him, Han. I wanted to ask you – but with the new baby an' all it never seemed a good time. Will you help him? Like you used to? If he could lick the headaches he'd feel well, a *whole* man again I'm sure of it."

The words came in a rush, Florence colouring with the effort. Watching Serena feeding tranquilly at the breast Hannah felt for the words.

"It's not always straightforward, Flo. Power, if that's what we're calling it, isn't turned on and off at will. I think it just hasn't *been* there this last couple of years. Maybe I wasn't right for *it*, these last years. There's so much I don't know." Her perplexed gaze rested on her dearest friend; Florence nodded, her brow creased.

"Sometimes I want nothing but to let it all go – you can understand that, can't you? But like I said, the choice is not mine in the end. When breath is poured into my old bugle it has no choice but to make a noise – same thing!"

Hannah smiled then, the delicious smile that had drawn Florence so strongly on their first day at school. "To tell the truth, I've thought about it quite a bit the last couple of weeks ... since the christening. It's as if a little breath is being blown back into the bugle."

She was right. Tensions eased, channels reopened;

whatever the cause, when Hannah asked Harry round and laid her hands on his head there came the old remembered heat. She found the black hole and her thumbs drew out the pian, which emptied harmlessly into the ground. When the heat faded she had been first tired, then pleasantly energised. Harry's smile had been livelier, his eyes more confident when she hugged him, and said he was to come each week. Afterwards, when Tom was doing the work she'd set him at the end of the table and chewing his pencil as he always did, Hannah suddenly wanted to write to Joe again. She got out the blue paper, the pebble and settled down opposite Tom. Half an hour, just for herself and Joe.

12 Incline Row
Nov 4th 1928

Not a month since I last wrote, dear, but I really wanted to. And reading in the paper today about all that dreadful business with the Stock Market brought you bang to the front of my mind again. I do hope you are not affected, Joe. Probably not – I don't suppose you're well enough off yet to get into stocks and shares! But it does sound, well, *serious*.

Chapter Fifteen

1929–1939

There was no quick recovery in sight for South Wales. The giant Dowlais Steelworks had shut in 1929, a death blow for the collieries that had served it. Twelve thousand men were out of work at a stroke. The steelworkers of Port Talbot became nervous, what had happened at Dowlais could be repeated. The flow of young men emigrating abroad became a flood and Harry's brother, Frank, finally abandoned hope of ever working again locally, turned a deaf ear to his mother's pleas and left to join the Welsh colony in Patagonia. With him went two of his long-term friends and his cousin Gareth, Auntie Lil's youngest. After a suitably boisterous family send-off, those remaining settled down soberly to work again – and heartily grateful they were to *be* working. In 1931 there were over two and a half million who were not . . . the same year that dole and means test payments were planned to be cut by ten per cent by the second Labour government under Ramsay Macdonald, MP for Aberavan. When his cabinet not unnaturally protested, though none more violently than every man on the dole in the borough of Aberavan, Macdonald called a general election and successfully formed a new national government, boycotted nevertheless by the great majority of Labour members.

For Hannah there was no time for protests, for politics. In January 1933 she took a very reasonable lease on a small premises in a decent area of Swansea. Raven Road climbed a hill as did so much of Swansea. A hairdresser's, a cleaner's, a chemist, an antique shop and a bank, two grocers and a specialist pork butcher were opposite or on either side, with a row of well-preserved villas just above and a public library on the corner below. There were laburnums and sycamores and wide well-maintained pavements, and the mess made by seagulls was cleaned up regularly. The property had failed as a cafe but Hannah believed she knew why; and believed she could turn the business round by going more up-market. The city of Swansea was suffering in the Depression just as was her smaller neighbour across the bay, but there was a great deal of money there and Hannah had seen an opening. The unemployment figures now topped three million but she sensed that things were now so bad that they could only start to get better. She held her nose, and jumped.

> "To market to market
>   to buy a fat pig.
> Home again, home again,
>   jiggety – jig."

Serena shouted with delight, pedalling the air as Hannah swung her round and round. "More! More!"

"You're getting too big for me," Hannah protested, laughing herself. "Four next week! There now, *cariad*, settle down or you'll not want to sleep."

"She never does," said Jonet primly from where she was filling in a colouring book at the table. "When you've gone she sometimes gets out of bed to look through the window. And she talks to herself." She selected a blue crayon and covered her sky with careful lines, neat little features a study in composed concentration. Hannah gave Serena a last swing and set her down with a hearty kiss.

"Does she now? Well, that's not too terrible. So long as she doesn't disturb you." She ruffled her youngest daughter's hair, thick and corn-coloured as she recalled Harry's had once been. Sunshine-coloured, exactly right for a sunshine child.

Hannah wrestled with the continuous fear of loving Serena more than Jonet, remembering her own childhood with its sad certainty that Betsy preferred Joe to herself. So Jonet was praised and encouraged generously, cuddled one for one; though the response cooled as the child's nature developed the watchful detachment that had always confounded Hannah in Betsy. She leaned over Jonet now, touching the dark bob lightly – no ruffling this smooth head or Jonet would pull away, complaining of being "untidied".

"That's a lovely picture. How good you are at colouring."

"It's easy. You only have to keep inside the lines."

"Even so. Let's get you ready for bed then so there'll be time to read."

Serena sat on the rug to take off her shoes and socks, trying to whistle as Harry was teaching her. Jonet continued to colour. "I have to finish the sky first. I can read for myself now anyway, you heard Miss Lloyd say. I'm the best in the class."

"Indeed. You can read to us then, if you'd rather." Hannah was finding Jonet's industry in school slightly disconcerting.

"When Dad comes in. He likes to hear me, he's always saying."

Hannah frowned. No "always" about it, Darrow saw very little of either girl. But Jonet clearly longed for his attention and approval. Hannah's voice was sympathetic.

"He'll be late tonight, dear. But Tom should be here soon; if you're washed and ready by then he'd love to hear you."

"He'd probably not follow it." Jonet sounded dismissive. "Alice Tonks says he's stupid." She laid her crayons in their shallow tin with orderly precision before closing the lid and securing it with a rubber band.

"Alice Tonks is the stupid one if she says that!" A surge of anger flooded Hannah's cheeks. "And very cruel, too. I hope you told her so," she added sharply. "It's certainly not a remark I like to hear you repeat, Jonet, since you know perfectly well your Uncle Tom's the sweetest, kindest man in the world!"

"What about Uncle Joe?" Serena chipped in from the mat where she was now busy pushing the button of one shoestrap through the buttonhole of the other. "Is *he* sweet an' kind? When will he come to see us, Mam?"

The warmth of the child's question drained away Hannah's anger. "Both your uncles are just lovely, Serry. It can't be long now before Joe comes home, then you'll see for yourself."

She darted to catch Serena as her daughter got to her feet wearing the shoes now buttoned to each other, teetered a few steps and collapsed, laughing. "Dying to see you both I know he is. Next year he'll come for certain, you just see."

Later, lying in the dark that was cut by rays from the street lamp, Hannah stared sleepless into space. Next year. She must have them out of here by then, with room for Joe when finally he did come. Like rabbits in a hutch now; Tom downstairs again sleeping in the parlour, Darrow in regal isolation in the back bedroom, she and the girls crammed into this one, them in the double bed whilst she occupied the one Darrow had once used. That left just the kitchen for everything else that went on. She'd earned the right for them to live better these past few years and she must see to it that they did. Last year she had felt sufficiently confident to return David Vaughan's loan. With it went a simple note of thanks and a hope that all was well with him. After a fight with herself she had added a request for him not to reply, regretting that the moment it was posted; but knowing it was for the best.

The shop was making a decent profit now and the new cafe in Swansea had taken off nicely this summer, keeping Florence busy full-time. They had decided jointly what was needed and as usual were in accord; gradually, the pretty room with alcoved walls and circular tables clothed in immaculate napery was upgraded to the point when it became less a cafe and more a restaurant. There were plenty of businesses and shops in the vicinity to supply customers for early coffees, through lunches to afternoon and high teas, finishing at six-thirty. Harry, too, had begun to work part-time for her. He drove well now and was making a good job of orders and deliveries in a small white van, bought secondhand by Hannah at a knock-down price and good as new. And Tom ... pray God that Tom would complete his bakery apprenticeship without upset. Then she could hope to take him too on the payroll, to give him the confidence of knowing he could hold down a job as well as any man.

It had been a fight to help keep Tom's head high through his childhood, in the face of remarks like that repeated tonight by Jonet. Hannah knew well enough that for every one she could field and hurl back, he must must have been hit and hurt by more. But they were winning; he could read, write and cope with simple calculations. More, he was caring and generous-hearted to man and beast.

Not virtues to guarantee a comfortable life, though. Hannah's head turned sharply on the pillow. Take Darrow: single-minded concentration on his own welfare, complete disregard of the needs of others and a good peppering of luck was how he got by. Though she had squeezed him into as small an area of her life as she could – he lived more in the style of lodger now and paid his expenses – it remained too big. What point in moving to a better place if he was included in the baggage? She may well be able to prove grounds for divorce; but not without revealing dark corners of their lives that never should see daylight and could only pillory the family she'd fought so long to protect.

In the girls' bed Serena heaved into her favourite position, bottom up and knees drawn to her chest. Hannah smiled at the small hump beside Jonet's neat flatness; this child could cheer her even when fast asleep. She slid from bed to kneel by her daughters, listening to the soft breathing, touching a hand curled on the pillow.

Thank heaven he left them pretty well alone now, after she made *that* the clear alternative to her disclosing the truth of his sexual preferences. Stupid, he was. Hannah smiled as she returned to her bed, but no fond smile of love this time. If he wasn't too scared for his own skin to think straight he'd know that she would never willingly broadcast the truth about him, for the simple reason that he was the father of her children. Too much to lose. So, just pray that he'd not force the issue.

Joe had never been told. Countless times she had verged on it, longing for the release of the truth, the whole truth; always she drew back from setting down the naked words. Once read, it could never be retracted;

and she'd no business anyway burdening Joe with her problems, he must have plenty of his own. When he came home, perhaps . . . when they were face to face. She longed to hear his own story of the past years. His letters, still regular, must, like hers, leave much untold. And still no mention of a girl, ever. Plenty of time for that, though . . . when he came home maybe, back to his own kind.

Thoroughly restless now she left her bed again to stand by the window, staring past the gaslight to where the familiar shapes of the mills stood starkly surreal against the glow of a furnace. *He* would be back soon. Her stomach muscles would tighten, hearing the scullery latch, the heavy footfall; following his movements about the kitchen below as he would take out his supper, scrape the chair up to the table. Every tread counted on the stairs, breath held as he reached the last one. Always, Hannah imagined a hesitation there and froze, still as a corpse under her sheet until she heard him turn to his room and close the door. Her breath would be released then, knotted muscles loosen as she curled into her pillow and allowed her eyes to close.

It had not been without a fight, gaining even this small measure of freedom. Not because he wanted her, that time had long since gone – if indeed it had ever truly been so. No, the struggle had been because he was determined to impose his will on the relationship and on her. But she had faced him out in her threat to expose him if he laid a finger on any of them again; and whatever tactics he employed, the last step to call her bluff was never taken. Darrow Bates could not be certain he would win, only be sure of what he stood to lose, and so co-existed in an uncomfortable and unhappy state of enmity. Hannah worked and planned towards the day when the pattern would break, never allowing herself to consider that it might not. They had nothing in common but their daughters, and never would have now. She could divorce, but the trauma of such an action, the distress to those she loved, caused her to turn from this extremity. She would from time to time retreat into her dream of David Vaughan's arms about her in the velvet dark. Hard, then, to wake to find him gone and she alone to face another day.

No, not alone. There were her daughters, her business, Tom, Flo and Harry. Dear Harry, saving hard these last years to set up home with Flo, and their wedding day actually fixed at last for three weeks ahead. Very quiet, just close family with Hannah as matron of honour. The reception would be at Florence's home and Hannah herself had made the cake from an old recipe of *Nain* Hywel's. Florence had made her own dress, cream satin cut simply on the cross with a deep collar of antique cream lace she found on a market stall. They had been urged to stay with Harry's parents until they had found a place of their own; Aunt Maggie had seen every child go now but this last son and Hannah knew how she feared for Harry's health.

She pressed her brow to the cold window, thinking how closely Harry had always been woven into her own life ... and now to marry her dearest friend. She remembered back to the war; the bright flame that had been Harry, always fascinating to the child Hannah. How she had loved him, hung on his word and opinion, basked in his golden warmth. She never had ceased to love him; never would.

Her dreaming eyes focused on the gaslight spilling over the pavement where she had seen Dorothea on that eventful first night of the war; a lifetime away, and so strange a pattern. Should she have repudiated her

powers for good after the dreadful night of the shipwreck in the bay, with a lifeboatman badly injured on
her account? Coming to terms once more with the gift of
healing that always set her apart had been a long slow
road. But she *had* helped Harry; had felt the strength
surge to her fingers as she touched his head. Animals,
too, the affinity there closer, simpler, and she had
worked to good effect with the veterinary surgeon who
was understanding of her powers and happy to avail
his patients of them. But traces of fear remained for her.
It was all too easy to be misinterpreted, or to have the
power abused, as in her dealings with Webber. She
could not afford to be wrong again. So her small
successes with healing remained unobtrusive; Harry, of
course, Aunt Maggie's arthritic knee, the shoulder
troubling her baker, and a quite sensational improvement in the leg muscle of a handsome carthorse who
had been on the point of being destroyed by the vet.
Premonitions, rare anyway now, were ignored, she
wanted no more of them. What would be would be,
without meddling from her.

That woman, though ... seen only once that May
evening in the company of David Vaughan. The memory of the phantom on the hill remained uncannily clear.
Hannah felt that one day she would face it again, be it a
vision of the past or of the future, and that then she
might learn its purpose; or its need of her.

There should have been nothing different about the
next day yet it had a bad feel to it. Hannah worked
through the routine of shop and bakery, as tension
increased in an unforgiving band about her head, and
cycling back home her legs moved with leaden reluctance. She breathed deep to steady the thudding

heartbeats. A cup of tea, a quiet sit down; all she needed. Nothing wrong . . . nothing.

But now she was pedalling harder, past Incline Row to turn instead into the back lane. Tom should be home by now and would have made Jonet's tea. Was Darrow back?

She saw then that he was ahead of her. He reached their wicket gate as Tom came through it with the big bowl for carrying back the week's eggs from Carreg Farm. He made to step wide of Darrow but the man halted and spoke, touching the boy's shoulder.

Hannah registered the scene in sharp focus: a gate slat poking out of line; pale strokes of grass against slate walls; a trodden Woodbine packet; Darrow Bates' hand sliding over Tom's shoulder to rest on his hip.

Sound swelled and burst through her throat. Bates swung round as she lunged for his face and gripped the hand reaching to claw at him. "I will kill you!" Her voice was unrecognisable. He stared, shaken by the look on the face of his normally self-contained wife; by the hatred exposed in eyes entirely strange to him. He had her pinioned now, but as Hannah's expression gradually lost its savagery he released her, stepping back to put space between them. She drew a shuddering breath and shook her head to clear it.

"Tom – will you fetch those eggs then?" She even managed a shaky smile for him. "Good fellow."

Tom disappeared gratefully down the lane at a fast trot. Hannah turned from Bates and shaded her eyes for a moment. When she faced him again she was fully composed.

"I warned you never to touch him again."

"Good God, woman, I gave the lad no' but a pat." Confidence returning, Bates pushed open the gate and strode up the path, swinging his snap tin. Hannah watched him in silence before his image blurred and she clutched the gate, dizzy and nauseous.

That had not been *her*. Not her voice, not her rage. Another time, another place sifted up from the past – Taibach beach on a November dawn and herself kicking at the body of the drowned German sailor after the news of Dada's death. She could recall the violence of her fury; and afterwards the leaden cold that had seeped into every pore. As now . . .

She had been possessed. God, how cold she was. Taken over by the avenging rage of another soul. Whose?

"God, keep me safe. Show me how. Help me. Help me."

After a moment Hannah picked up her cycle and turned back down the lane to fetch Serena from Aunt Maggie's.

Somewhere in the small hours came the nightmare. Darrow Bates, wrapped round by flames and screaming. Herself watching, unable to move. Thrown violently from sleep by the ferocious reality of the dream, Hannah had stumbled to her bedroom door before she came to her senses. She stared down the dark staircase, clutching her dried out throat. Nothing. No sound, no fire. She tiptoed to her husband's door and could hear his regular breathing. Only a cruelly tormenting dream, then. But she did not close her eyes again, sitting stiff and chilled in the rocking chair with her shawl pulled about her until it was time to waken Tom and begin the day.

The girls were still upstairs when Darrow left. No word had passed between them since last evening's scene in the lane, and now he cleared his breakfast plate without looking up, washed the food down with sweet steaming tea and counted out change for tobacco and paper. Watching him, Hannah could not think it possible that he knew nothing of what filled her mind . . . of last night's fearful vision.

"What are you doing today?" She could hear how stupid the words sounded, how stilted her voice. He did not look at her, reaching for the jacket on the door hook.

"Doing? What's that supposed to mean?"

"I'm not sure." Hannah hesitated, nervous but desperate. "Only, I had a dream. A – "

"Christ, woman, if you've nowt better to clap on about than some daft dream – " He slammed the door hard behind him and was across the yard when Hannah reached him and pulled frantically at his sleeve.

"Darrow, you must listen! It was dreadful!"

Bates knocked away her hand and when she tried to get between him and the gate, pushed her roughly aside so that she stumbled into the rosemary bush. Always the scent of rosemary would bring back the sense of fear that choked her now as her husband threw his last words at her.

"I don't give a tinker's cuss for your damnfool dream. Nor for you, neither."

Then he was gone. Hannah stood, one hand crushing rosemary leaves against her skirt, until his footsteps faded to silence. She'd not done enough – not after so vivid, so terrible a premonition. She must follow him, into the mill if necessary!

"Mam? Will I be late for school?"

Seeing Jonet's face at the door, Hannah gave up. She'd sworn to ignore premonitions so why should this be different? Only make a fool of herself again; and anyway, she had tried. She hurried inside to make breakfast for the girls.

*

She was making up an order for Harry to take to Swansea when two millmen came into the shop and stood awkwardly, manhandling their greasy caps. One, Perc Trevelyan from Chapel Terrace, chewed on a plug of tobacco and his straggling moustache moved rhythmically from side to side.

Hannah knew right away. She set down the custard tart with care; smoothed her hair and cleared her throat. "What is it, Mr Trevelyan?" He was still recognisable as the big boy with sandy hair and warts two classes above her at school. Perc looked to his companion, a lantern-jawed Scot who had appeared in the town a decade ago, but, getting no help, swallowed nervously round his tobacco plug.

"Your man, Missus. Hurt bad."

Hannah was perfectly calm. "You want me to come, then?"

"Aye. Right bad burn, one inch flat got his throat." Perc choked a bit over the Scot's bald statement but Hannah took her jacket from the stand with steady fingers and spoke quietly to Eileen behind the counter.

"Put four more of the cinnamon apple on the tray and don't lose the order slip. And ask Harry to come to my house when he's finished, will you?"

She walked to the mill with a man either side, not hurrying because she knew beyond doubt that Darrow Bates was already dead. Perc made efforts to explain the accident, spitting out his tobacco for decency's sake.

"More accidents in Light Bar than anywhere . . . one inch flats c'n miss them guide bars easy. All a body can do then is drop the tongs an' jump clear, see? Done in no time at all, tanglin' wi'a red 'ot flat."

"Coiled round his throat like a bloody snake." The Scot would not spare her. Hannah saw how blue and calm the sky was, how colours were warming towards

413

autumn on the hills. A kestrel hovered somewhere near the quarry where Norman Madoc had fallen that hot July day in 1921. Twelve years ago, Joe was twenty-four last month. She would love to see Joe, now.

She would write; ask him to come home. Get a decent place with a room for Joe, and a bathroom. And a garden, bursting with so many herbs and flowers you would smell them a mile off. Windows to open wide, the sun streaming in. A lawn for her girls to play on. She'd earned the money, the *right*.

She was free. But she felt nothing; simply numbness.

As Hannah stood by her husband's open grave at the close of the burial service, she had a thought so terrible that she all but cried out. She had, in the dark recesses of her heart and certainly unacknowledged until now, wished two people dead in her life: Norman Madoc and Darrow Bates. They had both died. Not through natural causes but violently, before their time. Were her powers, then, capable of working for evil as for good? Had *she*, Hannah, the seeds of great evil in her?

God, help me. Please let this not be so.

She had told the girls the truth, as gently as was possible; that their father had had an accident at work. They received the news calmly enough and Hannah realised that his past neglect of them now helped to minimise their loss. He had taken little interest in either Jonet or Serena, and this had been hard for her to forgive. Jonet, especially, was always hoping he would ask how she was doing at school, or want her to read to him. But the last years he had been no more than a lodger, and when he was in the house had buried himself in his newspaper, failing in any way to enter into the life of the family: a non-father, a non-husband, a non-marriage.

Hannah had discovered that whilst she could not forgive his neglect of his daughters she could forgive him his troubled sexuality, despite the anguish it had caused her. If he had been born so, how could he help himself? More difficult was to divine why he had married her; married anyone. She tried to put it into the past once he was dead, but would find her thoughts circling him again and again. Had he sincerely wanted the home and family other men had? Had he been attracted to her in some way and believed he might make the arrangement work? Hannah, in the end, thought it more likely that he had used the family's normal respectability as a cover for his undeniable leanings towards his own sex. As a driven, tormented man she mourned him; as a husband and father she could not wish him back.

Tom gradually became more relaxed; for him, Darrow Bates had been a looming shadow over his home, even threatening his relationship with his beloved sister. Now, little by little, came back happy normality. He could play games with Janet and Sorry without being belittled for it, spread out his books, speak when he pleased. Tom, rising sixteen, was coping well with his apprenticeship to a master baker in the town, but Hannah still encouraged him to improve his reading and numeracy and Tom would do anything to please her. Slowly, a step at a time, he was at last acquiring a degree of confidence.

Aunt Maggie said little about Darrow's death. This in itself was unusual in a woman who enjoyed communicating, and Hannah was grateful for her reticence. The family had turned out for the funeral as a matter of course but lips had been tight when the mandatory regrets had been expressed. Harry had perhaps shed some small light to his mother on the shortcomings of

Hannah's husband and word had spread. Aunt Lil, at the family tea following the funeral, had sniffed and said, "I told you so," though Hannah had simply smiled in reply, and of course Aunt Lil had told her nothing and had appeared to approve entirely of Darrow Bates.

Harry and Florence went ahead with their planned wedding at Hannah's insistence.

"If you're sure, *cariad*," Florence said, probing Hannah's face with a worried gaze. "It's a bit soon."

"If I say so, then do it. No one knew better than you and Harry the way things were." Hannah gave Florence's arm a little shake. "And I'm dying to get you married, you silly goose, so don't you dare put it off."

It was a beautiful day, an aura of quiet joy and peace for once united the whole family. Harry had always been universally popular and his patent happiness after the long years of pain and defeat were voted well deserved and about time, too. Florence bloomed into beauty as she took Harry for better or for worse. "It had *better* be for better," she laughed as they cut the cake. "I've waited too long to put up with the worse, I'm in my thirties now don't forget!"

Kissing her, Hannah thought of the fresh start they both were making now. Thirty-one seemed a good enough age to make it.

It was early summer of 1939 when Joe said he was coming. With every letter Hannah had asked *when* was he coming; with every reply Joe had told her soon, as soon as he could afford to. At first it had been the cash that neither of them could afford, she ploughing back the profits into the Swansea restaurant, extending the Taibach shop kitchen, buying a home for which she must take out a mortgage; Joe, building up an antique business from nothing having survived the Depression in New York by various and occasionally questionable means in the company of Alex Cline. When both of them had the price of a ticket with some over, it was the time that was difficult to afford. Joe had learned how easily a man could go under if he took his eye off the ball for one minute, and he had no intention of doing that.

It was with an air of unreality that Hannah read in July of his boat ticket having been purchased. He had tried for August, his quiet month, but the berths were full and he had settled for September.

Now, war talk was intensifying to a clamour throughout Europe and Hannah read of the German army on the march again with deep disquiet. Not again; it *could* not be going to happen again? She looked at Tom, at Jonet and Serena, around the age now that she herself had been the last time a war had exploded into her life. The madness *must* be halted now, before another generation suffered such loss and grief as she remembered. But she tried to push fear away; she could do nothing to change events. She fastened instead on Joe's visit; so longed for, over so many years. She talked to her family about it and about the man they were about to meet – a close kinsman but so far unknown. Tom asked time and again for details of his brother and pored over the few snaps Joe had sent to find in them some likeness to himself.

"He used to carry you around," Hannah told him. "And you loved best to be pushed in his cart, your great treat." And she would laugh herself at the memory, and a lovely warmth would spread through her as she thought of how they would take Joe back into their home and hearts.

She looked round Morfa Cottage and tried to see it through his eyes. A long road had been travelled by both since the morning in 1921 when she had read his pathetic note of farewell; they had had nothing in the world then but their own strength. Now she had this lovely stone cottage on rising ground above the Margam Road – she was a home-owner, the impossible dream attained by her own efforts. Florence and Harry had moved straight into her Incline Row house and had made themselves a comfortable home there by *their* own efforts. No babies, yet; but there was still time Florence would say optimistically.

For Hannah it was a full and satisfying life and she was happy. She had everything she could ever have wished for, the bad times were behind her; the memory of Darrow's death had faded in seven years. Except just now and again, in the quiet reaches of the night, she would stretch out her hand and find no one there; and become painfully aware of the one thing she did not have . . . never would have now.

Joe did not come in September.

"I have to tell you that no such undertaking has been received, and that consequently this country is at war with Germany."

Hannah stayed by the wireless after she had switched off Neville Chamberlain's announcement. Jonet was upstairs doing her homework. Serena was in the garden picking mint for lunch and playing with Wedgewood the cat. Tom, who had had his usual Sunday lie-in, sat at the kitchen table staring into his cup of tea.

She turned and ran upstairs, shut her bedroom door and walked to the window like a blind woman, bumping hard into the dressing table. The fine Sunday morning was still there outside the open window but blurred now with tears. Serena still played with Wedgewood but now . . . what faced them all now?

Hannah looked out at the hill. And would Joe not

come? How could he safely cross the Atlantic? Sick angry disappointment seemed to choke her for a moment . . . all the talk, the preparations, only ten days off his sailing now. She *couldn't* not see Joe!

She put a hand over her eyes. Night after night as the date marked on the kitchen calendar drew nearer she had enacted conversations with Joe in her head. So much to tell him that she could tell no one else, like the facts she had unearthed about the woman on the hill. She had kept that to herself for six years now, waiting until she could tell Joe that she had seen a spirit of a woman dead since 1768, whose name was Rachel Hywel. You aren't the only one who has discovered ancestors, she'd teased him in her mind. I have actually *seen* what I am certain must have been a forbear of ours! She had tracked down the record of Rachel's marriage in St Mary's church after a wearying but determined search not long after Darrow's death, when she had been struggling to reassess her life. Now, everything was shelved . . . all must wait upon this new, dark struggle, perhaps for their very survival. This time, not Dada but Tom? Tom, so ill-equipped by nature to take part in any conflict. And this time Albert and Daisy's son, young Al, called soon perhaps to fight his father's countrymen.

Hannah rinsed her face and powdered her nose, combed her hair and went downstairs, the broadcast words of the Prime Minister still echoing round her head: "And that consequently this country is at war with Germany." Tom was sitting where she had left him, hands absently turning his teacup round and round. She put an arm about his shoulder and bent to lay her cheek against his.

"Don't start worrying about it, dear. Nothing will happen yet."

419

She went to the back door and looked across the garden, rich in blossoming colour. It was a lovely morning, mild and tranquil, hovering between summer and autumn. Hannah knew she would remember for a very long time every detail of the moment she had heard the Prime Minister's announcement. She looked down at her hands; Darrow Bates' wedding ring was still on the third finger of her left hand. She would have preferred to take it off but thought it unfair to the girls, so had bought herself a thickish antique circlet that all but obscured it. The skirt on which her hands rested was of navy cotton twill with white coin dots, flaring over her hips, its bodice had a white Peter Pan collar and white buttons to the waist, two breast pockets, and a white leather belt. Over the back of the chair by the table was draped her light-blue cardigan. She had taken it off earlier when she'd come in from pottering in the garden, dead-heading the second flush of roses and picking parsley to dry for sauces.

"That's it, then." Tom was looking at her when she turned and she smiled at him, hoping to lift the anxiety from his eyes. He was twenty-one in December; of military age.

Serena came in with Wedgewood tucked under her arm and laid mint on the table. "How's that, enough?"

Hannah smiled again, this time at her sunshine girl, her beloved, lovely daughter. "That's fine, Serry. Thanks."

"They've just said we're at war." Tom told her and Hannah knew by his voice the depth of his apprehension.

Serena's beautiful dark-blue eyes widened as she looked at her mother, and she began to stroke Wedgewood's head with rhythmic little strokes. "On the wireless?"

"Yes, love." Hannah wanted to hug her but instead got up and took the mint to the sink where she stripped off its leaves.

"It'll be all right, though, won't it?"

"Yes, Serry. I'm sure it will be all right. Only you may be asked to carry your gas mask to school. D'you want to go and let Jonet know? Maybe you should."

Chapter Sixteen

September 1940

Serena and Jonet sat either side of Hannah; Jonet in the tubular visitor's chair and Serena on Hannah's bed. Hannah lay uncomfortably propped on the pillows and hoped Serena wouldn't bounce about. She had a thumping headache and her cracked ribs made it painful to breathe, except shallowly, which Sister had said not to do for fear of pneumonia.

"I don't think you're allowed to sit on hospital beds," Jonet told her sister, who offered back a good-tempered smile.

"There's only one chair and you're on that, they'll not mind." She gave the bed a reassuring thump and Hannah winced. Penitent, Serena at once stroked her hand.

"Sorry, Mam. When do they say you can come home?"

"When they're satisfied my head isn't going to fall off. A couple of days, maybe." Hannah held the offending head which, after the collision with her garden wall, felt as though it might indeed shatter at a touch. "Are you doing your homework?"

"She's not." Jonet was blunt. "She's getting all behind and says she doesn't care." Her full little lips folded down with disapproval; Jonet could not conceive of anyone not caring about getting behind with school-work. She had come out on top in exams for five consecutive terms now and would have stayed up all night to conquer a new piece of work rather than have it lie blurred on the outskirts of total comprehension.

"It's only algebra," said Serena cheerfully. "I'll never understand it so it's silly to use up any more brain cells trying to. I might need them one day for something important."

Jonet gave the heavy sigh of one whose patience is stretched beyond endurance before turning her mind to practicalities – she didn't want to stay too long because of getting her own homework done. She would be taking School Certificate in two years and passing all her subjects at Merit or Distinction grade was the vital first step in her Plan to better herself – Jonet always thought of her Plan in capital letters because it was the most important thing in her life. This accident of her mother's was most inconvenient just as the new school year was getting under way. But it must be coped with; though why a barrage balloon being struck by lightning and bursting into flames over their roof had panicked a generally unflappable person into running full-tilt against the wall was beyond her. Now she got down to business, consulting a list she'd put in her blazer pocket.

"Tom says we're almost out of coal. And it's Auntie Maggie's birthday tomorrow."

"Ask him to order ten bags from Morgan's in Kenfig Street tomorrow, he'll deliver same day. Or you could help out by doing that yourself, love, you go right by the coalyard on the way to school. If Morgan pushes the bill through the door I'll settle it in a day or two. You'll find Aunt Maggie's birthday card ready on the sideboard, it's missed the post but you can take it round after school tomorrow. Tell her I'll be out soon and I will see her then."

Jonet, who had no wish to go into Morgan's dirty coalyard in her school clothes – in any clothes – decided to ask Tom to go anyway. He could be stupid some-times but surely ordering a few bags of coal wasn't beyond him. She didn't mind popping the card round to Aunt Maggie, she could say about Mam's ribs and the concussion and Aunt Maggie might feel sympathetic enough to give her sixpence. Awful, the way Mum kept them so low on pocket money, saying they had to learn the value of it was just an excuse for meanness. Veronica Fisher got a shilling and Jonet felt certain that her Dad didn't earn half as much as Mam. It was bad enough having no father to pass her little extras now and again. At least Mam hadn't pressed her to look for a Saturday job like some of the girls had, Jonet was grateful for that extra study time. On the other hand she was expected to pull her weight with house chores, with Mam working so hard. She didn't like her friends at High School to know that Mam had once been quite poor – it didn't help to know that almost everyone's Mam had been in the same boat. She also sometimes felt ashamed on account of Tom who she was sure everyone knew was only nineteen and sixpence to the pound, though this was definitely not an opinion to be voiced in Mam's presence without fear of swift retribution. Now she nodded, kept her thoughts to herself and consulted the list again.

"Auntie Flo says not to worry about anything, she's found some extra help. And Uncle's Harry's seeing about the decorating estimates for Swansea and the van repair. She's calling in on her way home, actually, to ask if Sister will let her see you for a minute. Oh, and I need a new pair of pumps; last term's pinched my toes something awful in netball today."

"I'll have them, mine are pinching me." Serena screwed up her elegant little nose with its dusting of summer freckles. Hannah smiled and reached for her bag.

"Make sure they're the right fit." She handed two half-crowns to Jonet. "And you can share the change with your sister."

A bell in the corridor was signalling the end of visiting time. Hannah gingerly hugged her daughters. "Take care now. I may be home tomorrow. Tell Tom . . ."

Afterwards the ward was very quiet. She closed her eyes. Who could have imagined . . . Such a storm, the first of autumn's gales, to break adrift so many balloons in the bay. The tearing crack of a cable against roof tiles echoed through her head. Eyes tight shut, but still she saw the lightning, saw it touch and ignite the balloon directly overhead, remembered flames falling like rain and the fear that engulfed her at the sight.

Hannah forced open her eyes to escape back to the safety of the ward. But escape was impossible, the fear was too recent. The memory of it soaked her now as she lay neat and tidy with the nursing auxiliary pushing the tea trolley up past the old lady who kept asking for her teeth back.

A fool, to run like that. No real danger, nothing but a few broken tiles and a mess of charred fragments about the garden. But the fear had had the power of an old remembered nightmare. It had sent her flying down the stairs to tear open the door and pitch down the steps, pick herself up and run blindly into the wall extended by Tom to shelter her garden from the offshore wind. The storm had seized and buffeted her and she had slid to the ground and buried her face in her arms to shut out the sight.

Hannah accepted the cup of stewed sweet tea but left it skinning over. Not the best of years, so far. The winter had been appalling; frosts more severe than she could recall and snow blown into deep drifts by a wicked easterly that had made it impossible to carry on life save in the most basic terms. The Swansea restaurant had been closed for two days because Florence could find no way to get there, and deliveries were impossible. The foul weather had run through to April, crescendoing in hail-stones, by which time Hannah had had more than enough of trying to cycle to and from the shop and was exhausted. Evenings she spent filling in forms once she was licenced by the Ministry of Food, and as daylight increased, converting what was suitable of the garden to vegetables. As the Battle of Britain got under way she had begun to think seriously about air-raid precautions. Sam Warburton told her how the steelworks had solved the problem by sinking huge boilers into the damp morfa and filling them with seats. She thought harder when the docks were bombed; rushing to her bedroom window in the June dawn Hannah had seen the planes dive low over Taibach before climbing steeply over Margam mountain behind her. In July, the sirens had woken them so often that sometimes it scarcely seemed worth going to bed and locals agreed that they must be on a flight path to other targets. Jonet and Serena had become progressively more tired, more difficult to waken for school. Hannah had put her name down for an Anderson Shelter and meanwhile they made do with what protection the kitchen table could offer.

Then there was rationing; but that worked for her, not just against her. People were eating out more often to eke out food scarcities and as more items were rationed or disappeared altogether, the more she believed that would happen. But the paperwork seemed endless, like the shortages. The varieties of pastries and cakes they had been offering this time last year had diminished month by month and were now boringly narrow and denied the slightest sniff of extravagance. The types of bread were also restricted much to Tom's disgust; he had been quite getting into his stride with different flours as his confidence as a baker had grown under Hannah's guidance. Now they had simply flour. But women queued daily for whatever was on their shelves and the pretty little cafe she had adjoining the shop – a chemist's until old Mr Martin's retirement – was happily placed for women wishing to take the weight off their feet for a few minutes during the arduous business that was wartime shopping.

Taibach had quickly adapted to the needs of war for a second time. Full employment, good wages, long hours; blackout, shortages, separations, ARP patrols, the Home Guard, collections to buy a spitfire . . . Hannah smiled tiredly. Her daughters now took their money to school for National Savings stamps as she and Joe had done a generation ago. Just as well she never had time to feel depressed about the world seeming to have learned nothing; her days did not allow for luxuries, they were too crammed with practicalities. Only now and then, did Hannah miss a close helpmate, a loving companion. But she had so much; and no one could have everything.

When Florence called she was still lying almost hidden under the stiff white coverlet, staring wide-eyed at the ceiling.

"Well, then." Florence set down two brown paper bags on the locker and touched her lips to Hannah's cheek. "What on earth have you been up to? Falling about the garden in the middle of the night, Tom said. Because of the barrage balloons. So what's your story? If you wanted a few days off you could afford to go somewhere that does better food." She pulled a face at the smell drifting from the kitchens and opened out one of the paper bags. "Try these bakewell tarts. You look as if you need something in your stomach."

Hannah had a nibble to please Florence, discovered that she was hungry and began to eat.

"Lovely. Thanks, Flo." Florence watched the tart disappear with a satisfied nod and produced a second, which Hannah also ate. Her dark glossy hair, whose braided abundance Hannah had so admired in childhood, was now rolled and pinned in a horseshoe shape about her broad-cheeked handsome face. She had lately learned to pluck her thick brows so that they arched to give a look of witty surprise and matched her lips, which seemed always to be on the point of smiling at a secret joke.

Hannah finished the second tart and flicked a crumb off the counterpane. "Well; that's done for my supper in a big way! Whose batch was that, Flo? They were splendid."

"Hilda's. Not bad, eh? And now, answer my question because that firebrand ward sister could throw me out at any moment. What happened and how are you?"

"I simply panicked, Flo, don't ask me why." Hannah picked at Flo's handbag, embarrassed. She was reluctant to lie but was uncertain herself of the truth. "I was half asleep and obviously not in possession of my wits. I behaved like a total idiot. Fell down the steps and banged up against Tom's lovely wall."

"And the damage?" Florence pressed.

"A couple of bruised ribs and a touch of concussion. I'll be out of here tomorrow if I pass muster at morning inspection, and back at work the day after."

"That you'll not." Florence was brisk. "Show your face within the week and you'll be sent packing. What about the girls, are they okay? Shall we give Tom a bit of time off to do extra at home for a few days?"

"Not necessary, truly. The three of them will pull together fine and I'll soon be fit as a fiddle. Go now while you still have your head, sister's looking ominous."

"I did see." Florence settled her hat and drew on her gloves. "There's apple and cinnamon slices in the other bag, eat them while they're fresh. Harry sends love. And don't fret about a thing. The business won't collapse I promise."

She was at the foot of the bed when she turned. "Oh yes, I heard David Vaughan's home. His mother's quite ill apparently. I'll keep my eyes open for him though I doubt I'd recognise him if I fell over him after all these years."

Hannah sat on a bench in the arcaded walk outside her ward. Tom was coming for her after tea and she had been strolling up and down to organise her legs, still a touch unsteady. The gentle September sunshine was blissful after the ward and she was reluctant to leave the open view of chequered blue hills under a billowing sky. Barrage balloons floated like children's playthings over the steelworks; shining silver, comically jumbo-esque and benign. Hannah frowned.

She must never do that again . . . never be so afraid that she lost all sense of reason. A few roof tiles, Tom said, and a corner knocked off the chimney by the steel cable. Nothing really. Several houses had suffered worse. Just be grateful; not to be in the flight path of the air battles being fought daily over the south coast.

So different from last time. Hannah stared at a barrage balloon that seemed to hang over her father's old workplace. What would *he* say now, knowing it had all been for nothing, all to do over again? A year ago they'd said, "It will be all over by Christmas"; "We're

going to hang out the washing on the Seigfreid Line".
That was exactly what Dada, Harry, all of them had said
when it had started before. They'd been so confident; no
one could have dreamed then of the four years of
carnage and misery that had lain ahead.

The ranks of barrage balloons defending Swansea
Bay swayed back and forth on their moorings, gently
protective of her now. Could anything stop the Germans this time? Had they suffered and bled, Harry's
generation of young men, Dada's generation of older
ones, only to have the land for which they'd died finally
overwhelmed by the same enemy? After Dunkirk,
could anything halt them?

A plane raced over the town to curve up and away
over the hill. One had crashed nearby in June, killing
two of its three crew; at this moment, Hannah knew,
boys only months out of school were patrolling in their
little Spitfires to take on everything the enemy could
throw at them ... the last line of defence. Port Talbot
was busy now raising money for a Spitfire as were
towns throughout the land. But now the enemy's tactics
were changing and Aunt Maggie had lately read
Hannah an horrific report in a letter from Emily of a
massive raid that had laid waste London's dockland.

Not in trenches this time, then. Now young men were
falling from the sky in flames and cities were front line
targets. Flo and Harry had a ten-year-old evacuee from
Plymouth, a dark-haired skinny little boy called Raymond and more were scattered about, wetting their
beds and learning good Welsh swearwords. Airmen
from the camp on Stormy Down, looking almost young
enough still to be in short trousers were filtering into the
town, a few already had girls to take to the Walnut Tree
for a port and lemon, or to the Electric to see the newest
Gary Cooper, to sit in the back row and whisper,

holding hands. Local boys were thinning out. Some had not come back from Dunkirk.

And Tom had gone for his medical last week. She got up and began to pace the corridor again. How could they take Tom? She'd seen some of the troops stationed at Margam Castle doing extremely rigorous training in a field – Tom might not manage that. But maybe in the Catering Corps, doing what he knew . . . he was a first class baker after all.

Hannah turned and started back towards the ward, feeling tired; this was not the day to attempt to put the world to rights. A man in Air Force blue was walking in her direction and she moved nearer the corridor wall, tightening the sash of her blue velvet dressing robe. They were a few paces apart when she faltered and the breath stopped in her throat. Her immobile figure caused the man to look up; he halted, brows lowered over shocked brilliant eyes.

"You. Hannah?"

Her eyes closed for a second and she was aware of her knees starting to buckle. At once his arm was under hers, hand gripping her elbow. He half carried her to the next bench and lowered her onto it, chafing her hand between his as she sat with head down, feeling as though she had been kicked in the stomach.

"Are you ill? Shall I call a nurse?"

She looked up then and saw only David Vaughan's face. There was nothing in the world at that moment but the dark lantern-jawed features seen in her memory for fourteen years; eyes deep and vivid as she recalled, nose with the narrow bridge, long sensuous mouth. A scar on the chin had not been there before and the cropped auburn curls had receded to form a deep vee above the broad forehead. Now she saw there was grey round the

431

hairline; two lines between the heavy brows and more fanning the skin of his temples.

"Hannah?" He gave her arm a tiny shake. She smiled then, a tremulous curve of lips, and pressed the hand still gripping her.

"I'm fine. Simply very surprised." He smiled, too, at that and now she saw his brow bead with sweat. She waited to collect herself because the urge to kiss his lips, to wipe the tell-tale sign of weakness from his brow, was shockingly strong. Nothing had changed for her. She loved him as achingly, as deeply as on that last night fourteen years ago, running up Incline Row with tears scalding her cheeks after their goodbyes.

David Vaughan saw a fine-boned delicately beautiful woman, which was precisely how he had remembered her. There were shadows under the grey eyes and those eyes were tired. He wanted badly to gather her up, to stroke her cheeks and brow, her loosely waved nut brown hair . . . to kiss in gentle salute the soft pale lips. He wanted to lie down with Hannah Hywel, to love her and then to sleep for hours, for days and nights in her protective arms.

They searched one another's faces; began to speak, halted, smiled foolishly. Hannah saw the pilot's wings on his uniform . . . a brittle weariness behind the eyes. His second war. One too many for a man in his mid-forties.

"Why?" She said with sudden directness. "Why, David?"

"Because it's there." He made no attempt to misunderstand her. "Someone has to do it and I can do it, and I can do it well. Leave that for now. What are you doing here?"

She told him, making light of it, almost a joke. "Now

432

how do *you* come to be here? Oh, you're visiting your mother?"

"No, no. She's ill right enough, but in that nursing home on the Baglan Road. This was a cousin I was visiting, not seen him for years and he's just back from the east with a dose of malaria." He stroked her hand with a long finger. "I've thought so often, Hannah, wanted to write; only you'd said not to. I've been back twice; each time . . . well . . ." He picked up her fingers, gathered them into the palm of his hand. "I can only hope now that you're happy. It's amazingly good to see you – you look wonderful."

"I'm always at my best with a bruised cheek and my hair in rats tails," Hannah agreed. They smiled at one another, then began to laugh quietly with the pleasure of meeting. A nurse came from the nearest ward. Hannah sobered up and got to her feet.

"I have to go, I'm being discharged in a couple of hours, all being well."

"May I wait and take you home?"

He looked so set back when she shook her head that she added on an impulse, "Tom's ordered a taxi, he'd be disappointed."

"But I *will* see you?"

Pushing her hands deep into the pockets of her robe she said, "You're seeing me now, aren't you?" Now she smiled, but he was still anxious.

"Properly, I mean. To talk; so much I'd like to know."

She hesitated, then said slowly. "Very well, if you really want that. The day after tomorrow, perhaps, around seven-thirty?"

David Vaughan's face cleared again and he looked for a moment, a much younger man. He raised an eyebrow. "Your husband? He'd not object?"

"He died seven years ago, David," she said. "Have

you something to write my address on?" As she scribbled he watched her closely.

"Hannah, I don't know what to say. Except, will you have supper with me? And that I wish it was the day after tomorrow right now."

"Time will arrange that," she said with simple irony. She offered her hand, for the pleasure of touching his again. When he bent to kiss her cheek she was startled, and hurried back to her ward feeling its imprint hot on her skin. Glancing across before she pushed through the swing doors she saw that he was still there, watching.

"I thought we'd go to Porthcawl, there's this place that does a half-decent steak."

He drove fast, the Riley purring along the coast road in the early autumn dusk with slitted headlamps finding out an occasional rabbit. Hannah was quiet; so much to say, years of ground to be covered, yet now there seemed no urgency. She had been assailed by such a gamut of emotions earlier . . . excitement, fear, anticipation, impatience with herself for feeling *anything* – certainly for allowing David Vaughan to impinge on her safe and ordered life to any degree.

"Can you tell me how far away you're stationed, David? And when you're due back?"

"I've got five days' compassionate – three actually but I'd forty-eight hours due from way back and thought I'd tack it on before I lost it altogether." He lit a cigarette with one hand and she saw the tiny light reflected in his eyes. "I'm stationed about an hour's drive due west on the coast – when I can find the petrol to drive anywhere! It's far longer by rail. Coastal Command; too long in the tooth for Fighter Command, alas. But there's plenty going on."

"I can imagine." She could not of course, with only a

434

rough idea of what Coastal Command did. He reached over and lifted one of her hands to rest it on his thigh. Hannah swallowed and forced out the question that must be asked. "Are you still married?"

David Vaughan covered the hand with his own. She knew the answer of course. "Things much the same, I'm afraid." His voice was neutral. "Julia's ill a fair bit, days in bed here and there. She doesn't get out much ... counts on me to keep her in touch."

"So how did you – well, you must have volunteered."

"Yes." Now he sounded grimly humorous. "An opportunity not to be missed."

"That sounds cruel, David." It *was* cruel. Hannah tried to withdraw the hand warming between his thigh and his palm but he pressed it more fimly into the smooth barathea suiting. He swung the Riley into the hotel forecourt, parked and turned to face her.

"It does, doesn't it? Maybe it is. But I serve out my time year in, year out, Hannah. When a chance of parole comes along I'd be less than human if I didn't grab it with both hands. Quite apart from my natural inclination to settle with the bloody Huns. I've left her well looked after, you know; the best of everything for Julia. And for me."

He cupped Hannah's chin and stared into her eyes, before kissing her hard and sweet, full on the mouth. "For me, the chance I'd thought was gone for good. Christ, Hannah, you have no idea ..."

He bent his head again but Hannah turned hers away this time, shaken by the first meeting of their lips after so many years of dreams. "No please, David."

He breathed a rueful, "Sorry" as she was retrieved by the silhouetted bulk of the commissionaire coughing tactfully before he opened her door.

"What a handsome couple we make." David sat back in his chair to admire her. "You're like a good wine, Hannah. Every year improves you."

She tried to look suitably modest but succeeded only in blushing. The pleated dress of lavender crepe became her, she knew, as did the creamy pearls she'd bought last year with money Joe had sent for her birthday. She was doing well enough now to indulge herself sometimes; the days were past when the children or the business swallowed every spare pound. Her lavender court shoes of soft suede, the small veiled hat tilted at exactly the most fetching angle over shining nut-brown waves, the delicate pearl drop earrings, spoke of a woman who valued herself. But now she blushed like a gauche adolescent, eyeing David Vaughan with some severity over the rim of her glass.

"Never mind the flannel. Is this hotel the centre of a black market ring? It has absolutely no business serving such a meal in the middle of the war. I should know!"

"I phoned them," he admitted. "Forbade them bring a dried egg or an austerity sausage within hailing distance tonight. A very special lady I told them, and great efforts were called for."

He poured more coffee, refilled his own cup and lit them both a cigarette. They had a corner table under a soft amber light, with only two other couples left at the dozen tables in the quiet, high-ceilinged room. Hannah recalled another supper *a deux* in another war . . . and afterwards, two young lovers in the moonlit grass on Primrose Hill.

"Do you remember August 1918, David?" she asked suddenly.

He screwed up his face in a show of concentration. "Any particular bit?" he hedged. Hannah looked pained.

"Actually, yes. But don't wear out your brain cells. You're only a man after all and cannot be expected to recall boring incidents that seem overly important to silly women. Tell me instead about your job – or is that listed as careless talk? We've chattered our way through dinner and you've not mentioned it."

"The last thing a chap on leave wants to talk about is his job. It's simply a case of doing our damnest to keep U-boats off our shipping. I've only lately come down here; before that I was further north, liaising for the Canadian training scheme. There were efforts made initially to second me to the Air Ministry as an air transport advisor, but I resisted them like hell. Now we've lost our toe-hold in Europe I tend to think transport's not top priority. But keeping the western approaches clear is, and at this point we're desperate enough for pilots to include anyone out of a wheel-chair."

"Of course." Hannah looked serious now. "And your own business, you can shelve that for the duration?"

"Sure, no one's indispensable. And it's been going quite a while now, the initial air freight business expanded to include passenger schedules and it welded together pretty well. There's a good long term bunch running it, even allowing for those of us busy over here." He drained his coffee cup. "What say we make tracks? Does Cinders have to be in by midnight?"

"Before that, David. My daughters keep a close eye on me. And I'm still slightly convalescent, remember?"

It was raining as they made for the car, Hannah having bestowed a radiant smile of thanks on the impressive Gallic head waiter and David slipping a discreet note into an even more discreetly ready hand. She gave a tiny shiver in the first chill of autumn after the long weeks of hot dry weather and he laid a cream cashmere rug over her knees and held her for a moment, so that his warmth permeated the delicate fabric of her dress and jacket.

"That better, sweetheart?"

She was motionless in his arms as he stroked her face, touched her hair. A beautiful languor overcame her as his hands, his warmth, relaxed her in body and mind as she had not been relaxed for years.

"Let's get out of here." His voice was low as he eased back in the seat. He started the Riley and Hannah closed her eyes, just for now not caring where they went provided it was together. The car purred away into the night and she felt safe, cocooned, whilst aware on another level that the sense of security was entirely spurious. Where was security, flying through the rain in an expensive car with an Air Force officer of long and hopelessly romantic association? She recalled the child on a railway platform to see her cousin off to war so long ago, accidently prodded by a young man's umbrella. All these years on, and she could know him scarcely more now than she had then; almost all of their lives had been spent apart save for a few very brief glimpses when their paths temporarily had come together.

More than glimpses, though. Twice they had coupled, became one entity. How could they remain strangers after that? Hannah remembered as clearly as yesterday how it had been with David Vaughan inside her, moving further, with beautiful inevitability into the warm dark core of her until he reached her very heart and centre.

He had a wife. She had had a husband. Two separate lives, hopes, dreams, fears. But no, they could never be strangers after those times. And now she wanted that again, felt desire for him spread in liquid warmth across her stomach. Shocked, Hannah opened her eyes and realised he was speaking.

"So there'll be no one there. Won't you come; I could make you an – Ovaltine? Or something?"

She had to laugh then, thinking of David making her Ovaltine when nothing could be further from his mind; when making love was his urgent goal as she knew perfectly well. As it was hers, that was the appalling fact. It was to this they were reduced by their mutual passion, and there was not a thing to be done about it.

"David, whether there's anyone there or not is immaterial and you know it. Anyway, there must be someone; a servant? I know the size of your family home! It would become common knowledge then that I'd visited you. I cannot have that, I've two daughters to hear it. Please, understand that coming to your home is not possible."

"There's a war on ... doesn't that change all these confounded rules?" He sounded obstinate and Hannah remembered how used he was to ordering things the way he wanted them.

"Not my rules. Not for my family. I'm sorry."

He drew into a lane off the main road and sat despairingly, staring into the blackness. "Hannah ..."

"Don't try wheedling me round," she warned. Suddenly she saw the ridiculousness of it all – two middle-aged people acting like lovestruck children and desperately frustrated because they couldn't find a way to go to bed together. She smiled broadly; choked back a laugh, which made her aching rib cage hurt more. David heard that and turned, angry.

"Bloody warped sense of humour!"

Hannah laughed outright, putting her hand on his leg. "Darling, you're just like a man, honestly."

"That could be because I am one." His leg was stiffly

439

unforgiving under her hand. "I'll drive you home, then, if that's what you want." She laughed again at the absurdity of his being so utterly normal in his reactions. He stared at her then his mouth began to curve. "A madam. A tantalising madam, is what you are." Laughing himself now he shook her, but gently, before covering her mouth with his. It was a while later, when he had unbuttoned her dress to kiss her breasts, that Hannah pulled herself back to reality.

"David; you *have* to take me home now. It's been lovely, but we'll spoil it if we – I must go." She removed his hands and kissed them lightly. "If you want, you can call me tomorrow night – we can talk a little."

He watched her tidy herself up, then with a sigh of resignation switched on the light for her to comb her hair and put on her hat. "I'll do that, phone you. Latish, when I've been to the nursing home?"

"Fine." She switched off the light and they smiled at one another in the dark. David adjusted the brim of her hat a fraction and handed her her gloves.

"Perfect. No one would guess you've been touched." He kissed the tip of her nose, ran fingers through his tousled hair and started the car.

"You knew him when you were *my* age?" Jonet looked at her closely as though trying to imagine how on earth her mother had ever been thirteen.

"Well, slightly. He'd pushed me off a bench with his umbrella. By accident, of course. I was seeing your Uncle Harry off at the station."

"Off where?" Jonet always wanted to know precise details. She sipped her hot milk delicately, sitting up in bed. In the other bed, Serena made tiny puffing sounds in her sleep.

"To war, darling. The whole family was there, we

filled up the platform. Harry was the first of us to go and it was very upsetting. But rather, well thrilling, too."

Hannah sat at the bottom of the bed fiddling with the strap of Jonet's gas mask case hung over the rail. She felt tired and excited together, and nervous of Jonet's interrogation being over thorough. Not that she had committed any misdemeanor. So, why did it feel as though she had?

"Come on then, if you're finished." She took the empty glass and began to put rags into her daughter's hair, rolling under eight silky segments and tying them with firm little bows. In the morning they would brush out into the smooth pageboy that Jonet so admired on Joan Crawford, belling prettily about her neck. Once it had grown a fraction too long and Miss Crow, the science mistress, had mortified Jonet before the whole of Form IVa by tying it back with a bootlace. Jonet had never been held up to ridicule before and stayed white-faced at home next day, having told Hannah about a really bad pain she had on and off in her back. Now she took enormous care never to let her pageboy touch her collar.

"There. Settle down now, it's very late." Hannah pulled up the eiderdown and kissed her daughter.

"I'd have been asleep hours ago if I hadn't had to wait for you." Jonet pointed out. She enjoyed having the last word.

"Learn to put your own rags in and you won't have to," Hannah said with some astringence. "I can't really be expected to hurry back from wherever I am to do it." She put out the light and went downstairs, wondering how David Vaughan would view the putting in of hair rags as a reason for cutting short their first evening together for fourteen years.

Tom was mending a puncture in the kitchen, Serena's

bicycle upturned on the flagged floor. He had one of his beloved brass band records on the gramophone and whistled through his teeth as he stuck on the repair patch.

"Another blackthorn. They get through anything. Next time I think it'll need a new inner, this one's about had it." He took the bowl to the sink and poured out the water carefully. Tom never made a mess if he could help it. "Want a cocoa, Han?"

"Thanks, Tom." Hannah lowered herself into the small cushioned window seat and automatically checked the blackout curtain before stretching out her legs and yawning. She was tired now; with a small grim smile she thought perhaps she was getting a bit too old to be having her bodice undone in a car by a sexually deprived airman. Her ribs were also aching, and her head.

Tom noticed the smile. "Had a nice time did you?"

He took two cups off the dresser hooks, measured out the cocoa with his usual meticulous care. The tea set had been a wedding gift from Aunt Maggie, a set of four painted with yellow roses, and Tom had been concerned about using them everyday. But Hannah had said that pretty things were meant to be used, they gave more pleasure that way. Everything in the house was used, even the parlour, which she called the sitting-room. It was warmly welcoming with deep, chintz-covered chairs and a rich Turkey carpet. They had a fire there in cool weather in the big inglenook fireplace, making the brass fender and the copper coal-scuttle glow invitingly. The kitchen, too, was a friendly room. It looked over the garden and hill, with two diamond-paned windows and a neat little range where a fire burned low now, a cream gas cooker and, bought last year – and for Jonet, a huge status symbol – an

Electrolux refrigerator standing bulbous and self important between the windows. On the sheepskin hearthrug a black and white cat was curled with his back to the fire. He had come as a stray kitten three years ago and decided to stay, being christened Wedgewood because Serena had first discovered him wedged in the woodpile, trapped by his tail and mewing frantically to be freed. Next to the range was the guinea pig's cage. Serena had bought Towser for threepence from a schoolfriend but had lacked the long term commitment for the chores. Ownership had gradually passed to Tom who became devoted to Towser, made him a variety of wooden toys, and allowed him to play out in the kitchen some evenings. Jonet didn't care for Towser who had nipped her finger early on and who she said made the kitchen smell, but Tom absolutely refused to have his friend's cage transferred to the outhouse. The only other possible move would have been into Tom's bedroom and Hannah had drawn the line there.

She sipped her cocoa, watching Tom watching Towser play with a wooden ball, attempting to climb on it and slipping off, then pushing it along. He had become a slimly built, mild-faced young man whose calm grey eyes were deceptively observant; gently spoken and quietly mannered, he had the wide brow with light brown hair falling across it that Hannah recalled in her father. But he had a streak of Betsy's obstinacy and would not be pushed. He was nervous in unfamiliar situations and Hannah knew he must have been disturbed by his call-up medical last week. When he turned to her she knew what he was going to say.

"D'you think they'll take me, Han?" He looked at her steadily. She wanted to say of course they wouldn't, it would all be fine, he'd stay in the job he was used to now and in which he was confident.

"I truly don't know, Tom. I hope not, I'd miss you terribly. But we have to accept that they might. They must need lots of bakers in the Catering Corps and you're a good baker. We'll just hope, eh? And not fret about it in the meantime."

"Yes." She could see Tom making the effort not to fret and ached for him.

"I've just been to that hotel they made such a fuss about when it opened last year – you know, near this end of Porthcawl?" She tried to divert him. "A lovely place. How if we go there for supper on your birthday this year?"

"Oh, well, we'll see." That meant no; Tom felt more at ease eating at home. "That airman – you said he's an old friend? A Canadian?" Now he was trying to divert her. He washed their cups, dried them, and hung them with care on their hooks, then smoothed the tea towel straight over its dowel. Everything Tom did was methodical, as though he needed order to proceed through his life.

"He was born here. But has lived in Canada for years. He and a partner started a freight airline after the last war. I think he's done very well."

"D'you like him?"

Hannah was accustomed to Tom's naively direct questions.

"I do, yes . . . although of course he may have changed after so long. I didn't really have the chance to find out in the time tonight."

"So you will see him again?"

"I'm not sure. He's only here for another day on his leave. His mother's ill, he's visiting her every day." Hannah began to feel transparent.

"You'll see him again," said Tom in his flat voice. He riddled out the range then went outside to fill the hod

444

with coal for the morning; disturbed, Wedgewood stretched, scratched, and followed him out, rubbing against Hannah's ankle as he passed.

Creaming off her make up, Hannah watched her face dispassionately in her dressing-table looking-glass. Her headache showed round her eyes and there were tight little lines about her mouth. She suddenly felt enormously glad that Florence had vetoed her going to work tomorrow. One more day to get herself together. There'd been an air raid warning last night, one of many false alarms, and she hoped most fervently for peace to sleep through this night. Then tomorrow she'd clear up a backlog of paperwork and write some personal letters, most importantly one to Joe.

She did not want to do any of this. Since their meeting she had behaved like an automaton, keeping at bay, as though under orders, the only subject of any importance to her whilst attending to the minutiae of everyday life. What she craved now was to walk up into the hills, remain there for a long time and think of David Vaughan. It was still difficult to believe he had come back into her life. A couple of days ago she had not given him a thought, he was far away in the past, tucked away with other fading memories. Yet now his kiss seemed as warm on her lips as though freshly given, and she could almost feel the bulk of him beside her on the stool.

When she was in bed she curled up on to her side to stare at the moon through the open window. She never slept with the blackout curtains across, she felt unable to breathe unless she could see the night sky. The cottage stood apart on rising ground looking over the morfa and she could smell the gorse and bracken outside the sheltering wall. Slowly, Hannah passed her hands over her body; over her breasts that were soft as only a woman's breasts can be, over her flanks and the gentle curve of her stomach.

Would she see him again? Was it a mirage, disappearing as she stretched out her hand, or would he re-enter her life? For what?

She turned restlessly a few times then swung her legs over the bed and sat up. Things were probably better left. These last years she'd achieved a serenity undreamed of in her years of marriage and in the fight to survive them. She still worked hard but answered now to no one, and the satisfaction of success was sweet . . . almost as sweet as love.

Hannah brewed herself tea and wandered with it to the window, peering into the night. The rain had cleared. Were they hitting London again? Was Emily safe? She'd sent her children here to her mother last autumn, but the phoney war and Aunt Maggie's arthritis had decided her to have them back in London after Christmas. And David . . . in a couple of days he'd be back on duty, patrolling the western approaches in his Sunderland.

Yes; better left, their lives had no true parallels on which to run and little space for new relationships. She thought how it might be, to live with David Vaughan: to sleep by him at night, waking to find his face inches away; to see him shave, dress, lose his temper, need support; hear his worries; take his part; make love without a sense of desperation.

Her cup clattered in the sink – stupid, time-wasting conjecture. Hannah swept back upstairs, angry with herself; for whatever her future, she felt certain that David Vaughan would not feature in it.

On the edges of consciousness she saw Dorothea at the foot of her bed, smiling in the moonlight that had just broken through clouds. For just a second an unaccountable fear swamped her. The room seemed to be full of shadows that had human substance, they crowded in on her, whispering. But fear slid away as suddenly as it had come. Strange how Dorothea would come in moments of fear or crisis or – as now – deep uncertainty. Sometimes not for months . . . but then she would be there; smiling, loving and caring. She smiled back at Dorothea, turned over, and a sense of profound peace eased her at last into sleep.

Chapter Seventeen

September 1940

"It's for you, Mam."

Jonet stuck her head round the back door and called to Hannah who was trimming up her herb garden after the summer's growth. She came in reluctantly, jealous of her precious time outside as the days shortened and loving every second spent working in the first garden she had ever made. Jonet looked up from the kitchen table, cross at being fetched to the phone from her homework.

"Sounds like that man, the one who came for you last night." She managed to infer that her mother had been in the first place wrong in allowing herself to be come for, and again for sanctioning further contact with this strange man. Hannah ignored the inference, more concerned with her own reaction to David Vaughan which was ambivalent to say the least.

"Hello?" She spoke warily, sitting on the bottom step of the stairs the better to gather her thoughts: she had expected him to phone much later.

"Hannah?" He sounded alarmingly decisive. "Look, I've got to report back tomorrow evening. Can we meet tonight, say around nine?"

"David, I don't see –" Her limp wafflings were swept away.

"You don't have to. I'll pick you up later, then."

"No." Hannah summoned up her failing will power. "David, I've things to do here before I can get back to work myself tomorrow – I can't keep simply walking out of the house, you know. And anyway, I don't think it's a good idea for you and me to, well, to – "

"To what? All we're going to do is have a quiet drink together and talk. Is that not allowed in your cloistered little life? You run into an old friend after – however long it is – and you can't push the timetable around to accommodate him for a couple of hours? Shame on you, Hannah Hywel. Is this any way to treat a volunteer from far shores come to guard yours for you?"

"My name is Hannah Bates now. And spare me the sob story about the brave fighter off to war, I heard that in 1918." But she was starting to smile. "You haven't come over for any reason other than that you enjoy a scrap and it gets you out of the house, so let's call a spade a spade."

"Okay. So I'll pick you up around nine."

Laughing now at his persistence she capitulated. There could be no threat in one more meeting, so long as it stopped there. She could explain how she felt about it to him; he would understand.

Later it was Hannah who did not understand, when all she had to do was say no, they would not be meeting again; that he was married; that she did not care to be loved and then left to pine for what was absolutely not available. All she had to say was that she had a good life now; it may lack a man but that was not always a bad thing, there were other less hazardous pleasures to be found in work and family. So enjoy your war, David Vaughan, then go back to your wife where you belong.

So, why was she in his arms again in the dark intimacy of his car after only two small cocktails that could not possibly have clouded her judgment? Why was she not only enjoying his kisses but returning them in full measure?

449

"What I thought," he ran his hand down her throat to encircle her neck in a movement of smooth eroticism. "What I thought was that if I took a place somewhere near, just a flat maybe, we could be together there when the opportunity arose." He drew back the wave of hair and kissed her ear.

Hannah was still, shocked by the sudden appearance of the net closing about her and by her paralysing inability to cut her way out: her lack of serious wish to ... Pressing home his point David Vaughan's lips moved to the hollow above her collar-bone then down to the shadowed valley between her breasts. She pushed him away and sat up straight.

"Are you serious? Have you any idea – "

He turned her to face him, hands firm on her shoulders. "What I do know is this. We're only here once; this is no dress rehearsal, Hannah. I've seen enough men die to know how very dead they become at that point. You and I, we've meant a lot to one another and it's damn clear to me that we still do. I want you; I see no point in beating about the bush. I've never stopped wanting you and when we met a couple of days ago nothing had changed. I have this feeling it's the same with you, so why can't we allow ourselves at least *something*? Makes sense to me."

"And the devil take care of the future?" Hannah studied the dim profile. "Well for one thing, you stand to lose nothing and I could lose a great deal, like the love and respect of my whole family if they discover the affair. I'm a widow, I'm free. But do you think I'd feel good, helping you betray your own vows? Cheat an invalid wife?" She put it as brutally as she could to help herself, but with no serious hope of shaming him.

"Don't try to make me feel bad, Hannah." He was on to her. "I've danced to Julia's tune for years but even a dog must have his day. And who can say what will happen . . ."

"To Julia? David, don't wish your own wife dead for pity's sake. To you? Well, yes; but you cannot run your life as though every day is your last."

"Hannah, why don't you stop being so bloody rational? I can't tell you how depressing it is." He began to kiss her again, preventing her from answering, enveloping her so tightly that his tunic buttons cut into her breasts. When she broke away her voice was blurred and soft as the parted lips.

"I've two young daughters at home, David. I can't be away anywhere overnight. You have to see that?"

He was quiet, with a look of defeat. "Yeah, that's a tough one." He lit them each a cigarette. "But you could maybe get off for the odd evening? Just now and then, when I manage a spot of leave?"

"I'll think about that." She watched his smoke ring disappear into the gloom. This Canadian inflection in his voice was intriguing.

"Thanks."

They sat together in silence, separated by their thoughts. When he kissed her again it seemed to Hannah that a bond had been forged almost without her knowing.

Tom passed his medical and in November was ordered to report to a basic training camp near Cardiff. He had asked for the Army Catering Corps; no earthly reason why he shouldn't get it Hannah assured him, and herself. She helped him pack his small bag, tears so near the surface she scarcely dare speak. This was how it must feel, she thought, to have a son go.

"Nothing to worry about," she said yet again as he

looked round his room with a worried frown. He met her eyes with the clear straight look that she loved.

"Harry says the basic training is a bit grim."

Of course the basic training would be grim. Horrendous, for the unconfident young man who was not equipped for the extreme rough and tumble of drilling, assault courses, weaponry, even sleeping in a room with a crowd of young men from every quarter of society. Why the hell did he have to go through that when all he needed was to go straight to a bakery? That would be a valid enough contribution to the war; men marched on their stomachs, didn't they? Hannah swallowed down her rage, directed in advance against every man who would cause her brother trauma, fear, pain, in the next weeks and months. Why could they not have left Tom where he was . . .

"Just remember it will pass, Tom. Ride it out. Only a few weeks. Tick them off and they'll go, that's certain. I'll keep in touch and be at the station to meet you on your first leave; and then the worst will be over."

"Yes." He looked so stricken that Hannah wanted to fling her arms round him and say he shouldn't go, she would not allow it. But she could not stop it. And if she touched him now she would start to weep, and that would upset him more. "But you; I worry how you will manage without me."

"I shan't manage at all well." She may as well be honest about that. "You're irreplaceable so I shan't even try. You'll just have to catch up on all of the jobs I'm hopeless at on your leaves – so don't think you'll be lying around getting spoiled! And the girls will have to do a bit extra. I'll just tell 'em there's a war on and they can't have it soft any more. Serena's already knitting army socks when she should be doing her homework – I caught her at it in bed last night! Now, if that's everything we'd best make a move . . ."

She would have liked to take him in the car, in style. But every drop of petrol was needed for essentials, so they balanced Tom's bag on his handlebars and pedalled off past her Morris Eight towards the station, the sea wind smacking them sideways. Harry and Florence had wanted to come but they were short-staffed now; everyone was so busy these days, family needs ran a poor second to work.

"So first thing when I get leave, I'll put one in the garden."

"Surely we're not going to get many raids here?" Abstracted, Hannah realised Tom had been talking of the shelter he was determined she should have. He regarded her seriously as they wheeled their bikes into the station yard.

"How'd we know, with all these works? And the docks. You get one and I'll dig it in. Might just about fit in the lawn."

"I'd really like to put that down to vegetables anyway this autumn, Tom. I wish we still had the old allotment, though Harry's getting good use out of it." She took his arm as they reached the platform and a shadow darkened the day to make her shiver. She'd seen Harry off here, and Dada. She could hear Dada now; see his slight frame burdened with the unfamiliar khaki greatcoat and hung about with equipment, that last cold April morning in 1917. "You be a help to your Mam now, Princess. And see after young Joey for me till I'm back."

"I will, Dada. Of course I will."

Her eyes misted over and she stared into the smoky distance, then at Tom, putting his train ticket with great care into the wallet she'd bought him with his initials stamped in gold leaf. Dada had left her Tom to look after, too, though he hadn't known it at the time of parting. And she *had* tried. But now she must let him go; he would keep what she had given him over the years and Hannah prayed now for it to be enough.

"You give me a ring tonight if you get the chance, let me know the right address. And that you're okay." She brushed a thread off the sleeve of his good suit. "And don't forget the sandwiches, they're your specials."

"Great. Better not ask where you got the ham." He tried to smile but it wavered. He peered at his watch. "Due about now."

"Hasn't been a train on time since the war started." She tucked her hand into the crook of his arm and they walked up and down the platform, threading between young men in uniform and their kitbags; some alone, smoking and staring into space and others in nervously joking family groups.

Tom said suddenly, "I wish Joe was here. He should be here."

Hannah examined his pinched face. "I wish that too, Tom. But everyone has to lead their own lives. You know how each time he writes he says he'll be over the moment he's able. When this is all finished."

"He should be here now," Tom repeated with the mulishness to which he occasionally resorted. "He's my brother and I'd not know him if I saw him."

Hannah felt agitation shake him. Seeing a bench just vacated by a sailor and his girl she pulled him down beside her and took the cold hands between hers.

"It's not right you bein' on your own." He spoke jerkily. "There's bad air raids startin', not just London, all over."

She was quiet, concentrating on calming him. As her hands became warmer she became aware of a golden

454

tide running down through her veins, down her arms and into Tom's still fingers. They were enclosed together in a warm bright peace, an island in a shifting sea of strangers. Time became meaningless as Hannah healed Tom.

She released his hands very gently. He said nothing, but smiled at her, the innocent child's smile she would miss above all. When the train came in he gave her a hug, climbed into a carriage and bent through the open window to kiss her cheek shyly.

"Take care now, Han. I'll be in touch."

"See you soon, Tom dear. 'Bye."

She went on to the shop as soon as she'd wheeled Tom's bike home, anxious to push what he was doing to the back of her mind, anxious also not to start remembering that it had been almost four weeks since she'd had a call from David Vaughan. How would she know, if . . . There had been U-boats sunk in the west, that had been recently in the news; at what cost she had no way of knowing. All she could do was wait and feel guilty for caring one way or the other.

She parked her cycle outside the fresh white and blue frontage that never failed to give her a lift, though the pretty bow window was no longer as well stocked as she liked. Her food went out almost before it had a chance to cool and she'd started making plain oatcakes to plug the gaps. Some cakes were eggless, some took less sugar; every week she experimented. There was a good supply of local fruit for pies and jam this autumn but sugar remained a problem and fats were more uncertain with each delivery.

Harry drew up behind in the delivery van, back from Swansea. He pushed his cap to the back of his head and winked at her, and for a second she caught a glimpse of

455

the old Harry of her childhood in the middle-aged man with faded blond hair and a lined forehead.

"Laddo got his train then? I'd've liked to come."

"I know, Harry. He understood. A mite strung up, but he would be, wouldn't he? We'll hope for the best now and wait to hear."

"A good lad, Tom. He told me he was worried how you'd manage, him bein' gone."

"I know." Hannah smiled. "So we worry about each other. You're looking a bit tired yourself. Are you taking on too much, Harry?" He was heavy-eyed and his blue overall seemed looser on him than she remembered. Harry shrugged.

"Lost sleep last night, young Raymond had another of his crying spells just as we'd got off. I sometimes think he'd be best back in Plymouth with his mam and never mind the bombs. She's not bothered herself. Seems to forget all about the lad for weeks on end."

"I'm sorry about that ... he can come to me on Sunday if you like; help in the garden."

Hannah followed him around to the back of the premises and as always personal problems were shelved to focus on the business. She loved the kitchen behind the shop; the warmly fragrant smells, the comforting shapes of ovens and sturdy work tables and big oval mixing bowls, the shelves of coloured spice jars along the white walls. She enjoyed the gleaming copper and aluminium pans and trays, the capacious fridge that had taken her so long to choose but was proving worth every penny. The premises alongside had become the bakery and the front room of that was her recently opened cafe, with an archway through to the shop. Hannah was secure here; confident that she knew her job after the long careful apprenticeship beginning with the stall on the market, so long ago now. She enjoyed the Swansea restaurant, but her Taibach shop held pride of place.

Mrs Price, rubbing pastry at a table, looked up and smiled; a small thin woman, she'd raised a family of five and was only content when busy. Her fingers were light and quick, her tongue could be sharp, but she and Hannah had an honest working relationship. Washing patty-pans at the deep sink, sixteen-year-old Lorna was still a relatively unknown quantity, on approval for a month. Her predecessor had been allergic to work and she and Hannah had parted by mutual consent. Lorna was so far so good. Just as well since war work at Bridgend Arsenal was both more exciting and much better paid. A replacement would also soon be needed for Vera, peeling apples at the corner bench and awaiting her medical for the ATS.

"Morning, Mrs Bates. That dried egg didn't come. And Fletchers want their buns glazed if we've any sugar." Mrs Price scratched her chin with a floury finger. "Oh, and Ned'd like a word in the bakery when you're in."

Hannah took off her headscarf and gloves. "Right, Mrs Price. I'm in."

"It seems funny without Uncle Tom." Serena ate her toad-in-the-hole by carefully cutting around the two sausages to save them until last as she usually did. That came after the mashed potatoes and the runner beans were eaten first of all as she didn't much like them. Mashed potatoes had been lovely with butter forked into them but now they rated no more than middling. Chips were her favourite, but there wasn't often enough fat to fry them. She sighed; the war made a mess of everything. Now Uncle Tom.

"I expect he thinks it's funny without us." Hannah

carried a half-pint of custard to the table to have with the plums. It was the last of the custard powder and they couldn't spare the milk, but she felt they needed a treat and the custard was it. "He's going to phone if he can."

"My brakes are loose," said Jonet who'd cleared her plate and was eyeing the custard in anticipation. "We've not had custard for ages."

"And it may be ages before we have it again," Hannah pointed out. "Bring your bike into the kitchen after we've cleared, we'll have to do things like that for ourselves now."

The phone rang and Serena shouted, "That'll be Uncle Tom!" She pushed back her chair but Hannah was up already.

"I'll get it, we mustn't waste his money. Finish your beans, love." She hurried into the hall, smiling. Dear Tom . . .

"Hannah? David here."

She sat down. "Is he okay?" Serena called from the kitchen.

"It isn't him," Hannah called back and wished she'd shut the door. "David, are you all right?" She spoke quietly into the receiver but her voice seemed loud in the silent hallway. She felt part cross and part pleased, resulting in confusion.

"Yes, thanks. It's been a bit, well . . . can't say much over the phone; you know, walls have ears. Had a few days in sick-bay. And there's been some, well, reorganisation might be one way of putting it! The thing is, I've got twenty-four hours off, day after tomorrow."

"Oh," said Hannah in a cautious voice. She heard a chair scrape in the kitchen.

"And I want to see you. Hannah? Are you there?"

"Yes." She attempted to marshall the words chasing

458

one another round her head. "It's ... really difficult. Look, phone me when you get home, I'll see if there's – "

Jonet was in the doorway watching her and Hannah was glad the hall was in darkness. "I must go now," she said pleasantly. "Thanks for calling. I'm relieved that everything is all right there. Goodnight."

"The custard's got a skin on," said Jonet accusingly.

"Well, I'm sorry about that, but I can't really leave the phone ringing all night because of the custard, can I? It might have been Tom and then what? Anyway, I like the skin, so you can have the underneath."

"Who was it?" After a few moments contented silence whilst she spooned up every lick of custard with total concentration Serena was ready to rejoin the world. "Your voice went funny, did you hear it?"

"You shouldn't ask who's on the phone when it's not for you," Jonet rebuked her, but waited just the same for Hannah to tell them. Hannah strove for composure; hesitated. If she told them to mind their own business it would be much worse next time David phoned and would blow the whole thing up when she preferred it to be diminished.

"Oh, it was that airman, Mr Vaughan." She tried for a casual note without much success. "There's more plums, Jonet, but we've cleared the custard."

"Does he want you to go out with him again?" asked Serena, deeply interested.

"He did mention it." Hannah felt driven into a corner now. "But he's coming to see his mother. Jonet, will you take over the cleaning of Towser's cage whilst Tom's away? He was a bit worried about it so I told him I didn't think you'd mind."

"Well I do," said Jonet bluntly. "It's a horrid job. But I suppose I'll have to. So, when will he come, Mr

459

Vaughan? He's not a mister actually is he, in the RAF? What rank is he?"

Hannah realised she could truthfully say that she had no idea but before she did the air raid siren wailed through the evening. She hurried round the cottage to check the blackout whilst Serena called Wedgewood in and bolted the door. She always did this, though Jonet told her that a bolted door would make no difference at all to a bomb; Hannah sensed that her younger daughter was nervous of a raid, and as the throb of bombers swept overhead she kept Serena busy.

"Mam, d'you think Tom's safe?" The small oval face was pale. "That was terrible, what they did to Coventry. The wireless said – "

"Tom will be fine," Hannah said firmly. "He's not far, just along by Cardiff."

"When are we getting a shelter? Tom said we should have one."

"We're going to – though I don't expect for a moment we'll need it. I'll get the details from Harry."

"You won't be able to play in the garden," Jonet warned Serena. "It'll take up the whole lawn. Oh, good, the all clear. Can I switch the big light on now for my homework?"

When the girls were in bed, Hannah wrote to Joe. She'd meant to attack some of her Ministry of Food forms; but tonight she needed Joe. She sat at the kitchen table, with Wedgewood washing himself on the rug and Towser washing himself in his cage and the wind outside getting up off the sea. So strange, without Tom. He had not phoned but she knew that had been unlikely. She thought of him in a barracks full of strange men; thought of his room upstairs, tidy, empty. Thought of David Vaughan, what had been wrong to be in sick bay? But he was alive.

She started her letter, Joe's pebble smooth and warm in her hand.

They sat in the lounge bar of the pub on the outskirts of Swansea. Hannah had taken the table in the corner and sipped her sherry with her face shadowed under the down-curved brim of a russet velour hat. David's peaked cap lay on the table by his pint of watered-down beer and in the dim light his face had more hollows and sharp angles than she recalled, and his eyes were deep-set in khaki circles.

"You'll at least come and look at it?" He laid an anxious hand over hers. She saw the tremble, slight but tell-tale, and said urgently:

"David, should you be back on duty? You won't even tell me what – "

He brushed away the concern. "Because it was no big deal, just my shoulder wrenched trying to keep her on course. Down on power in two engines. Made a mess of the touch-down. Nothing, really."

"Nothing," she echoed. "David, isn't there a desk-job you should be doing at forty-four?"

"Ouch." He gave a sour grin. "I love you, too."

"Absolutely no offence. But you take longer to mend than a boy of twenty – that's logical."

"But better in an emergency, and at taking responsible decisions fast. And tons more flying experience," he countered. "This is a futile conversation. I do what I do. Now, come and see where this place is. Can't get possession till December, but we can look. It's quick for me by rail if my car juice runs out and by bus for you if yours does. Discreet, salubrious, Christ, Hannah, say yes!"

She turned the stem of her glass slowly. She wanted to get into bed with him and hold his bruised body close against her own – stroke it, heal it. And she wanted him to claim her then, to bury himself in her until she cried and melted and dissolved into him. Hannah swallowed.

"David, you know I cannot stay there. I have to stay in my home with my children. Please don't keep pretending not to hear. But I will come with you to look at the flat. If you decide to take it, that's your decision. You must know that I can make no promises about coming to it. And we both know I should not, anyway."

They sat in the car and gazed at the first floor window, a Georgian one with nets in a row of spacious villas mounting a hill. David felt for her fingers and tucked them into his palm.

"Why are you so cold?"

"Because I'm frightened."

"Don't be, sweetheart. There's nothing here can hurt you."

"I've heard that before." Hannah hunched her shoulders. The air raid siren howled through the November night and she snapped straight again. "Oh God – not another one. Please get me back right away, David – they're on their own."

She sat forward, tense, scanning the sky as they drove round the estuary as fast as the black-out allowed.

"I'm taking the flat." He sounded tired but dogged. "We might work something out – we will, if you really want to. You already know my side."

"Yes, I do. Well . . . take care. And any time you want to write – "

"Not a lot of time, love. But yes, I will. And the odd phone call when the lines behave. I'll be here whenever there's a chance; but things are hotting up somewhat and we can't afford to lose shipping on a big scale. For one thing, your rations would hit rock bottom." He smiled, then slowed to hear the aircraft overhead. "Not for us . . . some other poor sods."

"I'm trying to decide the best way I can help. I thought, maybe firewatching, but that means leaving the girls at night. Or Civil Defence. But maybe I'll need to settle for the WVS, to fit in the right hours."

They drew up outside the cottage as the all clear sounded. "Thank God." She turned and on an impulse took off his cap to kiss him. The feel of his cool firm mouth stirred her; she put a hand behind his head and drew it down again. When she pulled away they stared at one another, breathing hard.

"Lord, I hope it will be soon." David's voice was ragged. Hannah made no pretence not to understand him. At that moment it could not be soon enough.

The Luftwaffe must have had a couple of bombs left and jettisoned them on Port Talbot docks on their way home. They sounded terrifyingly close. Crouched under the kitchen table with Towser's cage, and Wedgewood clutched tight and squirming, Hannah and the girls agreed they wished that Tom was home.

"Just as well he's not, though," said Hannah after the all clear when they drank cocoa huddled by the stoked-up range before going back to bed. "Not really room for any more under the table – and there's no way he'd leave Towser out."

Hannah used grated carrot in some cakes now with a beautifully sweet and moist result, and decided to risk it in the Christmas cakes. She had an impressive plaster-of-Paris edifice made for her window but the cakes she sold could not be iced and there was no marzipan. The onions grown by Tom were worth their weight in gold in meat pies, as were all the mushrooms picked on the sloping fields behind Taibach and dried. Ranks of Kilner jars were filled with plums and tomatoes, blackberries, raspberries and the wonderfully mouthwatering dewberries from the morfa, and from Margam warrens, bought by Hannah for twopence per pound from willing small boys. The difficulty came with finding the fat to convert these into pies. Hannah could often buy chicken and rabbit from farmers she had known all her life, and sometimes fish from the docks; but pastry shortening was another matter.

Daisy, prostrate when Albert was interned, had been supported splendidly by her eldest, Albert junior, who filled his father's place in their cycle and motor-bike repair business. Now young Albert was called up, throwing his mother completely, and a further replacement was urgently sought. As the year drew to a close Port Talbot had drilled its Home Guard into splendid shape on the athletic ground. The Steelworks Wharf was permanently patrolled against possible acts of sabotage, the guards armed with a cargo of rifles from America. Dewi, now much in demand, took a job in the steelworks costing office, put himself in an ARP rota at his local post, and found it easier to forget the continual discomfort of his leg. Cousin Bella had quickly let David Vaughan's mother know that she must find a new parlourmaid. In her element once more, she was at Bridgend Arsenal along with thousands of other local women, earning such good money that she could easily put five shillings a week towards a rainy day and still put regularly into the Spitfire Fund. Auntie Lil disappeared into the Margam Works canteen and persuaded Aunt Maggie to do three mornings there, telling her briskly that it would take her mind off Daisy's troubles. Harry's father was called back to the steelworks and

Sam Warburton seemed to take on a new lease of life as these older men came into their own.

Hannah was busier than she had ever been. The Swansea restaurant had permanently full tables as her Christmas menus went up and the cafe in Taibach stopped serving only when it was closed. Fifty-nine-year-old Ned, who had taken over Tom's baking, needed attention as he settled in and the shop assistants and waitresses changed endlessly. But however occupied, Tom was rarely far from her thoughts. Her great fear was of bullying. Yet there was, she knew, absolutely nothing she could do now but wait and hope. Cycling back and forth she would worry, too, about David Vaughan if more than a few days went by without a phone call or a note. No one would notify her, of course, if . . .

Mines had been laid in the bay by enemy aircraft and a vessel taking a cargo of coal was blown clear out of the water by one. By day the morfa bombing and gunnery ranges made their own mayhem. Some days there were well over thirty barrage balloons up at once – Serena liked to count them, neck arched and squinting into the sun. But no matter how loud the blast of war blew in their ears, when Joe's Christmas parcel arrived – in a van since it was far too heavy for the post lady's satchel – all was forgotten but the excitement of opening it. They set it on the kitchen table and delved in turn into the carton . . . tins and packets, boxes and mysteriously shaped objects taped into brown paper. This year there were nylons for Jonet as well as Hannah, and white lacy knee-socks for Serena. They could make the tin of meat do for two dinners and the salmon and peaches were set aside for when Tom had his first leave. There was a box of chocolates, fragrantly scented soaps, a silk scarf, delicate balls of angora knitting wool and a tinned ham. And a letter.

When the girls were in bed Hannah sat by the fire and wrote to Joe. They seemed very close . . . she looked into the glowing coals and sent her love over the miles of bitter winter ocean to home in on him. This war could not go on for ever, not as long as the last, surely. Then he would come home. And then, perhaps, she would tell him about how it had been, all these years without him.

Chapter Eighteen

January 1941

When Cardiff was hit in January, Hannah could hear it. Not possible, Aunt Maggie said; no one could hear that far. Maybe it was heard with her mind and not her ears. The eye of her mind saw buildings crumble, smoke and dust bloom into the icy air. When Tom got to a phone two days later he said only that it had been "bad". She asked how close the camp was to the city and his answer had been "close enough".

"But you're all right?" Hannah strained to hear him over the bad line. His dutiful "Yes thanks, Han," failed to relieve her concern. "See you next week, then, we're looking forward to that, Tom."

Bristol sounded equally close when that was blitzed, and they spent hours under the table. "At least we keep warm this close together." Hannah had spread an eiderdown to lie on and blankets to drape down over the table against the flying glass. That was the night the pipes froze because Tom hadn't been there to lag them. Serena was looking wilted and Hannah had glimpsed her sucking her thumb under the table when a couple of bombs found Cwmavon, close to Uncle Jenkin's place.

She and Serena fetched Tom from the station in the car, throwing petrol problems overboard for this once. His train, of course, was late and they huddled under a rug in the car; preferable to the waiting room where there was no fire allowed. Consulting her watch, Hannah knew she should be at work; worried that the baking ovens might not get up to heat; and had the flour quota arrived and did Flo still have that terrible cold.

Tom looked different, bundled in a greatcoat and all the trappings, with the muffler Serena had knitted for Christmas over the lot. His voice seemed quieter as if he was too tired to speak, or even to smile with conviction. Everyone is always tired now thought Hannah and was suddenly angry, so furious with Hitler that she could have killed him herself and almost overshot her cottage thinking about it. Tom fell asleep the moment he'd finished the carrot and potato pie with sprouts, so Hannah sent Serena off to afternoon school and spent the afternoon on endless Ministry of Food paperwork and chopping wood, which she'd left in hopes of Tom doing it.

When he came to the door looking for her she was glad to leave it, the cold was bone-deep. "Cup of tea now, Tom? Or would you really like to get to bed? You still look a bit done in."

Tom smiled. "No thanks." He took one of her potato scones.

"It's potatoes with everything," she apologised. "We're encouraged not to use flour – I expect you're a bit out of touch with that sort of problem, though."

"Yes, we just eat what's given us."

"Tom?" Hannah hesitated. "Are you all right? Really?"

He finished the scone, never quick to respond. "Just about."

"But it will be easier now, with basic training over?"

"Should think so. I've done an interview for catering an' filled in the form. Bit of help from Len there – he's my mate."

"Oh, good." She was ridiculously pleased that he had a mate. "So, everyone's friendly?"

Tom paused again. "There's a few – well, they're real

468

roughs. You try to steer clear when they want their bit of fun."

"Of course." Hannah thought of the real roughs having their bit of fun with Tom. "But I'm sure it'll be better if you get bakery work. You'll let me know how you get on?"

"I'll try." Looking tired again, Tom took another scone.

He went back much restored but the lawn, too frozen to get a spade in, remained undug for the shelter. A few days later Swansea was targeted three nights in a row. Hannah covered the girls with her eiderdown against the blast as the world shook and roared about them; Wedgewood crept shivering between them and peed with fear. Each morning smoke billowed across the estuary from the stricken city and each morning Hannah and Florence took the bus to the restaurant. The second day they found the windows blown out. Florence went white.

"Jesi Crist! Well, they needn't think I'm not opening it *right away*, because I am! I'll show them who's boss!"

Hannah felt an insane urge to laugh. "Flo, I love you. Of course we'll open. But first we have to pick up those glass shards; then sweep up; then find someone to board up the windows till we can get them replaced."

"We could have it open air." Florence was turning pink again. "Only, it's a touch cold for that. Boards it is then. An' nice rosy lamps – what about we buy red shades? Look quite invitin' with our red velvet curtains drawn."

They were open by two o'clock, Civil Defence coming to give a hand with the boarding up. Florence printed BUSINESS AS USUAL on one board in buttercup yellow paint left over from the kitchen walls, above a menu of light snacks. They were quickly full and daylight had gone when Hannah rode out of the still smoking, dust-choked city, where people braced themselves against the possibility of another dose of the same. It came; this time three houses within yards of the restaurant were wrecked. The docks blazed, but workers poured into the battered factories for the dawn shift.

That afternoon Hannah made a detour on the way back to the Taibach bus. She picked through the debris to the road where David had shown her the flat. It was still intact on the brow of the hill, though nearby shops had suffered, and the tall windows glittered as they caught the last dregs of winter sunset. Hannah regarded it with thoughts chasing half-formed about her head; David had phoned last night with news of a forty-eight hour break, and wanted them to meet.

That night was worse. He rang again in the middle of it and Hannah ran into the hallway to make the bell stop, one noise too many. The girls had turned the wireless up to drown what was happening outside and Tommy Handley was being both funny and very loud.

"Hannah? What's that racket?"

"Hello, David. It's Tommy Handley. Or it could be the air raid. We have both."

"Oh God. Are you okay?"

"As okay as anyone is in an air raid. How about you?"

"Leave cancelled; our numbers are down a bit. I'm fed up, I want to *see* you." The line crackled as the explosions grew louder. "Hannah? Listen, I don't want you on your own out there with that circus going on. What a bloody awful business."

"I must go, David. The girls –"

"Sure. I may get next weekend. Or the next. Will you –"

"Yes." Hannah was surprised how certain she felt about that. "Yes, darling. And take care."

"And you. Love you."

She left her hand on the receiver for a moment after she had replaced it. That was the first time he had said that.

It was when magnetic mines were laid in the dock entrance channel, and the light plate mill where Thomas had worked was hit and an entire local family was wiped out that Hannah made the decision to evacuate the girls inland. Money would be found. Jonet was impressed; a boarding school was a perfect chance to distance herself from her working-class roots. Not so Serena.

"We can't leave you with everything to do! Uncle Tom would be furious! Who'd clean out Towser?"

"Tom would much rather know you were safe, Serry. You can do Towser when you're home, you'll get some weekends."

Hannah felt so sick at the thought of sending them from her that it was hard to sound convincing. "And I'll get on with my work much easier if I'm not worried about you. It may only be for a term, these raids are just a phase; you'll see."

She hung on to that, driving through the gates of a big stone manor house in a valley fold. They'd be safe here; and only a forty minute bus ride home. Serena stared at her with desperate eyes at the moment of parting but Jonet was already studying the notice board. On the way home Hannah stopped at a pub for a whisky, then went straight to the shop and began to beat ingredients at a furious rate for a tray of swiss rolls. Much later, before she let herself into an appallingly empty house, she went to the ARP post to enrol for part-time duties.

"You aren't allowed to cry when you're twelve," said Jonet. "Come on; use this to blow your nose, then we're all to go for a walk."

Serena took the handkerchief and blew, "I'm not crying." She offered the handkerchief back but Jonet shuddered.

"I'll have it when you've washed it. No more moping now, mind. And comb your hair before Miss Phillips comes."

"How d'you know her name? I didn't." Serena gave a last hiccup and abandoned herself to her sister's commonsense.

"Because I make it my business to know things that are going to be useful to me. Now look; you can't *possibly* have lost your comb already . . ."

When Hannah opened the door to David Vaughan she felt as awkward as an adolescent, and as confused . . . throat dry, eyes uncertain, her scalp tight with tension. He seemed awkward, too, fingering his cap on the doorstep while the wind made his trousers legs snap like dinghy sails. When she stood back he stepped quickly past her so she could shut the door and pull the blackout curtain over it. They faced one another then in the little hallway.

"You all right, darling?"

As she nodded he moved suddenly and they locked together. Hannah's eyes shut as he stroked her hair; arms tight about his neck she rubbed her cheek against his. They remained so for a while, folded tightly together, silent. Then David turned towards the stairs. Entwined, they went up, with Hannah pressed against the whitewashed wall each time he stopped to kiss her face and throat. In the bedroom they did not want the light. It was enough to feel each other's breathing warmth, fingers touching lips, eyelids, ears, hair. When he began to slide off her jumper she helped him and quickly garments were discarded about their feet as skin met skin. The ache of fourteen years was assuaged when Hannah arched to him, endearments like whispered benedictions between them.

Neither would wait. She drew him to her with a huge sigh and they moved together in an explosion of ignited desire. Hannah thought she cried out; nothing was clear but joy. When his seed spilled into her and he subsided damply against her shoulder she smiled in the dark and stroked his hair, cradling him.

It was a while before he spoke, voice muffled in her hair. "Hadn't meant to go at you like a bull at a gate. Sorry."

"Don't be." Hannah was still smiling.

"But next time, I'll be . . . well . . ."

"If you like," she said equably. She was heavy, boneless, thinking how lovely "next time" sounded. Moving slightly to free her other hand she stroked him some more and realised from his passivity that he was asleep.

She lay quiet, the warmth of his relaxed body seeping into her bones so that she forgot what cold was like, that it was below freezing just the other side of the window. How long passed before she started to think of Serena and Jonet she was not sure; only that the loss of the last days had begun to harden once more into a painful ball in her gut. She sighed. David stirred, lifted his head and kissed her.

"I seem to be something of a dead loss. So bloody tired." He tried to see her face, stroking hair from her temples.

"Of course you are. That's why you've got forty-eight hours, isn't it? Would you like some tea? There's a drop

473

of whisky, that could go in. And toast – how about toast and whisky tea? Oh, and there's some vegetable soup. We'll picnic in bed."

"Sounds wonderful, darling. Set me up for meeting Mama – she said I was to go straight in to her no matter how late. Damn sight easier when she was in the nursing home."

They ate like children at a midnight feast, with lamps low and the gas fire popping in a friendly fashion. They giggled over crumbs and licked one another's buttery fingers. Watching him reluctantly dressing she wanted to draw him back to her bed so they might love again, taking all the time they wanted; maybe till morning. She wanted to fall asleep with him there and have him still with her when she awoke. She knew what was happening to her, was powerless to stop it and would not have if she could.

"Let me do it." She fastened the tunic buttons, the belt.

"Put this on, you'll get cold." He wrapped the dressing gown about her and knotted the sash, then pulled her close again. "I don't want to go. Promise you'll be here when I come again?"

"I'll be here." They went down with arms entwined. He kissed her hands, face, then went quickly, shutting the front door with a bang that made her jump.

Hannah heard the car engine fade. Wedgewood rubbed at her ankles and she picked him up and cuddled him, pushing her face into the warm fur of his throat as she took him into the kitchen to feed. She switched the radio on and whilst Bruce Belfrage read her the news she squatted by Towser's cage, stroking his nose and offering bits of carrot.

When she went upstairs Wedgewood came with her, weaving back and forth round her legs, and she picked him up again for comfort. The house was agonisingly silent. In the bedroom she looked at the rumpled bed, the untidy tray, her clothes still on the floor, the whisky bottle on the bedside table. Hannah sat stiffly on the bed, considering the situation, which seemed to be out of control. None of it should have happened. She should never have allowed him to visit her here. It might be the war . . . the world had gone mad, as had she. All she wanted – far, far too much – was David. And her daughters.

Hannah stroked her cat, remembering berating David Vaughan outside the Electric cinema for trying to recruit more men, shouting at him that she already had father, uncles, cousins gone and wasn't it time to call enough. Now she wanted him; to love and to be a rock to which she might cling in a sea of care, of duty and responsibility for others.

Cold, she went to make more tea. It was all happening again. Where would it end this time? It seemed impossible that any man could come safely through two wars.

The air raid siren began to wail. Turning the radio on loud, Hannah poured the last drops of the whisky into her tea.

"We heard yesterday," said Florence, her voice hushed. "Mother, father, baby sister – all gone. And an aunt. Poor little lad." She frowned at the bread she was checking in. "This gets greyer by the week. I've said we'll keep him if he'd like to settle – Harry was all for it. I told him right away. He's been very quiet . . . didn't cry. He's with Harry now, doing the van rounds. He always likes that."

"Flo, that's terrible! Poor Raymond. I knew Plymouth was having a dreadful time." Hannah sat in the restaurant kitchen, tired after night shift at the ARP post.

"The man who came about Raymond says there's over thirty thousand homeless there. Terrible . . . Anyway, we'll keep Raymond. He's nowhere else to go, that much is certain."

Flo started one girl on vegetables and another on apple suet pudding. "You look as though you've not had breakfast." She looked sharply at Hannah. "I'll cut a sandwich. Take this tea through, I'll be right with you."

They sat in the corner of the restaurant with weak April sun stroking the white cloths and making the cutlery gleam. "Pity we have to open soon and get it all messed up, I love it like this." Florence sighed, inspecting her round tables and pretty chairs.

"Tidy *empty* tables won't pay the girls' fees. Nor the wages bill. We need to be full with this five shilling ceiling on meals. And if we don't give value they'll all trot round to the British Restaurant." Hannah drank her tea quickly, she had to receive a Ministry of Food official shortly at the bakery. Florence put down her cup.

"Look, love, I need to tell you."

"Tell me, then." Hannah ate her sandwich. "Lovely, Flo, thanks."

"I saw Dewi yesterday."

"Oh, is he okay? I've not seen him since he got married. I never thought he would, after all this time."

"Han." Florence tried again. "He was asking about David Vaughan and you. He'd heard, well, that you'd been seen together."

Hannah stared into her cup as though to read how she should answer in the tea leaves. Florence leaned forward.

"Don't fret about it, Han. Dewi passed it on so you

wouldn't be taken by surprise should anyone else bring it up."

"What did you tell him?"

"I made light of it. Said you'd had a chance meeting with him in hospital and had met him for lunch to chat about old times."

"But no one knew about any old times between me and David Vaughan, did they? Did he say anything else?"

"He asked if Vaughan's wife was over here, too," Florence said with some reluctance. "I said I'd no idea and changed the subject."

"Thanks for telling me, Flo." Hannah pushed back her chair, her face grim. "I wouldn't care but for the girls – I'll not have them upset by mischief makers." She bent to kiss Florence. "I'll catch Harry in Taibach if I step on it, I'll give him a cake for Raymond."

The night in London was impossible to resist. He had to go anyway, David urged, the Air Ministry brasshats were trying to get him interested in liaising with the Canadian Training Scheme. He'd no inclination for it but at least must go and say so. They could go up together by train, have dinner and a show, and a whole night together. All Hannah had to do was organise her end of it.

She had done, with a mixture of guilt, delight, excitement and trepidation that quite exhausted her. Meeting David was becoming more hazardous as winter's sheltering blackout turned to spring daylight, with less hope of keeping the affair from her family. The thought of being together openly for once sent her happy to bed for a week. Her spirits bubbled, helped by a sunny drift of daffodils in a garden corner not dug over for vegetables and buds everywhere, fat and promising. Having the girls home for Easter had been strange . . . both seemed taller, more mature, especially Jonet. Girls and teachers unknown to Hannah figured large in Jonet's conversations; when asked about them she would identify them by what their fathers did.

"That's nice," Hannah murmured when told that Pamela's father was high up in the Department of Health and that their house had two lavs; or that Edith's parents drove a huge car and her father had his own factory.

"She's a cry-baby just the same," Serena said from the rug where she was stroking Wedgewood. "Not my idea of a good best friend."

"That's what you think, silly!" Jonet was sharp. "She'd had the nail of her little finger almost torn off by a hockey stick – and she's not my best friend anyway. That's Shirley Carling," she explained to Hannah. "She's from London. All their windows have those lovely leaded lights."

"That's nice," Hannah repeated dutifully. "They're terrible to keep clean though, they catch all the dirt."

"Oh, well, their maid would do all that sort of thing." Jonet paused. "You could have a maid, Mother."

Hannah looked carefully at her daughter. "Mother" was new this Easter. She'd not remarked on it but noted with a tinge of sadness that the Welsh "Mam" had been relegated to the past along with playing on the beach and calling the midday meal dinner.

"Mrs Lloyd's Friday morning is plenty, dear. And I like her, she never needs telling what to do. Who's your best friend, Serry?"

Serena smiled up through the curtain of hair released from its pigtails. "Caroline. She has to miss games sometimes because of her chest, but she's really nice.

478

She tells me super stories after lights-out. She wants to become a poet."

"What does her father do?" Jonet asked. "Won't he mind her being a poet?"

"She's not told anyone but me yet." Serena kissed Wedgewood's velvet paw. "I don't know what he does, we don't talk about those things."

It was very quiet when Hannah returned from taking them back to school with her hoarded petrol. Serena had left a slipper on the stairs, and there was a note from Jonet in their bedroom requesting Mrs Lloyd not to dust her collection of glass animals. Hannah put the slipper carefully in the cupboard and removed the note; Mrs Lloyd must not think that anyone believed her remotely capable of damaging an ornament.

Struggling to put her daughters out of her mind she changed into her dark blue cotton overalls and took her helmet from its hook. She was wheeling her bicycle down the path when the phone rang.

"You sound breathless, darling."

"I was at the gate, David, it's a duty night."

"Ah. How was Easter?"

"Easter was okay, thanks. I've just taken the girls back. We had one night up; Swansea got it again. How about you?"

"It's been, well, busy. You know."

"Yes. But are you *all right*?" She tried to picture him and knew there would be fatigue lines around his eyes and mouth.

"I will be once we're on the Paddington train. Still on course?"

"Absolutely." Why mention that she still had to find a rota substitute for the warden post, that the shop accounting would go unchecked or that Harry had to come and feed Wedgewood and Towser? Hannah smiled. "No problems this end."

"That's my girl. Look, there's a damn great queue for this box. If I don't manage to call again it's the ten-fifteen into Swansea, got that?"

"Got it. Take care, darling."

Cycling to the wardens' post she was still smiling.

They had to stand until Newport. David had sprinted up and down the platform twice in search of a first class carriage before the guard informed him he was wasting his time.

"Not putting a first on this one till Newport, sir."

"So much for my warrant." Rueful, David swung up their luggage as the whistle blew. The train was packed with servicemen and women with kit piled into every carriage and corridor, where groups sat on it, smoking and laughing or hunched with eyes closed. Hannah and David swayed against one another for a while, smiling when their eyes met and clasping hands under cover of Hannah's coat. Then they threw dignity overboard and squatted on David's grip balanced on Hannah's case, backs against the compartment door for support.

There was a long wait at Newport for the extra carriage. At Oxford Hannah darted out for sandwiches, pushing her way back as the doors were slamming.

"Not sure what they are, darling." Wedged into their corner, they opened the bags. "I've got cheese and pickle. What about you?"

David took a bite. "I'm too hungry to care. Actually this one's spam, that's fair enough." He foraged further. "And a currant bun ... treasure trove." He pressed it and an odd expression crossed his face. Watching him, Hannah choked with laughter on her sandwich and earned a disapproving stare from a woman opposite in

WVS uniform who was knitting hospital blanket squares at a great rate.

There were two unexplained halts before Paddington and the train ran in over an hour late. A taxi miraculously unloaded its fare as they pushed from the teeming concourse and David won the fight, pulling her in after him with a triumphant grin.

"Not long now, darling." Hannah nodded. She stared out at devastated buildings being demolished by work-parties in blue overalls and helmets. A row of shops and flats had raw, splintered gaps and a bedroom was sliced in half, its chimney jutting bare and roofless. Fresh craters in roads and pavements were cordoned off and a department store had lost its front.

"It's worse than I'd imagined." Her voice was thin with shock.

"It's grim, no kidding. They've had a couple of scorchers lately." They were silent as the cab chugged past the burned-out husk of John Lewis. David tilted her chin. "You're not going to let it get to you, though?"

"Of course not, David. It just makes my Civil Defence stint seem a bit puny."

"Just feel lucky!"

"Yes . . ."

The Savoy was cool and courteous with an afternoon tea trio playing Mozart behind tasteful greenery, and officers with pretty girls chattering and laughing. Their room had sunlight filtering through embroidered nets at the long windows, quilted satin spread and drapes of pearl grey and a big gilded looking-glass over the marble fireplace.

When the bellboy had left Hannah looked round appreciatively, then buried her nose in a posy of roses on the glass-topped table. David encircled her waist and drew her to the window. They stood without speaking, gazing out at the Thames, then turned to embrace.

"You like it, darling?" His lips were against her temple. He took off her hat and dropped it on the rose brocade chair. "I want you to feel good, relaxed." His fingers pushed gently through her hair to cup her head whilst he kissed her closed eyes. Hannah leaned against him, tension seeping away to leave her light and boneless. "I want to give you the world for twenty-four hours. That way there'll be something to hang on to when it gets bad and I can't be there."

"I'll remember, David. Thank you."

They shared a bath, soaping off the journey without haste and afterwards showered one another with talcum. Nothing was said, but both resisted the urge to go to bed there and then. They had the night before them and it was a delicious pain to wait, knowing that. Hannah put on a dress of creamy linen with a garnet necklace in the scooped neckline and matching earrings that glowed against her pale skin. Watching the reflection of David brushing his damply curling hair, she had a second of unbelief. What was she doing here . . . Then she saw that he was tired, shoulders slumped momentarily under the fresh blue shirt, and she put down her own hairbrush to circle her arms under his.

"You're very smart." She kissed the tip of his nose. "What I should love now is some tea. That suit you, darling?"

"Absolutely." He kissed her back. "Provided we're not hard against the lady with the cello."

Afternoon tea stretched into cocktails whilst they ate tiny crustless sandwiches, sponge fingers and individual swiss rolls, and drank fragrant tea. Gaps in their knowledge of each other's lives were narrowed; Hannah drew out reminiscences of a struggle to carve a future in a new continent; of cut-throat competition and years on a tightrope between success and failure. Queries about life in Coastal Command bore less fruit. "Let's not talk shop now, darling." Bits of her own life were revealed – of Joe in America, of her own long fight for security for her family. She said nothing of her marriage and did not ask of his.

"Now, this evening." David leaned back in his chair, looking rested. "Has Modom any preferences? I'd thought to ask the desk which theatres are open this week."

"What I should really enjoy is to see *Gone With The Wind*." Hannah looked tentative. "I glimpsed the billboards as we came by. Would you?"

"Why not? A splendid idea." David was advised by a waiter that a performance would start in something over an hour. "We'll ask them to rustle up a taxi, then. And have a spot of supper when we get back?"

"Marvellous." She leaned over to kiss his cheek, suddenly grateful for the here and now and for the man who was sharing it. Arm in arm, they went to look at the river.

"This is not good."

They regarded the cinema queue which reached halfway round Leicester Square.

"Let's give it a try now we've got this far, darling," Hannah urged. They tacked on behind a quartet of East End nurses who kept them entertained with blackly comic patter of life on the wards of Guy's in the blitz. They had edged to within a few yards of the cinema canopy when a man in evening dress stuck his arm into the queue just ahead of the nurses.

"Sorry, ladies and gentlemen. That's it for tonight."

He dodged back into the foyer to escape some

colourful invective. Hannah and David looked at one another as the queue dissolved about them.

"Okay." David tucked her arm into his. "Plan B."

"Plan B," agreed Hannah. She laughed, simply because *Gone With The Wind* was small beer beside the pleasure of being alone with David Vaughan and knowing that they still had the whole night together. "What *is* Plan B?"

"We stroll back at leisure through this perfect spring evening to our hotel, stopping for liquid refreshment at the hostelry of our choice. We order the finest dinner available, accompanied by a bottle – or three – of the best champagne the Savoy can rustle up. We may take a turn about the dance floor if we're still steady on our feet. I shall then invite you to retire with me to our bedchamber, where I shall make passionate love to you until the maid brings in the morning tea." David steered her across Leicester Square and his face looked young and happy as he reset his peaked cap at a jauntier angle.

"That sounds rather nice." Hannah was beginning to feel nineteen rather than thirty-nine.

An hour later they were still pressed contentedly into a corner of a pub off Charing Cross Road, having first meandered arm in arm through the West End, window shopping. It wasn't until David tried to read a rude Victorian cartoon framed above Hannah's chair that he realised the light was fading.

"Drink up, sweetheart, it's time to find supper."

"Can we walk back along the Embankment, David? It's magic at twilight." As Hannah spoke the siren began to wail.

"Blast." David drained his tankard. "I'd hoped we'd get away with it tonight. Let's make tracks, sweetheart."

A warden appeared. "Nearest deep shelter, Charing

Cross Station. Don't hang about folks, this could be another big one."

David peered up at a full moon climbing into the deepening sky. "It's a bomber's moon." He put an arm about Hannah and began to step out. "The Embankment stroll's off; sorry about that."

"We don't have to go to Charing Cross, though?" She hurried to match her stride to his. "The Savoy's not much further and they showed us that comfortable basement place they've laid on for raids."

"Okay. But we must push on, things could get busy any minute. I know a short cut that'll help."

They lost rather than gained time on the short cut, with side roads shut off for demolition work. When the heel of Hannah's shoe caught in a grating, searchlights were probing the sky to the south and they could hear distant ack-ack fire.

"Christ!" David struggled with the trapped heel whilst Hannah balanced against the wall. "Who designed these damned things!"

"Heels or gratings?" The firing was getting closer.

"Both. Come on, you –' After furious manoeuvring he gave a last savage heave and the shoe parted from its heel.

"Oops, sorry."

She said gravely, "If you could take off the other heel now, maybe I can get going?"

David looked towards the noise, the steady drone of planes in the night sky, bright now with gunfire, searchlights and fires from the first incendiaries. Then the planes were above them. He pushed the shoe back on Hannah's foot and grabbed her hand.

"Do the best you can. Keep right in . . .'

They began to run, Hannah limping. When they heard the sickening crump of high explosives they

485

froze, silhouetted against fires blooming skywards ahead, beyond a narrow road junction. In seconds, a massive flash tore upwards from behind buildings on the junction's far corner. It was followed by a thunderous roar. In mesmerising slow motion the buildings spewed out in all directions before sinking into a miasma of dust and smoke, completely blocking the little intersection.

"Good God!" David shielded her with his arms as the blast reached out to rock them on their feet. Debris spilled from the stricken area and a pall of dust ballooned towards them; Hannah could already taste it. The noise was everywhere now and seemed to be deadening her brain, but she started to move forward.

"Not that way!" David shouted, pulling her back. "The road's blocked, can't you see? There, on the right, that should lead to the Strand. We'll run for it."

"David . . . we must help! There may be people –"

"Leave it to the experts. They'll be on the scene directly. What the hell d'you think *we* could do?" He urged her towards the side turning. "For God's sake, the shrapnel's coming down like rain! We've got to make for shelter!"

An air raid warden ran into view, paused to assess the damage and disappeared again. David gesticulated toward him. "There you are – *now* will you come?"

Hannah shook her head. "I can't, David. I'm not being difficult; it's just that I have to go *there*!" She struggled to free herself from him as more bombers swept overhead.

"You are utterly mad!"

Something cracked into the debris strewn road a couple of yards ahead and he pushed her into the nearest doorway. They watched as the warden reappeared with three others and shone screened torches into the murk. Scrambling about, their voices carried faintly through the noise and dust. One heaved aside a splintered door to grasp something, which when pulled free was a woman, who seemed to be alive.

Hannah evaded David and ran nearer. He caught up with her and pressed her into another doorway, but closer now to the wreckage of what appeared to have been a few shops with accommodation above. She strained to watch the wardens working, but David forced her into a corner, his body between her and the street.

"Hannah, what *is* this? You know if we don't reach deep cover fast we could be dead? This isn't a bloody game!"

"David, I know that. But I *have* to *stay*!" She nodded to where the wardens had been joined by a heavy rescue team. "I've no idea why. Look, you make for the hotel, no use our both staying. I'll join you soon, I promise."

"It's not this damned spirit business again is it?" He was angry now. "I've seen what it does to you; I tell you, it's a load of trouble!"

Hannah's mouth set. "And I tell you, David, I can't leave here until I'm free to go." She could scarcely be heard now over the noise of more planes, gunfire and explosions, the roar and crack of fires and falling masonry and the scream of sirens.

"What the hell d'you mean, *free to go*?"

Hannah craned her neck to see rescue workers bring out two more injured to an auxiliary ambulance that had just shot past them to back up close against the rubble. Instructions were being shouted; smoke was beginning to filter up into the choking dust. She faced him with desperate eyes.

"David. I beg you, hear me. I'm not even sure *what* I

mean! There's only this huge compulsion; something that *will* take me to that pile of rubble."

"Even if you're killed there?" He grabbed her arm. "Christ, love, I'm trying to understand." Another series of explosions drowned his words and she cut in, shouting again now.

"There's help I can give! That's it! Someone under there!" She tried to push past him again.

"What d'you think those men are doing?" he yelled back. "Don't you think they'll find them then? It's their *job*, damn it, it's what they *do* in this bloody place!"

Hannah broke free with a sudden twist and ran, shoeless now. Three bodies covered by blankets lay in the shadow of a broken wall and two women swathed in blankets were being passed mugs of tea from someone in a newly arrived car. Beneath the smoke there was an orange glow and Hannah could sense its heat. She halted, overcome by the old, shameful fear of fire.

David was beside her. Grateful, she felt for his hand. While they watched, the long grey auxiliary ambulance returned to reload.

"You see, love? They've got it all under control. You'd only be in the way."

She said nothing, standing trembling on the margins of the activity, but her face, illuminated by the strengthening glow from the ruins, was rigid under the smoky dust. The elegant cream dress was grimed, now. David took the shoes from her and eased them back on but she appeared not to notice, aware only of the drama taking place by the light of torches and fire, and the moon. Two nurses and a doctor were operating from the car; there had been cries from under one section of masonry and the nurse was kneeling there, talking.

"There's someone trapped." Hannah gripped his hand. "Two, I think."

The rescue men worked fast but carefully, lifting aside debris from what might have been a cafe or bar. Above, a slice of room sagged on its jagged boards and behind it flames were taking hold. When the fire engine arrived an adolescent boy was being eased clear. Moments later another older man became visible. His face was grey with dust and he grinned weakly at his rescuers as they burrowed round him.

"What's bin keepin' yer? Stap me . . . couln' 'arf do wi' a pint."

"Make do with this for now." A nurse held a mug of tea for him as gradually his legs were freed, then a trapped arm, and finally he was lifted clear.

"Bloody lucky," David murmured. Hannah took a step or two nearer the wreckage, straining to listen. The glare of a thousand fires lit the city now; guns, planes, explosions and the hiss of water on hot bricks piled sound upon sound as the rescue squad went over the area yet again, bending low to catch a possible whimper.

The fire crew played on the encroaching flames and not far off another building took a direct hit and disappeared in a great pall of smoke.

"That's about it, lads." The rescue chief stood up, rubbing at his dirty forehead under the steel helmet. "Time to move on. This lot's a death trap, the fire's only got to reach those fractured mains . . ."

"No!" Hannah ran forward, limping, to where the first ARP warden was taking a breather with his mug of tea. She faced him, balanced on the rubble in her ruined shoes.

"You can't go yet. There are people still buried – two at least. And a cat."

489

The warden gave her the full benefit of his bloodshot gaze. "Is that right, miss? And you would be – ?"

"I'm not anyone. I was just here. When *this* happened." She gestured. "Please hurry, the fire's taking hold!"

Not a big man, the warden yet had an air of being in full command. "I know a fair bit about fires takin' hold, Miss, by now. I also know every man, woman and child – if not moggie – on this patch; that's my job. An' I say we've accounted for everybody."

"I can't help that." Hannah was firm, though more terrified by the minute of the advancing flames. David joined her, seeing no hope of escape until whatever Hannah had to do was done.

"You should listen to this lady. She told me some time ago about these people, that's why she wouldn't go to shelter."

The warden looked at the rings on the squadron leader's sleeve, the wings above his jacket pocket. He hesitated another second, then turned back to the rescue team. "We'll have a last shufti then, lads. All ears to the ground." He looked hard at Hannah who was starting to work her way across a pile of timbers. "Out of our way now, miss, you're not kitted out for this business. Quiet everybody!"

"Don't waste time listening." Hannah pointed. "You should find them around there."

The warden gave her another piercing look, then signalled to the others. Some crouched over the place indicated and sought gaps in the jumbled mess through which to listen. The chief warden put an eye to a space between joists and shouted.

"Anyone down there?" He was still a moment. When he got to his feet there were signs of shock in his eyes. "It's not loud. But it's certain. Two of 'em."

There was immediate and feverish activity. Hannah touched David's arm.

"I'd like to go now." She looked as though she might fall down at any minute. He put an arm about her.

"You don't want to see them? After that amazing thing you just did?" She shook her head.

"I know they're okay. That's all that matters."

He helped her back to the road. When the warden came to ask how the devil she'd known, they were turning into the Strand.

They sat in the station buffet at Swansea drinking stewed tea and eating toast and bright red jam with pips like wood chippings.

"I still can't believe it." David lit a cigarette. "Our big night spent in an air raid shelter under the Savoy!"

Hannah looked pensive. "Everything went wrong, from when you couldn't get seats on the train."

"Through not getting in to *Gone With The Wind*. Not getting in to bed with you at *any* point – quite the worst disaster! Not even having my wretched interview. Then no damn trains out of Paddington!"

"One stroke of luck, that sweet Air Ministry man offering us a lift." Hannah licked jam off her fingers. "So, why does it feel as though the trip was a great success?"

"You tell me." David smiled through a smoke-ring. "I agree that's how it feels."

"Because we were simply together? Or because the things that went wrong drew us close? Tell again about your Ministry thing."

"Oh, pure Fred Carnot. Chaos. No way were little men in blue going to sit at tidy desks and conduct lucid interviews with the likes of me. Most of them were likely still dowsing incendiaries in their sitting rooms or

491

digging out mother-in-law from her Anderson or hiking miles to work with the rail system shot to hell. 'We'll send you another appointment for a more suitable time, Squadron Leader.' " He was suddenly sombre. "That was one helluva raid. The House of Commons was a mess; Winnie will not be best pleased."

"And we were holed up in the bowels of the Savoy eating a very passable tray of supper before rolling ourselves up in our top quality blankets. I loved the little waiter who said 'I will see what can be done, madam' when I told him we were starving, and ushered us across that basement as though to the best table in the house."

"What you did." He examined his nails. "I haven't a clue what you were at, sweetheart. It was of course extraordinary, saving two lives like that. Only – " He frowned. "I have to say I wasn't keen about it. Not for *you*."

She felt a small shock of disappointment. "Even though it did save two lives? Not to mention the cat's. Why, David?"

"It does knock you about so, darling. Remember that night back in '26 at my father's place? You were *terrified*. And that cannot be good."

"It wasn't." Her voice was low. "But that was – different. Not the same thing."

Travellers pushed around the little table and a sailor's duffel bag knocked David's cap sideways. He put it on the table and Hannah thought he looked older without it, the grey in his hair and the furrow between his brows more visible. She touched him, willing him to understand.

"David, I've wanted often to push it away; refuse it. I didn't ask for it. But once someone very dear to me begged me to accept this about me, as I accept the colour of my eyes, the shape of my body. Because I loved that person very much and always trusted him, I then knew I must try quite hard to do just that . . . to accept."

"Who was he? Your husband?"

"Absolutely not. It was my father. David, if I can accept, cannot you? If we are to mean anything to one another it could be important."

Hannah read the bafflement in his eyes. She took his hand, stifling her unease. "Don't worry about it now, darling. We'll talk again, preferably when we haven't spent a night in the middle of a mega-blitz! Your train can't be much longer, it's already fifty minutes later. Are you feeling totally shredded?"

"I'm used to losing sleep." He held her fingers. "Frustrated, maybe."

"About the interview?" she asked innocently. He grinned.

"Not that, so much."

She said intently, "Why don't you take up this idea of getting involved with the training scheme?"

He leaned back. "Why? I'm okay where I am. And I like Sunderlands."

"But you are looking tired. There are surely lots of younger men?"

"If there were enough experienced fliers in their twenties and thirties d'you think they'd be using old fogies like me? They sent up kids fresh from school in the Spitfires, you know."

"Yes, but –"

"But it's a tough job, hunting U-boats in the bloody Atlantic for hours on end. Good God, if you knew." He broke off and she saw that his hand was shaking.

"Why don't you tell me, then, David? So I do know?" He smiled then, lighting another cigarette.

"Mix business with pleasure? Not on your nelly." He

rubbed a hand over his face. "It's okay, sweetheart, no problem. When we're up to strength they'll kick us oldies out in short order. Then I'll maybe get behind a nice safe desk. Would that suit Modom?"

"It would," she said bluntly. "You can hate me for it, but that's exactly where I'd like you. Oh – that's your connection!"

She watched his train sweep from sight with a weight in her stomach the size of a big stone. Always it could be the last time. The last goodbye.

That night there was a raid. Four people were killed and nine cows. Hannah helped douse three incendiaries. Cycling home, stiff-legged with fatigue as the dawn sky turned orange over the mountain, Hannah recalled yesterday's dawn in the basement of the Savoy and it seemed a distant dream. The sea was slate grey, heavy and flat, with a convoy of ships threading along the horizon.

Where was he now . . .

Chapter Nineteen

December 1941

Morfa Cottage
9 December 1941

My dear Joe,

I could scarcely believe the news – that terrible thing at Pearl Harbor, and America at war. You'll know, of course, that we've long hoped for America to come in; we've hung on and prayed for that very day. Now it's come, and in such a frightful way that it is a great shock. But, please God, it may now serve to put an early end to this murder and misery. Oh Joe, if only we could be together in this. How will you be placed about a call-up? I know you have citizenship now; does that mean you will be drafted? Please let me know what happens about everything. I'll be thinking of you.

About us – Tom's just had another week's leave and made himself useful as he always does, catching some good mackerel for one thing; so many that we could serve them in the restaurant as well as having a big feed ourselves! Then he worked a bit in the garden, though the earth is sticky as tar this weather. He even repaired the roof – his coordination seems better than it was. So strange, telling you about this young man who you probably still think of as a small child! I wish he'd talk more about his life in the Army. But he never volunteers information, only answers my questions briefly; and I must not grill him. He misses the girls, he's always sorry that his leaves don't coincide with their visits home. I can only hope he is coping reasonably with his changed life.

Jonet is already swotting for her School Certificate mocks in spring. French is the only subject in which she feels she might have a problem. She's certainly a young lady with the highest aspirations – now she's in the Lower Fifth she's so busy I wonder she finds time to come home at all! Serry's just the opposite. It's a perfectly okay school she says and the girls are fine, but she likes it better AT HOME. I tell her that the minute the raids stop she can come and welcome; for in truth, Joe, I do miss that child. She's untidy, forgetful, and can be a torment when there's something that she absolutely has to do that minute – but she's just so, well, nice with it! You'll see what I mean when you meet her – which may not be long now that America's in. Won't our first Christmas together be wonderful? This one will be pretty utility though we're looking forward to your parcel of goodies again. I shall never cook another vegetable pie as long as I live when this lot's over.

Florence had a scare when Harry had to register. But I was pretty sure they would only need one look at his medical record; and mercifully I was right. They're roping people in at a great rate now but not, thank God, Harry. He's on a fire-fighting rota anyway and also works in his spare time doing salvage collections. They've taken all the railings from Incline Row, from everywhere, even taken the park gates! I sent our tin bath and lots of pans; and you'll notice this wretched paper; it's already been used once! But you'll get to know all about salvage drives soon.

We've had two ships sunk in the bay recently by mines, and another was dive-bombed so close in that we could see the German markings on the plane. But I don't want to waste more paper or time on the war – it takes over our lives if we allow it. When you come home I shall tell you tales of my nights at the wardens' post and we will laugh together; for truly, some of it is comic.

Joe, I've wanted to tell you something important for ages. I did not for many reasons. Now I want to, although I shall hate it if you feel burdened, or feel that I have no right to confide in you.

I have a lover. Wrong; I love someone. There is a difference is there not? I've known him since I was twelve – David Vaughan, the son of Vaughan Tinplate. We met again by accident, the September before last. He's over from Canada as a pilot, he volunteered. He has a wife. But I love him, Joe. His base is on the west coast but he has taken a flat in Swansea and when we can, we meet there. This is not easy, in any way. But our time together has become precious. I've waited so long to be loved, Joe. Can you understand? Perhaps not. In the world's eyes I am the wicked "other woman". But it does not feel like that; it is two people loving and needing each other. He cannot leave his wife, she is in poor health.

Why do I tell you this now? I suppose because I had to face up to Aunt Maggie today and there was an upset. I'd gone after work to give her old dog some healing for his arthritis. I thought she seemed a bit "off", and asked if she was unwell. Upset, rather, she said. Jenna – you know, cousin Jenna from Cwmavon – had called earlier and told Aunt Maggie she'd seen me yesterday morning in Swansea, leaving a house with a man in Air Force uniform. Aunt Maggie asked outright if it was David Vaughan, said she'd heard talk about us before but hoped it wasn't serious. I said I *was* a widow – she said, "And is he a *widower*?" Then she said she was glad my Dad wasn't alive to see me behaving like a loose woman. That was when I left.

I can handle this, I am not ashamed of loving him.

But it will be bad if the girls are upset by it. Please
don't mind my telling you. I should simply like to
have someone I love, understand.

I'll say goodnight now. It's past two in the morning
and my hands are very cold. I need a cup of hot cocoa
and a hot water bottle and sleep. Tomorrow I am
seeing the Ministry of Food man yet again over
quotas, for which I need my strength! Take care of
yourself, Joe dear. And although our cards have gone
already, I wish you again all the joy that Christmas
may bring.

My love to you
Hannah

She got up stiffly, pushing herself up from the
table, and went across to fill the kettle. Towser was
enjoying the nightly assault course set up for him by
Tom and, ignoring her, he made the sawdust fly.
Hannah filled her hot-water bottle, made cocoa and
climbed the stairs with her ankles and wrists aching
with weariness. When the light was out she curled
round the comforting warmth of the bottle, sighed
and closed her eyes.

It was no use: Overtired. Should she send that letter
or was it enough to have written it out? It had just
been so awful, Aunt Maggie hectoring her. She
needed to talk it over with someone. Only she really
had no business off-loading on Joe when he was so far
away and in no position even to advise, let alone help.
After all, she was, if she were strictly honest, actually
hoping that Joe would say – sure, Han, it's perfectly
okay for you to have an affair with a married man.
No; she should rewrite the letter, omitting that piece
about David. Perhaps just having *written* it was thera-
peutic, even if she now threw it out.

She wriggled further down the bed, the house

always seemed colder without the girls. They'd be home soon for the holidays, thank goodness. Too bad, Tom not getting Christmas leave, But thank God there was no sign yet of an overseas posting. Pearl Harbor ... what might that mean for Joe? Hannah fantasised briefly about his getting posted here – Americans might well come over here when it was sorted out what must be done. She could recall faintly when the Americans had come in last time; she had imagined that the war would end almost immediately then. But it had not. And when it *was* over this time, David Vaughan would go back to where *he* belonged. It was a month since they had been together now, and then very briefly. He'd asked her if she could go into Pembrokeshire, to *him*, but of course that was impossible.

It all seemed pretty impossible. Warmer now, Hannah drifted into a doze, just as she was deciding that come spring, she would buy some pullets. The girls would almost certainly be home by then ... freshly laid eggs for tea ... wonderful ...

The three of them did what they could to make Christmas festive. There were no balloons, crackers, streamers, tinsel silver paper, oranges, but Hannah bought a chicken from a contact near Cwmavon and they made the most of that. She showed a fascinated Serena how to make a haybox and they cooked a rice pudding in it. The idea of pullets was approved; but only for eggs they insisted. They could not eat the hens who would by then, in the natural way of things, have names and personalities of their own. They devoured most of the edible contents of Joe's parcel, sharing it with Harry, Florence and Raymond on

Boxing Day. Hannah, remembering the family gatherings that time and war seemed to have destroyed, thought of Daisy without her husband and eldest son – now in North Africa – and Frank and Gareth in Patagonia, and Joe. She looked round at the family she did have left, and though she wanted most to sit by the fire and tune in to Gert and Daisy in pantomime as the Ugly Sisters, she organised charades and pass the ring with forfeits, and consequences.

And she wished David Vaughan could have been there with them; accepted by them. He was up at his parents' home for forty-eight hours and there was no way, absolutely none, for them to meet she had insisted. She had been close to tears on the telephone on Christmas Eve when he said that it was ridiculous they were just a couple of miles apart and could not meet and she said it was ridiculous that he could not understand. She shut herself in the bathroom afterwards and, sitting on the edge of the bath, shed tears of exhaustion and frustration. She had worked twelve hours a day for the last ten days had only two precious days at home now before the bakery and shop opened again, and he had no business adding to her pressures. She felt quite bad enough about not seeing him without being made to feel worse.

The day after Boxing Day she and Jonet and Serena went to see the film of Shaw's *Major Barbara* at the Plaza. As they were coming out Mr and Mrs Vaughan were just in front of them; David's mother, noticeably frailer than when Hannah had seen her last, wore a fur coat and an expensively simple black velvet beret. She turned to smile at a friend and, in doing so, looked directly at Hannah for a second or two with eyes that held a certain resemblance to David's. Did she know? If her own family did, was it reasonable to expect that David's family would be less informed?

David Vaughan pushed open his bedroom door and threw his bag on the bed. He stood irresolute, brows drawn down. Bloody train had been even later than usual leaving Port Talbot. Maybe he'd just call it a day, get his head down.

He looked at his watch. Eleven-ten. The mess bar would still be open, it being Boxing Night. But did he want another drink . . . he'd had a skinful over the last couple of days.

Another look at the bed, immaculately made, not a wrinkle in sight. Davies did a good job, kept his gear in tip-tip order. He knew for sure his uniform would be hung neat and newly pressed in the cupboard, his towels would be fresh laundered and his shirts laid out in their drawer exactly the way he liked them. But not even Davies could make that narrow, pristine bed look inviting right now.

Vaughan swung round and walked back along the corridor and down the broad, blue-carpeted stairs. He signed himself in at the table in the entrance hall, adjusted his tie, and strolled to the tall double doors of the lounge.

The warm noisy room was four deep at the long bar, knots of airmen stood about the fire, and another group had collected about the grand piano where a portly admin type in spectacles was playing "Christians Awake' accompanied by a somewhat befuddled and highly indecent chorus. Vaughan knew only a smattering of the crowd, but his own squadron was on stand-down; and only a couple were in civvies apart from him. He stared at the crush about the bar . . . it all looked fairly hopeless.

"Anything I can get you, sir?" Recognising him as a generous member, a bar waiter had materialised at his elbow. Vaughan's face cleared.

"D'you think there might be a drop of cognac left, Bill?"

"We've a spot, sir. A double?"

"Fine. How's the ante room for space?"

"Better than this, sir. Still the odd chair."

In the ante room the atmosphere was appreciably calmer. One man was writing a letter, a couple were reading, one of whom was on the point of nodding off with his head fallen forward. A bridge school was in progress at a baize-covered table with a tray of drinks drawn up close by. Vaughan settled in a deep saggy leather armchair not far from the fire, stretched out his legs and closed his eyes with a sigh.

"Your drink, sir."

"Oh, right. Thanks, Bill."

The liquor ran warmly down his throat. The fire began to thaw out his feet which had been cold since the long wait on Port Talbot station. Vaughan cupped his glass and stared into the deep amber liquid. The man who had fallen asleep began to snore; the dummy at the bridge table said "Christ!" and went over to shake his shoulder.

A wasted exercise, really, might as well have stayed here. Could've saved that bloody tiresome journey. Christmas in the mess was fair enough and he'd have saved his old man's dissertations on the correct conduct of the war according to Penrhiw Vaughan.

He finished his brandy, considered having a second, and decided he didn't need it. He was warmer, more relaxed. That phone call had probably not been the best idea. If he hadn't jumped so fast he'd have worked out that Christmas Eve and Christmas Day were simply not on for Hannah. Work, girls and everything . . . a bit much probably to expect her to drop the lot, just like that.

Julia's Christmas at Neville and Kay's place would have been okay, of course, she'd seemed in reasonable spirits when he'd put through his call, bar the usual complaints about the snow. He'd long since given up asking what else she expected in mid-winter in Canada. Poor Julia, she had absolutely no idea how her endless whingeing could –

He got up quickly, fetched a magazine from the corner table and sat down again with it, frowning. If there'd been children, perhaps; something to hold them together. He tried to be sympathetic about her ailments, of course. But being sorry didn't actually make the situation easier to cope with. And now . . .

He'd no idea if it meant as much to Hannah as it meant to him, their being together. Vaughan thought of her naked in his arms, the scent and feel of her, and shifted in his chair. He'd really counted on it, thought about it, all those bloody hours over the Atlantic.

Even so, pressuring her like that was not constructive; he *had* to believe she'd have got away if she could. Hoped he hadn't completely blotted his copybook . . . He must give her a call tomorrow, set about making amends.

God, a bloody mess; all of it. He shouldn't let her think he didn't know that well enough. But it was so damned important to him . . . certainly would be hellish if he were finally to be forced into the London posting.

Hannah was grateful to take his call at a moment when the girls were out. She had hoped there might be one after the bad taste left from Christmas Eve.

"Hannah. Look, love, sorry about that last call. I'd really not got myself properly together."

"That's all right, David. I do understand."

"I believe you do. Well, I'll try to do the same, I honestly will."

"Thanks, darling. Now we'll look forward to it working out better next time."

"Yes. We'll do just that."

None of it, of course, was easy. She wished for the strength to make a clean break; final, as she had before her marriage to Darrow Bates. Soon, perhaps, then she could feel good, knowing she had done the right thing however hard. Only, she could not do it *quite* yet.

1942 got under way with a further spate of rationing on a points system: dried fruit, rice, semolina, pulses, canned tomatoes and peas. This increased Hannah's paperwork but also her trade, since it was now food and not cash that was in short supply. Her restaurant and cafe were allocated food on the basis of how many meals were served in an average week. The amount allowed for each meal was tied in to domestic allocations. Any off-ration meats – offal, chicken, fish, rabbits – that Hannah could find would mean more customers able to be fed and so would increase her meat allocation for the next period. To this end she set herself to cultivate a web of possible providers of such treasure trove, aided by various mates of Sam Warburton, Harry and her baker, Ned. In March when the private petrol ration was axed completely save for essential business needs, she was less concerned about that than about the resistance of her customers to the new flour. Wheat was now so scarce that it was to be milled to extract almost the entire grain. This Ministry

of Food edict was inflicting upon the already suffering British, a loaf of heavy putty-grey quality that
Auntie Maggie was insisting would not be
approached by a self-respecting duck on a frozen
pond. In April, breakfast cereals were added to the list
of foods on points rationing. Tom, home for Easter
with his own row of points and coupons, had them
pounced upon by Serena who was having a brief but
hectic love affair with porridge.

"It'll make you fat," he teased her. She laughed,
shaking the bright hair freed from its term-time con-
fines. At twelve and a half there was no sign yet of
that happening; willow-slim, with small neat joints
and movements full of grace, Serena had a quality of
air and light that could not allow for an excess of
flesh. Jonet, too, was light, neither girl had their
father's bulky frame. But Jonet's build appeared
sharper, more tightly knit. When she laughed it was
not with a happy toss of the head and a little jump,
but quietly, standing with her pretty legs neatly
together.

"Come for a bike ride, then, and we'll work off the
porridge." Serena took his hand and pulled him to his
feet. "I know we've all these seeds to plant out but we
can do that together afterwards. All of us."

Hannah saw Tom's face smooth out, saw that gentle smile she loved begin in his calm eyes. How long,
before they *would* all be together?

Hannah got up off her knees and stretched, rubbing
her back. The vegetables were looking good for May;
potatoes just showing, peas and onions well on the
way, two little rows of lettuce and now the runner
beans going in, just a bit late. More time was needed;
always more time. Right now she wanted to sit in a

deck chair and do absolutely nothing but watch the clouds blow white and soft across a cobalt sky, and smell spring rushing headlong into bloom.

She wanted to forget about food – growing it, filling in forms about it, eking it out, cooking and presenting it between permissable hours and in prescribed amounts, and continually hoping that next week would not bring yet another edict on the rationing of it. National loaves, Victory dishes, Woolton Pie, egg-less cakes ... Hannah stared at the sky. One cloud looked amazingly like a saucepan of milk boiling over.

"That okay, Mam?" Serena stood back to admire the freshly weeded row of carrots.

"Splendid. Thanks, Serry, you've not pulled up a thing you shouldn't have!"

"I should think not! I told you, I'm on the veg garden rota at school. I actually do know my onions!" She smiled broadly; her hair was tousled, there was earth on her neck where she'd rubbed it and her elbow had pushed through her jumper. Hannah would have liked to hug her. But Jonet, busy revising, might glance out of her window and it would not do. Instead she smiled back. "So this is a busman's holiday of a half term. Poor Serry."

"I like it. We help with a salvage shop in the village – that's fun, too. You know, old clothes, bottles and tins – anything tin – old records, books, paper. I'd really like to give *all* my maths books and my French. More use to the war effort than to me!"

"Don't you dare." Hannah sounded stern. "You'll find the penny will drop. Just keep plugging away, love."

They started on the path together, using old dinner forks to prise up weeds from the crazy paving,

Wedgewood overseeing from his bed on a pad of aubretia. When Hannah turned to stare at the sky the drone of the plane was only faintly discernable. Soon she saw it flying seaward from the direction of the training aerodrome. She pushed herself upright, the fork dropping from her hand.

Somewhere in a far away fog, Serena's voice was telling her about the fearful toad-in-the-hole she'd made in cookery. The small monoplane was losing height, dropping towards the far end of the morfa and Hannah could hear the engine choking, coughing like an old man. She heard her own voice then over Serena's, calling out, but could not tell the words for she was uncannily, in her head, closer to the plane than to the garden path. Ever closer . . . and then, close enough to *see* the pilot fighting for control, one man at his side and a third just behind, leaning forward and shouting.

The plane's fabric seemed to have become transparent, so clearly could she see inside in the seconds before it plunged nose-down into a dune. She watched in impotent horror as the pilot wrenched in vain at the buckled door, as the other two joined in the struggle, as a ball of fire shot suddenly up and engulfed the upended wreck.

Serena screamed. Hannah stared at the flames, sweat running down her ribs.

"Did he get out?" Serena shook her mother's sleeve. "Mam, the pilot's not still – he *can't* be!"

Serena stood on the path, sobbing helplessly. Hannah was still watching the conflagration, the plane invisible behind a wall of fire and smoke. When the girl's weeping seeped at last through the numbness she reached for her, stroked the corn-gold hair that was so like Harry's had been, once, before that other war.

"All over now, Serry. The petrol ignited, they had no chance. All over now."

"They?" Serena twisted to look into Hannah's face. "More than one? Oh, Mam!"

"Three." Hannah's throat closed. Too far away to hear, the dry crackle of flames was loud only in her head as she led the sobbing child indoors.

"Want to tell me?" Harry glanced at her then gave his attention to the road, he was a careful driver. A convoy of US Army trucks thundered past the van and he said when they had the road to themselves again; "Things getting on top of you a bit, are they?"

Hannah enjoyed the occasional lift to Swansea with Harry now her petrol ration had been axed. Snippets of news were exchanged but often they drove in companionable quiet, an oasis in the busy day. Their ties were strong as they had been since childhood. Hannah wondered what it would take to break them.

"If it's about David Vaughan that's okay." He glanced across again. "A very long time back, I told you about someone. Bet you've forgotten that."

"Brigid." Hannah touched his hand. 'I've not forgotten any of it, Harry."

She stared seaward, where the hulk of a vessel wrecked last winter by a German mine reared up by the south breakwater. All hands had been lost. How long since Dada had told her why she could see the mariners on *Amazon*'s deck? All gone, now. But now there was something else.

She shifted uneasily. On ARP duty two evenings earlier she had been patrolling the road above the dunes when the flames had come suddenly, shockingly in view. All was exactly as it had been that morning last week, in the garden; the little plane engulfed, devoured. But worse had been the faint cries from the inferno.

"It's not David," she said. "I wish things were different there, of course. For one thing I wish your mother wasn't so upset about it. But I know I must live with the family's disapproval. At least you and Flo don't judge me."

"Course not. The girls aren't frettin' you, are they? Seemed fine last week when they called by."

"It's Joe, Harry." It came in a rush now. "Every time I write I ask him: what about being called up? But he's not told me; almost as if he doesn't read that bit of my letter. Well, I heard from him this morning, and he's finally told me. And I think I wish he had not. He says he actually volunteered but has been turned down – medically unfit. He has a heart problem. *Joe* with a heart problem!"

Harry drove slowly, giving her time. She turned her face away and said in a cross shaking voice, "It's ridiculous. Tom was the unfit one and they took him and he's doing his best, bless him. While Joe, he was such a strong boy, Harry. You remember? Big for his age and never ill. That was Joe."

She read Joe's letter again when she got home, with Wedgewood circled on her lap and a cup of tea on the table beside her. Her day had been long. Her customers were still complaining about the bread and two more of her girls had been detailed into the Brigend munitions factory. But the new pastry recipe was coming good. And they'd served a record number of meals in the restaurant last week which meant their meat quota would rise yet again. She just prayed there'd be no air raid tonight so she could check the figures again to be certain.

When she put the letter down Hannah picked up the little stone Joe had given her when she was Serena's age. She turned it between her fingers, feeling its smooth curve warming to her. Tranquil evening light fell in a gold panel through the open doorway. What time was it in New York? What was he doing now?

She looked at the phone and hoped David would call. Where was he? He'd recently had a weekend leave cancelled. He must be so tired. She needed him tonight; needed to be held, caressed, loved.

Putting Wedgewood down on her chair she went to the dresser cupboard and drew out her father's bugle. She found the Brasso and polished it until it shone and trembled in the last ray of the sun. Then Hannah put it to her lips and blew; gently at first, then harder as the note wavered, centred, and held, small but true.

It all came back then: the last day with Dada, when she'd played to him on the hillside – the few inexpert bars that had taken many hours to master. The pain of their parting was so clear it hurt her *now*, this moment, the healing skins of many years peeling from the wound. Hannah lifted the bugle again and tried the notes of the simple tune, closing her eyes to concentrate. When she opened them, she thought a figure stood in the doorway; a silhouette against the sunset that was exactly how she remembered her father.

She blinked. It might have been the tears in her eyes. She ran to look outside but no one was there. But her loneliness had eased. She wrapped up the bugle and laid it on the table for company, turned the radio on to Itma, and started her paperwork. Apropos of nothing, she recalled that in a couple of weeks it would be June; and she would be forty.

Chapter Twenty

January 1943

Hannah was perched on a high stool in the kitchen behind the Taibach cafe revising the menu when Harry came in. He stood in the doorway, the stiff cotton work-coat hanging from his thin shoulders and she said at once: "What is it? Harry?"

"Daisy's young Albert, Han." He swallowed. "She's had a telegram."

Hannah took his elbow and led him back to the van and climbed in beside him. Then she waited.

"She's in a real state. He's dead. That's what it said. Killed in action. Just on his twenty-first."

"Oh, Harry." Hannah, shocked into silence, remembered Albert. He was a cheerful lad with his father's spare build and the blue eyes of his mother and Harry; the first of Daisy's four. Until his call-up he had been Daisy's mainstay in the miserable, on-off period of his father's internment as an enemy alien, helping her run the cycle and motor-bike repair business Albert Mens had carved out of nothing. He had started by buying an old bicycle for half a crown, had de-rusted it, rebuilt it, and sold it for nine and sixpence. With that he had bought two others, turned them out in spanking condition and resold then for fifteen shillings each. So it had gone: never overcharging, punctilious in his work-manship, but shrewdly not allowing cycles to leave his hands without payment. He would take sixpence a week if necessary. But only when the agreed amount was payed would he allow the customer to remove his property.

Young Albert had continued this sound practice. "Got his Dad's head for business," Daisy would say. "No one has a better son." And until the war few people had remembered that twenty years ago his Dad had fought on the wrong side and ended up a prisoner of the British. Even Aunt Maggie had long since ceased to hold that against the hard-working little man who had survived the depression better than most and clearly did well for their Daisy. This had all changed when he'd been sent to an internment camp; recently an appropriate committee had decided that Albert Mens was too useful to be left languishing and he had been released for war work with other aliens and refugees.

When his eldest son was called up, the cycle business had to be shelved for the duration. Young Albert was shipped to North Africa with the Pioneers, his father disappeared daily for long shifts into one of the great camouflaged steelworks sheds, and Daisy went to work at Brigend Arsenal where she could earn three pounds a week. She had lately shown Hannah a snap of her son taken in the desert. He had stood grinning widely, dwarfed by a gun emplacement, in voluminous khaki shorts with a bush hat slung around his neck.

Tears trickled down Hannah's face, looking at Harry's stony profile. "That's terrible, Harry."

"Daisy's sittin' there, just sort of staring at nothin'. Mam's gone round. Dad's fetching Albert from the works. It'll hit him hard, he thought a lot of young Albie."

"Yes." They sat quietly in the van, watching a queue move raggedly through the January wind towards a fishmonger who had very little on his slabs. "D'you want to go, Harry, to be with Daisy?"

"What could I do? Mam'll see after her; and there's Albert. I'd likely be more in the way. I'll go tonight, with Flo."

"I'll go tonight, too, then. Not that there's much we can do," she added wearily.

She had an incendiary fighting practice after work and it was late when she slipped through the door of Daisy's house in Forth Street. Aunt Maggie had gone, but Flo and Harry were still hovering, racking their brains for words that could be remotely comforting to the bereaved parents. The two children still at home of Daisy's four, Clementine, nineteen and waiting to be called up for the WRAC and seventeen-year-old George, a loader at Bryn pit, sat awkwardly at the table, at a loss to know exactly what to do. Their father, Albert Mens, sat by the fire, hands hanging limp on his thighs and despite the warmth of the range his face looked pinched with cold. His voice when he saw Hannah was expressionless, as were his eyes.

"Daisy's just gone up. She had a good cry a bit back, she might sleep now." Albert had but the merest accent left, twenty-five years away from the Fatherland. He made as though to push himself up, let his arms drop again. Florence, who looked relieved to see Hannah, could think only to offer the universal panacea and made for the kettle, but Clementine shook her head.

"He's been swillin' that all day, Flo, you know *Nain*. Could you fancy a sandwich, Dad? There's a tasty bit of cheese."

Albert shook his head. "Thanks, love. But I'll go up in a minute."

Hannah said quickly. "I won't delay you, Albert. I'd have been here earlier but for the fire-fighting practice." She indicated the navy-blue siren suit under her coat. "I only wanted to say how dreadfully sorry . . . I was so shocked when Harry told me. Is there anything at all I can do? Anything that Daisy might need; or anyone?"

She scanned the little room. No one moved or answered.

"That you, Han?" A reedy voice floated down from above.

Hannah opened the stairs door. "Yes, Daisy. Shall I come up?"

"Please."

The bedroom seemed cold despite the gas fire. It was a small square room with diamond-patterned wallpaper in beige and pink, tightly drawn beige curtains lined with blackout material and beige and pink mottled lino with Daisy's handmade multicoloured rug by the bed. Daisy's face was swollen and shiny in the unkind light as she lay flat under the covers. When she saw Hannah she raised herself on an elbow and her mouth trembled.

"Daisy, *cariad*." Hannah sat on the bed and put her arms about Daisy's plump shoulders, which began to shake. But Daisy made a great effort not to cry, searching Hannah's face with swimming eyes.

"Will you help me, Han?" She spoke in breathy jerks. "You can do these things, I *know* you can. Tell me how Albie is, where he is. Try to get him to talk to me, just this once. You can! I *know* you can!"

She gripped Hannah's arm. Hannah drew back and thought suddenly how cold the little room was, she was shivering cold in her winter coat.

"No, Daisy." She spoke as calmly as she could, holding her cousin's hot hands between her own. "I don't know what made you think I could do that. I couldn't. I absolutely could not."

"Somebody said you could. I can't quite think . . . years and years ago. But they were quite definite you could do it – bring loved ones back to the people they'd left behind. Han, you *must* do this for me! I never had a chance to say anythin' to Albie!''

Hannah remembered Maurice Webber; the seances in the darkened room in Swansea. Further back still she remembered the dead soldier, Rowland. She felt not only cold but as though she might be sick. She got up, moving away from the bed.

"I'm sorry; that's all wrong. Whatever you heard, it was untrue. And I wouldn't do that even if I could, Daisy.''

Daisy sat up straight and her poor blotched face took on a venomous glare. She pointed a trembling finger at Hannah.

"You've never given a tinker's cuss for the family, have you, Hannah Bates! Too good for us! You've never had any heart! We c'n all rot for you, Miss High and Mighty. Even sent your own girls away –''

"And what for?'' Hannah blazed back suddenly. "So they'd be safe, because I loved them!''

"Loved them my arse!'' Daisy was shaking with rage and delayed shock as she struggled to get out of bed. "You just wanted 'em out of the way so you could carry on with your fancy man! Your fancy *married* man!'' She jabbed her finger up close to Hannah's face.

Hannah, impossibly goaded, raised her hand to defend herself against the woman who was suddenly a menacing stranger.

"What the devil's goin' on? What's up, Daisy?''

Albert was in the doorway, keen little eyes flicking from one woman to the other. Daisy opened her mouth, paused, then collapsed sobbing against him. He stared at Hannah over his wife's heaving shoulder.

"What's upset her? You been sayin' something?'' When Hannah hesitated he added sharply: "You'd

516

better go." Patting Daisy's arm he led her back to bed. "Come on now, love, I'll not leave you."

Florence and Harry had gone. Daisy's children were staring at her in much the same manner as their father, but before they could say anything Hannah was at the door, buttoning up her coat.

"I'm sorry." She said it with no idea for what she might be sorry about. As she ran down the black tunnel of the entry and into the street she knew only that she wanted to put distance between herself and Daisy's desire for her to bring back young Albert. She all but fell over the kerb and fumbled in her pockets for her torch. It was so dark she could have been alone in the world. A bitter wind cut her face as she turned along Margam Road, the masked torch illuminating scraps of pavement before her hurrying feet. A house near the corner of Woodland Avenue was showing a sizeable chink of light, but she was some yards past before duty got the better of her longing to reach home and she turned back to knock the door hard.

"Will you check your blackout please, there's light escaping. Well, I'm sorry if the milk's boiling over but I'm not standing here in the cold for fun. I'm a warden and your blackout is very much my business."

Hannah lay curled against David in the bedroom of the Swansea flat, listening to the wind that roared up the hill to rattle the window regardless of where in the frame they pushed wedges of folded paper. The curtains were closed but the room was still cold, with the entrenched, relentless cold of early February. Except for the bed; that was deliciously warm. She burrowed deeper into the curve of David's body. He sighed and adjusted his arm to accommodate her head. She knew they would soon sleep but fended it off, reluctant to end these special and all too rare moments of relaxed intimacy.

"David?"

"Mmm?"

"Darling. Was it so obvious?"

"What, sweetheart?"

"That someone had . . . that I had –"

"That you weren't giving us your full attention?" He tucked her head under his chin to free his mouth, stroking down her hair. "I thought so."

"I am sorry." She paused. "I hadn't intended you to know."

"About your set-to with your cousin?"

"What it was she'd asked me to do for her. I didn't think you'd –"

"It wasn't a big deal, love, forget it now. You didn't want to be involved. Perfectly reasonable. I agree you'd have been an idiot to have gone along with her." He yawned and stretched a leg over her thighs to draw her closer. "Nice, the way we fit together, isn't it? Everywhere."

"It's very nice." She gave the skin of his throat a loving nibble. "What I'm not sure of, David, is *why* I got so angry. *Why* I turned her down straight off like that when she was so dreadfully upset.

She thought briefly of being honest and telling him what else Daisy had said; what she had flung out about David and herself. But again concluded there would be absolutely no point. She said slowly: "Did I refuse so fast because *you'd* said it wasn't a good thing for me to do?"

"Darling, if you really want to commune with spirits, far be it for me to complain." David was crisp. "I simply believe it does you no good, having seen the effect it can have on you. As for not being part of the family –

518

haven't those ties been loosening for a while now? Whether you mind or no is another matter." He took his leg from across hers and turned away his head.

Hannah leaned over to study his face in shadow from the warm light. "I'm sorry, David. I was stupid to have let you see." She broke off again. No use talking; she would sort it out herself given time. But she was apologising so often lately and was beginning to feel uncomfortable about it. Touching David's arm in a defeated little gesture she lay back, her shoulders cold. After a moment his hand reached across.

"I do see, sweetheart. And we should always talk about any problems you're having. Only," he turned to stroke her cheek, neck, down over her breast to span the curve of her waist. "Only, can it be when I get my four day break and we have more time? When we don't have to go our separate ways come dawn?"

He leaned over her. He kissed her closed eyes, her ear, and the hollow of her throat. By the time his lips found her nipples, Hannah had set the problem of Daisy to one side.

David Vaughan was more than ready to begin the return run. He was feeling slightly light-headed and felt in his pocket for the chocolate bar he'd retained from his last ration box. He knew from experience that he needed every ounce of energy the chocolate offered at this end of the shift, when it became perilously easy to relax concentration.

"I'll be reading the course for home in about seven minutes, Skipper."

The navigator's Suffolk drawl reached him down the intercom. David nodded, raising his hand. "Okay, Ron." He looked towards Sandy Firstone in the co-pilot's seat, whose lips pursed in a soundless whistle as he trimmed the Sunderland's nose back down to search pattern altitude. "I'll take over at the point of return then, Sandy."

"Right, Skip." Sandy held the seaplane steady, looking ridiculously small and slightly built to be mastering the controls of the big four-engined machine. David finished his chocolate before speaking again.

"How about a weather check from base, Doug?"

"Will do, boss."

The radio operator was already dialling base frequency. Vaughan stared at the empty Atlantic and smothered a yawn, flexing his stiff calf muscles. A frustrating day ... damn all to relieve the boredom since taking off northward at dawn in blanketing cloud. That had thinned after they'd cleared the Irish Sea to turn west into the cold wastes of the North Atlantic. Their brief was to sweep the path of two big convoys coming in from North America, ninety merchantmen in all with twenty escorting vessels split between them. The bad weather of early winter had broken up U-boat patrol lines and halved sinkings, but February had been disastrous, and the prognosis was that March could reach a new low. Sonar and radar equipment lacked range and the want of long-range patrol bombers left an area in mid Atlantic unprotected from the air. Here, U-boats were surfacing to attack in relative safety; air crews based in Britain, flying at the utmost limit of their range, did so in the knowledge that they might well find a convoy already badly crippled limping towards them.

"Coastal gales in the Irish Sea, boss." The radio operator bent over him with a slip of paper. "Could be a bit of a chop when we moor up."

Vaughan studied the report. "Thanks, Doug. Doesn't look too drastic." He fished a small apple from his pocket and demolished it in a few bites, to refresh his mouth before taking the controls. A long way back. Better to have been based with the Plymouth outfit operating over the Bay of Biscay. A short hop out and back compared to this, and loads of action over the shallow waters; reasonable chances of bagging a kill. He'd been in a few fights on this route, but no actual kill. The only plus was the proximity to Hannah – or as much proximity as they were likely to achieve in this situation. He knew she was anxious to have the girls back at home, which would make it more difficult to meet. Pretty bleak prospect, all told. He'd have had a much worse war without Hannah ... that was one above average lady to say the least.

Julia had been sounding sorry for herself again the last couple of letters; no more than par for the course, though. And his mother was going to need attention – the family business should be sorted out and sold while it was still profitable, with no one left who wanted to take it on. Thank God his own outfit was ticking over nicely, according to the figures he got each month from Toronto. Good heads on their shoulders, Neville and Reg. And Nev's cash had been absolutely crucial.

He wondered quite a bit lately if he would ever see Neville and Reg again. Or Julia. He was being overtaken a little more each day by a sensation of having run out of time. He'd gone through the trenches a generation ago against the odds, with no disabling wounds. And now he was in his third year of this show, and feeling every day of his age. Why should he get away with it? A useless sort of life really ... no kids to hand on to, no good done to anyone by his having been here at all. And who would he miss? Well; Hannah.

David Vaughan's heredity and upbringing both had forced his nature into a mould that in many ways stood him in good stead. He simply got on with events that

521

overtook him, turned those he could to good account and did not whine about those resisting manipulation. Having made his bed he was for the most part prepared to lie in it; but he saw no reason why it should not be as comfortable as he could arrange.

He could not have a permanent relationship with Hannah, one regularised by society. He had married Julia for a variety of reasons and the alliance had delivered the positive elements he had expected of it. The minuses must be accepted; he had never told Hannah different. That did not mean he would not take any comfort offered from her love . . . she was in turn able to take what she might need from him, knowing the limitations.

He dwelt for a few moments on the happy ease of a life shared with Hannah. Such fantasies, whilst being fruitless, did him no harm.

"Ready for the turn, Skipper."

David Vaughan settled himself back in his seat. "Right-ho, Ron." He glanced across at Sandy Firstone. "Okay, Sandy; I'm with you."

Three hours later, a watery March sunset lit the froth of white horses as he lined up for his approach. It was certainly choppy; the tender already laid by on the quay to pick them up was bouncing like a rubber ball. He was dog tired as he lowered the flying boat down, parched for a beer; and a sirloin steak would be just the job after debriefing. Some chance, corned beef hash more likely.

"Touchdown, fellas."

It was one of those set-downs when he wished devoutly for an undercarriage and simple honest runway, wihout the nerve fraying bind of manoeuvring on to a mooring. A crosswind lifted his starboard wing and his port float hit the water. He cursed; pulled on the controls; releasing his breath thankfully as the float came clear. The wings stayed horizontal and the giant boat continued straight to the end of the landing run. When finally he opened up the engines to taxi towards the mooring he found his arms were trembling.

Not a superlative landing. But it would suffice. He sat still, allowing the tension to seep from his muscles whilst the others gathered up their gear and opened the plane door, the tender bucketing up alongside. His crew were already aboard it when he reached the door.

He was never certain what happened. There was a spray as a wave slapped up the Sunderland's side and he seemed to be off balance for a second. Then he slipped, striking his shinbone against the gun'wale of the tender with an uncommonly loud crunch. He remembered looking up at the nearside props and thinking how huge, now they were still; how powerful. Then he heard Sandy say "Christ!" and he felt a great surge of relief, knowing he'd not be heading for the Atlantic tomorrow at dawn. Supported by Sandy and Doug he fell into the tender.

When Hannah bent to kiss him he caught her familiar scent, the slightly lemony bouquet with a hint of musk that he had come to associate with pleasure.

"I'm sorry not to have made it earlier, darling." She pressed his hand lying on the snowy hospital bedcover and drew the visitor's chair up close. He thought she looked beautiful, though her skin was pale and a little bruised under the eyes. She wore a white beret pulled over the nut brown waves, and a white roll-neck blouse under a heathery-toned suit, a wrought silver and amethyst brooch high on its lapel. "I've been making plans to come since the phone call, but something happened each day to make it impossible. Today I simply said I'm going." She smiled a smile of warm and delicious intimacy, as though there were not five other men in the ward, a handful of visitors, and two nurses going about their business. David gripped her hand, hoping its fragile strength would help him through the pain in his leg, which was considerable. There was a cage over it draped with blankets and he thought of the pain as a wild animal, captured, which must be tamed.

Hannah was watching his face intently. "Does it hurt a lot?"

He considered a lie. "Everything is relative. How about a fag?"

"Is that allowed?" But she lit one for him and saw by the way he held it low that it was forbidden. "Are you going to tell me how it happened?"

"I slipped, getting from the plane to the tender. Damned stupid."

"And now you're grounded." She regarded him calmly. "Good."

He stared at the coverlet, silenced by her honesty, shocked almost into telling her that he agreed; but not quite. He had not been taught honesty in his dealings with others at school, nor at home, nor had he yet managed to acquire it naturally, simply through living.

"So, how do you think it's doing?" She nodded at the cage.

"Seems to be a wait and see situation. I'm cheesed off with the waiting bit already. God knows how long it'll be before I can get to Swansea." He shifted his position to one that was no more comfortable, and Hannah winced in sympathy. She was feeling unsettled by seeing him here like this and being able to do nothing to help him.

"Darling, don't fret about that for now. I'll come down as often as I possibly can. Are your friends able to come in with the station news?"

"Sandy's managed a visit. Not easy, though." He stared at the opposite window and his jaw set. "The crews are getting a bit brassed off, actually."

"Because?" she prompted. She was trying to assess his emotional situation not by his words but by his face and body language. He stubbed out his cigarette with an angry jab.

"One of the convoys we'd been patrolling for was sighted the day after this leg business. It and its sister convoy lost over twenty ships. Bloody U-boats had it all their own way in mid-Atlantic according to the reports. We can't stretch cover that far." He looked at her, revealing the depths of his anger in the deepset eyes.

She said softly: "You must feel so frustrated." He shrugged, shifting his leg again.

"But you won't be flying again, will you, darling? Not with that fracture?" It had to be out in the open . . . whether David's war was over now.

David Vaughan looked morose. These last days, lying here, he'd thought to the exclusion of everything else about flying again or being grounded. He seemed to feel torn between relief and regret in equal parts, and this was adding greatly to his general discomfort. He looked at Hannah. He wanted them to be close, wanted her to love him despite his many imperfections. But he had never been truly relaxed with any woman; and he feared that if he dropped his guard Hannah might not accept what she saw. He knew he walked on perilous ground because of his wife; because there was no way to regularise their relationship. He had no claim of any description on her. She was free to turn her back on him at any time of her choosing.

"You're all mixed up about it, aren't you? Poor love." Her voice was low. For a moment, defences unexpectedly pierced, Vaughan actually felt the warmth of tears behind his eyelids. He could have cried the whole miserable business out of his system and admitted that yes, he was bloody mixed up, pissed off, you name it.

"There's nothing wrong with me that getting over to Swansea won't fix. Even on crutches. I'd be willing to bet that you've not been made love to by a man on crutches."

Seeing her begin to laugh, he forgot how nearly he had begun to cry.

Hannah had sensed the beginnings of hope in the air, those glorious hot summer months of '43. Air raids had dwindled throughout the year and talk of a lull had changed to that of a cessation. German planes still made tip and run raids but there was a steady drift of evacuees back to the cities and Hannah gave the girls' school notice for Serena to leave at Christmas. Jonet had begged to stay on in the Sixth Form, pointing out she would never get good enough Higher School Certificate grades for a decent university if forced to move now. Hannah was unconvinced, feeling pretty certain that Jonet would get exactly the results she intended anywhere if she set her mind to it. But she did seem content, had done well in School Certificate and just been made a junior prefect.

Serena on the other hand had never disguised her preference for home. Her current ambition was to be a nurse and she didn't need Higher School Cert or university for that, she told her mother with a relieved grin. She was cultivating a Veronica Lake hairdo this summer having decided that plaits were childish, and her smile lurked beneath a blonde curtain that obscured one half of her face – though she frequently lost patience with it and pulled it back with a rubber band. Hannah looked forward to the day when she would fetch this daughter and all her possessions back home, and take time getting to know her as she changed from child to young woman.

It would, she realised perfectly well, complicate her relationship with David. But she had to take that as it came. She loved David; she loved Serena; things must simply unfold as best they may. Her relief that David was no longer combatant had been one of the summer's bonuses; now on a deferred posting to the Air Ministry he was retained on temporary loan to his station involved in the conversion of aircrew to Sunderlands. He seemed reasonably content once he was flying again, enjoying his reputation as a hard taskmaster among the men under his instruction. He had shared the good news with Hannah when, in May, U-boat losses had soared.

"I think we've cracked it, sweetheart." They had sat together in the Swansea flat, sharing a snack lunch Hannah had brought in from the restaurant. His train had been late as usual and his grip was dropped inside the door with his tunic and cap. "These Liberators give just the long-range cover we lacked. Added to which," he lowered his voice and glanced around the room with a conspiratorial frown, "we've cracked their code for U-boat movements. And word has it, changed our own, not before time. So they must hunt real hard now for our convoys and risk being blown out of the Atlantic while doing so."

He bit into his chunk of meat pie with a satisfied smile, his aching leg propped up before him on a stool. Early summer sun poured through the open window and Hannah wished suddenly that they could be eating their lunch stretched on the mossy bank of a stream on Margam mountain. The primroses would be over, but there would be trefoil and harebells, bluebells lingering in the hollows and foxgloves ready to bud. They would lie back and gaze at the sky through a tender green haze, and there would be time to talk, and maybe doze, folded close in the sweet air and lulled by the comforting drone of bees in the gorse. She sighed. Life was not like that now.

"Darling, I must be back within the hour, we're short-handed again. You'll be going on to your mother anyway, won't you?"

"I've no option, love. I'll hop on a bus I guess. God, am I sick of this petrol business! You know she's going to demand I stay the night, don't you?"

Hannah had sighed again. Never enough time; their precious meetings always cut short by people and circumstances. But how could it be different? He only had this twenty-four hours because his mother had insisted she was very unwell.

"Does she ever mention us, David? She must surely know by now."

"Absolutely not. That would be admitting it." He lit them both a cigarette and patted the sofa. "We've still a bit of time to relax. And I'll call you if there's any chance of seeing you tonight. Actually, I might just force the pace with Mama, bring you into the open so to speak. I could trust her absolutely not to write to Julia, she would see no point. Could be easier for us, though. What say you, sweetheart?"

What she said was that he must decide that for himself, which was true of course; it was not up to her to force their relationship on his mother. But she had thought about it a great deal; also, increasingly, about the effect she and David were having on her own family.

As she and Florence were closing down for the day

she said suddenly: "You know Daisy hasn't forgiven me, Flo? For refusing to try for Albie?"

"She's still very upset, Han." Florence looked up from counting receipts. "Give her time."

"She is right, though, about my no longer being part of the family. I've drifted away from it, haven't I, over these last years. Except for you and Harry."

"Things change, *cariad*. People, too. You were ambitious and you worked very hard for what you have. And your hands were really full – first with Joe and of course with Tom. Then the girls. And Darrow didn't help."

"And sometimes there just hasn't been the time to give to other people? Is that what happened?"

"Maybe, partly." Florence regarded her with kind brown eyes. "David Vaughan's complicated things, too, hasn't he? Set you apart from . . ."

"Almost everyone?" Hannah finished with a rueful smile.

The words stayed with her as she worked in the vegetable garden until dusk. Her loyalties *had* shifted . . . she no longer felt welded to the larger family, to the district, as she had once. But that was natural enough with parents gone, Joe gone, Tom away, daughters away, no husband. Only her business to tie her here, now. Not that *that* was not important, of course. When the war is over David would be gone, too. David, scarcely a mile away right now and unable to be with her.

It was late when he phoned.

"I'm sorry, honey. No chance. She'd roped Desmond in for dinner. She's clearly not up to the mark, but even so she had her head full of queries for me to deal with. And a sheaf of papers to discuss and sign."

"Don't worry about it, darling. I'm up to my eyes in paperwork myself."

"Tell you what. If we can get a few days, couldn't we just disappear? Hole up somewhere quiet? Throw away our watches?"

"Sounds wonderful. Can't quite think how but it's worth a try."

She thought about it in bed that night – several days and several nights alone with David and absolutely nothing they had to do. Just for once, actually to come first with him, have his undivided attention as he would have hers. It sounded quite wonderful. She fell asleep smiling.

In July Dutch troops moved in and set up camp on Aberavan Beach, even more GI's piled into Margam Castle, the Allies invaded Sicily and Hannah and Florence were called upon to register. "It'll be the aircraft factory for both of you," Harry teased. But with Florence caring for young Raymond and cooking in the WVS canteen on Sundays and Hannah running a catering business and in Civil Defence – now gainfully employed assembling fiddling little parts to fit into aeroplane instrument panels around a big table in their scout hut post – both were deemed to be doing their bit. During August Jonet, almost sixteen, was pressed into service in Hannah's Taibach shop and cafe and retreated thankfully back to school for the autumn term saying she needed the rest. Serena joined a local youngsters' August harvesting camp and had a wonderful time, and also helped Florence with WVS pie making and fruit picking. And when the new term started neither she nor Hannah were upset, for this was to be the last and Serena had saved up an exeat for her fourteenth birthday weekend only two weeks into the term. Tom had a weekend pass due, too.

"I may find a chicken," Hannah said, starting a mental list of the farms she could approach in search of this luxury. "Or failing that, there may be some mackerel. And we shall have a cake. And all go to the cinema. It will be lovely."

David phoned the night before; almost certain of leave in four weeks and what could Hannah do about it? She promised to start forward planning and that, too, went on the calendar, but tentatively pencilled in, unlike Serena's exuberant red crayon for her birthday exeat. She went over his call again, waiting for sleep. Could these few precious days together actually be going to happen? The Allies' landing on Italy's mainland had brought home to her afresh the impermanence of their relationship. Those days away, that could be counted on the fingers of one hand, might be all they would ever have. She knew that she must come to terms with his inescapable return to Canada and to Julia, who was his wife and entitled to the loyalty he had pledged to her long ago.

Serena arrived before Tom, jumping off the bus and running to her mother, weekend case swinging against black-stockinged legs. She tugged off the elastic band to set free her curtain of hair.

"Did you get a chicken for tomorrow?" They hugged, laughing, and Hannah realised her daughter had grown again.

"Wretched child, always thinking about your stomach." Arm in arm they started towards home. "Yes, I did, I told you I would."

"Wait till Uncle Tom knows, chicken's his favourite. I can't wait to see him. Jonet sends her love, she hopes I'll

531

take her back a drumstick. Honest, Mam, the food's pretty grim there now."

"It's pretty grim everywhere, Serry. But I've collected a few treats for tomorrow, we might put together a parcel for poor Jonet. Tom's not going to be here until later, it takes him longer now he's further off in Gloucestershire. His train's due in at around ten. How about you and me going to the Regent before that?"

"Smashing!" Serena skipped with excitement. "What's on?"

Hannah's smile widened. "Three guesses."

"Mam, don't be mean!"

"Think of a film you'd really like to see."

"Any. Now tell me what!"

"How about *Gone With The Wind*?"

Serena gave a squeal of pleasure. "You're not kidding me?"

It was all they had imagined and more. They came out into the blackout, heads bursting with technicolour images and ears assailed by Tara's theme. Making their way to the station, readjusting to reality seemed difficult.

"I'd love dark hair like Vivien Leigh. It's so – so –"

"Dark?" offered Hannah helpfully and Serena giggled. She was diverted by the allure of the fish and chip shop and they shared a bag of chips, sitting on the bench waiting for Tom's train. "He'll be very tired," Hannah warned.

"That'll make two of us." Serena drooped with childish suddenness, sated with larger-than-life cinema and the chips. She was almost asleep before Tom's train came in, head lolling against Hannah, who hoped David would phone again soon. She wanted to tell him about seeing *Gone With The Wind* at last. Wanted just to talk.

Tom was indeed tired, drained of colour but for an angry red spot on his chin, and was clearly fit for nothing but bed. He slept till noon on Saturday and came downstairs with a guilty smile and a small brown paper bag.

"Happy birthday, Serry." He held out the bag. "I'm sorry I'd nothing nice to wrap it in."

"Don't worry about that, Uncle Tom. Oh, how pretty!" She held up the scarf, a square of rich stained-glass window colours that caught the September light and glowed. "Mam, look!"

"I got it at the church bazaar. I thought the colours were pretty," he said shyly.

Serena folded it to a triangle and tied it over her hair. "Gorgeous! Thanks a million. And wait." She ran to the sitting room. "This is from Mam. Don't they go beautifully?"

She put on the cherry red coat with patch pockets and a shawl collar and twirled before them, cheeks pink with pleasure. "It's taken all Mam's coupons – isn't it a knockout?"

"I couldn't resist the colour. Tom, the scarf is perfect with it. And look." Hannah, back from the bakery, set down her bag and lifted out a cake box. "It's not fancy, darling, because you know we're not allowed icing and things. But it should taste nice. And I still have just a little icing sugar here, enough to run a thin topping on it."

"Smashing." Serena lifted out the cake. "Can I do that, put the icing on? And did you get the sausages?"

Hannah waved a parcel at her daughter. "Pork and tomato. Don't ask how I came by them. Sausages and chips for tea, Tom? The birthday girl's choice."

"Lovely." Tom looked as though he needed more sleep.

"And chicken for dinner tomorrow. With thyme and parsley stuffing and all the vegetables. And apple pie." Serena caught his hand. "Does that beat your rotten old canteen food? Now come and see my cards."

They lingered on over lunch with a pot of tea. Joe's gift of fur slippers had arrived a week early and was now duly admired, with a red pokerwork purse from Sam Warburton who never forgot either girl's birthday.

"It's ages since I saw Mr Warburton, Mam. Maybe I'll just cycle round and thank him."

"Nice idea, Serry." Hannah smiled at Tom, who was looking more refreshed now. "I have to go to the ARP post for just a bit, Tom, we're falling behind with our quota of plane parts and it's a matter of pride that we keep it up – all the local posts are doing it. Why not put your feet up and listen to the radio?"

"And I'll cycle down to Harry and Flo. And do Mr Warburton on the way." Serena picked up the purse and slippers. "I'll take these to show them. Could I put on my coat and scarf, Mam?"

"You'll not get oil from the bicycle chain on your coat? It's longer than you're used to."

"Absolutely not." Serena knelt on the hearthrug, stroking Wedgewood until the cat began to purr luxuriantly. Watching her, Hannah thought of the four-year-old on the rag rug at Number twelve Incline Row, buttoning her shoe straps together then looking up to laugh. Where had a whole decade gone?

They cycled together towards town. The afternoon was wild and blustery; tendrils of hair escaped from Serena's new scarf and the red coat blew open to reveal bare knees working energetically up and down.

"See you soon," she called and peeled off at Sam Warburton's street, slippers and purse in her cycle basket. Hannah waved and accelerated down to the post. She would be finished within the hour with no time out for gossiping. Maybe a chance of a few quiet words with Tom before Serry got back for tea.

She had been assembling cockpit consoles for some time when she began to feel uneasy. She looked at her watch, inched up her work-rate. Almost three o'clock. She wanted to get back, that was all. But soon Hannah knew that was not all; a sensation of dread was settling in her stomach like cement. When the hour was up she still had work on her section of the table, but she pushed back her chair.

"I'm sorry. I'll have to go."

She hurried out, forgetting her cycle leaning against the wall. Up past the station and into Commercial Road; the wind had strengthened and she seemed to be fighting it as she ran, navy slacks snapping against her legs. Images were tumbling through her mind, a formless kaleidoscope; but when she saw Tom coming towards her it all crystallised with a dreadful finality.

"What's happened to her? Where is she, Tom?"

Then she saw his face, the colour of uncooked pastry, and wanted to stop her ears against what he would tell her.

"They've taken her to hospital. Sam saw it happen, he'd gone out to wave her off. Turned out of his road straight into a convoy of American trucks."

In the waiting room a US officer was standing with his back to the door, staring at a notice on a wall-board and smoking. The nurse invited Hannah to sit but she remained stiffly in the centre of the little room with Tom at her side.

"I'll fetch the doctor, Mrs Bates." Then she nodded at the American. "This officer came in with your daughter." She left them, closing the door.

"There wasn't a thing we could do, Mrs Bates." The young man stubbed out his cigarette and Hannah saw his hand shake. "She was under our wheels almost before we saw her. A train was passing down below and I think with the noise she didn't hear our boys coming. The driver said he thought she turned to wave to somebody. I just can't say how sorry –" He stopped. "The driver's in a helluva state."

"Yes," said Hannah in a voice that seemed to belong to someone else. Her mind seemed to be a complete blank now. After a few moments a middle-aged man wearing a white coat came into the room.

"Mrs Bates?"

When Hannah failed to answer, simply looking at him, he took her elbow. "Would you like to . . ." He led her out, Tom following closely. They walked in silence along a corridor and round a corner. When the doctor stopped outside a door with his hand on its knob Hannah saw inconsequentially that he looked tired, with a nervous tic in his cheek, and that he was overdue for a shave.

"Mrs Bates, I'm very sorry to have to tell you that we were unable to save your daughter. She died in the ambulance. She would have known nothing about it, if that's any comfort to you." He opened the door a fraction, then paused. "She's in there."

Hannah walked past him into the little room. Serena lay with a regulation white coverlet turned back neatly under her chin, and might have been asleep. Hannah stood by the bed looking at her daughter and none of it was real. Nothing was making any sense at all. When Tom gave a painful gasp and felt for her hand she took his, and its coldness surprised her.

"I hope her coat didn't get dirty," she said, and to her ears her voice seemed to come from far off. "Or her headscarf. That would upset her. They were both brand new."

Chapter Twenty-One

September 1943

"I shall be all right," said Hannah yet again. Tom was leaning from the train window; eyes pale with anxiety he continued to hold tight to her hand. Poor Tom . . . she stretched her mouth into a smile in an effort to reassure him.

"You'll go to Flo and Harry's like they said? You'll not go back home on your own?" He looked for the guard to start banging the doors, fearful on both Hannah's account and his own, his delicate equilibrium shaken almost beyond control. "And Jonet won't be long, here tomorrow."

"Yes." She made a supreme effort to steady him, caring for Tom was a habit that would not easily break. "Tom, try now, for me? I need to know you won't allow what has happened to make you ill. That's the very best way to help me."

The whistle blew and she saw panic rise in his eyes. Reaching up to kiss him she whispered, "You be strong for me now, love. I shall write to you in a day or two. I'm sorry you have to go back, but you have no choice."

"Okay, Han." He released her as the train moved. Hannah waved until he'd gone, her arm going back and forth like that of a mechanical toy.

Gone: the word echoed in her head as she walked from the station. Monday morning, a dull, overcast autumn day. She had work to go to. She had a daughter to bury. But there was still something other ... and it was eluding her.

She walked past the end of Incline Row. Florence had had no option but to go to Swansea as usual, the restaurant must function, but Harry had said he would return home to be with her as soon as his early deliveries were done. Aunt Maggie would be there anyway, just a few doors away, in case he was delayed. Hannah had nodded, grateful. He said that Daisy and Albert, too, had called with their condolences and would be back. She was aware in a detached way that there were arrangements to be made. But soon she turned inland towards Margam mountain and began to climb, legs moving automatically, though she still seemed to have no obvious plan in mind.

Her pace stayed steady as she walked higher and the winding road narrowed and became rougher. Soon the coastal strip had fallen away with its giant sheds, cylinders and tubes. The chimneys sent more grey clouds into the grey sky of this grey, blustery September day. She might have seen the gunnery range further off, and the bombing range on the Morfa, and the Dutch camp on Aberavan beach protected by a minefield, had she looked.

Hannah saw nothing. Her breathing was hard as she reached the shoulder of the mountain; soon after that there were the windswept pines that sheltered the tumbled stones of what had been Rachel Hywel's cottage. Anger began to rise in her like bile as she approached the place, bubbling through her gullet to foul her mouth.

"Where are you? You haven't gone, have you? You're still there?"

There might have been a shadow then, near where centuries ago had stood a stout oaken door. Hannah ran forward and her voice rose to a scream that echoed round the hills, round her head.

"What is it about, then? Tell me! Do you hear? *Tell me!*"

She was using the Welsh, the old tongue she had rarely used since childhood. It rolled from her throat as she ran and now she could see the figure more clearly.

"You're still angry, are you? Rachel Hywel? Well, *I* am angry, too!"

She fell over a rock and blood trickled through her torn stocking but she felt no pain. That was all inside her; a grotesque torrent that threatened to split her open with its force as it surged and boiled. Some fifty yards from the ruin she swayed and steadied herself against a stunted oak.

"What happened to you, that you cannot rest? Have you sworn vengeance for some dreadful wrong?" She pushed herself off the tree and moved a few more unsteady paces. Frowning, she tried to bring the figure of the woman into focus but it remained blurred, as though seen through heavy rain. "Well, *I* want vengeance, too," she shouted. "For my daughter, my Serena! What do you say now, Rachel Hywel? Answer me. *Answer me!*"

Her scream appeared to explode through the top of her skull, smashing it. Circling dizzily into unconsciousness Hannah was yet aware of an approaching shadow, and as she threw out a hand to save herself she had a sensation of a heavy woollen skirt brushing past it. She called out once and fell into black release.

Her eyelids were almost too heavy to lift. A fraction at a time she let in the daylight, bright enough to make her wince for the skies had cleared. Too weary to move for some time, she finally levered herself onto an elbow. God . . . *so* tired.

Getting to her feet was a supreme effort, as though she had been drugged, and her legs felt unreliable; she shook her head to clear it and rubbed at her cheeks. Then she wished for oblivion again, because she remembered that Serena was dead.

Hannah leaned weakly against a boulder and the salty wind blew back her tumbled hair. She had no inkling of why she'd come here; no idea what she wanted of Rachel Hywel, what she had hoped for. Gradually, achingly, she remembered the anger, a great formless destructive monster; gradually, became aware that she was no longer possessed by it.

She looked at the ruined walls in the fold of the hill. The gentle sunlight lent warmth and colour to the old stones and she sensed no air of menace now. If the troubled spirit of Rachel had departed it had left no trace. But in place of that fearful anger Hannah now felt a huge sadness seeping into every pore.

"Serry. Little love."

She laid her head on the fissured ancient boulder and felt the tears gather and begin to fall. They ran down the granite and on to her shoes. She had no idea how long she wept for her lost daughter; she curled on to the cropped grass and cried and cried, and the tears were the beginning of the healing.

When she lifted her head, Hannah saw through swollen, aching eyes that the shadows were lengthening. Pulling herself to her feet and stumbling with exhaustion, she began the journey back.

"Harry, you've not told anyone who Han's gone away with, have you?"

Florence handed Harry his tea and he wrapped his

hands around the cup in the way he always did, elbows on the kitchen table with its crisp yellow gingham cloth. He enjoyed their evening drink with Raymond tucked up and the day's work done, curtains drawn and the fire at its best with plenty of heart to throw out a comforting glow. Another November; the fifth of the war.

"Can you see me letting on?" He helped himself from the biscuit barrel, filled these days with misshapes from the bakery. "Come on, Flo, credit me with a bit of sense."

"Sorry, love. I know she always says she doesn't care who knows now; but no need to advertise is there? Han's hurt enough, with Jonet being so rude to David when he turned up for the funeral. I think it's best *she* doesn't find out. Not unless her Mam decides to tell her."

Florence drained her teacup and went back to turning the collar of Raymond's shirt. "In fact I could see she was pretty much hurt by the way the family in general took against him going to the funeral. I remember her saying that if they had any real thought for her they'd be glad she had somebody to *care*. Pity about your Mam makin' it so clear what she thought."

"It was a bit unexpected, Flo, you must admit." Harry lit his last Woodbine of the day and leant back to enjoy it. "Must've taken some nerve, I'll say that for him, turnin' up at church as if he was family."

"It gave her a lift, though, that he'd taken the trouble. She said afterwards that it helped no end." Florence squinted as she re-threaded her needle. "And I agree with how she feels now – that basically it's her own business and no one else's. I'm only glad she's managed to get these few days off. If anyone needed a break it's her."

"I still can't take it in some days, about Serry." Harry stared soberly at his wife. "Full of life . . . then."

"Han worshipped her." Florence's needle faltered and she frowned to keep at bay the tears that after weeks could still surprise her. "If she hadn't had her work I don't know what . . . It was too bad Joe couldn't get over, he'd have been a big comfort. Well, I for one am glad she's David Vaughan to turn to. Even though they can't . . . well, it can't ever *come* to anything. And of course the war will be over one day. Can't be that long surely, once they're into Europe again. Fightin' hard around Sangro, the paper says. I read about Italy in November being as bad for mud as the Somme was."

The Somme: Harry closed his eyes. The room, warm and familiar with the wife he loved sitting opposite him in her easy chair sewing Raymond's collar, had disappeared. There was darkness cut open by gunfire and Very lights and blood-red screams of men as they were blown to bits. There was the pain of trying to run another twenty yards to safety when your lungs were bursting and yellow mud sucked your legs down into hell, which was full of bloated rats who had drowned in the same mud.

His forehead wet with sweat, Harry forced open his eyes. Not his war. His war was over.

"Yes, Flo." His voice sounded almost normal though his head was still thudding. "Yes, they're fighting around Sangro. But there's a way to go yet."

"She did know he'd go back one day. Poor Han." Florence stared into the fire.

"Known that all along," agreed Harry. "There's the rub."

"It should have been longer." David Vaughan turned Hannah over and began to work on her back, kneading

543

outwards from the spine. "Four days has been nowhere near enough."

Hannah rested her head on her hands, sighing as she relaxed under his hard palms. The bedroom was warm and intimate, with thick velvet curtains drawn against the rough night and a gas fire popping in the hearth. November was not the ideal month to see the Cotswolds at their best, the hotel owner had told them on their arrival, and had proceeded to do everything to make them welcome, warm and well-fed.

"Longer would have been wonderful." Her voice faded as his fingers reached her shoulders to put in some vigorous work. "But I've been grateful for this. You were clever, finding such a marvellous hidey-hole."

"Personal recommendation, as I told you." He drew a final gentle line down her spine to bring his hands to rest on her waist. "If it was good enough for Sandy's honeymoon . . ."

"And the weather's been kind. I'd no idea the Cotswolds were so magical." Hannah rolled over, smiling in the soft peachy light. "Of course, the right company makes a difference."

"Ah, well, we're both lucky there."

He slid his hands under her shoulders and kissed her breasts, throat, mouth, with a tenderness that touched new depths. When he pulled away a little to study her face Hannah knew he would find shadows there now; lines speaking of pain and loss. But she lay quiet under his scrutiny, willing herself to trust him without reserve. All guile had gone. These days it seemed to her that their relationship had moved on a notch – though it may only have been on her part, for how could she presume that he had made identical progress? For her

544

part she felt stripped of artifice, pared down to elementals. So many things that once had carried weight now were of no importance. Serena's death had changed her values.

He went to the bar and returned with drinks, and hot milk and biscuits which he set down on the bed. Hannah lay against the pillows reading the paper, relaxed and warm.

"You are to eat *all* the biscuits. I've an idea they're black market. And there's whisky in the milk. That's most likely black market, too." He undressed and got into bed beside her with his own whisky and they shared out the newspaper. Sipping her milk, Hannah wondered if this was anything like being married, not counting being married to Darrow Bates, of course. If so, she liked it. Then she read about the campaign in Italy that seemed to be bogged down, and ongoing demands for a second front, and laid down her piece of the paper. David had been sounded out again about a job in transport . . . possibly in London. She felt that the Swansea flat period was approaching its end.

All the time there were endings. The end of this term and Serry would have left boarding school and come back to live. There would be an end one day to this appalling war, as there had been to the last. And then there would be an end to herself and David. Hannah lay by him in the warm bed and though her skin felt warm enough she was so cold inside she was shivering.

They made love with an intensity that bordered on dedication. Each carried the other along a deepening river that tossed and swept them with heady abandon to beach them finally, exhausted and damp, in one another's arms. Neither moved until their breathing and senses had steadied. Then David moved his lips against Hannah's face and found it salty wet.

545

"What's this, sweetheart?" There was no reply but her chest began to heave with unshed tears. "Hannah? Darling, tell me?"

With a sudden twist she fastened hard against him, palms spread over his back. "You won't go, David?" The words were thick and muffled with her face pushed into his shoulder.

"Now why should I do that?" He patted her back as he would comfort a child. "Why would I want to leave you?"

"I mean – " She drew a shaking breath. "Not ever. Not leave me. Stay . . ."

He stroked her murmuring endearments until she steadied and lay quiet. After a while he said:

"Hannah, you know there's nothing I'd like more. But I have to report back tomorrow night for duty the morning after. I've no choice."

"That's not what I *mean*, David." She turned to lie on her back, staring at a mushroom-shape on the ceiling cast by the shaded lamp. Their hands touched and he caught and held her fingers. "I mean – afterwards. That it would be to *me* you come back." After a moment she added: "If you actually love me, that is."

They lay still, joined now by their fingers. When he turned on to his elbow to lean over her Hannah tried to look back calmly, without more tears. She knew men hated tears, could not cope with them.

"There's nothing I want more than to live with you, Hannah. And since September, well, I don't go along in the least with leaving you." He traced down the line of her cheek with a gentle finger and Hannah remained still. "I can do damn all about anything till I'm back over there; you do see that? But I'll get things sorted out then. A divorce. She'll be well provided for. You could make a fresh start after all this, in Canada with me you'd not be reminded of what happened at every turn . . . every time you passed that spot. And Joe's just over the border in the US, you could visit him." He found as he spoke that he did want to believe what he was saying. He touched her lips with his. "There now. Feel better?" Hannah squeezed his fingers. "Good girl. Try to get some sleep now."

"One thing, darling."

"What's that?"

"I haven't actually told you, have I, what it meant to me? Seeing you at the church, at the funeral." She found it fearsome to say the words, confirming again that Serena was truly, officially dead. "It helped me so much."

"Just seemed a good idea to put in an appearance. A show of support if you like. Despite the odd black look from various of the congregation."

"They didn't understand, David. But that didn't matter. *I* understood . . . and I was grateful."

When she did sleep, her dreams were busy and violent. At one point she was running down a grassy slope pursued by men with spears. Inexorably the slope steepened and her momentum forced her on with increasing speed; faster and faster, until the ground dropped away beneath her and she tumbled into terrifying space. She woke, bolt upright, with the vivid sensation of flight and fear and stared about her. David did not wake, but she could feel his warmth and hear his breathing, and was calmed by them enough to sleep again.

Hannah's winter was survived a day at a time, by working until she was simply too tired to lie awake once she got to bed. There were no air raids but the local wardens all continued regularly with blackout inspections and fire practice and assembling aircraft consoles. She also did a Sunday shift in the precision engineering factory at Baglan alongside other women who worked all week at other jobs. She would cycle home in the winter blackout not having seen daylight, numb with the effort of ten hours' sustained concentration on the delicate instrument panels she had been assembling. She would scrape up just enough energy to feed Wedgewood and the now elderly Towser before pulling herself up the stairs with a glass of hot milk in lieu of supper. Her business boomed to new heights, rising successfully to the challenge of local British Restaurants in this fifth winter of the war. Wages were good, the district was crammed with British and foreign troops, and a meal out to stretch the rations held appeal equalled only by a trip to the cinema. She had found favour with enough fishermen to vary her menu with seasonal catches, and a small band of farmers would sell her what few chickens they could feed for the right price. Florence went from strength to strength and a vacant table in the restaurant was unusual, whilst Harry quietly absorbed numerous jobs that had not been within his remit. Mrs Price in the Taibach kitchen accomplished small miracles daily with the ingredients still allowed them by the Ministry of Food, and when in February one of her sons was wounded at Anzio, the blow seemed only to spur her to fresh efforts.

"They'll not get the better of us," she would mutter, fingers fluttering through her pastry; and if one of the girls left suddenly for a war job she would rustle up a member of her extended family to lend a hand between their own shifts. Young Raymond, secure in his adoptive home and growing like a weed, came on Saturdays to make himself useful and put his small wages thriftily into Savings Stamps.

Hannah had at first longed for Jonet to say she would come home, but ultimately had to accept that the idea simply had not occurred. At her sister's funeral she had been white-faced and silent, but composed, and Christmas had passed without any indication on her part that Serena's death had left a gaping hole at the centre of the family. Florence advised Hannah to simply *tell* Jonet she was leaving – she should have gone ahead as she had intended, a term's notice and home for Christmas, there'd be no more raids now. Hannah acknowledged that Flo may have been right. Yet somehow, seeing Jonet so content there, things going so well for her, she hesitated to make that demand despite her own need. Tom had said Jonet should come home, too. But he did not press her. He had had Christmas leave this year and had done his best to appear reasonably cheerful, but Hannah had felt an unmistakable relief when both he and Jonet left again. The huge effort of having to behave with any degree of normality slid from her, leaving her silent and lethargic. She worked automatically through each day, answered when she was asked a question but seemed to have no wish for company otherwise. Except David . . . she did long to be with him. That, she knew, was rarely possible. When they did manage a few hours he was usually tired and quiet and showing every day of his years.

By March her need to find Serena became uncontainable. David told her that he could be called to London at any time now, to do with air transport he said vaguely. Things were hotting up towards a second front and he had experience of shifting cargo from A to B. Hannah felt a sick jolt of anguish; turned her head so he could not see.

"You get up to London and we'll have that night at the Savoy we didn't manage last time," he encouraged her, her dismay too plain to hide from him. "And look at it this way, sweetheart. The sooner we organise this second front the sooner we'll have the whole damn thing finished and be able to get on with our lives again."

"But you will have to go back to Canada?" Hannah felt stupid then; of course he had to go back. A divorce took time to sort out. She apologised and said she would certainly try to organise London and that yes, she was certain it would all work out if they were patient. She cooked dinner for him and told him he was welcome to stay at Morfa Cottage since the whole place knew about them now anyway.

She said nothing about wanting to visit a medium to attempt to contact Serena, knowing that he would hate the idea and try to persuade her against it. After a couple of nights spent agonising over the decision, she wrote to a man in Porthcawl of long-standing reputation as a medium and asked for an interview. She felt quite sick, slipping the letter into the postbox. This was what she had refused to do for Daisy; an area she'd vowed she would never again touch. But Serena – simply to know something, anything ... she would manage her grief better, surely, after that. She had looked everywhere, all winter, hoping to catch sight of the bright little face; how could she spend the rest of her life in such a way? If she might only use her own powers ... But instinct told her she could work only for others, never for herself; she could only ever be the channel connecting two others.

On the bus to Porthcawl ten days later Hannah thought she might faint. Her knees threatened to melt as she walked slowly towards Temple Street; a slender, beautiful woman in a dark blue coat and matching hat with a half-veil that hid the pain in her eyes from passers-by.

There was no difficulty in finding Ambleside, a discreet Edwardian semi-detached villa with snowy starched nets at the windows and a vast hydrangea filling the little front plot. Hannah drew level with the house, faltered in mid-step; walked past. At the end of the road she kept walking, with no idea of direction until she reached the sea front and was hit by the March wind. She sat on a wrought-iron bench that faced the incoming tide, boiling and frothing up the deserted beach to leave a line of dark ragged seaweed.

It was not what she wanted . . . some disembodied spirit voice in a darkened room, coming through the lips of a strange man. Her daughter was not that. She would hear Serena in the scented June zephyr blowing through the gorse; in the soft contented purr of old Wedgewood and in the rhythmic slap of wavelets on the summer beach. She might catch her smile in a glowing fire, or glimpse a shadowy girl tumbling with the lambs in spring. If Hannah learned how, she could find Serena wherever she found beauty, generosity and joy. Not lost; not inaccessible. Just waiting in some fragrant garden where one day they could be together.

She became aware of someone beside her on the bench. It had been some time since Dorothea had come. Now Hannah turned, and when she smiled her friend of so many years smiled back, the wind lifting and teasing her long hair. A healing hand enclosed her heart and warmth stole through her chilled flesh. She lost the sense of isolation that had enveloped her all winter, never quite leaving her even in David's company. She sat there for a few minutes more, watching the gulls bob and dive in the heaving grey waves or fling themselves about the sky, scattering like tea leaves on a tablecloth. Then she returned to Temple Street and explained to Mr Ormond that she had made a mistake and would not now need him, and knew that was the truth.

Chapter Twenty-Two

June 1944

The excitement was tremendous. Mrs Price got her mix wrong for the currant buns and Ned singed his first batch of bread, running out to see the American troops swinging past in the blustery grey dawn.

Hannah, half-dressed, peered on tip-toe from her bedroom window at the unfamiliar vessels crowding the docks, the endless khaki columns snaking up and down the quays and ribboning back to the town. Far out in the bay an escort of destroyers and corvettes waited for the landing craft to take on their human cargo and join the armada bound for the beaches of Normandy.

"Not long now, then." Mrs Price was brewing up the strong tea clearly called for by the occasion. "They'll go through France like a knife through butter and it'll all be done come the Bank Holiday. We got Rome already, I heard it on the wireless. Only Berlin now. Well, there's them nasty little Japs but they'll cave in once Jerry's smashed."

Hannah envied Mrs Price her splendidly simplified over-view of the conflict. It might be only weeks now before David would follow these men still flowing towards the embarkation points. Pray God Tom would stay . . . not Tom, across France and into Germany, baking bread for the advancing battalions. Pray God those battalions *would* advance.

"Be quiet around here, with the Yanks gone." Noreen Jones, peeling potatoes for the shepherd's pies, sounded pensive. Mrs Price sniffed. Noreen's elder sister was known to be in an interesting condition due to her liaison with a gunner from Ohio. Little Peggy Way who had only been with them in the kitchen two weeks and didn't know about this, but who was walking out with a Dutch boy, giggled in such a suggestive fashion that Mrs Price glared at her and slammed down a pan for her to scrub.

Hannah said briskly: "I'll miss them for the very practical reason that they've been so good for business. But apart from that I think it's been nice having them around. They're a friendly, cheerful lot, aren't they?"

The silence that greeted her remark and Mrs Price's expression checked her. Well, of course Mrs Price must know about herself and David. She should have realised there would be no one even remotely connected with her who would not know. Funny, though, to think of him lumped in with the GIs and the rest. Maybe she was being lumped in with Noreen's sister and with young Peggy who cuddled in shop doorways with her Dutch boy! Was that how Jonet saw her, why there was this hurtful wall of antagonism dividing them? Hannah had felt it being slowly built for months and was finding no way to reach Jonet through it. Perhaps it was justly deserved, but it was painful to be so harshly judged by her own daughter without a chance to give her version of the damning picture. Probably only with maturity would Jonet learn not to judge others. Of course, she might never learn.

Walking that night along the hill, she watched the now diminished movement of men and vessels in the summer dusk. How many were dead already on the beaches of Normandy? The town itself seemed dead, emptied of its life force. As she turned homeward a blur of orange caught her eye. The vision of the wrecked plane in the dunes flared for a moment, weirdly, as it had on that bright May afternoon two years ago. Hannah shivered, pulling her jacket tight about her. She believed she heard the cries of the trapped airmen, faint in distant memory . . . a memory that included Serry, who had been with her that day as they'd weeded the garden together. If she were here now they would be listening to the radio together for news of how the invasion was going. Together; a beautiful word. She wished that David and she were together, that first night of the Second Front.

Summer, wet and leadened-skied, was quickly gone, centred round wireless bulletins or newspaper reports of a slow advance in one sector or a heartening push in another. When Montgomery entered Caen David phoned Hannah, excited as a boy, and when at the end of July the Americans broke out to pour through France he did so again, the line crackling with the feeling of great events unfolding.

"So it won't be long now? Before . ." Hannah paused, not wanting to ask what she could not bear to have answered.

"Oh, I don't know about that, sweetheart. Have to see how things go for a bit. Early days."

He'd been in London some weeks now, dangerously so as news of the unmanned, fearsome flying bombs broke. Hannah read descriptions of them and of the sudden death raining anew on London . . . and there was nothing to be done. Three months since they had been together. But, "I won't hear of you coming up till we see the back of these damn contraptions." He was adamant. And so August came; and Jonet.

"I really can't wear this," said Jonet. She frowned at herself in the looking-glass. The dusky pink crepe frock was Hannah's. It had a pintucked bodice with pink pearl buttons, pleats stitched to hip level then released to fall slimly to the knee; short cuffed sleeves with shoulder pads, a Peter Pan collar and a matching suede belt with curved clasp. Hannah had bought it in Cardiff the autumn war had started and it had been expensive. It fitted Jonet perfectly and suited her dark dramatic looks.

"Why not?" asked Hannah reasonably. "I think you look very nice."

Jonet twitched at the skirt, turned away and looked back over her shoulder. Her hair swung out, hanging smooth until it frothed in curls about her neck and with a bang turned under at the front. It was thick and glossy; watching her, Hannah recalled that Darrow Bates had had such hair. And eyes; big and dark under strong brows. Jonet never spoke of her father . . . and neither did Hannah.

"It really does suit you," she tried again. "And not a soul at the dance will have any idea it was mine. We've simply no coupons for anything else; anyway, mothers and daughters swap clothes all the time these days to have a change. I bet Gerald's sister and mother do."

Jonet's frown changed to a smile. "Not a chance. Mrs Francis is built like a tank and Pam's thinner than me." She pulled the belt in a notch, made a face and let it out. "We – e – ll . . . maybe."

"You can wear my garnet with it." Hannah bribed. "And I have a lipstick that goes beautifully. What time is Gerald coming?"

"Half past." Jonet patted the dress collar, sighed, and began to unfasten the pearl buttons. "He's nothing special, you know. Just Pam's brother; he comes to all the things at school, being nearby."

"He doesn't have to be special, as you put it, for you

556

to have a nice time at the dance. Any idea when you might be back?"

"He said it finishes at eleven, we'll have to leave early to get the last bus, won't we?" Hannah thought Jonet looked much younger than almost seventeen, standing in her vest and knickers. "I'm fed up with this war," she said with sudden venom. "No petrol, the blackout, trains and buses always late or cancelled. Everybody busy and having to do loads of rotten things we don't want to do."

"Like helping me out at work in the holidays? You're seventeen next month, lots of girls are working full-time in factories at that age. I'd have thought you were quite lucky compared to most – even counting the war. That's quite inconvenient for a lot of people you know."

Hannah checked herself, hearing the sharpness in her voice. She remembered that at just about Jonet's age she had been left alone, both parents dead and two brothers dependent on her. And that even younger she had gone to London to work in the munition factory . . . and had made love with David Vaughan one hot August night on Primrose Hill. She also wanted to say that Jonet was lucky compared to her sister. But what good would that do – that wound should be allowed to heal.

She sat on the bench in the garden when Jonet had departed in the dusky pink crepe dress with Gerald. It was almost dark, the garden was full of fragrance and a hunter's moon hung over the sea. There had been such a moon that night on Primrose Hill, in the last August of the last war, for her and David Vaughan. Hannah put out a hand to stroke Wedgewood, who had joined her on the bench. "Will this be the last August of this war, *cariad*?" she asked him. "Sometimes I can scarcely remember what peace is like." But Wedgewood kept his counsel, gazing at the moon with yellow eyes, and she buried her fingers in his velvet coat, lonely for contact.

It was David she wanted; David, to make her feel loved and warm. They should be lying together now under this lover's moon, as they had lain under it twenty-five years ago. Hannah seemed always to have been alone, and wanted at this moment never to be so again. Soon . . . she had to wait, be patient. One day, please God, one day, somehow, she might not be alone.

He phoned as she was coming in with an armful of mint to chop and dry.

"Darling?"

"David, I knew it, I've been thinking of you all evening." She could hear the relieved happiness in his voice bubbling across the miles and laughed. He laughed, too.

"Must've been telepathy. Couldn't put you out of my mind. Look, sweetheart; I've five days off. Next week, should be Wednesday or Thursday. You can't come here, these damn rockets are the devil still, but I'll come to you, okay?"

Hannah thought frantically. "Darling, could you possibly put it off – for just two weeks? It's Jonet, you see, home for August. It would be, well – "

"Difficult?" She heard the dryness in the word. "I do see that, of course. But Hannah; this isn't the sort of leave that can be postponed. You understand?"

Embarkation leave. Europe. Hannah kept her voice steady. "I do understand. Come of course."

"Great. Look forward to that, sweetheart. Looks as though we'll have to put off your London jaunt for the present, but it'll happen one day, I promise."

"Yes, David. One day. Take care now."

When Jonet came home Hannah was sitting at the kitchen table, her hands spread idly over the accounts books. Hearing the door she made a show of working, but the skin of her cheeks was tight with dried tears.

"How was it, then? Would you like a drink?"

Jonet threw herself into the rocking chair. She was breathing hard and her face was pink and Hannah hastily put on the kettle. "Well, if they are all like him, all I can say is I don't want to know!"

"Gerald, you mean? An all-round failure was he?" Hannah asked mildly. "Never mind, plenty more fish in the sea. Tea or cocoa?"

"I don't *want* more fish thank you! They're one big pain, boys. *That* one was more like an octopus, anyway. Seemed to have a dozen hands and they were all trying to undo my buttons!" Jonet's blush deepened becomingly.

"Ah." Hannah made tea at top speed and reached for the tin of gingerbread ends from the shop. "He's one of those."

"You mean there's another sort?" Jonet took her tea and stirred it so violently that it spattered the skirt of her mother's expensive frock. "Pam's asked me if I can stay with her a couple of days next week, but I certainly shan't if *he's* going to be there!"

"Why didn't you ask, dear? You could have found a tactful way, surely?"

"Oh, he was behaving himself then. It was only now, when we were coming home, that he started this . . ." Jonet met Hannah's eyes with sudden and disconcerting directness. "How can anyone . . . I mean, no one could, well, actually *like* being mauled around? Could they?"

She's talking about me. "Anyone" is *me*, with David. Hannah shaded her eyes for a moment, thinking of the pleasure of David Vaughan's hands.

"If Gerald had appealed to you in any way it

wouldn't have seemed so unwelcome, his wanting to touch you." She spoke carefully. "You do see that? I hope that sometime in the future, Jonet, you will get to know someone – special. And that you'll be happy when he touches you . . . and want to touch him. I really do hope that will happen to you."

Jonet said nothing, staring at the floor. Hannah opened her mouth to say more, to speak about her own relationship, to make Jonet confront and deal with it. Instead she swallowed her tea. Perhaps tomorrow. They were both tired now.

"Don't worry about it tonight, dear. Call Pam tomorrow – you can either tell her straight what happened and say you don't want that again or think of a tactful way of asking if he'll be home. It really will be easier after a night's sleep."

Hannah knew that situations weren't invariably solved by a night's sleep, even if sleep came. Whether Jonet was here when David arrived or at Pam's would alter nothing – it was time to talk, if only to lift this weight of secret guilt from her shoulders. Jonet was practically seventeen . . . almost a woman and certainly not a child.

A night's rest seemed to help Jonet at least.

"I shan't let *him* prevent me going where I want," she said flatly at breakfast. "I shall simply ignore him – and if he tries anything stupid he'll be sorry."

"That's my girl." Hannah was stuffing her paperwork into its envelope to catch the early post. "Which days will you go then? Only David has several days' leave before he goes to Europe and he's coming down Wednesday or Thursday. Would that be a good time to go to Pam's?" She was surprised to hear the words suddenly fall out, unplanned.

Jonet swallowed her porridge in a tight little silence. "I'll have to phone her. Why, will he be coming here?"

"Almost certainly. I naturally want to see all I can of him before he goes. I do love him you know," Hannah added with a sudden shy smile. Jonet said nothing as she reached for her jacket, but continued with her porridge. "Must go, dear. You know how busy Saturdays are – you'll not be far behind me, will you? Lock the door and take care on the road."

She dropped a kiss on Jonet's head as she went by. Wheeling her bicycle down the path she felt a huge relief. The wall had, she hoped, taken a big enough knock to help it crumble.

In the end of course it was not five days; not with Hannah. First there was the farewell to his mother. Hannah knew there was no way round that and did not attempt to find one, however desperate she might be to hoard these last hours for them alone.

Jonet had gone to Pam's and no more had been said on the subject of David. Abstracted by the knowledge that his train had already come in but that he would not be with her that night, Hannah decided to add nothing more herself for the present. She slept badly, tense and restless; went to the shop for a couple of hours, then came home at about eleven to prepare lunch for them. She had a couple of eggs from a good customer who kept chickens and planned an omelette with a few mushrooms she'd discovered in a field nearby and a slice of ham from the restaurant, donated by Florence.

"You'll want to give him something a bit special," Florence said, when told of David's coming. "I'll get Henry to bring it over on a van and leave it at the shop for you. I hope you have a lovely time . . . you make the most of it, now."

She had given Hannah a great hug. And it was a very fine slice of ham; Flo's offering of love for the farewell feast. Hannah understood perfectly and was thankful anew for the support.

The taxi drew up at about midday when she had been watching out for an hour between dashes to the kitchen and to comb her hair yet again. It had been raining hard but suddenly had stopped, and a weak sun cast light on the sea as she opened the door.

"Hi." He smiled, but she could see how tired he looked. In the three months since they had last met his hair had become greyer and the vertical line between his brows deeper. He was casually dressed in slacks and a blue sweater and carried a leather grip; more used to seeing him in uniform, Hannah had just a moment's uncertainty before drawing him inside and shutting the door.

"Hello, darling."

They looked at one another then moved together, David dropping his bag. As his arms went round her Hannah's eyes closed in gratitude; this was where she wanted to be. Now she willed time to pass very slowly. As they walked arm in arm into the sitting room their movements too were slow, with a dream-like quality. Even the familiar room seemed oddly unreal, the big bowl of scented phlox under the window almost artificial in its perfection, the long mirror across the dimmest corner reflecting a scene from a play.

They went to the window and stood quietly in each other's arms, looking out at the garden.

"We could go for a walk after lunch." Hannah put her head on his shoulder and caught a faint scent of him that she always associated with being happy. "Or are you too tired?"

"Suits me fine." He sounded relaxed. "Not tired. I

could do with some air after Mama's place – she doesn't go for open windows."

"Is she upset? About your going to Europe?"

He raised an eyebrow. "Hard to say, she's not a great one for showing emotion." He closed his eyes, lips against her hair.

Hannah said after a moment, "Darling, she must *know* about us." She paused, feeling her way. "Did you, well, was she aware that you were coming on here, to me?"

She waited. He was stroking her shoulder, light even touches. "Sweetheart, the time is long past when I need report my every move to Mama. Don't you agree?"

Hannah was quiet. He was not going to tell her. What he was saying was, this is not your area, what goes on between my mother and myself. She would never know for certain, should she come face to face with the old lady, what had been said or unsaid. And yet if he meant what he said about a divorce she would be a Vaughan herself one day.

For now, it must rest. What he did not wish to tell her she would not strive to know.

Every second was held and savoured, every word and touch stored away for times ahead when she would need them. Tears might so easily have spilled; but memories must be of smiles, and of the certainty of tomorrow. Nothing was held back. And when for the last time she twined fast about him and drew him deep into her loving flesh it was like bestowing a gift of everything she had ever possessed, complete and perfect.

"Hannah. Hannah . . ."

"I've got you, darling. Let go, you're safe with me." Afterwards, she wanted to say don't leave me, don't ever go. Instead she stroked him, murmuring, and held him long after he had laid his head on her shoulder and slept.

When he had gone, the final smile, the last wave, she felt slightly empty as though she had gone, too. Jonet came back from Pam's and asked no questions and Hannah had no words that would have been in the least suitable to explain what had happened or how she felt. So she helped to get Jonet's trunk packed to return for her last year, and listened to news bulletins, and early in September took Jonet back to school in a taxi with the trunk strapped to the boot.

She thought of the previous September. She bought a bunch of yellow roses and took them to where Serena lay, not far from Betsy. The late afternoon was tranquil and Hannah stayed for a while, remembering her daughter, the fourteen years of love. She wished for Joe to be there, and Tom, and most of all she wished for David Vaughan. Then she went to Incline Row and had supper with Florence and Harry and admired the balsa battleship Raymond was glueing together with Harry's help. The ice that had been threatening to numb her heart melted in the warmth of the small family's content. Florence and Harry walked with her back to Morfa Cottage where Wedgewood waited in stiff indignation for his food, and where a note from David had come by the second post, saying that he loved her and that she was to keep well and happy until they could meet again.

"That's what I must do then, isn't it?" she said to Florence, and found that she was laughing and crying at the same time.

By October, she was certain. Not just the missed period. The huge desire to remain in bed after the alarm, the longing for sleep after lunch and nausea at the thought of food were all unmistakable. She had taken her usual precaution. But that night had been dead in the centre of the danger days ... sometimes even a strategically placed diaphragm could fail in the face of nature's utter determination to multiply. She told Florence quite soon; there was no point in procrastination when much would need to be decided. And Flo meant so much to her; always loyal, loving, positive in looking for ways forward.

"Are you *certain*?" Florence looked so staggered that Hannah made her sit down. They had checked up in the restaurant after closing, with a few moments of privacy before they caught the bus home to Taibach.

"Of course I am, Flo." Hannah glanced at her watch and saw there was not time to steady Flo's nerves with tea or there'd be an hour's wait for the next bus. "About the middle of May if I've done my sums right."

"Well." Florence swallowed, staring at Hannah. She said weakly, "That's a bit of a turn up I must say." She gave a shaky smile. "And that's about all I *can* say. Not often you've managed to leave me speechless, is it?"

"The first time, I think." Hannah smiled back. "I was quite surprised myself." No point in telling Flo that surprise was currently the least of the welter of conflicting emotions ebbing and flowing about her entire body.

"Are you all right? Have you seen a doctor?" Florence strove to get her feet back on terra firma.

"Not yet. And if you call feeling sick all day and wanting desperately to fall asleep absolutely anywhere, anytime, all right – yes, I am all right, Flo dear. But I have to face that things are going to become, well, more complicated in the fairly near future." Hannah smiled again; the mask of the mature woman who could always cope with every contingency overlaid the near-panic of the frightened lonely girl.

"They certainly are, Han," said Florence fervently. "You're right about that. Does David know?"

"No one knows, only you. And no one must until I've decided what to do."

"What do you mean?" Florence suddenly looked stern. "You wouldn't . . ."

"No," agreed Hannah. "That isn't an option. I really could not destroy this baby, even if I knew how to set about it. But I have given adoption a bit of a thought these last days. And probably decided that's not on either. So . . ."

"The business," Florence said, and looked about the room with its pretty circular tables and light paintwork between panels of flowered paper; her particular, cherished domain.

"Yes. Tricky, isn't it? Then, even more tricky, there's Jonet."

They sat in silence before Florence said in a hushed voice: "Good Lord, Han, what on earth will you tell Jonet."

Hannah was still, looking at the neatly laid place setting before her. Her face seemed suddenly to run in downward lines from her shadowed eyes and when Florence put out a hand to cover hers she gripped it hard.

"I don't know. Not yet, Flo. But I must say something soon. Then there's David." She looked at Florence. "Could we talk some more after the weekend? Thank heavens I don't have to pussyfoot about finding the best way to tell *you*. Such a relief to come straight out with it. If only it could all be that honest and uncomplicated."

"What d'you want me to do about Harry?" Florence looked anxious; she was not good at keeping things from him.

"Well, I suppose tell him, Flo. He won't let it go any

further, will he?'' Hannah shook her head then, for of course *everyone* would know in a little while.

Hannah found increasingly that it was all far from straightforward, when what she wanted most to do was lie still with a packet of dry biscuits and fizzy lemonade to hand and not to think. This had to be resisted, for as she recalled from past experience the next thing to overtake her would be the safe, cocooning sensation that nothing was actually important but getting through each day with a minimum of trouble. Pregnancy's final stage, when she would feel full of energy and able to take as many decisions as came along, would be too late.

Too late . . . in her moments of near panic Hannah felt that whatever she could do now would be too late. David Vaughan's child was growing inside her and at the allotted time would be delivered. She, a respectable forty-two-year-old business woman, was having an illegitimate child. What on earth would David think when she told him? Would he panic, too? There was no way he could marry her before the baby was born. What would he want it registered under? And would he tell his wife? He might actually make this child the *reason* for divorce, rather than herself. . .

At no time did her situation leave her thoughts entirely, but some days it loomed larger than others, as in early November when Tom came on leave. She realised, seeing him jump off the train then turn to help down two elderly ladies that Tom was at last becoming able to cope. In the wake of the weary months of loneliness and trauma for him, Hannah glimpsed small signs of confidence and they were like gifts from heaven for her. The weight of seeing after Tom, her burden for so many years, lifted. She could tell him about the baby.

567

"I wanted you to know early, Tom, because it's a big thing to get used to – having a baby after such a long gap. For both of us." She smiled at him, walking arm in arm back to the cottage. "And you'll like it, won't you, a little niece or nephew to come home to again?"

He was silent, and she knew his thoughts were with Serena, whom he had adored.

"This won't be a replacement for her, Tom," she added quietly. "Don't ever think that. A *new* life. Someone else to love."

"I don't know anything, Han." He spoke awkwardly. "I mean, you're not, well, married . . . are you?"

"I do wish I were. That would be so much easier for all of us. But I shall marry him, as soon as he's free," she added, and her voice was firm. "Till then, Tom, we must not allow anything that might be said to upset us. You understand? People can be cruel; you learned that early, I know."

"Yes." They had reached the end of the houses and started up the slope towards home when he said: "But I shan't be here, shall I? If they say bad things about you?"

"That won't matter just as long as I know how *you* feel. That *you* support me. And Jonet," she added. And Perhaps beccause she sighed then, Tom said:

"I don't think she'll be pleased."

"No, I've thought a lot about that, Tom. She does have a tendency to judge people. She sets high standards for them, as she does for herself. And she's very aware of other's opinions. I have to think very carefully of the best thing to do for her."

"What can you do?" asked Tom simply.

He waited quietly while she sorted through her bag for the door key, and when Wedgewood appeared from nowhere to rub round his ankle he lifted the cat and held it against his cheek. In the kitchen, he looked at once to where Towser's cage had always stood.

"Tom, I'm sorry. He died a few weeks ago. He was really very old though, wasn't he? He'd done awfully well."

"I suppose so." Tom stared bleakly at the space left by Towser's cage. Hannah dropped her things on the table to hold him, her hands warm and comforting on the cold nape of his neck.

"Oh . . . love." Hannah found that absurdly her eyes were full of tears, and when she stood back she saw that Tom's also were suspiciously bright. She hugged him again.

"Thomas Hywel. I do love you. Thank God *you've* not been posted to Europe – well, escaped so far at any rate! And now I will make some tea."

She wrote to Joe, kept it for a couple of days, then burned it. Was she ashamed? She wrote to David on Sunday evening after her factory shift, with her feet up on the sofa and firelight rosy in the burnished fender. After two attempts had been screwed up and thrown into the hearth Hannah sat staring into the flames for a long time, chewing on the end of her pen.

She had no idea why it should be so difficult. She needed him to know. And surely he had every right to know. Yet – this was the strangest part – she did not want to tell him. When, exasperated and overtired, she went to make herself a drink Hannah was beginning to realise that she intended keeping her pregnancy a secret from him, at least for the present.

Why? Because she did not fully trust him to keep his promise? Was she punishing him? Or protecting him? If so from what – bad news? Would a child of theirs be bad news? He'd never said if he wanted one.

She wanted to turn on the wireless, listen to a show, a play; anything rather than buckle down and work out what she was going to do. A child was growing in her belly, she was forty-two, and her whole life would be split open and reassembled in the next months. She had committed a cardinal sin and not only she but the baby would suffer for it, being illegitimate. For a moment Hannah thought wildly of writing to David Vaughan and insisting that he came back right away to marry her and give his name to the child. That would make him a bigamist. She choked on the biscuit she was nibbling.

"You certainly have made one hell of a mess, Hannah Hywel," she told her reflection in the looking-glass above the mantel. "Your family will never want to own you again, and women will whisper behind their hands as you pass. It's one thing for young girls . . . they know no better and get taken advantage of, carried away, their silliness is forgiveable in wartime. But an all-above-board, sensible middle-aged widow with her own business and a daughter of seventeen already . . ."

She frowned at herself, pushing back her hair with unkind fingers. If only Jonet didn't stand to be harmed she could ride out the storm herself; put up with being a nine days' wonder, the local scandal of the month. But Jonet would never forgive her. Even when she married David it would make no odds; the damage would have been done. Just the thought of telling her daughter made Hannah feel ill enough to sink back onto the sofa. How *could* she have been so insensible to the danger of conception? Had she stupidly supposed, hoped, that she had passed the age? *Why* that one time; the *last* time?

She remembered then that once, long ago, after that August night on Primrose Hill, when David Vaughan had left her as now to go to France, she had actually, stupidly, hoped to be carrying his child.

"Have you been to the doctor yet?" Florence asked her. "You're very pale. And at your age – "

"Quite a few women have babies at my age, Flo. My own mother was only a year or two younger when she had Tom. Has Hugh promised the rabbits for sure?"

"Six brace for Monday, yes. Don't you think you should go, Han? To the doctor." Florence would not be deflected.

"I will, soon. But I'm really fine. Is Mavis still leaving us at the end of the week?"

" 'Fraid so. You know how good the wages are at Blacks and she can't stop talking about being a welder. Han, have you told Jonet yet?"

"Not yet. But I'll be going there on Saturday, it's the school play. I'll tell her then. Flo, will you put an advert in? We absolutely must get a replacement for Mavis right away." Hannah was desperate to hang onto, and solve, any problem possible of resolving.

"I'll pop in tomorrow – I'll try for a fifteen-year-old. Have you heard from David lately?" Hannah had to smile at Florence's tenacity.

"Not very lately. He must be up to his eyes organising freight on such a scale. I'll try old Muffin's boy tomorrow for some more mackerel, it's worth paying over the odds to jolly up the menu. Mrs Price says if it's to be eggless Christmas cakes again she's going into the tank factory!"

"I can only wait for her to make the decision," Florence said to Harry after they'd switched off Itma. "I've told her I could manage perfectly well. Otherwise it's selling everything up. I think it's going round and round in her mind . . . she'll be ill if she's not careful."

"Maybe she'll feel easier when she tells Jonet tomorrow. That's been hanging over her. I wouldn't fancy the job myself."

Harry shifted the van's spark plugs and ignition leads off the table to make room for his night drink; if anything needed repairing these days it was a question of getting on with it yourself as best you could, on a corner of the kitchen table if necessary. He sighed. One of his headaches, rare these days, had come on when Flo had told him about Hannah's trouble and he couldn't seem to get it out of his mind now. He thought it might perhaps have been best to have gone to somebody, got it over with. He knew how these things could happen in a war, when everyone's lives were turned upside down.

He thought for the first time in years of Brigid Davies; of her rich red hair and brilliant brown eyes, and of her proud breasts that he could just encompass with his hand. His son would have been thirty, he was certain it had been a boy. He would be fighting in this war. Harry, remembering what had happened to Brigid and her baby, changed his mind about what Hannah might be wise to do. Whatever difficulties there were to sort out she should never have to end up like Brigid, just because of public opinion. Times were changing anyway and this war would change them further still.

"So I've no idea when she's going to tell him, now." Florence set the iron on the hob and looked at him with worried eyes. "It might at least give her a bit of moral support for him to know. Even if he can't do anything – not till he gets back home and gets that divorce. I honestly think she's nervous of upsetting him or something. She keeps saying how dangerous it must be over there, and how hard he must be working. But it's not as if he's in the front line, is it? I mean, he'll have enough food and a bed to sleep in."

"More than we had." Harry's voice sounded odd and Florence glanced up from the ironing. He sat with idle hands and his eyes had an absent, dull expression.

"Harry?"

Harry did not hear. He was listening to the whine of mortars, the drone of overhead planes. He heard the cough of machine guns and men shouting and screaming. His head began to throb. His fingers spread, feeling oily mud and splinters of bone and the soft bodies of rats. And there was a smell . . .

"Harry!" Florence's face swam into focus. He felt her hand on his shoulder and lifted his own, which seemed heavy, to cover it.

"I'm glad I'm not in France now, Flo." No more than a whisper but she caught it.

"So am I, love. Drink your tea now before it goes cold."

There was nowhere private to talk. Hannah went through the motions of drinking tepid tea in the hall whilst parents, teachers and pupils milled about her.

"You really didn't notice?" Jonet sounded incredulous. "Practically half of the second act, Mother! She took the wrong cue and wham, half the act gone! They all sorted themselves out pretty well afterwards considering. Honestly, trust Connie Mildmay to muff it."

"It seemed very good to me." Hannah did her best to inject interest into her voice. The back of her neck was stiff with tension and she felt sick. "Oh, may I – " She snatched a biscuit off a passing tray. "I don't suppose you have anything cold to drink, Jonet? And fizzy, perhaps?"

"We're not allowed fizzy drinks." Jonet looked

round. "Have you seen Alison anywhere? I'd like you to meet her parents, they have this really big house near Southampton, I've seen a snap."

"Darling. Is there somewhere quiet we can go? To talk?"

Jonet looked doubtful. "There's the library. Shouldn't be too many there . . . a few catching up on prep. Oh, Alison's over there by the stage, see?"

"I have to speak to you, Jonet. Alison must wait." Hannah's voice had an edge of desperation.

They ended up in the sixth form changing room, a hostile cubicle with shiny butter-coloured walls lined with narrow benches and a small high window. "We took the blackout down at last – before that it was nailed up and we never saw daylight."

"Yes." Hannah looked round.

"We shan't be long, shall we?" Jonet stood in the middle of the room, poised for flight. "I don't want to miss Alison's people."

"It needn't take long at all. But I think we should sit down." Hannah subsided onto a bench and straightened her back, waiting whilst Jonet perched on the end of the one opposite. "It's simply that I'm having a baby next May and I think you should know sooner rather than later."

The words fell out as if by accident; after them, Hannah shut her lips tight and her heart thumped loudly against her ribs so that she thought Jonet would notice her jacket shaking. But Jonet just stared at her.

"What did you say?"

"You did hear me, dear. I'm having a baby next May. I'm very sorry indeed to give you this shock."

Jonet got up, walked up and down, then came to stand in front of Hannah: "Sorry? Mother, what are you talking about, *sorry*?" Her laugh was a dry harsh sound.

574

She turned her back on Hannah and stared at the wall and when Hannah tried to touch her, flinched away. Then swung round.

"Whose is it, Mother?"

"Should you need to ask?" Hannah's voice was very quiet.

"That David Vaughan's? He's married, everyone knows that!"

"Yes."

"You can *do* something, can't you? There's something . . ." The girl leaned closer as she spoke, her breath harsh and uneven.

"You couldn't mean that. When you're not so upset, you'll – "

"When won't I be upset? When everyone finds out my mother's pregnant, having been a widow for years and years? And having an affair with a married man? And when I've to tell my friends I have an illegitimate brother or sister? Is *that* when I won't be upset?" Jonet laughed again but her eyes were big with distress. Hannah began to feel as though she'd been kicked in the stomach.

"Jonet, *cariad*."

"Don't *cariad* me! You wouldn't have done this if you'd cared the smallest bit about me!" Tears gathered and fell then and Jonet brushed them angrily away. "You won't have it at home, will you? At least you'll go away? You could have it adopted . . . maybe not tell anyone?"

Hannah got up slowly, defeated by her daughter's violent reaction. "I must do the best I can for everyone Jonet. I can only say again how truly sorry I am that you feel this way. That you're so upset."

She sat up far into the night. Another letter to David

was begun and thrown into the fire. Needing desperately to tell him, she needed the other thing more . . . to know that when at last he did make the move to free himself and come to her, it was above all his own willing choice. To complicate it with duty to a child, or to her, would be never to know her true value in his life. She'd waited so long; now she must know for certain that he wanted her and loved her enough. No more mistakes; not on the Darrow Bates scale.

Jonet . . . that relationship was in tatters. She could only tread carefully there; hope that time and maturity would blunt the edge of Jonet's anger. At least after what she'd endured in that dreadful little changing room the reactions of the family at large could hold no terrors. If *Nain* had been alive . . . but it seemed to matter little now, what the others thought of her. Damned beyond redemption, she supposed. So be it.

That just left Joe. How long ago Joe seemed, these days. What would he think of her? No opinion either way perhaps, of so distant a part of his life. How could she expect him to care? For her own need though, she would tell him. Strange, how she could recall the child, the able, cheerful boy, when she had need to. She would welcome a son like Joe.

"So that's what I have decided, Flo. If you're still happy about your part?"

"Why not? We'll keep in touch and sort out details as they may arise. You've the bakery running like clockwork under Ned; and Mrs Price is worth gold. She can dig up staff from nowhere and knock 'em into shape in no time. And Harry, he's just tickled he can do something to repay you for all *you* did over the years. And you know I can cope perfectly well here. It's no problem at all for me." Florence touched her hand. "As for Jonet, I'm real sorry, Han. I don't think she should have – "

"She had every right to be hurt, Flo." Hannah leaned forward, anxious to convince not only Florence but herself. "She's always tried to better herself. And I've encouraged her. So now . . ."

"I could say that you've as much right to your life as Jonet has to hers. I could say she should rate you too highly to judge you." Then Florence grinned. "Let's be honest, Han, your only crime's gettin' caught. Not exactly a major offence; folk do it all the time!"

"It's still up to me to minimise the damage to her, Flo."

"But does it have to be London? With all those buzz-bombs?"

"Don't confuse me when I've laid plans," Hannah said firmly. "I was up there in the last war, it won't hurt for just a short while. I'll go up and find a place; then sometime after Christmas slip away. One thing, Flo, a very important one for me. It's likely she'll refuse, say she's grownup now and likes managing for herself – which she does – but will you ask Jonet to stay at your place if she comes home for Easter? Of course, she may opt to go to that friend of hers; to Pam. Now, let's go get ourselves a drink, a proper one at the Lamb. I'm suddenly very thirsty."

Chapter Twenty-Three

December 1944

She should have known that finding somewhere to live in London would be next to impossible. She had looked north of the river first, not too far from Paddington and trains home, but all she seemed to find were bombed sites, or rows of damaged homes covered by swarms of builders. Further south, strolling along Chiswick Mall, she coveted a room overlooking the river or perhaps bordering Ravenscourt Park. She may as well have asked for the moon: local papers, property agencies, even police stations; all avenues were fruitlessly explored.

It was Aunt Maggie's Emily, living in Fulham now with her husband Geoffrey, who told her of the room in Clapham about to be vacated by Geoffrey's brother and his wife whose house had been repaired after damage from a V2. Hannah, just returned home for the second time and prepared to admit failure, was given no chance to decide whether or not she wanted to be in Clapham.

"Just off Abbeville Road, Han." Emily always shouted on the telephone. "Turn up Elms Road and you're on the Common. A nice room, it's been plenty big enough for Oswald and Ida. Only, you'll have to say by tomorrow. You know what it's like."

Hannah did indeed know what it was like. After a sleepless night when she reviewed her limited range of options one last time, she sent up a month's rent in advance. Just ten days off Christmas and up to the armpits in work she could give her future no more attention – if Clapham proved untenable she would give notice and leave; she did have a home after all and could have her baby there if all else failed. But she had personally chosen not to, though for reasons that in her more practical and clear-headed moments she now suspected may not be altogether sound.

She wrote next to David, from whom she had had a couple of notes saying little but that he was very cold and very busy. Hers was an uncomfortable letter mentioning that in the new year she might try London for another business, she'd heard people were pouring back to the city as fast as their homes were made habitable. Hannah thought about that, sipping her evening drink . . . what may be a palpable lie at the moment of writing could well bear the seeds of truth. Why should she not? David's divorce could take ages, even when the war ended and he eventually went home. The war, indeed, seemed far off ending, with the new German offensive in the Ardennes. Staring at it on the map Hannah tried to imagine where David might be in the bitter cold of this midwinter; a deeper, more penetrating cold than any she remembered. Swathed in assorted scarves and woollies as she cycled daily through the flaying wind, she looked at the grey houses, the tired streets of Taibach, the flame throwing, smoke-belching, man-eating monster that was the steelworks spread between houses and grey icy sea, and felt more than ready for a change.

Christmas brought an uneasy truce with Jonet, who spent hours in her room to emerge thinner, darker, more intent each day.

"I need to catch up," she gestured vaguely at a pile of books on her bedroom table whenever Hannah ventured near. "Don't want to leave it all till the spring."

579

"No, but what about the kitchen table?" Hannah noted the pinched face. "You can't concentrate if you're freezing. And I don't believe there's an oil stove to be had in the district – I've tried for an extra one for the restaurant. How odd it will seem if we are ever again in a position to *buy* things that we need."

Jonet refused to budge from her room, wearing the woolly mitts Hannah had bought at the church bazaar, two pairs of black stockings and, on the cruellest days, an old balaclava of Tom's. Florence, Harry and Raymond came for Christmas dinner but the atmosphere was sober and they left afterwards for the ritual tea at Aunt Maggie's. Hannah sat with her knitting and the radio whilst Jonet drifted restlessly before disappearing upstairs to her room yet again. Aunt Maggie had, of course, invited them both; Jonet said she simply did not want to go, leaving her mother – who did not want to go either – to make what lame excuses she might. Knowing that cousin Daisy, still grieving for her dead son, would be there Hannah wanted anyway to keep a low profile. And there was her pregnancy. Most likely they all knew about it by now but she wanted no confrontations over her wickedness.

The second Christmas without Serena . . . Memories crowded, of other happier Christmases. Tom; he should be here today, his square, gentle face creasing with pleasure as he followed Itma on the radio, head cocked. He'd been denied Christmas leave this time but at least he was still in Gloucestershire rather than Europe. The stool he had made for four-year-old Serena stood against the wall by the fireplace; one of its three legs had worked loose. No one used it now; would anyone again?

Abruptly, Hannah dropped the jumper she was knitting for Jonet. A brisk walk, then; sitting trapped in the past helped no one. Well muffled, she decided to call on Sam Warburton. She had missed seeing him about for a while and wanted to tell him her own plans. The brief day was fading and the streets were deserted with lights coming on in rows of front parlours to make a brave show of carefully hoarded streamers and paper chains and little Christmas trees in buckets covered with fading pre-war red crepe paper. At the corner of Sam's street she averted her eyes from the spot where Serena . . . She almost ran the few yards to his house and down the passage to the back door.

It was easy to see the house was empty. She heard voices in the kitchen of the next house and opened the gate into its yard where an old black cat was hunched, waiting to be let in.

"Oh." The woman stood awkwardly, a plate of sandwiches balanced in her hand and the cat moved soundlessly in between her feet and disappeared. "Well, I'm sorry, Mr Warburton died. Day before yesterday. Very quick – his heart. Mrs Warburton's gone over to her sister's till the funeral."

Hannah went on down the street towards the railway lines and the massive bulk of the mill sheds, with cranes and hoists rearing behind, black against the reddish purple sky. She felt sick with shock – she should have come before . . . and she felt very, very alone.

It had changed; but perhaps, this oldest part of the works was not vastly different from when she had watched her father and Sam coming towards her at the end of their shift, snap boxes swinging and Thomas laughing at one of Sam's outrageous quips. The last time Sam had scooped her up to hug she'd been fourteen, and pink cheeked with the indignity. He'd smelled of engine oil and cinders, had set her down and doffed his greasy cap, and his eyes had disappeared into the leathery crags and fissures of his face. Her true friend . . . her father's closest friend. One more link with the past was broken.

It was then that she felt the first movement, high in her stomach, nothing more than a flutter. But then again; a shade stronger this time.

She pushed her hand inside her coat and pressed it to the place in an answering signal. This was the future, telling her which way to look. Hannah turned up her coat collar and began to walk home.

It was February before she went. Her pregnancy was still difficult to detect in the loose coat and baggy jumpers, and floral work smocks completely disguised what was, as Florence described, no more than a neat little football. She had offended Florence by refusing to go to the doctor, but promised to register the moment she moved to London.

"It's just false pride," Florence said sternly. "I'm really surprised you can't get the better of that for the sake of your baby. You could be giving it rickets, not having your orange juice."

"Flo, it's simply that I haven't the *time*." Hannah spread her hands. "You know the hours it takes trying to see the doctor. And I'm feeling fine or I'd go, truly. Now, stop bullying me and let's go back to work." She consulted the list, pencil poised. "We'll do the quota forms next – they're a dreadful bore but if you make a hash of them . . ." She drew her fingers across her throat.

"Have you fixed up with Dewi to see to the books? That's the one thing I chicken out of."

"I invited him and his wife to supper to broach it and he seemed actually pleased. I think he'll be glad of a spot extra, cash in hand."

Hannah was developing a talent for finding ways to get things done. Bureaucracy might have gone mad these last years of the war but there were still ways to clear paths through the undergrowth given the will and much tenacity, and she lacked neither. Cousin Dewi, with his 1918 disability pension had found things improved since his late marriage in '39. Not only did he have someone to sympathise over his artificial limb giving him gyp, but his wife had a small bequest that had eased their finances. Even better, she was also doing war work, and of course Dewi was now earning a decent wage in the steelworks offices. He was aware, though, that come the war's end and demobilisation the pendulum might swing against him again, and he welcomed the chance to do something for Hannah. She was, after all, on the way to becoming a rich relation . . . never mind about her debatable morals.

She stretched her arms above her head and arched her back. "I'll make us a pot of tea, lashings of tea is essential for these quota forms; preferably tipped over them. How about a piece of toast? I'm ravenous. I had a letter from David," she added almost casually.

"About time, too." Florence brought her down to earth. "So what's he got to say for himself?"

Hannah put the kettle on the hob then lit the oven grill, sliced bread and laid it on the wire rack. "Oh, that he's very busy. And how cold he is. And how there's no food about in the countryside. He can't say much about what he's actually doing."

"Does he talk about – afterwards? Getting his divorce?" Florence probed.

Hannah looked in silence at the pat of butter that must cover two slices of toast. Then she said: "Flo, we don't talk about it. I can't say for certain why he doesn't. I don't because I want no problems for him right now other than getting through the winter, and then to the end of the war. All the other stuff can wait. Everything's waiting, isn't it, just for the war to be over?"

"Your baby isn't," said Florence.

Hannah remembered Florence's words that night as the baby began to exercise just as she was arranging herself for sleep.

"No, my little friend, you certainly won't wait. Well, you're going up to London town next week and that should keep you quiet for a bit." She shivered then, a frisson of sudden excitement. Nothing could ever be the same again. Another child . . . a new life.

Harry came with her. He would not hear of her making the journey alone and she capitulated gratefully, worn down by last-minute traumas. She had packed and unpacked her cases, finally cramming in everything she felt she could not possibly live without. Wedgewood was to go to Florence and Harry, Raymond was red with pleasure given charge of his feeding. The businesses were fully staffed and Mrs Price boasted that she still had the odd relative in hand for emergencies. Hannah knew that by now everyone would have heard about the baby; she handled the situation with quiet directness. When she called to say goodbye to Aunt Maggie the old lady was clearly in two minds about her attitude. The official family line was disapproval of someone who should have known better; but this was her favourite brother's daughter . . . and one who had done so much to help her Harry when others had written him off. Her struggle was both transparent and oddly comic, and as Hannah took pity on her and made her excuses she found herself suddenly pressed to the pillowy blue jumper.

"Take care then, *cariad*."

"I will, Aunt Maggie. And I'll give your love to Emily, I'll be seeing her as soon as I can."

Jonet was invited to spend the Easter holidays in Clapham but had so far declined, preferring to be left alone to revise.

"I'll hope to see you, even so," Hannah told her. "I know you can manage perfectly on your own at home, and you'll want to spend most of the time revising for Higher. But if you fancy a break we could go to a show. Tom's put in for Easter leave this year; he doesn't usually ask for special times but he was hoping to have half the week at Morfa Cottage with you then come to Clapham. You know of course that Flo and Harry would love to have you stay with them." She ignored Jonet's look of pained exasperation . . . the road back to acceptance by this prickly daughter would, she knew, be long and bumpy.

The journey was slow after a late start, the train crowded, littered and cold as all the trains were now, and Hannah and Harry alighted stiff and hungry at Paddington. Clapham seemed to be still so far off.

"A cuppa and a sandwich then we'll try for a taxi," Harry said cheerfully but his face was white with fatigue, it was only his second ever visit to the capital. There were no seats left in the buffet, invaded by a noisy batch of French sailors and half a dozen Polish airmen loaded with kit. Watching them as she sipped stewed tea, Hannah imagined where they might be going; perhaps even to David's airfield, wherever that was. If he operated from an airfield, not at some central headquarters. She smiled at one of the Poles and he smiled back; a hollow-cheeked hawkish young man who stood apart in the crowd of his compatriots. She would have liked to speak to him. But even as the thought shaped she turned quickly to Harry with a sudden certainty, for she knew without doubt that the young man would die soon.

"Oh Jesus." The tea was like bitter aloes in her throat. "Harry, can we go?"

They pushed towards the door and joined a queue for taxis. Harry looked anxious. "Are you all right, Han?"

"Only tired." But it was more. She felt defeated, helpless, under the weight of this power that other were spared, that could split the normality of her life apart in a second. She moved forward in the queue, wanting to be no different from the other travellers jostling towards their goal. And she wanted one more thing – Hannah wanted, at that moment, with surprising urgency, to have Joe here. She remembered then that the Polish airman had looked just a little like Joe.

It was dark, of course, but it seemed a nice enough road, quiet and tidy. The taxi drew up outside one of a row of pleasant, solid villas, which was all that could be discovered of them in the blackout. The landlord opened the door, Mr Perrot was a large man with thick spectacles and a genial smile. The room was on the ground floor, high-ceilinged and spacious as Emily had said, with a window overlooking the tiny front garden. Further along the narrow hall was a tall slice of kitchen with a tall slice of bathroom opposite that – both to be shared, they were told, with a nice single lady named Miss Mallow. Mr Perrot showed them the cooker, the kettle, and had a jug of milk for Hannah. Other things could be had from the corner shop where she would be able to register for her rations. He had been unable to bring her bread as his ration was already used up. But ushering them back to the big room, he pointed out a brown carrier bag on the table under the window. A lady had left that around tea-time, the one who had taken the room on Hannah's behalf.

Mr Perrot, having initiated them into the mysteries of the slightly temperamental gas fire, informed them that he lived on the top floor should they need him again and departed, smiling more genially than ever.

Hannah sank into the chair by the fire. It was old, deep and soft, with the feel of a friend; which was just as well as she was by now in a state of near exhaustion. She looked at Harry. He leaned against the table, smiling at her, and was clearly as done in as herself.

"There's things here from Em." He opened the carrier bag and peered inside. "With a note."

Emily had invited them to Fulham for the night, but they had decided against the offer. "I want to get you settled in your place, Han." Harry said. "And we don't want to be cartin' your stuff all over London for a couple of days. I can always go to Em's on my way back, she tells me there's a bus from here."

Hannah took the note from him.

Dear Han, here's just a few things to keep body and soul together til you get your rations. When you do, maybe you can spare me the tea and butter back, we get short of them all the time. Roll on the end of rationing! I do hope you like the room, I thought it was very nice when I came over with these after school. Come to see me as soon as you like, I'm not back late from school.

There was a screw of tea in some greaseproof paper secured by an elastic band, another of sugar, an ounce of butter securely wrapped and a small piece of cheese; a quarter of a loaf, two apples, and a small vegetable pie in an oval dish.

"This is kind of her." Hannah turned the pie dish thoughtfully. "Shall I heat it through for you? I really feel a bit tired to eat much myself tonight."

"Don't think I could manage it either. But I tell you what." Harry felt in his Macintosh pocket and drew out a bag. "Flo made these for us . . . she said we'd be bound to want something during the day." He opened the greaseproof paper inside the bag and there were two rounds of sandwiches, only slightly squashed. He sniffed them. "Spam. Very nice, Flo makes a really good spam sandwich with a bit of chutney on. A round of these'd do me a treat, now we've the makings of a pot of tea to go with 'em. How about you?"

"Lovely." Hannah pulled herself out of the chair. "Trust Flo to get it right. Come on, love, let's make the tea."

They felt even more sleepy after the sandwiches and tea and the comfortably popping fire that had made an excellent job of thawing them out. Forcing themselves to keep going, they unpacked the bags and cases and Hannah had most of her possessions stowed away before she said slowly, "Harry, we've nowhere for you to sleep. We just didn't *think*."

She stared at him, eyes glazed with the effort to stay awake. Harry stared back.

"Well," he looked at the bed screened across the corner beyond the window. It had four pillows, three folded blankets and a fawn satin eiderdown.

"You have that an' I'll take your chair . . . that okay by you? I'm whacked enough to sleep on a clothes line now."

"Me too." Hannah was yawning. "Let's just roll ourselves in those blankets then for tonight; I'm past getting the bed made up, that can wait."

They made for the bathroom in turn, then turned off the fire. Hannah kept on her dressing gown and selected a blanket for herself and one for Harry, who kept on everything but his jacket. She heaved herself wearily on the bed.

"Good night then, Harry dear. Thanks so much for all you've done today." Her eyes were already closing. "Sure you're comfortable?"

" 'Night, love. I'm fine."

It must have been a while later that she was roused by Harry's fidgeting. Hannah peered over her blanket to see the vague shape of him struggling to get comfortable. She sat up; the room had become extremely cold.

"Harry?"

"Mm-m"

"Come here. Bring your blanket. That's right, now get in here; I'm not having you messing around in that chair another second."

She made space for him. Harry climbed obediently in beside her and shuffled himself into place.

"If you're sure you don't mind. Oh-o-o, great."

They lay side by side in the bed, swathed in their blankets. After a moment or two Harry turned onto his side and almost at once Hannah could tell he was asleep. She turned then too, smiling in the dark, pushed her back up against his to feel the companiable warmth of it and closed her eyes, still smiling.

Hannah had been in Clapham for two and a half weeks when she took the job in the British Restaurant. She found that she needed to be both busy and tired in order to bear the homesickness that clawed at her day and night, a sharp unexpected pain. She wanted her home, her garden, her place. She missed the small inviting rooms of her cottage, their uneven colour-washed walls and deep windows looking over hills, fields, skies and seas. Missed her garden, the paths overgrown with thyme, rosemary, lavender and eau-de-cologne mint so that fragrance was brushed into the air as she passed. She longed to see the honeysuckle and clematis, the dog roses entangling the hedge beyond the vegetable patch, and imagined them putting out early shoots now the days were lengthening. She wanted to watch delphiniums, hollyhocks and lupins pushing strongly through the earth; up, up until they burst in glorious profusion far above the sheltering wall to mingle their colours with those of wild foxgloves. And she missed the familiar shapes of the steel mills, the massive cylinders and the chimneys that could throw flames sky high, the railsheds in front and docks behind ... never silent, never at rest. Her roots were woven into every contour, every blast, of the end-of-shift hooter, every leap of a furnace flame, and she felt the tearing of them. She wanted the old church near Castle Street where her mother and baby brothers lay with Serena in the quiet shade of ancient yews and where every name on every headstone was familiar. She'd left money with Harry for fresh flowers ... but these people were *hers*.

She even thought of the restless lonely spirit on the hill; of Rachel, clinging for centuries to her ruined stones, waiting for Hannah knew not what. That was when she had pulled herself together and marched into the British Restaurant near the Common. If she was becoming maudlin she needed a job and fast.

She got it, experienced caterers were hard to come by in the last spring of the war. The hours were long and achingly hard but the work was well within her capabilities. War-weary, overworked Londoners queued patiently for their self-service meal of two nourishing courses and a cup of tea for a shilling. When Hannah finished she was more than ready to hurry back to her room for hot milk and a sandwich, to turn on the wireless or read the paper with her feet up on a stool. It was even an effort to write to David; and on Sundays she studied the weekly report from Florence, made notes, and replied to it.

She liked her room more each day, with its big bay window overlooking the road and holes in the paving of the front garden for strong shiny daffodil leaves. From her favourite chair she could see across the road to a pretty young chestnut tree and a house with cheerful yellow curtains. These curtains seemed almost to glow on dull days, and Hannah's curtains being a subdued stripey beige, she felt that being able to see them was the next best thing to owning them. She threw over the boring square table under the window, a bright paisley shawl she'd brought from home in case she should feel cold in bed. She had, in the first days, but had put on a jumper rather than deprive the room of its gay table cover. She also brought fresh flowers once a week to put in the window bay, colourful mixed bunches to catch cheerful rays of morning sun. She quickly became familiar with the tall thin kitchen with its window overlooking the wall of the next pair of houses, but her use of it was largely confined to making tea as she could eat at the British Restaurant. She met Miss Mallow briefly after her third week; small, unassuming and quietly friendly, with silver hair pinned back with a tortoise-shell slide like an elderly schoolgirl, Miss Mallow was clearly not going to present problems. She had just been down to Seaford to visit relatives she told Hannah and offered advice on the best shops, most convenient buses, prettiest walks across the Common.

These March days, a spirit of half-fearful anticipation began to ripple over the crowded tables in the

British Restaurant. The Americans had crossed the Rhine, and when Monty and his men reached it and struck deep into the heart of the Ruhr Hannah could almost hear the releasing of a relieved, collective breath. Then the sirens at last fell silent and April came; weary eyes scanning the skies for signs of death saw only birds swooping and tumbling against clean spring clouds. Hannah left work then, the hours of standing on a concrete floor made her ankles swell, her back was aching, and she needed to pay attention to herself and the baby.

For the first time ever she got up when she pleased. Some mornings she would make toast and tea and climb back into bed with her tray, pulling aside the screen so she could see the window with the yellow curtains. Other times she would be up early to write letters, then she would tidy the room quickly and walk to post them. She visited Emily every other week, taking a bus over Putney Bridge to Fulham in time to meet her from school and walk home together for tea. By tacit arrangement this was on days when Geoffrey went directly from school to a pupil's house for private tuition. There was nothing wrong with Geoffrey; Hannah simply preferred him not to be there, watching with his sharp brown eyes and smoothing a densely freckled hand over his bald pate when he spoke. Geoffrey was small-boned and plump, with a high-pitched voice. Hannah had no idea if Emily was happy with him, the cousins chatted of everyday things whilst revealing nothing of their private selves. Emily did not even make references to a possible father of Hannah's child and avoided the fact of the pregnancy altogether with some degree of determination. Poor Emily ... Hannah played along with her inhibition, recalling Em's own hurried marriage and "seven-month" pregnancy of her son back in '26. The time in Poplar, the horror of the bombed school, was not mentioned either. It seemed that Emily had no wish to re-live the past.

She had more time to write to David now. Every time she hesitated . . . the urge to tell him the truth was often unbearably strong as the time approached for her to deliver his child. His only child. Would he not above all be delighted? Then Hannah would dig deep into her reserves of strength to resist the temptation to put the ball in his court. The reason for her decision remained as valid as ever – she wanted him to return for *her*, not for his child, or what secure foundation was there on which to build their future?

Hannah came to know the Common, the paths, the ponds, the brick strong point defending the anti-aircraft battery, the bandstand. Sometimes she would walk to its southern tip to stare at the hospital where her child would be born; the doctor she had found in Clapham Park Road had vetoed her idea of its being delivered at home. Some days she regretted her move here, a stranger in a strange land; but usually she was content. This was the least she could do for Jonet.

Jonet had excused herself for Easter but Hannah continued to write each week, aware that the effort must come from her. Tom had come for two nights just after Easter and had insisted on sleeping in the big chair.

"It's a waste of money, Han," he had said with his gentle smile when she wanted to book a room in a nearby hotel. "I'm fine here and we'll see more of each other."

"How was Jonet?" She tried to keep her voice

casual, eyes fixed on the baby's nightgown she was stitching.

"Just fine." She looked up to make certain he was telling the truth and he nodded reassurance. "She cooked a good dinner and the place was in apple pie order. You've no cause to fret. She's just workin' hard for those exams."

"Yes. And you, Tom? D'you think maybe it won't be long before you're home for good?"

"Not too long. Or so the talk goes. Then you'll be home again too, Han, and things can be like they were."

They were quiet then, Tom's words seemed to echo in their heads, for of course things never could be as before. Serena was gone. Jonet would be away. And there would be a new child, probably for Hannah to take to Canada without Tom. Oh, not leave Tom. Hannah pricked her finger hard and a drop of blood fell bright on the creamy flannelette.

"Damn!" She was on the verge of tears. Head averted so Tom should not see, she rose clumsily and hurried to rinse off the blood. When she came back she was smiling again, carrying a plate of chocolate biscuits she had saved from Joe's last parcel.

Since the British 2nd Army's operation Plunder took off in March, David Vaughan had known the end must be in sight. Plunder was part of a gigantic drive across the Rhine to flood into the Ruhr, beginning with the dropping of two divisions of the Allied Airborne Army behind the German defences on the Rhine's east bank. He was aware, by the sheer enormity of the freight logistics now being handled, that into this massive advance were being thrown millions of the best prepared and equipped troops the world had seen.

His own effort was directed north-east in conjunction with the Canadian 1st division. Amphibious craft were required in addition to vast loads of regulation supplies and his usual Dakotas were supplemented by more from the American 9th on their southern flank. The winter offered no let-up and the workload increased as their supply lines lengthened. Finally, in the lonely reaches of dawn on Easter Sunday, he was forced to confront himself. He had turned and heaved the night through, dreaming of enormous crates falling towards him from a plane with its freight doors open, and had shot to sudden conciousness wet with sweat, and with a numbing headache.

He was too old for the job. Men half his age were showing the strain; at forty-eight, with two wars behind him, he was played out. He craved peace, order and sanity, light years from this doomed rubble-strewn continent, these endless files of refugees, the truck-loads of sullen prisoners.

He walked stiff and aching from his quarters to stare at the ruined walls of the town. There should have had church bells ringing now to signal Easter Day, so burghers would smile and put on their good clothes to celebrate winter's end and the Divine Resurrection.

David Vaughan thought of Hannah, this Easter morning. He'd had no time to write for weeks. Lately her image had blurred to that of someone he'd known in another part of his life. Would she have gone home for Easter? He was vague as to what she was up to in London, but that was maybe just the letters. He remembered a sort of peace about her, that he found wonderfully attractive. Several times he tried to clear his tired brain to think about their situation; what he must do when this lot was done with, when he was demobbed. What he must do about Julia. But nothing ever became resolved; and finally he acknowledged the plain fact that nothing would be, for the present. He must make an effort to put a letter together, though. Not easy, when the only important topic on his horizon, the race to encircle the Ruhr, was *verboten*.

He got the day over in some sort of order and was studying the reports on aircraft availability when his aide, Wilmot, scuttled into the office, face mottled with excitement.

"That's it then, sir, they've done it!"

"What've they done, Dickie? And who's 'they'?"

"Monty's 21st and Bradley's 12th, sir. The pincer's closed! Some place called Lippstadt, they linked up at around 1530, it's loud and clear on radio." He paused expectantly. When he got no response but a weary stare he added; "They're talking about four thousand square miles, sir, and maybe a third of a million Jerries in the cage."

David Vaughan rewarded him then with a grim smile. "Let's hope they don't all want feeding, Dickie. Now will you be a good chap and see if Stanway's still about for me."

He closed his eyes when Wilmot had gone. Four thousand miles ... the heart torn clean out of the Ruhr. A third of a million men ... how many still on their feet and equipped to hold out? How long ... weeks? Months? When Stanway reported his eyes were still closed, and Stanway had to cough before he opened them.

Hannah read the paper avidly and listened to every

596

news bulletin. In mid-April there was a letter from David. She read it a dozen times, but got little from it but that he was busier than ever, had billets with bugs in the walls and had learned a few words of German. He hoped she'd had a nice Easter, he had thought of her on Easter morning. He'd fancied going to church himself, but there were none left standing for miles around. He ended by saying that he didn't think it would be long now, and sent her his love.

She felt the baby thrust out a fist and grimaced; *that* wouldn't be long now, either. Could he possibly be back before . . . Not realistically. But she followed the Allies' progress ever more closely as what was once the mighty Third Reich was reduced to a strip a few miles wide, crushed from west and east between two massive and vengeful armies. She went to the cinema each week where she saw thin Allied prisoners released from camps in their hundreds, and Germans filtering into barbed wire pens in their thousands. She saw the horror of the concentration camps and was without sleep for two nights, unable to erase the shocking images; saw the funeral of President Roosevelt, dead on the eve of his triumph. She saw Russians and Americans meet finally on the Elbe; the ruined city of Berlin and its grey-faced inhabitants, the Italian dictator and his mistress hanging upside down, and turned away as though to protect her child from the sight.

The suitcase was packed ready now by the door, alongside the number of the taxi firm. Miss Mallow had shown an increasing interest in her condition through April but in a completely uninquisitive way that Hannah found endearing. In early May she invited Hannah to take tea in her restful, gracefully furnished room overlooking the garden. The table was set with delicate china on a lace cloth, and a Victoria sponge with butter cream that must have made inroads on her week's rations. Hannah, who had been seriously off sweet things for eight months, politely ate a large slice, because she had found that she really liked this lady.

"And you will let me know if you should *need* anyone?" Miss Mallow looked straight at her with round honest hazel eyes, escorting Hannah to her door.

"I will," Hannah assured her, shaking the proffered hand.

"I was an air raid warden for four years. And we had lots of bombs." Miss Mallow smiled broadly, perfectly aware of her fragile, lady-like appearance.

"Oh? Well!" Hannah was as surprised as she was meant to be, Miss Mallow simply did not seem an obvious choice for a warden, with her delicate heart-shaped face and small build.

She had to hurry now to post Tom's letter; although one week off full term, Hannah's hurrying had become more of a quick stroll. On the way back she bought an evening paper and sat on a low wall to read it. MONTY TAKES SURRENDER OF ALL TROOPS IN NORTHERN EUROPE.

Almost there. She was filled with an elation that seemed to lift her off the wall – it was all but over. She looked at the residents of Clapham going home from work, expecting to find them smiling, if not actually laughing, with sheer relief. But they appeared much as usual, striding along with vacant faces. Hannah would have liked a drink, a dry sherry perhaps, a celebration. But not alone ... and she felt tired now anyway – a bit past all this hurrying. Instead she walked slowly to the telephone box at the corner of her road and dialled the Swansea restaurant.

"Flo? I thought I might catch you cashing up. I've just read that they're all surrendering and suddenly wanted – " Hannah found herself unexpectedly speechless.

"Are you okay, Han?" Florence's voice crackled in her ear.

"Yes, yes, I'm just fine; fine! I simply thought how lovely to have a few words. Have you had a good day?"

"Busy, yes. It's always busy! But you, love, not long now, is it? I wish – "

"Soon, Flo. And you are not to worry, everything's going along nicely. I just wish you were here. I'd so love a good talk. Damn, I've run out of change! Sorry –"

She almost swore with frustration as the phone disconnected, and stood for a while clutching it against her chest. Then she laid it carefully back and eased herself from the booth. Tomorrow she would buy herself a bunch of lilacs ... they would be out at home, now. Tomorrow, the war in Europe might be over.

Not tomorrow, but early the day after Eisenhower imposed a general surrender; and the day following was designated Victory in Europe day and a public holiday. That was the morning Hannah went into labour; and when the Prime Minister broadcast to the nation at three o'clock in the afternoon she was too occupied to give it her full attention.

The hospital had put out flags and whatever bunting it could muster. Nurses flirted with doctors and laughed a lot and one told Hannah that it felt like Christmas, and that as soon as she went off duty she was going up west with her friend to see all the floodlighting and the crowds.

"That will be fun," said Hannah, sweating freely as she made an effort to compose herself between contractions. The nurse had come to see how she was getting on and, as she pressed Hannah's stomach, another contraction descended to turn it hard as a cannonball and cause Hannah to open her eyes very wide and fix them on a light switch.

"That was a nice one," said the nurse cheerfully, pulling up the sheet. Hannah who had thought it not in the least nice, took a sip of water and composed herself again. But the contractions were leaving her less and less time for this as the afternoon crawled on, and the light switch became more indistinct each time she searched for it. By the time the midwife came to examine her she was very tired and had had more than enough of stage one, and said so before being sick in her kidney bowl.

"May well be time to push then, Mrs Bates. We'll have a look, shall we?" The midwife, a short but powerfully built woman with peppery red hair, thrust a large hand into Hannah, who gasped with pain.

"Two fingers." The midwife said with a disparaging sniff. "I thought you'd've done better than that by now."

"You try, then," Hannah snapped when she had control of her voice. "I'd just like to go home." She squeezed the bedrail frantically as another contraction enveloped her and shut her eyes this time, quite beyond looking for the light switch.

"We'd all like to do that," the midwife pointed out. "With it bein' VE night an' all. But you can't go yet awhile, you've a job on. I'll look in again."

Hannah had lost track of time when she felt the first

urge to push. She heard the sounds of many people in some faraway world outside the window; there was a band somewhere and singing. Later the intermittent bangs and whizzes of fireworks. She was sick again. At some point the midwife returned and explored her stomach with big warm fingers, head cocked like a blackbird listening for worms in the grass.

"Now . . . push. Come on, Mrs Bates, *push!*"

Hannah tried to say she *had* pushed. But she was too tired now to make her lips work in the right sequence; too tired even to be sick again. She heard a man's voice some time afterward but then no more than snatches of reality were piercing the fog of red and black pain.

"Mrs Bates? Are you listening, Mrs Bates? You *must push* – it's important. Are you *listening*?"

But Hannah was in another place, drifting in an inescapable spiral down a dark tunnel, with a gentle wind blowing the hair from her brow. She felt only a welcome numbness, the pain had dropped away and she closed her eyes in relief at the escape.

The tunnel was long, dark, but the sensation of floating faded gradually as space opened out, lightened. Finally it was behind her and she was in a garden, her feet touching cool grass.

She sensed the garden before her eyes opened. As they did, she saw the colour . . . flowers everywhere, in all conceivable pinks from palest shell to magenta, and every flower was fragrant. Perhaps the garden lay behind a tinted veil? The sound of water tumbling over stones merged scents and hues in a harmonious whole; and now, Hannah could see children beyond the flowers, playing.

Serena . . . she was certain that one of the children was Serena. Smiling, she began to move through the fllowers, filled with a sense of peace, of tranquil joy, such as she had not dreamed possible.

"Mrs Bates?" Someone was tapping her on the hand. She pulled it away, wanting nothing but to remain for ever in the garden with the laughing children.

"Leave me alone. Don't want . . ."

The tapping again, this time on her arm. "You will when you see what you have here."

A hand guided hers. Her fingers touched another hand, so small, so soft, that Hannah was drawn to consciousness by the surprise of it and by minute fingers that found and gripped hers. She lifted her eyelids a fraction. The image of the garden was still strong but it began to pale as her eyelids let in the light.

"That's better. Look, here she is. Your new daughter. Bring Mrs Bates a cup of tea now, will you Jean?"

Hannah moved her head to see the small face in the cocooning shawl. Her fingers explored the creased forehead, the downy cheek. She pushed back the shawl a little. The baby's hair was dark copper and on either temple was an indented bruise.

"What . . ." Her voice was a little slurred. She coughed and winced as her muscles clenched.

"Don't worry about the forceps marks, they'll soon fade. She'll be a picture in a couple of days. You concentrate on getting your strength back. We'll try her on the breast when you've had a cup of tea and a little rest. What're you going to call her?"

The nurse popped a thermometer into Hannah's mouth and took her pulse. Hannah stared at the little face and at the finger still curled fast about her own. She was still staring when the tea came, strong and life-reviving, and she sipped it thankfully, propped on one arm.

A daughter: that was strange, she'd been fairly certain of a son. David would surely be happy with either. She wanted to tell him about it now, at once, and watch his reaction. But she contented herself with composing a few sentences in her head, for when she wrote. "I think I should tell you, darling; you have a daughter." Or perhaps. "This will come as a surprise I know, but on VE Day I gave birth to our daughter." She mentally crossed out both efforts, set down her teacup and sank back against the pillows.

VE Day ... she certainly hadn't seen much of *that* after looking forward to it for so long. The clock above the ward door said two-thirty, which must be early on VE Day plus one. Later maybe a nurse would phone Florence for her. Hannah felt she simply had to tell someone about her daughter, even if it could not be David.

What could she call her? Drifting on the verge of sleep she thought Elizabeth would be nice, after her maternal grandmother. Betsy; Dada would like that. Yes, Elizabeth. But the garden ... she would have loved, above all, to have stayed in the garden with the flowers, the cool water, the voices of children. She would find that garden again ... one day.

Hannah wheeled her baby along the paths of the Common every day. Trees burst into summer above their heads and blackbirds flew low over them carrying grubs for their nestlings. She continued to compose letters to David, but failed to commit them to paper. The agreement she had made with herself months ago overbore her longing for him to know about their daughter. First he must decide to make his commitment, without pressure from her, for only then could she feel secure in his love. She wrote often to Jonet, wishing her all luck in her exams, and was grateful for the few brief notes in return. And she wrote to Joe, begging him to come and see his new niece the moment the Atlantic reopened for business. Tom, soon to be demobbed, managed a brief visit, Hannah taking a taxi to meet him with the baby in her arms.

"She's lovely. Very little, though." Tom looked awstruck when Hannah put the sleeping child in his arms, going back to Clapham.

"She's bound to be at only four weeks, silly." She laughed at the expression on his face, also because she was pleased to see him. He grinned himself, then said:

"You look well, Han." He coloured a little, not given to making personal remarks, and ducked his head to study the baby. Hannah touched his sleeve.

"I'm fine, love. And better for seeing you. Let's just hope you're demobbed *fast*."

She did look well; smooth, rounded, with shining hair and a pearly lustre to her skin; nowhere near almost forty-three years old. It seemed that late motherhood must suit her. All manner of problems lay ahead – how and where she would live, if and when she would return to Taibach; how her business would develop in the aftermath of the war; David, Jonet. Jonet was never far from Hannah's thoughts. She had written to her each week without fail, always saying how much she looked forward to seeing her and hoping now to show her the newest member of their family. But Jonet's replies were never more than notes; now she was taking her exams and was incommunicado. After that? Well, she *would* persevere.

But Hannah could live only in the present, now. A day at a time. David, Jonet, the restructuring of her life, nothing could be forced, by however strong a will. Above all she must establish a secure and loving base for her baby – for Elizabeth, or Liza as Hannah was beginning to think of her. This child must never want for love.

The day after Tom's visit, a letter from David. No more than a few hurriedly scrawled lines, to say that he was being flown back to Canada direct in a couple of hours. Something vague; transport liaison from the home base. He would be in touch.

About four weeks' later came a longer letter, three sheets of expensive vellum with the big spaced-out scrawl. Hannah read it quickly, standing by the open window with her free hand rocking the handbar of Liza's pram to lull her to sleep after bath and breakfast. When she had done, Hannah lifted her head and gazed for a long moment at the yellow curtains in the window across the road, and at the bright splash of summer flowers in the vase between them. She moved the pram aside and sat down, spread out the pages and read the letter a second time, slowly.

My dearest Hannah

I've known for a few days that this letter must be written. I should very much like to put off writing it but today that seemed to be not only cowardly but a downright cruel way to behave towards the woman I love. For I do love you and you must never doubt that.

I finally got to have a talk with Julia, having tried to choose the best possible moment – when she felt fairly well, and not worried by anything much. I told her that I wanted my freedom; a divorce. That I would make a generous settlement – she is of course a rich woman in her own right – and always stay in touch, but that I wished to marry a lady I had loved for many years. To say that she was upset would be an understatement.

The next day she was taken to hospital with breathing difficulties. She is still there. I have had a talk with her doctor. He says that not only is her physical health volatile, with the angina getting worse, but her mental health is volatile, too. I levelled with him about us; he said the responsibility must be mine, but I should bear this talk in mind. Some help he is.

Hannah, how can I be responsible maybe for the death of someone I vowed to protect all those years back? Simply to gratify my own wishes? You, who are so very strong in every way, cannot imagine, I guess, how it is with someone like Julia. But I do not believe that you would wish me to do her ill, so we could have *our* way.

What can I say, but that you have made these last years happy and fulfilling; the war years that I shall never forget. You will be always in my heart, my sweet Hannah. And when I am free I shall come and find you.

God bless you and keep you safe
Ever yours
David.

She sat for a long time. She would have liked a drink of water. Her gaze shifted from the pages on the table to her flowers, set on the window ledge in the small jug Serena had bought her one birthday from a stall in Taibach market. It held a bunch of sweet williams, and the scent came to her as a gentle benefice on the movement of air from the open window. Hannah sat still, breathing in the fragrance, and outside the street was as side streets should be, peaceful, with one side in bright sun and the other in purple shadow.

She supposed that he was right, thinking of her as strong. Maybe that was only because she'd had no option, once she had reached fourteen and Dada had gone to the war. Since then, there had been no one to be strong for her. Now he had made his choice and there was no one again. So ... just as well if she *were* strong.

She tilted back her chair and looked at David's daughter, sleeping with the deep abandon of the newly born. Her hair was showing a distinct hint of her father's auburn and already her jaw had the squared firmness of Hannah's. Her lashes, long for so young a baby, curled dark and dewy on the cream-soft skin. The nurses had been right; this was a perfectly lovely baby, particularly when she opened her brilliantly blue eyes.

Hannah looked intently at the unusual peaceful face. "Just you and me then, sweetheart." Elizabeth stirred, opened her eyes and looked straight at her mother. Hannah looked back; and for the first time it occurred to her to wonder if this child would inherit the gift.

"No." Her voice was soft as mother's and daughter's gazes held. "Better for you, my little girl, if you do not ... so much better."

The baby yawned prodigiously, closed those brilliant eyes and, with the preliminary snuffling and shifting about of all small animals, slept again.

Hannah sat in the sunny window for a while longer; it was warm and pleasant, there seemed to be nothing that simply had to be done that minute, and anyway she was feeling quite tired. She read the letter once more.

It would never have done. How could she ever

607

have hoped for happiness on the back of another woman's misery? It had all been a dream, never rooted in reality, that was perhaps why she could not cry now. Although she did not doubt there would come a time to cry.

The cold truth had rarely been submerged for long by her love for David Vaughan. She had glimpsed it in an unguarded moment but had turned her eyes away, reluctant to kill the warmth of a perfect moment by acknowledging its presence. Now the fact that she had never, ever trusted him completely spread like a shadow through the little room. She had never been quite certain that if she leaned too hard on the structure of their delicately poised relationship, it might not crumble beneath the demand made of it.

Hannah began absently to rock the pram again. The dream had been so constant . . . of herself and David together. It had not encompassed sites, or interiors, or day-to-day minutiae of any description. The relationship alone had filled the dream completely; and now it was over. She knew that when the shock had worn off she would begin to hurt as if that cold, terrible core of truth, that she could not ever have trusted him absolutely, had not existed.

The sleeping child gave a little mew and yawned, settling deeper into her shawl. Hannah watched, smiling at the ridiculous new perfection of her. She had already raised two daughters single-handed; now she would start again. It did not cross her mind to tell David about this child now, for it would change nothing.

Some months later, after the baby had been christened Elizabeth, Hannah recalled quite unexpectedly that Elizabeth had been the second given name of Rachel Hywel, the woman on the hill.

Chapter Twenty-Four

August 1946

"Hannah?"

She had picked up the phone at once because Liza was in the deep middle of her morning nap in the pram just outside the open window. She knew anyway who it must be and was already smiling with delighted anticipation as she snatched at the receiver.

"Joe! Oh, *Joe*. You've made it!" She was barely coherent with pleasure.

"Sure have. So how're you doin'?" She did not, of course, recognise the voice with its American accent; but how *could* she after twenty-five years? Hannah's smile widened

"I'm doing fine, Joe. Especially now. I knew I couldn't really count on it till I actually heard your voice, even when you cabled from the boat." She had a sudden terrible thought. "You *are* in Southampton?"

"Of course." The laugh was a warm brown one. "Now, I get into Victoria at two thirty-five and – "

"I'll be there," Hannah cut in breathlessly. "Right at the end of the platform. And there's a nice room for you in the private hotel just up the road where Flo and Harry and, oh, everybody stays."

"Fine. See you then."

"Bye, Joe dear. Two thirty-five, I'll be waiting."

Hannah stared at her reflection in the looking glass over the fireplace. She pushed at the wave that dipped over her forehead, stroked down the skin of her neck.

Twenty-five years. She had been nineteen . . . a woman could change so much between then and now, particularly when the now was forty-four.

Leaning forward she examined the fine lines fanning from her eyes. Well, they were laughter-lines, weren't they. *That* was okay. Her eyes were still good and clear; and her skin. Teeth were still her own. And there were no more than half a dozen grey hairs so far.

Hannah laughed suddenly and put out her tongue at her reflection. For heaven's sake, she was in good shape! And this was her *brother*, not an examination committee for *Youth and Beauty* magazine. Joe, a successful New York antique dealer; Joe, with whom she'd shared her childhood and the hard years of her adolescence. And he *would* go home to Wales . . . he *must* be ready now to beat his fear.

Just time for a cup of tea before Liza woke. Hannah carried it back to her room and sank down in a beam of summer sunlight with a contented sigh. She loved Sundays. From time to time she would sit quiet on a Sunday morning and try lazily to figure out exactly why she was still here in a bed-sitter in Clapham. Not that this wasn't fine as bed-sitters went . . . she had her own sunshine-yellow rep curtains now and a pair of good docket-free armchairs with flowered covers from a local second-hand dealer. The same man had searched out for her two carved Edwardian wall-mirrors to reflect the light from the window and a set of three pale, beautiful Victorian water colours. A rug she had bought at an auction of bomb-damaged stock of lustrous, light washed-wool lay before the handsome hearth, masked now by a huge jar of marguerites. But comfortable as she was here, this was *not* home . . . not Morfa Cottage. Some days it made no sense at all to her. On others she recalled exactly how it had been – the stresses and strains of last year, the weeks of indecision after David's letter, when she had seemed to spend the whole summer pushing Liza around the Common trying to think clearly about her future.

Come home, Florence had urged. All right, you have an illegitimate child – maybe the Port Talbot Chamber of Trade will be a mite glassy-eyed around you for a while. Maybe there *will* be a slight drawing aside of skirts as you pass in case you're catching. You can deal with that. Come back where you belong. Harry and I and Tom will support you a hundred per cent and I believe Daisy would, and Aunt Maggie after she's held the baby a few times. Maybe even Aunt Lil when she's over the shock!

Jonet: she had been a factor, that could not be denied. Had *she* not been so ashamed, so desperate to hush everything up for fear of what people would say, Hannah might have brazened it out. But she had been so very aware of the damage she had done to Jonet. She had wanted only to mitigate it in any way left to her. Losing Jonet's love – it that was what had happened – was a sadness at the very core of Hannah's life.

Another thing. Tied up with her drop in confidence after David's letter were her doubts about the businesses. Once rationing was over might people *want* to eat out so much? Or might there be a post-war depression as there had been last time, when there was no longer money in people's pockets for that luxury? How could her businesses then be certain of supporting herself and daughters, Harry, Florence and Tom?

Hannah had been poor once, and she would never want to be so again. She had only to recall the struggle after the last war to be certain of that. If she lost the security that money could bring now, she would have nothing and no one to fall back on.

She guessed, of course, that she only needed to write to David; only tell him of his child and cash would flow freely across the Atlantic in support of Liza. But that would be a last resort, which was certainly not in sight.

She had still been indecisive when last November she'd noticed the card stuck to the glass door of the tea-rooms in The Pavement. "Experienced caterer required. Apply within." Hannah had put on the brake of Liza's pram and gone inside; it had seemed entirely logical to make an interested enquiry. In fifteen minutes she had come out with the offer of a job. The elderly Colliers had been worn down by bombs and blitzes and still saw no end to constant shortages and endless paperwork. They wanted to retire and move out to Devon where their son farmed. For a start they wanted a manager, but would ultimately hope for their shop lease to be taken off their hands.

Hannah had talked it over that evening with Miss Mallow who had, since Liza's birth, become a liked and trusted friend. When Hannah had remarked now how good she was with the baby, Ursula Mallow had divulged that she had spent many happy times looking after her sister's babies and then those of her favourite niece. The experience was obvious anyway when Hannah had a short sharp bout of flu in September and Ursula, taking charge of Liza, had made an excellent job of it. Fragile she might look, but she was in fact both fit and tough.

Did Hannah want to manage the tea-rooms, she had asked? If so, she would be delighted to help out with Liza. Life had been interesting enough as a warden but now *that* excitement was over she would welcome another small challenge that was also a large pleasure.

After a night of heart-searching, Hannah had taken the job. She'd argued that little could be lost by casting herself out on a new venture. Business was still excellent in Swansea and in Taibach, and everyone content with what they were doing. Tom was happy at Morfa Cottage, with the garden to work in at weekends and Mrs Lloyd to do the cleaning on Fridays. Hannah had asked for a six month trial for all concerned at Collier's with weekends off, and finishing at four on weekday afternoons . . . trade was quieter in August with residents on holiday out of London, so it fitted when Joe asked to come then; and Mrs Collier's niece agreed to stand in for two Mondays to allow Hannah extra time with him.

Perhaps it really *did* have mostly to do with Jonet. Not that she was around now, she had completed her first year at Durham University and had a holiday job in Scarborough. She *could* have come to Morfa Cottage . . . but had come only once, last Christmas, when Hannah and Liza were there.

Hannah went to the window to check on Liza, tucked in under the cat-net stretched across the hood of the high maroon pram. Her eyes darkened, thinking of Jonet. There had been no public rift; after the scene in the changing room at Jonet's school there had been – nothing. Simply coolness, and a marked disinterest from Jonet in her mother's affairs. Perhaps she saw that as the most successful way to hurt Hannah.

So often Hannah had striven to improve things. She had taken the car for the final collection of Jonet and her possessions from school to Morfa Cottage last July, leaving eight-week-old Liza with Florence to Flo's great delight. But on the first sight of her infant sister that evening, Jonet had been unable to produce the graceful word or gesture. She had looked at the sleeping child without expression and Hannah had felt the air pulsate with tension. She had wanted to beg the perplexed girl not to lay blame where there was only innocence, but in the end had simply waited. What could she say that would not reopen wounds?

"Her skin is very pale," Jonet had said in the end, mindful that some remark was expected of her.

"That's because she is deeply asleep." Hannah had stopped then, at a loss herself.

"Oh, I thought perhaps it was the colour of her hair that made it appear so."

The dark auburn hair; a feature of David Vaughan. Hannah had said no more, feeling wretched about the situation. And Jonet made no overtures, did not pick up the baby or touch her. She spent hours in her room in correspondence with universities before telling Hannah in August that she had accepted a place at Durham.

"Such a long way." Hannah had felt the sudden shock of loss. Jonet gave a little shrug.

"It was my first choice, I really enjoyed the interview. Places have been hard to come by with so many being saved for people getting demobbed."

"I know, love. You've done splendidly to get your first choice. Now, I'll give you something on account and you get whatever you need with it."

"It will be books mainly." Jonet had paused, then added awkwardly, "thanks. I could help out in the shop now, till late September. Or with Flo, in Swansea. Whatever needs doing."

Hannah had felt a rush of compassion for the tied-up, intense girl who had not learned how to forgive. "Thanks, dear. I'll have a word with Mrs Price and with Flo – a few hours a week would be welcome I'm sure. And we must sort out the allowance you'll need for your first term."

The devastating possibility, had occurred then, that she was trying to buy Jonet's love. She had moved blindly to the door of the cottage, knocking her hip on the table and stumbling down the steps to sit on her corner bench by the roses. The great yellow King's Ransom that Serena had chosen was in full flower, it had more than fulfilled her hopes. Oh Lord; if Serena could just see this rose now. Coming home, as she did whenever she could manage, was always a source of peace and renewal. But together with that was pain, brought back by memories of Serena's death.

Now, Hannah looked out at Liza's pram. Of course it would all have been different with Serry . . . she and Jonet had been dissimilar in so many ways. Jonet was – as she was. And what was so terrible about trying to buy love if it would not come any other way? She most probably never would stop trying and hoping. She thought it unlikely that Jonet would live at home again after three years at university. But distance, and time, might do what proximity could not, so she would wait, there was nothing to do but wait.

The pram rocked a little. Then a fist shot up to clutch at the coarse cotton webbing of the cat-net and the pram rocked quite violently. Hannah leaned out of the window and smiled at her daughter, pink and freshly awake and raring to go.

"Mama . . . Mama! Out!"

"All right – hang on a sec, I'm coming."

Her mouth was dry with anticipation, waiting at the platform barrier. Liza wriggled in her arms, diverted in first one direction then another by people and noise. At fifteen months she was indeed a beautiful child; the auburn curls framed a face whose enchanting baby curves were dominated by eyes exactly like her father's . . . a penetrating green-blue under strong brows, framed by long dark lashes. Liza looked, and was, a handful. "Down! Down!" she demanded now and pushed herself strongly away from her mother's shoulder with hands already sticky in the humid London air.

"Well, you can try." Hannah lowered her to the ground and took a firm grip on the baby's blue leather reins. "But you can't really walk far. Uncle Joe will be here any time now."

"Go, Mama," Liza leaned hard against the reins, her face pink with the effort to become mobile. She had begun to stagger about under her own steam at thirteen months and hated the confining reins insisted upon by Hannah.

"In a minute," Hannah scooped and lifted her quickly again as the express steamed slowly towards them. "Here, darling – here's Uncle Joe's train!"

She knew him of course; though *how* she could not say. He smiled, waved, a handsome, healthy-looking man of above average height with thick brown hair and lively brown eyes. Then he was at her side. The interminable years of war and separation fell away and as they clung together, with Liza struggling on the perimeter, Hannah closed her eyes in bliss and tears of happiness slid under her lids.

"Oh, you're here! *Here*. Oh, Joey, *cariad*."

"Han . . ." Joe held her and Hannah feel his heartbeat under the fine cotton shirt. Then his niece pushed him hard in the ear with the small celluloid doll clenched in her hot hand.

"Go 'way, man."

Joe released Hannah and leaned back to inspect her daughter. Liza stared back eyeball to eyeball, the fingers of her free hand circling the doll's arm and moving it gently back and forth on its elastic. The doll's blue and white gingham dungarees were, he now saw, a tiny version of Liza's own, and he touched them with an approving finger.

"They're pretty. Yours, too." He touched Liza's round little chest. "Very nice."

The toddler stared at him a moment longer, then thrust the doll towards his face. "Iggy."

"Oh, is that so?" Joe looked to Hannah for help.

"Iggy's her name," Hannah told him, wanting either to laugh or cry, or do both at once. She stared at Joe as Liza had, searching his face for clues to twenty-five years of living.

"Oh, right. That's a real nice name," he told Liza, nodding approval. "My name's Joe. Can you say that?" They continued to regard one another as the travelling public milled around them in the sweaty mid-summer heat.

"Man," Liza said finally, as though that clinched matters.

"Have it your way." Joe picked up his case and began to pilot them forward. "So, now let man see about a cab for us all."

They went for a walk on the Common in the early evening. It was still humid, but cooler; Joe had had a bath and changed into an open necked shirt and light slacks that looked indefinably different from the clothes of the Londoners taking Sunday walks with their families. He stared at the bomb sites, grown over now with dusty late summer weeds and grasses and noisy with sparrows and finches scavenging for seeds.

"Did this all happen before you came, Han?"

She nodded. "Miss Mallow, Ursula, told me a few stories, she was a warden. She had a narrow escape one night when a block of flats in the Kings Road was demolished by a direct hit. She was searching for survivers with another warden when a section of wall started to fall and she jumped clear in the nick of time."

Then Hannah looked at him. "Joe, you *are* all right? You never talked about it after that one letter when you told me; you know, about failing your medical."

"I'm okay, Han." He put a hand over hers on the handle of Liza's pram. "I just carry these tablets around and if I get to feel a mite strange I swallow a couple. Nothing to it, honest."

"Good. Only it was rather on my mind."

Somehow it was easier to talk outside, under the trees. Children were playing round the pond, some with boats on pieces of string. One father had rolled up his trouser legs and waded in to rescue two boats whose strings had tangled. Liza began to bounce up and down, watching them, and Hannah's breath was suddenly caught with the sadness of *her* not having a father to help sail her boats on the pond. She thought of how different her own childhood would have been without Thomas and was for a moment overcome by guilt for what Liza would be deprived of because of *her*. She reached blindly for Joe and he turned, frowning as he saw the unhappiness in her eyes.

"What is it, Han? What's wrong?" Hannah shook her head, trying now to smile.

"Just a goose walking over my grave, Joe. Sorry."

"Show me the goose and I'll shoot it," he said. "You know that, don't you?"

"I do, Joe. Thanks. I'm so dreadfully sorry – sad – that you can't meet Serry."

"Of course you are." He pressed her hand, the warm comforting hand she'd so longed for in the bad years. "I am, too. And I know what she meant to you, Han. But maybe it'll help if you tell me all about her, now I'm here. And there's still Jonet – and this one."

"Of course." When the time was right she would try to explain what had happened between Jonet and herself. "You *will* come home to Wales?" she added in a little rush. She had meant to say nothing until he did, but there it was, said. They walked for a few paces before he answered her.

"Yes, I'll come. When do we go?"

Hannah gave a little gasp and, standing still in the middle of the Common, began to weep silently, tears trickling freely down her face. Too late to see Serena, and Jonet wouldn't be there. But he *would* come home. Overwhelmed by the currents of emotion that had run through her day, Hannah held fast to his hand and struggled with the tears.

"Hey." He fished a handkerchief from his trouser pocket. "That's no way to show you're pleased!"

"I know." She choked, laughed. "It's *stupid*." She wiped her face. "If you were married though you'd know it's all perfectly normal."

Liza had lost her patience now and was struggling to squeeze out of her pram strap to make for the pond. "Out! Me out!"

Hannah lifted her from the pram and, hooking her on to her reins, handed them to Joe along with a little tug-shaped boat from under the pram cover. "I'll follow with the transport," she promised. "And don't lose the string unless you fancy a paddle."

She sat on the bench and watched them. Liza might be only fifteen months but she was already alarmingly female, ordering Joe about with small imperious gestures backed up by single-word commands. He was surprisingly good with her, treating her as a perfectly reasonable human being which, had he ever had children of his own, he would not have expected her to be. Studying them as they went about the business of

619

getting the boat into the water without Liza going with it, Hannah speculated on why Joe had no children, no wife. Maybe there was no single reason . . . she would wait to see if he told her before she jumped in. Maybe he would make it clear to her in the days they would spend together. When he went home with her.

It had been raining when they left Paddington on Friday afternoon, cluttered with umbrellas, pushchair and baby paraphernalia; Liza clutching Iggy in one hand and a ragged segment of cot blanket in the other, without which it was out of the question for her to sleep as Hannah explained to Joe.

"It's the ribbon binding, you see. It has a nice sharp little corner at the end. She eases that corner under the nail of her little finger, then sucks the thumb of her free hand. Works like a charm."

"Whadya' know." Joe shook his head. "Come to think, young Carl – Alex's boy, remember? – he used to tote a piece of old undervest! Got to be a terrible colour; but Carl would not have that bit of cotton washed, screamed blue murder if they tried to have it off him. Wouldn't do to mention all that now of course . . . not to a young man all of nine years old!"

The further west they travelled the quieter Joe became. At Cardiff the sun came out, but by then he had closed his eyes, leaning back in the carriage seat with folded arms. Hannah watched him, sitting opposite with the sleeping Liza warm against her. She knew he was awake, but that his eyelids were shutters, indicating a desire to be left alone with his thoughts. What those thoughts were she could only guess. Joe had seemed happy to talk on any subject but that of his return home after twenty-five years . . . about how the man of almost thirty-eight felt to be retracing the steps of the twelve-year-old, desperate boy. But men rarely were forthcoming about personal emotions. Perception told her after just this brief time with him so far that Joe was guarded in the extreme – that emotional shutters would come down like the closed lids against anyone seeking more from him than he was willing to reveal. Hannah could only hope that behind those shutters he was not reliving the lonely terror of that last night, when he had finally crept away from his home and from her to face a hostile world alone.

"Joe, oh, *cariad*." She found herself whispering the words, watching the composed features that still bore traces of the boy she had loved so much and laboured so hard to protect and cherish. As though he had heard the old childhood endearment Joe opened his eyes; brother and sister regarded each other across the dusty motes of sunlight slanting through the carriage windows.

"Will it be okay, Han?" He spoke with an air of quiet, stripped-down simplicity that made Hannah long to gather him close, to reassure him and offer him her strength and love as she had so long ago, when she had gone with him in the dark to dispose of Norman Madoc's body. Instead, she smiled at him, and gave a little nod.

"It will be, Joe. I'm certain of it."

Joe continued to look at her and Hannah could see uncertainty in his eyes that were so like Betsy's. He sighed, then, and turned to watch the Welsh country-side slide past in the blowy early evening light, with busy, biscuit-coloured clouds running together and parting in chaotic dances. The little walled fields sloping up the hills and down the valleys were sometimes dotted with creamy flocks of sheep, sometimes with black Welsh cattle; were sometimes dark gold with ripely waiting corn, or striped with pale gold lines of stubble. Grey farmsteads sat with their crescents of protective oaks and pines, and above them the hills thinned out in colour with rocky outcrops and deeper smudges of heather, and always the drystone walls that had for centuries climbed over the same contours. Seeing them Hannah was homesick for her own hills, for the wall crannies sheltered from sea winds where she might find harebells and thrift, primroses and violets. Not long, not long, not long ... the carriage wheels drummed out the rhythm. She recalled the Madoc's farmstead stretched along its fold of hill. Old Gideon must be dead by now, and poor old Matty. Norman's brothers would have taken over. Hannah's spirit shrank from the memory of Norman Madoc ... of the dreadful weight of his body pushing her down into the barley straw. She *had* wished him dead, and could not ever rescind that wish. She must live with it – and its possibly dreadful consequences – until she died. Although she had not struck the blow that had sent the man tumbling to his death, Hannah could not shake herself free of the fear of complicity – it was perhaps fitting that she could not.

And complicity in *one* death might well suggest involvement in the second, equally terrible. Thirteen years ... yet still there was scarcely a week when something, somewhere did not resurrect the shadow of Darrow Bates. Hannah glanced at her brother's face, behind which lay *his* guilt, and thought it unlikely now that he would ever learn of hers. She stared out at the welcoming land, her land, and prayed again as she so often had that no power of hers had contributed to the downfall of the man she had vowed to love and cherish till death did them part.

Joe became increasingly nervous as they steamed toward Port Talbot. Even Liza, bouncing up and down between their knees and climbing over first one then another, failed to divert him. Hannah had told him details of Tom's life to date, to make the twenty-eight-year-old man he had left as a small child seem less than a stranger when they came face to face. Now she could only hope that the family reunion would not place more stress on Tom than he could take. She put a hand on Joe's arm as he swung their bags off the rack.

"He's still there, you know, the little boy you left. You'll find him if you look."

Joe squeezed her hand. "I'll find him, Han. Don't you fret now."

Tom was at the station. He had put on his good suit with a maroon and blue striped tie Hannah had bought for him. He stood quietly, watching the doors open. Hannah stepped down first with Liza and he started towards her with a broad welcoming smile.

"Tom." She hugged him with her free arm, kissed his cheek. As he straightened he looked past her and found Joe. Hannah saw tears gather in his calm grey eyes; she stepped aside and the brothers hesitated for a moment, then walked into each other's arms.

"We must drink to this special occasion," said Harry and filled up their glasses with ginger wine made regularly by his mother for as long as anyone could remember. Tom had taken Joe and Hannah straight from the station to Number twelve Incline Row for Florence's welcome home supper. They fed generously on her steak pie and topped up with rasberry trifle smothered with the best mock cream recipe in South Wales. They were all still seated round the table, save for Raymond who was playing in a Taibach versus Aberavan Junior XI cricket match, and Liza who had fallen asleep over her evening bottle and was tucked up on the sofa in the front room.

"To Joe," Harry raised his glass. "Cousin Joe, home with us after so many years. May this be the first visit of many . . . always welcome, boyo."

"Indeed." Florence turned to give Joe a firm kiss on the cheek. "Our home is yours, Joe."

They all drank, watching the newcomer in their midst. Joe smiled, his gaze travelling round the room again as it had often in the past hour. He may have been searching for signs of his past, but the warm friendly little room offered few clues to that; Florence and Harry had made it their own as far as utility furniture and dockets had allowed. But the table, covered now by a cream damask cloth embroidered by Florence's grandmother thirty years ago, was the one on which Joe had so often sorted his precious collection of pebbles. He believed he could recognise it by its shape. Then his gaze went down to the legs and he knew for certain; could recall that crescent-shaped burr where a flake of coal had shot out of the fire . . . the scuffs at the bottom that had been made by his own boots.

He became conscious that they were waiting for him to speak and gathered his thoughts. He was affected by several emotions, but strongest by far had emerged a sense of family. Often, through the quarter of a century that had slipped by since he last sat in this room, he had believed that gone for ever . . . the warmth, the comfort of belonging somewhere, to someone, had been no part of his life in America where he had functioned always as a single entity. The price of running from his nightmare had included that of forfeiting this precious facet of his childhood. Even with parents gone, he had had Hannah, Tom, his own place in the world he knew.

Now, looking at the faces turned to his, Joe felt again

that he belonged. The warmth of it flooded him, flooded through his veins to drown the fear still lurking there; flooded his cheeks with colour. He looked at Tom, the brother he had played with on the ragrug in front of the fire, pushed around in his cart for a treat. Tom was watching him with love in the eyes so like his father's. And Hannah . . . Han.

"I just want to say it's great to be home." His voice was husky. "It's great to be here with you, with my family. Thanks a million for making me so welcome. It sure does mean a lot."

"Sit down then and I'll make us all a cup of tea." Florence blew her nose, moist-eyed. A contented marriage and the success of the restaurant she managed with equal doses of commonsense and flair had brought her to a maturity glowing with healthy confidence and sharp good humour. The babies had not arrived; but Raymond was as much a son as any mother might wish for Harry, too, at almost fifty, seemed less fragile than in his twenties or thirties. His gaunt frame had filled out under Florence's vigilance, headaches were rare, and he shared with young Raymond all the natural bonds of father and son. He smiled now at the inevitability of Florence's pot of tea and Joe thought he caught a glimpse of the dashing cousin he had hero-worshipped as a little boy.

Hannah helped clear down the table while the kettle boiled, carrying the dishes into the bright little scullery with its fresh yellow paint and new gas cooker.

"There's talk of putting in bathrooms soon as things get back to normal," Florence told her, attacking the washing-up with speed and vigour. "And extendin' this scullery out into the yard to take it. Make a nice little kitchen then, wouldn't it? An' Harry says he'll build me in some cupboards once he can get the wood. You know; we'd all gone without things six years and somehow that was okay because there was a war on . . . but that's been over a whole year now an' we're *still* goin' without! That rankles!"

"It would be marvellous to be free of rationing, Flo, it's given us such headaches. Yet we both know the business it brought us."

"*And* the paperwork!" Florence dunked a last stack of dishes in the bowl then wiped her hands. "There's the kettle ready. Oh." She lowered her voice. "Han, old Mr Vaughan died over a week ago, I cut it out of the paper for you. And David was at the funeral."

Hannah dried a plate slowly, running the cloth twice round the rim. Liza's grandfather, dead. One grandparent left now; and it was highly unlikely they would ever meet. Liza would not even meet her own father unless Hannah herself made the decision to allow it. Was she entitled to play God in her daughter's life? Or in David Vaughan's? Was she honestly protecting herself and Liza from further hurt and disappointment, or was there a touch of malice involved in her refusal to tell him of his child? A punishment for letting *her* down.

She stared into the August evening, out into the familiar little yard to the brick wall between the houses. She was sorry Mrs Rees had moved from next door – gone to her married daughter, Florence had said. They'd not been that close; but Hannah recalled her kindness when Betsy was so ill and afterwards, when she, Joe and Tom had been left alone she had brought bits of food round for a while like a hen bird feeding abandoned chicks.

Nothing stayed the same. And no one. How much was left in *her* of that bereft young girl of seventeen whose ambition had been to get herself and her brothers through each day. Who had already lain in David

626

Vaughan's arms one magic night on Primrose Hill and yet who would, a much changed, successful and mature woman, give herself to him again in another war. Some part of her had stayed the same, had loved one man for a long time, however circumstances had changed.

Hannah hoped that he had gone from here – that there was no danger of meeting. She was slowly attaining a degree of serenity, of acceptance; working to make her life complete without him, so that finally she could let him go with her whole heart. It would then remain for her to offer Liza everything possible to mitigate *her* loss, as she had tried to limit the hurt to Jonet.

"I said, your tea's poured." Florence's head poked round the scullery door. Hannah, still gazing out of the window, jumped. Florence relieved her of the plate and cloth and whispered, "Don't think about him, *cariad*. He's yesterday's man – okay?"

"True, O wise one." Hannah hooked her arm through Florence's. "The only men *I* need are right here, swigging your tea; let's join them."

Hannah and Joe climbed slowly up the hill, each with a hand on the bar of Liza's pushchair. Since he had to get up at four-thirty Tom had gone straight to bed after Harry had driven them home to Morfa Cottage in Hannah's Morris Eight – on permanent loan to himself and Florence – but brother and sister sat up late. Joe had begun to talk, and finally had leaned forward to touch Hannah's knee.

"Will you come with me? To the quarry?"

"If that's what you want," Hannah replied calmly, but her stomach had tightened in anticipation.

"Not what I *want* exactly. But maybe what I need."

627

Joe's eyes closed for a moment and he swallowed painfully.

"I understand. So, Tom has to go to work, Saturday's a busy morning at the bakery. We'll go right after breakfast, shall we? Then we've plenty of time to look at my shop, and go to Swansea for a late lunch with Flo. All right?" Hannah put on a brisk everyday voice to disguise the truth of their pilgrimage to the quarry being far from everyday.

The weather was still humid, mitigated here by a light wind off the sea. The old track had lately been tarmaced and the walking was easier. Joe was quiet, looking about him at the hill; Liza, who had been given a bracken frond, waved it about in a strange game of her own, muttering and crooning. Hannah was debating if she should ask Joe how he felt or wait for him to tell her.

"It was a sticky day." He spoke suddenly. "A bit like today. I remember wishing I had a drink."

"We're almost there." Hannah encouraged him. They rounded the curve and Joe recognised the boulder about a yard off the tarmac where Norman Madoc had sat twenty-five years ago, cursing his boot. He slowed as they passed it and Hannah saw beads of sweat on his forehead. Then they were there.

The passage of time had given the quarry a changed aspect. What had been undergrowth had become trees. Ash and birch and oak stretched their necks up from the shaley slope, spindly in the trunk and elongated. The floor of the quarry was no longer visible under a new generation of seedlings and thick mats of bramble, with a few straggly arms of yellow gorse. Joe leaned over the push-chair handlebar and his face looked so strange that Hannah wondered if he might be sick. She said nothing, but stood alongside and her hand closed over his. A blackbird called from the top of the birches and it was taken up by another, lower in the quarry. Apart from the bird calls it was quiet; enclosed by the dark heavy foliage of late summer they were masked from sight or sound of the massive spread of industry below them, or of the lonely slopes above.

"I shouldn't have run," Joe said quietly after some time. His pale blue shirt was dark with sweat across his chest but the hand covered by Hannah's felt cold to the touch.

"Easy to be wise from this distance, Joe. Try to let it go now, leave it in the past where it belongs." She pressed his hand, willing acceptance into his body and brain.

"Are they still there, the others? Up at the farm?" He could not leave it yet.

Hannah nodded. "I believe so. The two sons work it now."

They subsided again into silence. Then he said slowly: "D'you think some things are *meant* to happen? And would happen in spite of anything? It's a thing I've never . . . well, been able to work out, no matter how clearly I've tried to consider it."

Hannah looked down at her daughter who had stripped her bracken down to its spine and was bending that up concertina fashion.

"If we knew the answer to that I think we'd know just about everything. Sometimes we want to believe that events are pre-ordained but other times we want to feel that our destinies are for us to shape. We may have to wait till we're dead, Joe, to know for sure how the system works. Or we may never know."

"You're very sure about *something* continuing after death, aren't you?" Joe gave a little smile. "What if Norman Madoc's waiting out there for me so he can get his own back?"

"I don't know that either," she said honestly.

"But you have – *seen* things?" he pressed.

She nodded again. "Oh, yes."

"That woman you told me a bit about in a couple of letters a while back . . . is where she appeared nearby?"

"Not far." Hannah's tone was abrupt, for the truth was that Rachel Hywel had been dominating her mind since last evening. Lying in bed she had seen the blur of that pale narrow face behind her closed eyelids; had been perturbed to hear her own thoughts whispered in the old Welsh, the language she had not used for years, the language of Rachel Hywel. Thoughts and images had been pushed away with all her strength but would not retreat far enough to reassure her that she was in command. And here on the hill, the pull had become stronger.

"I'd sure like to see that place. I thought a lot about what you told me." Joe was fastening on the idea, perhaps as a means of cutting off from his own ghosts. "Have we time to walk there now?"

"Oh, Joe." Hannah ran a despairing hand through her hair. "Is that a good idea?" Yes, the voice inside her head told her, a good idea.

They pushed the pram together up the hill, not speaking. Liza, who had slept little yesterday and woken early, fell into sudden oblivion with the ruined bracken spine slipping from her uncurled fist. They left the trees behind; ignored the fork leading to Madoc's farm. Now Hannah decided she wanted to get there quickly and then leave, have done with it. They were both breathing hard as the old pines came into view. Hannah's mouth dried out and at this point she made a huge effort to gain control of her own will, deliberately slowing the pace.

The last time had been immediately after Serena's death. She recalled screaming out her pain, demanding of the shadow by the stones that she be told *why*. That pain drenched her again now; the longing for her lost daughter was fierce as a knife in her guts and she bent over the pram as her muscles clenched against it.

"You okay, Han?" Joe put a hand on her shoulder.

Hannah straightened. "Yes, thanks. It's up there, by the trees."

So little had changed for her. The pines had been full grown for years. Wind and poor, shallow soil limited other growth, save for a gradual increase of mosses and lichens over scattered rocks. Ivy covered what was left of the cottage walls but rabbits kept the brambles at bay and the grass trimmed well down. The land breathed quietly around them. The air was tangible in its sweetness, the coastal connurbation hidden by the mountain's shoulder. It could not have been so very different up here two centuries ago, save that the cottage then would have had four stout walls, a good roof, and a chimney with hearth smoke drifting from it.

"That was the house?"

Joe stopped. They looked together at the ruins and Hannah had an absurd desire to close her eyes. She wished hard to see nothing but what was there now . . . wished to have laid to rest her own ghost; for if Joe knew that, it would surely give him confidence to know a long-time burden had been lifted from both their shoulders.

"I'd like to take a look. Coming?" He started forward again, picking his way.

"I'll stay here, it's rough going for the pushchair." Hannah watched him approach the main fall of stone and as he did, saw from the corner of her eye a flickering shadow. Her chest tightened painfully; she tried to turn away her head but it, and her eyes, were immovable.

"Just a whole lot of nettles and things." He threw

back the words over his shoulder, standing a few feet from the shadow that had materialised to become Rachel Hywel. Hannah's breath died in her throat. She leaned on the pushchair over her sleeping daughter and knew she had lost the battle this time. *Why?* What more was needed?

Joe turned and made his way back toward her. Hannah, watching the woman's image, wanted to ask her what was to be done. But her throat would produce no sound.

"Can *you* see anything I can't?" He raised an eyebrow at her. Hannah did not take her eyes away until Rachel's shape had quivered and slowly faded. Then she transferred her gaze to him and found her voice.

"Nothing, Joe. Not a thing."

'That's good." He smiled and his relief was patent. "Maybe now we can both turn over a fresh leaf, eh?"

"I do hope so," said Hannah devoutly. She felt slightly nauseous and quite spent. "Now let's go."

On Joe's return to New York he wrote to thank Hannah for looking after him so well.

I do realise that the visit was certainly long overdue! And no doubt it resolved problems that have badly needed attention for years – I'm sure you know about them, you seem to know me so well despite the long separation. For that, too, I thank you, dear Han. I would also like to think that *your* ghost might have been laid to rest? I really want to get over again next August; that's a dead month here anyway and those Jacobean oak chairs I found in Wales have paid for this trip. No reason why I shouldn't do the same next year.

Hannah smiled, reading the letter. That was, she

believed, the first time she had ever deliberately lied to Joe. She hoped it would be the last.

By spring of the following year she was beginning to build a profitable business in Clapham. The Collier's tea-rooms had simply not attracted sufficient notice; they were unassuming, even dull. With bomb damage being made good, shops were beginning to brighten their images after the long hard war with its impossibility of refurbishing. She had long discussions with Mrs Collier about various options but the old lady was not inclined to do much forward thinking. "You take on the lease, Mrs Bates, then you will have a free hand and the satisfaction of making profits for yourself."

But certain improvements were agreed to, involving relatively small sums. The kitchen facilities were good but under-used and Hannah up-graded the "light lunch" menus to attract local businessmen. The shop front was repainted and bright new curtains put up; she found a dozen more comfortable chairs in a local saleroom to augment the supply of polished wheel-backs and enlisted a new and excellent supplier of breads and pastries.

As she worked, she considered Mrs Collier's words. Ursula Mallow was superb with Liza, handling the toddler with a winning formula of love and firm discipline, so that boundaries of permissible behaviour came to be recognised and accepted. At a time when women had laid down the tools of war industry for the second time and disappeared back into their homes to have babies, Hannah was aware that she was a maverick. One letter to David Vaughan and she would, she felt, not have to work again to support Liza; but for *her* that could never be the road to travel.

Also, she was increasingly aware that she really *wanted* to take up the challenge of Clapham – make it work for herself and Liza, make a success of a new venture away from the stresses of her old life. Her businesses were running smoothly, profitably, under Florence and a first-class manageress in Taibach, good back-up staff and of course Tom in the bakery where he most enjoyed being. Harry, too, was happy rising to the challenge of greater responsibility. Perhaps having Liza had been the overriding factor at first; but Hannah felt less sure that was still so – perhaps now she had more confidence and simply wanted to prove she was good at what she did, like Tom. She could always go back to Wales, when she was ready. But then the enigma of Rachel would present itself again. She had felt so certain that Rachel had gone, after Serena; to have found herself wrong had left her for a while in a turmoil. Perhaps advancing years were increasing her sensitivity to Rachel? But here in London she felt safe from that unquiet, turbulent spirit. Would she ever know *why* Rachel came to her? It seemed not, since the poor soul never spoke; that would remain an enigma.

As spring finally came after the longest, hardest freeze-up Hannah could recall there was daylight to take Liza to play on the Common in the early evening. There were late daffodils under the trees, and clumps of primroses among the brambles coming into tender pale new leaf. Liza, almost two, chattered incessantly and between bouts of pushing her pushchair would run from one object of immediate interest to another. Laughing with her, enjoying her, Hannah remembered the April two years ago when she had trodden the same paths as a stranger, with her lover fighting out the last days of the war in Europe and his child kicking lustily under her belt. No stranger now; she had Ursula for a friend, she was on Christian name terms with the girl and her young son in the house with the yellow curtains, and often shared a joke with the retired post-master and his wife in the upstairs flat. And there was Emily in Fulham.

So, time to decide. Absorbed, Hannah allowed Liza to run too far, too fast, so that when she tripped, fell flat on her face and began to roar with indignation at her cruel fate she was nearer to someone else than to her mother. A tall, lanky man kicking a football about with two boys strode over and scooped her up. For a moment she went stiff with surprise, staring at his smiling face. She started another yell, to abandon it as the man began to talk to her and stroke her rigid little back. When Hannah reached them, picking up the pushchair on the way, the man had pulled out a big white handkerchief and was wiping Liza's nose, still talking.

"Play with boys now," Liza told him. "Play with boys' ball."

He set her down and she trotted rapidly to where the boys were laying out goal posts of rolled up jackets. Seeing Hannah with the pushchair he smiled again, a wide lop-sided smile that exposed his large teeth and completely transformed his slightly lugubrious features.

"Nothing hurt but her pride."

"There isn't usually." Hannah smiled back. "But thank you even so. If you hadn't worked fast the Common would still have been reverberating, her lungs have always been remarkable."

"My first was the same." The tall man pointed to the fairer of the boys. "We were asked to leave our first flat. Oh dear . . ."

Liza had picked up the football that the smaller boy was about to kick between the posts. Holding it with difficulty in front of her stomach she bore it away.

"No, Liza. Give it back," Hannah called.

"My turn," Liza called back pleasantly but firmly. Setting it down she aimed a kick at it, missed and fell over the big ball. Laughing at her, the smaller boy ran over to claim ownership but Liza, roaring again with fury at being ridiculed, spreadeagled herself over the ball.

"Me kick it! You go 'way."

The boy gave his father a look of mute appeal. Had this been a boy his own size he would have done the obvious thing and engaged in physical combat for possession of his football, but he had no experience of very small creatures who made a racket out of all proportion to their size.

"You get up and stop that silly noise." Hannah squatted by the mutinous toddler. "Then ask the boy if you may have a kick. I think he'll say yes if you get up right away."

Liza considered her position, saw that she was being offered a reasonable way out of the impasse and heaved herself off the football.

"Why do their noses *always* run when they cry." The man pulled out his handkerchief again and Liza, surprisingly, allowed him another wipe of her nose. "Give her a kick then will you, old son?"

The boy sighed. "Okay."

"Now," the man positioned Liza carefully just far enough from the ball. "You're allowed one practice shot. You swing back your leg like this – " he lightly grasped the small knee – "then you *push* forward fast, like this." He shot the leg forward and Liza's foot connected with the ball and sent it rolling a few yards. She beamed, ran after it and belted it across the grass.

"Not bad," called the dark haired boy. "Kick it to me, then."

"That was kind." Hannah turned to the man. "How old are they?"

He frowned for a moment, then smiled widely again. "Eleven and thirteen, I think. Time goes so fast I have a job keeping tabs. I have to write their birthdays down or I'd forget those, too."

"I'm sure they wouldn't allow that." She laughed back at him; he possessed a slightly disorganised, naive quality that made her want to laugh. "Now, if I don't extract Madame you'll all lose patience with her."

"That's okay, it goes without saying that they're total savages at that size. Two, is she?"

"Next month."

He nodded. "I recall it was quite interesting, watching them learn in fits and starts to restrain – or cover up – their uninhibited animalism."

Hannah laughed again at this tall relaxed man wearing clothes that seemed to have been picked up at random from a pile and put on without thinking, and whose thinning untidy grey hair was due for attention from a barber.

"Aren't they still going through that process? It's quite a long one."

"Well, yes. But they become more adept at disguising their savagery under a veneer of civilised behaviour. Nick and Jake aren't bad, actually. Quite human for boys . . . considering."

They watched the play for moment. The boys had decided to get some fun from Liza since she'd foisted herself on them and had put her in goal, where she was clearly in some physical danger. "Did I say human?" Their father sighed and set off to rescue Liza.

"I have to go now anyway." Hannah caught up with him. "She's got to be tired by now, she might well nod off on the way home. What time does your wife like to have yours upstairs?"

"I organise that. My wife was killed by a V1."

"Oh." Hannah stopped. "Oh, I am sorry. How dreadful for you all."

"We weren't the only ones." He spoke with a moving simplicity. "There's a helluva lot of families all over London like us. It will be three years in June."

"I know a little of how you feel," she replied quietly. "I lost a daughter the September before that – September '43. It wasn't a bomb, but it was certainly because of the war. Our town was full of troops gathering for the Second Front; she was hit by an American truck."

"God, that's terrible, to lose a child." He looked down at her with such concern on his strong, open features that Hannah felt tears constrict her throat as she always did when she was offered sympathy.

"It's terrible to lose anyone you love. Now I must collect that infant." She spoke briskly to force back her emotion and held out her hand. "It was nice talking to you. I'm Hannah Bates."

"Matthew Sturton." His hand was big, dry and warm. Hannah's felt comfortable inside it and she was sorry to have to remove it so quickly. "We'll allow Liza one more kick shall we? If she agrees to get in her pushchair without ructions?"

She smiled. "You understand children quite well, I must say."

"Not bad. For a man." He tried to sound modest,

failed, and laughed again. His ruse did not work. Hannah turned the pushchair towards home with a backward wave and she thought that for Matthew Sturton, laughter probably came no less honestly for coming easily. It also occurred that she could not recall ever having shared laughter with her own husband.

It was the extra room becoming available that finally decided her. It was impossible to find anywhere with more space; hundreds of thousands of houses were having to be built in London simply to replace those destroyed. Street after street had been demolished and landlords had no need even to advertise accommodation; people materialised from nowhere and fought for every box room. Ursula Mallow, a close friend now besides a wonderful part-time carer for Liza, heard first about the extra room next to her own at the back.

"Been used as a storeroom for years," she told Hannah, visibly excited as though she had stumbled across buried treasure. "When the van came on Tuesday and men began trundling all manner of odds and ends along the hall I did wonder. Then a man in overalls with tins of paint turned up on Wednesday. And today, a roll of carpet. You would be wise to see Mr Perrot immediately."

Hannah did, and the landlord disclosed that the room was indeed being prepared for letting and hinted that it was already spoken for. Negotiations were brief but to the point; Mr Perrot wanted hard cash and Hannah wanted the room. She offered six months of the asked-for rent in advance and, recognising a good thing when he saw it, Mr Perrot accepted.

A bedroom: Hannah and Ursula stood in the doorway and surveyed the square empty room, both beaming with satisfaction.

"Facing east over the garden, Ursula, perfect for a bedroom. And that lovely tall window for the morning sun. And what a pretty little iron grate, I shan't cover that up." Hannah moved across to the window. It looked out on to a long narrow garden, undoubtedly untidy but with the nostalgic charm possessed by most semi-wild, enclosed gardens. A patch by the window was paved, with forget-me-nots blooming through the cracks and purple pads of aubretia hugging two chipped old urns, and foaming down three steps onto the lawn. An ancient double lilac swept low over this; it was more moss than grass and Hannah thought how spongy and soft it would feel to bare feet. Either side of the garden was fenced, though that had disappeared under the luxuriant May growth of unpruned shrubs and climbing roses, honeysuckle and clematis twisted together in tumultuous love. Across the bottom of the garden were trees in new leaf, and a wooden shed huddled in one corner with a tabby cat sitting on the roof washing its ears.

"He doesn't mind tenants in the garden," said Ursula, seeing Hannah's delighted face. "I think he always hopes someone will do a bit in it."

"Lovely. And I'll get a new bed for myself and a small one for Liza, she's ready to leave her cot. This carpet's neutral so I can get lovely flowery curtains and covers. And our bathroom is right opposite. Ursula, it's a really good idea!"

"So you think you might decide to stay on for a bit?" Ursula Mallow's heart shaped face with its petal-soft, finely-lined skin and round hazel eyes looked expectant. Hannah and Liza had opened up for her a life that had been in danger of closing in after the long camaraderie of the war years. She loved books and paintings and making beautiful samplers and dried flower montages, but she also liked people, movement and variety in her days. Hannah smiled at her now.

"I'll talk to Mrs Collier. I'd quite like to spend a year or two turning that place into a success. I'm not absolutely sold on this wallpaper ... how if I painted over it? A soft, happy, sunshine yellow."

"You and your yellow." Ursula smiled back. "And big yellow sunflowers on the curtains – don't tell me. I'll keep an eye open for something while Liza and I are pottering about."

Mrs Collier was putty in Hannah's hands, so eager was she to be relieved of the lease. "You will find an excellent firm of solicitors on the corner of Crescent Lane. And I shall include all the fixtures and fittings and pay the electricity bill to the end of this quarter."

Hannah phoned Tom from the call box by the cinema on the way home before she could be tempted to change her mind.

"I shall still come to Morfa Cottage every couple of months, you know how I count on my weekends there, and seeing you all."

"Of course, Han. You do whatever's best for you and the baby."

"And Joe hopes to come again in August. And this time maybe he'll meet Jonet – I do hope so."

"Yes, that would be good."

Dear Tom. Now Hannah wanted to get the next train out of Paddington to be with him; she felt a sudden harsh yearning for them all, for Morfa Cottage, for home. *Why* did she feel driven to exile herself like this? It was not too late, she really should give it more careful thought – did she truly want to commit herself to several more years in London, possibly for no better reason than that she had an illegitimate daughter?

Now she was approaching Marlborough Lane, it was the way she went home ... lovely Georgian and Victorian houses set back from the road with graceful lime trees. That solicitor ... Hannah walked across to read the engraved brass plate. It was raining, soft rain of early June and the brass plate was blurred with raindrops. She was peering to read it, wiping off the rain with her finger, when a man came out of the door, paused and spoke.

"I'm afraid we're closed. I'm the last out."

Hannah looked up. It was the tall man with the footballing sons. She looked again at the brass plate and a long finger pointed to a name. "That's me. I'm perfectly reliable."

She burst out laughing, recalling then that this same man had made her laugh a few weeks ago on the Common.

"I'm sure you are. How are the boys?"

"They're fine, I think, or I'd have heard." Matthew Sturton smiled down at her. He looked different with his bowler hat on but had raised it now and his hair at once blew into untidy strands as she remembered it. "They are away at school; they've an exeat on Sunday so I shall have their news then, which is usually that their pocket money will simply not go round. How is your electrically operated toddler?"

"Still sparking. Now she's two she thinks she has *carte blanche* to be twice as naughty."

"Two is a fearsomely naughty age," he agreed solemnly. "And with red hair, too, is that from her father?"

"Auburn," corrected Hannah. "Yes, it is. Well, look, I won't keep you now as you're closed anyway. I had not realised the time, I must get home myself. And please put your hat back on, your head's getting wet," she added. Matthew Sturton obediently clapped on his hat which, with his dark suit, stiff white collar and formal tie made him a more possible, but still unlikely, solicitor. Hannah realised this was almost certainly because she had seen him first playing football, in his casual clothes; he was nevertheless far from the stereotypical lawyer.

"So will you call tomorrow for an appointment? I shall be delighted to be of service to you."

"I will; thank you. Good afternoon then." Hannah began to walk on to find he was walking with her, his stride long and leisurely.

"I'm in the same direction, on the way to Clarence Avenue. Where are you Mrs – er – ?" He smiled affably. "Oh dear; and I really hoped I would recall your name, I'm so sorry."

"It's Hannah Bates. And people rarely do remember a name just dropped out once, that's nothing to worry about. I hadn't remembered yours until I read it on the doorplate."

"That's good. A pair of duffers." He sounded so pleased for her not to have recalled his name that Hannah wanted to laugh again. Matthew Sturton had the unerring knack of "tickling her funnybone" as *Nain* would have said. He seemed to be so completely at ease with himself that it was impossible for him to be awkward in another's company. What a happy gift. She imagined that the marriage split apart so cruelly by a V1 flying bomb had included a good deal of happiness.

"I miss the boys a lot," he was explaining. "But I

simply could not do justice to their daily care. And at the time when Myra was killed I was away quite often ... the army."

"Surely they didn't lose their mother and go immediately away to school?" Hannah sounded horrified, then stopped, fearful of appearing judgemental.

"Lord, no. I sent them to their maternal grandmother in Surrey. They like her enormously and they all helped each other so it worked well. It wasn't too far off and I saw them myself at every possible opportunity. All very difficult even so ..."

His voice tailed off and for Hannah those few simple words masked a huge core of suffering. She had to restrain a strong, instinctive urge to reach for Matthew Sturton's large hand and hold it, a gesture of understanding for his loss. At the same moment he looked down at her. His blue eyes were calm and deeply kind; and Hannah could have sworn he read her thought.

"You must have heard, Mrs Bates, how people say 'I wish I had done more' when they speak of someone who has gone. I'm sure that is always absolutely true. But I do know that I valued her more than I can say. Now the best I can do is bring up our sons in the way she would have wanted. And continue to be as happy as I can be."

Hannah swallowed. The rain was stopping, the cloud was breaking up and a patch of blue hung over the spire of St Mary's church. Matthew Sturton looked up then took off his hat, he was clearly not fond of it, and smiled at the bit of blue sky.

"You are absolutely right," Hannah said suddenly. "You see, my husband died ... it was an unhappy marriage so my feelings can be nothing like yours. But

644

although I felt very sad about it initially and wondered if things could not have been different, I too have come to see that I did all I could within that marriage. My knowing that he would die so soon could have changed nothing. So, like you, I too would like to be as happy as I can be now." She smiled then. "Is it not most odd to be holding this conversation with a comparative stranger?"

"It is sometimes easier to talk openly with a stranger. Not that you seem in any way a stranger to me." He smiled back at her.

"I feel the same," said Hannah simply. "Tomorrow is my birthday. And if you have a free appointment I shall come to see you about beginning a new phase in my life."

"What better day to make a new beginning than on a birthday?" His smile broadened to show his big even teeth. "I recall that I am free at twelve fifteen. If you come then would you allow me to take you to lunch afterwards to celebrate the birthday, if you have no previous engagement?"

'I should be working, but I'll see what can be arranged. I should enjoy that; thank you, Mr Sturton." When Hannah looked about her she realised that she had passed the turning for her road and she was smiling again.

Chapter Twenty-Five

April 1949

When it was time for Hannah to decide about Matthew Sturton she went to Morfa Cottage; to think carefully and to speak to Tom, Florence and Harry. She and Liza went as usual by rail from London, always a treat for Liza whose idea of heaven was a train journey long enough to include refreshments. This time there was to be a proper sit-down lunch in the dining-car and she requested tomato soup and egg and chips.

"Soup's not easy on a train," Hannah warned with an eye to her daughter arriving with red rivulets down her cream jumper, but Liza was adamant as only a red-head of rising four can be. After the rivulets had flowed the waiter who, in common with most of his sex had fallen under Liza's spell, took away the jumper with the promise to rinse and return it in a food bag. Liza negotiated the egg and chips successfully then curled up and slept like a sated cat, the auburn curls that were her father's legacy falling away to reveal her white fragile neck.

Hannah leaned back to watch the countryside unravel. April, a magical month with its certainty of fresh beginnings and rebirth. And on the horizon a new decade; the second half of the century; perhaps a propitious time to start another chapter in her life.

She smiled, thinking of the gentle, companiable delight of this courtship. From the first meeting there had been an ease between them that both recognised as unusual . . . from the first lunch date, a warm liking that had grown steadily with further meetings. Hannah had told him about Liza right away and he had appeared undismayed, saying that the war had forged a great many unexpected relationships.

"Which war?" she had smiled wryly. "I met Liza's father in the first weeks of the *last* war – I was twelve at the time and he pushed me off a bench with his brolly. Accidently, of course!"

"There you are then, what did I tell you?" He had laughed, finishing off his lemon sponge pudding with obvious satisfaction, and Hannah had felt a little light-headed with relief at not being considered a loose woman. After that it had been frighteningly easy to trust him. She had tried to remind herself often to keep her distance – that she'd trusted before and been in trouble for it. But it was almost impossible not to relax with this man. Ultimately, not to trust him completely; not to like him enormously.

Two years had slipped effortlessly by, busy and rewarding. The new business took up as much of her time as Hannah allowed it to and it thrived; but she kept her hours there firmly in check, leaving time always for Liza. Ursula Mallow took her to kindergarden two mornings each week now and in September that would become five mornings, leaving Ursula with "Time on my hands" screwing up her face in mock horror. They had been allowed to use the garden; they had hooked a rope and an old tyre over a tree branch for Liza to swing on and made a small sandpit from a disused cold frame. The women had cleared off bindweed and ground-elder, dock and dandelion, allowing old peonies to breathe and flower; rediscovering lupins and delphiniums and starry little scillas in unexpected places. Matthew sometimes came on Sunday afternoon with his long-arm pruners to cut back and tidy up, then afterwards would sit on the uneven old steps with his long legs stretched out, drinking tea. He always had bits of leaf or bark in his hair by then, often a smudge of earth on his face and grass stains on his trousers. Hannah could never quite equate the soberly suited solicitor with spotlessly scrubbed nails and well-combed hair with the lanky, falling-apart, off-duty persona. When she remarked on this, Matthew gazed down at his scuffed "at home" shoes and frowned; he invariably gave her comments due reflection.

"I think *this* is me," he finally admitted. "Why? Don't I suit?"

She laughed then at his solemn expression and pushed gently at his chest. "You suit very well, silly man."

Sometimes she took Liza to his graceful Georgian house with its big garden of dim mysterious curtains of willow, and deep drifts of rhododendrons falling over mossy paths, and a swing. He would push the little girl who shrieked "More, more", pink with pleasure as she soared high over the daisy-strewn grass, her hair flying out in bright streamers.

It was at the bottom of Matthew's garden that he had proposed to her . . . last Sunday, a gusty showery April afternoon when they were planting onion sets in the vegetable patch. He had been squatting over the bulbs as he pushed them one by one into the soil with a forefinger, and had looked up at her as she was counting how many they had left in the bag.

"Hannah, I don't ever want to plant onions on my own again. Is there any good reason why we can't get married?"

Hannah had lost count of the onions and knelt down by him. She put a hand to her ear, trumpet-fashion, and bent her head sideways. "What was that? Can you speak up a bit?"

Matthew had burst out laughing, overbalanced, and sat down on the onions. "You rotten thing! What's up, did I not do it right?"

"I'd just like a re-run if you can manage it. It's not often I get a proposal in an onion-patch after all, by a man with a tear in his trousers and mud on his ear. You know, Matthew Sturton, you must be the only man south of the river who can find mud when there seems to be absolutely *none* for miles around."

Hannah reached over to pull his muddy ear and collapsed laughing on top of him. Matthew set her upright again.

"I'm very hurt. I really am." He eyed her sternly. "Have you no sense of romance, woman? Good grief, you've just been proposed to and all you can do is waffle on about torn trousers and ears! It's enough to take the heart right out of a chap."

"Darling," Hannah smoothed back his untidy hair and kissed him. "I'm terribly impressed. Honestly. Particularly if it actually was a proposal."

"It was." He was suddenly serious. "Absolutely; no doubt about it. Now, I *can* do it again; say when I've cleaned up, changed, and got you listening attentively in the sitting room. Only the boys and Liza are in there playing records and I thought it better with just the two of us."

"It *is* better," she said, serious also. "And how kind of you to think of it that way." They were silent for a moment as the strains of "My Old Man's a Dustman" percolated down the garden from the sitting room. Matthew coughed and looked anxious.

"Shall I say it again anyway? I should be very happy, dear Hannah, if you would agree to marry me. I should quite likely dance all over these freshly planted onions, in fact."

Hannah sat back on her heels on the old red brick path.

"I'd love to say yes right away. I enjoy so very much our times together – I'm sure you know that after two years." She hesitated, trying the find just the right words. He nodded

"That's how I feel. I enjoy being with you. So, if it's been like that for both of us for quite a while, what's the problem?"

"I suppose . . . that I have to be one hundred and ten per cent certain this time, darling Matthew. I have not been brilliant at choosing partners to date. And I'm not always the only one to pay for my ill judgement. So would you understand if I said, may I think this over for a few days?"

"Of course, sweetheart. How many days?" He looked so expectant that Hannah laughed, getting to her feet and looking down at him.

"As few as I can possibly make it, you may be certain. Tell you what, I hope to go to Morfa Cottage next weekend. Can you give me till then? That would give you time to take a cool look at us, too, just in case this proposal came in the heat of the onion planting."

He unfolded himself and drew her close. Hannah stood in the circle of his arms, her cheek against his hard ribby chest, and she felt safe and comfortable. After a moment she raised her face to his and when they kissed his lips were sweet on hers, warmly loving, so that she closed her eyes and gave herself up to the enjoyment of them.

She smiled now at her reflection in the train window. Thinking of Matthew always did cause her to smile. And she recalled the incident on the Common a couple of weeks ago, not far from the place where they had first met. Jake and Nick had been there, too, and Liza had fallen off the crossbar of Jake's bicycle. She had sat on the grass and howled and Matthew had hurried over, picked her up and rubbed her leg, talking quietly. The child had listened, her hand resting on the man's shoulder. When he had produced a handkerchief to dry her eyes Hannah had seen the trust on her daughter's face, the confident nod when she was set down to rejoin the big boys' game. It had reminded her of that first April, their first meeting, when he had comforted Liza in a similar way, with a natural instinctive gentleness.

They would surely both be safe with Matthew. No broken promises, no violence: a stable, loving relationship for her, which was so much more than she had ever thought to find. And for headstrong, emotional little Liza, a family environment in which to put down roots. Those times on the Common, and other times too, she had watched Matthew do for Liza what Dada so often had done for *her*. But on its own that would not suffice . . . this relationship had to mean more, she had to make it work for them both. It must not be on the rebound from David's agonising rejection or, as with Darrow Bates, because she had yearned for a family of her own; to belong, to be loved. Hannah must make certain this time – as certain as fallible humans ever are – that there could be no mistake.

Joe had not met Matthew yet. Last summer he had still been officially no more than her solicitor, although quickly becoming her good friend and trusted adviser. Wonderful, to see Joe each August now. This August she would tell him about this lovely man who had brought so much laughter and content into her life already. She would try to look at their relationship coolly this weekend – she had made wrong judgements

651

before and she could not afford another. But she *did* feel good about Matthew.

Liza stirred, opened the dazzling aquamarine eyes briefly and closed them again with a little sigh. So like David . . .

Hannah still searched her conscience about this, about David's right to know. She stared out of the window, seeing his face as it had been that last time. Right or wrong, it was past. Maybe Julia was dead now . . . maybe he had a new wife, a younger woman to give him children. Liza was *hers*. If she was honest, one of her reasons for living in London may perhaps have been a reluctance to risk meeting David again. But once she'd heard his mother was dead she had felt safer, coming back to the district that was still 'home'; the people that were 'hers'.

What a long way she'd come from the small girl in the terraced house in Water Street . . . when a penny, or the lack of it, was so important. And those dreadful years after Mam died when the buck had stopped with her to feed herself, Joe and Tom. She had not felt secure for years after that, either financially or emotionally. Financial security had come with the success of her shop; but the other had evaded her continually, until now. With Matthew, had she perhaps reached harbour?

Maybe she should rethink the business ties, though, if she was marrying. Florence might jump at the chance of buying out Hannah's half-share of the restaurant and going solo. And the bakery and shop would quickly find a buyer. There was Tom, of course, nothing must put his job at risk. But it may be right to let go, if there was to be truly a fresh start.

"Well now!" Tom helped his niece from the train, then Hannah, smiling hugely. He had broadened out these last years and was losing his hair early. Though still a man of few words, and these simple ones, Tom's eyes were content, and whatever scars the army had inflicted appeared to be healing. It could have been so much worse; if he had been posted to Europe or the Far East Hannah doubted he could have survived mentally. Perhaps sensible decisions had been made higher up to limit him to Cardiff and Gloucester.

"Flo and Harry want us to eat at their place. I've a taxi waiting." He put his cheek against Hannah's and she could smell the yeasty, bakery smell of his working life on his skin. He squatted before Liza, touching her hand with a gentle finger.

"You are getting a big girl. What's your dolly's name, then?"

Liza clutched her doll tighter, uncertain and travel-weary, but Tom waited quietly, not fussing her. She bestowed upon him a little slanting smile.

"Binny." The whistle blew; the waiter leaned from the dining car to wave to her and she waved back. "He washed my jumper," she told Tom. "It's in a bag. Will you dry it?"

"I certainly will. Soon as we're home I'll put it on the kitchen rack, okay?" He offered her his hand and after a moment's hesitation Liza took it. Tom smiled over her head at his sister, picked up the suitcase with his free hand, and they started towards the footbridge.

Florence poured sherry for herself and Hannah.

"We've earned this."

The living-room of the refurbished Number twelve Incline Row, Florence and Harry's home for fourteen years now, bore small resemblance to the little house Thomas and Betsy Hywel had moved to with such a sense of achievement in 1913. The scullery had been extended to make a kitchen and above it, pinnacle of luxury, a bathroom with inside lavatory and hot-water tank. A cream kitchen cabinet stood in place of the old copper boiler, and a gleaming new sink and drainer topped yellow formica cupboard doors, next to the cream gas cooker. In what was now the "living room" the black-leaded range still gleamed comfortably and a kettle sang on the red coals. Seventeen-year-old Wedgewood toasted his flabby stomach on the hearthrug, testament to Raymond's tender care.

Hannah held up her glass. "We've been together now for forty years," she quipped.

"And it don't seem a day too long." Florence downed her sherry. "It's more than forty, come to think. We were five . . ."

"A sobering thought, Flo. Maybe it would help if we weren't sober." Hannah stared reflectively at her glass.

Florence refilled and they sat back, smiling at one another. Harry and Tom had gone for an hour's snooker with Raymond and Liza was asleep under a blanket on the front room sofa. Hannah relaxed, yawning. The room was familiar, yet different. Its four walls had witnessed so much of her life. The table where Joe had nightly sorted out his pebbles, where she had helped Tom to read and write, had bunched herbs, hulled fruit, mixed innumerable bowls of pastry and rolled out pie-crust by the mile had finally gone. Gone, too, Dada's old rocker – though she had that safe at Morfa Cottage. Also the little dresser with the toffee tin where Betsy had stowed the insurance and rent money each payday. That room lived only in memory now; but this room was bright with good vibrations, warm with love.

"You'd better tell me about him quick, they'll be back presently," Florence prompted. "Why you've played him so close to your chest all this time beats me. Not got two heads has he? Or cauliflower ears."

"Neither. But I didn't want any of you trying to make up my mind for me! With my poor record I needed lots of time."

"Point taken. So, I know he's a solicitor, a widower, two boys, fifty-two." Florence looked expectant.

"Well, tall, over six foot, thinnish, hair greying from light brown, getting a bit sparser." Hannah paused. "Is that the sort of thing?"

"Only partly. "What's he *like*? Himself?"

"That's harder. He's, well, he often makes me laugh, which I really noticed first about him. Forgetful; he writes lists. I like his humour so much I think because he often directs it against himself. And he is kind and considerate. And he seems to understand me amazingly well."

"With those last three you're basically home and dry," Florence said promptly. "Provided he's not faddy about his food."

"He's not complained about mine. Nor made a restaurant scene in my company. Is that okay?" Hannah was laughing now.

"It'll do. And how did you meet this paragon?"

"He's not that, Flo, what on earth would I do with a paragon? He was the solicitor I'd had recommended when I wanted the restaurant lease checking out. It was strange . . . we seemed to be friends right away. He asked me to lunch when I mentioned it was my birthday and it seemed perfectly natural to go on seeing one another after that. We grew quite close quite quickly. He started having lunch at my place a couple of days a week and when he found the food was good he brought his clients. He even invited me to a concert by a Welsh choir, in case I was homesick! All fairly ordinary I suppose."

"The nicest things often are." Florence topped up

their glasses. "So, your happiness, Han love. Long may it last."

"Yours too, Flo dear. May you never look worse than you do now, which is pretty good." It was true, Florence's broad, handsome face was refusing to sag at forty-eight, the grey in her abundant hair was minimal and her body, always more sturdy than Hannah's, was only slightly more so now. She pulled a face, pleased with the compliment.

"Don't know about that. I do seem to be fonder of putting my feet up evenin's! D'you reckon we'll have to think of retirin' one of these days? Matthew hasn't said anything about you selling up? Some men can be funny about their wives workin', though they weren't heard complaining through the war!"

"It hasn't come up, so far." Hannah decided not to take on the restaurant issue tonight.

"It well might, love. After all, you'll have no need now, will you?" Florence paused. "Does he, well, did you tell him – about David Vaughan?"

"I'd no choice, Flo, with a bouncing toddler! But it came out easily enough, very early on. I didn't bore him with all the miserable details . . . no need."

"No. All behind you now. And she's a little smasher." Florence stared into the fire. "I'd have loved a daughter. But Raymond's a good lad; he's courtin', you know, Amy Powell, a Baglan girl, seems nice. Wouldn't surprise me if he didn't buy her a ring next pay-rise. But a place to live, that'd be another thing, this town's packed to the gills as it is."

"These new Abbey mills can't be far off finished, surely? The site looks more gigantic every time I see it."

"It's certainly making a job of covering the morfa. I read in the paper . . . what was it?" Florence frowned.

656

"Sixteen hundred acres in all I think it said. Seven bridges. It took months to stabilise the dunes."

The women were silent, remembering how it had been when they were small – just the Port Talbot mills by the docks and the morfa to play on, searching out wild flowers and shells. Then, after the first war, the Margam works; and *that* had seemed big alongside the sheds where Thomas Hywel and Sam Warburton had sweated. And now . . .

"What *would* Dada think." Hannah sounded doubtful.

"Maybe that the world had gone mad," said Florence crisply. "What with posh canteens with menus, and washrooms, an' all the sports clubs and facilities, the shows and talks and things goin' on all the time. And good wages on top! Your Dad'd have a fit."

Hannah remembered Dada's old snap tin and tea bottle, his face when she would meet him off his shift, streaked grimy-grey; the smell of sweat and dust and dirty cloth.

"He might well, Flo. Sam, too. All of them."

She was in the garden early next morning, poking round for her favourites. Daffodils were past their best but there were other delights pushing into the new season, plant jostling plant and some winning at the expense of others.

Hannah leaned on the wall, gazing down at the vast connurbation of the Steel Company of Wales, soon to extend into the new works under construction. She felt part shocked, part exhilarated by the panorama that in its way was as stirring and emotional a sight as that of the hills behind her. For the first time she regretted that it would mean nothing to either daughter, and that her brothers, too, were uninvolved. The steelworks had remained at the centre of life for many of her cousins and their children, but *her* branch had grown away.

Jonet. If only Jonet ... To the family, Jonet was a success story. A first in English from Durham last summer in the teeth of competition from thousands of newly demobbed students clamouring at every university gate. "You must be so proud," Aunt Maggie had said. She had been, of course ... but how infinitely preferable to have had a good relationship with her daughter.

Hannah walked over to the roses and touched a glossy young leaf of King's Ransom. There seemed small possibility of any closeness now with Jonet. She had gone up to Durham last June for the degree ceremony, staying overnight and coming back alone. Jonet had remained to work in the city until September when she had started a permanent job in Bristol reference library. Hannah failed to see her in August for her twenty-first birthday and could only send a generous cheque and a letter. She had wanted to talk to Matthew about it; still did. Well, so she would, if she and he ... Oh dear, might that put her worse in the black with her daughter? How could *any* personal relationship of hers possibly meet with Jonet's approval after the David Vaughan debacle?

Poor closed-off Jonet. Now she was already studying hard for the next step up the long ladder to her ultimate goal of a senior position at the British Library. At least she had promised to make herself available to meet Joe this summer. Hannah had written a carefully composed letter saying how disappointed Joe had been the last two visits, and that Jonet simply must do the civilised thing by him this August.

She went indoors to make herself tea and toast and listen out for Liza sleeping off her late night. All she could do about Jonet, she knew, was what she had done for the last four years; wait and hope.

Feeling suddenly depressed, Hannah dialled Matthew's office.

"Darling? Just to say we're here in one piece. Sorry I didn't reach you last night – we were with Flo and Harry and by the time I had Liza bedded down here again I simply fell into bed myself."

"Don't worry about that, Hannah, I knew you'd be tired." Matthew was using his "I-have-a-client-with-me" voice, pleasantly modulated but impersonal. "May I call you back later?"

"No need, dear, there's no problem. But if you like, of course. 'Bye."

She found she was smiling now; it *was* good, knowing he was there for her. A relaxed warmth tinged the remainder of the day. She took Liza into the shop and to see the bread ovens, then to Aunt Maggie's before they came back to potter on the morfa while Tom took his tea-time nap. Liza picked thrift growing low in the coarse grasses and small yellow trefoil and a bag of bright pebbles, and watched with awe as flames shot skywards from an ignited works furnace.

Hannah was soaping her in the bath when the phone rang.

"For you, Han."

"Thanks, Tom, would you stay with Liza for a minute?"

Hannah ran down, smiling; it would be Matthew. Next time he might come to the cottage with her.

"Hello?"

"Hannah? David here. Hello."

She stood in shocked silence; considered putting down the instrument but it had welded itself into her palm. Upstairs she could hear Liza's happy splashing and Tom's laughter. In the hall the old clock struck six-thirty.

"Hannah? Are you there?"

She took a deep breath. "Yes, David."

"Look, I know what a shock this must be. Forgive me if it's thrown you. I saw you this afternoon – only a back view as I drove past but I knew it was you, going into your bakery. That threw *me*! I'd been told you lived in London."

"I do." Her mouth was still dry.

"Hannah, please, can I see you? I must – "

"Not a good idea, David, to rake things over." She was speaking at random, whilst she tried to think. Impossible, with Liza and Tom chattering and laughing upstairs and David, David . . .

"No raking, I promise. But do allow me to call tonight, Hannah. I must see you."

"How long are you here for?" Still she played for time.

"Maybe two weeks. Winding up the estate and things. May I call on you around half-eight?"

Did he know? Had he seen Liza with her this afternoon? Had he known for some time? Common knowledge in Taibach . . . but somehow she had thought, hoped, that no one would actually have found the words in his small circle.

"Hannah, don't be upset. Just let me see you tonight."

"Very well. Tom will be here," she added pointlessly.

"Fine. I'll come at around eight-thirty then."

She leaned against the newel post feeling unwell, confused, angry with herself for not giving an unequiv-ocal 'no'; *very* confused. He could have said straight out if he knew about Liza, but if he'd known for some time why wait this long to make it an issue? He could have reached her through the bakery, through Flo. If he did not know about Liza, what reason for this urgent call?

Staring at the red and blue patterns on the hall rug, Hannah was unnerved by a sensation of dangerous insecurity. She struggled to think of Matthew, but could not recall his features. She was on her own again.

In half an hour Liza was in bed and asleep and now she had to tell Tom about David Vaughan.

"That's all right, Han." He helped himself to a plateful of vegetables to supplement the little medallions of pork Florence had filched for them from the restaurant. "I want to do a bit to my bike anyway. And George's cage needs a clean."

"I don't know what he wants, Tom." Hannah sounded apologetic. "But he won't stay long, I'll see to that."

"Don't worry about it," Tom said calmly. "I'll not be long out of bed anyway. You leave these dishes, now. An' I'll fill the coal scuttle for the room, okay?"

"Thanks, Tom dear. You are a darling man." Hannah gave him a sudden kiss and Tom coloured with pleasure.

In her room she looked over the clothes she had with her. There was the New Look suit she'd come down in with its pinched waist and calf-length skirt; too formal. A crepe dress with a bow-tie neck; too dressy. And April was too cold for cottons. She finally stepped into the suit skirt and added a pansy blue lacy jumper Florence had bought her to celebrate the end of clothing coupons. She decided against earrings, not wishing to look as though she had made an effort. Frowning into the looking-glass she could not think why she was concerned anyway about how she looked for David Vaughan, since she was almost certainly marrying

Matthew Sturton very soon. Why she was feathering in her eyebrows with a soft pencil, outlining her lips in Dusky Rose, brushing her hair till it shone and hoping the grey was not too apparent? She had even reached for her Chanel before frowning again, turning her back on her reflection, and going into Jonet's old room to check on Liza. If only she did not have this shaky, queasy feeling.

She *was* a beautiful child. Lying on her back with her head drooped towards her shoulder and arms thrown up so that her curled hands rested on the pillow, Liza had all the heart-stopping perfection of the unconscious young. Could she see David Vaughan tonight and keep from him the knowledge of this child? Or was he in possession of the truth already and coming to claim paternity?

Hannah lifted a tendril of bright hair from her daughter's cheek, checked that the night-light was safe, and went downstairs.

When she opened the door to him her mind was blank.

"Oh ... come in." Hannah fought for calmness, control, and wished to be anywhere but here.

He remained on the step for a few seconds, hat in hand. The night wind tugged at his hair and she could see from the light above the door that it was now completely grey, but scarcely thinned and still curly. She could also see that the presence, the charisma, was undiminished. This is just a man, she was telling herself. A part of your *past*. He means nothing to you now, you can surely be objective about how charismatic he still is.

"Good evening, Hannah." His eyes were the piercing aquamarine she had remembered and knew in his daughter, but were now hooded. She coloured under their scrutiny and stepped aside. He came indoors then,

662

put both hands on her shoulders and kissed her cheek. Surprised, Hannah's foot went back and she stumbled over the little rug in the hallway so that he cupped her elbow in his palm to steady her. The unexpected warmth of contact unnerved her further and she turned quickly to the sitting-room where Tom had built up a good fire and lit the lamp behind the sofa. When she pulled across the curtains she turned and he was in the doorway, watching her. She gestured to a chair by the fire.

"Do sit down, David. Can I get you a drink?" The words were so stilted that she wanted to take them back and begin again. She saw then that he was nervous also; he sat down with an abrupt movement but got to his feet again to feel for his cigarette case.

"A drink would be fine, thanks."

He offered the cigarette case. She hesitated, then took one. As he bent over it with his lighter Hannah knew he was willing her to meet his eyes, and with a huge effort lowered her lids until he moved aside and she could go to the drinks cupboard. When she handed him the whisky he was still standing by the fire. Hannah sat down and tried to compose herself and after a moment he sat opposite, putting his glass on a small table.

"I was sorry to hear of your mother's death." She attempted to pitch her voice evenly.

"Thanks. She'd been ill quite a while."

"Do you still have the business?" Hannah sipped her sherry with a sensation of struggling to swim in treacle.

"Desmond and I are selling out. We seem to have a fair enough deal going; an amalgamation."

"Oh. Well, that will save you further bother this end, won't it?" She leant back, having reached her conversational limit. He must take over now.

663

"How about you, Hannah? You kept these businesses? But live in London?"

"I've a half interest with Florence in the Swansea restaurant. And a manageress here in the Taibach shop and cafe." She shifted, nervous of his questioning.

"You prefer to stay in London? Is that long term?"

"I managed a restaurant in Clapham owned by an elderly couple who'd had enough of London. I was offered the lease."

He nodded. "And you're happy there?"

Hannah began to feel irritated now, not only uncomfortable. Had he simply come for an update on her life and times? "Why not?"

"No reason," he said gently. "You deserve to be happy, for sure." In the silence that fell she looked into the fire and David Vaughan looked at her.

"What I wanted to come for," he said suddenly, "is to say personally what that last letter of mine was damnably inadequate to explain."

Hannah wondered for a moment if he had needed the whisky for courage. At the same time a load lifted from her mind, it was now obvious that he knew nothing of Liza. This was followed by the realisation that the ball of whether or not to tell him was back in her court.

"David, there's no need to explain anything. It's all done with; what happened was a long time ago. You were right anyway; any other course would have been unfair to Julia."

"And that course was unfair to you." He stood up, a hand rammed into the pocket of his suit. "Don't think I wasn't aware of that. You'd given me so much. I'd taken then walked away."

"If you must castigate yourself to feel better about this do so by all means, David. But please don't think you will be doing *me* a service. On the contrary."

Hannah's voice was cool; she felt a lick of anger for having been put through this exercise in order for him to unburden himself of his guilt. As the tension of uncertainty faded, she wanted only for David Vaughan to go while she was still even tenuously in control of herself and the situation.

"Mummy?" The voice was small but penetrating.

"Excuse me one moment." Hannah hurried to the door.

"Yes, dear?" She called softly from the bottom of the stairs and her stomach was knotting again.

"Can I have some water?"

She was about five minutes settling Liza; when she came down again David Vaughan was by the open door of the sitting-room.

"Who was that?"

She walked past him into the room, closed the door, then turned to face him, trying to breathe deeply to steady herself. "It was my daughter, David. Liza."

He stood with both hands on the back of the chair. "Was that the small girl I saw holding your hand this afternoon?"

"Yes." Hannah picked up her sherry and drained the glass.

"How old is she?" David's voice was quiet.

"Liza will be four next month."

She sat down. David Vaughan stood perfectly still. After some time he asked even more quietly: "Is she ours?"

Studying her empty glass, Hannah thought not for the first time what a warm companiable word "ours" was, projecting images of sharing as it is longed for in lonely dreams. She thought of David and herself seeing the little girl upstairs as "ours". Now she knew absolutely that this was not so. In the true sense of that word

Liza was hers; *her* responsibility to nurture in mind and body until the child became the young woman and took on that responsibility for herself.

She had the choice now of telling a direct lie and saving herself all further involvement, or of telling David Vaughan the truth, which was that he was indeed Liza's biological father. She remembered the months, years, when she had dreamed of him coming to claim her and their daughter. For so long she had wanted above all to belong *herself* to David, her love. But the most faithful dreams must fade with time.

She poured them another drink and handed him his glass. "You are her father; yes."

He exhaled, a long low sigh. Sipping her drink, she heard Tom's footsteps cross the hall on his way to bed. "Why did you not tell me, Hannah? *Why*?"

"Because I needed you to make up your mind about *us*, you and me, with nothing to cloud the issue."

"She wasn't *nothing* – she was my only child, for God's sake? It would have changed everything – can't you see?" His voice rose and Hannah put a finger to her lips to remind him.

"That's what I was afraid of, David. I needed you to commit yourself to *me*, not simply your child. That's what I had waited for. But as I said, it would still have been wrong; because of Julia."

"Julia's dead, Hannah." As he spoke she had a second of disbelief almost . . . too late now.

David Vaughan came over to Hannah's chair and gripped her shoulders to bring her to her feet. "There's nothing to keep us apart now, that's what I came to tell you."

"That's not true!" She pulled away from him. "You came to sell your business – you just told me. Then you saw me in town and thought you'd like to come along to explain your letter of five years ago in person. At least make your story consistent, David!''

His voice rose again. ''You gave me no time to finish, to tell you about Julia!''

''When did she die?'' Hannah asked softly. He turned back to the fire and took out another cigarette, making a visible effort to keep control.

''About six months . . . last fall. I've been – ''

''Busy? I'm sure you have. But I do recall your letter, David. If ever you became free you wrote you would come for me. Yet when you *were* free, you found it more convenient to wait six months until you had to come anyway! And would you have bothered to look for me then? Or did you catch sight of me and think – oh, goodness, there's that woman I had an affair with in the war, maybe I should look her up!''

She turned away, not wanting to disclose that she was close to tears. The warm little room was silent.

''Hannah. Oh, God! Look, will you allow me to see her? I shan't disturb her, I promise. Just a look.'' He ran a distracted hand through his hair.

Surpised at his apparent meekness after her outburst, Hannah turned back to him. They looked at one another. ''I don't know. Tom's up there now, he goes to bed early. And what if she woke?''

''I wouldn't let her see me. Please?''

Hannah rubbed the back of her neck in a tired gesture. She held all the cards – David had absolutely no rights over Liza. Knowing that made it easier to show generosity and finally she moved to the door.

''You won't wake her?''

''I've said so.''

Tom's door was shut, as always. David Vaughan followed her into the little room next to hers where Liza was lying on her side with an arm encircling a knitted

667

rabbit. She was asleep again, a pinkly sucked thumb fallen from her slightly open lips.

David approached the bed soundlessly. The night-light cast a glow over the child's face and threw highlights across the auburn curls. He stopped, one hand on the bedhead and gazed down at his daughter. Hannah remained by the door, aware of a sense of intrusion as the importance of this moment for David Vaughan became increasingly apparent to her.

The room was quiet, a tableau of three motionless figures. As Hannah watched David Vaughan watching his daughter she saw a tear roll down his cheek. Shocked, she averted her eyes, and after a moment retreated downstairs.

When he came down she was attending to the fire. He drained his whisky and lit another cigarette. "What beats me is how you could wittingly have deprived me of the chance to know my only child. God, Hannah, I thought of you as too generous for that!" He regarded her with red tormented eyes but she rounded on him, remembering the penetrating loneliness after his letter, the pain of the sleepless nights.

"I had to do the best I could for Liza, and for me, David. You'd made your decision and I had to rebuild my life on the basis of it. What would you have done had you known about her? Tried to adopt her? Take her to Canada and put her in the care of a nursemaid? Or demanded that she be sent over once a year? How could you have told Julia about her? You couldn't tell her about *us*! Above all I wanted stability for Liza; children *need* that."

He threw his cigarette into the fire. "Hannah, I am sorry. For the whole damn mess. But look . . ." He held out a hand. "She can have stability now – the lot! I'm free to take you both!" He gave an embarrassed laugh.

"I can't get over how she has a look of me; that hair an' all! What colour are her eyes? God, I can't wait to see her awake!"

Hannah picked up a figurine of a clown from the mantel and examined it before she answered. Her head, which seemed to have been full of stormy, fast moving clouds, cleared suddenly. She set the figurine back on the tiles with a sharp click.

"I'm sorry, too, David. But it's too late now. You see, I'm getting married."

He stared at her in disbelief. "You can't be – not now! Not when we . . . and her . . ."

"I'm sorry," she repeated. "Sorry that you saw me today so we might have saved all this. But you *have* to understand that it is too late now – I love Matthew. And he will be good for Liza."

"Not as good as her real father!" he shot back. "I could give her everything."

"David." Hannah went up close to him and put her hands on his shoulders. "Hear me now. I want to marry Matthew and that is what I intend to do. I was here for you in 1918. I was here for you in 1926. Here for you again in 1940. I am *not* here for you now. Three times you have left me. Now I have to leave you and that is what I am doing. There is nothing to discuss here, David, because I am marrying another man. Very soon, possibly next month. Please, will you go now because I'm quite tired."

She sat down. David Vaughan stood where she had left him. In a while he put both hands on the mantel and stared down into the fire.

"I shan't give up. This man may not measure up to your expectations." He swivelled to face her. "Meanwhile, will you at least *tell* her about me? When is she four? I shall send her a birthday gift. Hannah, you won't try to stop me seeing her? Later on? Surely I have *some* rights?"

"You have no legal rights. I don't want to stop you seeing her when she's old enough – believe me, I'm not trying to punish you. You'll just have to leave this with me for now, David. I shall need to think about it all."

"You'll give me your London address? I have to know where she is. Hannah, you *will* tell her about me? So she at least knows who her father is?"

"All I can say right now is that I shall do whatever I think is best for Liza. Of course I'll tell her what she wants to know, when the time comes to talk about it. If she wants to meet you that will be her decision. Now you must go, David, please."

He stood in the hallway, turning his hat brim in nervous fingers. "When do you return to London?"

"Tomorrow, I have to be in the restaurant on Monday."

"What does Liza do while you are working?"

"She goes to kindergarden twice a week. And my friend looks after her."

"What about evenings?"

"David." She was suddenly at the end of her tether. "Don't cross examine me! What you are inferring is that I may be neglecting my daughter and that is insulting in the extreme."

"Profound apologies." David Vaughan took her hand. "Make allowances for me, dear Hannah; I've never been a father before and it's quite unnerved me."

She smiled weakly. "Apology accepted."

"So may I phone you before I leave for Canada? I imagine that will be in around a week's time."

"Very well. Goodbye now, David."

When he was gone Hannah looked at the stairs and wondered how she was going to climb them, for her strength seemed to have drained away down her legs and into the floorboards. She set the fireguard in the hearth, cleared ashtrays, picked up the glasses and took them to the kitchen, moving stiffly like an automaton but with her mind a blank. She would have plenty of time to see Tom in the morning before getting the afternoon train back ... at least it was Sunday and he wouldn't have to be up by four o'clock. Was it too late to phone Florence? Probably. She and Harry weren't late-nighters.

But not Matthew. He had already called her back but now she dialled his number again and so urgent was her haste that her fingers were clumsy and trembling.

"Matthew? Just to say goodnight. No, nothing wrong, darling. Oh, she's well away. I'm going up myself now. Oh, that was nice, did they enjoy it? Yes, I shall see you tomorrow evening then, at Paddington. And Matthew? Dear, dear Matthew. I will marry you if the offer is still open."

Cradling the receiver she conjured up his image the long bony face, the way he pulled his ear lobe when he was listening to her, the friendly, light-blue eyes below level brows. When finally she went upstairs Hannah was calmer. In her own time she would tell Matthew about tonight. He would listen with quiet attention and afterwards they would discuss the options; and she would have no fear of being misunderstood. In the same way, she would tell him about her gift – how she had struggled with its demands, its responsibilities and consequences over so many years. Oh Matthew, thanks for loving me.

Lying in the bedroom under the eaves, the spring night clear and full of stars, she thought again of David Vaughan. She had cared so much, for so many years, and never until now had she felt pity for him. Perhaps that was a fitting end to desire. Always she had thought of him as having so much; born to privilege and plenty when so many had so little. But tonight, when she had watched him weep over his only child, Hannah had been shocked by how little he had actually possessed of value. He might, had he come to claim them six months ago, have had Liza and herself. But would she ever have been confident that it was herself he loved, or the beguiling idea of a child of his own? Could she ever have trusted him completely; as she trusted Matthew?

She recalled how hard it had been – how impossible – for David to accept her gift of second sight as an intrinsic part of herself; how he had failed to understand the dilemmas that could stem from it. Perhaps Matthew also would not understand; there was still so much to tell him. But Hannah believed that he would. More, she already could be confident that he would not press her to deny the irrevocability of these powers and their place in her life. Matthew . . . she smiled into the dark.

By four-thirty rest had evaded her and she was padding to the window to look for signs of dawn. The stars were gone; the light came now from a furnace being fired down at the works, giving Hannah the same thrill of excitement it always had as flames soared free to the heavens. She went into see Liza who lay on her front with her bottom in the air, covered her securely against the pre-dawn cold, and went quietly down to make tea. She took it back to bed and sipped it with eyes closed. The warmth crept through her stomach; but there was a chill deeper than that and it would not be comforted.

It *had* to be her . . . Rachel Hywel. Hannah's fingers clasped the warm tea-cup for reassurance. She had not slept and the thoughts that had prevented her had even dispelled the memories of last evening . . . ultimately,

672

even of her new-found happiness in Matthew. Increasingly her mind had been peopled by strangers ... by shadowy unfamiliar faces. They had spoken in the old tongue and Hannah had answered them. And one face *had* been known to her; that of Rachel Hywel.

Almost two years ... on Joe's first visit home. That was the last time she had had any sign either of her powers or of Rachel's. For almost two years there had been no intrusion to mark her out as the possessor of this gift. So why *now*? That day, Joe's request had forced her to go to the ruined cottage and confront the vision of Rachel. Must that be done again today? Was she never to be abandoned by this sad, searching spirit?

Ridiculous. She *must* have slept and dreamed it all. She pushed back the bedclothes and went to wash, towelling herself vigorously as though to exorcise these stupid vapourings. Perhaps the old Welsh hymns she had heard yesterday on the wireless had been responsible; evocative, they were, working powerfully on the senses. She went back downstairs and made toast; took it to the kitchen window seat and watched the new day emerge, grey and still.

It was not the hymns. She knew with certainty that it was Rachel Hywel. She had not been near the ruined cottage since the time of Joe's first visit almost two years ago. She had thought about her, though, increasingly, over the last months. And last night, continuously. Now why should that be? Had coming here now, to decide about Matthew, made her vulnerable again to this unquiet spirit? But why? What could she do?

Hannah pulled a jersey over shirt and skirt, laced up flat shoes. If she started now she could be there and back in plenty of time, but she scibbled a note for Tom anyway should Liza wake earlier than normal. It had not been a dream – she only wanted to believe that. She hesitated once before locking the door behind her and sliding the key under the second flowerpot on the left. Each time she had been to that old ruin, that place, she'd seen something, someone. Was she prepared to face the prospect yet again?

Hannah looked at the house she loved, the garden she had created, waking up to another spring. This woman – or whatever she was now – had not been good for her. The first time, with David in the car; *she* must have been responsible for the dreadful nightmare afterwards, ruining what would have been a rare evening of happiness. And the bouts of fury, so uncharacteristic, unaccountable, that had several times turned her into another being; that was obscene. The being she became was Rachel Hywel, of that she felt certain; there *had* to be a link. And yet . . . when she had run there in her extremity, when Serry had died, she had found strange release up there on the hill . . . a first step of ultimate healing. For that she had been grateful. Was she required now to return that help in some way?

It must be resolved; she closed the gate and started up the track. She wanted to be free now, after so many years. Whatever Rachael Hywel's tragedy, it should not be visited on *her* . . . she was determined to have some peace. Surely to God she had earned that? Peace, with Matthew; what she had been seeking all her life.

It was a longer climb than she'd recalled. When she came in sight of the old stand of pines Hannah was ready for the night's sleep she had missed on account of this – whatever – and in no mood to suffer more. She sat on a cracked little boulder and wished she had a drink with her; the sun was dispersing the cloud cover as it rose and was already warming her back. She looked at her watch. Seven o'clock. Come on then; if you want me I'm here. Hannah fixed her eyes on the tumbled stones

674

that had once been a home and made a conscious effort to let go.

She certainly was tired. When her vision appeared to blur she rubbed her eyes and straightened her back, this was no time for a nap. But the blur became more defined; took on a vague shape. As Hannah concentrated she had the impression it was raining, although with logic knew perfectly well that it was not.

"Rachel?" Her voice was strange to her ears, seeming to reverberate in her head. "Rachel . . . why can you not rest?"

The shape was slightly more firm now, about where the cottage door would have been. Hannah tried again.

"What happened to you, that was bad enough to hold you here for centuries? Why cannot you free yourself?"

There, the silhouette remembered from last time. The features were unclear but the set of the head was unmistakable as she had first seen it when Dorothea had come and gone, that unforgettable night of the fire. Dazed and in pain though she had been, standing outside her home whilst the bedroom fire was doused, yet Hannah could recall as clear as yesterday the vision of a woman she had seen in the doorway of her house . . . the cloud of dark hair blowing in the wind, the pale oval of a face, a hand clutching long skirts. This *was* the woman; the *same* woman . . .

"Is it vengeance you seek – is *that* what holds you back from your journey?"

She had no fear. Hannah leaned forward, putting every ounce of power she had into the effort to communicate. The vision did not move, yet she was certain contact had been made. Beads of sweat pricked her forehead and neck.

"Vengeance is pointless, Rachel Hywel. It is ultimately destructive to the avenger. And I never harmed

675

you; so why do you blight my life by entering my body and filling it with hate when you are able? I know you have done this, there is no other explanation for what happens to me. Why do you want me now? How can I help you?''

Hannah wiped the sweat from her face. She saw nothing on the mountainside now but the image of Rachel Hywel, motionless before her home.

''I would help you if I could, believe me. But there is nothing I can do but beg you to seek peace, not vengeance – and to give *me* peace. Nothing, now, can undo the harm that was done to you in another, far off time; I certainly cannot. If you destroy me it can only serve you ill, of that I am certain. So, go now . . . I shall pray for you; and that, truly, is all I can do. Rachel, go in peace. Accept, and find rest.''

How tired she was . . . Hannah's head drooped on her chest

When she awoke there was nothing; only the tumbled stones, a stand of pines, the sun climbing an April sky and the call of the seagulls. Hannah walked up to the place where the woman had stood and there was only coarse grasses and ancient, moss-covered stones with little ferns sprouting in their shade. Bees hummed about a clump of primroses and grasshoppers chirruped in a patch of sunlit gorse. The air was fragrant, tranquil. Go in peace, Rachel Hywel, go in peace.

''What's this, Mummy?'' Liza drew the bugle from the dresser cupboard which she was excavating in search of an old story book Hannah thought might be there. She unwrapped it from the protective scarf and turned it about, fingering the stops and peering into the bell. Hannah knelt and ran an affectionate hand down the gleaming brass. The instrument seemed far from inanimate; it spoke to her of love, and of effort and hardship in the name of love. Of courage; of Dada.

She lifted up the bugle and the sun glanced off its mellow gold patina and lit the little room. "It's my bugle, Liza. Your Grandad Hywel gave it to me a long time ago. He played it well."

"Does it still play? Can I try?" The little girl put her mouth to it and blew until she was red in the face but the bugle remained mute.

"Come on." Hannah took her head. "I'll show you. But not in here."

They went into the garden where Tom was putting in broad beans and peas. He smiled at them, leaning on his fork.

"Got the old bugle out, then? You ought to play it more regular, Han, keep it in trim."

"I'd like to, Tom; maybe I will. I don't like it played indoors, though."

She opened the garden gate and walked a few yards up the hill. The bugle was heavy and warm in her hands and gave her a sense of excited anticipation.

"Why don't you play it in the garden?" Liza put her hands on her hips and stared at her mother.

"I'm not sure," said Hannah truthfully. "I only know I like playing it best on the hill. Where I played it for Dada," she added softly.

She braced herself, lifted the bugle to her lips, and closed her eyes. It seemed impossible . . . but the notes sang out sweet and true. The simple, age-old melody, learned with such difficulty that bitter winter of the war as a departing gift to her father, streamed in a beautiful evocative ribbon of sound over the hill. To Tom, watching the slight figure of the woman who had so lovingly nurtured him from babyhood to manhood,

Hannah appeared to blossom and grow as did the notes. They swelled to a small crescendo before fading, melting into the gentle air. Hannah remained motionless for a further moment before she looked at her daughter, then at Tom, and there were tears in her grey eyes.

I *will* accept, Dada. I will be myself, as you asked. I will accept and use my gift where and how I am asked now, for the good of whoever has need. And I will not be afraid.

She felt boneless, relaxed, gazing through the carriage window with Liza's head heavy against her arm. Always sad, saying goodbye to Tom, to Flo and Harry, but she would come again very soon, this time with Matthew. She could never stay away for long; always the hills would pull her home. One day, for sure, she would live at Morfa Cottage again, this time with Matthew.

Hannah put a hand into her bag and felt the hard shape of the bugle, and smiled. London was not really the place for it but she had wanted to bring it and explain to Matthew what it meant to her. And when they came back to Morfa Cottage she would play him her old Welsh song, as she had today.

A person's life was perhaps a little like a song . . . some parts might be fast and bright, some sad and slow; some loud, others soft. The tune was always special to one person, no two ever quite identical.

Liza stirred and Hannah studied her sleeping face. Almost four, too soon to know yet what song this child would sing. If she, if Liza had been with her this morning on the hill would *she* have seen Rachel? Were embryo powers already invested in her? Hannah's grip tightened on her daughter. Time alone would reveal that and Hannah would be watchful.

She would tell Matthew about Rachel Hywel. It would be her choice; to reveal herself fully to him now because she trusted him. They would go over everything together and would perhaps see reasons and patterns evolve.

He was at Paddington when she stepped off the seven-fifty, waiting by the barrier. He smiled broadly as they reached him; took Hannah's arm and bent his head to kiss her lips then picked up a drooping Liza and the bag.

"I have a taxi. I should love you both to come to my place for some supper. But judging from this young sleepy-head we need to get her home to her bed."

"I'm not tired," protested Liza, pummelling his arm to prove it then fell asleep as the taxi drew away.

"You could come round for a drink once she's bathed and away." Hannah slipped her hand into the crook of his arm, reminded again how wonderful it was to have Matthew around. He wore his weekend sports jacket and flannels which she infinitely preferred to the dark, formal business suits. His persona changed with his attire; his sports-jacket self was relaxed and humorous as his professional self was attentive and scrupulously precise. Best of all, Hannah enjoyed the face revealed by Matthew when he was painting. Last autumn, her happiest hours had been spent in the countryside with him and Liza, watching his watercolours take shape with little apparent effort but delightful results. It would always be a source of deep pleasure, sharing their leisure hours.

He lifted the sleeping child from the taxi. Liza woke and stared grumpily at them, picking hairs from her rabbit's tail.

"She'll be out like a light again once she's in bed. I'll see you a little later darling." She reached up to kiss him. As he turned at the corner to wave, the perplexities of the weekend finally slid away. A life shared with Matthew would bring peace and love, and a full measure of laughter. It was a great deal to have found, a treasure house, and she would guard it well.